WILLIAM CULLEN BRYANT

CHARLES H. BROWN

WILLIAM CULLEN BRYANT

CHARLES SCRIBNER'S SONS, NEW YORK

CONTENTS

WILLIAM CULLEN BRYANT

1

LIGHTS AND GLOOMS OF CHILDHOOD

WILLIAM CULLEN BRYANT DIED AT 5:30 ON THE MORNING OF June 12, 1878, after an illness of two weeks at his home at 24 West Sixteenth Street in New York City. The news quickly spread throughout the city from the newspaper offices, where bulletins were posted early in the forenoon. As the word got about, Mayor Smith Ely ordered the flags flown at half-staff at City Hall and on the plaza at Union Square, business firms lowered their flags, and by midafternoon Bryant's portrait draped in black or adorned with flowers appeared in show-windows on Broadway.[1]

If this display of mourning had been for a President, or even for a lesser official, it could have been expected. But Bryant had never held public office except for serving as village clerk and justice of the peace in western Massachusetts more than half a century before. He was merely a newspaper editor and poet in a time when the powerful ones in America were the robber barons of business and finance. But in sermons from the pulpit, in newspaper editorials, and in resolutions of civic and literary groups he was described as not only New York's first citizen but also the country's. That he was New York's first citizen was undeniable. For ten years no large public affair had been considered complete unless Bryant spoke or was on the rostrum with other notables. That, having lived beyond the age of threescore and ten, he sometimes dozed through the ceremonies did not matter. He was there in person and that made the event.

His death, as a matter of fact, came about because of one of these appearances. The Italians of the city had chosen him to be the orator at the unveiling of a bust of the patriot and revolutionist, Giuseppe Mazzini, in Central Park on the West Drive opposite Sixty-seventh Street. During the preliminary speeches Bryant sat hatless on the platform exposed to the late May sun on this sultry day. While he was giving his oration, a friend noticed that he appeared to suffer from the heat and held an umbrella over his head. Though visibly fatigued after speaking, Bryant remained for the rest of the ceremony, going afterward to the home of James Grant Wilson, an editor, biographer, and celebrity-hunter, to partake of refreshments. Proud of his vigor in his old age, Bryant refused to ride in a carriage and walked to the residence at 15 East Seventy-fourth Street. Leaving Bryant on the stoop, Wilson went ahead to unlock the inner door of the vestibule of the house. As he inserted his key, he heard a sound and turned to see Bryant fall backward, his head striking the edge of the top step. Bryant, insensible, was carried inside but soon recovered and went by the horse-cars, rather than by a private carriage, to his own home. But he had suffered a concussion and lived for only two weeks, most of the time in a coma.

The press, of which Bryant had been a member for more than fifty years, paid immediate tribute to its most distinguished representative. His own paper, the New York *Evening Post,* signalized his death by the conventional funerary trappings insofar as the building was concerned—the entrance was draped with black cloth. But it failed to honor him in the way papers customarily honored a notable at his death—by turning the column rules. On the *Evening Post* the practice of separating the page-one columns by heavy black lines had been abolished by Bryant himself years before, though many thought this showed lack of respect for the dead. But one of the *Post'*s evening rivals, the *Express,* appeared on the day of Bryant's death with turned rules, and the next day his obituary dominated the newspapers.

In the near-century since Bryant's death he has been known almost solely as a poet, the first authentic American voice to sing of native birds like the brown thrasher and bobolink rather than the skylark and nightingale, of the spicebush or the late-blooming fringed gentian rather than Britain's gorse or primrose, of the grandeur of his country's mountains and broad prairies rather than the curried and combed landscape of England. It was as a poet, too, that he was best known at the time of his death.

It could hardly be otherwise, as the New York *Tribune* said in its obituary in reference to his most famous work, "Thanatopsis": "There are few people in the country who have not read it; almost every school reader contains it; few students . . . finish their studies without learning it by heart." With Bryant, the two most celebrated literary men of the day were Henry Wadsworth Longfellow and Ralph Waldo Emerson. The telegraph brought newspaper readers statements from them about Bryant. "He was my master in verse . . . ," Longfellow said. "His first little thin volume of poems, containing his 'Thanatopsis' and other youthful performances, lies on my study table today." And from Emerson: "It is certain that Mr. Bryant has written some of the very best poetry that we have in America."[2]

But in 1878 Bryant was equally well known as an editor, a reputation afterward so forgotten that the historian Vernon Louis Parrington was led to write in the 1920's: "Since his death a serious injustice has been done him by the critics, who have dwelt too exclusively on his work in the field of verse to the neglect of other work in fields perhaps quite as significant. The journalist has been forgotten by the poet, the later democrat who spoke for American liberalism has been displaced by the youthful versifier who described American scenery."[3] To the contemporaries of Bryant, his work as editor of the *Evening Post* could not be overlooked.

The New York *Times* pointed out the contradiction between the poet, who loved the quietude of nature, and the editor, who had to face the "vigorous brutalities of the daily press." It felt that his "fibre was too fine, his mind too pensive" for the controversy that delighted Horace Greeley. This was not the opinion of the editorial writer on the *Tribune,* often in Greeley's time the target of Bryant's editorial wrath, who noted that he could write with a vigorous and vitriolic pen: "Beneath a lithe and delicate physical organization . . . he concealed an energy of purpose, a strength of will, a power of antagonism, which made his presence felt, and not unfrequently feared. . . ." The *Herald* considered him preeminently a political editor: "Although Mr. Bryant's enduring fame will rest chiefly upon his productions in verse, poetry was only his recreation. . . . He was an editor of the *Evening Post* for fifty years, and during this long period his influence was always actively felt in the politics of the country." The Brooklyn *Times* recognized that Bryant had superior qualities of strength and militancy as an editor but that his character saved him from many of the faults of his rivals: "In an era of bitter rivalries, of fierce personalities and ruthless partisanship, he set a conspicuous example at once of dignity and independence, teaching his contemporaries how wrongs might be redressed, and great principles asserted, without intolerance or the cruel violation of the security of private life."

But more than as a poet and editor, a defender of personal freedom, a fighter against corruption, a supporter of art, music, and literature, Bryant in the eyes of his contemporaries was the exemplar of the noble man. Almost every tribute—in the pulpit, in the press, in the resolutions of organizations—recognized that he was a man of character. The poet Edmund Clarence Stedman summed up this feeling of the country toward Bryant in an assessment of his life two days after his death: "He grew to be not only a citizen, journalist, thinker, poet, but the beautiful, serene, majestic ideal of a good and venerable man."

II

The story of William Cullen Bryant began late in the previous century among the beautiful highlands of western Massachusetts, where he was born on November 3, 1794. It was the proper setting for the birthplace of the poet whose "proper praise," as Ralph Waldo Emerson said, was "that he first, and only he, made known to mankind our northern landscape—its summer splendor, its autumn russet, its winter lights and glooms."[4] The best depiction of this region as it was in the days of Bryant's boyhood is found in his poems—from minute descriptions of wild flowers, tiny brooks in the dells, chirping squirrels in the woods, and throngs of insects trying their thin wings, to the dark mysteries of deep forests felt by one who had walked in their solemn shade or climbed the shaggy mountains and viewed from above their green and rolling tops.

The village of his birth, Cummington, was in the 1790's an isolated place. By New England standards, it was a frontier settlement, the first family having moved there only in 1770. Its pastor, the Rev. James Briggs, the boy's mentor in school as well as in church, began preaching there in 1771, and three years later his grandfather, Ebenezer Snell, moved there with his family and began clearing away the oak, beech, and birch trees from land to be devoted to growing Indian corn and wheat, and grass for grazing cows and sheep. Cummington was situated, as Bryant wrote, among hills

> Broad, round, and green, that in the summer sky
> With garniture of waving grass and grain,

Orchards, and beechen forests, basking lie,
While deep the sunless glens are scooped between,
Where brawls o'er shallow beds the streams unseen.[5]

These hills and valleys form a spur of the Green Mountains of Vermont that, extending south into Connecticut, subside into a gentler, rolling countryside as Long Island Sound is reached. In Massachusetts the western half of the highlands are in Berkshire County and the eastern half in the three counties of Hampden, Franklin, and Hampshire, in which Cummington is found. The area about the village is one of hills and dales and hundreds of streams, small tributaries of the Westfield River, which in turn feeds the Connecticut. Bryant's birthplace was a cabin two miles from the hamlet, built either of logs or roughhewn timber and situated, Bryant wrote in an autobiographical fragment in his eighties, "amid fields which have a steep slope to the north fork of the Westfield River, a shallow stream brawling over a bed of loose stones in a very narrow valley."[6]

It was a region of enjoyment and wonder to Bryant as a boy. "I was always from my earliest years," he wrote, "a delighted observer of external nature—the splendors of a winter daybreak over the wide wastes of snow seen from our window, the glories of the autumnal woods, the gloomy approaches of the thunderstorm, and its departure amid sunshine and rainbows, the return of spring, with its flowers, and the first snowfall of winter." Late in life he recalled his boyhood in an autobiographical poem, "A Lifetime," consisting of shifting scenes conjured up in memory:

I sit in the early twilight,
    And, through the gathering shade,
I look on the fields around me
    Where yet a child I played.

And I peer into the shadows,
    Till they seem to pass away,
And the fields and their tiny brooklet
    Lie clear in the light of day.

A delicate child and slender,
    With locks of light-brown hair,
From knoll to knoll is leaping
    In the breezy summer air.

5

The joyous time seen in these stanzas, however, had its darker cast in the experiences growing out of the gloomy Calvinistic religion to which the boy was exposed. There were visual reminders of human mortality and the threat of eternal perdition in the graveyard across the way from his birthplace, a graveyard in which the boy was aware slept "some of those who came to Cummington while it was yet a forest, and hewed away the trees and were the first to till its fields." This dark spirit, the shade rather than the sunshine of Bryant's youthful habitat, is more familiar to readers, because of the popularity of "Thanatopsis," than the "gayer hours" he also sang of in many of his verses. Actually, "Thanatopsis" was written after the poet had found in nature a philosophical reconcilement with his fear of "breathless darkness, and the narrow house." In his boyhood the graves must have had a more hideous aspect for one who had been taught from the first days of his awakening intelligence

> a fearful creed
> That God forgets his creatures in the grave
> And to the eternity of darkness leaves
> Thought and its organs.[7]

The boy, charmed by the sparkling waters of the rivulet by the schoolhouse or the yellow of a violet thrusting its head above the brown leaves of the previous autumn, was not shockproof to such a sight as this:

> Naked rows of graves
> And melancholy ranks of monuments
> Are seen . . . where the coarse grass, between,
> Shoots up its dull green spikes, and in the wind
> Hisses, and the neglected bramble nigh,
> Offers its berries to the schoolboy's hand,
> In vain—they grow too near the dead.[8]

There were other sights that, while not so frightening as the graveyard with its crop of headstones and hardy berries, also did not hold great appeal for a boy—places where the settlers had cleared the forest to grow their vegetables and grain and to pasture sheep for their fleece and raise flax for the homespun cloth cut and sewn into household linens and clothing. Bryant confessed his dislike for farm work, to which he was put early under the direction of his grandfather, "who taught me to plant and hoe corn and potatoes, to rake hay and reap wheat and oats with the sickle." But the experiences later formed images in the poet's inward eye in scattered descriptive phrases like the tall corn that in the advance of a summer wind "rolls up its long green leaves" or in more extended pictures like that of the pioneer settler who

> hewed the dark old woods away,
> And gave the virgin fields to the day;
> And the gourd and the bean, beside his door,
> Bloomed where their flowers ne'er opened before;
> And the maize stood up, and the bearded rye
> Bent low in the breath of an unknown sky.[9]

There were vestiges, too, of the Indians who had hunted deer in the forests and fished in the streams of this onetime wilderness, so mysterious and sinister to the early Pilgrims. Few Indians then remained in Massachusetts, and none at all apparently amid the scenes of Bryant's boyhood. Earlier in the century, in 1735, the remnants of the western tribes had been gathered about a mission some miles away at Stockbridge, but they had left in 1785 to settle in New York. There were, however, many relics to feed the imagination of a boy. Of influential American writers, Bryant was attracted more to Indian themes than most, turning to them again and again in his poems and tales. Some of these expressed the Romantic concept of the noble savage, but more significantly they were for him a symbol of the transitoriness of man and the inevitability of historical change. As a boy he felt the brooding immanence of these forest dwellers of olden times, as in the poem, "A Walk at Sunset":

> They who here roamed, of yore, the forest wide,
>   Felt, by such charm, their simple bosoms won;
> They deemed their quivered warrior, when he died,
>   Went to the bright isles beneath the setting sun;
> Where winds are aye at peace, and skies are fair,
> And purple-skirted clouds curtain the crimson air.

III

William Cullen Bryant was the second son of a physician and surgeon, Dr. Peter Bryant, who only a little more than two years before Cullen's birth had gone to Cummington to establish a practice, and of Sarah Snell Bryant, a daughter of one of the first settlers. Cullen's birth is recorded in an entry of fewer than a dozen words in the mother's diary which, starting in 1794, she kept more than fifty years: "Nov. 3rd. Stormy; wind N.E.; churned; seven at night a son born." In a frontier household in which the members had to toil early and late to maintain existence, births and deaths hardly broke the rhythm of daily life. The next day Mrs. Bryant noted: "Clear; wind N.W.; got up; Hannah Cobb came; Mamma went home." By the next day the interruption to the mother's work by the birth of a son had practically ended, her diary saying: "Clear; wind N.W.; made Austin [her first-born child] a coat. Sat up all day; went into the kitchen. . . ."[10]

On both sides of his family Bryant could trace his ancestry to the early settlers of Plymouth colony. The founder of the Bryant family in America was a Stephen Bryant, who came from England about 1632 and whose wife was a Plymouth woman, Abigail Shaw, who had come to the colony about the same time. Bryant's mother was a descendant of family branches that sprang from the Pilgrims who arrived in 1620 on the *Mayflower.* Among her ancestors were Captain John Alden and Priscilla Mullins, whose story was romanticized in Longfellow's poem, *The Courtship of Miles Standish.* For the most part the family on both sides seems to have been made up of plain folk brought up in the Puritan traditions of piety and austerity. None of the ancestors rose to great distinction, but a number were prominent in their local communities.[11]

Dr. Peter Bryant was born at North Bridgewater, Massachusetts, on August 12, 1767, the son of a physician and surgeon, Dr. Philip Bryant, and of Silence Howard Bryant. His childhood was an unhappy one, according to his own account,[12] for after the death of his mother his father married again, "a thrifty woman" who "thought boys ought to be kept out of idleness," which she identified with reading and study. One of eight or nine children, the boy Peter was kept at work on the family farm until he was twenty years old. His early education consisted of attendance at a grammar school about three months during four winters, where he "acquired some knowledge of writing, arithmetic, and the rudiments of Latin." He may have exaggerated his educational deprivations, however, for Cullen Bryant said that young Peter in the household of his own grandfather, Dr. Abiel Howard (Cullen's great-grandfather), had access to a good library and there "indulged that fondness for study which continued through life." A part of his study was learning Greek, and at the age of nineteen he passed an examination to qualify as a teacher. His story relates that, rebelling at the age of twenty, he was permitted to enter Harvard College, but he was soon recalled home to study medicine under his father. Additional instruction from one Lapriléte, a French physician exiled from the West Indies, and attendance at medical lectures at Harvard resulted in his being qualified at the age of twenty-three to practice with his father. "At the age of twenty-five, with my small stock of book-knowledge, without experience in the ways of the world, my whole property consisting of a horse, a few books, and about twenty-five dollars worth of medicine," he wrote, "I launched out into the wide world to begin business, and established myself where I now reside."

Dr. Bryant's adverse view of his boyhood may have been due in part to the fact that his interests were more scholarly and literary than medical. Just as his son Cullen was to do while studying for the law, Peter sometimes neglected his books on diseases and their treatment to write poetry. Most of his verse seems to have been written between 1788 and 1791 while he was studying under Lapriléte at Norton, Massachusetts. Among the family papers is a manuscript booklet of fifty-one poems, titled *Poems, Miscellaneous and Morceau, by Peter Bryant, Student in Physic.* Several of his verses were published anonymously in the *Massachusetts Magazine* in 1790 and 1791. His models were the poets of the Augustan school of Pope. He wrote love poems in the artificial mode of the time, placing his fair mistress in pastoral settings populated by nymphs and swains, and satires on town life, attacking "busy scandal" that "rules the female tongue" and the prevalence of "private pique" and "party spirit."[13]

In launching out "into the wide world," Dr. Bryant was probably led to Cummington because it was settled by former folk of North Bridgewater, including his father-in-law-to-be, Ebenezer Snell, in whose home he became a boarder. Small and remote though Cummington was, it already had a doctor, who resented the new competition and became an enemy. When Dr. Bryant went there in 1792, a faction of the community sought to prevent Squire Snell from being recommissioned as a justice of the peace. It is likely this was a popular move, for the squire, a stern Calvinist, had perhaps eccentric ideas of justice; but Dr. Bryant, in a letter to a state senator in Boston on June 9, 1792, defended him. He said the opposition was led by "a certain physician highly affronted in consequence of Snell's receiving him into his family as a boarder." The charges that Squire Snell did not render impartial justice were "lies" and "slanders" uttered by the physician.[14] After a year and a half in Cummington, Dr. Bryant nevertheless had built up a busy practice, he wrote his father, but he was not making much money. This was due in part to his competitor, who was "determined to root me out if possible" by charging lower fees. But even without the competition, Dr. Bryant would have found it hard to obtain cash: "It is a very good place, for a physician, who is well qualified, to get

9

business but a very bad one to get his pay——The doctor's bill is commonly the last thing attended to."[15]

Dr. Bryant now needed money, for early in 1792 he had married Sarah Snell, daughter of the squire, and their first child, Austin, had been born on April 16, 1793. The details of the romance between Dr. Bryant and Sarah are not clear from family records. Bryant's son-in-law and official biographer, Parke Godwin, related that Dr. Bryant wandered into the Cummington area seeking a place to practice and became smitten by Miss Snell's charms.[16] This makes a pretty story but it can be accepted as probably more true in spirit than in fact. It is more likely that Dr. Bryant had known her in North Bridgewater, probably on visits she made to relatives, for his manuscript booklet of poems contains an ode written to her in 1790 titled "The Farewell, Addressed to a Lady." The "student of physic" had also written, in 1791, another poem to a member of the Snell family, "Elegy Sacred to the Memory of Miss Mehitabel Snell."[17]

Dr. Bryant was by temperament and learning out of place in Cummington. A cultivated man as interested in books as in disease, who read the Latin and Greek classics as well as the English poets, who could turn out respectable verse himself, and who delighted in music—he played the violin and once constructed a bass viol—he was, as Bryant described him, of "a mild and indulgent temper." His manners and his appearance, too, set him apart. Bryant remembered him as wearing the dress of "a Boston gentleman" and having "a certain metropolitan air," and his manners were those of an aristocrat though he "had always a bow and a kindly greeting" for those he met. He was a conscientious physician, riding horseback in all sorts of weather to visit his patients widely scattered among the hills and valleys and being frequently aroused in the middle of the night by demands for his presence at the bedside of a sick person. He kept up with the latest developments in medicine and surgery as they became known in Boston, carried on a large correspondence with other physicians, and contributed to medical journals. He may have had the idea that his second son would grow up to follow medicine, for he named him after a famous Scottish physician, Dr. William Cullen.

In contrast with Dr. Bryant, his wife was more interested in practical affairs than in literature and learning. Her diary seldom mentions anything outside her own immediate family concerns. Bryant in his autobiographical fragment described her as "a careful economist, which the circumstances of her family compelled her to be." This is something of an understatement. The diary entries reveal that she spent her days in constant industry. She wove the cloth for the breeches, coats, pinafores, and pelisses worn by the family, even the green broadcloth suit of her physician-husband, dyeing the fabric from extracts of wood and weeds. Her diary is filled with such items as these: "Spun four skeins of tow"; "Spun thirty knots of linen"; "Made a pair of breeches"; "Wove four yards and went a-quilting"; "Made a dress for the boy"; "Sewed on a shirt"; "Spun and wove." There was, of course, a multitude of other tasks. She cooked the meals and cleaned the house; washed and ironed; gathered and prepared straw which she braided into hats; raised geese and plucked them for pillows and featherbeds or used their skins for tippets; made twine and of the twine a harness. The daily chores were almost endless—tending bees and gathering the honey, brewing beer, cleaning tripe, making sage cheese and sausage, molding candles and soap.

As with most diarists of the last century in an agricultural region, Mrs. Bryant's entries invariably noted the weather. The direction of the wind, the cloudiness of the sky, the fall of rain or snow—these were recorded almost with the meticulousness of a ship's log; and she noted the outlook for crops—a noble year for apples or good sap weather. Though unimaginative and severely practical, she perhaps sometimes felt the touch of the poet, mentioning the coming of the leaves, the blooming of the lilacs, or the appearance of starlight on snow. But fundamentally her life could be summed up in phrases recalled by her youngest son, John. She constantly admonished her children: "Never be idle; always be doing something" or "If you are never idle, you will find time for everything."[18]

IV

Within a year after Cullen's birth disaster struck the family. The full details are not known, but Dr. Bryant seems to have risked some capital in a merchant ship, money raised by loans, and had to flee from Cummington and go into hiding to keep out of debtors' prison. He wrote his wife from Newport, Rhode Island, on September 29, 1795, that he had wished for a long time to hear from her "but durst not write, lest my letters should miscarry, and by that means discover the place of my residence." He continued:

Ah! my dear, if you knew what I have suffered since I saw you, by a long
illness, you would pity me—but such is my folly, I confess I do not deserve

it—— I see my folly, and sincerely repent it & if I live to return I shall put my affairs into such a train as to pay every man his honest due—— But I will not judge rashly—— As for the vessel I expected to be engaged in, I have heard nothing of it—— My spirit would not brook returning to you without anything—— I have therefore engaged surgeon on board a vessel from New York, for a voyage of ten months, to sail round the Cape of Good Hope, to a Portuguese settlement called Mozambique.

He bewailed the separation from "the dear pledges of our affection," writing that "it brings tears into my eyes whenever I think on them." He bade his wife to "be tender and respectfull to your worthy & honoured father" and regretted "too late the loss of his counsel, which had I not been obstinate, I might have profited by."[19]

Offered good terms as ship's surgeon, Dr. Bryant hoped to clear five or six hundred dollars from the voyage. But he was to continue to suffer misfortune. War between Britain and France had led the two nations to issue decrees that neutral ships would be taken into custody if they broke their voyage to a neutral port by stopping at either a British or French port. The French captured Dr. Bryant's ship, and he was detained on the Isle of France (Mauritius) for more than a year. The detention was not without benefit. Dr. Bryant practiced in the island hospital and learned the French language. On his return trip to the United States, he stopped for awhile at the Cape of Good Hope, where he got together some surgical instruments and botanical specimens. But the voyage that had begun with Dr. Bryant in high hopes of recouping his losses was even to have a more disastrous ending, for the few possessions he had been able to gather were lost by some accident when they were about to be landed at Salem.[20] Of the trip, Dr. Bryant wrote: "Suffice it to say that I returned with more knowledge of men and things, but from several unlucky incidents without having added anything to my property. I was truly and literally poor." Through the aid of Squire Snell, however, Dr. Bryant was able to arrange his affairs so that he could return to Cummington and resume his practice.

In writing Mrs. Bryant on the eve of his departure from Newport, Dr. Bryant urged her to "spare no pains" in the instruction of their children. This was a task that she was able to do despite her household chores and lack of formal education for, as John Bryant recalled, she had made "a creditable progress in all the rudimentary branches of learning." Brought up in a Calvinistic household, Squire Snell serving as a deacon in the Congregationalist church and conducting morning and evening prayers for his family, she devoted her initial efforts to Austin and Cullen's religious instruction. "My mother and grandmother had taught me, as soon as I could speak, the Lord's Prayer and other little petitions suited to childhood, and I may be said to have been nurtured on Watts' devout poems for children," Bryant recalled. Grandmother Snell enlivened the instruction of the two boys by drawing pictures in chalk on the kitchen floor, a favorite of Cullen's being "a human figure, but with horns and cloven feet and a long tail," which she called Old Crooktail. Bryant's recollection was that he was considered to have been a precocious child, being able to walk alone on his first birthday and to recite the alphabet at sixteen months; but not the equal of Austin, who began reading the Bible in his third year and in his fourth had gone through the Scriptures from beginning to end. Bryant recalled making his first appearance at church about the middle of his third year and starting school the next year.

The effect of this early religious indoctrination at home and at prayer meetings was to make something of a precocious little zealot of the boy by the age of five years, for he delighted in mounting a chair formed when the one-leafed table that served for meals was folded and pushed against the wall and engaged in what his mother called "preaching." This took the form of declaiming the heavily metered hymns of Isaac Watts. But the appeal may not have been so much the religious sentiment as the boy's delight in rhythm and rhyme. These songs, as well as the prayers he heard, were his introduction to poetry, and he was influenced by both in writing his own verse. He recalled that the descendants of the Puritans in their prayers "culled from the Hebrew Scriptures the poetical expressions with which they abound, and used them liberally in their devotions" so that they were often poets in their extempore prayers.

When Dr. Bryant returned from his sea voyage in September, 1797, he established a home in the nearby village of Plainfield, but this was for a few months only. In May of 1798 he returned to Cummington, taking a house in town. This move permitted the four-and-one-half-year-old Cullen to attend the district school, though with no great regularity because he was so young. Bryant had few memories of his first days at school. "I only recollect gathering spearmint by the brooks in company with my fellow-scholars," he wrote, "taking off my cap at their bidding in a light summer shower, that the rain might fall on my hair and make it grow; and that once I awoke from a sound nap to find myself in the lap of the schoolmistress, and was vexed to be thus treated like a baby."

Cullen, despite his early instruction in religion, obviously did not understand many of the doctrinal tenets taught him, and the Westminster Catechism, on which the pupils were interrogated at Saturday school exercises, was the one subject in which he did not do well. "I was an excellent, almost infallible speller, and ready in geography," he recalled; "but in the Catechism, not understanding the abstract terms, I made but little progress." But the gloomy doctrines of the Calvinists infected his imagination, and among the poetical expressions from the Scriptures that he remembered strongest in his later years was this: "Let not our feet stumble on the dark mountains of eternal death."

A year after Cullen began attending the district school, the family moved, in April of 1799, into the Snell house, which was to be the boy's home until he left permanently at the age of twenty-two to begin the practice of law and which much later, as a prosperous New York newspaper publisher, he purchased and restored as a summer residence.[21] Squire Snell, despite certain injunctions in the Bible, had no qualms about laying up treasures on earth. Becoming well-to-do if not wealthy, he sent one of his two sons to Dartmouth College and gave a farm to the other, purchasing the homestead east of it on which to build the large house into which the Bryant family moved, now increased to five members with the birth of a third son, Cyrus, on July 12, 1798.

The house was situated on an eminence with fields dropping away to the valley where the north fork of the Westfield flowed unseen toward the Connecticut. It was approached in two directions by avenues of fine sugar-maples, an apple orchard had been planted, and at the northwest on the edge of a rivulet was a semicircle of evergreens—spruce, pine, hemlock—which formed a screen from the blasts of winter. The stream was one of Cullen's favorite spots, and he later wrote of it in the poem "The Rivulet":

> This little rill, that from the springs
> Of yonder grove its current brings,
> Plays on the slope awhile, and then
> Goes prattling into groves again,
> Oft to its warbling water drew
> My little feet, when life was new.

Another place familiar to the boy was the forest later described in "Inscription for the Entrance to a Wood," whose "calm shade" invited the sick of heart to enter and "view the haunts of nature."

Squire Snell, with Dr. Bryant's sons under his own roof, was in a position to take an important part in their upbringing, perhaps in a better position than their father, who was kept busy in his practice and who, after his election to the General Court, or legislature, at Boston, was often away from home. The squire had read widely in theological literature and he was an enthusiastic exegist of doctrine. A man guided in his actions by strong religious beliefs, a magistrate who upheld justice according to Puritan principles, and a firm believer in discipline and hard work for children, Squire Snell was not, however, without his own "remarkable pleasantries" of character, a form of crude wit in repartee. On one occasion the squire was told by a farmer somewhat noted for his excessive thrift and a tendency to boast:

"Today I am going to kill the biggest hog in town."

"Hold, hold!" Squire Snell answered, "don't talk of self-murder."

On another occasion, a medical student in Dr. Bryant's office, in a discussion, said to the squire: "My uncle maintains that thought is the soul. He says the soul thinks; therefore thought is the soul." Squire Snell in reply to this variation on the Cartesian logic of *Cogito, ergo sum* snorted: "Poh, poh! the man spits, therefore the spittle is the man."

Although concerned with the souls of his grandsons, the squire did not neglect their education in practical matters. As soon as Cullen was able to handle the lighter implements of farming, he worked in the fields under his grandfather's supervision. "In raking hay my grandfather put me before him, and, if I did not make speed enough to keep out of his way, the teeth of his rake touched my heels," Bryant related. Because of Cullen's delicate health and nervous temperament, the hard field work brought on sick headaches, which his father treated with a little soda dissolved in water.* Thus Cullen stood in awe of his grandfather but never held him in affection.

The discipline in the district school was also rigid. It was an age when elders did not spoil children by sparing the rod, and Schoolmaster Briggs, when his pupils were remiss, helped the course of instilling knowledge by

---

*When Cullen was three years old, he was ill with a fever from which his parents did not expect him to recover, and there were other serious illnesses. Dr. Bryant, to strengthen his frail son, subjected him to cold baths in a spring near the house, an application of the new medical theory of hydropathy. These treatments gave rise to a probably false story that Dr. Bryant, disturbed because of Cullen's large head, dipped him in the pool to reduce its size. The story appeared first in a book by Julia Hatfield, *The Bryant Homestead Book* (New York, 1870), p. 69. It was repeated in newspaper stories at the time of Bryant's death and in numerous biographical articles about Bryant, in one as late as 1959 in Louis Untermeyer's *Lives of the Poets* (New York).

a smart stroke of a birchen twig. "I got few of these reprimands, being generally absorbed in my lessons," Bryant related. But if Cullen gives something of the impression of being a little prig, with his sermonizing at home and excelling in his school work, he at times chafed under the discipline. The township minister regularly appeared at the school to hear the pupils, dressed in their Sunday clothes, recite their lessons and to examine them in the catechism. He always preached a little sermon on the educational advantages afforded the young people and exhorted them to work hard, since their parents made many sacrifices to send them to school. "I remember being disgusted with this illustration of parental kindness which I was obliged to listen to twice at least in every year," Bryant wrote.

With his parents, however, Cullen was on happy terms. One reason was that they shared a common interest in books. Dr. Bryant had collected a good library, and the boys spent the long winter evenings in reading, lying on the floor with their heads toward the fireplace to get the light from the burning logs. A favorite book of Austin and Cullen was Pope's translation of the *Iliad*. "My brother and myself, in emulation of the ancient heroes, made for ourselves wooden shields, swords, and spears, and fashioned old hats in the shape of helmets, with plumes of tow, and in the barn, when nobody observed us, we fought the battles of the Greeks and Trojans over again," Bryant related. At just what age Cullen encountered various books cannot be determined from the volumes reported as being in Dr. Bryant's library. On trips to Boston, Dr. Bryant almost always brought back a new book or books to add to his collection. Bryant's son-in-law, Parke Godwin, compiled a list that included such works as those of Hume, Gibbon, Plutarch, Spenser, Milton, Dryden, Pope, Akenside, Goldsmith, Thompson, Burns, Cowper, and others of this quality, but there were also books likely to appeal to boys of not so literary or intellectual bent—Scott's novels, *Robinson Crusoe, Sanford and Merton, Little Jack, Pilgrim's Progress,* and Watts's *Poems for Children.*[22]

The community was not without its public amusements, for many practical activities were turned into social affairs—house and barn raisings, when milk punch and grog flowed freely and inebriation was not unknown; the boiling down of maple sap for sugar, when the boys tested the sirup as it thickened; cornhuskings in the autumn, which ended with refreshments of pumpkin pie and cider; and apple-parings in preparation for the making of cider when a single farm might store a hundred barrels whose contents with the passing of time became intoxicating and must have led many a New Englander to become something of a toper.

Thus passed the first years of Bryant's life, years devoted to work, study, reading, attending church, and games. "I cannot say, as some do, that I found my boyhood the happiest part of my life," Bryant wrote. "I had more frequent ailments than afterward, my hopes were more feverish and impatient, and my disappointments were more acute. The restraints on my liberty of action, although meant for my good, were irksome, and felt as fetters that galled my spirit and gave it pain." He had, however, an inner defense against these problems in his developing kinship with nature, whose beauties and consolements even in his early years found expression in the poetry which he soon began to write.

2

APPRENTICE POET
AND POLITICAL SATIRIST

WITH THE SPIRITED HYMNS OF ISAAC WATTS AND THE
sonorous phrases of the Bible ringing in his ears, it is little wonder that
Cullen Bryant developed a love of words and attempted to string them
together in verses of his own making. He recalled that he was consciously
writing poems by his eighth or ninth year and that, since he had been
taught that God hears and answers prayer, he included in his devotions
a plea that he "might receive the gift of poetic genius, and write verses
that might endure."[1] The poem, "A Lifetime," tells of his beginnings as
a poet:

> I look again, and there rises
>   A forest wide and wild,
> And in it the boy is wandering,
>   No longer a little child.
>
> He murmurs his own rude verses
>   As he roams the woods alone;
> And again I gaze with wonder,
>   His eyes are so like my own.
>
> I see him next in his chamber,

> Where he sits him down to write
> The rhymes he framed in his ramble,
> And he cons them with delight.
>
> A kindly figure enters,
>   A man of middle age,
> And points to a line just written,
>   And 'tis blotted from the page.

The kindly man of middle age was Cullen's father, who, since he himself loved poetry, was interested in his son's efforts. But if he took pride in the lines by his precocious son, he did not allow himself to lose his critical judgment. Bryant, characterizing some of his early verses as "utter nonsense," recalled: "My father ridiculed them, and endeavored to teach me to write only when I had something to say." A few years later, however, when Cullen had learned to turn out lines that scanned and rhymes that matched, Dr. Bryant saw to it that his poems got into print.

Dr. Bryant had a taste for satirical verse, of the ancients preferring the odes of Horace and, of the English poets, Alexander Pope, who was tremendously popular in America. In the neoclassical vein, Dr. Bryant's poems include stanzas to a fair mistress, a Stella or a Chloe; pastoral verses in which the Massachusetts countryside is peopled with shepherds and shepherdesses and in which bullocks skip or lambkins play; and lampoons on city life.[2] Cullen, too, copied the neoclassical writers, but he was to outgrow their influence and to portray the real New England countryside and to achieve more variety in his poetic forms than their heroic couplets and Hudibrastic lines. The first of his verse that has survived was written in heroic couplets, an eighty-eight-line paraphrase of the first chapter of the Book of Job, for which he received from Grandfather Snell a Spanish coin, then called a ninepenny piece. Bryant quoted the opening lines of this exercise in his autobiography:

> His name was Job, evil he did eschew,
> To him were born seven sons; three daughters too.

Dr. Bryant denounced this as doggerel, but under the grandfather's urging the boy continued reducing the sonorous cadences of the Bible into neat couplets with a fifty-six-line paraphrase of Psalm 104.

In the spring of 1804, when Cullen was ten years old, he received his first public acclaim as a poet. This was a fifty-four-line poem which he declaimed at the annual school exercises before the dignitaries of the community and parents. The poem begins with a description of the closing of the schools during the Revolution when

> Affrighted Science cast a backward look,
> Clapt her broad pinions and the states forsook

and continues with a report on the advances in education since then. Tribute is paid

> to the Gentlemen assembled here,
> To see what progress we have made this year

and thanks rendered to heaven for the improvement made by the scholars in their studies. Then, in a solemn valedictory, the poet addresses his schoolmates:

> My comrades! tho' we're not a num'rous train,
> 'Tis doubtful whether, we shall meet again;
> For death's cold hand may aim th' unerring blow,
> And lay, with heavy stroke, the victim low;
> From this frail state, th' unbodi'd soul will fly,
> And sink to Hell, or soar above the sky.
> Then let us tread, as lowly Jesus trod,
> The path that leads the sinner to his God;
> Keep Heaven's bright mansions ever in our eyes,
> Press tow'rds the mark and seize the glorious prize.

This pious work spread Cullen's reputation beyond the confines of tiny Cummington, for it was published, on March 18, 1807, in the Northampton *Hampshire Gazette* and was often recited in school exercises elsewhere in the area for several years.[3]

While writing verses of model piety and urging his schoolmates to follow in the steps of Christ, Cullen carried on a war with fellow literati fought with Hudibrastic shafts: "I wrote," he said in his memoir, "various lampoons on my school fellows and others." There was, it seems, a touch of the waspish Alexander Pope in the boy.* The lampoons, however, were but byplay in the development of the young poet. Under the influence of his grandfather, Cullen continued to write religious verse, and under the influence of his reading of the neoclassical writers he developed a pastoral

---

*None of these metrical attacks have been preserved, but their nature is indicated in the replies of one of his opponents, Jacob Porter. In one Porter challenged his rhyming enemy:

> Step forward with poetic cap on,
> Which I shall tear, in heat of action;
> Don't spatter, Cullen, (how you scare us,)
> The muddy puddle of Pierus.

vein. One of the more interesting of his *juvenilia* is a first effort in blank verse, a form in which Bryant later became a master. This is a thirty-line version of David's lament over Saul and Jonathan, based on II Samuel, 1: 19–27. The poem is badly done, but it does mark a desire to get away from the mechanical beat and rhyme of tetrameter and pentameter couplets, a definite advance in his development.* It begins:

> The beautiful of Israel's land lie slain
> On the high places. How the mighty ones
> Are fallen! Tell it not in Gath, nor sound
> The tidings in the streets of Ascalon. . . .[4]

The years 1806 and 1807 were fruitful ones for the young poet. In June, 1806, occurred a total eclipse of the sun, which inspired him to write a thirty-two line poem "On the late Eclipse." A manuscript version in the poet's own hand reads in part:

> The late Eclipse was an occurrence rare,
> As ever visited the fields of air.
> How awfully sublime, and grand to see,
> The lamp of day, wrapt in Obscurity!
> To see the Sun remove behind the moon,
> And nightlike darkness shroud the day at noon,
> The birds no longer felt his genial ray,
> But sat in mournful silence on the spray.
> A solemn gloom and stillness spreads around,
> Reigned in the air and brooded o'er the ground.[5]

Bryant said that his father commented on the effusion: "He will be ashamed of his verses when he is grown up." Still under the sway of the awe aroused by the total eclipse, Cullen later in the year used it as a basis for his description of the Day of the Last Judgment in another poem:

> Begin, O muse! and sing the end of Time
> A theme tremendous, awful, and sublime,

Apparently Cullen emerged as the victor, for Porter ended his poem:

> I once had courage, but as I say now,
> I will take shelter in a haymow.

In later years the two maintained relations on a friendlier basis, and Bryant composed an epithalamium on Porter's marriage and an elegy on Mrs. Porter's death. Tremaine McDowell, "The Juvenile Verse of William Cullen Bryant," *Studies in Philology,* Jan., 1929.

*Cullen returned twice to the theme of this poem, writing in rhyming couplets, no doubt a greater challenge, in his view, to his poetic facility. One was published in the *Hampshire Gazette,* May 16, 1810, and the other in the Pittsfield *Sun,* Nov. 4, 1818.

No more the darkened Sun shall cause the day,
No more the stars their twinkling beams display,
No more the moon her silvery brightness wears,
But red as crimson to the eye appears.
Primeval Night her empire now resumes,
Midst countless horrors and attendant glooms.[6]

From his earliest days a lover of nature, Cullen as he grew older and became acquainted with books found that his reading increased his appreciation of his surroundings. "The poets fostered this taste in me," he wrote, "and though at that time I rarely heard such things spoken of, it was none the less cherished in my secret mind." It was inevitable, therefore, that he would write about nature, influenced by what he had read. On December 26, shortly after composing the Judgment Day poem, he found a congenial subject in a pastoral piece, "The Seasons," and a few days later, on January 6, he wrote "The Thunderstorm." Though his poetry was influenced by his reading, it nevertheless sprang from personal experience. The lines titled "Drought," dated July, 1807, doubtless were based on actual conditions:

> Plung'd amid the limpid waters,
>   Or the cooling shade beneath;
> Let me fly the scorching sun-beams,
>   And the south wind's sickly breath!
>
> Sirius burns the parching meadows,
>   Flames upon th' embrowning hill;
> Dries the foliage of the forest,
>   And evaporates the rill.
>
> Scarce is seen a lonely floweret,
>   Save amid th' embowering wood;
> O'er the prospect dim and dreary,
>   Drought presides in sullen mood![7]

Cullen seems early to have worried about his literary reputation, even at the age of twelve, a concern reflected in stanzas written in 1807, "The Reward of Literary Merit," in which an imagined poet speaks out in "plaintive strain":

> "Ah me! neglected on the list of fame!
> My works unnotic'd, and unknown my name!"

This poet's solution to his distress was one that Bryant later found when he himself on occasion decided the world was too much with him:

> "I go, base world! where rural scenes are spread,
> Amidst retirement's shades, to hide my head;
> Where health and peace diffuse a lenient balm,
> And soothe the weary to a pleasing calm!"[8]

II

Shortly after expressing the fear that he might suffer neglect as a poet, Cullen won acclaim that would have elated an adult and that, for a boy, was extraordinary. Dr. Bryant, among his numerous interests, was a politician, a Federalist, and he was elected to the first of several terms in the legislature in 1806. His two older sons were infected by his political enthusiasms. From Boston, Dr. Bryant wrote letters home that told of issues debated in the assembly, and this news was relayed to the community. Precocious in most intellectual matters, Cullen had been reading the newspapers—those in the Bryant household were Federalist organs—from the age of five. One of his first political poems was written upon the death of General Jonathan Woodbridge, a leading Cummington lawyer and Federalist. Dr. Bryant suggested his death as an appropriate subject for a monody, and in very Popean lines the young poet wrote:

> The word is given, the cruel arrow flies
> With death-foreboding aim, and Woodbridge dies.
> Lo! Hampshire's genius, bending o'er his bier,
> In silent sorrow heaves the sigh sincere;
> Loose to the wind her hair dishevelled flies
> And falling tear-drops glisten in her eyes.

"My father read it," Bryant recalled, "and told me that it was nothing but tinsel and would not do. There were only four lines among all that I had written which he would allow to be tolerable."

But one of the boy's efforts found greater favor.[9] The nation was aroused by the blockades established by England and France in the Napoleonic Wars, these interferences with trade being the subject of violent controversy among the people and the press and Congress. American ships were seized and American seamen impressed into the naval service of England. There were cries for war to protect American commercial interests and to defend the nation's honor. President Jefferson established a policy of neutrality, and to bring the two belligerents to terms decided

23

to use economic pressure through an Embargo Act, passed by Congress in December, 1807, that interdicted practically all seaborne commerce with foreign nations. New England and New York commercial interests were most severely harmed, and in New England, the stronghold of Federalism, the objections to the embargo reached a stage almost of insurrection. The battle raged in town meetings, in newspapers, and in pamphlets. Jefferson was vilified not only for his political principles but also in his personal life. The embargo was also hotly discussed in the Bryant household. Dr. Bryant in letters to his wife described the agitation in Boston. Of Jefferson he said that his *"Honour"* had exceeded his powers and violated the Constitution and should be impeached. He was delighted when his son showed him a few lines attacking the President in the terms of calumny prevailing in speeches in Cummington and in the editorials, squibs, and poems in the *Hampshire Gazette* of Northampton and the *Repertory* of Boston read in the household. The thirteen-year-old boy addressed the President:

> And thou, the scorn of every patriot name,
> The country's ruin, and her council's shame!
> Poor servile thing! derision of the brave!
> Who erst from Tarleton fled to Carter's cave;
> Thou, who, when menac'd by perfidious Gaul,
> Didst prostrate to her whisker'd minion fall;
> And when our cash her empty bags supplied,
> Didst meanly strive the foul disgrace to hide;
> Go, wretch, resign the presidential chair,
> Disclose thy secret measures foul or fair,
> Go, search, with curious eye, for horned frogs,
> 'Mongst the wild wastes of Louisianian bogs;
> Or where Ohio rolls his turbid stream,
> Dig for huge bones, thy glory and thy theme;
> Go scan, Philosophist, thy * * * * charms,
> And sink supinely in her sable arms;
> But quit to abler hands, the helm of state,
> No image ruin on thy country's fate!

Bryant's own account of the composition of the poem is:

I had written some satirical lines apostrophizing the President, which my father saw, and, thinking well of them, encouraged me to write others in the same vein. This I did willingly, until the addition grew into a poem of several pages, in the midst of which the lines of which I have spoken took their place. The poem was published at Boston in 1808, in a little pamphlet entitled "The Embargo; or, Sketches of the Times, A Satire; by a Youth of

Thirteen." It had the honor of being kindly noticed in the *Monthly Anthology*, a literary periodical published in Boston, which quoted from it the paragraph that had attracted my father's attention.

Cullen's expansion of his lines on Jefferson, begun in December, was completed in January, 1808. When Dr. Bryant went to Boston for the session of the legislature, he showed it to friends, who were enthusiastic over it. The feeling over the embargo is conveyed in a letter Dr. Bryant wrote his wife on February 6:

> Memorials are pouring in upon us from all parts, praying for relief—— But I know not what we can do. Our executive will be obstinately against us. The port of Boston is again blockaded and I know not what will be the consequences—perhaps Mobs and insurrection—— You will see by the Papers what measures have been taken. I think it will be proposed to have immediately a day of fasting and prayer, to implore the divine being his protection in this awful crisis in our affairs.

Three days later he revealed that he had undertaken the publication of Cullen's work, writing:

> His poems will be out the beginning of next week. I shall inclose you a copy by the mail to Worthington as soon as it comes out. I think the edition will sell very well—— We shall put the price at 25 cents—— I got a Gentleman in Town, Mr. Whitwell, to assist me in revising it—— He is a Poet and Scholar and I assure you my Dear, thinks very highly of *Cullens performance* and literary attainments. . . .

The Mr. Whitwell was Benjamin Whitwell, a fiery Federalist, a hater of Jacobin influences in America from the time of the French Revolution, and an enemy of Bonapartism. Dr. Bryant could be flattered by his interest in Cullen's effort, for, a satirist of some skill himself in the vein of Pope, Whitwell had delivered a poem, "Experience; or Folly As It Flies," before the Phi Beta Kappa Society at Cambridge in August of 1806. On February 13, Dr. Bryant was able to send to Cummington a copy of Cullen's poem —244 lines of invective in a twelve-page booklet—and on May 27 to report that it was popular: "Tell Cullen his poem is very much admired in Boston, and I can hardly persuade them to believe it possible that so young a lad should have had any hand in it—— They however on the whole give him the credit of being a very extraordinary genius——"

In reviewing the satire for the *Monthly Anthology*, Alexander Hill Everett, a young lawyer and littérateur, also expressed doubt that a thirteen-year-old could have written the poem—a doubt that disturbed both Cullen and his father. Everett began his review: "If this poem be really written by a youth of thirteen, it must be acknowledged an extraordinary performance. We have never met with a boy at that age, who had attained to such a command of language and to so much poetick phraseology. Though the poem is unequal, and there are some flat and prosaick passages, yet there is no small portion of fire and some excellent lines. . . ." Everett then quoted several passages selected for their eloquence and merit. After again expressing skepticism as to the authorship, Everett predicted: "If the young bard has met with no assistance in the composition of this poem, he certainly bids fair, should he continue to cultivate his talent, to gain a respectable station on the Parnassian mount, and to reflect credit on the literature of his country."[10]

The Embargo begins, according to neoclassical convention, with an address to the Muse of Satire and an appeal that she "hurl thin arrows at fair Commerce's foes," and reference is made to an obscure "stripling" who if his powers were "equal to his zeal" would make these "dastard foes" smart under his "keen reproach." Succeeding lines describe how the embargo brought suffering to the sailor and the farmer and then relate the tyrant Bonaparte's progress in putting Europe under his "galling yoke." Americans who, under the leadership of Washington, "brav'd Britannia's power" are beseeched to rise against the President, "the *willing vassal* of imperious France." This appeal is followed by the invective against Jefferson that had so pleased Dr. Bryant. Then came attacks upon three Democratic newspapers distributed in New England, the Pittsfield *Sun,* the Boston *Independent Chronicle,* and the Northampton *Republican Spy,* whose distribution by the postboy spreads a "dire contagion." Then, for some fifty lines, "Columbians" are exhorted to rise to resist France's "bullying mandates, her seductive smiles," and a picture of the peace and prosperity that will result is given.

Bryant in later life was irritated whenever *The Embargo* was mentioned, but as a youth who had already thought about "the reward of literary merit" he must have been elated by its reception. Certainly members of the family were. Squire Snell had Cullen read from it when visitors called, and Schoolmaster Briggs had him deliver it before his classmates. There was one thing, however, to cloud their cheer, the *Monthly Anthology's* questioning the authorship as well as the doubts expressed by Dr. Bryant's Boston acquaintances. Even within the family there was one skeptic, Dr. Bryant's uncle, Gamaliel Bryant of New Bedford, who avowed, when visited by his nephew and grandnephew in 1809, that while he thought Cullen was uncommonly talented he might have had some help in writing the poem.[11]

Appearing when the controversy over the embargo was at its hottest, the book quickly sold out, and Dr. Bryant and Cullen prepared a new edition. The satire, revised and enlarged to 420 lines, and several of Cullen's earlier poems as well as new ones written after the appearance of the first pamphlet were included. It was printed, under a copyright dated February 8, 1809, as *The Embargo; or, Sketches of the Times. A Satire. The Second Edition, Corrected and Enlarged Together with The Spanish Revolution and Other Poems.* Two days before, Dr. Bryant had written his wife: "Cullen's poems are now in the press, and will soon be published—— I think if the sale should be as rapid as we expect they will clear him at least 100 dollars——"

In the new volume of thirty-six pages the name of William Cullen Bryant appeared on the title page as the author. In a preface which the boy wrote, dated October 25, 1808, at Cummington, he justified the new edition and the expansion of the poem on the grounds that since the first edition "our political prospects are daily growing more and more alarming,—the thunders of approaching ruin sound longer and louder,—and *faction* and *falsehood* exert themselves with increasing efforts to accelerate the downfall of our Country." He seemed to be of two minds about the *Monthly Anthology*'s criticism of the first edition, apologizing on the one hand for crudities in a poem written by one so young and on the other hand stating that he would seek to benefit from "fair criticism." Reflecting the first point of view is the following:

> Should the candid reader find any thing in the course of the work sufficiently interesting to arrest his attention,—it is presumed he will not grudge the trouble of labouring through a few "inequalities," a few "flat and prosaic passages."
>
> The poem is intended merely as a sketch of the times. The nice distinctions, the adequate proportions, of *light* and *shade,* which give life and beauty to the picture, require some abler, maturer, and more skillful hand.

But he could not quite bring himself to accept criticism without some remonstrance and added: *"Fair criticism,* he does not deprecate.—He will consider the ingenuous and good-natured critic, as a kind of school-master, and will endeavor to profit by his lessons."

Preceding Cullen's preface was an "Advertisement" for the volume attributed to "friends of the writer." Referring to the *Monthly Anthology*'s skepticism about the authorship, the boy's defenders stated:

> They, therefore, assure the public, that Mr. Bryant, the author is a native of Cummington, in the country of Hampshire, and in the month of November last arrived at the age of fourteen years. The facts can be authenticated by many of the inhabitants of that place, as well as by several of his friends who give this notice; and if it be deemed worthy of further inquiry, the printer is enabled to disclose their names and places of residence.

The statement about Cullen's age was, of course, literally true, but there is a question about the absolute truth of the implication of the advertisement that the poem was completely the work of a thirteen-year-old-boy. The "friends of the writer" did not state outright that he had no help, and in this they committed no falsehood; but their "testimony" that he had reached the age of fourteen only in the past November at least may be considered equivocal in view of the fact that Benjamin Whitwell as well as Dr. Bryant had done some polishing work on the poem.

The revised version of *The Embargo* consists mostly of additions of new matter and amplifications of themes already stated rather than extensive changes in individual lines, a total of about 175 lines of fresh material. There are minor alterations in punctuation and spelling but relatively few in wording that would make the lines more polished. These minor changes in phraseology may be merely the substitution of a word, as when the Muse of Satire is asked to "quit the meaner game" rather than the "lesser game" of the first edition, or occasionally a recasting of entire lines. The additions often clarify themes stated in the first edition or make them more logically convincing, but quite as often they constitute mere padding. One of the interesting additions, because of New England's concern with manufacture, is mention of the mechanic along with the sailor and farmer as people hard hit by the embargo. These lines are:

> In vain Mechanics ply their curious art,
> And bootless mourn the interdicted mart;
> While our sage *Ruler's* diplomatic skill,
> Subjects our councils to his sovereign will;
> His grand *'restrictive energies'* employs,
> And wisely regulating trade—destroys.

A new villain is introduced into the piece in the person of John Quincy Adams, senator from Massachusetts from 1803 to 1808, who is described:

> Unhappy he, by glare of *office* lur'd
> Renounc'd the truth, and federal faith adjur'd!

With fine spun sophisms, and inflated style,
Strove to mislead, bewilder, and beguile;
O'er presidential error gently spread
The flimsy veil, perverted reason made.

In this passage Cullen elevates to his honor roll of opponents of the embargo William Coleman, editor of the New York *Evening Post* since its founding as a Federalist organ by Alexander Hamilton in 1801. Eighteen years after publication of *The Embargo* Bryant was to be employed as Coleman's assistant on the *Evening Post* and a short time afterward to succeed him as editor. Attacking Adams's efforts to defend Jefferson by the "flimsy veil" spread over presidential error, Cullen refers to Coleman:

Virtue abash'd beheld th' apostate's zeal,
And freedom trembled for the public weal;
Til Coleman rose, by honest anger led,
And at his touch the gay delusion fled;
The evil disparts, the painted bubbles burst,
The splendid fabric crumbles into dust!

In a few years Bryant was to become an apostate to Federalism, adopting the principles of Jeffersonian Democracy and subsequently, when he was editor of the *Evening Post,* converting it into an organ of Jacksonianism. Parke Godwin reported that in Bryant's maturer years he was ashamed of his early political lampoons as poems and as expressions of opinion. Asking him if he had a copy of *The Embargo,* Godwin received this testy reply: "No, why should I keep such stuff as that?" Later, told by Godwin that he had borrowed a copy from a friend, Bryant said: "Well, you have taken a great deal of trouble for a very foolish thing."[12] John Bigelow, Bryant's partner in publishing the *Evening Post* from 1848 to 1860, said that after Bryant became a champion of Jeffersonianism the Federalist press delighted in quoting his lines about Jefferson as an example of his inconsistency.[13] While Bryant may have been embarrassed in his maturer years by his youthful invective against Jefferson, *The Embargo* is not such a contradiction to his later beliefs as it might first appear. The poem is as much a salute to the principles of liberty, with which Bryant was indoctrinated as a boy by men who had taken part in the Revolutionary War, as it is an attack on the embargo, for much of it is devoted to assailing Napoleon and his "murd'rous war" to bring all Europe under his sway.

Throughout his life Bryant as a poet and editor was a defender of liberty, and he praised those who took up arms to withstand tyranny whether it was the Greek people against their Turkish oppressors, the Protestant people of the Waldenses in the Alps defending their right to worship as they pleased, the Swiss hero of liberation William Tell, or an African chief captured by slave-traders. The second edition of *The Embargo* contained the first of his many poems celebrating freedom, a 138-line work in heroic couplets on the uprising of the Spanish against Napoleon's puppet king, his brother Joseph, whom he had put on the throne at Madrid, and their war to drive the French from the peninsula.* The first four lines of "The Spanish Revolution" state the theme of the poem:

> A bard, in science young, unskill'd in song,
> Essays to tell, how, rous'd by gathering wrong,
> Iberia, rising from disgrace and chains,
> Repuls'd th' Usurper from her native plains.

Americans are asked to

> Think of your fathers, how in tragic hour,
> They burst the fetters of Britannia's power

and exhorted to aid the Spanish victims of Napoleon for

> My country! think what injur'd Spain endures
> Her righteous cause is *liberty's,*—'tis yours!

Besides "The Spanish Revolution," written in August, 1808, the second edition of *The Embargo* contains three other new poems written that year, "Ode to Connecticut River," dated May, 1808; "The Contented Ploughman," dated June, 1808; and an undated "Translation from Horace," written after Cullen left home to be tutored in Latin. The last-named piece must have been added to the collection just before it was printed, since it comes last and has no page number. The remainder of the poems are of the year 1807, "The Reward of Literary Merit," "Drought," and "Enigmas," riddles propounded in quatrains imitated, a footnote explains, from English translations from the Latin appearing in the Boston *Repertory.*

The ode, phrased in the artificialities of neoclassical diction, describes

*Bryant's interest in Spain continued throughout his life. He studied the Spanish language and literature, translating a number of poems into English, and visited the country twice. One of the few poems of his last years was "Christmas in 1875," which deals with a civil war then going on over succession to the throne, and the last poem he ever wrote was "Cervantes," written at the request of Spanish residents of New York for a celebration honoring Cervantes held on April 23, 1878.

"fair Connecta" winding its gentle way through the countryside. "The Contented Ploughman" is similarly literary, for Cullen, galled when put in the furrow by his Grandfather Snell, knew better than to believe that tilling the soil was the ideal life, as he has his rural hind singing in the poem.

Within five months after Cullen had celebrated the contentment of the ploughman with his "homely cot" and "His coarse attire and frugal fare," the poet was embarked upon a road that would remove him permanently from the agricultural sphere. Bryant reported the new turn in his life as follows: "It was decided that I should receive a college education, and I was accordingly taken by my father to the house of my mother's brother, the Rev. Dr. Thomas Snell, in North Brookfield, to begin the study of Latin." This was November 8, 1808, five days after he had observed his fourteenth birthday.

3

THE BARD AT SCHOOL

DURING THE YEARS WHILE CULLEN WAS ATTENDING THE
district school and trying his poetical wings, Dr. Bryant was able to repay
Squire Snell the money borrowed to keep out of debtors' prison. Though
he had become one of the substantial citizens of Cummington, representing Hampshire County in the state assembly, and had gained a reputation
as an advanced physician, cash was not plentiful, and sending Cullen away
from home to prepare for college created a problem.

In 1800, when Cullen was six, Dr. Bryant wrote his father of differences
between him and Snell, leading to local gossip that the squire intended to
live with his son on the neighboring farm. This turned out not to be so,
and Dr. Bryant wrote: "Harmony here is now generally restored among
us, although we have never differed much, except in opinions." He felt
that Squire Snell thought him "more beholden" to him than he was
willing to allow. He had spent money in enlarging and improving the
house, and mentioned paying $200 for land and $100 for a carriage for
the squire's daughter and son-in-law. Of his growing professional reputation, Dr. Bryant said that Williams College had honored him with an A.M.
degree, "unsolicited on my part," and that he had been elected a fellow
of the Massachusetts Medical Society.

A year later Dr. Bryant wrote that, during the summer, he had completed his barn and made additions to the house—a back kitchen, a wood-

house, and a two-room construction at the front to be used "for medicine room and study." Two years later, in 1803, he seems to have become entirely independent of his father-in-law, writing: "I have settled with Squire Snell and paid him 400 dollars, which he has put into his son Ebenezer's hands." He ended his letter: "I can hardly, however, reconcile myself to the idea of spending my life in Cummington—— If the Squire should go to live with his son I think I shall quit Cummington." This is the first mention in his letters of his dissatisfaction with western Massachusetts. Later on he frequently wrote of his desire to leave the area, especially after his health became bad. He was a victim of colds that sometimes confined him to the house for several days and developed what he called a "disagreeable cough," the first stages of the consumption that was to result in his death at the age of fifty-two. His rough life as a country doctor made him wish for a milder climate and a less arduous practice.[1]

The differences in opinion between Dr. Bryant and the squire may well have been chiefly over religion. Spending a part of the year in Boston, Dr. Bryant—he had formed a medical partnership that permitted him to leave his patients—was exposed to the new winds of liberal doctrine blowing through the metropolis. He was a Federalist, as were the merchants and professional men of Boston, but in the disguise of the religious heresy of Unitarianism some of the ideas of French liberalism began to enter the New England mind. Dr. Bryant became a Unitarian, one of several in Cummington who attended the Congregationalist church but who kept their seats when the members rose to sing the Trinitarian doxology.[2] Thus Cullen's religious instruction seems to have been tempered by William Ellery Channing's gospel of goodness and love, the perfectibility of man, the validity of reason, freedom of will, and the assumption of moral responsibility. Dr. Bryant's heresy—and very likely his scientific cast of thought—may explain why Cullen escaped joining the church as a boy—in fact, never joined any church until 1858, when he was baptized as a Unitarian. Like Dr. Bryant, he could attend, as he did, the Congregationalist church, or that of other faiths, without committing himself to whatever dogma was preached.

Looking back on his childhood while writing his autobiography, Bryant did not have much to say that was favorable about his education in the district school: "Reading, spelling, writing and arithmetic, with a little grammar and a little geography, were all that was taught, and these by persons much less qualified, for the most part, than those who now give instruction."[3] Perhaps it was not so bad as he remembered. Schoolmaster Briggs, narrow though his views and scanty his knowledge of ideas and literature, nevertheless respected Cullen's ability and put him on display at academic exercises. Cullen was not alone among these backwoods boys in his liking for literature, for at least one of those against whom he directed his poetic lampoons, Jacob Porter, was able to reply in turn.

Cullen's schooling was enlarged by his own explorations of nature and the books in his father's library. "In the long winter evenings and the stormy winter days I read, with my elder brother, books from my father's library—not a large one, but well chosen," Bryant wrote. And remote and rural though Cummington was, Cullen had a window to the outer world in Dr. Bryant's reports on Boston and in the talk of the students who prepared to practice medicine in his office. There were three of them as early as 1801 and in later years as many as ten at one time.

With the meager resources of the district school exhausted when Cullen was thirteen years old in 1808, he and his father were faced with the problem of what he was to do. Cullen's intellectual bent and his fame as the author of *The Embargo* clearly indicated one of the learned professions and hence attendance at college. The eldest boy Austin offered no problem, for it had been arranged for him to take over the management of the farm. The other children—there were now seven altogether, five boys and two girls—were too young at this time to cause Dr. Bryant worry about their future.* The decision was therefore reached that Cullen must learn Latin and Greek and the other subjects that would permit him to enter college.

In those days youths preparing for college went to live in the household, with several other pupils, of an educated man who coached them in Latin, Greek, mathematics, and other subjects. The choice of Cullen's uncle, the Rev. Dr. Snell, was the logical, almost the inevitable one, for Dr. Bryant. Dr. Snell was a graduate of Dartmouth and a former tutor at Haverhill Academy, he lived only fifty miles away at North Brookfield, and he was unimpeachable in religion and politics. Thus, when Cullen set out for his uncle's home on November 8, 1808, in his homespun suit, a boy extremely shy with people although with a mind filled with ideas and knowledge beyond his years, he was not entering an alien environment.[4] He found that Dr. Snell shared the dogmatical religious beliefs of Squire Snell; he was "a rigid moralist, who never held parley with wrong in any form, and . . . an enemy of every kind of equivocation." The aunt,

*The Bryant children and their birth dates are: Austin, April 16, 1793; William Cullen, Nov. 3, 1794; Cyrus, July 12, 1798; Sarah Snell, July 24, 1802; Peter Rush, afterward called Arthur, Nov. 28, 1803; Charity Louisa, Dec. 20, 1805; and John Howard, July 22, 1807.

however, "was a lady of graceful manners and gentle deportment," and there were two children, a son and a daughter, of "amiable dispositions." Cullen developed an absorbing interest in the Latin language, starting with the grammar, then going to the *Colloquies* of Mathurin Cordier, and next embarking upon the New Testament. Once his uncle, turning by accident to several pages beyond the daily assignment, read an unfamiliar text which Cullen was able to translate correctly. Gratified by this ability to translate at sight, Dr. Snell advanced him to reading the *Aeneid*.

Dr. Bryant, in Boston preparing the second edition of *The Embargo* for the printer, wrote to Cullen at North Brookfield favorably about the book's prospects and urged him to translate passages of his Latin reading into English verse. One of the results was the "Translation from Horace. Lib. I. Car. XXII," printed as an addition to the poems collected for this volume. On April 4, 1809, Cullen sent his father two translations from Virgil, done in the heroic couplet, with a letter containing the apology: "You will doubtless find in the enclosed lines much that needs emendation and much that characterizes the crude efforts of puerility. They have received some correction from my hands, but you are sensible that the partiality of an author for his own compositions, and an immature judgment, may have prevented me from perceiving the most of its defects, however prominent. . . . "[5] In his autobiography Bryant said he received no commendation from his father, whose opinion was that "the lines were cramped and the phraseology clumsy."

One of the translated passages was that of a storm that wrecked Aeneas's ship and the other an account of the blinded one-eyed giant Polyphemus. Both passages dealt with the kind of awesome manifestations that only a short time before had inspired Cullen to write his stanzas "On the late Eclipse" and "On the last Judgment." Of the storm that launched its fury on Aeneas's ship Cullen translated the lines giving a dramatic account of the fear of the sailors, the sinking of the ship, and the resulting horror when

> o'er the waves, in thick confusion spread,
> Rose arms and planks and bodies of the dead.

The passage about Polyphemus gave the young classicist even more of an opportunity to revel in ghastly description:

> I saw the monster when supinely laid
> Along his cave, and shrouded in its shade,

Ferocious, grasping in his mighty hand
Two from the number of Ulysses' band.
He dashed them on the rocks, the foaming flood
Poured thro the den, now floating with the blood;
Convulsed on the earth their quivering limbs I saw;
And flesh yet warm beneath his cruel jaw.[6]

Considering the subject matter of the passages chosen for translation, perhaps Dr. Bryant had a reason other than their poetic merit in withholding his praise: he may have felt that they showed an unnatural interest in death and destruction. Nevertheless, he was proud of Cullen's progress in Latin as well as a new interest Cullen had developed in art. Writing his wife on July 1 after visiting his son at the home of Dr. Snell, he said: "Cullen makes surprizing progress—— He has gone through the 12 books of the Aeneid, the Pastorals and part of the Georgics—— He likewise makes great proficiency in drawing—— I shall bring you some specimens of his skill." Later in the month he wrote: "I have several specimens of Cullen's painting to bring to you. It is thought here by good judges that had he suitable instruction he would make an eminent painter."*

Dr. Snell's instruction may have been narrow and uninspired, but it had its recompenses. Shortly after sending his father the Latin translations, Cullen wrote a rhymed epistle to his brother Austin telling of his new life:

Once more the Bard, with eager eye, reviews
The flowery paths of Fancy, and the Muse
Once more essays to trill forgotten strains,
The loved amusement of his native plains.
Late you beheld me treading labor's round,
To guide slow oxen o'er the furrowed ground;
The sturdy hoe or slender rake to ply,
'Midst dust and sweat, beneath a summer sky.
But now I pore o'er Virgil's glowing lines,
Where, famed in war, the great Aeneas shines. . . .[7]

But Dr. Snell's program did not allow much scope for the flowery paths of fancy. To him, reading was for edification and not for pleasure. He borrowed for his pupil's benefit Lord Teignmouth's *Life of Sir William*

---

*No drawings or paintings by Bryant seem to have been preserved. His interest in art continued throughout his life and among his close friends were painters and sculptors.

Jones, the English jurist and orientalist. Bryant related afterward that reading the book probably led him to be more assiduous in his studies and that it perhaps inclined him to take up the profession of law when he had to decide on an occupation. A book Cullen found in a closet and started to read with interest that grew stronger as he proceeded brought a rebuke from his uncle. It was one of Mrs. Radcliffe's Gothic tales, *The Romance of the Forest.* "These works," his uncle told him, "have an unwholesome influence. They are written in an interesting manner; they absorb the attention, and divert the mind from objects of greater importance." For some days Cullen let the book alone, but his interest had been so aroused that he resumed the story. Before he could finish it, the volume disappeared. Although Dr. Snell considered reading novels for their story or poetry for its beauty an unedifying pastime, he did not deny Cullen the pleasure of country walks, which he took in company with a fellow-student, Amasa Walker, later a professor in Oberlin College. Bryant related:

> As the spring came on, I wandered about the fields and meadows, where I missed some of the early flowers of the highland country in which I was born, and admired others new to me. The hickory, the oak, and the chestnut trees, as they put forth their young leaves, were new acquaintances to me. As the summer came on, my attention was attracted to an elegant plant of the meadows—a wild lily—with whorls of leaves surrounding the stem. I watched impatiently the unfolding of its flower-buds, in hope that I might see it in bloom before I went back to Cummington, but in this I was disappointed.

Cullen's first extended trip away from home ended on July 9 when, after an absence of eight months, he returned to Cummington. Except for achieving a familiarity with Latin literature, the experience had not contributed greatly to his intellectual growth; for Dr. Snell was not one to neglect his responsibility to see to it that his young charges maintained their belief in the dogma of Calvinism. But there were gains that Bryant noted. For one thing, his health had improved; the headaches that had tormented him had ceased, and never afterward did he suffer from them. For another, his view of the physical world had expanded; objects in Cummington had diminished in size. "The parlor, the kitchen, my father's office," he wrote, "all seemed to have shrunk from their former dimensions; the ceilings seemed lower, the fields around seemed of less extent, the trees less tall, and the little brook that ran near the house gurgled with a slenderer current."

II

The return home meant a resumption of farm work, and Cullen spent the next month and a half with the haymakers in the field, being taunted at times when he paused to rest by Squire Snell, who would say: "Well, Cullen, making varses again?" But this was an interlude only. Arrangements were made for him to learn Greek at nearby Plainfield under the Rev. Moses Hallock beginning in August. Plainfield, only three miles away, was within sight of the Bryant home; Parson Hallock was an intimate friend of Squire Snell, of whom he was accustomed to say, "I value Mr. Hallock; his life is so exemplary"; and the cost was not great, only one dollar a week for instruction, board, and lodging. Parson Hallock's school was known as "the bread and milk college" from the staple fare given the boarding students. Of the nominal charge made, he was wont to say, "I can afford it for that, and it would not be honest to take more." Yet in a way it was a distinguished school. Established in 1793 and conducted until 1824, it turned out 132 men of whom fifty became clergymen. What was significant for Cullen's future, however, was that it was a feeder for Williams College, and sometimes as many as one-half the entering class was made up of students Hallock had taught.[8]

Cullen's mastery of Greek was as rapid as his mastery of Latin, and again it was the result of rigid application. "I was early at my task in the morning, and kept on until bed-time," he wrote; "at night I dreamed of Greek, and my first thought in the morning was of my lesson for the day." At the end of October, when this period of study ended, he knew the Greek New Testament "from end to end almost as if it had been English."

It was now decided that Cullen would go to Williams College and that, to save money, he should concentrate on the studies that would enable him to pass an entrance examination and enter as a sophomore with the opening of the next term in October of 1810. With the exception of two months in the spring, when Cullen returned to Plainfield to receive instruction in mathematics under Parson Hallock, he worked at home reviewing his Latin and Greek, taking up French, which his father knew because of his year spent on the Isle of France, and broadening his knowledge of English literature and philosophy. This schedule did not give him much time for writing; but two poems are known to have been composed at this time. In one he attacked the menace of Napoleon, whose "dire career" had put Austria under his "conquering hand" and erected a throne for tyranny "In hapless Sweden's fallen land." Fearing even an invasion of the New World, Cullen invoked a spirit, "the Genius of Columbia," frequently found in the patriotic poems of the time, who urges Americans to arouse themselves to their danger from Napoleon:

> With quick repulse, his baffled band
>   Would seek the friendly shore in vain,
> Bright Justice lift her red right hand,
>   And crush them on the fatal plain.

This forty-line poem, dated January 8, 1810, was printed the next week, January 17, under the title, "The Genius of Columbia," in the *Hampshire Gazette.*[9]

The other poem, "The Spring's Walk," shows an advance in Cullen's poetic development. In it he writes with some freshness of language of the New England countryside. This may mark the first influence of Wordsworth on his poetry, for *Lyrical Ballads* was brought home from Boston by Dr. Bryant in 1810.* Richard Henry Dana, later Bryant's most intimate literary friend, related that Bryant told him that, upon opening the book "a thousand springs seemed to gush up at once into his heart, and the face of Nature, of a sudden, to change into a strange freshness and life."[10] Bryant describes his walk in spring:

> Again the vivid green I tread,
>   With garments fluttering in the gale;
> Or stretched beneath the deepening shade,
>   The balmy breath of Spring inhale.
> Scared at my distant footsteps, fly,
>   The chittering sparrows from the brakes;
> The wandering wild-bee murmurs by,
>   The frightened bird her nest forsakes.

He indicates that he has grown weary of the artificialities of Pope and other neoclassical writers and was on the verge of embracing Romantic spontaneity and enthusiasm in these lines:

---

*Parke Godwin said that Dr. Bryant purchased a copy in Boston in 1810 and took the book home but that since Cullen was in school he did not read it immediately. *Biography,* I, 61. Arthur Bryant recalled reading the book as early as 1810. Letter to Godwin, Nov. 21, 1879, Goddard-Roslyn Collection.

I love the poet in whose song,
A poet's animation glows,—
Fresh as the gale that breathes along
The dwellings of the morning rose.

After the summer of study, Cullen and his father went to Williamstown to enter him in Williams College. He passed what he called an "easy examination" and was admitted as a member of the sophomore class for the term opening on October 8. Dr. Bryant was worried about the costs, writing his father:

> I hardly know how I shall be able to meet the expenses of his education in the present scarcity of money and with my present means; without doing injustice to my other children; who will all, especially the boys, have equal claims—— But I thought, as he had exhibited a genius, and a taste for literature, rather above the ordinary level it would be almost criminal not to gratify him as far as I could, if I could possibly struggle through the expenses. Whether his acquirements will benefit *himself* or *society,* or whether I shall ever have the gratification to see him such as I wish him to be, are points which must be left to the disposition of that *Providence* whose ways are inscrutable and will unquestionably order all for the *best* and worst ends——[11]

Bryant left no record of his first impressions of the college, but doubtless he had few other than the outward appearance of the village, which he did not find attractive, and the two campus buildings.[12] Williamstown contained only a few houses facing undrained streets. One of the attractions of the college to the pious New Englanders who sent their sons there was its "sequestered location, and the high moral character of the surrounding community, presenting few inducements to extravagance and dissipation." The older of the campus buildings, known as the West College, was a structure of four stories. It had been built in 1790 and in Cullen's time housed the chapel, library, recitation rooms for the freshman and sophomore classes, and a dormitory for students, two to a room. It faced the highway, and a passageway through its center led to the East College, erected in 1798. Also of four stories, the East College contained the recitation rooms for the junior and senior classes and thirty-two suites of rooms for students. But if the town and campus were unimpressive, the countryside must have struck Cullen by its grandeur. Williamstown is situated among some of the loftiest mountains in New England, its most imposing height known, in those times, as Saddle Mountain, so called because of its double peaks rising 2,800 feet above the surrounding land.

The higher of the peaks was called Greylock because of the appearance of the frost visible on its sides during the winter months. Cullen was to learn that climbing to the summit of Greylock to spend the night was expected of all students at Williams College at least once during their period of attendance.

Aside from proximity, Williamstown being only twenty-five miles across hills and valleys from Cummington, and the low cost, Williams College satisfied at least two other requirements for Cullen's education. To Squire Snell its appeal was that of religious orthodoxy: surely Cullen would not fall into bad company if his associates were young men like those educated by the exemplary Parson Hallock. Dr. Bryant may have had some qualms about the academic standards, but at least the college was politically acceptable, being known as a stronghold of Federalism, though a few years before the editor of the Pittsfield *Sun,* an anti-Federalist paper, had waxed indignant over the partisan commencement orations of the graduating class and warned "Republicans to beware how they trust the education of their sons on the burning sides of a political volcano." But Cullen's mentors might have hesitated before sending him to Williams if they had known the situation that existed within the college walls. For a youth like Cullen, breathing from his first years a stern moral and religious atmosphere, who accepted with only occasional resentment rarely overtly expressed the precepts of his elders, who repressed his own boyish inclinations at a look or a word from them, it must have been a shock to meet young men who violated in thought and action much that he had been taught was God-given and inevitable.

Williams College had accepted its first students in 1793 with the aim of offering an inexpensive education in a place that because of its remoteness would "prove favorable to the morals and literary improvement of youth." The first president, who served until 1815, was Dr. Ebenezer Fitch, a graduate of Yale. In its early years it had been criticized as being dominated by the "infidel" principles of French libertarianism and French philosophy to the extent that "it was very unpopular for a sinner to be convicted of sin, or to be converted or say or do anything on the subject of experimental piety." But these influences weakened after a religious revival that swept the campus and community in 1806. This reform did not last long, however, and when Cullen entered the college "a lax morality and want of religious principle" had crept in. Student conduct was so bad that "it became a trial to live in college, especially in the building occupied by the two lower classes," and the number who professed religion was only twenty, of these several being described as "inefficient as Christians." There were reports that atheists had burnt the chapel Bible and that there had been a mock celebration of the Lord's Supper.

The academic situation was equally bad as the result of a student revolt in 1808. It arose when the sophomore class petitioned the trustees for the dismissal of two tutors. A vacation intervening, nothing was done. At the opening of the new term the rebellious class gave no more trouble until the professor of mathematics and natural philosophy, Gamaliel Olds, obtained from the faculty of four—himself, the president, and the two tutors —a resolution directing the juniors to sign a paper acknowledging that they had been in the wrong. Not one member of the class signed. When President Fitch, feeling he had been misled by Olds, upheld the class, the professor and the two offending tutors resigned. Without teachers, there was nothing for the president to do but close the college until a new staff could be employed. The incident almost wrecked the institution. From a graduating class of 115 in 1808, the number fell to about twenty in each of the four following years.

It is unlikely that Cullen, even with the ability he manifested in later years of steering a straight course in gales and rough waters toward a port determined by his own principles, could have been unaffected by what, in his own innocence at the age of sixteen, must have seemed the human depravity he encountered among certain of the students. If not, it was a tribute to the power of Calvinism, which taught that mankind was damned from the start in any case, or perhaps he knew little of what was going on because of the students he chose as intimates. At any rate, he never alluded, so far as is known, to the indifference to or scorn for religion of some of his classmates. He said in his autobiography: "The students of Williams College were at that time mostly youths of a staid character, generally in narrow circumstances, who went to college with a serious intention to study, and prepare themselves for some of the learned professions, so that I have no college pranks to relate."

When Cullen arrived at Williams, he was, as a sophomore, assigned to a room in the West College. One of his classmates, Charles F. Sedgwick, later to become a close friend, remembered him as being tall and slender with "a prolific growth of dark-brown hair." His achievement as a poet, even a prodigy, was already known. He first met members of his class gathered in one of the dormitory rooms. Another classmate recalled: "A friendly greeting passed round the circle, and all seemed to enjoy the arrival of the young stranger and poet. News of Mr. Bryant's precocious intellect, his poetical genius, and his literary taste had preceded his arrival.

He was looked up to with great respect, and regarded as an honour to the class of which he had become a member, and to the college which now received him as his *alma 'mater.''* Members of the senior class, however, were not quite so ready to credit him with superior poetic powers, express-ing doubt as to his authorship of *The Embargo.* On the whole, he made a good impression. Sedgwick said of him: "When spoken to in relation to these poetical effusions he was reticent and modest, and in fact his modesty in everything was a peculiar trait of his character."

When Cullen became acquainted with the college offerings, there can be no doubt that he was disappointed. His prescribed courses included geography, arithmetic, logic, and algebra, subjects hardly likely to have great appeal to one of his literary and linguistic bent. In his autobiography he said: "The course of study in Williams College at that time was meagre and slight in comparison with what it now is. There was but one Professor, Chester Dewey, Professor of Mathematics and Natural Philosophy, a man of much merit, who had charge of the Junior class. The President of the college, Dr. Fitch, superintended the studies of the Senior class, and the Sophomores and Freshmen were instructed by two tutors employed from year to year." Thus Cullen was not exposed to the two members of the faculty who might have helped him. He described Dr. Fitch as being "a square-built man, of dark complexion, and black, arched eyebrows," whose manner with students was "kind and courteous." Cullen heard him preach on Sundays, but found "his style of sermonizing was not such as to compel the attention." Cullen was more receptive to the sermons of Professor Dewey, who had graduated from the college in 1806 and served as tutor for two terms before succeeding to a full professorship when Professor Olds resigned during the troubles of 1808. The tutor for the sophomore class was Orange Lyman, who had graduated from the college only the year before. A young man already stiffly formal and self-satisfied, he apparently had little character that could interest Cullen and little knowledge that could inform him. But Cullen, at this time, was not the type to cavil at circumstance. "I mastered the daily lessons given out to my class," he recalled, "and found much time for miscellaneous reading, for disputations, and for literary composition in prose and verse, in all of which I was thought to acquit myself with some credit."

The intellectual dreariness of the curriculum and instruction was re-lieved somewhat by the library facilities and the two literary societies. Jointly, the two organizations were known as the Adelphia Union, which maintained a library on the fourth story of the West College; since 1795 it had been split into two societies, the Philologian and Philotechnian. Of the books available, Bryant wrote: "The library of the college was then small, but was pretty well supplied with the classics. The library of the two literary societies . . . was a little collection, scarcely, I think, exceeding one thousand in number. I availed myself of it to read several books which I had not seen elsewhere." As his roommate, John Avery, belonged to the Philotechnian Society, Cullen joined this group in whose literary exercises he recalled taking a great interest. These programs also afforded Cullen an opportunity for debate and discussion—the current term was "disputation"—and he remembered many years later several students noted as elocutionists to whom, when they spoke, "every ear was open."

Cullen was not thrown entirely among strangers, for several boys prepared under Parson Hallock whom he may have known were also in attendance. Of a retiring nature, Cullen was not one to seek out friends or to attract people on short acquaintance. "During his stay in college," Sedgwick recalled, "he associated with the more orderly and studious scholars, and was very modest and unobtrusive, though pleasantly familiar with his personal friends." Of these, the only real intimate seems to have been his roommate, who was older by several years.

No examples of Cullen's prose written while at Williams have been preserved, but several poems exist. Under the tutelage of Parson Hallock, Cullen had concentrated on Greek grammar; at college, as he had done earlier with Latin, he experimented with English translations from the Greek. One of these, a translation of Anacreon's ode on spring, he recalled with pride. The ode had been done into English by Thomas Moore, and Avery, liking Cullen's version, copied the two translations and submitted them to two juniors of some literary judgment to determine which they thought the better. They chose Cullen's. Bryant related in his autobiography "that they evidently supposed my translation to be that of Moore, and spoke of the other in an encouraging manner as quite creditable on the whole." Another translation was a poem printed in Bryant's collected works, "Version of a Fragment of Simonides." This is the first of Bryant's youthful poems that he cared enough about to preserve along with his maturer work, but only after several reworkings. It was first printed in the *Hampshire Gazette* of April 23, 1817; a revision appeared in *The North American Review* in March, 1818; it was revised again for the 1821 edition of Bryant's *Poems.* His other Greek translations include a spirited version of a chorus in *Oedipus Tyrannus,* which, after Cullen left Williams, he enjoyed declaiming with his younger brother Arthur while roaming among the hills about Cummington. He imitated the strophes of his translation of the dramatic chorus in a poem, "Indian War Song." In it a chief, in resounding phrases, threatens the enemies of his tribe:

> Ghosts of my wounded brethren rest,
>   Shades of the warrior-dead!
> Nor weave, in shadowy garment drest,
>   The death-dance round my bed;
> For, by the homes in which we dwelt,
> And by the altar where we knelt,
>   And by our dying battle-songs,
> And by the trophies of your pride,
> And by the wounds of which ye died,
>   I swear to avenge your wrongs.[13]

By March, six months after entering the college, Cullen saw its short-comings clearly, and voiced his opinion in a satire, *Descriptio Gulielmopolis,* read before the Philotechnian Society. It is a sweeping arraignment that begins with an adverse picture of the college's location,

> Hemmed in with hills, whose heads aspire,
> Abrupt and rude, and hung with woods,

and continues on to assail the climate and the ambiguous time of the year between winter and spring. He describes the extremes of drought and storm that left the land at times "a frozen desert" and others "a sea of mud," and denounces Williamstown as a place where "morbid exhalations rise" and "Disease unseen directs her way." Some of Cullen's harshest invective was directed at the dark and dingy buildings

> Where through the horror-breathing hall
> The pale-faced, moping students crawl
>   Like spectral monuments of woe,
> Or studious seek the unwholesome cell,
> Where dust and gloom and cobwebs dwell,
>   Dark, dirty, dank, and low

The discipline enforced by the faculty was more that of a prison than of an institution devoted to learning. Almost every action of the students was governed by laws that had continued almost unchanged since the college's opening, when penalties or "mulcts" were imposed, ranging from one penny for tardiness at prayers to ten shillings for "cursing, fornication or singing obscene songs." Students were confined to their rooms from sunset on Saturday to Monday morning, except for attendance at meals and religious services, and the tutors inspected the rooms every night. Cullen chose not to dwell upon this, writing:

Yet on the picture dark with shade
Let not the eye forever gaze
Where lawless Power his nest has laid
And stern Suspicion treads her maze.

The satire was well received and well remembered. At least two versions recorded by listeners at the time were subsequently printed, one in *The Christian Union* of June 25, 1891, and one in *The Independent* of January 7, 1904.

Cullen's disappointment with what Williams College had to offer was reinforced by his roommate and by another friend, Theodore Clapp, of Easthampton, both of whom were planning to withdraw to enter Yale College in the fall. With the incentive of their example, Cullen wrote his father for permission to do the same and was delighted when it was granted. He left at mid-term on May 8 for a reason not explained in his autobiography, which states merely: "Accordingly, in the year 1811, before the third term of my Sophomore year was ended, I asked and obtained an honorable dismission from Williams College, and, going back to Cummington, began to prepare myself for entering the Junior class at Yale."

Cullen's opinion of Williams College, as expressed in his later comment on his seven months spent there and in his satire *Descriptio Gulielmopolis*, was chiefly negative. Any bitterness he may have felt was diluted with the passage of time.* When a friend, many years afterward, suggested that his satire should be printed he replied: "Oh, no! it was one of my boyish pranks. I have no copy of the lines, nor do I remember much about them. At the time, I believe, I did not like the dark rooms, the low-lying land, and the rigid college regulations, and I suppose I so expressed myself in the verses." Any positive benefits he received can only be surmised or inferred from the writing that he did immediately afterward. For a boy who had scarcely known anyone outside his family or encountered minds, except his father's, that were not hidebound by narrow theological dogma, the experience of being exposed to other youths and young men with different backgrounds and beliefs must have been salutary. He made no lasting friendships for, as he wrote, his "stay in college was hardly long

---

*After Bryant achieved fame as a poet and newspaper editor, he was considered an honorary alumnus and attended several class reunions at Williamstown. In 1863 he wrote a poem, "Fifty Years," for the fiftieth anniversary of the class of 1813, the year he would have graduated if he had remained at Williams.

enough to form those close and life-long intimacies of which college is generally the parent." But the freer thinkers among them may have weakened the hold on him of the Calvinistic faith and made it possible for him, as he did a few years later—perhaps a few months later—to arrive at more liberal beliefs as to the relationships between God and man and nature. His resentment of the tyranny of the faculty over the thoughts and persons of the students must have also reinforced his love of liberty. Finally, although he did not write much verse, his study of Greek literature and his translations imbued his poetry with the spirit of order and proportion, of harmony and simplicity, of controlled imagination and passion, that are considered to be classical. He might have arrived at all these values in any case but the few months away from dominating home influences perhaps helped.

4

O'ER COKE'S BLACK LETTER PAGE

SHORTLY AFTER CULLEN RETURNED TO CUMMINGTON EARLY in May of 1811, his mother's diary records that a calf was killed. Her entry does not indicate whether it was done to celebrate the return of the sixteen-year-old prodigal,[1] but his homecomings were always welcome events to his brothers. The youngest brother John reminisced: "When I was yet a child, I well remember that his return home was always an occasion of joy to the whole family, in which I warmly participated. . . . He was lively and playful, tossed me about, and frolicked with me in a way that made me look upon him as my best friend." Arthur recalled that they roamed the hills, on occasion declaiming poems, Cullen shouting a strophe of a chorus from *Oedipus Tyrannus* he had translated and Arthur responding with the antistrophe.[2]

But in leaving Williams expecting to be admitted to Yale in the fall, Cullen knew that he must buckle down to study for the entrance examination. Thus, as he wrote in his autobiography, he pursued his studies with "some diligence" though "without any guide save my books." His curious mind led him also to take up some other pursuits that he considered merely a pastime:

> While I was engaged in the studies of which I have spoken, the medical
> library of my father being at hand, I read, in a very desultory manner, of

course, portions both of the more formal treatises and of the periodicals, and became much interested in the medical art. . . . The science of chemistry had, not long before that time, been reformed and reduced by Lavoisier substantially to the system now received, and provided with a new nomenclature. By the aid of experiments performed in my father's office, with the chemical agents which a country practitioner of medicine was obliged to keep at home, I became a pretty good chemist as far as the science, since that time vastly enlarged and extended, was then carried. I also acquired some knowledge of botany from works in my father's library, in which the Linnaean system was explained and illustrated. These readings and studies formed an agreeable relaxation, if I may call it, from my more laborious academic studies, but I have never regretted the time which I gave them.

Though the hardships of a physician's life, as Cullen saw them in the case of his father, disinclined him to take up medicine, he later adopted the principles of homoeopathy (the treatment of disease by drugs which produce in healthy persons symptoms similar to those of the disease), headed for years the Homoeopathic Society of New York Physicians, served as a director of the society's hospital, and treated members of his family and friends according to the principles of the system. He later on also kept himself informed of scientific developments, particularly the new science of geology, in which he found support for his beliefs in order and change. But the science he knew best was botany. He studied the subject formally and in later years experimented at his country home with raising varieties of plants gathered from many parts of the world. His own poems on flowers and trees and his other descriptions of nature reveal that he was botanically accurate as well as poetically imaginative.*

In these months of study, broken by excursions in the countryside, Cullen also found time to follow his literary interests—he read, as he recalled, all the poetry that came his way. At this age the poetry he discovered that did not relate to his studies of Latin and Greek must have had a great impact upon his mind, helping him no doubt to form his own theories and reform his own practices. It is not without reason, then, that scholars have emphasized the significance of this paragraph in Bryant's autobiography:

---

*The naturalist and writer John Burroughs praised Bryant for "closely studying Nature as she appears under our own skies." Yet he had some quibbles, saying that Bryant "sometimes tripped upon his facts, and at other times he deliberately moulded them, adding to, or cutting off, to suit the purposes of his verse." "Nature and the Poets," in Complete Writings (New York, 1924), VII, 90–6.

About this time my father brought home, I think from one of his visits to Boston, the "Remains of Henry Kirke White," which had been republished in this country. I read the poems with great eagerness, and so often that I had committed several of them to memory, particularly the ode to the Rosemary. The melancholy tone which prevails in them deepened the interest with which I read them, for about that time I had, as young poets are apt to have, a liking for poetry of a querulous cast. I remember reading, at this time, that remarkable poem, Blair's "Grave," and dwelling with great pleasure upon its finer passages. I had the opportunity of comparing it with a poem on a kindred subject, also in blank verse, that of Bishop Porteus on "Death," and of observing how much the verse of the obscure Scottish minister excelled in originality of thought and vigor of expression that of the English prelate. In my father's library I found a small, thin volume of the miscellaneous poems of Southey, to which he had not called my attention,* containing some of the finest of Southey's shorter poems. I read greedily. Cowper's poems had been in my hands from an early age, and I now passed from his shorter poems, which are generally mere rhymed prose, to his "Task," the finer passages of which supplied a form of blank verse that captivated my admiration.

This is the last paragraph of Bryant's autobiographical fragment,** a circumstance that scholars have regretted, with Parke Godwin, who said that it ended "just at the time when the poet was going to tell us of the

---

*Arthur Bryant recalled in a letter to Parke Godwin, Nov. 21, 1879: "I have reason to believe that my father disliked Southey's poetry—he had only a small volume of him in the library." Goddard-Roslyn Collection.

**An additional paragraph is contained in a manuscript in the Goddard-Roslyn Collection. It is quoted by William Cullen Bryant, II, in "The Genesis of 'Thanatopsis,'" *New England Quarterly,* June, 1948: "I cannot say precisely whether the poem entitled Thanatopsis was written in 1811 or 1812, probably the latter—before I had completed my eighteenth year. I find that I was at Cummington at the time, and that and the Inscription for the Entrance to a Wood were written about the same time. My father found these two poems at Cummington while I was living at Great Barrington, took them with him to Boston, and had them published in the North American Review, then a magazine, in the year 1817. By some misunderstanding it happened that the Thanatopsis was taken for my father's till I afterward claimed it."

On other occasions Bryant also said that the poem was written when he was seventeen or eighteen years old. He told his friend and biographer James Grant Wilson that he was "much inclined to think it was in my eighteenth year." *Bryant and His Friends* (New York, 1886), p. 36. This could mean as late as 1813, since Bryant was born on Nov. 3, 1794. The "Inscription" is dated 1815 by Godwin; if, as Bryant said, the two fragments were written at the same time, the first version of "Thanatopsis" could have been written as late as this year. *Poetical Works* (Godwin, ed., New York, 1883), I, 24. William Cullen Bryant, II, accepts this year. He also writes that it is probable that Cullen began his reading of the "graveyard poets" in 1813 rather than 1811, for among the Bryant manuscripts are a number of poems and fragments on death dated 1814 and 1815, obviously derived from the English poets "of querulous cast." It is equally probable, of course, that Bryant first encountered these poets in 1811 and continued his reading of them over the following years.

various influences under which his 'Thanatopsis' was written."[3] For it has generally been held that Bryant's reading of these "graveyard poets" led him to muse about death, and, in answer to questions they posed, to adopt the beliefs expressed in the lofty blank-verse lines of his major achievement. Thus, if Bryant wrote the poem before his birthday on November 3, he would have been but sixteen years old, or, if afterward, seventeen. Poetic genius is, of course, frequent in young people—perhaps more commonly found in youth than in age—but even so the writing of such a poem at so young an age would be remarkable. The fact is, however, that the writing of "Thanatopsis," even in its first fragmentary versions that exist among the Bryant manuscripts, cannot be definitely assigned to the year 1811; and, if it could, the poem went through so many revisions before reaching its final form in 1821 that it would be wrong to assert it was the product of a precocious juvenile. The seed may have sprouted in 1811 but the plant needed several years of growth in which to mature.

If Cullen was having thoughts at this time of "the last bitter hour" that blighted his spirit, he soon had another reason to grow sick at heart, for his father reached the unhappy decision that there was no money to send him to Yale. He was now confronted with the momentous problem of what he should, or could, do with his life. As a way of making a living, literature, his consuming interest, was no answer. No one at that time was a fulltime professional writer, and a related field, journalism, either on magazines or newspapers, was so little developed that it held out little promise. Medicine, of course, was a possibility. It is a tribute to Dr. Bryant's sympathy with the desires of his son that he did not press him to become a physician, following the course of several paternal ancestors. This choice would have solved the financial problem, for training could be obtained in Dr. Bryant's own office. But the hardships of the profession and the scanty financial rewards, as well as his own literary interests, deterred Dr. Bryant from asking Cullen to pursue it. The ministry, even if Cullen had had an inclination for it, was out of the question, for it required a college education. The law, of the learned professions, therefore seemed to be the most practical as well as the best to which the youth could apply his talents. The decision was made: he would read law in a lawyer's office to prepare for being admitted to the bar.[4]

II

Sarah Bryant's diary records on December 3, 1811, that, after the washing and mending, she cut out a coat for Cullen; four days later she writes that it was completed; and on December 9 she says in a sentence: "Cullen went to Worthington to tarry awhile." The entry meant that he was beginning a career in which he had no interest, only four or five miles from home in a village where he would have to apply himself to tedious legal tomes and learn the practice of law under a friend of his father, Samuel Howe, who had been admitted to the bar in 1807 and had maintained an office for a time in Stockbridge before moving across the hills to Worthington.

Cullen expressed his disappointment in a letter to his friend Avery in December,[5] writing that Worthington had nothing to offer better than "a blacksmith-shop and cow-stable, at either of which places he might be found, while the only entertainment afforded was bound up in the pages of 'Knickerbocker.' "* But he did not give up hope that he might yet go to Yale, for on January 9, 1812, he wrote Avery asking if it would be possible to enter at the beginning or middle of the next term. He added, with the Worthington smithy in mind: "However, if I should not enter *this time* I shall quit study and go to farming or turn mechanic. Would not blacksmithing be as good a trade as any for the display of one's abilities? Vulcan though the son of Jupiter and *sleeping partner* of Cytherea, gloried in his skill in *hot iron* and forging the thunderbolts of Eternal Jove."

The Freudian implications of the last sentence are evidenced also in the next paragraph:

> "Much study," says Solomon, "is a weariness of the flesh," and I think Solomon perfectly in the right. Yet, without this "weariness of the flesh," I conjecture that Solomon would never have attained to what reputation for learning and wisdom that he possessed. You may perhaps smile at my gravity when I add that all the learning and wisdom of Solomon did not prevent him from going "after strange women and idols in his old age."
> ————Bacon notwithstanding he was the wisest brightest was yet the "meanest of mankind." The government of passion rather than the acquisition of science ought to be the study of man. Of what benefit is it that the understanding and imagination should be cultivated when the heart, the fountain of all noble and infamous actions, lies, like a garden covered with weeds whose rank luxuriance chokes even the plants that are natural to the soil.————Learning only points to the easier gratification of our sensualities and teaches us to conceal our passions, only to give them vent when the shackles of law and disgrace are removed. All the dark deliberate, and subtle machinations of iniquity, every plan that has ever been formed against the

*The reference is to Washington Irving's *Knickerbocker's History of New York.*

peace and prosperity of the human race, by confederated art and villainy, have been organized and directed chiefly by mean of learning. . . .[6]

It requires no great psychological insight to see that in this confused letter Cullen's stirring adolescent sexuality had been brought almost to the surface of his consciousness by the setback to his college career.

Avery disagreed with Cullen's conclusions. After telling him that nothing except failure to pass the entrance examination would prevent his entering Yale, he commented on Cullen's outburst about the dangers of learning: "I approve of your philosophy, in general, that it is more noble to rule the passions, than to penetrate the depths of mathematical science, or shine in the department of literature. But what of all this? Cannot a man be virtuous and learned too? He certainly can, and where learning is accompanied with virtue, it is a source of rational enjoyment."[7]

An adolescent is likely to suffer the extremes of elation and depression, and no doubt this was true of Cullen at Worthington. While he was telling Avery of his despair in not getting to go to Yale and his discontent with Worthington, he wrote more favorably of his situation in a short poem "Ad Musam":

> So long neglectful of thy dues,
>   And absent from thy shrine so long,
> Say, wilt thou deign, Immortal Muse,
>   Again to inspire thy votary's song?
> The time has been when fresh as air
>   I loved at morn the hills to climb,
> With dew-drenched feet and bosom bare,
>   And ponder on the artless rhyme;
> And through the long laborious day
>   (For mine has been the peasant's toil),
> I hummed the meditated lay,
>   While the slow oxen turned the soil.[8]

The escape from farm work, even if it meant studying law, no doubt had its compensations.

There were other compensations, for Cullen was not Howe's only student. He formed friendships with two others, Elisha Hubbard and George Downes, and the three corresponded for several years after each had hung out his shingle in different Massachusetts towns. One of Cullen's letters reveals that the blacksmith shop where Vulcan forged his thunderbolts was not the only Worthington place he frequented. He also discovered the haunts of Bacchus. Comparing Worthington with Bridgewater, to which he went in 1814 to continue his study of law, he wrote Downes: "I am certainly as well contented with this place as I could be with any, and I would not exchange it for Worthington if the wealth of the Indies were thrown into that side of the balance; yet I must acknowledge that, when I think of Ward's store, and Mills's tavern, and Taylor's grogshop, and Sears's, and Daniels's, and Briggs's, &c, &c, such cool, comfortable lounging-places, it makes me rather melancholy, for there is not a tavern in this parish."9

Eros was another god that entered Cullen's life in his first spring and summer in Worthington, for among the poet's papers are poems and fragments indicating that he had fallen in love.10 Parke Godwin was at first inclined to consider these mere literary exercises suggested by a reading of the love poems of Paulus Silentiarius, Anacreon, Bion, and Virgil— some of the verses were paraphrases of these poets—and perhaps Byron and other English Romantics. But some showed a depth of feeling that led Godwin to suspect there was an actual object of Cullen's affection. He wrote that he was confirmed in this suspicion by recollections of Arthur Bryant, who said that, while Cullen was at Worthington "a distinguished friend of their father came from Rhode Island on a visit to Cummington, bringing with him a beautiful and accomplished daughter, who fascinated the poet, so that for some time afterward they maintained an earnest correspondence." Since the facts of the case are not known, Godwin's reconstruction can be considered plausible, for Cullen would have had to be an abnormal youth not to be attracted by girls and if he did not fall in love, or fancy himself in love, he should have at this age. But the verses, written over a period of two or three years, follow so closely the conventions of poetic love that one is led to believe Cullen's emotions were probably as much literary as real. Godwin carefully chose the poems to tell a tale in which he exercised a great deal of license: worship from afar at first, then a more intimate expression of admiration, the poet's resistance to the "syren song" of his beloved and his capitulation, the separation of man and maid, and finally his disillusionment with one who proved guilty of "fraud and guile and faithless art." Another story could be woven from the same materials, one in which the beloved died and the poet, in the convention of the writers of a "querulous cast" who appealed to him, visited her grave where "cold clods press" upon her and where also are "darkness and the worm."

Though the biographical importance of these poems may not be great, they have an interest in the development of Cullen's prosody, for in them he broke away from the stiff iambic couplets he had been wont to write and practiced in more various meters and stanzaic forms. Some of them, though imitative, are pleasant and musical statements of conventional Romantic love:

> There is a charm of heavenly birth,
> A charm of mystick name,
> Of power the virgin's laughing eye
> To light with lovelier flame,
>
> That bids the rose-enamelled cheek
> A riper blush assume,
> To beauty gives a fairer grace,
> To youth a deeper bloom.

Others, however, take on a more somber cast, perhaps influenced by Cullen's reading of Henry Kirke White. In one the poet speaks of the death of a beloved:

> Alone in the moonlight I knelt at the grave
> Where slumbered of Ellen the all that could die
> And the tears that to bitter remembrance I gave
> Gleamed mixed on the turf with the dews of the sky.

In another verse he sees the dear face of his loved one among the "Shades" of his friends who have died:

> It was my love—that form I knew—
> The same that glazed unmoving eye;
> And the pure cheek of bloodless hue,
> As when she slept with those that die.

But these funereal stanzas must be considered in connection with another body of verse written at Worthington that has a greater relevance to Bryant's growth than a passing love affair, fictive or real. These poems have to do with his dread of death, taught him in his childhood by his Calvinist elders. They constitute a remarkable psychological document of the youth's gropings through doubt and despair to reach a final affirmation in the poem "Thanatopsis."

III

The romantic interlude that can be manufactured from the love poems written at Worthington is a beguiling one that would adorn the biography of any poet but especially that of Bryant, whose character was considered by many people a cold one. Equally attractive, from this view, are the hints in Bryant's letters to his fellow law students that he was abandoned enough as a youth to lounge about in grogshops and taverns, to get off his dignity once in awhile and be one of the boys. Bryant was never an outgoing person but his aloofness may have been not so much that he maintained an inner check because of his rectitude but that he was merely shy. Certainly he was a diffident youth at Worthington, since, with the exception of his few months at Williams College, he had never familiarly associated with any people other than the members of his family and even to have had no boyhood companions other than his brothers. Mr. Howe's bride, whom he brought into the household in Worthington in 1813, perceived this in some reminiscences.

> The first time I saw Mr. Bryant was in the autumn of 1813; he was then a student in my husband's office, and about nineteen years of age. He was quiet, reserved, and diffident, so that I formed but little acquaintance with him; but I learned from my husband that he was a diligent student, not only of his profession, but all the good books he had time for, including the classics and botany. He was a practical botanist, going to the woods and fields for his specimens. My husband feared that Bryant would be backward about speaking, and, I think, wrote to him afterward to accustom himself to the practice. I doubt if he ever satisfied himself in that branch of his profession.[11]

By this time Cullen had become somewhat reconciled to the law, or at least had some good things to say about it in response to a letter from Avery who mentioned that he was considering it as a career. Cullen wrote on March 27, 1813, that he was happy to hear Avery express "so favorable an opinion" of the profession, "the more so because it was something different from what I expected." "It has been called dry," Cullen added, "but you are doubtless acquainted with a class of people to whom drudgery and labour are synonymous."[12]

Mr. Howe discouraged Cullen in activities that did not pertain to the law. Discovering him one day reading *Lyrical Ballads,* Mr. Howe warned him against wasting his time.[13] Cullen took the advice seriously, for in one of his poems of the time he wrote that he had forsaken poetry but was inspired to return to it by the wedding in March of 1813 of his childhood friend and duelist in rhyme, Jacob Porter. The poem ended:

> O'er Coke's black letter page,
> Trimming the lamp at eve, 't is mine to pore;
> Well pleased to see the venerable sage

56

Unlock his treasur'd wealth of legal lore;
And I, that lov'd to trace the woods before
And climb the hill a play mate of the breeze
Have vow'd to tune the rural lay no more,
Have bid my useless classic sleep at ease,
And left the race of bards to scribble, starve and freeze.

Farewell.—When mildly through the naked wood,
The clear warm sun effus'd a mellow ray
And livelier health propell'd the vital flood,
Forgot the cares and business of the day,
Forgot the quirks of Littleton and Coke,
Forgot the publick storms, and party fray;
And, as the inspiring flame across me broke,
To thee the lowly harp, neglected long, I woke.[14]

The "publick storms" refer to the clamor in Congress to go to war with England over the seizure of ships and impressment of sailors in her conflict with France. Upon the request of President Madison, Congress did declare war on June 18, 1812, members from New England and other northern maritime states voting against it. Cullen took note of it by a request, made through his father, that he write a Fourth of July ode for the Washington Benevolent Society of Boston.* But in Cullen's patriotic stanzas Napoleon was the enemy and not England:

Should Justice call to battle
The applauding shout we'd raise;
A million swords would leave their sheath,
A million bayonets blaze.[15]

For more than a year Cullen remained personally uninvolved in the war, though he wrote Avery in March, 1813: "Amidst the awful concussions and changes which are taking place in the moral, political and physical world I must doubt whether the good man can find any better consolation than that the hand of an over-ruling and all directing Providence will prescribe the course of revolutions, mark the bounds of war and slaughter and recall from the hot pursuit his ministers of vengeance."

If Cullen seemed to be untouched by these "awful concussions and changes," it was probably due, not to a love affair but to events that turned his mind to thoughts of "breathless darkness, and the narrow house." One of these events was an epidemic which swept Worthington described in

*Henry S. Gore, editor of the *Hampshire Gazette* in the 1880 s, reported that the poem was printed on July 15, 1812, with an indication that it was to be sung to the tune of "Ye Gentlemen of England." The 1812 editor introduced it: "Want of room last week obliged us to delay the publication of the following elegant and patriotic ode, from the pen of Mr. William C. Bryant, son of Dr. Bryant of Cummington." *Bryant Centennial/Cummington/ August the Sixteenth/1894* (Springfield, Mass., 1894), p. 74.

the letter to Avery: "A strange species of the typhus accompanied in most but not all cases with an infection of the lungs . . . has visited us with the most alarming ravages. Three or four die in a week nor does the disorder seem much to abate. . . ."[16] Shortly after this two other deaths struck home to the youth. The first was that of the bride of Cullen's friend Porter. On May 24, Porter wrote Cullen from Plainfield that she was "very much out of health." "If she fall," Porter said, "I hope your lyre will not be silent on the occasion."[17] Her death aroused Cullen to write in July a threnody that began:

> Alas! When late for thee I twined,
> And thy lost love, the bridal wreath,
> I little thought so soon to bind
> The cypress round the urn of death.[18]

The second was the death of the stern and retributive figure of Cullen's childhood, his Grandfather Snell, on August 2. Squire Snell had walked to church on Sunday and had gone to bed that night as well as usual so far as the family could tell. But the next morning, when someone went to his room to see why he was late for breakfast, he was discovered dead in bed.[19] The stanzas for Eliza Porter were the first of a number of mortuary verses which Cullen began to write at this time reflecting for the most part a stark fear of death.

Godwin assumed from the closing paragraphs of Bryant's autobiographical fragment mentioning his reading of the Rev. Robert Blair, Bishop Beilby Porteus, and Henry Kirke White that he was inspired in the fall of 1811 to compose "Thanatopsis." According to his account, Cullen in his walks about the countryside was led to muse upon the questions raised in their poems and saw a correspondence between human mortality and the "tokens of decay" in nature and conceived of the earth as being a great sepulchre. One afternoon Cullen hurried home and wrote the poem for which, Godwin said, he coined a name from the Greek, "Thanatopsis."[20] This version has been accepted by most literary historians. The circumstances surrounding the composition of the poem and Bryant's age at the time have been the subject of so much discussion, however, that it is worthwhile to consider the history of the poem in some detail.

Bryant himself on several occasions when he was asked about the poem said it was written when he was seventeen or eighteen. But he was in his sixties when he replied to the questions, and the circumstantial details had grown dim in his memory, as he once confessed: "I cannot give you any information of the occasion which suggested to my mind the idea of my poem 'Thanatopsis.' It was written when I was seventeen or eighteen years old—I have not now at hand the memorandum which would enable me to be precise—and I believe it was composed in my solitary rambles in the woods. . . ."[21] But there is conflicting documentary evidence, one a "Copy of a Memorandum found among Mr. Bryant's papers—Mrs. Bryant's Handwriting," which lists the date of the poem as 1813. Thus, if one must speculate on the date of the poem, it might be well to trace the development of the young poet's ideas on death in the funerary verse he wrote in 1813 and 1814. This process leads to the conclusion that the poem was composed later than the date usually given and that it was the outgrowth of a real emotional upheaval.

The view that Cullen was led to ponder upon death by his reading of the "graveyard poets" is plausible, but it is just as likely that he was led to study them to find an answer to the questionings aroused in his own mind by his firsthand experience of death during the summer of 1813. There can be no quarrel with the interpretation, however, that "Thanatopsis" was written in part in response to his readings, for the influence of the poems he read is clearly seen in his own poems.

In his autobiographical fragment Bryant said that he considered Blair's *The Grave* superior to Porteus's *Death*. A comparison with his own poems, including "Thanatopsis," reveals how greatly Blair, the "obscure Scottish minister," affected him, so much so that his own lines show close similarity not only in themes but also in phraseology. He was appalled by the sense of death and gropingly sought some belief that would deny what he knew to be a universal truth, or if not this, a way in which man could approach it with equanimity. At this time he could find no consolation in the conventional Christian view that the soul of man upon dying would go to heaven if he had faith or to hell if not.

The Grave contains some seven hundred lines written in a vigorous blank verse and in strong, simple language.[22] Blair begins by saying that his task is "To paint the gloomy horrors of the tomb," and he succeeds, conjuring up dire images of ghosts in the graveyard:

> Roused from their slumbers,
> In grim array the grisly spectres rise,
> Grin horrible, and obstinately sullen,
> Pass and repass, hush'd as the foot of night.

But while Blair portrays the ghosts as troubled spirits shrieking from "the hollow tombs" and the grave as a dread place "Furr'd round with mouldy damps and ropy slime" Cullen, in a poem, "A Chorus of Ghosts," obviously inspired by him, looks upon it as a place where restless man may find peace. His ghosts speak to man:

59

> Come to thy couch of iron rest,
>   Come share our dreamless bed;
> There's room, within the grave-yard bounds,
>   To lay thy weary head.

Blair's schoolboy passing the graveyard, "Whistling aloud to bear his courage up," finds this echo in the "Chorus":

> There, as he seeks his tardy kine,
>   When flames the evening sky
> With thoughtful look, the cottage boy
>   Shall pass thy dwelling by.

But though Cullen sought to accept the idea that death brought the peace of the grave he could not bring himself to do so and argued with himself in lines written about the same time:

> It chills my very soul, to think
> Of that dread hour when life must end.

The most significant outcome of Cullen's grappling with this problem of man's annihilation and his greatest indebtedness to Blair are found in the middle portion of "Thanatopsis." Cullen, as does Blair, develops the theme that it is the common doom of all men to die, but where Blair devotes several hundred lines to the subject Cullen distills it into only forty-nine lines. Blair's is the method of elaboration; Cullen's, that of abstraction. His method has been described by the poet William Ellery Leonard:

> Bryant wonderfully visualized and unified the vast scope of the racial move-ment and the range of natural phenomena. His "broad surveys," as they have been called, are more than surveys: They are large acts of the combin-ing imagination, presenting the significance, not merely the catalogue. These acts take us home to the most inveterate habit of his poet-mind. . . . The task is . . . not to make a list, but to make the right list; a list not by capricious association of ideas, but by the law of inner harmony of mean-ing. . . .[23]

Thus Cullen's catalogue of those that must lie down "all in one mighty sepulchre" takes only three lines. Blair's poem enumerates the same hu-man characters, and many more, each described in ten, twenty, or thirty lines.

Cullen's view that the world is "one mighty sepulchre" or "the great tomb of man" is a close echo of Blair, who writes:

> What is this world?
> What but a spacious burial-field unwall'd,
> Strew'd with death's spoils, the spoils of animals
> Savage and tame, and full of dead men's bones?
> The very turf on which we tread once lived;
> And we that live, must lend our carcases
> To cover our own offspring; in their turns
> They too must cover theirs.

Many other echoes of tone and expression can be found, but when it came to answering the question posed by Blair—how "to learn to die"—Cullen was at a loss. Blair's answer, the Christian belief that a day of Resurrection will come when all will go to heaven, was unacceptable to Cullen, though no doubt he appreciated the beauty of Blair's final lines:

> We make the grave our bed, and then are gone.
> Thus at the shut of even, the weary bird
> Leaves the wide air, and in some lonely brake
> Cowers down, and dozes till the dawn of day;
> Then claps his well-fledged wings, and bears away.

Cullen's conclusion to "Thanatopsis," though affixed some years later, denies this expectation of an after-life—there is no mention of dawn and an awakening after sleep. The poem ends:

> approach thy grave,
> Like one who wraps the drapery of his couch
> About him, and lies down to pleasant dreams.

But this stoical acceptance was one that Cullen could not achieve when he first wrote the fragment.

The influence of Porteus, bishop of London, upon Cullen's verse is less apparent, though the essential question, "How should man approach death?" is asked and answered in different ways in poems composed at this time. Cullen agrees with the bishop's view of man's innate resistance to death, in which man is portrayed

> unwilling to be wrench'd
> From this fair scene, from all her custom'd joys

but he was unwilling to accept a direct appeal to the "Almighty Father" to "smooth the restless bed" and calm all fears until the soul

> Bursts from the thralldom of encumbering clay,
> And on the wings of ecstasy upborne,
> Springs into Liberty, and Light, and Life![24]

Henry Kirke White's life, as well as his literary remains, must have had a melancholy appeal to the young Bryant, for their circumstances were not unlike. A member of a poor family, White, like Cullen, was articled to the law; and though addressing himself industriously to learning his profession, he too expressed his hopes and fears in verse. Through the aid of friends, White was able to go to Cambridge University; but, his health weakened by zealous devotion to study, he died with his poetic promise unfulfilled at the age of twenty. Young poets are traditionally gloomy, but White must have been one of the gloomiest that ever lived, for hardly a poem of his deals with anything other than death.

Bryant found him a kindred spirit, his lines on Eliza Porter reflecting in manner and substance White's ode to the rosemary:

> Come, thou shalt form my nosegay now,
> And I will bind thee round my brow;
>   And as I twine the mournful wreath,
> I'll weave a melancholy song;
> And sweet the strain shall be, and long,
>   The melody of death.

The opening of "Thanatopsis" in which Bryant says that to the lover of Nature she speaks "A various language" may also have been suggested by lines by White:

> Yet nature speaks within the human bosom,
> And, spite of reason, bids it look beyond
> His narrow verge of being. . . .[25]

During 1813 and 1814, then, Cullen grappled with the question of death and sought to calm his fears though rejecting the answers he found in his reading of the poets as well as the Christian reassurance of an afterlife. But among his poems at this time was a forty-nine line fragment in blank verse which constitutes the middle portion of "Thanatopsis" as it is known today, beginning with the half line:

————Yet a few days, and thee,
The all-beholding sun, shall see no more
In all his course. . . .

Although satisfied with what he had written about the universality of
death, Cullen had not, however, answered the questions nor quieted the
fears that had caused him so much mental turmoil. Thus, as the fragment
begins with an imcomplete line of verse, it also ends with an incomplete
line that says that all must leave

Their mirth and their employments, and shall come
And make their bed with thee!————

Testimony varies as to exactly how this fragment reached print in the
North American Review in 1817, though it is known that it was submitted
to the editors by Dr. Bryant and not by Cullen. The most commonly
accepted version is Parke Godwin's, that Cullen did not take it to his father
for criticism but instead placed it in a pigeonhole of the doctor's desk, on
which it was written, possibly fearing an adverse reaction because the lines
were irreligious in not considering death the penalty of man's disobedi-
ence of God but rather a part of universal nature. This supposition, considering Dr. Bryant's liberal religious views, seems to be farfetched and is
inconsistent with the statement that, finding it with some other verses on
death, he submitted them to the magazine. Godwin's account would have
Cullen dashing off the fragment in a few moments of inspiration and
putting it aside to complete later. But Bryant's practice in composition,
even in writing letters, would indicate otherwise; his manuscripts show
that he labored over his first drafts, making frequent changes, and that he
carefully recopied them when he considered that he had achieved a satisfactory form. The fragment that Dr. Bryant found was not something done
in a poetic frenzy but the result, as the evidence of the other poems written
at the time indicates, of more than one attempt. Cullen had finally
achieved a statement that satisfied him, and he put it aside expecting to
return to it later, being prevented from doing so because, being away from
home, he did not have the fragment at hand. Composing a beginning and
an end to complete the work as to poetic form and philosophical substance
came several years later when his attention was attracted to it by publication in the *North American Review.*

IV

After two and one-half years of application to law books under Mr. Howe, Cullen in June of 1814 went to Bridgewater to get his office training under William Baylies, a well-known attorney and a member of Congress since 1808. His versifying on love and death continued for the first few months after he left Worthington, but gradually he became more personally involved in the war with England and in politics and devoted himself less and less to the Muse, possibly because Mr. Baylies during his absences in Washington left the office in the charge of his assistant. Cullen kept Mr. Baylies informed in letters of the public sentiment in Bridgewater and in turn Mr. Baylies wrote him in detail about what was happening in the capital, information that Cullen relayed to the local people. The youth had wanted to complete his training in a Boston law office, but this was ruled out on the ground of cost, Dr. Bryant telling him that $400 had been spent on his education in Worthington and there were other children to be launched into careers.

Within a month after going to Bridgewater, Cullen responded to the request of the Washington Benevolent Society for another Fourth of July ode.* In it he referred to the American military defeats in the poorly conducted campaigns against Canada:

> Our skies have glowed with burning towns,
>   Our snows have blushed with gore,
> And fresh is many a nameless grave
>   By Erie's weeping shore.
> In sadness let the anthem flow—
>   But tell the men of strife,
> On their own heads shall rest the guilt
>   Of all this waste of life.

Then, as he had done two years before in his Worthington ode, he attacked Napoleon's military depredations and, reflecting a broad cross section of New England opinion, lauded England, "Queen of Isles," for holding back the Gallic scourge.[26]

That Cullen had acquitted himself creditably in his studies is revealed by the fact that in August he was examined by a bar committee at Plymouth which recommended that he be admitted to practice at the August

---

*Printed in the *Hampshire Gazette,* July 12, 1815, with this introduction: "The following ode, the production of Mr. William C. Bryant, a young gentleman to whom we have been repeatedly indebted for his elegant and poetic effusions, was received at too late an hour to occupy the place it so well deserves in our festivals. We cannot, however, refrain from giving it to our readers." *Bryant Centennial/Cummington/August the Sixteenth/1894,* p. 74.

term of court in 1815. His diligence had reduced the usual five-year training period to four. To his former classmate at Worthington, Elisha Hubbard, now in Northampton, Cullen expressed satisfaction with his situation at Bridgewater, in a letter dated August 30. He praised Mr. Baylies: "Everybody, even those who entertain the greatest dislike to lawyers in general, concur in ascribing to him the merit of honesty. You, who know how much calumny is heaped upon the members of our profession, even the most uncorrupt, can estimate the strict and scrupulous integrity necessary to acquire this reputation." He then went on to dilate on the fair ladies of Bridgewater, there being many more of them than at Worthington.[27] Hubbard replied on September 13 that Cullen's "situation in one respect must be tolerable, surrounded as you are by so much beauty." The difficult part of it was brought out by Hubbard: "This universal love answers well for philosophers, brought up in the school of Zeno—but for a man of your temperament, so many objects, equally dear, and still desirous of choice is perplexing."[28] If Cullen did have a love affair with a visitor at Worthington, he got over it quickly at Bridgewater.

Cullen's other Worthington friend, George Downes, wrote him saying that he had encountered Dr. Bryant, who had mentioned his desire to finish his studies in Boston. Downes protested that Cullen would not like Boston and that after three months in the "metropolis" he "would be pleased with a retreat even in Worthington." Downes recalled a conversation in which he had advised Cullen to go to Boston "two or three months before you practiced for the purpose of attending courts and engaging a little in the pleasures of the town to wear off a little of your rusticity as you were pleased to term it."[29]

Cullen replied that Downes was mistaken in thinking he had asked his father for permission to go to Boston: "The plan in the first place was proposed by him and I wrote merely to enquire his wishes, mentioning next winter, because I thought it the only eligible time to reside there." He reported in some detail on his social life, which was such that he would not exchange Bridgewater for Worthington "if the wealth of the Indies were thrown into that side of the balance." He described a ball, which had been postponed several times because of bad weather: "At last, despairing of ever having a clear sky, we got together in a most tremendous thunderstorm, and a very good scrape we had of it." The ball lasted until three o'clock in the morning. The next day he set out with five other couples for a sailing party at Middleborough about thirteen miles away. Although rain threatened, the weather cleared and a delightful day was had. "Mine host and hostess," he related, "were very accommodating; they gave us some fine grapes and peaches, a good dinner, and tolerable wine."[30]

Cullen soon had more serious things to think of than balls and boating parties, for the war was reaching into Bridgewater. Massachusetts opposed "Mr. Madison's war," and Cullen, in letters to Mr. Baylies, who had returned to Washington early in September, was wont to refer to the President as "his Imbecility." In July, Sir Alexander Cochrane, commander of the British naval blockade, issued orders to destroy and lay waste towns along the coast. The result, Cullen wrote Mr. Baylies on September 30, was a call upon the Massachusetts militia to protect the coast. Bridgewater militiamen were ordered to Plymouth. "This draft," Cullen said, "takes all the militia from this parish. . . . Our streets are now very solitary—the place is a perfect desert. . . . The people here grumble heartily at the affair, and seem angry that the general should think the safety of his pitiful village of more consequence than their corn and potatoes. . . . We are very anxious hear to hear from Congress; our paper of to-day, in which we expected the President's message, failed. I believe everybody knows what kind of talk to expect from the mouth of his Imbecility, if he may be so titled. . . ."[31]

Writing his father on October 10 of the exodus of the young men, Cullen said: "I was . . . almost ashamed to stay at home when everybody besides was gone, but was not a little comforted by the reflection . . . that the place was in no danger, that the detachment was entirely unnecessary, and, therefore, I might as well stay as go." Then he broached the idea of his volunteering for service in an army to be formed to defend Massachusetts. Objecting to the war, a number of towns, early in the year, had sent memorials to the legislature calling for a convention of the states to amend the federal Constitution. The people felt that it had been violated and the state's sovereignty infringed upon by the calling up of men to fight a war they opposed. It was the duty of the state to interpose its authority for the protection of its citizens. With these memorials in mind, Cullen wrote his father asking if it would be proper for him "to have anything to do with the army which is to be raised by voluntary enlistment for the defence of the state." He pointed out that the force might not be "altogether employed against a foreign enemy" but "in the defence of dearer rights than those which are endangered in a contest with Great Britain." He recognized that if control at Washington was thrown off, the state would "revert to an independent empire," but felt that such action would lessen the probability of bloodshed on the ground that the administration "awed by our strength" would not attempt the subjection of the state.

Besides these abstract reasons for joining the army Cullen had some personal reasons:

If I enter upon my profession next year I shall come into the world raw and rustic to a degree uncommon in most persons of my age and situation in all the greenness of a secluded education without that respect which greater maturity of years would give me. Now as I understand the matter the objection which is made to my spending five years in the study of the law is not upon the grounds that I shall not come soon enough into business but that the expenses attending my education would be greater than you could meet without injuring the interest of the family. In this reason I have always concurred and this it is that has led me to endeavour to shorten the term of my studies as much as possible. If I should enter into the service of the state I should procure the means of present support and perhaps with prudence, might enable myself to complete my studies without further assistance. I should come into the world likewise with my excessive bashfulness and rusticity rubbed off by a military life. . . .[32]

No immediate decision was made, and Cullen continued his work in Mr. Baylies's office.

On October 21 Elisha Hubbard wote Cullen saying that his latest letter "excited a wish that I could participate with you in your unalloyed pleasures," and he advised his friend: "As you in your present situation are surrounded by Dianas do not prove an Endimion and kiss them by moon light."[33] But shortly Cullen was compelled to forsake his pleasures and studies. He had lost weight and probably there were indications he was threatened by consumption. Therefore, sometime in November, he returned to Cummington to get his health back.

He was still possessed with the idea of joining the army, however, and on November 16 petitioned Governor Caleb Strong "for a lieutenancy in the army about to be raised for the protection and defence of Massachusetts."[34] Perhaps his illness also intensified his concern with death, for several of the funerary poems and fragments among his unpublished works are dated at this time.

Cullen's recovery was rapid, and by December 20 he was back in Bridgewater and writing his father that he weighed ten pounds more than when he had left in November. In a rough draft of a letter found among Bryant's papers the youth broached what Dr. Bryant would probably consider a frivolous project: "There is a dancing school about to be kept in the neighborhood, two evenings a week. . . . You will decide for me whether it would be proper to take advantage of the opportunity." Dissatisfied with this, Cullen made another attempt: "It has been whispered to me that I should do well to attend. You will decide for me. I should like to know your opinion soon, as it is to commence in a few days." He also noted that he had not received a response from the governor about his petition for an army lieutenancy: "I have not heard from my country to know whether it is her pleasure to accept my services or not. I begin to suspect that the jade is determined to take no notice of me." This unfinished letter, like many of the scraps found among Bryant's papers when he was playing with ideas to set down in writing, ended with some doodlings—quite often Bryant wrote his name over and over in fancy calligraphy—and ended with a translation of Fontaine's "The Oak and the Reed."[35]

During the first months of 1815 Cullen's thoughts were concerned with the Hartford Convention, called in response to a proposal by the Massachusetts legislature for a meeting to consider such matters as states' rights, the war, and the peace negotiations between the United States and England at Ghent. On January 25 he heard from his brother Austin that Dr. Bryant had been ill for a month and that there had been no word from the governor about Cullen's military commission. Austin said that Cummington Federalists were disappointed with the Hartford Convention; they believed that the delegates "dared not adopt any energetic measures, but would go on in the old way of supplication till the chains that were preparing to bind them to the earth were riveted."[36] The convention's proceedings indeed did not reflect the views of the extremist wing of the party, since the resolutions adopted merely called for protection of citizens of the states against military conscription unauthorized by the Constitution; use of federal revenue collected in these states to provide for defense of their territory; and an interstate defense machinery independent of the federal government for repelling enemy invasions. In a long reply dated February 5, Cullen repudiated the stand of the Cummington extremists and defended the convention: "Shall we attempt by force what we may perhaps obtain peaceably? The plan proposed by the convention, if it should meet with success, certainly appears competent to secure the interest of the eastern states at the same time that it preserves the Union."[37]

Cullen's adverse opinions on the war were confirmed by the Peace of Ghent proclaimed by "his Imbecility" on February 17, 1815. Writing Mr. Howe on March 19, Cullen commented that it had blown his own "military projects* to the moon," and said that he feared it would cause the Federalists to relax their exertions against the encroachment of the Republicans on the people's freedoms.[38] As to the treaty terms, he shared the

---

*A commission dated July 25, 1816, as an adjutant in the Massachusetts militia was finally sent to Bryant. He held it for less than a year, resigning Feb. 8, 1817. Godwin, *Biography*, I, 136.

sentiments of Mr. Baylies, who had written him from Washington just before the treaty was ratified by the Senate: "I believe we have not obtained even *one* of the objects, for which, it was said, we waged war—but such was the situation, to which we were reduced by the war, that peace on almost any terms, would have been considered a blessing."[39]

The time of his studies at Bridgewater drawing to an end, Cullen began thinking of his bar examination in August. On April 27 he wrote his father giving an accounting of his expenses at Bridgewater. So far his board covering forty-eight weeks at $2.25 a week amounted to $108. If admitted to the bar in August, the period of his training would comprise fifty-seven weeks—from June 10, 1814, to August, 1815—at a cost of $129.25. He added this request: "It would be convenient for me to have an additional pair of thin pantaloons this summer. If my mother should think proper to send down a pair by you next June I should like to have them middling large. . . ." He related that he had been tormented with boils on his face, commenting: "I pity poor Job if he had worse ones or more of them than I have had."[40]

In a draft of a letter dated May 24, 1815, Cullen gave a clue to Dr. Bryant's financial situation in writing that he had heard that his father "has half a score of pupils and has bought another farm and that matters at Cummington are going on in high style." "At Bridgewater, on the contrary," he wrote, "nothing is taking place to diversify the dull uniformity of existence—except that a neighbouring house caught fire yesterday—which I helped to extinguish—and brought away water enough in my clothes to help put out the conflagration of a city."[41]

By June Bryant was looking upon his entrance into the practice of law with some apprehension. He wrote his friend Downes:

> You have everything in your favor in entering upon the practice of law, accommodating your conversation to every sort of people, and rendering yourself agreeable to all. The maturity of your manners will add much to the respect you will receive upon entering into life, and the natural placidity of your temper will enable you to contemn the little rubs which will, of course, attend the young practitioner. But I lay claim to nothing of all these, and the day when I shall set up my gingerbread-board is to me a day of fearful expectation. The nearer I approach to it the more I dread it.[42]

Cullen's first mentor in the law, Mr. Howe, wrote congratulating him on his soon becoming "one of the brotherhood" and making an estimate of the young man's abilities designed to give him confidence: "From your habits and progress in your professional studies while with me I hesitate not to predict you will become a distinguished member of the fraternity."* But he also adverted to the weakness of which Cullen was extremely conscious: "I hope you have availed yourself of every opportunity to accustom yourself to speaking in publick." He told him that success as a speaker came from habit and advised: "Some persons acquire this habit more readily than others yet no person was ever able to speak gracefully and powerfully upon a first attempt. I hope also that a want of complete success in the first instance will not be suffered to discourage you."[43]

Cullen replied thanking Mr. Howe for his remarks but respectfully arguing that eloquence depended upon more than "mere industry," that it also depended upon natural gifts. "I never could believe that the maxim, *orator fit,* holds good in its full extent," he said. The letter reveals that Cullen had no definite plans for his future after being admitted to the bar. "Next week, by the leave of Providence and the Plymouth bar," he wrote, "I become a limb of the law. You inquire in what part of the world I intend to take up my abode. I have formed a thousand projects: I have even dreamed of the West Indies. After all, it may be left to mere chance to determine. . . ."[44] Thus in mid-August, two and one-half months before Cullen would reach the age of twenty-one, he returned to Cummington an accredited lawyer but with his next step undetermined.

*Bryant also received reassurance from his friend George Downes, who wrote him: "Some parts of your letter led me to suppose that you were giving way to low spirits. You express great anxiety concerning your future prospects. I think you do injustice to your talent and application. If I were conscious of possessing those qualities in the degree you do I should have no fear for the future. . . . Stand up my friend and look the world boldly in the face and they will soon acknowledge your worth." Letter of July 6, 1815, Bryant-Godwin Collection.

5

THEMIS OR THE MUSE

THOUGH CULLEN HAD BEEN IN A HURRY TO COMPLETE HIS law training, taking four rather than the customary five years, he did nothing immediately to commence his career when he returned to Cummington in August of 1815, "lounging away," he wrote a friend, "three months at my father's."[1] There were several reasons for this. He was young, two months short of coming of age, and he dreaded the thought of appearing in court. This terror he recalled more than sixty years later in the poem, "A Lifetime":

> And next, in a hall of justice,
>   Scarce grown to manly years,
> Mid the hoary-headed wranglers
>   The slender youth appears.
>
> With a beating heart he rises,
>   And with a burning cheek,
> And the judges kindly listen
>   To hear the young man speak.

Another reason was that he needed a rest after his studies at Bridgewater. But the chief reason probably was that he did not know where to locate and what he would live on while he built up a practice. Since Dr. Bryant had friends in Boston, he could have aided his son in making contacts there, and Mr. Howe and Mr. Baylies could have given him recommendations in various towns. But any place he chose would have to involve an advance of money that Dr. Bryant, now in ill health, must have felt he could not spare.[2] He himself was looking for ways of leaving Cummington to avoid the severe winters. A year before, on February 4, the elder Bryant had written his own father proposing a removal to North Bridgewater, where he could assist his parents in their declining years, his own farm to be left in the charge of Austin. Five months before Cullen's return home, he had written his father despairingly of his health, adding: "God however has been very gracious to me in raising me up so far, for I had very little expectation once that I should ever get well."[3]

During the autumn Cullen continued to write verse in a burst of creativity that produced many random lines and incompleted poems but also a number of finished works. One scholar has suggested that the fragment constituting the first version of "Thanatopsis" was written at this time.[4] Another blank-verse fragment, later printed as "Inscription for the Entrance to a Wood," is believed also to have been written then,[5] since it is so similar in tone to the earlier fragment that it might be a companion piece. One of the most popular of Bryant's poems about flowers, "The Yellow Violet," belongs to this period. It reveals a characteristic Bryant attitude in that it is not merely descriptive of the flower but contains a moral—the didacticism in his work that later readers have found repellent. He believed, as he said in "Thanatopsis," that man held communion with nature. Thus he addressed the flower and obtained from it a message:

> Oft, in the sunless April day,
>   Thy early smile has stayed my walk;
> But midst the gorgeous blooms of May,
>   I passed thee on thy humble stalk.
>
> So they, who climb to wealth, forget
>   The friends in darker fortunes tried.
> I copied them—but I regret
>   That I should ape the ways of pride.

Parke Godwin says of the poetic production at this time: "Fragments and sketches mostly, they resemble those rough outlines which artists are in the habit of making in preparation for larger canvases. He hums to himself of flowers, groves, streams, trees, and especially of winds which abounded in the region where he lived."[6] But there are none of the gloomy verses on death that had preoccupied Bryant at Worthington and Bridgewater. In one poem Bryant laments that he can never feel again the high delight experienced when he began writing poetry but hopes that these moments will return. He recalls his first poetic ardor:

> I cannot forget the high spell that enchanted,
>   Nor the visions that brightened my earlier days;
> When verse was a passion, and warmly I panted
>   To wreathe my young brows with unwithering bays.*

This happy thralldom gave way to more somber experience, for the young poet has "mixed with the world" and been "stained" by its follies (a moralistic twenty- or twenty-one-year-old, Bryant could exaggerate his misdoings) and he cannot return to the earlier days. He hopes, however, that this situation will not be permanent:

> Oh! leave not forlorn and forever forsaken
>   Your pupil and victim to life and its tears;
> But sometimes return, and in mercy awaken
>   The glories yet showed to his earlier years.

II

The decision to start making a living could not be postponed longer, and Cullen decided to begin his practice at nearby Plainfield, walking across the hills on December 15, 1815, to the hamlet** to make arrange-

---

*This poem was first published in the *New-York Review,* Feb., 1826. Bryant revised the first stanzas, making them less spontaneous and revelatory, in the opinion of some scholars, when he included the poem in a book. The first lines of the rewritten poem are:

> I cannot forget with what fervid devotion
>   I worshipped the visions of verse and of fame,
> Each gaze at the glories of earth, sky, and ocean,
>   To my kindled emotions, was wind over flame.

**Parke Godwin said that Bryant's "To a Waterfowl" was inspired by the walk across the hills to Plainfield when the flight of a bird in the sunset suggested that the power that guided it would also lead his "steps aright." Godwin dated the poem as being written at Plainfield in Dec., 1815 (*Poetical Works,* I, 27), but an early draft in Bryant's handwriting in the Goddard-Roslyn Collection dates the poem "Bridgewater, July, 1815." Godwin's account seems unlikely since the question comes to mind why Bryant, since he could have walked to Plainfield in an hour, did not leave in the morning rather than late in the day when he would reach his destination after nightfall. Another reason for questioning Godwin's version is that a bird migrating in December would be flying south to its winter home and not to "find a summer home, and rest," as it is reported doing. See William Cullen Bryant, II, "The Waterfowl in Retrospect," *New England Quarterly,* March, 1957.

ments for an office.[7] Though not a place that could have been his first choice, it had certain advantages, chiefly that he knew it and was known there. The Bryant family had lived there for a short while and Bryant had prepared himself for college there in 1809 and again in 1810 in Parson Hallock's "bread and milk" school.

After Bridgewater, where Bryant had enjoyed the company of lively fellow law students and the young ladies of the town, Plainfield was depressing. Writing Mr. Baylies on January 13, 1816, to tell him of his move, Bryant complained of the hamlet and its people. He received a reply urging him to take a better view of things. "I am glad that you have commenced business and have no doubt you will succeed at Plainfield, or at any other place," Mr. Baylies wrote. "Your talents, I hope you will not suspect me of intention to flatter, ought to inspire you with *confidence.*" Then, referring to Bryant's complaints, Mr. Baylies advised: "I suppose from your description that Plainfield does not furnish a very *polished society.* If the people are honest and industrious, it is sufficient. Indulge not in any *over refined* taste. It is an enemy to our peace, a destroyer of our comfort. Experience will teach you that it is from that class of society, sometimes denominated the lower, as much probably or more than from any other, you can expect zealous support and disinterested friendship."[8]

Within six months Bryant was offered an opportunity to get away from Plainfield when a young lawyer at Great Barrington, George H. Ives, sounded him out on establishing a partnership. By then Bryant had decided he had "little prospect of ever greatly enlarging the sphere" of his business at Plainfield, he wrote a Bridgewater friend; he had found the people "rather bigoted in their notions and almost wholly governed by the influence of a few individuals who looked upon my coming among them with a good deal of jealousy."[9] Thus, when the overture came from Ives, Bryant expressed an interest, and on June 26 received from him an account of the Great Barrington practice. Ives, who had been admitted to the bar in 1810, gave a year-by-year report on the cases he had handled, saying that alone he obtained from his practice about $1,000 annually above his expenses. Since his business often forced him to leave his office, he believed that if he had someone there at all times to see clients the income could be increased to $1,500 or $2,000 a year.[10]

Bryant accepted the offer and set out for Great Barrington, on the Housatonic River about twenty-five miles over the mountains in the southwestern corner of the state, about October 1. He had gone to Plainfield reluctantly; he went to Great Barrington eagerly, delighting in the village and its surroundings at first sight, as he recalled later:

The woods were in all the glory of autumn, and I well remember . . . how much I was struck by the beauty of the smooth, green meadows on the banks of that lovely river . . . the Housatonic, . . . whose gently-flowing waters seemed tinged with the gold and crimson of the trees that overhung them. I admired no less the contrast between this soft scene and the steep, craggy hills that overlooked it, clothed with their many-colored forests. I had never before seen the southern part of Berkshire, and congratulated myself on being a resident of so picturesque a region.[11]

Though Bryant felt that he was better placed at Great Barrington than at Plainfield, the life of a young attorney, even with good prospects, was not the fulfillment of his dreams. Perhaps his feelings were influenced by the fact that, as he wrote his friend John F. Howard of his Bridgewater days, he was "wasted to a shadow by a complaint of the lungs" when he arrived at Great Barrington though he soon recovered.[12] He wrote Mr. Baylies in January of 1817 that "this is a pretty little village in a very pleasant part of the world" and that if it did not have every advantage he could wish nevertheless he ought perhaps to be satisfied.[13] Had he been eager to attain success as a lawyer, he would have expressed more enthusiasm than he did when, as he wrote his father on May 28, Ives decided to give up his practice. "I made a very good bargain with him and got it for a mere trifle," Bryant said.[14] He wrote Mr. Baylies of his feeling toward the law: "You ask whether I am pleased with my profession. Alas! sir, the Muse was my first love, and the remains of that passion, which is not *rooted out* nor chilled into extinction, will always, I fear, cause me to look coldly on the severe beauties of Themis." He said that, even with the departure of Ives, he expected the office to continue to bring in $1,000 or $1,200 a year, "as I am very well patronized and have been considered with more kindness than I could have expected." He concluded: "Upon the whole, I have every cause to be satisfied with my situation. Place a man where you will, it is an easy thing for him to dream of a more eligible mode of life than the one which falls to his lot. While I have too much of *mauvaise honte* to seek opportunities of this nature, I have whipped myself up to a desperate determination not to avoid them."[15]

If Bryant were loath to buckle down to the law because of his enchantment with poetry, he nevertheless developed an incentive to do so, for it is likely the thought of marriage entered his mind. As Bryant had done at Bridgewater, he attended the social gatherings of the young people. At one of these he met a Miss Fanny Fairchild, and he was immediately interested. Fanny was nineteen years old, "a very pretty blonde, small in person, with light-brown hair, gray eyes, a graceful shape, a dainty foot, transparent and delicate hands, and a wonderfully frank and sweet expression of face." She was the daughter of a farm couple who had died of a fever, and Fanny was living with a sister, Mrs. Allan Henderson, in Great Barrington.[16] Shortly after Bryant met her, she went to East Bloomfield, New York, to stay with another sister. The Bryant papers contain a draft of a letter dated March 31 in which the serious young barrister was prompted to write her, playfully suggesting the idea of her marriage:

> It is so long since we have heard from you that some of us begin seriously to doubt whether there was such a young lady as Frances Fairchild. Others pretend to say that the reason we hear nothing of Frances Fairchild is that she has changed her name to Frances Wells but I am pretty certain that if you were either dead or married or run away you would let us know it. I have been disappointed of the high gratification I anticipated in hearing that you had become the bride of some illustrious western Sachem—Wall-in-the-water or Split-log, for instance. I expected much pleasure in learning how you appeared in your new dignity, wearing the wolf-skin, bedizened with wampum, and brightened up with bears-grease; but since your hand was not solicited on your first arrival among them, I have abandoned all hope of your being elevated to that splendid station. Upon the whole, I believe that you may as well give up all expectations from the Indians and return to Great Barrington. . . .

The lovely Fanny was still on Bryant's mind five months later. In an incomplete draft of a letter dated September 13 Bryant wrote that since she had not returned to Great Barrington he would "put you to the trouble of reading another of my epistles—that is, if you are disposed to do it." He continued:

> It is whispered here that you have lost much of the interesting pensiveness of countenance that you used to exhibit here so often in the morning and that you have become as rosy and plump as a cherub. What particular virtue there is in your western air that might produce this effect I know not, nor am I willing to impute it to any such cause. . . . Is there no young *Adonis* of the west who is permitted to whisper soft things in your ear . . . ? This is a delicate enquiry and I will press it no further. . . .

Two weeks later Bryant again was tempted to let Fanny know his feelings, and revised this missive to improve its literary quality.[17]

Bryant may not have got up enough nerve to mail his effusions to "Dear Frances," but apparently the thought of getting married caused him to decide to forget poetry and to settle down to his practice with the aim of making money to support a household.* This is indicated in a reply to a letter written him on November 8 by Mr. Baylies, who expressed his pleasure that Bryant's situation was now "so promising." "It is not surprising," Mr. Baylies continued, "that you should meet with difficulty in breaking off all connection with the Muse, as your love has ever met with so favorable a return. I do not, however, condemn your resolution. Poetry is a commodity, I know, not suited to the American market. It will neither help a man to wealth nor office."[18] That Bryant had fixed his eye on becoming a success is further indicated in a letter to one of his former fellow-students in which, urging the need for adopting "habits of diligence" in the practice of law, he said: "Our profession may be a hard taskmaster, but its rewards are proportioned to its labors, which is as much as any way of life has to say for itself."[19]

III

In the meantime Dr. Bryant had set in motion a train of events that were to revive his son's poetic ambitions and to cause him more than ever to regret the time devoted to the law. In Boston for the session of the legislature opening May 28, Dr. Bryant chanced upon a young Hampshire acquaintance, Willard Phillips, who had lived in Cummington and visited at the Bryant home to study in preparaton for college with one of the doctor's medical students.[20] Phillips had gone on to Harvard, where he was a tutor while studying law. He was a member of a literary club which had sponsored the magazine, the *Monthly Anthology,* and had assisted with the publication of another, the *General Repository.* In 1815 the club estab-

---

*One of the love poems which Bryant never printed may have been inspired by Miss Fairchild's trip to the West. Bryant imagines her facing the eastern sky and recalling her friends:

> The memory of thine earliest home,
>   With feelings which no words can speak,
> Like a soft spell shall o'er thee come
>   And tears shall gem thy rosy cheek.
>
> Oh, often may those thoughts return;
>   And oft thy moist and glistening eye,
> While sunset's fading splendours burn,
>   Be turned upon the eastern sky.

See Tremaine McDowell, *Representative Selections* (New York, 1935), p. 353.

lished, under the editorship of William Tudor, the *North American Review and Miscellaneous Journal,* modeled after the Scottish and English reviews. Tudor withdrew after a year and the club took over the responsibility of bringing out the magazine. Phillips was one of the editorial board. Others included Edward T. Channing, brother of the more famous William Ellery Channing and the "responsible editor"; Richard Henry Dana, a lawyer; and Jared Sparks, a Harvard tutor. In June Dr. Bryant wrote Cullen that Phillips wished him to contribute something to the review: "Prose or poetry will be equally acceptable. I wish, if you have leisure, you would comply, as it might be the means of introducing you to notice in the capital. Those who contribute are generally known to the *literati* in and about Boston."[21]

Bryant, bending his will to make a success at the bar, did nothing at once, and Dr. Bryant decided to submit on his own some of his son's poems that he had on hand. These included the two blank-verse fragments, later titled "Thanatopsis" and "Inscription for the Entrance to a Wood"; four untitled quatrains dealing with man's fear of death, beginning "Not that from life, and all its woes"; and a translation and an imitation of Horace. Dr. Bryant called at Phillips's home, and not finding him in, left the poems for his consideration. This circumstance resulted in a mix-up in which the *North American Review* editors were led to believe that the "Thanatopsis" fragment was written by Dr. Bryant when they published the five poems in the September number of 1817, unsigned, as was the policy of the magazine.[22]

What happened seems to be as follows: Dr. Bryant had clean copies in his son's hand of the "Inscription" fragment and the Horatian poems, but he had recopied the two pieces on death, although later in explaining to Cullen he mentioned recopying only the "Thanatopsis": "With respect to 'Thanatopsis,' I know not what led Phillips to imagine I wrote it, unless it was because it was transcribed by me; I left it at his house when he was absent, and did not see him afterward. I have, however, set him right on the subject. . . ." But since the two poems on death were published under the heading "Thanatopsis," the editors must also have thought the verses in quatrain form were also by Dr. Bryant. Apparently, then, they were also in Dr. Bryant's handwriting. Perhaps he did not bother to mention the poem in quatrains, for it was forgotten in the enthusiasm of the editors for the blank-verse fragments.

For the poems were immediately recognized as being the work of an exceptional poet. Dana wrote later that Phillips turned the contributions over to Channing, who read them to him one day when he had gone into

Boston. During the reading of "Thanatopsis," Dana interrupted: "That was never written on this side of the water." He thought this belief was natural enough "considering what American poetry had been up to that moment." Dana has also related the story that when he was told that the Hampshire senator, Dr. Bryant, was the author of the lines he was so overwhelmed that he went to the statehouse to see the prodigy. He found Dr. Bryant to be a man with "a finely marked and highly intellectual-looking head," but nevertheless told himself: "That is a good head, but I do not see the 'Thanatopsis' there."

The confusion over the authorship persisted for some time. Writing Cullen in December, Phillips said: "Your 'Fragment' was exceedingly liked here, among others Mr. Channing spoke very highly of it. All the judges here say your fragment and your father's 'Thanatopsis' are among the very best poetry that has been published in this country." Dr. Bryant wrote his son in February, 1818, that he had set Phillips right on the subject, but Channing was still under the delusion as late as March, 1819, when he wrote Cullen expressing the hope that the *North American Review* might have "more pieces from you and your father."

The question of the authorship of the blank-verse fragment on death is not the only curious circumstance in the publication of this group of poems. Another is that the title "Thanatopsis" appeared over the two poems on death. First came the lines of "Not that from life and all its woes" followed by the blank-verse lines, without the typographical separation of a dash. Some scholars have suggested that the editors may have supposed them to be a single poem, the rhymed quatrains forming an introduction to the blank-verse portion, but the two pieces are so unlike in form, mood, and thought that they clearly do not belong together. They are related only in that both deal with the theme of death. The forest poem was titled, or labeled, "A Fragment," and the Horatian poems also bore names.* The editors could not, apparently, publish the two other poems with no headings at all. Therefore, they coined from the Greek the term "Thanatopsis," meaning a view or contemplation of death, as a general heading for the two untitled pieces on the same theme. Thus, the arrangement on the page may not have been a mistake or oversight, as usually

---

*One of the Horatian poems, "Horace, Ode II. B. I. Translated," was prefaced by a note to the editor: "I know not that the attempt has ever been made, by any of the various translators of Horace, to give his *Sapphics* an English dress in the same metre.—I send you the following rather as a *curiosity,* than as a specimen of elegant poetry. . . ." The other poem from the Latin was headed "Horace, Book I. Ode IX. Imitated" and had the subtitle: "To a discontented friend."

it has been interpreted. Bryant himself, despite what has often been said, did not originate the word "Thanatopsis" probably influenced by Henry Kirke White's similar titles, "Thanatos" and "Athanatos." Bryant's poems that the *North American Review* editors saw, he stated in later life, "bore no title in my manuscript—that was supplied by an editor who knew Greek."[23]

Dr. Bryant in urging Cullen to contribute to the *North American Review* had suggested that publication there would bring him to notice in Boston, but the circumstances of his appearance in the magazine were such that he received no immediate credit. First, of course, the poems were printed anonymously; and, second, the one that most clearly bore the mark of genius was attributed to his father. Though new numbers of magazines were frequently mentioned in newspapers, noteworthy contributions being commented on or quoted, neither Boston nor New York newspapers carried a notice of the September *North American Review.* Bryant, when an early version of probably his finest poem appeared in print, did not—like Byron—awake one morning to find himself famous.

The immediate effect of Bryant's first appearance in print, aside from his *Embargo* and the pieces carried in the *Hampshire Gazette,* was that he was prompted to help form a literary club in Great Barrington. In October he sent Phillips a subscription in the name of the club with some information about himself, perhaps recalling earlier days in Cummington. Phillips replied on December 2, saying it gave him great pleasure "to receive your letter, as I recollect the epitome of your present self with regard and have recently renewed my acquaintance with you through your father." But even an esteemed contributor was not to get a free subscription to the magazine, for Phillips suggested that Bryant's father, when he returned to Boston in the winter, could pay the $2.50 which was the charge.

In this letter Phillips thanked Bryant for encouraging the magazine by subscribing to it and expressed the hope that he would "also encourage it by writing for it."[24] Bryant did not hurry to do so. Late in December or early in January he went to Cummington for a short visit. On his return to Great Barrington, he got together some verses, which he sent his father. In a letter on January 10, he wrote that since his visit home he had "not enjoyed perfection of health," and continued: "I have sent you a correct copy of my version of 'The Fragment of Simonides,'* and another little

---

*This was published with the title, "Translation of a fragment of Simonides." Bryant had first translated the passage while at Williams College and had recently revised it and published it in the *Hampshire Gazette* of April 23, 1817, before sending it on to the editors of

poem which I wrote while at Bridgewater, which you may get inserted if you please. . . . I would contribute something in prose if I knew on what subject to write."[25] Dr. Bryant answered from Boston, saying that he had given the poems to Phillips, who told him that "they were approved and admired."[26] The record is not clear about these contributions. The *North American Review* for March printed "To a Waterfowl," the Simonides translation, and "To a Friend on His Marriage," which Bryant had written at Worthington and not at Bridgewater. It could be that the "little poem" written at Bridgewater was his later famous "To a Waterfowl." It is curious that Bryant would submit the ode to the marriage of his friend Jacob Porter, who had printed it at Cambridge in 1813 in a pamphlet after his wife's death, *To the Memory of Mrs. Betsey Porter.* It may be that he did not. His father could have added it to the two poems Cullen sent him, or the editors, finding it difficult to obtain good poetry, could have decided to reprint it from the pamphlet. Cullen and Porter were in contact at this time, for Porter knew that his friend had forsworn poetry and remonstrated in stanzas titled "To William Cullen Bryant, Great Barrington." He exhorted Bryant:

> Such merits in thy poems shine,
> Such beauties grace thy matchless line;
> To spread thy fame, then, ne'er decline,
>   But court the muses,
> And a bright breathing chaplet twine
>   Sans all excuses.[27]

Shortly after sending off the poems for the *North American Review,* Bryant got himself involved in delivering a public address on the Bible at the request of the Bible Society of Great Barrington. He spoke on January 29. The address was published in the *Berkshire Star,* and Cullen wrote his father of it:

> It was hasty and imperfect, and I was reluctant to suffer it to be published, and should not have consented but for the solicitations of Mr. Wheeler, our parson. The good man was so importunate and so confident that it would be good on account of the quarter from which it came, it not being common for young lawyers in this part of the country to harangue upon such subjects,

---

the *North American Review.* The translation, with minor changes, appeared in the first collection of Bryant's poems, published in 1821, and in all subsequent volumes of his complete poems.

that I could not well refuse him, but stipulated that the production should appear without my name. It was, however, by some mistake, printed as the work of William C. Bryant, to which was carefully subjoined attorney-at-law.[28]

That Cullen was prevailed upon to speak in public indicates that he was overcoming the fear that filled him when several years before he dreaded the time when he would hang out his gingerbread board.

IV

Bryant's offer to do something in prose for the *North American Review* if he had a subject prompted Phillips to suggest one to Dr. Bryant on February 14. Phillips said that he had noticed there had recently appeared a book, Solyman Brown's *An Essay on American Poetry . . . Sentimental, Moral, Descriptive, and Patriotick,* and added: "I think it is a very good subject for Cullen. If you think so too send it to him and if he has the means give a short history of and criticism of our poetry."[29] He followed the letter to Dr. Bryant with one April 2 to Cullen, saying that since he wanted the article for the July number the review would have to be in his hands by the middle of May. "If anything prevents your undertaking it," he said, "have the goodness to let us know."[30] Cullen replied on April 14 agreeing to do the article. In a second letter on April 20, Phillips indicated some worry over the article and put the deadline forward to June 1.[31]

Phillips had conceived of the article as being a critical essay on American poetry and not merely a review of Solyman Brown's work, but it was not an easy undertaking for Cullen because of his lack of library facilities. In writing his father on February 20 saying that he would do the article he mentioned his difficulties: "This place is like most other villages in this country—there are not many who suffer an excessive passion for books to interfere with other employments or amusements, and they encumber their houses with no overgrown collections." He mentioned the poets with whose work he was familiar—he knew, as it turned out, all of them of any importance and most of them of none—through his reading in his father's library and asked Dr. Bryant for his suggestions.[32] Bryant was able, as he wrote his father on another occasion, to obtain Brown's book in the neighborhood. He considered it a bit of luck, as he found it "poor stuff" and "escaped throwing away my money on it."[33] He was able to use his father's books on a visit to Cummington from April 27 to May 1 and to consult with him on his opinions on the poets to be discussed.[34]

The essay was completed in time to meet Phillips's deadline and duly appeared in the July *North American Review*.

Bryant's first piece of literary criticism revealed an almost fully developed prose, style that did not change materially during his life. It was a style, in its force and frankness, modeled on that of the critics writing for the *Edinburgh Review* and *Quarterly Review*. Like Bryant's poetry, his prose was marked by lucidity and logic—in this he belonged more to the eighteenth century Enlightenment than to nineteenth century Romanticism—and it was elevated without ever being turgid. Later when Bryant wrote so much and so rapidly to meet the requirements of daily journalism, his style became simpler and had a quicker pace; but in his first essay the characteristics of his editorial mode of writing are to be found: the maintenance of a balance in ideas and sentence structure, the ability to make his point at once, and the possession of a somewhat mordant wit that made him a master of irony and at times trenchant sarcasm.

Bryant began by attacking the chauvinism that had made Americans too touchy about criticism of their literature from abroad and too generous to their own poets. He urged the nourishment of a national literature that was American and not European but continued:

> On the other hand, it is not necessary for these purposes—it is even detrimental to bestow on mediocrity the praise due to excellence, and still more so is the attempt to persuade ourselves and others into an admiration of the faults of favorite writers. We make but a contemptible figure in the eyes of the world, and set ourselves up as objects of pity to our posterity, when we affect to rank the poets of our own country with those mighty masters of song who have flourished in Greece, Italy and Britain. Such extravagant admiration may spring from a praise-worthy and patriotic motive, but it seems to us that it defeats its own object of encouraging our literature, by seducing those, who would aspire to the favour of the public, into an imitation of imperfect models, and leading them to rely too much on the partiality of their countrymen to overlook their deficiencies. . . .

He himself bestowed no unmerited laurels in his essay. With only one exception, his mainly adverse judgment on the poets who had written before 1818 is the same as that of critics a century later. The exception is the work of Philip Freneau, of whom, in a discussion of the poets of the Revolution, Bryant said that he was a "writer in verse of inferior note." His pen, he added, "seems to have been chiefly employed on political subjects" and with the production of occasional verse that was distinguished chiefly "by a coarse strength of sarcasm." Bryant seems not to have known Freneau's nature poems, which made him a predecessor of Bryant himself in writing about the American countryside.

The most highly esteemed poets when Bryant wrote were the Connecticut group—John Trumbull, Timothy Dwight, Joel Barlow, David Humphreys, and Lemuel Hopkins. Still fired by the spirit of the Revolution, they wrote poems eulogizing the new nation and conceived and, what is worse, executed grandiose epics they hoped would glorify its beginnings like the epics of Greece and Rome. Influenced by Pope, they also wrote satire that gained them the name of "the Hartford Wits." Their spirit of nationality and patriotism, Bryant said, "at times gives a certain glow and interest to their manner." But this was about all he could allow them. Of Trumbull's popular *McFingal* the best that Bryant could grant it was that it was "a tolerably successful imitation" of Samuel Butler. "The work of Trumbull," Bryant remarked, "cannot be much praised for the purity of its diction." Of Dwight he said respect was due because of his learning, his piety, "and long life of virtuous usefulness," but added: "We must be excused from feeling any high admiration of his poetry." Of Dwight's major poem, *The Conquest of Canaan,* Bryant noted its singular quality— a versification "remarkable for its unbroken monotony." The work, he said, "will not secure immortality to its author." Bryant considered Barlow's "Hasty Pudding" a good specimen of mock-heroic poetry, but of his serious epic, *The Vision of Columbus,* Bryant said it was "utterly destitute of interest."

In closing his survey of American poetry before taking up Solyman Brown's book, which had inspired the critical foray, Bryant noted that there were probably some names of which he was not aware that were "equally deserving of notice." If so, the authors were lucky, for the chances are that nothing very favorable would have been said of them. For other names omitted Bryant excused himself: "Some we have passed over, because we were not willing to disturb their passage to that oblivion, towards which, to the honor of our country, they are hastening."

Of the Boston literati to whom Dr. Bryant wanted his son to become known the only one with whom he had been in contact was Phillips. In two letters Phillips had reminded him that Edward T. Channing was the editor, and, in urging him to contribute, said this fact "is a security for the character" of the magazine. On September 3, Channing wrote expressing his delayed thanks for the essay on American poetry. He sought Cullen's continued support:

You know how important it is that those, who have helped to give a character to a work of this sort, should continue their exertions. There is in this part of the country a notion that all American periodical publications are and must be short-lived, and it is one of our objects to remove this impression, and secure the confidence of readers by a steady adherence to the principles on which we started, and, if possible, by making the book better and better every number. Excuse me then, when I ask you to spend a little time from your profession, and give it to us.

Channing asked for something for the November number, a book review or an essay, and added: "I have not spoken of our poetical department—we are anxious to support this, as it is next to impossible to have it uniformly respectable."[35]

Though Bryant's small literary successes may have fed his ambition to become better known, his law practice was constantly interfering and his health was still poor. In June his business required him to make his first journey outside Massachusetts, to New York City. He wrote his father that the trip, which took two weeks, had improved his health. He went by boat down the Hudson River, and it was a rough trip sailing against a strong headwind. Bryant, suffering from the motion of the vessel, spent three days flat on his back in his berth. Later in life Bryant was an inveterate traveler, but he never became much of a sailor and was almost always seasick when on the water. "While in New York," he related, "I kept running about continually, and this constant exercise, together with being rocked and tumbled about in the vessel, operated on me as a restorative, and since my return my pain in the side and night-sweats have left me." He said that the need for devoting himself to his business would not permit a visit to Cummington. Besides his own law office, there was another firm in Great Barrington and, Bryant now revealed, his former partner George H. Ives had resumed practice. "My several absences of late render it proper," he wrote his father, "that I should now give a little attention to my office, and, as I have taken off the tether from Major Ives and let him loose into the field of practice again, it has become necessary that I should use some diligence to prevent any part of that share of practice which I have obtained from falling into his hands."[36]

In response to Channing's request for more contributions, therefore, Bryant could make no firm promises. Of Channing's praise for the essay on American poetry, Bryant said he was happy "if I may be esteemed to have done anything to raise the literature of my country." But he apologized for not being able to write more for the *North American Review:* "In the mean time I may occasionally attempt something for your journal, and lend such assistance as might be expected from one situated as I am, *Musis procul, et Permesside lympha,* distant from books and literary opportunities, and occupied with a profession which ought to engage most of my attention." He said he was working on an essay for the next number but was not satisfied with it—it was probably "The Happy Temperament," which appeared in the June, 1819, issue. Wanting anything else to send, he enclosed "a small poem which I found by me, and which you may give a place in your journal, if you think it will do." The poem was "The Yellow Violet."[37]

Bryant was able to rework the essay to his satisfaction, submitting it for publication in the March, 1819, number. Channing wrote him March 8, apologizing for holding the essay over to the July number and for not printing "The Yellow Violet." Of the poem, he said: "The 'Lines' would take up so little room that I am unwilling to put them in alone and unless you will supply some more, or get some other poet to work who will be worthy of your company, I fear our poetical department must be given up." He then asked a question that surely delighted Bryant—when a book might be expected from him. "The author of the 'Waterfowl' and 'A Fragment' is under higher obligation than any American bard to do more," he wrote. His letter closed with a suggestion that Bryant do another essay or a review of James Kirke Paulding's poem, *The Backwoodsman.*[38]

Realizing that his poetic output was not great enough for a book, even a small one, Bryant replied: "Had you seen more of those attempts of mine, concerning which you express yourself so favorably, your opinion would, perhaps, have been different." He said he would try to obtain a copy of Paulding's poem to review for the June number or, failing this, would send some article for the miscellaneous department. Then he returned to the thought of a book of his own: "I may, perhaps, some time or other, venture a little collection of poetry in print, for I do not write much—and, should it be favorably received, it may give me courage to do something more. In the mean time, I cannot be too grateful for the distant voice of kindness that cheers me in the pursuit of those studies which I have nobody here to share with me."[39]

Instead of being a paean to "uninterrupted cheerfulness," the essay "On the Happy Temperament" is a prose meditation on the inevitability of evil and death, somber topics with which Bryant had sought to come to grips in many of his poems. In his poetry he had not resolved his thoughts into a philosophy; he approached one in this essay. He found that "the happy temperament" did not enter into the character of the "truly wise and good man, the man of feeling and reflection." "The temperament of unbroken cheerfulness," he asserted, "is the temperament of insensibility." In his poems Bryant had repeatedly expressed his fear of dying. In this essay, for the time being at least, he was able to attain an affirmative acceptance of death. Fundamental in Bryant's philosophy was his recognition of the inevitability of change, of life's transience. Death was a part of this change, he knew, and in this essay for once he saw that it was something that need not be regretted; indeed, it was something to welcome: "As awful as the prospect of death justly is, he, who has thought of it most, will perhaps recollect, that he has sometimes felt a thrill of wild and strange delight as he contemplated this great change of being."

Bryant was to have two more contributions in the *North American Review*. One of these was an essay he resurrected from his papers, "On the Use of Trisyllabic Feet in Iambic Verse," perhaps sent as a substitute for a review of *The Backwoodsman,* a copy of which he was unable to obtain. It was printed in the September number in 1819. Parke Godwin said that he may have written portions of the essay as early as 1811 and probably reworked it in 1815.[40] The essay is a technical discussion of metrics, in which Bryant defended the use of an occasional foot of three syllables in iambic lines, as in the last foot of the line:

> To scorn delights and live labor-*i-ous days.*

This was avoided in the usually metronomic verses of Pope, but Bryant maintained, citing examples, that too strict adherence to rule resulted in "the frequent sacrifice of beauty of expression, and variety and vivacity of numbers." Godwin based his belief that the essay was written some years before it appeared in print on the fact that Bryant cited only older authors —Spenser, Shakespeare, Milton, and Dryden—who comprised his reading before he discovered Wordsworth. This need not be the case, for Bryant declared his purpose was to show that the trisyllabic foot "is an ancient birthright of the poets, and ought not to be given up."

After this essay, Bryant contributed nothing more to the *North American Review* for more than a year. On August 4, 1820, Phillips wrote asking him to do a review of James A. Hillhouse's five-act poetic drama, *Percy's Masque.*[41] Bryant complied immediately, and his article appeared in the October number. He discussed the story and the characters, but his most interesting comments were on the language, which he found to be defective: "There is occasionally a stiffness in the language, and too great a license of inversion to suit well with the flow of dialogue. Indeed, if we might be permitted to interpose our humble judgment in this matter, we should say, that most of the tragedians in our language, for the last hundred years, have adopted a diction much too florid and stately, and too far removed from the common idiom of our tongue." Though in his own verse Bryant never went so far as Wordsworth in believing that the actual language of man should be used—he was never colloquial, for instance— he did, as he urged Hillhouse, employ a style that was usually "idiomatic and easy" and free of "capricious departures from the natural construction."

Despite the praise of the editors of the *North American Review* for his poetry, Bryant's first two years at Great Barrington were largely unproductive of new work. Everything he sent to the magazine had been written earlier. Only two poems that he cared to print later in his books were written at this time. One was another blank-verse meditation on death, a fragment titled "The Burial Place." In this he regretted that the pilgrims did not follow the custom of their English sires in planting trees and flowers at the resting places of their dead, but left them

> Naked rows of graves
> And melancholy ranks of monuments

without the softening touch of yew or willow tree. The other was "Green River," a stream feeding the Housatonic which was one of the haunts he enjoyed when he felt the need to escape his life's daily pressures.

But Bryant's neglect of poetry helped him professionally. When admitted to the bar, he was qualified to practice only in the common pleas court. At Great Barrington he was admitted to practice before the supreme court, and by appointment of the governor became a justice of the peace with the authority to hear and try minor cases. Young though he was, he won the respect of the community. On March 9, 1819, he was elected one of the tithing men, the duties being to enforce the Sabbath rules. Shortly afterward he was chosen town clerk, a position he held for five years. The job was chiefly honorary, for it paid only five dollars a year, but it marked Bryant as one of the responsible men of the town.

6

A VOTARY AT SUNDRY ALTARS

IN THE VEIN OF THOUGHTS ON DEATH EXPRESSED IN THE essay "The Happy Temperament" Bryant in 1820 began a blank-verse poem entitled "Hymn to Death." In contrast with the poems setting forth his dread of dying he took an altered view in the new work:

> Raise then the hymn to Death. Deliverer!
> God hath anointed thee to free the oppressed
> And crush the oppressor.

Reflecting an Old Testament attitude, Bryant saw death as striking down the tyrant, the scoffer at God, the perjurer, the reveller "Mad in the chase of pleasure," the evil man in all guises. This dithryamb broke off suddenly after some one hundred and thirty lines, all the brave utterance seen as vainglory:

> Alas! I little thought that the stern power,
> Whose fearful praise I sang, would try me thus
> Before the strain was ended. It must cease—
> For he is in his grave who taught my youth
> The art of verse, and in the bud of life
> Offered me to the Muses.

Death, the punisher of evil, was indiscriminate and had struck down also the man of worth, the poet's father, Dr. Peter Bryant.

Years of exposure to the snows of Massachusetts winters and the winds and rains of other seasons had weakened Dr. Bryant's constitution. His letters to his father had contained clinical discussions of his ailments; he was ill with the disease that carried off so many New Englanders at that time—consumption. In July of 1819, accompanied by Cullen, he went to the seashore to recuperate. Cullen wrote the family on August 3 from Newport that his father had on one occasion become so ill that another physician had to be called in.[1] The father returned to Cummington but soon became worse and in a few months had to take to his bed. He died on March 20, 1820. Cullen, writing his aunt Charity Bryant of her brother's death, was glad that Dr. Bryant did not linger on for months, that it was not "his fate to wait the gradual extinction of life which is the usual termination of the disorder under which he labored." "A man so honest and upright in his conduct," Bryant continued, "so gentle in his temper, so forgiving of injuries, so full of offices of humanity—to which he sacrificed his health and perhaps his life—must be of those whom God rewards with felicity."[2]

The death of Dr. Bryant left Mrs. Bryant at home with five of her children. Austin, twenty-seven, the eldest, had gone into business, and Cullen, twenty-six, was of course at Great Barrington. The next boys, Cyrus, twenty-two, Arthur, seventeen, and John, thirteen, worked the farm, Cyrus teaching school in the winter. Mrs. Bryant still had the problem of sending the two younger boys to school though Cullen later assisted them as much as he could. Sarah Snell, Cullen's favorite sister, was eighteen, and the other girl, Charity Louisa, was fifteen.[3]

Despite the shock of his father's death, Bryant did not give way to morbid grieving. He was now at an age when he had a man's place to fill in the world. Moreover, he had a new interest, for his early attraction to Frances Fairchild had turned into a strong love which she returned. As a poet, Bryant expressed his deepest thoughts and feelings in verse, and the output of this period includes several poems to or about Miss Fairchild.*

---

*The story of his wooing is related in one of the unpublished poems, "Housatonic":

Oh, I shall love, till life depart,
    That stream so sweet, that scene so wild;—
For the dear maid, who stole my heart,
    There listened to my vows and smiled.

Only one of these did he include in his published collections, the popular anthology piece that begins:

> Oh fairest of the rural maids!
> Thy birth was in the forest shades;
> Green boughs, and glimpses of the sky,
> Were all that met thine infant eye.

The poems give a charming picture, not uninfluenced by the conventional attitudes toward romantic love of the time, but they do not reveal the depth of the mutual regard that brought the two together and was to endure until death separated them. Their holy dedication to each other was expressed in a premarital vow or prayer of the year 1820, one of the most unusual documents about love to be found in literature:

May Almighty God mercifully take care of our happiness here and hereafter. May we ever continue constant to each other, and mindful of our mutual promises of attachment and truth. In due time, if it be the will of Providence, may we become more nearly connected with each other, and together may we lead a long, happy, and innocent life, without any diminution of affection till we die. May there never be any jealousy, distrust, coldness, or dissatisfaction between us—nor occasion for any—nothing but kindness, forbearance, mutual confidence, and attention to each other's happiness. And that we may be less unworthy of so great a blessing, may we be assisted to cultivate all the benign and charitable affections and offices not only toward each other, but toward our neighbors, the human race, and all the creatures of God. And in all things wherein we have done ill, may we properly repent our error, and may God forgive us and dispose us to do better. When at last we are called to render back the life we have received, may our deaths be peaceful, and may God take us to his bosom.[4]

> Bright river! thy fresh banks may fade,—
>   The axe may lop the tree and vine,
> The winding avenue of shade,
>   Through which thy waters steal and shine!
>
>   .   .   .   .
>
> Yet with me shall thy image stay,
>   And wear undimmed its living hues;
> While love's warm pencil, every day,
>   The tints retouches and renews.
>
> As green thy bowers shall flourish there,
>   As bright thy glimmering current run,
> And thy wild banks shall bloom as fair
>   As when my blushing maid was won.

One of the drawbacks of Great Barrington, as Bryant had written his father and Edward T. Channing, was the lack of a literary and intellectual society. His need for this sort of company was met when he formed ties with the Sedgwick family at nearby Stockbridge. The founder of the family was Theodore Sedgwick, who had been sent to the Congress at Philadelphia and was a friend of President Washington. Five of his children were to become friends of Bryant. Bryant had met his first Sedgwick, Charles, the youngest son, while a student at Williams College. Charles was a member of the Berkshire bar, and Bryant had resumed their acquaintanceship when he first went to Great Barrington. Bryant wrote of him later that he was "a man of most genial and engaging manners and agreeable conversation, as well as of great benevolence and worth."[5] Another brother, Theodore, who practiced law at Albany, New York, spent the summers at the family home, retiring there permanently in 1821 when ill health forced him to give up his profession. Also at Stockbridge was the youngest of the three sisters, Catharine, who before long after meeting with Bryant was to become a novelist. Two other brothers, Henry D. and Robert, were lawyers in New York City.

The Sedgwicks were a cut above other families of the vicinity not only in wealth but also in cultural interests. "I was reared in an atmosphere of high intelligence," Catharine once recalled. "My father had uncommon mental vigor. So had my brothers. Their daily habits, and pursuits, and pleasures were intellectual, and I naturally imbibed from them a kindred taste. Their 'talk was *not* of beeves,' nor of making money; that universal passion had not entered into men and possessed them as it does now, it was not in the sanctuary of our home—there the money-changers did not come."[6]

It was in this home that Bryant became a frequent visitor beginning in May of 1820. The first occasion was on an invitation from Catharine, who wished to persuade him to write some hymns for a volume being collected for the Unitarian Society of Massachusetts by Henry D. Sewall. Bryant called in the afternoon after his attendance at court, and agreed to contribute to the collection. Miss Sedgwick, then thirty years old, liked Bryant at first sight. "He has a charming countenance," she wrote her brother Robert, "and very modest, but not bashful manners. I made him promise to come and see us shortly. He seemed gratified; and, if Mr. Sewall has reason to be obliged to me (which I certainly think he has), I am doubly obliged by an opportunity of securing the acquaintance of so interesting a man."[7] Bryant was equally pleased with Catharine. He recalled that she "was well formed, slightly inclined to plumpness, with regular features, eyes beaming with benevolence, a pleasing smile, a soft voice, and gentle and captivating manners."[8]

Writing hymns for a Unitarian songbook, though he was a pewholder and tithingman in the Congregationalist church of Great Barrington, created no religious conflict in Bryant's mind. He had been brought up in the Calvinist faith, but its grip on him had loosened over the years. Dr. Bryant, from his trips to Boston, had brought the doctrine of Unitarianism to Cummington, and at Williams College Bryant had been thrown among youths scornful of religious orthodoxy. In studying Greek and Latin literature he had found many elements of belief that attracted him, especially stoicism; and his reading of the poets and philosophers of his own time had inclined him toward deism. Thus he was not much in sympathy with dogmatic religion, and at Great Barrington he was "terribly prone," it was said of him, "to pick the sermons all to pieces."[9] He might perhaps have allied himself to the new religion if there had been a Unitarian society in the village. Bryant wrote five hymns for the collection, all Unitarian in spirit, though in later life in prose and poetry he paid tribute to the Christ and, in 1864, revised one of the 1820 hymns to mention the Son:

> And lead us all to learn of Him
> Who died to save mankind.

His hymns pleased Sewall, who wrote him on August 29 asking for more and suggesting two or three subjects not treated of in the collection. After some delay, Bryant answered that he could not undertake to supply additional hymns.[10]

While Bryant was working on the hymns, he engaged himself in another project at the request of the Sedgwicks—preparation of a Fourth of July oration to be given at Stockbridge. Because of Bryant's appearances in court, he by now had overcome much of his fear of speaking before the public but he lacked mastery of the fervid oratory that audiences of the time loved. Nevertheless, his restrained and dignified delivery was well received. A friend of later years, William Pitt Palmer, recalled that Bryant gave in the Old Church at Stockbridge "a very chaste and appropriate oration." "Mr. Bryant's delivery," he continued, "was modest and graceful. I got a position in the gallery quite near the speaker, and have not yet forgotten how fair and large and prominent his forehead appeared to me, under the brown locks that curled, if I mistake not, around it."[11]

Only a few months before, in March, Congress had agreed on the Missouri Compromise by which Maine was admitted to the Union as a free state and Missouri as a slave state and slavery was excluded from the Louisiana Purchase north of the line 36°30'. In his oration Bryant condemned the compromise as "extending the dangerous and detestable practice of enslaving men into territory yet unpolluted with the curse." In his youthful patriotic verse he had attacked the tyranny of Napoleon; now for the first time in a long life devoted to the defense of freedom he spoke out, as he was to do repeatedly as a New York editor, against the oppression of American Negroes. He attacked the 1820 law as a compromise with evil brought about through party bargains and, with his deadly sarcasm, hoped that the people of Missouri would have too much good sense and kindness of heart to accept the pernicious privilege granted them by the nation.[12]

III

Bryant's courtship of Frances Fairchild had progressed to the extent that they had decided to join their lives, very likely late in the year signing their own marriage compact before God and deciding on the conventional ceremony for January 11, 1821.* As town clerk, it was Bryant's duty to publish the banns in the church, which he generally did by reading them aloud. In his own case he avoided this embarrassment by pinning the notice on the door of the church vestibule.

The wedding took place in the home of Frances's sister, Mrs. Allan Henderson, before several of the bride's relatives and a few friends. None of Bryant's family attended, perhaps because it was in the dead of winter and travel would be difficult. After Bryant's early childhood, he never had the close relationship with his mother that he had with his father, and this may account for his choosing to write her about the wedding in a mock-serious vein. He related that several people were assembled at a house in the village. "At last," he wrote, "came in a little elderly gentleman, pale, thin, with solemn countenance, pleuritic voice, hooked nose, and hollow eyes." The audience stood while he prayed, and then most of them sat down. "The gentleman with the hooked nose," the letter continued, "then muttered certain cabalistical expressions which I was too much frightened to remember, but I recollect that at the conclusion I was given

---

*Godwin erroneously gives the date as June 11, 1821, an error that has been perpetuated by later writers. *Biography,* I, 169.

to understand that I was married to a young lady of the name of Frances Fairchild, whom I perceived standing by my side, and I hope in the course of a few months to have the pleasure of introducing to you as your daughter-in-law, which is a matter of some interest to the poor girl, who has neither father nor mother in the world."[13]

The couple did not begin housekeeping until April 1, when, according to an autobiographical fragment of Mrs. Bryant's, they rented part of a house that had been erected by Bryant's former law partner, George Ives.[14] They had two rooms, a parlor and bedroom, and shared the kitchen with other occupants. They paid thirty dollars a year in rent. Their expenses during their first few months of married life included such items as seventeen cents a month for pasturage of a cow, eleven cents for a bushel of potatoes, fifty cents for two bushels of corn, and $2.01 for sixty-seven pounds of beef.[15]

Of Bryant's own family he was fondest of his sister Sarah, and shortly after setting up his own household he invited her to visit at Great Barrington. They had exchanged letters since September 6, 1817, when Bryant wrote her expressing the hope it would be the start of a regular correspondence. "You are now at the most interesting period of your life," he said, "at a time which impressions are easily taken and a thousand circumstances are busy in forming and settling the character. . . . Next to her parents a young lady ought to consider her brother as her best friend. . . ." She suffered from the pulmonary complaint that had carried off Dr. Bryant, and in welcoming her visit in a letter on May 5 Bryant tried to reassure her: "I am much concerned at the account you give of your health. I hope, however, that you have not all the cause for apprehension you suppose. I myself at your age and all along since till within two or three years, was occasionally afflicted with symptoms just as you describe, and I have known others to be so, who yet escaped the consumption. I think therefore that though there is every reason for prudence and caution in everything that affects your health yet that you ought not to give way to despondency." He then went on to express pleasure over her interest in botany and said she could continue her study at Great Barrington, since he had several books on the subject.[16]

Bryant had begun his study of botany when he learned the nomenclature of Linnaeus years before from the books in his father's office after withdrawing from Williams College. Intermittently while practicing law he had continued his studies, which he shared with Frances. In 1820 they had the opportunity of taking a course with Amos Eaton, author of several manuals which Bryant owned. From 1817 to 1824 Eaton was an itinerant lecturer in New England, sometimes stopping long enough in a village to conduct classes for a few days or weeks. It was in one of these classes that he came to know Bryant. On June 21, 1833, he recalled this in a letter to Bryant written to let him know the pleasure that his volume of poems had given him. He remembered walking the banks of Green River, where he showed Bryant the windflower and "traced its tender organs." Bryant replied, saying he was flattered "to obtain the voluntary and even extravagant commendations of a veteran and distinguished votary of science." "For the guidance in my botanical studies to which you allude," Bryant continued, "I have ever held myself your debtor."[17] Bryant was a collector of specimens, which lent an odor of forest and field to the musty atmosphere of his law office. He was also, as he said in "Green River," a "simpler" who with "basket and book" sought on its low banks "herbs of power."

IV

Bryant's contributions to the *North American Review* had been so well received at Boston that his admirers succeeded in getting him invited to write a poem for the Phi Beta Kappa Society to be read at the Harvard College commencement in the fall. He had been chosen "by a unanimous vote of the fraternity," the secretary, W. J. Spooner, wrote him. Bryant replied, on April 26, that he was gratified by the honor but that he was unfamiliar with the proceedings. He asked for details to prevent his "doing anything *outre* or getting foul of an interdicted subject."[18]

Spooner took his time in replying but finally on May 29 wrote a letter of several pages of instructions. He explained that the session began at noon, and since the chaplain probably would require fifteen minutes this would leave about an hour and forty-five minutes to be divided between the orator and the poet. It would not be a good idea, he said, for the program to last beyond two o'clock, for this was the usual dining hour of Bostonians. He suggested that a poem lasting only twenty minutes would not be considered very short while one lasting forty-five minutes would not be considered very long. Only if Bryant had a voice that would carry in a crowded church could he safely speak beyond three quarters of an hour. In the past party politics was held to be a reasonable subject, but this would hardly do for the modern "era of good feelings." Satire went well if not personal even though not of the highest kind. "As you will have ladies among your auditors," Spooner said, "you may be pathetick, if you are of a weeping temperament. You will speak before scholars, and so may safely indulge your classical enthusiasm, if you chance to feel it, when writing." Generally, Bryant was advised, he would be safe to write upon a literary topic, as the audience was a literary one, "and more particularly American literature."[19]

All this must not have been very encouraging to Bryant, worried about his unfamiliarity with polished and literary society, but he felt that the occasion was an opportunity he should not miss. Disregarding Spooner's caveats, he chose a philosophical theme, to endeavor "from a survey of the past ages of the world, and of the successive advances of mankind in knowledge, virtue, and happiness, to justify and confirm the hopes of the philanthropist for the future destinies of the human race."[20] He worked at it during the summer, writing a friend that his effort had "come near" to making him sick.[21] In recent years Bryant had composed little poetry and only when the spirit moved him, and he found the going rough, particularly as he had chosen a verse form which he had not attempted before—the nine-line Spenserian stanza. He may have been led to adopt this form for a philosophical poem because it had been used successfully by one of his favorite boyhood poets, Byron, in *Childe Harold's Pilgrimage.*

Shortly after agreeing to write the Phi Beta Kappa poem, Bryant received a letter from Edward T. Channing, who said that he had quit the *North American Review* and that he and Dana were planning a miscellaneous periodical to be published in New York and to "come out as the editors' health and other considerations will admit." He asked Bryant to send something, prose or poetry. He referred to Bryant's marriage, of which he had heard from friends: "I remember you once resolved to give up the muse, but a friend's marriage made you break the vow, and surely your own should have equal efficacy, if you have formed another such unrighteous resolution."[22] This was not to be a magazine in the sense of a review, such as the *North American Review*, but, primarily Dana's project, was conceived of as a personal organ to be called *The Idle Man.*

Bryant contributed four poems, all printed anonymously, to the two volumes of the short-lived publication. One was "Green River," which he had written the previous year. His second was "A Walk at Sunset," of which, in sending it to Dana, he wrote: "You see my head runs upon the Indians. The very mention of them once used to make me sick, perhaps because those who undertook to make a poetical use of them made a terrible butchery of the subject. I think, however, at present, a great deal might be done with them."[23] The poem was not really about Indians, however, but was on a theme that now occupied his mind: historical change. The sun setting "o'er the western mountains" recalls to the poet the Indian legend that

> the quivered warrior, when he died,
> Went to bright isles beneath the setting sun

and the poet is led to muse upon the passing of the "war generations" and upon the fact that he, the "offspring of another race," stands where they once dwelt. He concludes that the sun's rays

> Must shine on other changes, and behold
> The place of the thronged city still as night—
> States fallen—new empires built upon the old—

in subsequent cycles of time. His third contribution, "Winter Scenes," later titled "A Winter Piece," was Wordsworthian in tone, celebrating his release from worldly cares by communion with nature. It begins with a description of the delights of the woods in spring, summer, and autumn but for the poet winter too has its splendors. The somber forest of other seasons in winter is turned into a "fairy palace"

> Where crystal columns send forth slender shafts
> And crossing arches; and fantastic aisles
> Wind from the sight in brightness, and are lost
> Among the crowded pillars.

His final contribution was "The West Wind," a minor effort in quatrains in which the poet finds an underlying note of sadness in the zephyr that he addresses as the "Spirit of the new-awakened year."

Struggling to get his Phi Beta Kappa poem written, Bryant's worries were increased by a well-intentioned letter from Phillips on July 13. In it Phillips emphasized the importance of a good reading of the poem, warning that "however good your poem unless it is well delivered it might as well be a bad one." Phillips told him that the best poem given before the society was "almost a total failure" and one of the worst "went off with great eclat." "In the good poem," he said, "the subject was not obvious and so the audience was a little puzzled and though it was full of high poetry in thought and language yet none but the very attentive saw their connection and there were no convenient pauses and points and antitheses and spirited sallies brought out with effect to set the clappers in motion."[24]

The Harvard commencement was scheduled for August 30, and Bryant set forth from Great Barrington on the twenty-fourth. Frances saw him off on the first leg of the journey, Bryant seated "on a rough board laid on the top of a crazy wagon, whose loose sides kept swinging from right to left, with a colored fellow at my right hand and a dirty old rascal before me who kept spitting all the way." His first view of Boston after two days of travel was at midnight when he saw "the rows of lamps along the great western avenue, and beyond them those of the Cambridge and Charleston bridges." Taken in hand by his friends on the *North American Review,* Bryant met many of the distinguished people of the city and was shown the sights. He was impressed by a wealthy merchant's country home that he described in detail to Frances: on the estate were growths of the mountain ash of Europe, the English beech, and the Chinese sumach, a greenhouse with pineapples and exotic grapes, and "thousands of other curious matters."[25] This country home may have been in Bryant's mind years later when he built his own at Roslyn on Long Island and experimented with all sorts of plantings with the practical and scientific knowledge of a nurseryman. This letter written during Bryant's first separation from his wife was typical of those he wrote on similar occasions in the years to come. His letters were seldom personal. It was as if the two were so well attuned that it was unnecessary for him to express his love for her. Thus, like any prosaic husband writing to his wife, Bryant might say that he missed her, and this was about as close to any expression of emotion that he allowed himself. He preferred poetry for the statement of his deeper feelings. His letters on his trips were travelogues, in which he described the people he met and the places he saw.

Of the Boston literati whom Bryant now met the most significant for him was Richard Henry Dana. The meeting marked the start of Bryant's most enduring literary friendship, one that was to last for fifty-seven years. Born at Cambridge on November 15, 1787, Dana was now thirty-three years old, Bryant's elder by seven years. Dana, like Bryant, had been trained for the law, and, like Bryant, he had found it distasteful. Literature was for him his whole life and not a pastime for a gentleman, as it seemed to be in the case of the young poetasters and critics of Boston. He had assisted Channing in the publication of the *North American Review,* admiring the Romantic poets of England—Wordsworth, Coleridge, and Byron, anathema to most of the members of the club sponsoring the magazine. When Channing resigned to become professor of rhetoric and oratory at Harvard, Dana expected to become editor. But his championship of the new poetry was opposed by the conservative majority and Edward Everett, noted as an orator and scholar, was chosen instead.[26] Dana thereupon withdrew and began publication of his *The Idle Man*. Bryant considered his forced resignation a misfortune for the national letters, saying that if the *North American Review* "had remained in Dana's hands he would have imparted a character of originality and decision to its critical articles which no literary man of the country was at that time qualified to give it."[27] The correspondence that began when Bryant was asked to contribute to *The Idle Man* continued until his death in 1878. Dana lived on for another year, "the sole survivor," he remarked after Bryant's death, "among my literary friends and contemporaries—Channing and Allston, Cooper, Irving, Halleck, Percival, Verplanck, and now Bryant."[28] Although Bryant was by far the finer poet, he looked upon Dana as a mentor, perhaps as a replacement for his father, and sought his opinions on his poetry, and accepted them more often than not in the scores of letters that passed between them in subsequent years.*

At the Phi Beta Kappa program in the Old Congregational Church, Bryant followed the orator, John C. Gray, in reading his poem, "The Ages." Phillips in his letter advising Bryant to give attention to his delivery, had written that he wished for him to "come off safe, for which you have one advantage as Mr. Gray who gives the oration will not probably set it off greatly in the utterance." Neither the oration nor the poem created a sensation, the Boston *Daily Advertiser* commenting in a sentence: "These interesting performances commanded the deep attention, and received the high approbation, of a very numerous and select audience." Many years later two persons who were present remembered Bryant's quiet delivery. One of them, the orator Gray, wrote: "I said to myself at the time, 'If Everett had read this poem, what a sensation it would have produced!' " The other, Miss Eliza Susan Quincy, recalled that Bryant's "appearance was pleasing, refined, and intellectual; his manner was calm and dignified; and he spoke with ease and clearness of enunciation."[29]

By Bryant's admirers among the literary set "The Ages" was greeted as a work of the highest merit and they urged its publication, persuading him, if he needed persuasion, to let them undertake the task of getting it,

---

*The literary historian Van Wyck Brooks says of Dana: "Alas for Dana, born too soon, not strong enough to break his own path and yet the symbol of a rising world where other poets of a tougher grain were to find their audience waiting. A sensitive dreamer, diffident, self-distrustful, with all the shy and solitary ways that marked the romantic poet as a type, he was to become an ancient Nestor, the only man living, decades hence, when even the Civil War was growing dim, who could still remember Washington's death." *The Flowering of New England* (New York, 1936), 115.

together with other poems he had available, into print. This high opinion of "The Ages" has not been shared by later admirers of Bryant. Poe, who held him to be a genius, though not of the "loftiest" sort, maintained that "The Ages" was not a poem at all—it was too long and did not deal with a poetic subject—though he granted that there were good images and even good lines in it.[30] Bryant himself in later years did not regard it as his best poetry, but, considering it an important statement of his credo and his hopes for his country, he placed it first in all his collected volumes, followed by "Thanatopsis."

The poem sets out to answer a question that Bryant asks of God, whether in creating man, now spread over the earth, He will leave "a work so fair all blighted and accursed." In dignified and elevated stanzas Bryant traces the dreary and sometimes monstrous history of civilization, finding somehow that the end of each age has marked an improvement over the one that preceded it, that when evil triumphed in one place and time good appeared elsewhere. After this survey of the ancient world and Europe, Bryant casts his eye over America's past and discovers a similar progression and extols the land where

> the free spirit of mankind, at length,
> Throws its fetters off. . . .

Such freedom has not been won in Europe, which

> is given a prey to sterner fates,
> And writhes in shackles.

But his own country, Bryant says in a peroration that may have stirred even his learned Boston audience despite a lack of fervor in his delivery, has before it a future, unfettered and free, whose duration no man could foretell.

Before Bryant left for home, Channing, Phillips, and Dana arranged for publication of "The Ages" with other poems, and the little volume of forty-four pages with brown paper boards, entitled *Poems by William Cullen Bryant,* appeared the first week in September. The Phi Beta Kappa poem led the volume, occupying pages seven to twenty-four. The poems that followed were "To a Waterfowl," "Translation of a Fragment of Simonides," "Inscription for the Entrance to a Wood," "The Yellow Violet," "Song" (later called "The Hunter of the West"), "Green River," and "Thanatopsis." With the exception of "The Ages," the poems are printed in the order of their composition. It may be significant that Bryant placed

"Thanatopsis" last, since his final revision consisting of a beginning and an ending was completed while he was in Boston. He would seem to have considered that its date of composition should be in 1821, when it was completed, rather than an earlier year when it was started.

Dana sent Bryant a copy of the book on September 8 "as a glass for you to look into," he wrote, "and see how handsome you are in print." He hoped that Bryant would not be offended by some liberties—mostly restorations of earlier wording—taken in printing "The Yellow Violet" and "Thanatopsis." Bryant had revised the flower poem while in Boston, but his editors preferred the first version sent for publication in the *North American Review* but never printed. They agreed "that the town atmosphere must have got into your upper regions when you made that and other changes." The other alterations were certain phrases in the fragment of "Thanatopsis" that had appeared in the *North American Review* in 1817. Over the years Bryant had tried several beginnings and endings for the poem, but achieved nothing that satisfied him until, apparently, his most recent attempts in Boston. It was now in its final form except for minor changes made in later reprintings. In objecting to some of the changes, Dana expressed his Romanticism in the remark: "I believe that a poet should not be allowed to alter in cold blood; he grows finical." Bryant replied that he submitted "as quietly as you could wish to your restoration of the altered passages."[31]

Phillips wrote Bryant shortly afterward "about the fate of the *Poems,*" saying that they had "sold well in Boston but have not been sent away to other places." He had written a review for the *North American Review,* as well as one for the Portsmouth (N.H.) *Journal,* and copies of the book would reach other places about the same time as the magazine. "I have no doubt," he predicted, "that the present edition will be mostly sold."[32] Though there was apparently no widespread distribution of the book, the venture resulted in Bryant's receiving attention in New York from a leading literary figure, Gulian C. Verplanck, later to become a close friend. Verplanck wrote Bryant on October 5 that he had received a copy of the poems from Dana and was inclosing an issue of the New York *American* containing a review. But Bryant's seeing his praises in a New York newspaper had to be postponed. He wrote Verplanck on October 10: "Whether you think highly of my poems or otherwise, I hope, at least, that you think more of them than I was able to find in the paper you sent me. On unfolding it, I found the two inside pages entirely blank, through some blunder, I suppose, of the press." Another copy was quickly dispatched, and Bryant could derive satisfaction in reading that his poems were remarkable for "their exquisite taste, their keen relish for the beauties of nature, their magnificent imagery, and their pure and majestic morality."[33]

Bryant, in telling of the composition of "Thanatopsis," said that the portion printed in 1817 was written in his "solitary rambles in the woods." "The rest of the poem—the introduction and the close—was added," he said, "some years afterward, in 1821, when I published a little collection of my poems at Cambridge."[34] Manuscripts of early texts of his poems, however, reveal that this was not entirely the case. He wrote at least two versions between 1817 and 1821, when he put the finishing touches on the poem while in Boston. His main problem had been to find an introduction and conclusion for the middle portion. An earlier introduction was:

> It was his better genius that was wont
> To steal upon the bard what time his steps
> Sought the repose of nature, lone and still
> And unfrequented walks—and in his ear
> To whisper things of which it irks the mind
> That clings to the dear fallacies of life
> To think:—and gravely with his graver hours
> Oft the benevolent and heedful one
> Could thus commune.—"Yet a few days, and thee
> The all-beholding sun shall see no more. . . ."

These lines show that Bryant was groping his way in darkness. The concept of the inner spirit speaking to the poet, his "better genius," is not clearly developed. The passage, in fact, does not make sense, as though the young poet had an idea in the back of his mind that he could not verbalize. Through some process of creation that can only be surmised Bryant conceived the idea of changing the speaker in the dialogue from the better genius to nature, which in his own experience he had found to be the great teacher. This solved his problem and the lines began to flow:

> To him who in the love of Nature holds
> Communion with her visible forms, she speaks
> A various language; for his gayer hours
> She has a voice of gladness, and a smile
> And eloquence of beauty, and she glides
> Into his darker musings, with a mild
> And healing sympathy, that steals away
> Their sharpness, ere he is aware. . . .

103

Finding a fitting conclusion was easier than finding a fitting beginning, for the idea was already there in the metaphor of the bed that receives all mankind. In the various poems and fragments that Bryant had written on death he had sought an answer that could appeal to the mind of man so that he could face his end with dignity. His answer was in these lines:

> So live, that when thy summons comes to join
> The innumerable caravan, which moves
> To that mysterious realm, where each shall take
> His chamber in the silent halls of death,
> Thou go not, like the quarry-slave at night,
> Scourged to his dungeon, but, sustained and soothed
> By an unfaltering trust, approach thy grave,
> Like one who wraps the drapery of his couch
> About him, and lies down to pleasant dreams.

Many who have found consolation in "Thanatopsis"—during Bryant's lifetime he received numerous letters from people telling how they had been helped by it—have regarded it as a religious poem, and the critic Carl Van Doren said that once it was held to be "half an act of worship to learn" it by heart. But some ministers have not agreed, because it does not mention God nor offer hope of immortality. Henry Ward Beecher, for example, denounced it from the pulpit as a pagan poem,[35] and Alfred P. Putnam significantly omitted it from his collection, *Singers and Songs of the Liberal Faith,* though he included, besides Bryant's hymns, his "The Past," "The Conqueror's Grace," and "The Death of Lincoln," which were not written primarily to express a religious view. Yet it is not the denial of the Christian faith that some critics have held.* Though Bryant while writing "Thanatopsis" had composed other poems in which he could not reconcile his fear of death with the promise of the rewards of heaven, there is little indication that he disbelieved the Christian doctrine. "Thanatopsis" was not written to deny the consolations of religion but to appeal to the rational man. As a recent critic, Alfred F. McLean, Jr., has written: "The

---

*A critic for the *American Athenaeum* in the issue of Oct. 20, 1825, considered "Thanatopsis" as perhaps the best of Bryant's poems but attacked it on a religious ground: "Whether [Bryant] intended it or not, he has adopted the old doctrine of materialism in its full extent; and there are few thoughtful readers who would not rise from its perusal with painful feelings of dissatisfaction." He went on to say that the poem "inculcates but too plainly those ancient doctrines which lead at last to atheism and annihilation. We are sorry to asseverate such a charge, because Mr. B. has written many minor pieces which are replete with entirely different sentiments."

problem successfully attacked in 'Thanatopsis' is not what happens to the soul in death but to the human mind.''

The publication of Bryant's little book ended a period in his life in which, had it not been for the urging of his friends on the *North American Review,* he might have entirely given up his poetry. Between 1817 and 1820 he had contributed eight poems and four essays to the magazine, and he was further prodded into composition by their urging him to write for *The Idle Man* and to accept the invitation to give the Phi Beta Kappa poem. Bryant remembered the importance of this support late in life when, on September 20, 1873, he wrote Dana on the occasion of Phillips's death: ''The publication of the poems which you mention, through his agency, was properly my introduction to the literary world, and led to my coming out with the little volume which you and Channing encouraged me to publish, and which he so kindly reviewed in the *North American.* To me he was particularly kind—unconsciously so, as it seemed; it was apparently a kindness that he could not help.''[36]

Phillips's particular kindness is shown in the fact that he took upon himself the promotion and sale of the *Poems,* making reports to Bryant during the next two years. On February 17, 1822, he wrote Bryant that he believed the poems ''would pay for themselves'' but added: ''For want of that pushing which a good thing seems to need more than a bad one among us, your book will not sell so well as it deserves. But as far as reputation is concerned, as I told you before, you have nothing to complain of, and this was the ground I presume of all your calculation on the subject.''[37] But the book had not paid for itself by October 21, when Phillips wrote that $14.92 was still owing the publishers, Cummings & Hilliard.[38] At last, on May 5, 1823, Phillips informed Bryant: ''Though the book has finally given you an established reputation yet that is all you will get from it.'' He attributed the small sale in part to the split between the old editors of the *North American Review* and the new editors, who were enthusiastic over a volume of similar nature poems from the pen of the New Haven poet and physician, James Gates Percival. Percival's volume was favorably noticed by Edward Everett in the *North American Review.* Phillips explained how Bryant's book had suffered: ''The reason why it did not sell as well as it ought to have done, was that it did not at first *take* with the admirers of Percival and of others inferiour to him. These people at first obtained a very considerable vote and seemed almost to put us in the minority, and my notice in the N.A. Review was thought to be a friendly rather than a fair article. . . .'' The slightness of the book, Phillips continued, also hurt the sale, for booksellers were not interested in a volume on which there was only a small profit because of the low price.[39]

The division among the Boston literary set had the effect of closing for the time being the *North American Review* as an outlet for Bryant's writings. A review he had written for it of *The Idle Man* was "suppressed," according to Phillips's letter of February 17. "It was gravely settled that you praised the Idle Man *plus grano salis* and more than would go down," he wrote.[40] A place for the article was found in the Boston *Columbian Centinel* of November 27, 1822. Bryant was not again to be invited to contribute to the *North American Review* until 1824, when Jared Sparks resumed the editorship.

The *North American Review* period, however, could not by any means be considered as one marked by a great burst of creativity, but it did serve to keep alive the poetic fire that Bryant had attempted to put out. Even the publication of his book did not serve to renew the flame, for he wrote almost nothing in the next two years. Not until 1824 was the fire of poetry in him to blaze up again, and he enjoyed perhaps his greatest year of creativity when he wrote and published about twenty new poems, some of them among his best.

7

RECALLED TO THE MUSE

RETURNING HOME AFTER GIVING THE PHI BETA KAPPA POEM, Bryant had need to attend more zealously to his practice. The sales of his book, as he soon learned, did not improve his financial situation, nor was it likely his poetic reputation would assist his career in Great Barrington. As Mr. Baylies had told him some years earlier, poetry was a commodity not suited to the American market. It was imperative now for him to get ahead as a lawyer, for his wife was with child. The birth took place on January 2, 1822, a girl, named Frances after the mother. The parlor and bedroom in the Ives house were inadequate for a family of three, and on April 1, Frances recorded in her autobiographical fragment, they moved "into the south part of Mrs. Barstow's house."

Besides caring for his own family, Bryant felt he should help his younger brothers get their education as he had been helped in getting his. Since Dr. Bryant's death, they had farmed the family acres, but agriculture in a mountainous area did not bring in the cash needed to send three young men to school. One of them, the fourth son, Peter Rush, then twenty years old, on a visit to Great Barrington tentatively decided upon his future, Bryant writing his mother on September 15 that his brother had decided to apply for admission to the United States Military Academy. "I am not certain that West Point would not be a good place for him," Bryant said. "The learned professions are getting to be a poor way of making a livelihood, and he will at least have the advantage of being able to choose the military profession if he should happen to like it."[1]

A diversion from the law for Bryant was politics, largely because of his association with the Sedgwicks, particularly with Theodore Sedgwick who had retired to Stockbridge. Bryant was still a Federalist, as were the Sedgwicks, and he worked for the party, attending meetings, serving on committees, and discussing candidates and issues in newspaper articles.[2] But the grip of Federalism, after the War of 1812, had loosened, even in New England, and the *Columbian Centinel* of Boston, noting the decline of partisanship, had given the period of President Monroe the name, "Era of Good Feelings."

It is likely that Theodore Sedgwick influenced Bryant to take up the study of political economy. He read Smith, Say, Thornton, and Ricardo and adopted their laissez-faire principles that were to dominate his thinking as a New York newspaper editor. Sedgwick, who later wrote extensively on political economy, was working out his ideas, the first statement of which he put in a book, *Hints for the People, with Some Thoughts on the Presidential Election,* published in 1823 under the pen name "Rusticus." Yet even without this influence, Bryant no doubt would have been prompted to examine economic questions, brought into political prominence by the movement for a protective tariff and internal improvements, given the name the "American System" by Henry Clay in a speech in Congress in 1824. Bryant's studies led him to reject both and facilitated his later transfer of political loyalty to the Democratic party.

These distractions from poetry were regretted by Dana, who urged Bryant to undertake a major project. "We talk of you a great deal down at my brother's, and want you to write a poem as much longer than 'The Ages' as may please you," Dana wrote. "Fix upon a subject, and turn over the plan in your mind; get as full of the matter as you have leisure to be, and write as you find time."[3] Later he wrote again: "There are men of talents enough to carry on the common world, but men of genius are not so plenty that any can afford to be idle, neither can any man tell how great the effect of a work of genius is in the course of time. Set about it in good earnest."[4] The appeals had little effect. Bryant continued his poetic silence and made good progress in his law practice, informing Mr. Baylies of his situation in 1823 in writing to obtain his aid in getting his brother an appointment to West Point. Mr. Baylies replied on December 26: "I am glad to hear of your *welfare* and *goodly prospects.* I think I am justified in using this language, by your own account of yourself. You are no worse off, as to wealth, than when you began the practice while you have increased very much, I have no doubt, your means of happiness."[5]

II

Unexpectedly from Taunton, Massachusetts, Bryant received a letter late in 1823 that led to a new publishing association and his resumption of verse-making. Under the pressure of his financial needs Bryant had given up the Muse, declaring:

> I broke the spell that held me long,
> The dear, dear witchery of song.
> I said, the poet's idle lore
> Shall waste my prime of years no more,
> For Poetry, though heavenly born,
> Consorts with poverty and scorn.[6]

On December 19 he received from Theophilus Parsons, editor of the *Free Press* at Taunton, a letter saying that Cummings & Hilliard of Boston was to establish a periodical, the *United States Literary Gazette,* which he would edit. Contributors would be paid, or as Parsons put it politely, the terms were such that he would be able "to make pecuniary compensation for whatever assistance I may need." "If you can confer upon me this favour," Parsons continued, "will you have the goodness to inform me, how much money I may have the pleasure of sending you for ten or twenty pieces of poetry . . . in the course of the ensuing year?" He mentioned that "most of the best writers in Boston . . . have promised me their aid, and I am very anxious that the work should have, in some measure, the support of your talents."[7]

Bryant, in reply, mentioned no specific payment, suggesting as suitable the terms offered "other gentlemen" who would contribute. On February 14 Parsons proposed a figure that overwhelmed Bryant looking for ways to increase his income. "We are sensible of the strong necessity of obtaining your aid," Parsons wrote, "and of the *pecuniary* value your contributions bear to us, but, I fear, we are constrained to offer, for the present, compensation not adequate to their value." But after this discouraging preamble he went on to say that Bryant's work would be so necessary to the success of the magazine that he should be paid at a higher rate than other contributors and ended with this offer: "The result to which we come, is that we ask you to furnish us an average of about 100 lines a month, and receive for it $200 a year. Less than this we could not offer, and more we cannot afford."[8] To Bryant, who was clearing only about $500 in his law practice, this was such a windfall that he quickly disavowed his pledge to poetic silence.

The first number of the *United States Literary Gazette* appeared on April 1, 1824, containing a long review of Bryant's book published two years before and a seventy-four-line poem based on the story of Rizpah in II Samuel, 21:10, the daughter of Aiah who, when her children were slain by the Gibeonites, stood guard over their bodies in the wind and rain to protect them from vultures and wild beasts.

The review was not signed but it may have been written by Dana, since it called upon the poet to try a greater flight than any undertaken in his short poems—"one poem long enough to task all his powers, and good enough to reward his severest toil." "We are not afraid of praising Mr. Bryant too much, but of praising him injudiciously," the reviewer wrote. "We are in little danger of giving the public too exalted an opinion of his poetic powers and works, but we feel that there is much in this little volume, which it is difficult to measure by any usual criterion, or to class with other works of kindred character." Though some of the lines reminded him "too strongly of the Lake School," the critic continued, he nevertheless found little British influence in them— there were no imitations of Goldsmith, Scott, Byron, and, "worst of all," Moore—and he was delighted to be able to say "that they were American poems."

"Rizpah" is not one of Bryant's better poems but it is interesting for its experimentation in versification. The subject may have appealed to him because the Biblical tragedy recalled similar stories in the Greek drama. His poem is a dramatic monologue in which Rizpah, mourning "her children slain," vows:

> "I hear the howl of the wind that brings
> The long drear storm on its heavy wings;
> But the howling wind and the driving rain
> Will beat on my homeless head in vain.
> I shall stay, from my murdered sons to scare
> The beasts of the desert, and fowls of the air."

Because the prevailing taste still favored the regularity of the Augustan poets, the schism on the *North American Review,* for example, having been caused when conservatives like Everett won out over liberals like Dana, readers seeing on the page the rhymed couplets of "Rizpah" that looked like those of Pope must have been shocked to discover that the lines did not scan. Bryant indeed had done something unusual, creating a meter of four accented feet with the unaccented syllables varying in number in the lines. He had pushed to the extreme his theory of avoiding too strict regularity by employing an occasional trisyllabic foot, set forth in his early essay on versification. Even his friend Phillips had remonstrated with him on this point in a letter telling of his notice of Bryant's poems written for the *North American Review:* "I think on the whole you have too great fondness for trisyllabics."[9] Now Bryant flung in the face of readers a poem in which the trisyllabics ran wild. The meter offended even Poe, who said that the "mingled Iambuses and Anapaests, is the most positively disagreeable of any which our language admits, and, having a frisky or fidgetty rhythm, is singularly ill-adapted to the lamentations of the bereaved mother."[10]

Bryant was quick to supply Parsons with additional poems, sending him "The Old Man's Funeral," "The Rivulet," which he had written late in the previous year, and "March." Parsons acknowledged receiving the "three delightful pieces" on May 5, saying that he would "so economise as to make them answer for the second and fourth numbers" of the magazine. He added: "But I endeavor to keep as far ahead as I can and shall be glad to receive a further supply as soon as it may suit your convenience to send it." He invited Bryant also to contribute some prose, suggesting a rate of pay of one dollar a column, for something to be used in the "Miscellany" department of sketches and informal essays. "The most acceptable answer I could receive . . . would be not merely an affirmal," he said, "but an instance of the affirmative."[11]

"The Old Man's Funeral" appeared in the issue of April 15. It was written out of personal experience, the funeral of a Cummington patriarch. The poem's message is put into the mouth of an aged man who speaks over the bier, urging those in attendance not to mourn and comparing death with the harvest of grainfield and of orchard as a part of the natural order, a favorite theme of Bryant's. The next poem, "The Rivulet," describes the stream that flowed past the Bryant homestead and beside which he had played as a boy, written in lilting tetrameters copying the rush of the water. The poet recalls his early childhood when

> My truant steps from home would stray
> Upon its grassy side to play

and his boyhood when

> Duly I sought thy banks, and tried
> My first rude numbers by thy side.

111

But viewing the rivulet as a man he is led to muse on the melancholy thought that the stream will flow on when he is dead:

> But thou, unchanged from year to year,
> Gayly shalt play and glitter here;
> Amid young flowers and tender grass
> Thy endless infancy shall pass;
> And, singing down thy narrow glen,
> Shalt mock the fading race of men.

The poem "March" is Bryant in a more cheerful mood in which he welcomes this "stormy" month when winter ends and spring begins.

III

On April 1 of 1824 the Bryants moved again, into the north part of the house of a physician, a Dr. Leavenworth, and late in the month Bryant made his second visit to New York. Through his association with the Berkshire Sedgwicks, he was welcomed by Henry D. and Robert Sedgwick, both prominent lawyers and leaders in social and literary circles. As their guest, he met some of the Knickerbocker writers—James Fenimore Cooper, Fitz-Greene Halleck, and Robert C. Sands. The occasion for the trip seems to have been a suggestion of Henry D. Sedgwick, who believed that Bryant could form a magazine connection that would earn him a living.[12] Just what the prospects were is not clear, but Catharine Sedgwick, visiting her New York brothers, described, in a letter to her brother Charles at Stockbridge, her pleasure at seeing Bryant: "I never saw him so happy, nor half so agreeable. I think he is very much animated with his prospects. Heaven grant that they may be more than realized. I sometimes feel some misgivings about it; but I think it is impossible that in the increasing demand for native literature, a man of his resources, who has justly the *first* reputation, should not be able to command a competency."[13]

Bryant had been brought to the attention of the New York Sedgwicks the year before when Charles submitted for their criticism a farce written for the stage. Bryant's play, "The Heroes," was suggested by a duel between two southerners that had been widely discussed in the press. The elaborate protocol established for a gentlemanly duel led him to believe that he had a fit subject for satire. Charles Sedgwick had doubts about the play, as did Bryant himself, and wrote him on February 14, 1823: "Your feelings in regard to the farce are just what I supposed they would be. It is perhaps one of the best properties of a superior mind to estimate justly its own performance. In regard to the satire of the play we both know that it is excellent. As to its success neither you nor anybody else can tell beforehand." He thought it should be judged by someone familiar with the New York stage and promised: "My brothers will hear it in a few days and will do their best with it." A few weeks later, on March 23, Bryant was told of the adverse reaction in New York. Charles added that he was "rather amused" at Henry's surprise in reading a farce written by the author of such a serious work as "Thanatopsis."[14]

Besides looking for a magazine connection in New York, Bryant could justify the trip as one taken to promote the sale of his book of poems. He had written Phillips that the Sedgwicks thought two hundred copies might be disposed of in New York. Phillips wrote Bryant on March 25, saying he had sent seventy-five copies to New York and would dispatch additional ones as soon as these were sold. He inclosed a copy of a letter he had written the Sedgwicks in which he said: "I have told Bryant repeatedly that he ought to write something more, that with these poems would make a small volume of a size to be bound and published as soon as these are sold. I think he ought not to have them republished until he has enough to make such a volume fit for binding. I wish you would enjoin the same things upon him if you think it right, for I am apprehensive that he grows careless of poetry, and will let his talent sleep."[15]

Bryant had planned to stay in New York only a few days, but he wrote Frances on April 24 that he thought he would remain a little longer: "The weather has been so bad that I have seen little of the city as yet and as there is no knowing when I shall be here again I think I had better take time to look about me before I leave this place. Miss Sedgwick has undertaken the charge of getting a bonnet for you, but as the weather has been rainy for two or three days past she has not been out, and I do not intend to come away till the bonnet is bought." He told of meeting Cooper, Halleck, and Sands at a dinner party given by Robert Sedgwick. "Mr. Cooper engrossed the whole conversation," he wrote, "and seems a little giddy with the great success his works have met with."[16] He also met Jared Sparks, who only a short time before had resumed the editorship of the *North American Review*. This chance encounter resulted in Bryant's being invited to contribute to the magazine again.

On Bryant's return to Great Barrington he received the disquieting news from Cummington that his favorite sister Sarah, who was now married, was seriously ill. Her imminent death inspired his next poem in the *Gazette*, a sonnet "To ———," later entitled "Consumption," which ends with this melancholy thought:

Death should come
Gently, to one of gentle mould like thee,
As light winds wandering through groves of bloom
Detach the delicate blossom from the tree.
Close thy sweet eyes, calmly, and without pain:
And we will trust in God to see thee yet again.

Poe, who believed that the death of a beautiful woman was the ideal subject for a poem, thought the sonnet was perfect with "the exception of harshness in the last line but one."

Bryant's worry over Sarah was increased when he received a letter from his brother Peter, now a cadet at West Point, saying the family had written that her condition was worse. On July 30 he wrote his mother: "Frances and myself feel a great deal of solicitude upon this subject; and intreat you to write immediately and let us know how Sarah does." He said that he had thought of visiting Cummington during the month but could not since "Frances's health is at present extremely infirm."[17]

Sarah's illness progressed to its fatal conclusion in the autumn. In the sonnet Bryant was unable to rise above sentimentality, even bathos in the last line, but the next year he achieved a triumph in a transfiguration of his feeling of loss at Sarah's death in the poem "The Death of the Flowers." It is a poem that, because of the poet's commonplace ideas and the banality of his imagery, could easily have been maudlin. Somehow it escapes this. One of his dominant poetic themes is the passage of time leading to death and decay. He saw as a natural symbol of this the transience of flowers, blooming lovely in the spring but doomed to die with the frost. It is this hackneyed theme that he develops in his elegy. He speaks first in general terms:

Where are the flowers, the fair young flowers, that lately sprang and stood
In brighter light and softer airs, a beauteous sisterhood?
Alas! they all are in their graves, the gentle race of flowers
Are lying in their lowly beds, with the fair and good of ours.
The rain is falling where they lie, but the cold November rain
Calls not from out the gloomy earth the lovely ones again.

For four stanzas the poem expresses a general regret that the lovely flowers—the windflower and the violet, the brier-rose and the orchis, and all the others that bloom from spring through summer until autumn—are felled by the frost. Only in the last stanza is the true subject of the elegy revealed:

114

And then I think of one who in her youthful beauty died,
The fair meek blossom that grew up and faded by my side.
In the cold moist earth we laid her, when the forests cast the leaf,
And we wept that one so lovely should have a life so brief:
Yet not unmeet it was that one, like that young friend of ours,
So gentle and so beautiful, should perish with the flowers.

IV

Although Bryant's regularity in contributing to the *Gazette* showed that his poetic pen was not rusting through disuse, his output of short poems was not satisfactory to Dana, who wrote him on July 4: "I doubt whether it is well for the mind to work much in this way—to write from some occasional thought, or chance object." Again he urged Bryant to undertake a major work, something "sketched out on a large scale": "A man does not feel himself completely till he grapples with something that will *hold him in* tug."[18]

To Dana's inquiry on whether Bryant had written anything except what he had furnished Parsons, he replied on July 18: "Nothing at all. I made an engagement with him with a view, in the first place, to earn something in addition to the *emoluments* of my profession, which, as you may suppose, are not very ample, and, in the second place, to keep *my hand in,* for I was very near discontinuing entirely the writing of verses." He explained why he could not undertake such a project as Dana desired: it would interfere with his law practice but most of all he could not hit upon a good subject. He had, however, begun the past winter "a poor story about a Spectre Ship" but gave it up on finding that the legend had also been used by Washington Irving.[19] A few hundred lines of the poem in manuscript reveal that the story was based upon a report by Cotton Mather of a ship, *Magnalia Christi,* which sailed with a group of colonists returning to England and was never heard of again. It was a good story subject, since it was used later by Longfellow and Whittier, but probably not for Bryant, whose talent was for descriptive rather than narrative poetry.

In the letter to Dana, Bryant commented disapprovingly on the kind of verse that was popular at the time: "The only poems that have any currency at present are of a narrative kind—light stories in which love is a principal ingredient." Though unwilling to complete a long narrative, Bryant nevertheless, as he wrote Dana, considered it a misfortune "to write what nobody can read," and produced two story-poems on Indian themes for the *Gazette.* In 1816 while at home after being admitted to the

115

bar he had begun a tale based on Indian legends with the hope of doing for America what Scott had done in his highland poems. Now in casting about for subjects which he thought would be popular he returned again to the idea. The result was two tales in verse, "An Indian Story" and "Monument Mountain." This interest in an American subject also produced "An Indian at the Burial-Place of His Fathers."

In "An Indian at the Burial-Place of His Fathers" Bryant wrote another version of his favorite theme of mutability. An Indian, viewing the burial spot, laments that the white men have obliterated the graves of his forefathers, turning the ground into a place for sheep and cattle to graze and plowing up the bones of the dead. But as the Indians vanished, he predicts, so will the race of white men

> And leave no trace behind,
> Save ruins o'er the region spread,
> And the white stones above the dead.

"An Indian Story" is an attempt to write a ballad "in which love is the principal ingredient." It is a sentimental tale in which the Indian Maquon goes into the forest to kill a deer for his bride and on returning to their "bower" finds that she has been stolen away. He pursues and slays the ravisher and brings the bride home, who "smiles at his hearth once more."

"Monument Mountain" is a more significant work in which the drama of a human tragedy is played before a backdrop showing the awesomeness of nature. In an explanatory note Bryant said that Monument Mountain was a craggy precipice overlooking the valley of the Housatonic. The legend was that an Indian girl fell in love with her cousin, an attachment forbidden by the laws of her tribe. Overcome with feelings of guilt, she climbed the mountain in company with a friend and, after spending the day singing songs and repeating prayers, leaped from the cliff at sunset. The legend of Indian lovers committing suicide by jumping off cliffs—it usually was a youth and a maid—is one of the most persistent and widespread of the white men in America, to judge from the number of "lovers' leaps" in all parts of the country. Bryant's was not only among the first but also among the best literary talents to make use of it. The dark attraction of these stories for the white men has assumed mythical proportions. The reason may lie in Bryant's "An Indian at the Burial-Place of His Fathers," which expresses a sense of guilt for what they had done to the Indians:

They waste us—ay—like April snow
 In the warm noon, we shrink away;
And fast they follow, as we go
 Toward the setting day—
Till they shall fill the land, and we
Are driven into the Western sea.

After writing a number of poems in various meters and stanzaic forms, Bryant returned to his measured blank verse in "Monument Mountain." It begins with a long description that sets the tone for the tale and introduces the theme. On the precipice height man's spirit is uplifted:

There, as thou stand'st,
The haunts of men below thee, and around
The mountain-summits, thy expanding heart
Shall feel a kindred with that loftier world
To which thou art translated, and partake
The enlargement of thy vision.

The story of the Indian girl is then told, in the process of which her feelings of guilt over her incestuous love for her cousin are transformed into a symbol of the sins of all mankind.*

Coming out twice a month, the *Gazette* laid heavy tribute on Bryant's creativity to produce a poem for each number. Most of those written and printed in this year were nature poems in which Bryant revealed his technical virtuosity and his enjoyment, both visual and emotional, of the Berkshire landscape. One critic has said: "Breezes blow almost constantly throughout his poems."[20] Among Bryant's best on this theme is "Summer Wind," which Poe praised because it made "the sound the echo of the sense." The poet, lying languidly in the shade on a sultry day, wishes for the wind to come. When it does he is aroused to lyrical ecstasy:

See, on yonder woody ridge,
The pine is bending his proud top, and now

*The publisher James T. Fields, visiting Nathaniel Hawthorne at Lenox in the 1850's, recalled a picnic on Monument Mountain attended by, among others, Herman Melville, Oliver Wendell Holmes, David Dudley Field, and E. A. Duyckinck. These literati offered a toast to Bryant: "Then we all assembled in a shady spot, and one of the party read to us Bryant's beautiful poem commemorating Monument Mountain. Then we lunched among the rocks, and somebody proposed Bryant's health, and 'long life to the dear old poet.' This was the most popular toast of the day, and it took, I remember, a considerable quantity of Heidsieck to do it justice." *Yesterdays with Authors* (Boston, 1893), pp. 52–3.

Among the nearer groves, chestnut and oak
Are tossing their green boughs about. He comes;
Low, where the grassy meadow runs in waves!
The deep distressful silence of the scene
Breaks up with mingling of unnumbered sounds
And universal motion. He is come,
Shaking a shower of blossoms from the shrubs,
And bearing on their fragrance; and he brings
Music of birds, and rustling of young boughs,
And sound of swaying branches, and the voice
Of distant waterfalls.

The poet writes of another aspect of the wind in "After a Tempest," describes "Autumn Woods" that have "put their glory on," and, in one of his few sonnets, "November," reluctantly views the coming of winter:

Yet one smile more, departing, distant sun!
One mellow smile through the soft vapory air,
Ere, o'er the frozen earth, the loud winds run,
Or snows are sifted o'er the meadows bare.
One smile on the brown hills and naked trees,
And the dark rocks whose summer wreaths are cast,
And the blue gentian-flower, that, in the breeze,
Nods lonely, of her beauteous race the last.
Yet a few sunny days, in which the bee
Shall murmur by the hedge that skirts the way,
The cricket chirp upon the russet lea,
And man delight to linger in the ray.
Yet one rich smile, and we will try to bear
The piercing winter frost, and winds, and darkened air.

In another sonnet, "Mutation," he deals again with a favorite subject and concludes:

Weep not that the world changes—did it keep
A stable, changeless state, 'twere cause indeed to weep.

These two poems indicate that Bryant had not mastered, or perhaps did not care to master, which is the more probable, the conventions of the Italian or English sonnet forms. He held that the Italian model "possesses no peculiar beauty for an ear accustomed only to the metrical forms of our own language." Thus he was content to consider his work in this form as being merely "poems in fourteen lines" rather than sonnets.[21]

In the poetically productive year of 1824 Bryant, besides taking care of his law practice, wrote for the *Gazette* seventeen poems totaling more than nine hundred lines. In addition he contributed two critical articles to the *North American Review* and composed an ode for the Howard Benevolent Society of Boston.[22] One of Bryant's reviews was of Catharine Sedgwick's novel *Redwood*. Two years before Miss Sedgwick had introduced a note of realism in American fiction with the publication anonymously of her first novel, *A New England Tale*, designed to "lend a helping hand to some of the humbler and unnoticed virtues" and to describe the rustic scenes of the Berkshires. She followed this in 1824 with *Redwood*, which she dedicated to Bryant. In a somewhat coy letter to Charles Sedgwick on July 10 Bryant wrote that the word from Cambridge was that the book was held "in such high esteem there that it is absolutely dangerous and unsafe not to admire it." He added: "In the midst of these acclamations of praise which I hear from all quarters, it is a matter of no small pride to me that the unexpected and flattering honor which the author had done me in dedicating the work to me has permitted me to

'Pursue the triumph & partake the gale,'

as Pope says."[23] Later in the summer, on October 16, Jared Sparks asked Bryant to review the book for the *North American Review*.[24]

Bryant's article, which marked his return to the magazine which had first discovered his talent, appeared in the April, 1825, number. He used the occasion not so much to praise his friend's work, since it was dedicated to him, but to advocate the writing of fiction on American themes by American authors. Cooper had shown that the nation's past could be used for the romantic tale, his work revealing to "the literary world into what beautiful creations those materials may be wrought." But Bryant also insisted that, as Miss Sedgwick's novel demonstrated, "the writers of works of fiction, of which the scene is laid in familiar and domestic life, have a rich and varied field before them in the United States." He denied that "the habits of our countrymen are too active and practical" to have "leisure for that intrigue, those plottings and counter plottings, which are necessary to give a sufficient degree of action and eventfulness to the novel of real life." He did not believe that "the distinctions of rank, and the amusements of elegant idleness" were necessary for interesting fiction and he appealed for fiction dealing with American democrats. In Europe men lived out all their life in the condition in which they were born; this destiny prevented the development of character. This was not so in the United States: "Whoever will take the pains to pursue this subject a little into its particulars, will be surprised at the infinite variety of forms of character, which spring up under the institutions of our country." Moreover, change was characteristic of the United States: "Each little hamlet, in a few seasons has more events and changes to tell of, than a European village can furnish in a course of ages."

Six years before, Bryant in his review of Solyman Brown's versified essay on American poetry, had condemned "a sickly and affected imitation" of British poetry. Now he was able to perceive progress in the development of the national letters and to note that American writers were being recognized abroad. Of Cooper's success in England, he wrote Dana: "I hope it is the breaking of a bright day for American literature. . . ."[25] In a letter to Charles Sedgwick about Catharine's novel he said that he was "gratified at seeing so many handsome things said of it on both sides of the water" and that he thought it could not "fail with the English public," because it was a "faithful picture of our domestic manners, drawn by a writer of genius" and therefore "must have with English readers, the . . . piquant and popular attraction of novelty."[26]

Bryant himself was beginning to be noticed abroad, Dana writing him that *Blackwood's Magazine* had carried an article about his work, though he must have been more chagrined than pleased when he read it. John Neal, in the issue of September, 1824, commented that Bryant's poetry had found "its way, piecemeal, into England" and had "met a little of our newspaper praise." He himself did not find much to praise, declaring: "Mr. B. is not, and never will be, a great poet." "He wants fire—he wants the very rashness of a poet—the prodigality and fervour of those, who are overflowing with inspiration," Neal continued. "Mr. B., in fact, is a sensible young man, of thrifty disposition, who knows how to manage a few plain ideas in a very handsome way."

V

Bryant was finding the law more and more irksome. Had it brought in the income he needed, he might have been content, dividing his life into two compartments—his practice by which he made his living and his poetry by which he lived. But it did not. Hence, during 1824, he gave more and more thought to the suggestion of the Sedgwicks that he might be able to earn a living by literary journalism in New York. Later, after he had determined upon the change and moved to New York, he explained to Dana that besides his distaste for the law "my residence in Great Barrington, in consequence of innumerable quarrels and factions which were springing up every day among an extremely excitable and not very enlightened population, had become quite disagreeable to me."[27] Bryant is ordinarily portrayed as being of a calm—even cold—temperament. If he often appeared unmoved, it was because of his self-control. At Great Barrington he sometimes lost his temper, on one occasion bouncing out of the courtroom and exclaiming of his adversary: "If old Whiting says that again, I will thrash him within an inch of his life."[28] Repeated provocations became intolerable, as he wrote Dana: "It cost me more pain and perplexity than it was worth to live on friendly terms with my neighbors; and, not having, as I flatter myself, any great taste for contention, I made up my mind to get out of it as soon as I could and come to this great city, where, if it was my lot to starve, I might starve peaceably and quietly."

In many respects Bryant had the abilities needed to succeed in the law. He had a logical mind that could distinguish among the issues in a case, disentangling the relevant from the irrelevant, and that could marshal evidence and citations of precedents to reach cogent conclusions. But this was not enough for him: he believed that the function of law was to achieve equity; therefore, he could not willingly undertake a case unless his client was in the right. But court decisions were often not on the side of the right. He cited, for example, a slander suit which he won in the Common Pleas Court but lost on appeal. A man named Tobey had said of Bryant's client, one Bloss, that he had burned down his house to collect the insurance money. The lower court decision was reversed on the hair-splitting interpretation that an action for slander could not be sustained unless the utterance were of such a nature as to make it clear that the burning was unlawful. Commenting on the case, Bryant said: "Thus, by a piece of pure chicane—in a case the merits of which were with my client, and which were perfectly understood by the parties, the court, the jury, and everybody who heard the trial, or heard of it—my client was turned out of court, after the jury had awarded him damages—and so deprived of what they intended he should receive."[29]

Bryant often discussed his attitudes toward the law with Charles Sedgwick, who had reservations about his quitting the profession. On November 5, 1824, Sedgwick wrote Bryant: "The law is a hag, I know, wearing the wrinkled visage of antiquity, towards which you can feel no complacency. Though it comes to us fraught with the pretended wisdom of ages, it wears an ugly drapery of forms, and the principles of practice and the simple perceptions of truth are so involved in the clouds of mystical learning and nonsense that the finest mind must needs grope in obscurity and be clogged with difficulty—besides, there are tricks in practice which

121

perpetually provoke disgust." On the one hand, Sedgwick thought that Bryant should prove that "his genius which delights the world can surmount the barriers of the least inviting and most laborious profession." On the other, he thought that if he were of Bryant's mind with "a very prevailing desire for literary occupations I should run the hazard of indulging it." He offered to engage the help of his brothers in New York to further Bryant's interests and ended his letter: "Whenever and whatever you decide, may God help you."[30]

By December 24 Bryant was more firmly decided on quitting the law. On returning from New Haven, where he had gone twice as a witness in an action against one of his neighbors, he wrote Charles Sedgwick: "I am fixed to leave this beggarly profession." In New Haven, he had seen the poet-dramatist, James A. Hillhouse, whose new work, *Hadad,* a play based on a Biblical theme, had just been published. Hillhouse had only recently left New York, and he assured Bryant "there would be no obstacle in the way" of his attaining success there. Bryant told Sedgwick that he would "reconnoitre the ground in the spring."[31]

Bryant's first step toward this end was to write Henry D. Sedgwick on January 15, 1825, of his plan to visit New York. But in the meantime, Charles Sedgwick had broached the idea to his brother, who, before he received Bryant's letter, had written inviting him to spend a week or fortnight as his guest while he looked about "to see what could be done." Mentioning certain advantages of New York, Sedgwick said: "Life is here so miscellaneous that any description of talent may find not only occupation but diversity of application."[32] A week later he wrote Bryant of more definite prospects and urged him "to lose no time in coming here" for the time was "peculiarly propitious." There was "a rage," he said, for the Athenaeum, a library and reading club which had just been formed, and there was talk of its sponsoring a journal. He wrote that the *Atlantic Magazine,* which had been started in May, 1824, by Robert C. Sands, "has pined until recently when it has begun to attract attention and favour." It had just been taken over by Dr. Henry J. Anderson, "who indulges the pride (or whim) of supporting himself although his father is a man of wealth." He was planning to change it from a literary magazine to a more general review. "I do not believe, however, that he will be able to conduct the work alone," Sedgwick continued. "I have not yet been able to see him and learn his views—but I do know that the proprietors (Bliss & White) would like to have you associated with him. They now give him $500 a year and allow him the same sum in addition to pay other contributors." He thought that if the *Atlantic* were remodeled and associated in some way with the Athenaeum, with Bryant's name added as one of the editors, "a great circulation might be obtained." He continued: "Any deficiencies of salary, moreover, may be eked out by teaching foreigners, of whom there are many in New York, eager to learn our language and literature. In short, it would be strange if you could not succeed where anybody and everything succeeds."[33]

So promising did these prospects sound that Bryant went to New York in February to see what he could arrange. He wrote his wife on February 18 of his arrival and three days later of plans underfoot for the Athenaeum to establish a literary paper under his direction. The details were not all worked out, but he told Frances definitely: "At all events, I shall make the experiment."[34]

8

A LITERARY ADVENTURER

WHEN BRYANT WROTE FRANCES FROM NEW YORK THAT HE was committed to undertaking the editorship of a magazine, he was being too optimistic, for he was unable to conclude negotiations for the project. He had felt confident because he not only had the support of the Sedgwick brothers but also of the poet James A. Hillhouse, Gulian C. Verplanck, one of New York's leading littérateurs as well as a member of Congress, and, as Bryant wrote to his wife in practicing his French, "beaucoup d'autres savans de New York."[1]

Disappointed, Bryant returned to Great Barrington, where he found two letters awaiting him that increased his desire to escape from his law practice and the intellectual limitations of the village. During the past year his dissatisfaction had been somewhat lessened by his association with the *United States Literary Gazette* and the $200 a year addition to his income. The letters announced a change. One, dated February 18, was from Theophilus Parsons.[2] He acknowledged receipt of Bryant's "beautiful hymn" ("A Forest Hymn," with its memorable opening line, "The groves were God's first temples.")* and announced that he was turning over the edi-

---

*Parke Godwin's account of the composition of "A Forest Hymn" says that Bryant wrote it in April, 1825, on a brief trip to Great Barrington to arrange his affairs for moving to New York City. *Biography,* I, 214. The fact is that the poem was written some weeks or months earlier. Theophilus Parsons, as his Feb. 18 letter shows, already had received the poem before Bryant went to New York to negotiate for the editorship of a magazine, and the poem appeared in the April 1 number of the *Literary Gazette.*

torship to James G. Carter, a Harvard graduate who had attracted attention by newspaper articles on educational reform. Parsons said that Carter wanted Bryant to continue as a contributor "unless the compensation now given shall be deemed by you wholly inadequate." But the other letter, from Carter, contained the bad news that the *Gazette* publishers, because of the small subscription revenue, were compelled to economize. They proposed that Bryant receive one-half the payment he had been receiving for one-half the quantity of verse.[3]

Bryant wrote immediately that he could not continue to contribute to the *Gazette* under the terms suggested.* He received answers from Parsons and Carter regretting the decision. Parsons said he had hoped the magazine could continue to have "the benefit of your name" and suggested that Bryant bring out another book of poems: "Perhaps my connections with the press may enable me to know better than you, how much they are demanded. I am sure that a new edition of your volume, with all those published in the Gazette & as much more as may be added, would be very acceptable to the reading public and would be made very profitable to yourself."[4] Carter asked Bryant to "contribute a piece now and then" and added: "We think the literature of our country is deeply interested in what may be your decision as to writing. . . . The public begin to look in our works for the best poetry published in the country, and we shall be ambitious to meet their expectations."[5]

The news that the *Gazette* had not been able to make expenses was not a favorable augury for Bryant's New York project. Nevertheless, his desire to leave the law was so strong that he returned to the city to resume negotiations. He wrote Frances on his arrival on March 23. He had gone overland from Great Barrington to Hudson, New York, which he reached in "a damp great coat and pantaloons" because of having to ride through a heavy rainstorm, and awoke the next morning "giddy and almost blind with a cold." He was unable to get passage on a steamboat until noon the next day; it was a rough journey of about eighteen hours down the Hudson River. "Here I am trying to starve myself well, going hungry amid a profusion of good cheer, and refusing to drink good wine amid an ocean of it," he said. "But all will not do; I am continually in the steamboat. Sitting or standing, I feel the roll and swell of the water under

---

*Bryant's appearances in the *Literary Gazette*, however, did not end immediately. His contributions in 1825 were "The Murdered Traveller," Jan. 1; "Hymn to the North Star," Jan. 15; "The Lapse of Time," Feb. 15; "Song of the Stars," March 1; "A Hymn" (later titled "A Forest Hymn"), April 1; and "The Grecian Partizan" (later titled "The Greek Partisan"), May 15.

me; the streets and floors of houses swing from side to side as if they were floating in a sea."[6]

Over the years New York literati had started several magazines, all of which had been short lived. A bustling place of about 180,000 people, the city had outdistanced Boston and Philadelphia as a commercial center. It looked forward to still greater growth, since the Erie Canal, the "Ditch" of Governor De Witt Clinton, to be completed in October, would open up a vast trade with the interior. But in literature New York lagged behind her sister metropolises.

The city now had three magazines of no great distinction, the *Minerva, or Literary, Entertaining and Scientific Journal,* the *New-York Mirror and Ladies' Literary Gazette,* and the *Atlantic Magazine.* The *Minerva* had been founded by George Houston in 1822. He had as his junior editor the young poet James G. Brooks, who was in charge of the literary and poetical departments. It was a well-printed miscellany of sixteen pages octavo appearing every Saturday. The *Mirror* had been founded the next year by George Pope Morris; the editor was Samuel Woodworth, famous for "The [Old Oaken] Bucket," which had been published in 1817. A weekly, the *Mirror* was also a well-printed publication, a quarto of eight pages. Both carried book reviews, though not extended critiques like the British quarterlies, tales, poetry, familiar essays, notes on the arts, and notices of plays performed at the Park and Chatham theaters. Their material, however, was not all original, some of it being copied from other American as well as British publications. Planned to be an American version of the English and Scotch quarterlies, running to eighty pages octavo, the *Atlantic* had been started only in 1824 with the precocious and learned Robert C. Sands as editor. Sands's reputation rested on his coauthorship of the romantic narrative poem, *Yamoyden; a Tale of the Wars of King Philip,* which had created a fashion for Indian narratives and plays. He was also known as a wit, one of the poetasters and essayists who had enlivened the city since Washington and William Irving and James K. Paulding had brought out their sprightly satire *Salmagundi* in 1807. Sands, however, had given up the *Atlantic* after six months, and the editor was Dr. Henry James Anderson, who despite his interest in literature was chiefly a scientist and who was in November to be appointed professor of mathematics, analytical mechanics, and physical astronomy at Columbia College.

But as Henry Sedgwick had written Bryant in January, the *Atlantic* still fell short of being a "review," and to improve it Anderson needed assistance. At this time the words "review" and "magazine" had connotations as to content that have long since been lost. A "review" was a publication on the order of the *Edinburgh Review* that contained long discussions, serious and learned, suggested by a book under consideration by the reviewer. A "magazine" was a repository or storehouse containing a variety of matter—verse, tales, essays, biography, history, and news about science, the arts, and government. The founders of the Athenaeum, as had literary, art, and scientific clubs before it in other cities, wished to get out their own magazine, and Bryant was wanted for this project also. He drew up a draft of a prospectus, on March 30, 1825, for a weekly magazine to be called the *Gazette of the New York Athenaeum,* which said in part:

> A mine of rich and various materials will be found in the numerous publications from the presses of Europe and America received at this institution. A brief analysis of these works as they appear will furnish a general view of the state of literature and science, and a record of their progress in the different countries of the world. . . . There will be interesting abstracts from the literary journals of England and France. . . . The paper will be furnished with a department in which will appear miscellaneous notices of information on all subjects connected with the state of literature, science and the arts in our own and other countries. . . . In this department will be found a journal of all the proceedings of the Athenaeum and a weekly list of all the publications received at the institution. . . . There will also be a department of original matter consisting of such articles from the pens of mature writers that will not in the judgment of the editor disgrace the selections in whose company they appear. . . .[7]

Conferences between Bryant and the interested New York parties—members of the Athenaeum and the publishers of the *Atlantic,* the firm of Elam Bliss and Elihu White at 128 Broadway, led to the decision to unite. An agreement was signed by the firm and the two editors, Anderson and Bryant, for a monthly publication to be called the *New-York Review and Athenaeum Magazine.*[8] By the double title, the publication would serve two purposes: that of a "review" and that of a "magazine." It would be likely to appeal to a broader readership than if it were one or the other.

Under the agreement, Bryant was to receive $1,000 a year, "no great sum, to be sure," he wrote Dana on May 25, "but it is twice what I got by my practice in the country."[9] He was under no misapprehension that the salary would continue for long. Bliss & White had paid Anderson $500 a year for editing the *Atlantic,* and he was in addition allowed $500 to remunerate contributors. Bryant's employment merely meant that the publishing house was willing to spend money at the start in the hope that in joining the *Atlantic,* which had only about three hundred fifty subscribers, with the Athenaeum project a successful enterprise could be developed.

II

Little in the history of United States magazines and reviews indicated that success was likely. Publications were almost entirely local, being supported by subscriptions obtained preponderantly within a single city and by contributions by coteries of resident literati. In Philadelphia the *Port Folio* under Joseph Dennie, the "American Addison," at one time had a circulation of two thousand copies at five dollars a year, but this had been phenomenal; in 1825 it was on the verge of being suspended and was two years later. The *North American Review* had about five or six hundred subscribers. Sands had noted in the first issue of the *Atlantic* the danger of starting a new publication when the field was littered by "past abortions and rickety, short-lived productions."

If magazines suffered from a lack of readers, they suffered also from a lack of contributors. The letters to Bryant at Great Barrington from the editors of the *North American Review* and the *Gazette* beseeching him to submit poems and prose reflect the sparsity of literary talent. Authorship was not a profession, many who engaged in it being gentlemen who wrote merely for personal pleasure, a relaxation from their regular pursuits. There were of course writers like Bryant and his rival in popularity as a poet, James Gates Percival, who wanted to make a living by authorship but they were few.* It might be expected that when magazines began paying contributors, as did the *Gazette* and the *Atlantic* when they were started in 1824 and the *North American Review* the same year, writing as a profession would be encouraged. But this was not the case, for payment was so low that no one could live by his pen alone. Moreover, some magazine contributors refused to accept pay. Sands commented on this in the *Atlantic:* "Those who are able and willing to assist us must accept their honorarium for the principle of the thing. . . . As to false delicacy, we will obviate its scruples by forwarding every contributor's dues to any address given in his communication."[10]

---

*Several years before, in 1821 or 1822, friends of Percival, as Bryant's friends were now doing for him, had tried to find a means for him to make a living by authorship in New York. When they proposed that he bring out a volume of poems, Percival replied "that circumstances had put it out of his power to devote himself to poetry, and had compelled him to accept employment in that most degrading and disgraceful of all occupations—the editorship of a party newspaper." James Grant Wilson, *The Life and Letters of Fitz-Greene Halleck* (New York, 1869), pp. 288–9.

Despite this recent magazine history, Bryant hoped for success and wrote a prospectus for the *Review and Athenaeum* to go to potential subscribers. On March 30 he sent copies to Dana and Phillips in Boston, asking them to "show it to such persons in your neighbourhood who will be likely to subscribe." His accompanying letter to Dana said: "I have given up my profession, which was a shabby business, and I am not altogether certain that I have got into a better. Bliss & White, however, the publishers of the N.Y. Review, allow me a compensation, which at present will be a livelihood for me, and a livelihood is as much as I got from my profession."[11] If Bryant had thought everything was settled when he issued his prospectus, he was quickly disillusioned. Within two weeks he found himself the center of a war that involved dissidents from the dominant group in the Athenaeum and rival magazine editors.

One of the dissidents was George Bond, who on April 21 issued a magazine using the second half of the name adopted for the one planned by Bryant and Anderson. Bond called his publication the *American Athenaeum, Repository of the Arts, Sciences, and Belles Lettres*. The Athenaeum society had been formed in May of 1824 by fifty-eight of the city's leaders, men devoted to scientific and literary pursuits. They issued an address to the public inviting members, but the response was slow until the late fall, when the society's first sponsored lectures proved to be greatly popular, drawing attendances of more than six hundred persons. Applications for membership poured in at such a rate that, a historian of the society wrote, the subscriptions appeared likely to reach $100,000. But the founders, in attempting to maintain some exclusiveness in the membership, turned down many of the applications, and the society was rent by disputes.[12] One of those at odds with the majority faction was Bond, who, in spite, started his magazine using the society's name. In one article he attacked the Athenaeum as a society got up by "a few select persons to honor themselves."[13]

Another row involved George Houston's *Minerva*, which was published by Bliss & White. Now committed to publishing two competing literary magazines, the *Minerva* and the *Review*, the firm dropped Houston's name as editor in the issue of April 23 and announced that all orders, remittances, and communications should be submitted to the publishers. On the same date Houston issued an "extra" accusing Bliss & White "for reasons best known to themselves" of assuming "a right of property, which never belonged to them" and of offering to sell the establishment. The two parties to the dispute, however, settled their differences and Houston continued as editor until May 28, when the *Minerva* carried a notice that the junior editor, James G. Brooks, had purchased it from Bliss

& White and Houston and that subscribers would receive it until the completion of the current volume in September. The name then would be changed to the *New-York Literary Gazette and Phi Beta Kappa Repository.*

This publishing warfare resulted in a contretemps for the sponsors and editors of the *Review.* They decided, however, to continue with the magazine as planned with the exception of changing the spelling of *Athenaeum* to *Atheneum* to avoid confusion with Bond's weekly. The new spelling was also adopted by the society. The first number would be published on June 1.

Bryant then returned to Great Barrington to close his law office and to plan for his wife and daughter until he could arrange for them to move to New York. Sending them to Cummington to spend the summer, he was back in New York by the middle of May. He found awaiting him letters from Dana and Phillips. Dana, who had never written any verse, enclosed a poem, "The Dying Crow," as a possible contribution. He was in doubt as to its merit, asking: "Does the movement offend thee, thou veteran in verse?"[14] Phillips, out of his experience on the *North American Review,* was apprehensive over the prospects of the magazine, saying "that the risks and perils are certainly not trifling." He advised that it was "absolutely essential to permanent success" that "editors should not be in the power or under the control of the publishers."[15]

At home Bryant and Frances had spoken French, teaching it also to Fanny, and his letters to his wife frequently contained passages written in the language. To learn to speak it better, he obtained board and room with a French family, that of a M. Evrard, who lived on Chambers Street within view of the North River. "The family speak only French," Bryant wrote Frances on May 24, "and what is better, very good French; and what is better yet, are very kind and amiable people." A devout Roman Catholic, M. Evrard attempted to convert him to the faith. "I have been so far wrought upon by his arguments," Bryant wrote, "that I went yesterday to vespers in St. Peter's Church; but my convictions were not sufficiently strong to induce me to kneel at the elevation of the host." Nevertheless, he planned to ask the favor of being permitted to attend the family prayers. "In the meantime," he continued, "I have become a great church-goer; I went three times yesterday, including the Roman Catholic service, which is more, I believe, than I have done before these ten years."[16] The church of his attendance was the Unitarian, which had been established by the Rev. William Ware in 1821. This began a friendship with the minister that lasted until his death in 1852.

III

The first issue of the *New-York Review and Atheneum Magazine* appeared the last week in May. It was a neatly printed octavo in two parts, the first or "review" part consisting of eight articles discussing books and the second or "magazine" part consisting of five poems, several letters, and some notes on literary topics. The names of the editors did not appear nor was there an introductory announcement of their purposes and standards of selection. Bryant sent a copy to Frances at Cummington, remarking that he thought it was "a pretty good number." He said that the subscription list was "going pretty well," with five hundred in the city and one hundred in the country besides the Boston subscribers.[17] The subscription rate was six dollars a year, and this would mean a revenue of more than $3,600, a good start for a magazine but not enough to insure its continued existence.

Bryant had three contributions in the issue, the lead review on *Hadad, a Dramatic Poem,* by James A. Hillhouse; a notice of Catharine Sedgwick's tale for children, *The Travellers;* and a poem, "A Song of Pitcairn's Island." What gave the magazine editorial éclat, however, was the first publication of Fitz-Greene Halleck's stirring poem *Marco Bozzaris* on a hero of the Greek revolution against the Turks. Halleck was known as a clever versifier and man-about-town, who a few years before had created a stir when, with his friend Joseph Rodman Drake, he had contributed to the *Evening Post* a series of topical poems satirizing local men and events under the name "Croaker" and had followed these poems with an extended *jeu d'esprit* of his own, *Fanny,* which delighted New Yorkers with its exposure of current foibles and its lines describing such familiar places as Weehawken, Saratoga, and the Falls of Cohoes. Writing Dana about the June number, Bryant said he thought *Marco Bozzaris* "a very beautiful thing," continuing: "Anderson was so delighted with it—he got it from the author after much solicitation—that he could not forbear adding the expression of his admiration at the end of the poem. For my part, though I entirely agree with him in his opinion of the beauty of the poem, I have my doubts whether it is not better to let the poetry of magazines commend itself to the reader by its own excellence."

Bryant spoke also of the difficulty of finding entertaining material for the *Atheneum* part of the magazine: "A talent for such articles is quite rare in this country, and particularly in this city. There are many who can give grave, sensible discussions on subjects of general utility, but few who can write an interesting or diverting article for a miscellany." In printing

Dana's "The Dying Crow," Bryant transformed the bird into a raven. He thought Dana had given "too many magnificent titles to a bird" not generally highly thought of. "I can speak also of his character from my own experience," he said, "having once kept a tame crow, and found him little better than a knave, a thief, and a coward."[18]

In reviewing *Hadad,* Bryant addressed himself to the question of how far "subjects drawn from the sacred writings are proper for narrative poetry," citing the objection that such treatment might tend "to impair our reverence for the history of our religion." Bryant felt that any such scruples were unnecessary, since the "human persons mentioned in sacred history must be considered as actual human beings, subject to the common passions and infirmities of our race." Of Miss Sedgwick's *The Travellers,* an account of a trip to Niagara Falls and the Great Lakes of two children with their parents, Bryant was happy to see his friend employ her talents in writing a book for young people. Such books designed to educate as well as entertain children, he said, were an important responsibility of writers.

Although Bryant was glad to escape from the bickerings and other unpleasantnesses that made practicing law intolerable, editing a magazine was not the fulfillment of his heart's desire. Even while working on the first number of the *Review,* he wrote Dana: "The business of sitting in judgment on books as they come out is not the literary employment the most to my taste, nor that for which I am best fitted, but it affords me, for the present, a *certain* compensation, which is a matter of some consequence to a poor devil like myself."[19]

Nor did Bryant easily adapt himself to city life. After some weeks in New York, he wrote Frances on June 3 that he liked his "boarding-house better and better" and that though M. Evrard was a "bigoted Catholic" he found it "almost impossible to conceive of a man of more goodness of heart and rectitude of principle." Catholicism he thought mistaken in many of its doctrines but nevertheless he considered the religion much more "amiable and cheerful than that of many sects." "On the whole, I think that a *good Catholic* is quite as good as a *good Calvinist,*" he declared.[20] But he missed the Berkshire countryside. Writing again ten days later, he said: "I envy you very much the pure air, the breezes, the shade, and the coolness which you must enjoy in the country, while I am sweltering under a degree of heat which I never experienced in my whole lifetime for so long a period." Preparing the July number of the *Review,* he was able to get some work done during the morning but at noon he barely could call up "resolution enough even to read." He found there was no escape outside the city: "Yesterday, in the afternoon, I rode a few miles into the country; I found it worse, if possible, than the city. The roads were full of carts, barouches, chaises, hacks, and people on horseback passing each other; and a thick cloud of dust lay above the road as far as the eye could follow it. It was almost impossible to breathe the stifling element."[21]

For the July number of the *Review* Bryant was laboring over a critical article of more than 8,500 words on the lives of the troubadour poets by Jehan de Nostre Dame, a book written in 1575 which had just been reissued in France. The review was a notable performance, showing Bryant's mastery of the French and Provençal languages and the wide scope of his reading. It also revealed the high seriousness with which he viewed his editorial function and his role as a critic. Though Bryant shared the belief of other critics that the country must develop a literature that reflected truly its people and places, he did not permit this to influence his judgment of books, to praise a book by an American just because he was an American. Other editors had declared one of their purposes to be that of refuting the aspersions of the British quarterlies against the literature of the United States, typified in the famous question asked in the *Edinburgh Review*, "Who reads an American book?" Bryant had shown an opposite attitude years before in his survey of native verse for the *North American Review* when he condemned American poets he considered pedestrian. In editing a journal himself, he would deal with books on their intrinsic merit. Although nationalistic in politics, he considered literature to be international. His study of the troubadours was the first of his examinations of the literature of other nations that led him to give space to foreign works in the periodicals he edited and to translate poems from the Spanish, German, Italian, and Portuguese.

In beginning his review, Bryant took the occasion to satirize current literary criticism. John of Nostradamus, he said, wrote before there were any critical magazines and his work was not "made the subject of an elaborate article in the ponderous literary journal" and there was no one to have him stand up in public "as a school-master summons his pupil." But though he lacked the "inconveniences" of having someone to point out his misspellings and bad grammar, he enjoyed some advantages: "If he could not expect that an ingenious literary friend should lift it into public favor by a cunning exposition of its latent merits, and an artful selection of fortunate passages, so neither could he apprehend that any ill-natured critic should injure its circulation by caricaturing its defects and making a bouquet of its absurdities and mistakes." From these animadversions on current reviewing, it is evident that Bryant thought criticism should be interestingly written; that it should not dwell at length on minor faults at the expense of more important matters; that it should not consist of puffery inspired by friendship; and that it should not be the product of the ill will of a person occupying a place of authority from which to condemn. Bryant's own review showed that he had thoroughly prepared himself to point out the merits and defects of John of Nostradamus, illustrating them by apt citations (the English translations of the Provençal poems quoted were his own), and to describe the quality of the work in a readable way.

The July issue, however, did not maintain the standard Bryant had set in his article on John of Nostradamus. The fault was not his. Rather, it was the lack of good books on which to comment. A review of Henry R. Schoolcraft's *Travels in the Central Portions of the Mississippi Valley* could be expected to interest readers but not one on a work on mathematics by a professor at Columbia College or two discourses on the duties of American citizens by a minister delivered at the First Baptist Meeting House in Boston. The *Atheneum* part of the magazine also fell below the quality of the June number, which had carried Halleck's *Marco Bozzaris*. It opened with an essay, "The Literary Trifler," probably by Paulding, written in the leisurely vein of Irving but without his style or humor; and it contained two mediocre poems besides Bryant's own mediocre "The Skies" and two translations, one from Goethe and the other "Paraphrase of the Hymn Sung by the Hierophant, at the Eleusinian Mysteries." The translation from Goethe, "The Indian God and the Bayadeer," was sent in by the head of the experimental Round Hill school at Northampton, Massachusetts, George Bancroft, who later became Bryant's friend and achieved fame as a statesman and historian.

Bryant was compelled, as he wrote Frances on June 20, "to be pretty industrious," but he thought this was well enough. "In the mean time," he said, "I am not plagued with the disagreeable, disgusting drudgery of the law, and what is far better am aloof from those miserable feuds and wranglings that make Great Barrington an unpleasant residence, even to him who tries every method in his power to avoid them." He had planned to go to Brooklyn to look for a place for his family to live but had been unable to get away from his desk. He advised Frances in getting her things together for moving to put her name on every article of clothing she was likely to have washed. In his own laundry just returned to him he discovered one cravat, two pairs of stockings, and a flannel wrapper that did not belong to him while two cravats of his own and two pairs of stockings were missing.[22]

With the July number of the magazine out of the way, Bryant was able to go to Cummington to see his family. As he was ever to find after going to the city, a visit to the country refreshed his spirit. With Fanny, now four years old, he explored old haunts and was moved to write his "Lines on Revisiting the Country":

> Here have I 'scaped the city's stifling heat,
>   Its horrid sounds, and its polluted air,
> And, where the season's milder fervors beat,
>   And gales, that sweep the forest borders, bear
> The song of bird and sound of running stream,
> Am come awhile to wander and to dream.

IV

By the last week in July, Bryant was back in New York, busy with his editorial chores. The poetry obtained often did not meet his standards of correctness, and he took the liberty of rewriting lines to remove crudities. He also had to rework some of the prose material, for James G. Carter had criticized the writing in the first issue of the magazine, saying: "We think the editors are not always sufficiently impressed with the importance of preserving the purity of the language, not sufficiently careful to exclude slight errors in construction, or unauthorized words. . . ."[23]

Because of the unusually hot weather—Bryant wrote Frances that the thermometer during one week had never registered below eighty degrees day or night—private social gatherings as well as public entertainments were held to a minimum. But with the arrival of autumn the country lawyer was to wine and dine with the city's illuminati; to enjoy the Italian opera popularized by the Venetian expatriate Lorenzo da Ponte, who had written the librettos for Mozart's *The Marriage of Figaro, Don Giovanni,* and *Così fan tutte;* to attend the plays at the Park Theatre which William Dunlap had managed for twenty-five years; and, before the year's end, to become a member of the young artists' set that was beginning to revolt against the conservatism of their elders.

At the homes of the Sedgwick brothers Bryant was introduced to the intellectual and artistic life of the city, homes where sparkling conversation flowed with the wine and ideas were assimilated with the excellent food. Both Henry and Robert Sedgwick were philanthropists and reformers, dedicated to improving society but "without the faults which too often make that class of persons disagreeable," and, although supporters of all worthy projects, "did not fatigue people with them." Their homes "were the resort of the best company in New York, cultivated men and women, literati, artists, and, occasionally, foreigners of distinction."[24]

It was at this time that Bryant's friendship with Cooper began, one that was to continue more than a quarter of a century in which, as Bryant said later, "his deportment toward me was that of unvaried kindness." Cooper's fame as a novelist had begun in 1821 with the publication of *The Spy*, and he had come to New York to be near his publisher, Charles Wiley. The bluff and hearty Cooper, who had served in the navy before settling down to be a farmer at Scarsdale, intimidated Bryant. Shortly after his arrival in New York, Bryant, meeting Cooper casually on the street, was brusquely invited:

"Come and dine with me tomorrow. I live at No. 345 Greenwich Street."

"Please put that down for me," said Bryant, "or I shall forget the place."

"Can't you remember *three-four-five?*" asked Cooper bluntly.[25]

Writing to Dana on September 21, Bryant mentioned seeing Cooper again. "He is printing a novel entitled *The Last of the Mohicans*," Bryant related. "The first volume is nearly finished. You tell me that I must review him next time myself. Ah, sir! he is too sensitive a creature for me to touch. He seems to think his own works his own property, instead of being the property of the public, to whom he has given them; and it is almost as difficult to praise or blame them in the right place as it was to praise or blame Goldsmith properly in the presence of Johnson."[26] But he became a member of the Cooper coterie that frequented the back room of Charles Wiley's bookstore, christened "the Den," where the novelist held forth to an admiring audience. He was also welcomed into Cooper's Bread and Cheese Club, which met at the Washington Hotel at Broadway and Chambers Street. It was popularly called "the Lunch," and was attended by the city's leading writers and artists.[27] The young Samuel F. B. Morse, just arrived in New York from England to set himself up as a portrait painter, was taken into the club at the same time as the poets Bryant and Hillhouse, writing his parents expressing his gratification at being accepted.[28] Members were admitted by a bread and cheese tally: if a name was proposed and any cheese was found on the plates when the candidate was voted on he was rejected.

At the Sedgwicks Bryant also first met the painter Thomas Cole, "then in the early promise of his genius," as he recalled. Cole had joined his family in the spring, painting in the garret of his father's house on Greenwich Street. A picture exhibited in a store window attracted the attention of the connoisseur G. W. Bruen, who bought it and financed Cole on a trip up the Hudson River to paint the landscape. One of the three pictures completed was of Catterskill Falls, which Bryant later celebrated in a poem. Soon, through the Bread and Cheese, Bryant came to know others among the city's artists—the aging John Trumbull, painter of the Revolutionary War pictures hung in the Capitol at Washington, and the younger artists, Asher B. Durand, Henry Inman, John Vanderlyn, and John Wesley Jarvis as well as Morse and Cole.

As a youth preparing for college at his uncle's home in North Bridgewater, Bryant had shown some talent for drawing and painting. This early interest, which he had let lapse, was revived through his association with the artists he met. Since shortly after the turn of the century, the city's art circles had been dominated by the New York Academy of Fine Arts, headed after 1818 by the now aging and testy Trumbull. Domineering and sensitive to imaginary slights, Trumbull alienated the younger painters, who were turning away from the huge historical canvases with which the older painters had celebrated the founding of the nation to landscapes expressing new concepts of nature and man's relation to it, concepts already voiced by Bryant in his poetry. On November 8, the younger artists met in rooms occupied by the Historical and Philosophical Societies and formed the New York Drawing Association, with Morse presiding. Whether Bryant attended the meeting is not known, but he was sympathetic to the movement. Early the next year, the informal drawing association was organized as the National Academy of the Arts of Design, and a short while later Bryant was elected its "Professor of Mythology and Antiquities."

Besides his literary friends, Verplanck, Halleck, Paulding, Hillhouse, and Sands, and the artists, Bryant became acquainted with William Dunlap, the guiding genius of the New York theater who was also a painter not without distinction; with such leaders at the bar as Chancellor James Kent, before long to edit his *Commentaries* on American law, and Thomas Addis Emmet and Edward D. Griffith; such merchants as Charles A. Davis and Philip Hone, whose *Diary* later became one of the most fascinating sourcebooks of New York history; and with the scientists and natural philosophers gathered at Columbia College—in short, a stimulating and varied group whose talk was learned yet entertaining, friendly yet provocative.

The life of the city was concentrated in the southern tip of Manhattan Island, the space occupied with houses, Bryant was to recall later, extending a little beyond Canal Street.[29] Farther on were a few straggling houses and then orchards and farmlands, leading to the villages of Greenwich, then popular as a summer resort, Carmansville, Yorkville, and Harlem. Parke Godwin, who had been born in 1816, recalled hesitating to cross Canal Street "in dread of imaginary savages, or of the press gangs that stole little boys and carried them out to sea."[30] But New York was a booming, bustling place, and fortunes were being made in real estate. "Whichever way we turn," the *Evening Post* editorialized, "new buildings present themselves to our notice. In the upper wards particularly entire streets of elegant brick buildings have been formed on sites which only a few years ago were either covered with marshes, or occupied by a few straggling frame huts of little or no value." The newspaper printed the observations of a visitor from Boston who praised the Broadway stores as having "more splendor and magnificence than any I have seen." He commended the paving of some of the streets and considered the new City Hall a show place with its Turkey carpets, crimson silk curtains, and eighteen imposing portraits of warriors and statesmen.

The *Evening Post's* praise of this elegance was offset by editorials condemning the dirt and squalor of the town, for, as the blunt Cooper was wont to annoy the citizens by saying, it was a "hobbledehoy metropolis, a rag fair sort of place." William Coleman, the *Evening Post's* founder in 1801 and its editor for a quarter of a century, campaigned against letting pigs roam at large and the garbage in the streets. He sarcastically invited residents to observe select views: "The collection of filth and manure now lying in heaps, or which has been heaped in Wall, Pearl, Water, and Front Streets, near the Coffee-House, and left there, will astonish those who are fond of the wonderful, and pay them for the trouble of a walk there."[31]

The population was a mixture of the countrified and the cosmopolitan. Many of the merchants had come from farms, and still followed their rural habits, though they were able to be as smart as others in business enterprise. The Dutch influence since the days when the city was Nieuw Amsterdam still could be seen in the high-pitched roofs and yellow brick walls of older houses and even in the customs of the descendants of the island's first settlers. Of these Gulian C. Verplanck was a representative. At the family mansion in Fishkill, Verplanck celebrated holidays according to the old Dutch usages, for, as Bryant noted, "with all the ancient customs and rites and pastimes pertaining to them he was as familiar as if they were matters of today."[32] Verplanck never forgave Irving for his burlesque *Knickerbocker's History,* feeling that it belittled the Dutch contributions to liberty in the New World. The older inhabitants still maintained their liking for English manners and furnishings, but New York being a trade center attracting people and products from over the world, the old dominance of the mother country was on the wane. The British traveler Mrs. Trollope noted, in 1830, that "everything English is decidedly *mauvais ton,*" New Yorkers having for years become addicted to things French. French exiles of the ancien régime had come to the city during the time of Napoleon, and operated dancing schools and confectionery and pastry shops. Bryant in seeking a place to live had gone into the home of M. Evrard, for the French expatriates also went into the boarding house business. The emigré Lorenzo da Ponte, who settled in New York as a teacher of Italian, created a rage for Italian music and letters. He had already translated into Italian verse the dramatic poem *Hadad* of "Signor Giacomo A. Hillhouse," the subject of an article in the July *New-York Review,* and in the same number appeared the first of three articles by him under the title "Critique on Certain Passages in Dante"; the December issue contained an article, probably written by Anderson, on the Italian opera in New York. Before long Da Ponte was to translate some of Bryant's poems into Italian. To New York, too, came visitors from Latin America, where the countries were in revolt against Spain, and Bryant met the famous Cuban poet, José Maria Hérédia, whose poems he translated into English and whose acquaintanceship led to the further study of the literature of Spain and his interest in Latin America during the rest of his life. Thus, the city was heterogeneous in its people, even polyglot, with English merchants, Dutch bankers, French exiles, Italian singers, and South Americans as well as Irish, Poles, Swedes, and even Chinese mingling with the native New Yorkers, the newcomers from the farms roundabout, and Yankees from New England at the wharfs, on the streets, in the boarding houses, and at places of public amusement.

By about the first of August Frances and Fanny were able to join Bryant in this city that was proving to be so exciting to the country lawyer from Great Barrington. They lived somewhat unsatisfactorily at the home of M. Evrard for about a month, when, because of the late summer heat and the crowded situation in the home of the French family and the difficulty of finding lodgings in the growing city, Mrs. Bryant went to Jamaica on Long Island, remaining there for about three weeks.[33] Finally, on September 17, Bryant was able to report he had obtained rooms with a Mrs. Meigs at 88 Canal Street.[34] It was the beginning of a series of moves from boarding house to boarding house for the Bryants in the next several years until in December of 1830 they at last were able to set up housekeeping on their own.*

---

*Mrs. Bryant's autobiographical jottings of this period in her life reads: "We took lodgings

Toward the end of the year Bryant discovered that he ranked as an equal in the new cosmopolitan society he had entered. When the prospectus for establishing the Athenaeum was issued, one of the stated purposes was to foster science, literature, and art through a series of public addresses. The first series began in December, 1824, with an address by Professor Clement C. Moore of Columbia College, author of "A Visit from St. Nicholas." His first lecture was attended by barely a hundred persons but as the series progressed the crowds increased until they overflowed the hall.[35] Later addresses proved to be equally popular. Bryant therefore could feel gratified on November 25, when he received a letter from the recording secretary notifying him that he had been unanimously elected a lecturer on poetry for the ensuing winter.[36] He immediately began to work on the addresses, his first and, as it turned out, most extended statement of his poetic principles.

---

at Monsieur Evrard, in Chambers St., where we staid one month. Then we went to Jamaica on Long Island. I boarded at Mr. Lords three months. [She must have meant three weeks, since, according to a Bryant letter of Sept. 17, 1875, he wrote her instructions for getting to their new lodgings at 88 Canal Street.] Then we went back to town and took lodgings with Mrs. Meigs in Canal St. The next May 1826 we moved to Laight St. with Mrs. Meigs. In June we went to Orange Springs. Staid a month with Mr. Hillyer. Then I went to Cummington & Gt. Barrington and home to Laight St.

"The next May 1827 I moved with Mrs. Meigs into Thompson St. The summer I spent at Fishkill at Mr. Tellers & Wyatts. Fanny had the hooping cough, age 5 years. In the autumn we returned to town and took lodgings with Mrs. Tripler, corner of Market St. and Broadway. In March 1828 we removed to Mr. Salazars in Humbert St. and in May we removed with the Salazars to Hudson St. . . . In May 1829 I moved into Varick St. with the Salazars. June 1830 I went with Fanny to Watertown. . . . I then returned by the way of Gt. Barrington to Varick St. In December I commenced housekeeping in Broome St. between Hudson and Varick. . . ." Goddard-Roslyn Collection.

1. Bryant at the age of thirty, by Samuel F. B. Morse.

2. Dr. Peter Bryant

3. Sarah Bryant

4. The Bryant homestead in Cummington. A view of the house after Bryant's renovations.

5. Williams College, which Bryant attended briefly.

6. Miniature portrait on ivory of
   Frances Fairchild Bryant,
   by an unidentified artist.

Thanatopsis.

To him who, in the love of Nature, holds
Communion with her visible forms, she speaks
A various language. For his gayer hours
She has a voice of gladness and a smile
And eloquence of beauty, and she glides
Into his darker musings with a mild
And healing sympathy, that steals away
Their sharpness ere he is aware. When thoughts
Of the last bitter hour come like a blight,
Over thy spirit, and sad images
Of the stern agony and shroud and pall,
And breathless darkness and the narrow house,
Make thee to shudder and grow sick at heart,
Go forth, under the open sky, and list
To Nature's teachings, while from all around—
Earth and her waters and the depths of air
Comes a still voice. Yet a few days and thee.
The all-beholding Sun shall see no more
In all his course, nor yet within the ground,
Where thy pale form was laid with many tears,
Nor in the embrace of ocean shall exist—
Thy image. Earth, that nourished thee, shall claim

7. Autograph manuscript of "Thanatopsis,"
owned by Samuel J. Tilden.

THE

EMBARGO,

OR

SKETCHES OF THE TIMES:

A

SATIRE.

✦✦✦✦✦✦✦✦✦✦✦✦✦
BY A YOUTH OF THIRTEEN.
✦✦✦✦✦✦✦✦✦✦✦✦✦

BOSTON:
PRINTED FOR THE PURCHASERS.

1808.

8. *Above right:* Title page of
    The Embargo, 1808.

9. *Below right:* Title page of
    Poems, 1821.

POEMS

BY

WILLIAM CULLEN BRYANT.

CAMBRIDGE:
PRINTED BY HILLIARD AND METCALF.
1821.

11: Two views of New York around the time that Bryant settled there. *Top:* Broadway. *Bottom:* The Washington Hotel, where writers and artists met regularly for lunch.

12. *At left,* Washington Irving's circle of friends. *Left to right, standing:* Holmes, Hawthorne, Longfellow, Willis, Paulding, Bryant, Kennedy. *Seated:* Simms, Halleck, Prescott, Irving, Emerson, Cooper, Bancroft.

13. *Below, left to right:* Samuel F. B. Morse, a self-portrait; Asher B. Durand; Richard Henry Dana; Catharine M. Sedgwick.

14.   Asher B. Durand's famous *Kindred Spirits* shows Bryant (right) and the painter Thomas Cole contemplating the beauties of nature.

9

IN A BANK-NOTE WORLD

THOUGH BRYANT WAS STIMULATED BY HIS NEW LIFE IN THE city and its intellectual and artistic community, he began to realize early in 1826 that, after eight months struggling with the *Review and Atheneum,* its future was doubtful. He wrote Dana on March 10 that the circulation was increasing but added: "If I keep to it I may possibly find it a source of some profit in time, but these things you know are built up slowly, and no man must expect in this country to grow rich by literature."[1]

His income, if it continued, was sufficient to meet the needs of his family. Frances described their situation at Mrs. Meigs's boarding house at the upper limit of the city on Canal Street in a letter to Bryant's mother on January 12. The Bryants occupied opposite the dining room a small parlor and an adjoining bedroom which they had furnished themselves. They paid $10.50 a week for their rooms and board, and in addition had to provide their own heat at a cost of twenty-five dollars for the winter by a coal-burning Dutch stove. It was a crowded household. Mr. and Mrs. Meigs had two daughters, and also living with them were two brothers and a sister of Mrs. Meigs. Besides the Bryants, the boarders were "two young gentlemen" from Stockbridge, another from Newburyport, and "a French lady born in New York." Frances wrote that she led a lonely life among these strangers. Her health, which had been bad in the fall when she went to Jamaica, was now improved and she was able to return social calls, usually between one and two in the afternoon and nine and ten in the evening. They were a formality only, lasting about fifteen minutes.[2]

Bryant was not happy with the quality of the material in the magazine, particularly in the *Atheneum* section. To Dana, who had commented on the lack of "literary entertainment," Bryant wrote in January on the change from the preceding decade when such sprightly writers as the Irving brothers, Paulding, Halleck, Verplanck, and Sands had contributed to the gaiety of the city. Washington Irving had gone to England in 1813, and the other members of his convivial set had become older—and more staid and respectable. Bryant complained that though there were clever men in the city "they are naughtily given to instructing the world, to elucidating the mysteries of political economy and the principles of jurisprudence, etc.; they seem to think it a sort of disgrace to be entertaining."[3]

Unable to get contributions of an amusing sort, Bryant attempted to meet the want himself, writing two humorous poems, "To a Musquito" and "A Meditation on Rhode-Island Coal," and his first prose tale, "A Pennsylvania Legend." He thought enough of the poems to include them in his collected work, but even his greatest admirers have not had a good opinion of them. Bryant possessed a native cleverness revealed in hundreds of pointed and amusing remarks scattered throughout his prose and an anecdotal gift for selecting entertaining illustrations to point up his editorial and critical articles, but his humorous poems have been generally found to be "painfully facetious."[4]

In his tale, "A Pennsylvania Legend,"[5] Bryant gave neither Irving nor Paulding cause to worry about their public. Bryant's story attempted to do for the Pennsylvania Germans what Irving had done for the Dutch in the Catskills and, as he said in an introduction, to show that there were American legends suited for literary use. "Let the European writer gather up the traditions of his country; I will employ a leisure moment in recording one of the fresher, but not less authentic, legends of ours," he said. The story, as related by the beldames among the Pennsylvania Germans, tells of Caspar Buckel, a hunchback who is an object of ridicule. Receiving the pity of a woodland sprite, he is transformed into a handsome youth who marries and becomes wealthy through a store of gold to which his fairy guardian directs him. But Caspar is a profligate and spendthrift and his greed destroys the magic source of gold and he disappears. "As for Caspar," the tale ends, "he was never heard of again; but the old people say that the woods north of his widow's house are haunted at twilight by the figure of a hunchbacked little man, skipping over the fallen leaves, and running into gloomy thickets as soon as your eye falls on him, as if to avoid the sight of men." A nation that had taken Rip Van Winkle to their hearts could not do as much by Caspar Buckel.

Original poetry for the *Atheneum* was also lacking. Dana sent in another poem, which, after some changes, Bryant was able to print; it was "The Little Beach Bird," to become one of the best known poems of the century through being printed in school readers.[6] From Yale College Bryant received some stanzas by a student, Nathaniel Parker Willis, in a few years to become a popular poet and essayist. But he received nothing from the major poets of the time who were contributing to the magazines, the young Henry Wadsworth Longfellow, whose verse was appearing in the *United States Literary Gazette* of Boston, James Gates Percival, or John G.C. Brainard. More and more, with the exception of Bryant's own poems, the *Atheneum* carried, rather than original verse, translations from the Italian, German, and Spanish. Under the pressure of writing reviews and carrying on his editorial chores, Bryant was unable to write poetry himself and dipped into his files to find something to publish, the poems "Hymn to Death," "The Death of the Flowers," "The Indian Girl's Lament," "Stanzas" ("I cannot forget the high spell that enchanted"), and, indicating that he had reached the bottom of the barrel, "Chorus of Ghosts," which he had written in the depth of his youthful despair about death in 1814.

II

The invitation from the Atheneum to deliver a series of lectures was the spur for Bryant to organize his ideas on the nature and functions of poetry which he had been developing from his boyhood. In the early essay on "Trisyllabic Feet in Iambic Measure," he had attacked the metrical rigidities of the school of Pope and urged a revolution in taste to break away from them; and in his review of Solyman Brown's *An Essay on American Poetry*, which the poet and critic William Ellery Leonard called America's "first declaration of intellectual independence, antedating Emerson's *American Scholar* by nineteen years,"[7] he had condemned his country's imitative versifiers. More recently, in his reviews of James A. Hillhouse's *Percy's Masque* and *Hadad*, of John of Nostradamus's lives of the Provençal poets, and especially of James G. Percival's *Poem: Delivered before the Connecticut Alpha of Phi Beta Kappa* he had gone further in advocating a wider freedom. Commenting on Hillhouse's dramas, he had asked for a more natural diction in dramatic verse, and he praised Percival's poems for the "exuberance of the author's imagination":

143

To us there is something exceedingly delightful in the reckless intoxication with which this author surrenders himself to the enchantment of that multitude of glorious and beautiful images that come crowding upon his mind, and that infinity of analogies and relations between the natural objects, and again between these and the moral world, which seem to lie before him wherever he turns his eyes. The writings of no poet seem to be more the involuntary overflowing of his mind.

The lectures and Bryant's reviews and especially his own practice in poetry were highly important, for, as the literary historian Robert E. Spiller has written, they "served both major and minor poets for many years as a gauge of what poetry should be and do," Longfellow and Lowell, among others, following his prescriptions, "and his influence extended down the century to form the main stream of American verse."[8] But Bryant's esthetic theories influenced not only the poetry of his time but also the painting. Among the members of his audience were the young artists revolting from the older school of painters and looking for new ways to view man and nature. Bryant expounded a philosophy that provided them not only with themes but also with the methods for developing them. So impressed were the artists with Bryant's concepts that they arranged for him to lecture before their newly formed National Academy of the Arts of Design in the fall, and he was to continue as a welcome instructor for the next few years.[9]

Bryant's theories set forth in these formal lectures when he was a man of thirty-one can be traced to his reading as a youth before entering Williams College. The two most important sources were Archibald Alison's *Essays on the Nature and Principles of Taste* and Edmund Burke's *A Philosophical Inquiry into the Origin of Our Ideas of the Sublime and Beautiful.* Other sources were Wordsworth's preface to *Lyrical Ballads,* which Bryant had read after becoming acquainted with Alison and Burke, and essays by other Scotch critics and rhetoricians. These ideas were reinforced by his favorite reading among the poets.

Bryant followed Alison closely in certain parts of his explication of the nature of poetry. Poetry, he said in his first lecture, was a suggestive art, unlike painting and sculpture, which were imitative arts: "Its power of affecting the mind by pure suggestion, and employing, instead of a visible or tangible imitation, arbitrary symbols, as unlike as possible to the things with which it deals, is what distinguishes this from its two sister arts." Bryant followed Burke in his statement that poetry by the symbol of words suggests both the sensible object and the association. Because language was inadequate to express fully the "mighty and diversified world of matter and mind," giving only "here a gleam of light, and there a dash of shade," poetry must appeal to the imagination. Thus he defined poetry: "Poetry is that art which selects and arranges the symbols of thought in such a manner as to excite it the most powerfully and delightfully." But even more than exciting the imagination poetry must touch the heart, and the "most beautiful poetry is that which takes the strongest hold of the feelings." Nevertheless, for Bryant emotionalism was not enough: poetry must also gratify the understanding and therefore "requires intellectual faculties of the highest order." This led him to his major point: that poetry was valuable in proportion to "the direct lessons of wisdom that it delivers." Here we find an expression of the didactic principle that some readers have considered a defect in Bryant's own practice—the moral tags attached to many of his poems.

In this lecture Bryant raised the question of the distinction between poetry and prose, since the uses of language by the poet to affect the mind were also open to the prose writer. The answer, he said, was one easy of solution. It was simply this—that poetry, unlike prose, made use of metrical harmony and excluded all that disgusted and all that was too trivial and common to excite any emotion whatever.

To one who as a boy had been warned against reading merely for pleasure and who as a man had been confronted with the indifference of what he called "this bank-note world" to verse, Bryant felt called upon, in his second lecture, to address himself to "the value and uses of poetry." In reviewing Percival's Phi Beta Kappa poem Bryant had disagreed with the view expressed that "a good poet . . . is good for nothing else than to write poetry." In his lecture he expressed the opinion that the poet was good for more than this, for he was the teacher of the highest moral lessons. "All moral lessons which are uninteresting and unimpressive, and, therefore, worthless," Bryant said, "poetry leaves to prose; but all those which touch the heart, and are, therefore, important and effectual, are its own." Echoing Alison and Wordsworth, Bryant found that among the most important influences of poetry was "the exhibition of those analogies and correspondences which it beholds between the things of the moral and of the natural world." In this belief we find explained Bryant's constant drawing upon nature in his own poetry to find illustrations for moral ideas, a practice followed by Thomas Cole and the other painters of the Hudson River school in their use of symbolism and allegory.

One of the current explanations of the lack of development of American literature was that the nation had no past that would provide subjects for poetry. Thus, as Bryant said in his third lecture, American scenery might be beautiful but "it is the beauty of face without expression," lacking "the associations of tradition which are the soul and interest of scenery." As Bryant had stated earlier in his defense of the adequacy of American material for fiction, he found the argument untenable. If traditions were all that were needed for poetry, then it could be expected that "a multitude of interesting traditions will spring up in our land to ally themselves with every mountain, every hill, every forest, every river, and every tributary brook." He did not dwell at length on this theme, but turned to a related theme, that the present age was too materialistic, science and the useful arts having "a tendency to narrow the sphere of the imagination," to call forth poetry of the quality of the ancients, who were inspired by the mystery of nature as yet not investigated. Bryant found in Wordsworth a refutation of this, for Wordsworth had argued that the poet "will be ready to follow the steps of the Man of science." It was well enough for the ancients, who supposed the earth to be a great plain, the sun a moving ball of fire, the stars a multitude of little flames, but Bryant saw more mystery and wonder in the fact that the earth is an immense sphere, one of an army of worlds that move in ordered revolutions through the boundlessness of the skies.

In his fourth lecture Bryant was faithful to his classical training in maintaining that all fine poetry was built upon the past, that it was an art "not perfected in a day" but one that was developed "by slow degrees, from the first rude and imperfect attempts at versification to the finished productions of its greatest masters." He was unsympathetic to some aspects of the Romantic movement in England and strongly so to the metaphysical poets of Milton's time, whom he condemned for their excesses in their striving to be original. He considered originality, of course, one of the delights of poetry, saying, in paraphrase of Wordsworth, that "it consists in presenting familiar things in a new and striking yet natural light, or in revealing secrets of emotion and thought which have lain undetected from the birth of literature." But this striving for novelty had led some poets astray:

> They have been led, by their overeagerness to attain it, into puerile conceits, into extravagant vagaries of imagination, into overstrained exaggerations of passion, into mawkish and childish simplicity. It has given birth to outrages upon moral principle, upon decency, upon common sense; it has produced, in short, irregularities and affectations of every kind. The grandiloquous nonsense of euphuism, which threatened to overlay and smother English

literature in its very cradle, the laborious wit of the metaphysical poets who were contemporaries of Milton, the puling effeminacy of the cockney school, which has found no small favor at the present day—are all children of this fruitful parent.

Though Bryant believed that the best poetry must develop out of tradition and though he believed that the passion for originality had produced "weeds among the flowers" of poetry, his final lecture ended with an attack on orthodoxy. In science the authority of great names, he said, had long since been shaken off, and the same was true in literature. A narrative poem no longer need be written on the model of the epic, a lyric in the manner of Pindar or Horace, a satire after the fashion of Juvenal. If asked which was the more likely to produce poetry that would live, an age marked by too careful imitation or one marked by "an excessive ambition of originality," he would favor the latter. When "a tame and frigid taste has possessed the tribe of poets, when all their powers are employed in servilely copying the works of their predecessors," Bryant declared, "it is not only impossible that any great work should be produced among them" but "the period of a literary reformation, of the awakening of genius, is postponed to a distant futurity."

Bryant's lectures on poetry are not among the great critical statements in American literature perhaps, but they are important. The circumstances of their composition and delivery prevented their being a fully considered expression of his beliefs, perhaps explained why he spoke with a "divided voice," being unable to make "the choice between self-reliance and conformity."[10] As Parke Godwin pointed out, he was asked to address a popular audience, not "adepts or even students." Therefore, in talking about poetry, "he confined himself to a brief consideration of its nature, its influences, and its relations to the general progress of mankind."[11] For his audience, Bryant was right in choosing to explain the nature of poetry and to justify its influence "on the welfare and happiness of our race."[12] Just as Bryant's own reading of Alison and Burke had prepared him for the *Lyrical Ballads,* so his lectures could help his hearers appreciate the new poetry. Romanticism needed defense then, too, for it was under attack. Bryant's friends Dana and Phillips had been ousted from the *North American Review* only a few years before because of their espousal of it; and Bryant himself was to be attacked a few years later, in 1832, for imitating those "perverters of literature," the Lake School of English poets.[13]

147

III

Although Bryant had written Dana on March 10 that the *Review and Atheneum* might in time become profitable, before the month was out he was looking about for other opportunities. The country was undergoing a business setback, and the currency situation in the city was chaotic. The financial district was rocked by frauds by managers of the Fulton Bank, and there were runs on other banks. The *Evening Post,* in a series of editorials, blamed the monetary situation on the failure of the legislature to license institutions as banks that had indirectly assumed the functions of banks. Worried about the outlook for his magazine, Bryant obtained a license to practice in the New York courts.

On March 11 Bryant's two rivals in the literary market place, James G. Brooks, publisher of the *New-York Literary Gazette,* and George Bond, publisher of the *American Athenaeum,* merged the two magazines,[14] the combined publications to appear every Saturday. This may have suggested to Bryant the idea of associating the *Review* with the *United States Literary Gazette* of Boston. It must have appeared obvious to him that a first-class journal, or even one at all, could not be published by relying chiefly on the support of a single city. The alternative was to get out one of national scope. This had been the aim of the editors of the *North American Review* and the *Literary Gazette,* as well as editors of earlier publications, but the aim had not been realized. Such a union was an attractive one, since Bryant's literary tastes and those of his New York associates were the same as those of James G. Carter in Boston.

Bryant's proposal of merging the magazines received a favorable response from Carter, who wrote him on April 11: "I have mentioned the plan of uniting the two works to the other proprietors of the Gazette and find that the idea strikes them favorably. They think there would be no difficulty in having it published, if it were made a monthly, simultaneously in Boston and New York and do not protest so vehemently as I feared they would being booksellers, to having a double imprint in the form of the principal Scotch reviews and journals." He asked Bryant to submit detailed plans, adding that the "whole advantage to be expected from the union depends upon the perfect and cordial cooperation of the literary gentlemen of your city."[15]

Plans for the merger were developed during the next two months, but there were many obstacles. In a letter of April 26 Bryant mentioned the difficulty of two editors living in different cities and suggested that Carter might remove to New York. Carter replied, on May 3, that the majority of the subscribers would be in Boston and that he feared he could not "carry *all* Boston" with him if he left. Though there was literary rivalry between the two cities, he did not consider this a ground for "gunning opposition." He felt that he and Bryant could work in harmony, since they had no interests to promote in politics or religion. His proposal was that if Bryant could obtain five hundred or more subscribers he would be entitled to one-fourth the stock with a salary of $800 annually if he became one of the editors. The salary would be increased $200 a year besides one-fourth of the proceeds if the total circulation went above 1,700. Two weeks later Carter informed Bryant that the price for his one-fourth interest would be $500. He suggested that the publication be called the *United States Literary Gazette and Monthly Review* or the *American Monthly Review*. Bryant replied suggesting that the name be the *United States Review*, but Carter objected on June 1 that "Gazette readers would not be familiar with it while the subscribers of the N.Y. Review would see at once that they had before them the same thing with only a new name."[16]

Late in June, Harrison Gray, one of the Boston owners, visited Bryant in New York to complete the sale of a one-fourth interest to him. Meanwhile, Carter and Bryant in exchanges of letters discussed materials for the first number of the merged magazine to appear in July. They compromised on a name, the *United States Review and Literary Gazette,* but financial matters had not been satisfactorily arranged. Carter wrote on June 22 that the *Gazette* proprietors regarded his salary as "a pretty high one" and that Bryant's in addition would be more than the magazine could sustain. He said that it was a matter of indifference to him whether he remained or quit—indeed, he preferred to quit since he could employ his time otherwise more profitably than as an editor of the *Gazette.* He would remain, then, as "responsible editor" until his place could be filled "at a cheaper rate."[17]

While these negotiations were being carried on, Bryant continued to get out the *Review.* For the April number he wrote an article on Robert Benson's *Sketches of Corsica,* in which he said of Napoleon Bonaparte, whose conquests he had attacked in several juvenile poems, that "if the world must have a master, Corsica was not unworthy to give it one." His humorous poem, "A Meditation on Rhode-Island Coal," also appeared in this number. The May number, to which Bryant contributed only a review of Henry Wheaton's life of William Pinkney, the Maryland statesman who had served his country on several important diplomatic missions, completed volume two of the magazine. It was the last issue. After one year in New York, Bryant must have felt that he had failed in his literary venture. To be sure, he would with the July 1 number become the New York editor of the *United States Literary Gazette,* but the *Review and Atheneum,* which he had helped found with such high hopes had lost its identity—to be a nameless part of the Boston magazine, now converted to a monthly, until it completed volume four, when out of the union would emerge the *United States Review and Literary Gazette.*

IV

While Bryant was struggling to solve his financial problems, his family affairs also caused him some worry. In May the Bryants made another of their frequent moves during their first years in New York, when Mrs. Meigs gave up the house on Canal Street and took one on Laight Street. Ever thoughtful of his wife's comfort, Bryant sent her out of the city in June to avoid the heat. She first went to a resort, Orange Springs, where she boarded for a month before going on to visit at Great Barrington and Cummington.[18] Thus during a period of extreme trouble Bryant lacked the reassuring presence of Frances.

Unexpectedly, at this juncture, a new opportunity was opened to him. One of the leading newspapers in the city was the *Evening Post,* which Alexander Hamilton and other Federalists had established in 1801 as a party organ with William Coleman as editor. About the middle of June, 1826, Coleman was injured when he was thrown from a gig by a runaway horse, and Bryant, responsible only in part for the content of the *United States Literary Gazette,* was able to accept temporary employment as an assistant in getting out the paper. It is not quite clear when Bryant began work, but it seems likely that it was in July.* A comparison of the issues during this month with those of the preceding months indicates that there was a change for the better in the paper—in cleaner typography on the principal news page and in longer and more carefully written editorials than were characteristic of Coleman's work.

One reason why Bryant accepted the *Evening Post* employment may have been that arrangements for the merger of the *Literary Gazette* and the *Review and Atheneum* had been further complicated by a proposal that the idea of simultaneous publication in Boston and New York be dropped, the magazine to carry only the Boston imprint. It was made by Harrison Gray, but Bryant rejected the plan, being supported by Carter, who wrote

---

*On the removal of the *Evening Post* to a new building on July 1, 1875, an editorial said it marked to the day the fiftieth anniversary of Bryant's joining the newspaper.

him on July 30 that he would have been "exceedingly sorry to have had you answer the proposition in any other manner" as it was "contrary to the spirit of the agreement by which the works were united." Carter said that success of the magazine depended on its being as much a New York publication as a Boston one. He pointed out that Boston already had the *North American Review* and that he had "always supposed that the ultimate effect of our union would be to transfer the United States Review to your city" since "New York must have a journal." He saw no future for the magazine unless it could be "divested of all local character."[19]

Coleman may have asked Bryant to join the *Evening Post*, because, being a member of the same set, he doubtless knew of the difficulties involving the union of the two literary journals. Moreover, he was an admirer of Bryant's poetry, and he probably had an interest in the younger man because both had come to New York from practicing law in the same area in western Massachusetts. The poem "Green River" very likely was a favorite of Coleman's since he had once built a home overlooking the stream in Hampshire County. Since Bryant's arrival in New York, the *Evening Post* had reprinted several of his poems and had commented favorably on the *Review and Atheneum.*

The *Evening Post* was a four-page publication with six columns to the page. The first page was devoted entirely to advertisements, except when it carried in full a President's address or a notable speech in Congress. About two columns were taken up with shipping advertisements giving schedules of arrivals and departures and passenger and freight rates. Other advertisements were services and sales—marble mortuary monuments and chimney pieces, boats, tea, clothing, lamps and oil, china, silks, dental work, insurance, coffee, opera cloaks, fireplace grates and fenders, boarding houses, help wanted, sales of church pews, loans, and to-let notices. Advertisements, set in small type and separated by a horizontal rule, were contracted for on a long-term basis from a month to a year and appeared unchanged from issue to issue. The only illustrations were woodcuts indicating the nature of the object for sale or the service offered—a steamer or sailboat for shipping notices, a house for real estate sales or rentals. Occasionally there were other illustrations, a new kind of stove or in one instance an instrument of torture, "A new and elegant corset, with patent metallic eyelets, warranted never to cut through." Page two was the news page. In the first columns usually appeared copious extracts from British papers and miscellaneous reprints from American papers. Coleman's contributions in the form of comment and news notes were carried under the *Evening Post* flag and were differentiated from other material by being leaded, that is, having extra white space between the lines of type. Other material on the page consisted of letters to the editor, reports from the state legislature and Congress, and additional items from other newspapers. Both pages three and four, like page one, were given over almost entirely to advertising and legal notices.

In his first writing for the paper Bryant devoted himself to a topic far removed from his literary interests—the state of the currency, the chief subject treated editorially during the month and one he was equipped to discuss because of his study of economics while a lawyer at Great Barrington. His editorials were longer and more thorough treatments of a subject than Coleman usually wrote and they have the marks of Bryant's clear and forthright prose. On August 2 Bryant wrote an account of the Columbia College commencement, which he mentioned in a letter to Frances at Great Barrington.[20] The letter reveals that Bryant not only seemed to like work on a daily newspaper but also was inclined to consider it a way of making a living:

> I shall send you a number of the Evening Post . . . containing an account of the Commencement of Columbia College and will also mark with a pencil such paragraphs as are written by me. I have got to be quite famous as the editor of a newspaper since you were here and some of my friends—Mr. Verplanck in particular—are quite anxious that I should continue it. Some compliments have been made to me about the improvement in the Evening Post. . . . The establishment of the Evening Post is an extremely lucrative one. It is owned by two individuals—Mr. Coleman and Mr. Burnham. The profits are estimated at about thirty thousand dollars a year—fifteen to each proprietor. This is better than poetry and magazines.

There is little interest in the commencement report, which gives in detail the day's program, except for Bryant's criticism of the orations. Reflecting his concern about the proper use of the language, he noted that the speakers had a habit of "sinking the letter 'r' when it follows a vowel." Instead of pronouncing the consonant, he said, speakers, "especially in the east and most particularly Boston, merely prolong the vowel." A second fault was the misuse of "shall" and "will."

In the letter Bryant gave an indication of his desperate financial situation in mentioning the receipt of forty dollars from Frances, who was settling some of his affairs at Great Barrington, and revealed plans for a trip to Boston to arrange matters in connection with the magazine but also to carry out a commission from Coleman. Of receiving the money, he said: "I could have made a shift to get along without it, for Coleman pays me enough to go to Boston with; but now I shall have enough to settle with Mrs. Meigs, and something to get us all to New York again." He had been asked by Coleman to sound Dana out about joining the *Evening Post,* but found him reluctant to do so since he would have to leave Boston and asked that the offer be kept open until he heard "what could be done nearer home."[21]

From Boston, Bryant went to Cummington, where Frances joined him, and on October 2 he set out with his family for New York.[22] On his return he went back to work on the *Evening Post* as an assistant to Coleman at a salary of fifteen dollars a week.[23] Coleman was proud of Bryant's association with the paper, and published several laudatory articles about the *Literary Gazette.* On September 5 he published a translation from the French *Revue Encyclopédique* praising the magazine as being "full of taste and talent" and commenting: "But the principal attraction of this journal, to us, is the exquisite and finished beauty of the little poems from the pen of W. C. Bryant, under the head of poetry." The article attributed to Bryant the discovery that the New World contained material for literary treatment:

> Ancient history and popular tragedies, enveloped in the cloud of past times, are the subjects which most address themselves to popular favor, and which seem to be the most fitted for the genuine poet. But the poet of Green River (le Barde de la Rivière Verte) tendered a great and true service to literature in thus spreading the dominion of the muses over the scenes and events of the history of his country.
>
> He has destroyed (and it is an effect of no small importance) the too commonly received error, that the moral and physical features of the new world are too cold and serene for the glorious visions of poetry.

V

Bryant's hand is not especially discernible in the numbers of the *Literary Gazette* appearing during the interregnum before the start of the new magazine in October. He wrote no reviews himself though there are several indicative of New York origin. His poetry contributions were "From the Spanish of Villegas," "Midsummer," "The Two Graves," and "The Conjunction of Jupiter and Venus." These issues differed in no significant respects from the magazine's former entities, living up to the promise of the editors in an "advertisement" annexed to the numbers appearing before the consolidation. They had pointed out that the two former journals "resembled each other nearly in their plan and objects," though they had "contracted something of a local character, in consequence of deriving the contributions to their pages principally from the neighbourhood of the cities in which they were published." The main objects of the editors had been "to furnish a seasonable and *complete* view of the progress and state of our national literature" and this object was not essentially changed.

As James G. Carter had written Bryant in June, he planned to remain with the magazine only until a successor could be obtained. The successor was a young classical scholar who was serving as librarian at Harvard, Charles Folsom. He and Bryant had come to a working agreement on Bryant's trip to Boston, and an extensive correspondence between the two men having to do with the magazine began September 8 when Folsom wrote Bryant asking what he might expect from New York for the first issue. A second letter from Folsom reveals that Bryant was the "responsible editor." Folsom wrote that one Edward Wigglesworth, who was employed in the Boston office, complained that he could not fill the space expected of him, the labor involved being greater than he had anticipated. Folsom also expressed the opinion that the fund to pay contributors should be increased to $400. He said that the matters were for Bryant and Gray to decide, as they were the "principal proprietors."[24]

During the last four months of 1826 Bryant was kept busy writing reviews and other material for the magazine, seeking contributions from his New York friends, and corresponding with Folsom over publishing problems. Questions to be settled were such matters as the allocation of space, the merits of contributions, decisions on the books to be reviewed and the selection of reviewers, and typographical arrangement. The lack of money to pay contributors resulted in some complications. In a letter of November 9, for instance, Bryant wrote in connection with printing some verses by Grenville Mellen that "Our *concern* is too poor to buy much poetry" and expressed the belief that Mellen could do better elsewhere "than he could by writing poetry for us at the rate we can afford to pay."[25] One notable contributor that Bryant was able to obtain was Fitz-Greene Halleck, whose poem "Burns" he secured in December for the January number. Writing Folsom, he said it was "altogether the noblest monument that has been erected to the memory of him whom it celebrates" and requested that it be given first place in the poetry department, adding: "It will have a great run here, as everything written by Halleck is sought and read with the greatest eagerness. Halleck of all the literary men of the age except the author of the Waverly novels is the most universal favorite with the New York public." Bryant also sent a poem,

"My Native Village," by his brother John, still at Cummington undecided about what he wanted to do but hoping to go to college if the eldest brother, Austin, could furnish the money.*

Aside from several reviews, Bryant's own contributions to the fall and early winter numbers included three poems, "The African Chief," "The Damsel of Peru," and a sonnet, "October," and two translations, "Mary Magdalen," by the Spaniard Bartolomé Leonardo de Argensola, and "Niagara," by the Cuban José Maria Herédia, which Bryant felt was "the best which has been written about the Great American Cataract," and his second prose narrative, "A Border Tradition."[26] The tale, written in imitation of Irving's recounting of the legends of the Catskills, is interesting because of its prose descriptions of the Massachusetts countryside that Bryant also portrayed in his poetry. It seems to have been inspired by his summer visit to Cummington and Great Barrington.

Bryant was thus fully occupied after a troubled year which had seen the failure of his first magazine project and the strenuous effort to preserve it in part through a merger with its sister publication in Boston. The prospects for making a financial success of the *Review and Literary Gazette* with its divided management between Boston and New York must have seemed highly dubious. He was one of the proprietors, to be sure, but his income had been reduced by the new publishing arrangement and he could not be assured of any increase from his share unless the magazine at least doubled the number of subscribers. Since room and board alone at Mrs. Meigs's place amounted to $540, Bryant's earnings from the magazine would not have supported his family in New York, and his job on the *Evening Post* was essential. Handicapped by inadequate funds to pay contributors to the magazine, he realized that whatever success it might attain would be largely through his own efforts. The fall and early winter numbers indicated that he was doing his best.

---

*This is the first of John Howard Bryant's poems, written when he was nineteen, to appear in a magazine. Subsequently William Cullen Bryant printed many of his brother's verses in the *Evening Post*.

10

POLITICS AND A BELLY-FULL

IN TAKING OVER THE ASSISTANT EDITOR'S JOB ON THE *Evening Post,* Bryant evidently felt that if he could not support his family by literary work newspaper work was preferable to returning to the law. Except for getting admitted to the New York bar and associating himself with Henry Sedgwick in one case,* he did not consider worshiping again at the altar of Themis. Of the eight or so daily newspapers in the city, the *Evening Post* was probably the best from his standpoint. Founded as a Federalist organ, the paper had been known to him since his boyhood when it was received by Dr. Bryant, and Cullen in *The Embargo* had praised its editor, William Coleman, who in "honest anger" had led the assault on President Jefferson.

Coleman in his early years had been embroiled in the controversies between the Federalists and Jeffersonians and had warred with the opposition editors James Cheetham, of the *American Citizen* in New York, and William Duane, of the *Aurora* in Philadelphia. The battles produced the memorable squib in the *Evening Post:*

---

*The case was a suit to recover money improperly used or diverted in the campaign to raise funds to help the Greeks in their revolution against the Turks. Godwin, *Biography,* I, 228.

Lie on Duane, lie on for pay,
     And Cheetham, lie thou too;
More against truth you cannot say,
     Than truth can say 'gainst you.

But name-calling was a mild way of carrying on political and editorial fights in the early 1800's. When the *American Citizen* printed a charge that Coleman was the father of a mulatto child, he challenged Cheetham to a duel. The impending encounter became known, and the two editors were brought into court and enjoined to limit their weapons to ink and type. An ardent Republican, a Captain Thompson, spread the story that Coleman had allowed the news of the duel to get out so that authorities would intervene to prevent it. Coleman thereupon challenged Thompson to a duel. It was conducted at a secluded spot known as Love Lane, later Twenty-first Street, and the captain was fatally wounded.

In 1826, however, much of Coleman's belligerency had softened, Bryant related in a reminiscent article on the paper. Coleman had suffered a series of paralytic attacks in 1819 which resulted in loss of the use of his legs. His health was further impaired when a minor public official, whose scandalous conduct was exposed in the paper, fell upon Coleman driving to his office in a small wagon and beat him unmercifully with a cane. When Bryant met Coleman, he was a man "with a broad chest, muscular arms, which he wielded lightly and easily, and a deep-toned voice; but his legs dangled like strings." In conversation Coleman expressed himself energetically and decisively, but in writing his editorials he had the habit of revising his first drafts to weaken their force.

Coleman's partner, Michael Burnham, had been with the paper from the start as its printer. Coleman had no skill as a business manager, being prone, if he had money, to spend it freely, lend it without security, or give it away. Several years after the founding of the paper, its finances were so confused that an arrangement was entered into whereby Burnham became a part owner with full charge of the business end. "From that time the affairs of the journal became prosperous," Bryant wrote; "it began to yield a respectable revenue; Mr. Coleman was relieved from his pecuniary embarrassments, and Mr. Burnham to grow rich."[1]

The disintegration of the Federalist party had deprived the *Evening Post* of its position of political influence by 1826, when it was no longer the vehicle for the opinions of such highly placed men as Hamilton. Coleman's political tenets in the past decade had become more personal than partisan. In 1816 he had given only tepid support to the Federalist candidate for President, Rufus King, against the Republican Monroe. When the *Aurora* in 1819 attacked Monroe, Coleman flew to the President's defense. By the time of the presidential election of 1824, when the old party distinctions had dissolved and the principal nominations were made by state legislatures, Coleman supported the Republican William H. Crawford in a field that included John C. Calhoun, Andrew Jackson, Henry Clay, and John Quincy Adams. Coleman hated Adams because he had supported the embargo acts of the Jefferson administration. Thus, as the historian Allan Nevins has written, the *Evening Post* in 1826 was half-Democratic or Republican.[2] Bryant's own personal political history had somewhat paralleled the *Evening Post's*—at first strongly Federalist he had become more and more of a Jeffersonian so that when he joined the paper he too could be described as half-Democratic.

One of the attractions of the *Evening Post* to Bryant was Coleman's long association with the literary men of the city. In 1809 he had collaborated with Washington Irving in perpetrating the hoax which introduced his *Knickerbocker's History* to the world. The paper printed a news item reporting that an old gentleman named Diedrich Knickerbocker had disappeared from his lodgings and information was sought as to his whereabouts. There were subsequent accounts of the search and finally a report that he had left "a very curious kind of written book" at his hotel. The story said that if he did not return to pay his bill the manuscript would be disposed of to satisfy the charges. With public interest in the mystery now at its height, advertisements of the book appeared—the two volumes of the *Knickerbocker's History.*

As did other editors, Coleman reprinted poetry and literary articles from the magazines, both American and British, but he was also hospitable to original material. Fitz-Greene Halleck's first published poem appeared in the *Evening Post,* and when Halleck and his friend Joseph Rodman Drake concocted some satirical lines on "Ennui" they took them to Coleman. He printed them as being from an unknown correspondent who called himself "Croaker," and promised that they would be followed by other "poetic crackers of merit." There came a series of poems lampooning New York people and happenings, and, as Bryant wrote, "the town laughed, the subjects of the satire laughed in chorus, and all thought them the best things of the kind that were ever written."[3]

Bryant has been credited with bringing to the management of the *Evening Post* "a new and vigorous hand" in the winter and spring of 1826–1827, but this is not indicated by the files. He was employed as Coleman's assistant, a part-time one at that since he was also editing the

United States Review and Literary Gazette. His chief duty was probably choosing the literary material and perhaps rewriting the news in British papers arriving in the transatlantic packet ships. In a letter to Dana, he said: "I drudge for the Evening Post and labor for the Review, and thus have a pretty busy life of it. I would give up one of these if I could earn my bread by the other, but that I cannot do."[4] The editorials early in 1827 were mostly short ones and hence probably written by Coleman, since he seldom discoursed at length on a topic, and they reflected long-standing views. Thus the lead editorial on January 4 attacking almost two hundred lotteries being conducted in the city as a "ruinous species of gambling" was but the continuation of a fight that Coleman had begun in 1818. Likewise, the paper's increasing expression of favorable opinion of Jackson was also Coleman's work. The support was first indicated on April 30 when Jackson was mentioned as being "a more suitable man and more capable of conducting" the office of President than "the one who now holds that envied and elevated station." This was but another statement of Coleman's ancient dislike of John Quincy Adams. On May 29 Coleman defended himself against an attack in the *American,* which had said of it: "The *Evening Post,* the old, and in its day, the able champion of federalism is, it cannot be doubted, only for Jackson, because he is the rival of John Quincy Adams—as it was for Mr. Crawford—and would be for Mr. Anybody on the same ground."

Though the paper's support of Jackson was the work of Coleman, its discussions of another raging political issue—the tariff—seem to have been by Bryant. Bryant wrote of the paper's stand on the tariff: "Immediately after Mr. Bryant became connected with the *Evening Post,* it began to agitate the question of free trade."[5] This, however, was not a sudden shift in policy. The paper had always been friendly to the commercial interests, and many leading merchants opposed a tariff. The tariff of 1824 had failed to eliminate British competition, and in 1827 wool-growing and textile interests sought higher duties. A bill was introduced in Congress that would have made importation of woolen goods almost prohibitive. The editorials on the question were stronger than Coleman would probably have written and their style is typically Bryantesque. For example, on February 12 the *Evening Post* editorialized:

> The provisions . . . are such that they should call forth a general cry of indignation from Maine to Florida. Their effect will be a legal robbery of that part of the community whose interests are most entitled to protection. The members of Congress wear fine broadcloths, and those among them

who support the new tariff have friends among the noisy and hungry manufacturers besieging the doors of Congress whose activity may have some
influence on their own popularity at home.—What do these members care
for the consumers of cheap woolens? Nothing at all. Their own interests are
safe, and they will be able to buy fine clothes about as cheap as ever, and
their manufacturing friends will get rich and send them again to Congress.
They feel nothing of the distresses of the poor, but they hear the clamors
of the woolen manufacturers, and to pacify them, they will set themselves
to work without remorse of conscience to double the burdens of the poor.

An editorial several days later, marked by Bryant's waspish sarcasm, attacked Daniel Webster and Edward Everett for not speaking out against
the tariff. These "two gentlemen . . . have been at all times remarkable
for their ready faculty of speech on every important occasion," the
editorial said, but on this important question they "tamely sink down into
silence and content themselves with uttering a drowsy syllable."*

II

While Bryant was becoming embroiled in politics on the *Evening Post,*
he was trying to keep partisan matters out of the *Review.* On January 11
he wrote Charles Folsom opposing a review of a pamphlet by Cooper on
the Constitution relating to a question that divided the two parties. "I
think it had better not be meddled with," he said. He hoped that Everett,
in a review of Clay's speeches, would also stay clear of the Constitutional
question.[6] When the review appeared, Bryant wrote Folsom that printing
the Everett article had put "a heavy load" on his shoulders and that he
had to resort to "some dexterity in parrying the attacks made upon me for
it." For his part, Bryant said, he had considered Clay's appointment as
secretary of state "a very bad one—never having much respect for Mr.
Clay's principles nor a high estimate of his political knowledge."[7]

In the advertisement for the union of the *Literary Gazette* and the *Review
and Atheneum,* Bryant and Folsom had promised to provide readers with
"a greater variety of matter" than either had been able to do singly.
Containing eighty pages octavo, the magazine was a large undertaking that
taxed the editors' abilities. Bryant exerted strenuous effort in supplying a

*Of the *Evening Post's* editorials opposing the tariff on woolens in 1827, Martin Van Buren
said: "To the very able exposition of the [protective] system and the assaults upon its injustice
and impolicy by the New York *Evening Post,* the country is more indebted for its final
overthrow, in this state [New York] at least, than to any other single influence." *Autobiography* (Washington, 1920), p. 169.

great deal of the material himself. He did not confine his reviewing to fiction and poetry but also considered works on such diverse topics as science, agriculture, education, and travel. These reviews gave him the opportunity to write extensively on the art of fiction and poetry, the state of literature, the purpose of education, and the progress made in various branches of knowledge.[8] Short narratives being hard to get, he wrote two tales for the magazine, and he contributed to the poetry department five original compositions and three translation from the Spanish. Only twice did he have to search through his files to obtain poems to print, "The African Chief," written in 1825, and an extract from his unfinished narrative about the lost ship *Magnalia Christi* written in 1824 and published under the title "The Parting" in the issue of March, 1827.*

Bryant had protested to Dana, who had suggested that he review Cooper's *The Last of the Mohicans,* that the novelist was "too sensitive a creature for me to touch." He was brave enough now to comment on *The Prairie,* which he found showed no loss in Cooper's power of narration.[9] Bryant had more to say about the art of the novel in a review of the anonymous *Adventures of a Young Rifleman . . . Written by Himself,* the story of a German soldier in the armies of Napoleon in 1806. He expressed a preference for older novels, which consisted of a series of adventures not bound together by the thread of plot. He admitted that the new novels attained unity through the plot but he considered this artificial. Frankly, he was bored with feverish plots artfully contrived to achieve suspense. Though Le Sage's *Gil Blas* had no regular plot, he found it unfailingly amusing, as he did *Robinson Crusoe,* "the delight of all countries, a book for readers of all classes and ages, a book which is put into almost as many hands as the Bible."[10] In a review of *The Atlantic Souvenir,* a gift book or annual for the year 1827, Bryant praised tales by his friends Catharine Sedgwick and James Kirke Paulding.[11]

In poetry, there was little of significance published this year for Bryant to review. Of the poems in the *Souvenir,* he particularly liked some stanzas

---

*Bryant's contributions other than the reviews are as follows: "A Border Tradition," "Sonnet" (later titled "October"), and "Mary Magdalen" (from the Spanish of Bartolemé Leonardo de Argensola), Oct., 1826; "The Damsel of Peru," Nov., 1826; "The African Chief," Dec., 1826; "Niagara" (from the Spanish of José Maria Hérédia), Jan., 1827; "The Parting" (from an unfinished poem), March, 1827; "Spring in Town," April, 1827; "The Life of the Blessed" (from the Spanish of Luis Ponce de Léon), May, 1827; "Is This a Time to Be Cloudy and Sad" (later titled "The Gladness of Nature"), June, 1827; "The Disinterred Warrior," Aug., 1827; and "A Narrative of Extraordinary Circumstances That Happened Twenty Years Since" and "Sonnet" (later titled "Midsummer"), Sept., 1827. Bryant also printed John Howard Bryant's "The Traveller's Return" in the Aug., 1827, number.

161

by Percival, but Washington Irving's lines on "The Passaic Falls," he considered to be "such as a gentleman and a man of taste might be expected to write" and there was "much less poetry in them than is to be found in a great deal of his prose."[12] He was happy to be able to review Halleck's *Alnwick Castle, with Other Poems,* though he regretted that the book was so small, only sixty pages. His praise of Halleck's musical versification and his graceful, irrepressible humor was tempered by an adverse criticism of the correctness of his diction.[13] As to American verse in general, a great deal was being published, almost every month producing "several thick volumes," but it was "indifferent poetry." One of the new poetic voices was that of a young South Carolinian, William G. Simms, Jr., whose *Lyrical, and Other Poems* Bryant praised. He wrote that there were many imperfections in the verse but there were also passages which showed "the possession of no ordinary degree of poetical talent."[14] Simms and Bryant were later to become close friends, visiting each other in their New York and Charlestown homes until the Civil War caused a break in their relations.

Before long to become editorially involved in controversy over New York City schools, Bryant's attention to education was attracted by Charles Fenton Mercer's *A Discourse on Popular Education.* Detesting much of his own schooling, Bryant recommended state legislative action for establishing boards of education to prescribe courses of study and the nature of the discipline to be employed. He said education "ought to be a preparation for the world" and hence recommended that schools be not sequestered refuges for pupils but places where they learned the true nature of society and themselves.[15] His interest in botany was reflected in a well-informed review of John Torrey's *Compendium of the Flora of the Northern and Middle States,* in which he declared that botany was a branch of science with which "no well educated man should willingly remain entirely unacquainted."[16] He treated of other scientific topics in an article on lectures delivered before the New York Lyceum,[17] in a review of *An Essay on the Art of Boring the Earth for the Obtainment of a Spontaneous Flow of Water,*[18] and in a review of *Communications of the Agricultural Society of South Carolina.*[19]

In September of 1827 Bryant wrote Folsom that he was sending an uncompleted tale "which has given me much trouble to write," promising to forward the ending during the next week.[20] It was his fourth prose tale, "A Narrative of Some Extraordinary Circumstances That Happened More Than Twenty Years Since." Like his earlier stories, it had a poorly constructed plot and the characterizations were not well realized, but his love of the New England countryside and his power of description are revealed in his pictures of farms with their fertile fields of oats, wheat, and Indian corn, of the mystery of the forest depths, and of the approach of winter as the trees shed their leaves and the transparent blue sky thickens into a dim white haze "through which the sun seemed to labor his way, like a traveller wading through the deep snow."[21]

In acting as the chief editor of the *Review* and as the assistant editor of the *Evening Post,* Bryant severely taxed his strength during the summer. He wrote Frances of his difficulties in completing the tale, "A Narrative of Some Extraordinary Circumstances": "I am yet hard at work writing my tale for the next number of the Review. It is a story of man killed by an explosion of fire and water from the ground like that which happened at Alford a few years since at Otis Patterson's farm. I hope I shall get it finished in the season but I find it slow work."[22] As usual during the summer, Frances had left the city, lodging at Fishkill on the Hudson. Earlier, on June 10, she had written her mother-in-law that after boarding with Mrs. Meigs for more than a year they were "pulling up stakes," Bryant to live during the summer, at a cost of five dollars a week, in the boarding house operated by a Mrs. Tripler at Broadway and Market Street, where she and Fanny would join him in the autumn.[23] Frances had hoped to get out of a boarding house into a place of their own, but their income would not allow it. In reference to renting a house on Walker Street, Bryant in his letter about the tale said: "I undertook to see the proprietor for this and having learned of him that he intends to ask $400 rent I dropped the conversation."

Bryant was depressed by the knowledge that, though the merged magazine was a better one than either had been singly, the endeavor was not proving a financial success. But developments during the summer on the *Evening Post* offered a way out of his difficulties. Coleman's health had steadily declined after the carriage accident in which he had been injured. He and Burnham made an offer to Bryant that would enable him to purchase an interest in the firm and assume the editorship. Since the *Review* was failing, Bryant proposed to Folsom that it should be suspended with the September number, which would complete the second volume, and the plan was agreed upon by the Boston owners.

Bryant's financial arrangements for purchase of his interest in the *Evening Post* are not known. His biographer John Bigelow reported that he had been told Henry Sedgwick lent him two thousand dollars for this purpose.[24] If so, it was not sufficient to cover the entire amount, for Bryant shortly after becoming one of the owners wrote Dana that he owed the firm money, being able, it appears, to apply his dividends to the original purchase price. He explained his situation in a letter of February 16, 1828: "I am a small proprietor in the establishment, and am a gainer by the arrangement. It will afford me a comfortable livelihood after I have paid for the *eighth part,* which is the amount of my share."[25] Early account books of the newspaper reveal that it had a net profit at this time of between $10,000 and $15,000. This would assure Bryant an income of more than one thousand dollars a year from the property.[26]

III

Relieved of his worry over being able to support his family, Bryant now entered upon a period which was to be one of the gayest and most lighthearted of his life. Through his work on the *New-York Review and Atheneum,* he had been associated with the sprightly and learned Robert C. Sands, who in 1827, after several years of engaging in varied literary projects, had joined the *Commercial Advertiser* as assistant editor. Another friend was the jolly Dutchman Gulian C. Verplanck, now serving in Congress but as interested in literature as when he had given Bryant his first New York recognition with the review of his 1821 little volume of *Poems* in the *American.* These three sympathetic spirits joined together in the fall to get out a book on the order of the gift annuals that were popular in England. The first to appear in America was *The Atlantic Souvenir* in 1826, which Bryant had written about in the *United States Review.* Designed for the Christmas book trade, the annuals were attractively bound and decorative miscellanies containing poems, tales, and essays by different authors.

The bookseller Elam Bliss proposed to Sands that he undertake the editing of such a volume, but he declined. Later, however, in a conversation with Verplanck and Bryant, a regret was expressed that the old fashion of Queen Anne's time of publishing collections by two or three authors had lapsed. Such volumes, one of the three pointed out, had an advantage over magazines in that they could be more selective and distinctive in content and did not require the time and toil of getting out a weekly or monthly. "One of the party," Verplanck related, "proposed to publish a little volume of their own miscellanies in humble imitation of the English wits of the last century. It occurred to Sands to combine this idea with the form and decoration of the annual." The three collaborators got down to work at once "without any view to profit, and more for amusement than reputation."[27]

Theirs was an unusual collaboration in which ideas were spontaneously born during rambles about New York City and the picturesque hills and woods on the Jersey side of the Hudson near the hamlet of Hoboken, where Sands still lived in his father's house, which became the headquarters for the trio. In the city they liked to visit out-of-the-way places and those with historical interest—the spot on Wall Street where Washington was inaugurated president, the shores of the North River where Jonathan Edwards strolled while thinking out his sermons to be delivered in the Wall Street Church of which he was the temporary pastor, or the porticoed house at Varick and Charlton Streets where Vice-President John Adams entertained foreign ministers and the leading members of Congress. These walks resulted in the joint writing of "Reminiscences of New York." The rambles in the vicinity of Hoboken offered a different kind of pleasure—the study of nature in the tangled undergrowth along the river between Jersey City and Weehawken, peaceful moments stretched out on the sunny rocks on the Palisades commanding fine views of the river and the city, and learning the local folklore from talks with people met by chance. Again, the walks were productive of literary material—tales based on incidents of the past and descriptive poetry and essays.

Back in the Sands home at Hoboken, the three friends would reduce the talk of their strolls to paper. Verplanck disliked the manual labor of writing, and, an inveterate and fluent speaker, he would balance his chair on its back legs, rest his arms and feet on other chairs, and dictate to his collaborators in turn as fast as they could write. Bryant wondered when Verplanck "found time for the studies by which his mind was kept so full of useful and curious knowledge."[28] A slow and judicious writer himself, Bryant also marveled at Sands's fluency: "His fancy was surprisingly fruitful of new and varied combinations of ideas; and if his vein of humor, peculiar and original as it was, had any fault, it was only that of excessive and unrestrained exuberance. His conversation was full of wit and knowledge, and the quaint combinations of language, and grotesque associations of ideas, that seemed to suggest themselves to his mind unsought, made him an amusing, as his learning and originality of reflection rendered him, an instructive companion." Whereas Bryant thought out his ideas in isolation, often on walks in the woods and about the countryside, Sands preferred human companionship, being disposed to make writing "a social and not a solitary enjoyment."[29]

Bryant described this "joint-stock authorship" as not "simply putting together in one whole, parts prepared separately, nor the correcting and enriching by a second hand of the rough materials of the first author, but the literal writing in company." So true did this seem to the three that when they came to issue their book they decided to present it as the work of one man, Francis Herbert. Their introduction was a tongue-in-cheek affair in which Herbert confessed that he was no writer by profession but had kept a journal of his worldwide travels. He had studied the philosophy of the Orient and was so impressed by its necromancers that he had chosen *The Talisman* as the name for his work. Its contents were written with a swan quill plucked from a fowl that he caught with his own hands on the banks of the Avon. The table on which he wrote was covered with the skin of a tiger he had slain at Madras. All the typesetters were born "in the planetary hour when words and signs have power o'er sprite." In the choice of a publisher one was found whose very name augured the most *Bliss*-ful result.

Each author was chiefly responsible for about one-third of the content, though the hand of the others can be detected in the prose contributions. Bryant was the principal author of three of the tales. Material for one, "The Cascade of Melsingah," a retelling of an Indian legend of the Hudson River country of Dutchess County, no doubt was supplied by Verplanck, whose father had retired to that vicinity. "The Legend of the Devil's Pulpit," whose setting was New Jersey, very likely came from Sands. Bryant's third tale was a completely imaginary one, "Adventure in the East Indies," an account of a miraculous happening that took place on a tiger hunt. The tales are so confused in plot and so carelessly put together that they betray their group authorship—a not quite successful meeting of the minds.

The Talisman had a popular reception, at least locally. On December 28 Bryant wrote Verplanck, who had gone to Washington in advance of the new session of Congress, that it had been "cordially noticed" in the *Courier, Commercial Advertiser,* and *Journal of Commerce,* adding that he had done what he could for it in the *Evening Post.* "On the whole if the Talisman should not succeed," he wrote, "it must be because puffing does not help a book on."[30] A part of the local interest, of course, was in the question of the authorship of the various pieces in the book.

Bryant carried over into the *Evening Post* some of the frolicksome spirit that had enlivened the sessions of the light-hearted triumvirate in their labors at Hoboken in getting out *The Talisman.* A contributor to the *Commercial Advertiser,* one Matthew Paterson, had chided the *Evening Post* for an incorrect Latin quotation. Bryant in collaboration with Sands concocted a riposte suggesting that Paterson consult a work entitled *Virorum Illustrium Reliquiae* and he would find the words were as originally quoted, .being addressed by Pope Alexander VI to his son Caesar Borgia. There was no such work. Delighting in this erudite joking, Bryant wrote Verplanck: "Did you see a learned article in the Evening Post the other day about Pope Alexander VI and Caesar Borgia? Matt. Paterson undertook to be saucy in the Commercial as to a Latin quotation in it, so we—i.e., Sands and myself—sent him on a fool's errand." Another intellectual sport that Bryant carried on with Sands, Henry J. Anderson, Lorenzo da Ponte, and others was translating a set of familiar verses into as many languages as the participants knew and printing them in the paper. They were signed by a fictitious "John Smith." Writing Verplanck about this, Bryant said: "We look upon it here as a very learned *jeu d'esprit.*"[31]

If Bryant had any rough edges when he left Great Barrington as a country lawyer to take up residence in New York, they were by now so smoothed off that he had a metropolitan air. He so impressed a young newcomer to the city's journalism, William Leggett. A hot-tempered man with an unruly tongue, Leggett had been court-martialed by the navy two years before for engaging in a duel. He had published a volume of verse, *Leisure Hours at Sea,* in 1825 and now was trying his hand at journalism. He was commissioned by George Pope Morris to do a series of articles for the *New-York Mirror* on the leading poets of the day.[32] Of Bryant he wrote:

> In person, Mr. Bryant is rather above the middle size; his face is of a pleasing character, and his eyes are lighted up with an expression of great intelligence. His manners are easy and urbane; his disposition open, generous, and sincere; his habits those of a gentleman; his pursuits those of a scholar; and his principles those of a man of honour. His conversation is "rich with the lore of centuries"; though of his learning he makes no parade, keeping it rather for use than show: and those who have the happiness of an acquaintance with this gifted man, find not, as is too often the case, a disparity between his written sentiments and the actions of his life.

A panel of engraved portraits of the nine poets honored illustrated the articles. In the center was the portrait of James Gates Percival and surrounding this in ornately decorated ovals were those of Halleck, Bryant, and the others. The portraits did not commend themselves to Halleck, who wrote Bryant about the "Illustrious Obscure" who had been singled out by Morris for recognition. "He has made me what I ought to have been, and very possibly shall be—a Methodist Parson. . . . The barbershop sort of immortality with which this engraving honors us is most particularly annoying, but how could we help ourselves?"[33] The engraving of Bryant was one copied from a painting by Samuel F. B. Morse done in 1825. Bryant had a high forehead, heavy eyebrows above piercing eyes, a large bony nose, and well-shaped lips. His profuse hair lay in loose ringlets that covered the top part of his ears and his collar at the back. He wore sideburns that extended to his chin; otherwise, he was clean shaven.

IV

When Dana had learned of Bryant's joining the *Evening Post,* he warned him against getting involved in the "vile blackguard squabble" of politics. Bryant replied: "I do not like politics any better than you do; but they get only my mornings, and you know politics and a belly-full are better than poetry and starvation."[34] But developments on the *Evening Post* made it impossible for him to remain aloof. William Coleman's health continued to get worse, forcing him to spend more and more of his time at home, and Bryant shared the burden of writing editorials during the presidential election year of 1828.

The course of the paper in the campaign had been set forth by Coleman the year before. He was prepared to defend "every prominent act" of Jackson. The *American* in one of its frequent potshots at Coleman declared this was inconsistent, and cited an article in the paper in the year 1818 attacking the general. Coleman did not deny this, saying: "We perfectly recollect what we thought at that day and what we, in the sincerity of our hearts, wrote and published. Far different views have presented themselves to us since that time, as we became more intimately acquainted with the facts and circumstances, as shall be made to appear—and all in proper order." Bryant found no difficulty in supporting Jackson, and his motives were probably purer than those of Coleman, whose rancor against Adams was well known. In the first place, Bryant shared Jackson's views, insofar as they had been expounded, opposing a protective tariff and Clay's program of internal improvements. In the second, he admired Jackson's personal character—his simplicity and frankness, his honesty, his sense of justice. These were qualities that had endeared the general to other literary men—Irving, Cooper, Bancroft, and Verplanck.

Because of Bryant's friendship with Verplanck, the two worked together in support of Jackson—Bryant in New York and Verplanck in Washington. Jackson's friends, to start the campaign year with hoopla, had declared January 8, the anniversary of the general's victory at New Orleans, as a date to be marked by celebrations. For the occasion, Bryant wrote an ode to Jackson, which was sung in the Masonic Hall in New York and recited by Verplanck at the Washington festival. Writing Bryant on

January 9, Verplanck said he had read the ode "with due emphasis, and a little theatrically." He received an ovation: "Vice-President Calhoun nodded approbation. Van Buren was in ecstasies, so was the Speaker [John W. Taylor], and Kremer [George Kremer, representative from Pennsylvania] shouted clamorous delight." The representative from South Carolina, Robert Y. Hayne, summed up the opinion of those at the dinner: "that the Jackson cause had all the poetry as well as all the virtue of the land."[35]

The campaign was fought mostly over the "corrupt bargain" issue raised in 1824 when, so the Democrats said, Clay had supported Adams for president in return for the promise of being named secretary of state. But the Democrats also exploited the tariff issue to discredit Adams and with Satanic guile—it was chiefly Calhoun's—framed a measure with such excessively high duties that it would harm even New England manufacturing interests and be so objectionable in other sections of the country as to insure its defeat. To the surprise of everyone, it passed the House on April 23 and the Senate on May 13. Bryant probably had a hand in framing the bill, since Verplanck, as a member of the Ways and Means Committee, was one of its sponsors. Nevertheless, when it passed the House the *Evening Post* inveighed against it, describing it as a "pernicious bill," and continued to attack it in subsequent editorials. Bryant had written Verplanck on February 16 that he was amused to observe how papers received the bill. "The Jackson papers . . . seized upon it as proof that the Jackson party was friendly to manufacturers, or at least willing to give their friends fair play," he said. "The Adams papers preserved a dead silence for a while, and then the storm broke." He agreed with Verplanck's prediction—erroneous as it turned out—that the New England members of Congress would be forced to vote against it.[36]

So closely did Verplanck work with Bryant that he was practically the *Evening Post's* Washington correspondent. As a matter of fact, he suggested to Bryant that he need not have a representative in the capital. Bryant could get the regular news from the Washington papers and Verplanck would supply him with inside information. "When anything occurs of value for the Post's correspondence I will not neglect you," he promised. On one occasion Bryant wrote Verplanck: "We are greatly obliged to you for such oracular hints, for so they are received, as you have occasionally given us since you went to the capital. They are copied everywhere, even in the American." Verplanck's dislike for the manual labor of writing, however, made him a somewhat unreliable correspondent. The irregularity of his letters caused Bryant to complain: "Why do you not write? The Evening Post is in eclipse since you have withdrawn the light of your countenance. The other papers are ahead of it in the revelation of State secrets and the mysteries of policy."[37]

In June the *Evening Post* took delight in reporting the difficulties in Boston over getting support for a dinner honoring Daniel Webster, who had voted for the tariff. It remarked of Webster's speech that it was a "poor thing" and in its attack on the Democrats relied upon "obvious untruths" and "as an harangue for popular effect" it dealt with topics "only worthy of a demagogue." Surveying opinion in the South, the paper on July 16 said that antitariff meetings were multiplying so fast that there was not enough space to report them. But its editorial concluded: "We have been looking over their proceedings with a view of seeing whether they recommended any of those projects of insurrection and disunion about which the administration papers in this quarter, have made such a clamour, and which they talk of as being very generally entertained at the south. We find no evidence of the existence of these treasonable plans." On July 23 the paper reiterated the charge that the Adams papers were trying to foment disunion with their assertion that "disunion is the creed of Jacksonianism." Finally, on October 31, in declaring its support of Jackson for President, Calhoun for vice-president, and Van Buren for governor, the paper declared: "The battle is about to commence and we therefore thus raise our broad pennant and nail it to the mast. We sink or swim with the ship." Victory was by no means a sure thing in New York, but the anti-Masons in the western part of the state and the Adams men split their vote, bringing about a narrow victory for the Democratic ticket. In the city, however, Verplanck and his fellow Democrat, Churchill C. Cambreleng, won their seats in the House by good majorities.

V

Bryant and Verplanck in the salutations of their letters during the year often addressed each other as "My dear Francis," in playful reference to their merged egos with Sands in the person of the author of *The Talisman*. The first volume had proved so popular that Elam Bliss prevailed upon Francis Herbert to write another. On May 9, 1828, Bryant reported to Verplanck that the demand for the volume was still continuing and urged him to do "your share for another year." The artist Henry Inman had done a design illustrating a poem by Clement C. Moore, author of "A Visit of St. Nicholas," on the Dismal Swamp and wanted the drawing to appear in *The Talisman*. Bryant asked Verplanck to obtain from Virginians some particulars of the swamp "which some of us may weave into a narrative, or make a florid description."[38] For the new volume the collaborators invited Fitz-Greene Halleck to contribute, suggesting the topics of Wee-hawken or Red Jacket, chief of the Tuscarora Indians who was being put on display at various museums to recount his life. Red Jacket's portrait had been painted by Robert W. Weir, and this inspired Halleck to write his lines paying tribute to the spirit of the disappearing Indians.

Bryant's contributions were chiefly poetry, though he wrote one tale for the volume, "Story of the Island of Cuba." As the pretended traveler Francis Herbert, he also penned "Recollections of the South of Spain," which prefaced his translation of a ballad, "A Moriscan Romance." He also wrote one original poem on a Spanish topic, "The Lament of Romero," a tribute to a warrior who, when King Ferdinand returned to the throne after the fall of Napoleon and renounced the liberal constitution, broke his sword and vowed not to use it until it could be employed again in the cause of liberty. These compositions reveal Bryant's deepening interest in Spain and its language and literature and in Latin America. Just as on first arriving in New York he had boarded with a French family the better to learn the language, he had now, in March, taken up residence in a Spanish home, that of the Salazars on Hubert Street.[39] The material for the tale of Cuba was obtained from Cuban visitors entertained by the Salazars.

As Weir's portrait of Red Jacket had suggested Halleck's lines on the Tuscarora chieftain, another of his portraits suggested Bryant's poem, "The Greek Boy," written to accompany an engraving of the painting. The subject of the poem was C. Evangelides, whose parents had died in the Greek revolution. He had been brought to America by a ship's captain to be educated, and had been lionized in the campaign to raise money to help the revolution. The other poems by Bryant were a romantic development of an Indian theme, "The Hunter's Serenade"; a short lyric, "Upon the Mountain's Distant Head"; and "The Past," another statement of his view of death. A deeply personal poem, "The Past" differs from "Thanatopsis" in that it promises a reunion of loved ones in the afterlife. Referring to his father and sister, Bryant says:

> And then shall I behold
> Him, by whose kind paternal side I sprung,
>   And her, who, still and cold,
> Fills the next grave—the beautiful and young.

Bryant considered "The Past" one of his best poems, an opinion shared by Verplanck and Dana,* and in later years often complained that reviewers ignored it in their discussions of his work.

*Godwin reports that Julia Sands recalled Verplanck rushing to the Sands's home one afternoon and exlaiming: "Oh, Sands, I've got such a poem! Gray's 'Elegy' is nothing to it. I picked it up at the publishers and all the way across the river it has been ringing in my brain." He then recited the complete poem, "The Past." *Biography,* I, 239–40.

11

VILE BLACKGUARD SQUABBLES

WHEN BRYANT JOINED THE *Evening Post*, EDITORS WERE POL-
iticians, serving as spokesmen for parties, whose leaders often furnished
the money to establish papers and, when in office, aided in their support
by awarding them the public printing. Their role was to change and to
become more important during the Jackson revolution, which ended government by succession with offices being filled by members of a reigning
elite. With Jackson, the government became a people's government, and
therefore more obedient to public opinion than before. Debates in the
press became more influential than debates in Congress in decision-mak-
ing. In joining the *Evening Post,* Bryant, as he had written Dana, had
chosen politics and a belly-full to poetry and starvation. The choice be
came more meaningful in July, 1829, when William Coleman died and
Bryant succeeded him as editor.

An article with turned column rules and black borders on July 14
announced Coleman's death of an apoplectic stroke the day before.
Bryant's tribute was not only an expression of personal regard but also
partly a statement of his own views on the qualities of a good editor.
Though mentioning Coleman's "boldness of character" and his "acute-
ness in controversy," Bryant praised him chiefly for his "disinterestedness," conceded even by his enemies: "He might commit errors, but they
never arose from any sordid motive. No person was ever more ready to

retract a mistaken opinion, when convinced of the mistake, no person was ever more happy to do justice to those whom he had unintentionally wronged, and none ever did it with a better grace. He seemed to have an utter disdain of that false and foolish pride which, veiling itself under the notion of consistency, refuses to retract an error, or repair an injury."

Bryant then apparently had only his one-eighth interest in the firm, the principal owners being Michael Burnham and, with Coleman's death, Mrs. Coleman. Nevertheless, the division between the editorial and business offices was continued as when Coleman was in charge. Thus Bryant, at the age of thirty-four with only a brief experience in journalism, was placed in a position to determine the policy of one of the most influential as well as most profitable of the city's dailies.

Bryant chose for his assistant a man four years his junior in age, William Leggett, whose work as editor of the literary weekly, *The Critic,* had commended itself to him. Coming to New York in 1826 after resigning from the navy under the cloud of a court-martial for insubordination and fighting a duel, Leggett had written for the *Mirror* and other publications. Two years later he had established his own magazine but had been unable to make it pay and it expired after six months. *The Critic* had been a one-man operation, Leggett writing the literary reviews, the notices of the drama and the arts, the essays, the tales, the biographical sketches—all except the poetry although about one-half the verse had been his also. This, as Bryant wrote later, was "an extraordinary instance of literary industry and fertility." But more important, Bryant had seen in Leggett's work "the dawnings of that fervid and eloquent style of discussion which afterwards, transferred to subjects in which he took a deeper interest, was wielded with vast power and effect."[1]

In contrast with Bryant's sedate life, Leggett's had been one of travel and adventure. He was born in New York City on April 30, 1801, the son of a businessman, and at an early age entered Georgetown College in Washington, where he "mastered the prescribed studies with such ease that they seemed rather a pastime than a task." Leggett's father, having suffered business reverses, moved his family to Illinois in 1819. There young Leggett became acquainted with frontier life, obtaining material which he used in his popular tale, "The Rifle," published in *The Atlantic Souvenir.*

Appointed a midshipman in the navy in 1822, Leggett was assigned to the U. S. S. *Cyane,* which sailed to the Mediterranean in 1825. The captain, according to testimony at Leggett's court-martial, appears to have been a tyrant whose kicking and cuffing of a marine resulted in the man's death.

Outraged, Leggett railed against him in the midshipmen's quarters. This led to words with a shipmate and a challenge to a duel, fought one night when Leggett was on duty and left his station to uphold his honor. The next day, appalled by his action, Leggett attempted to commit suicide. One of the charges against him was treating "his superiour with disrespect." On one occasion, Leggett, in the presence of other officers and in the hearing of the captain, alluded to the court-martial "in a jocular and deriding manner" and quoted verses of "a highly inflammatory, rancorous, and threatening import" against the captain. One quotation was from a play by Byron: "O! had I him on the ocean, with but one plank between us and eternity; that with these desperate arms I might throw him in the flood, and see him gasp his last." The court-martial found Leggett guilty and recommended his dismissal from the navy, but in view of his long confinement before the trial the penalty of dismissal was remitted. Leggett, however, resigned his commission in April of 1826.[2]

Such was the young firebrand that Bryant brought into the editorial offices of the *Evening Post*. At the time—though he was to change violently and soon—Leggett had little interest in government except for his hatred of despotism and oppression like that of the poets he admired, Byron and Shelley. One of Leggett's stipulations was "that he should not be asked to write articles on political subjects, on which he had no settled opinion, and for which he had no taste."[3] Unlike Bryant, Leggett had rushed into print: he was already the author of two volumes of poems, *Leisure Hours at Sea* (1825) and *Journals of the Ocean* (1826), and a volume of prose, *Tales and Sketches of a Country Schoolmaster* (1829).

II

Although the defeated National Republicans of Adams were despondent over Jackson's election and what they believed would prove to be the extinction of the republic when the mob took over—the local politicians, the war veterans, the editors, the ragtag and bobtail who swarmed into Washington for the inauguration—there was little in the *Evening Post* before or immediately after Bryant's assuming the editorship to indicate that the paper would become, as it did, a radical spokesman for the common people, the laborers and mechanics in the city and the small farmers in the country. No one was sure, in the first year of Jackson's term, what his program would be. Bryant had admired the President as a person and had accepted him as a free-trader because of his ambiguous statement about supporting a "judicious" tariff—which Bryant assumed would not be a protective one—but Bryant had seen enough of the common people, in Plainfield and Great Barrington and New York, to have no illusions about them. On the contrary, his editorials in 1829 seemed to mark him as an opponent of the rising labor movement, which was influenced in part by theories of the Scottish philanthropist Robert Owen and the Scottish agitator Frances Wright.

In January Miss Wright lectured at the Masonic Hall, drawing enthusiastic crowds of working people and reformers. She was then a notorious character. A few years before she had carried on an experiment at Nashoba, Tennessee, to educate emancipated Negroes. She attributed her failure to the clergy, who had corrupted the American people by a false system of education. Then she took part in Owen's experiment at New Harmony, Indiana, which shocked the country because of its communist practices, its opposition to sectarian religion, and its rejection of the conventions of marriage and family. Miss Wright served as co-editor of the *New Harmony Gazette,* which she and Owen moved to New York in 1829, calling it the *Free Enquirer.*

Conservative in his attitudes toward women, Bryant, in an editorial on January 10, wrote of Miss Wright that "female expounders of any kind of doctrine are not to our taste." He felt that the "privacy and delicacy of their education" and "their natural turn for those pursuits which embellish society" disqualified them for "conducting public metaphysical disputes."* Nevertheless, Miss Wright's being a woman did not save her from ridicule in a satirical ode, which called her a modern Aspasia with "a touch of old Xantippe." Bryant took delight in the fact that the satire created a great deal of talk and, as he wrote Verplanck, had "passed for Halleck's among the knowing ones," several papers reprinting it in the belief that it was another example of the "Croaker's" wit.[4] When Bryant on January 26 heard that she had rented the Park Theatre for a series of six lectures, he was struck "with utter astonishment" and wrote stingingly of "the singular spectacle of a female, publicly and ostentatiously proclaiming doctrines of atheistical fanaticism, and even the most abandoned

---

*The editorial on Frances Wright did not represent Bryant's full views on women and their education. The *Evening Post,* Jan. 8, 1831, carried a four and one-half column article urging reforms in the attitude toward them. It said they should be trained in business affairs to enable them to understand finance in the case of the death of a husband; condemned the circumscribed position of women that "allows no expansion of intellect"; advocated their employment in retail shop keeping; and recommended scholarships for them, not to prepare them for teaching, but "for the respectable maintenance of well-educated women." The article, which was not signed, drew much press comment and, the *Evening Post* noted on Jan. 15, extra copies struck off were immediately exhausted.

lewdness." The next day, another editorial contained the information that Miss Wright had offered "to let us have her lectures to peruse, to convince us that they contain nothing lewd or immoral . . . an offer of which we must beg to decline to avail ourselves."

On February 9 Bryant wrote Verplanck that the topic of common talk had changed from Miss Wright to Jackson's health, about once a week a report being bandied about that he was dead. He believed the general's death would cause more vexation than if Adams had won the election: "We should all think it very unkind of him, after all the trouble we have been at on his account. Besides, you know that everybody is in an agony of curiosity to know whom he will put into his cabinet. If he should slip off to another world without solving this riddle, we should never forgive him."[5] Two weeks later he commented humorously about the cabinet appointments—views that did not appear in the *Evening Post*. How could Verplanck have allowed Jackson to make such choices? The selection of Martin Van Buren for the Department of State was well enough, but "how comes [Samuel D.] Ingham to be the secretary of the treasury?" Though not exactly in favor of the tariff, Ingham was "a tariff man, infected with the leaven of the American system." Bryant had no objection to John H Eaton in the War Department or to John M. Berrien as attorney general, but John Branch, the navy secretary, was little known in New York "and that little does not give us a high opinion of him." "I allow," Bryant said, "that the cabinet is as good as the last . . . but where are the great men whom the general was to assemble round him, the powerful minds that were to make up for his deficiencies?"[6]

III

In quitting Great Barrington, Bryant had written Dana that the law had become intolerable because of the "innumerable quarrels" in which his practice involved him. As editor of the *Evening Post,* he was quickly drawn into quarrels with different factions in the Democratic party, with supporters of the tariff and the internal improvements program, now in disarray because of the defeat of the National Republicans, and with editors of rival newspapers.

The city's newspapers were roughly of two types, mercantile and political, though in some it was hard to detect any difference. With subscriptions at ten dollars a year, the papers were beyond the means of working people, and their readers were confined to well-to-do business and professional people. Little news in the modern sense appeared in either the commercial or political papers. Proceedings of the corporation council of the city, the state legislature, and Congress were reported in the form of minutes, and presidential messages and major political speeches were printed in full. Overseas publications provided the foreign news, there being lively competition to obtain copies of papers from arriving ships. Domestic news consisted of reprints from other papers. The party organs in Albany and Washington supplied the official political news and their articles were printed verbatim. Political figures communicated their views through speeches, which were printed in full, and through letters addressed to friends with the idea that these would be given to the papers. Public affairs were discussed not only in the editor's own articles under the flag on page two but also in letters, many of them quite long, from officials and politicians. These were usually anonymous, the contributors using noms de plume, frequently of Latin origin. The space not filled by commercial or political news was given over to copious literary extracts from the magazines or books.

The *Evening Post* under Coleman had been nominally a political paper, yet it did not differ much from the dailies that had "commercial" or "advertiser" as a part of their name. It devoted three-fourths of its space to advertising and it printed a great deal of commercial news, which Bryant soon increased. The best of the "commercial" papers was the *Commercial Advertiser,* edited since 1820 by Colonel William L. Stone. Stone, as Coleman had been, was a Federalist, but he supported the National Republicans and became a Whig when that party was formed. Two years before, in 1827, the *Journal of Commerce* had been founded by Arthur Tappan, a prominent merchant and reformer, opposing slavery, Sabbath-breaking, and intemperance. In 1828 it passed into the hands of Gerald Hallock and David Hale. Both had Tappan's religious bias, but were enterprising newsgatherers nevertheless; they were Democratic in politics. There were three other commercial papers in 1829, but these were not in the forefront of the journalistic warfare: the *Daily Advertiser, Gazette and General Advertiser,* and *Mercantile Advertiser.*

In the first year of the Jackson administration a rift developed among the New York Democrats between the conservatives and reformers. Until Van Buren relinquished the governorship to go into Jackson's cabinet, the reformers had dominated through Van Buren's close control of the Albany Regency. With his departure, the conservative wing took over. As the Democrats began to form alignments among themselves—the fight for power between Jackson and John C. Calhoun of South Carolina was soon to break out into the open—editors wanting to be party oracles were engaged in shifts and ploys to get the approval of Washington. The intra-party name-calling among the Democratic sheets soon became as rough as that coming from the opposition press.

As one of the city's oldest newspapers, highly regarded for its literary quality and its independence, the *Evening Post* was the chief Jackson paper. But the new administration brought new Democratic papers in its wake. One of these was the *Courier and Enquirer,* established in the spring of 1829 by the consolidation of two papers by the bellicose Colonel James Watson Webb, who had fought in the War of 1812 and had reenlisted to take part in the warfare against Indians in the Northwest; his martial record included two duels with fellow officers. The *Morning Courier* had been established in 1827 and came almost immediately into the hands of Colonel Webb. The other paper in the merger, the *Enquirer,* had been founded in 1826 by the colorful Mordecai M. Noah, a brilliant writer who some years before had named himself "Judge and Governor of Israel" and planned a community, Ararat, for the settlement of Jews on Grand Island, in the Niagara River. With Noah and the newspaper property came a member of the staff, one James Gordon Bennett, a squint-eyed Scotsman whose fanatical drive for journalism was to make him in a few years, the foremost American editor of the country save for Horace Greeley. Noah and Bennett had been associates on the *National Advocate,* which had been established as a Tammany organ in 1812. Noah left the paper in 1825 after quarreling with the editors; Bennett succeeded him as editor, but he left in 1827 when the owners backed Adams for President. The *National Advocate* did not continue for long, expiring in 1829. Another new entry in the Democratic field in 1829 was the *Standard,* established by John M. Mumford. Mumford had started the *Telegraph* in 1826 but suspended it to travel in Europe. Seeing the opportunities open to an ardent Demo-cratic paper, he soon made the *Standard* an outlet for the Washington administration. Against this array of Democratic papers, the cause of Adams and Clay had as its chief spokesmen in New York the ultra conserv-ative *American,* established in 1819 by Charles King and still edited by him, and Colonel Stone's *Commercial Advertiser.*

Bryant entered the political fray by attacking Henry Clay, mildly at first and then with increasing fury, defending President Jackson against "mis-representations" in the opposition press, and abusing the editors of the *American* and the *Commercial.* The onslaught on Clay was provoked by the acquittal for murder of one Charles Wickliffe, who, objecting to articles in the *Kentucky Gazette* at Lexington, called on the editor demanding the authorship and when the name was refused shot him dead. Clay was involved because he was one of Wickliffe's attorneys. On July 15 Bryant wrote: "It should seem that it is impossible to execute the law against a murderer in Mr. Clay's state, if the ruffian happens to have strong political connections." Both the *American* and *Commercial* replied vitriolically to the slur on Clay, and the interchange of insults continued for some weeks, Bryant complaining indignantly of the "extraordinary and indecent exasperation with which we have been assailed."

Bryant was not convinced by Clay's statement, after the election of Jackson, that he had withdrawn from public affairs "to recruit his health amidst the labors of agriculture," as the *Evening Post* phrased it. In the fall, Clay began rebuilding his political fences by addressing large crowds gathered at barbecues. Bryant was especially incensed that Clay, in reference to the talk of disunion in the South over the tariff, had said that highly as he regarded the Union he would not value it at the expense of the American system and that if the minority were determined to secede he would not be opposed. Calling the speech sedition and demagoguery, Bryant declared that faced by "such a spectacle of the infatuation and inconsistency to which mad ambition may lead" he scarcely knew "whether to weep or laugh."

In other editorials, Bryant attacked "the low and unprincipled mode of warfare pursued by the opposition journals against the present administration." It was marked by "coarseness and vulgarity" that was ill concealed by "the unsuitable garniture of pompous words." He declared that he could not "turn aside from our high and commendable object to enter into private warfare" and then went on to engage in it with these words: "The continual clamor which is kept up against the executive, when even the keen and jaundiced eye of political inveteracy and disappointed ambition, can see not a shadow of real cause for complaint, is an evidence at once of the imbecility and flagitiousness of the defeated party."

But a new element was beginning to appear in politics, a labor movement inspired when working men's parties were formed in New York and Philadelphia in the fall of 1829. The New York group entered slates in the local elections and established its own newspaper, the *Working Man's Advocate.* Although basically sympathetic to labor, Bryant was frightened by some of the views expressed because they seemed to reflect the extremist ones of Owen and Frances Wright on property and threatened American democracy by class warfare. On November 14, he urged "the really worthy mechanics" of the city who had joined the party to withdraw now that its "designs and doctrines" are known. "These designs," he warned, "are of too absurd and Quixotic a nature ever to be carried into practice."

Four days later he returned to the subject, asking why the clamor for "repartition" of property when there was a natural law at work in the social organism by which "wealth is taken away from the undeserving and turned over with unfailing poetic justice to the laborious and the thrifty." Bryant was further disturbed when the party had some success in the election, but his fears were somewhat allayed when he noted in an editorial on December 2 that a number of journeymen mechanics had adopted a resolution disclaiming the extreme demands of the Working Man's party.

Bryant's opposition to the working man's movement cannot really be considered a serious blot on his liberalism and humanitarianism. He believed that the laws of economics, as he had learned them, would operate to the best advantage of all and that there were no bars to rising in the world for the industrious who saved their money. His editorials did not attack such ameliorations of the laborer's lot as shorter hours and higher wages, only the methods by which they might be attained if they meant violating established procedures for change, if they endangered the American republic. He had opposed the protective tariff, because it worked hardship on the working people while the rich could still afford their fine broadcloths. His editorials on the banking situation had pointed out that workers suffered when their wages, paid in bank notes, could be discounted for whatever the buyers of the notes wanted to pay. The party with which he was allied had fought against imprisonment for debt and for extension of suffrage, and it had at Albany pushed through the safety-fund act of 1829 to regulate banking.

IV

The Bryant family were still unsettled in New York, still living in a boarding house. They made their usual yearly move on May 1—the regular moving day on which thousands of citizens exchanged residences —when the Salazars took a house on Varick Street. Mrs. Bryant, with Fanny, left soon afterward to spend the summer at Great Barrington.[7] A friend, Miss Eliza Robbins, wrote her on July 24, relating that Bryant had taken her to the exhibit of the Academy of Design, where Morse's portrait of him was on display. She did not care for it: "I think it indifferent—pale and chalky—not in character—too much like a common man—Mr. Morse never could have understood and felt his genius, or he would have disposed his mind to some tone of thought, that would have given the most striking expression to his features."[8]

Bryant's new duties on the *Evening Post* did not prevent him from collaborating with Verplanck and Sands on a third edition of *The Talisman*, though the previous volume, despite its being critically well received, had done poorly in sales. Reporting this to Verplanck on February 9, Bryant had written that "poor Bliss is very much disappointed."[9] Bryant's contributions to the new work included three prose tales, a half-dozen poems and translations, and a retelling of a story that he had run across in the book on the Provençal poets by John of Nostradamus.

Only one of the tales is of any interest, "The Indian Spring," an evocation in prose of the spirit of the Indians that, as Bryant had written in several of his poems, seemed to be immanent in areas from which they had long disappeared. The original poems, all in Bryant's collected work, were "The Evening Wind," "When the Firmament Quivers with Daylight's Young Beam," "The Innocent Child and Snow-White Flower," "To the River Arve" (composed to illustrate a scenic engraving of the stream at the foot of Mont Blanc), and "To Cole the Painter, Departing for Europe."

Bryant admired Cole for his portrayals of an unmistakably American landscape. Recalling his first enthusiasm for Cole's paintings of the 1820's, Bryant described them as carrying the eye "over scenes of wild grandeur peculiar to our country, over our aerial mountain-tops with their mighty growth of forest never touched by the axe, along the banks of streams never deformed by culture, and into the depth of skies bright with the hues of our own climate; skies such as few but Cole could ever paint, and through the transparent abysses of which it seemed that you might send an arrow out of sight."[10] The sonnet is an admonition to the artist to view the different places he will visit in Europe through the eyes of his American idealism. Cole's canvases have pictured

> Lone lakes—savannas where the bison roves—
> Rocks rich with summer garlands—solemn streams—
> Skies, where the desert eagle wheels and screams—
> Spring bloom and autumn blaze of boundless groves.

In Europe he too will see "Fair scenes" but they will be different

> everywhere the trace of men,
> Paths, homes, graves, ruins. . . .

And he is exhorted in the climaxing couplet:

Gaze on them, till the tears shall dim thy sight,
But keep that earlier, wilder image bright.

Bryant had more than done his share in supplying the content of the
1830 volume of *The Talisman*, but as editor of a daily newspaper he was
forced to give up such original literary work. The annual had run its course
in any case. Francis Herbert—Bryant was kept busy on the *Evening Post*,
Sands on the *Commercial Advertiser*, and Verplanck in Washington—had
little time to continue the project, which he had undertaken for pleasure,
and decided to give it up. The decision also suited the publisher Bliss.
Bryant wrote Verplanck on January 11, 1830, that though sales during the
last days of the year had been more than expected Bliss would still lose
money on it.[11]

V

The year 1830 was marked by continued struggle among the Democratic newspapers for ascendancy within the party. The *Evening Post* was
a partial loser in New York state when James Watson Webb of the *Courier
and Enquirer* proposed to the legislature that his sheet be given the printing of all legal notices in the city as a reward for "political merit." Bryant
objected, in an editorial on January 9, pointing out that the *Evening Post*
had supported the party longer than Webb, who only the year before had
opposed the ticket in the city. "If the legislature acts according to the
proposal," Bryant wrote, "it will deprive us of a very considerable and
profitable patronage arising from legal notices sent us by persons who
prefer our paper, by personal friends, or by those who like our mode of
doing business. This patronage the establishment of the Evening Post has
earned by a long course, we believe we may say without vanity, of diligent
attention to the duties of a commercial advertising paper." The editorial
gave the paper's circulation as 1,728 daily. This was about one-half that
of the *Courier and Inquirer*, which had led the city since the consolidation
in 1829. The national organ of the Democratic party was the Washington
Globe, established in 1830 by members of Jackson's Kitchen Cabinet. In
Albany, the Regency organ, the *Atlas*, continued. A new opposition paper
entered the field when Thurlow Weed established the Albany *Evening
Journal*, at first as an anti-Masonic organ but subsequently to become one
of the nation's leading Whig journals.

Although engaging in the political controversies of the day, Bryant did
not neglect the news side of the paper. During January and February of

1830 he printed the complete Webster-Hayne debate, which, beginning as an inquiry into the question of temporarily restricting the sale of public lands, had turned into a profound discussion of the Constitution and states' rights. He followed this by devoting five closely printed columns each day from February 15 to 17 to the tariff report of the House Commerce Committee, headed by the New York Democratic representative Churchill C. Cambreleng. Another long public document carried in full was a grand jury presentment attacking "the great and growing evil of lotteries," whose ticket sales, Bryant editorialized, exceeded nine million dollars yearly, much of it coming "from the pockets of the laboring and poorer classes." Finally, in December it printed the inaugural address of Governor James Hamilton of South Carolina and in an editorial denounced the doctrine of nullification. Editorials continued to support a reduction of the tariff and attacked opponents for their tactics in keeping the measure off the floor of the House; opposed a state law to forbid masquerades because of their impropriety as an instance of "excessive legislation" on matters that should be left to public opinion; and defended the government plan to remove the Cherokee Indians from Georgia to the West, condemning at the same time the "mistaken zeal" adopted in their interest by northern sympathizers.

But Bryant also published editorials on less serious topics, among them descriptions of nature as he saw it in the city, and in his only poem written during the year, "Hymn to the City," he developed the theme that natural evidences of the Deity could be perceived among the crowds on the streets as well as in the solitude of forested valley or mountain:

> Thy Spirit is around,
> Quickening the restless mass that sweeps along;
>   And this eternal sound—
> Voices and footfalls of the numberless throng—
>   Like the resounding sea,
> Or like the rainy tempest, speaks of thee.

During the year Bryant increased his holding in the *Evening Post* to a one-quarter interest, and when the books were balanced on November 16, as they were annually, he could congratulate himself on becoming prosperous. The net profits had risen to $13,466 from $10,544 of 1829, and Bryant's share was $3,366.51.[12] Mrs. Bryant had spent the summer staying at boarding houses or visiting friends in several New York and New Jersey towns. She went to Trenton Falls with her brother in August, when she was joined by Bryant and they traveled to Cummington. In

December, after having lived in boarding houses for several years, the Bryants with their new affluence were able to move into their own place —"commenced housekeeping," as Frances put it—in Broome Street between Hudson and Varick Streets.[13]

So prosperous had the *Evening Post* become that in December a new Napier press, manufactured by Robert Hoe & Company, was purchased. It enabled the newspaper, with the first issue of 1831 on January 3, to appear in a larger format, the number of columns increased from six to seven. An editorial boasted that papers could be printed at the rate of twenty copies a minute and if necessary at the rate of twenty-five, or one thousand five hundred an hour. New departments added to appeal to the commercial interests were tables of commodity prices not only in New York but other cities as well, a report of sales on the stock exchange, and listings of letter bags received from ships in addition to the long-published marine log of ship arrivals and departures. A little later in the year two more departments were added, "Police and Court Proceedings" and "Occurrences of the Day." On the same day appeared an announcement that Charles Burnham and William Leggett had been taken into partnership, but the business would continue to be conducted under the firm name of Michael Burnham & Company.

VI

At eight o'clock on the morning of April 20, 1831, the wealthy retired merchant Philip Hone was shaving at his fine home on Broadway when he was the observer of "a disgraceful affair" on the street which he recorded, as he did almost everything else that passed before his eyes for a quarter of a century, in his diary.[14] It was an encounter between Bryant and Stone of the *Commercial Advertiser,* in which Bryant inflicted corporal punishment on his rival editor with a cowskin whip.

The row had its origin in a jocose editorial which Bryant wrote on April 5 about a dinner got up by Adams and Clay supporters in honor of Senator Tristram Burgess of Rhode Island. The senator's speech had been carried in National Republican journals, requiring five or six closely printed columns to get it all in. The delivery, according to Bryant's editorial, "consumed an hour and three quarters." The squabble was continued next week when Bryant alluded to a toast given at the dinner directed against the city's leading Democratic papers: "The Evening Post and Courier and Enquirer—stupidity and vulgarity." The toast had been printed in the *Commercial* but the name of its proposer was not given. In reprinting the insult, Bryant attributed it to Stone. Stone wrote Bryant a note disclaiming the authorship, but Bryant could not believe this was so, stating that it seemed unlikely that Stone, one of the arrangers of the dinner, did not know who had proposed the toast. Stone was greatly incensed when the Albany *Argus* reprinted the *Evening Post*'s account of the affair, and he published a reply in which he said he had dispatched a second note to Bryant "giving the charge a solemn denial under our own signature, and leaving the brand of a significant word spelt with four letters, which it would outrage polite ears to repeat, to blister upon the forehead of William C. Bryant if a blister can be raised on brass."

Apologizing for the affray on Broadway, Bryant wrote on April 21, citing the latest article in the *Commercial:*

> In this paragraph it will be seen that Stone . . . boasts that he has bestowed upon me, by name, the most insulting epithet that can be applied to a human being—an epithet never before, to my knowledge, connected with my name. . . . The article was published in the Commercial on Saturday last. I did not see it until Monday, when the question became what course I ought to pursue on the occasion. On the one hand, it occurred to me that no glory was to be gained from personal contests between editors—and least of all from one with the individual in question—that scenes of violence were in the highest degree alien to my tastes, and that to have been engaged in them, was productive of the most unpleasant kind of notoriety. On the other hand, the most outrageous possible insult had been offered me, and if I submitted to it it would probably be soon repeated.
> The latter consideration determined me to inflict upon him personal chastisement for a personal outrage, approaching him fairly and giving him ample opportunity to stand on his defence. This I effected as soon as I fell in with him. . . .
> In conclusion, I feel that I owe an apology to society for having, in this instance, taken the law into my own hands. The outrage was one for which the law affords no redress. It was attended with circumstances of peculiar malignity; and I hope, if the propriety of my course be admitted, that the retribution will not be thought excessive. . . .

The *Commercial's* account of the altercation declared that Bryant had attacked Stone from behind without warning. This was denied by William Leggett in his account, carried along with Bryant's, in the *Evening Post*. Leggett related that he accompanied Bryant when he left the office to look for Stone, whom they saw walking down Broadway with his brother-in-law. Bryant called out to Stone, who turned around. Thereupon, Bryant took off his hat, withdrew from it a cowskin whip, and advanced upon Stone, who carried a bamboo cane. Simultaneously Bryant struck Stone on the shoulder and Stone struck a blow with the cane. The bamboo splintered and the cane was revealed to be a sword cane, with which Stone made several thrusts parried by Bryant with his whip. The sword was struck from Stone's hand, and the cowskin was wrested from Bryant by three "stout onlookers." Leggett related that he repeatedly prevented the brother-in-law from aiding Stone, once throwing him to the pavement. Since published versions of the fight vary—Hone, for example, saying that Stone took the whip from Bryant and carried it away with him—the exact details cannot be determined. But for once, at least, Bryant's ability to keep his temper in check was lost.

VII

During the year, Bryant continued to write editorials against the political opposition and the forces behind the tariff. On one occasion, he resorted to political satire in verses titled "The Bee in the Tar-Barrel." A bee buzzing angrily in the barrel is imagined as being upset by matters political: the halfway measures taken to reopen to direct trade the West Indian ports which England had closed, the question of the removal of the Cherokee Indians, and the replacement of federal office holders by Jackson men. Bryant's facility for topical verse, as in his "Ode to Miss Frances Wright," is shown in his description of the angry bee buzzing in protest:

> " 'Twas a crime to fill the land with groans,
>   'Twas a deed," he said, "most foul and ugly,
> To turn out poor unfortunate drones
>   From the public hive, where they lodged so snugly."

In April Bryant was named by the city's literary men to head a committee to arrange a dinner honoring Verplanck for his success, after several years' effort, to get Congress to pass a copyright law. The measure provided for a twenty-eight-year copyright that could be extended for an additional twenty-eight years. Among the toasts drunk, as reported by the *Evening Post,* was one by Bryant: "Engraving—the art which is to painting what printers [*sic*] is to letters; it brings into the cabinet of private gentlemen, the treasures of the Florentine galleries and of the Vatican." Bryant's care for correct language and typographical accuracy is shown in the fact that two days later the paper carried a correction changing the word "printers" to "printing."

As a matter of fact, Bryant commented frequently, as he was to do in future years, upon the use and abuse of the language. Accepting the Wordsworthian principle of plain language in poetry, Bryant made fun of the flowery tropes and euphemisms in the journalistic prose of the day. He considered "watery grave" an inaccuracy, since the person drowned "might be fished up again and decently interred in dry ground." People cannot merely be said to like flowers, he complained; they are referred to as "lovers of flora." Nobody in a newspaper ever dies; he "only resigns his breath." "By the same rule," Bryant continued, "nobody is ever married, but people are made ten times as happy by being united in the pleasing bonds of Hymen."

The family of Dr. Peter Bryant had remained pretty well intact at Cummington since his death. The younger boys had managed to attend college at intervals and, for a time a few years before, Cyrus had worked in New York and in Columbia, South Carolina, as a clerk; but they were never long away from the homestead. Now, however, things were changing. In 1830 Arthur had gone to Jacksonville, Illinois, to take up farming; and he was joined in 1831 by John Howard, whose poems Bryant printed from time to time in the *Evening Post.* John's letters from Illinois to his brother, the first of which the paper printed on April 5, were for the next few years a regular feature, dealing first with the opportunities afforded in the frontier West and later with the state's politics. In the fall of 1831 Cyrus emigrated to Michigan, where a number of Cummington families had settled, and the next year he was to join his brothers in Illinois. But he was now in Northampton teaching school, and met Ralph Waldo Emerson, who had delivered some sermons in the town. On June 19, Emerson wrote his brother William Emerson in New York:

> Do you know Mr. W. C. Bryant? At Northampton I saw a brother of his
> —a farmer & botanized with him a little for the sake of learning about his
> brother & family. A remarkable race sons of the soil yet chemists botanists
> poets.—Why had not Cullen the grace to go back to corn & potatoes and
> spit at
> > "dirty & dependent bread
> From pools & ditches of ye Commonwealth"
> I talked to his brother Cyrus about your man's folly in leaving poetry, in the
> hope it mt reach him that his verses have ardent and all unprejudiced
> admirers. He should know at least of Ellen's suffrage.* The "Death of the
> Flowers" was meat & drink to my noble flower.[15]

*The reference is to Emerson's first wife, who died, not like Bryant's sister, who perished with the flowers in the autumn, but in deep winter on Feb. 8, 1831.

In the spring Bryant exchanged letters with his mother to arrange for her coming to New York.[16] The visit—the first apparently for her with her son and daughter-in-law—was made to assist in the household, since Frances was in the last three months of a pregnancy. The family made their usual May 1 move, this time to the corner of Fourth Street and Broadway. On June 1 Frances went with her mother-in-law to Cummington, where the Bryants' second child, Julia, was born on June 29. Frances returned to New York in September with her two children and Bryant's sister, Charity Louisa.[17]

When the *Evening Post*'s books were closed on November 16, the net income had increased above that of 1830 by about $1,000 to $14,429, earning for Bryant $3,507.24 as his share. On the same day the paper announced that Michael Burnham had resigned from the firm, a wealthy man with a net worth comparable to that of some of the city's leading merchants, and that a new partnership had been formed by Bryant, Leggett, Charles Burnham (Michael Burnham's son), and Thomas Gill. Gill had for a number of years been employed as a clerk in the counting office and with Charles Burnham was to manage the paper's business affairs while Bryant and Leggett would continue as the editors.

Several years before when Bryant's admirers in Boston Richard Henry Dana, Theophilus Parsons, and Willard Phillips—had urged him to bring out a second volume of his poems, he had declined. One of his reasons had been given in a letter to Dana on March 10, 1826: "What reputation I have depends in good measure, I have no doubt, upon my having written so little. I began to write a great while since, and I have no doubt that if I had written voluminously at first I should have given the public a surfeit at once. I hold therefore that my best way of keeping in favour with the public is to appear before them rarely."[18] But now, ten years after the printing of his first thin volume of forty-four pages after the reading of his Phi Beta Kappa poem, he was ready to bring out his second book. During 1831 he worked over his poems and in December had chosen eighty-eight for publication as compared with the seven that had appeared in the first book.

12

HIS COUNTRY'S FOREMOST POET

ALTHOUGH BRYANT'S POEMS HAD NOT BEEN GATHERED into a single volume, being read only as they appeared in magazines and newspapers over a period of fifteen years, he was acknowledged to be the country's foremost poet. In the new book poetry lovers, not only those of the United States but also those of England, for he had arranged for publication there, had spread before them the work by which he wished to be known in a duodecimo volume of 240 pages. For the first time critics had a means of assessing his whole achievement.

A writer for the *New England Magazine* wrote that though Bryant had "been placed by common consent at the head of the list of American poets" he did not conform to the popular image of the lonely rhymster communing with the Muse.[1] Instead, during the business hours of the day, the poet could be seen in "a lower room of a large printing establishment in one of the most crowded streets in New-York, distracted by the countless duties and vexations to which the editor of a daily paper is exposed, and encompassed by the most unpoetical sights and sounds." He was a man "rather under the middle size than otherwise, with bright blue eyes and an ample forehead, but not very distinguished either in face or person." His manners were "quiet and unassuming and marked with a slight dash of diffidence" and his conversation was "remarkably free from pretension, and . . . characterized by good sense rather than genius." It was an occupation that the author of the article, as did many other persons, regretted:* With the same hand that wrote "To a Waterfowl" he was "scrawling political paragraphs" and offered "no longer to nature, upon her mountain altars, a sacrifice of song."

Bryant's delay in waiting until he was thirty-seven years old to collect and publish his verse is a remarkable instance of self-restraint, of humility before the Muse, especially for a poet so precocious in his youth. There is no contradiction to this in the fact that *The Embargo* was printed when he was fourteen and his 1821 *Poems* when he was twenty-seven. He can hardly be credited with the impulse to display these scant garnerings, for the first was prompted by his father and the second by his Boston friends. His purpose might now be that he felt he owed it to his admirers to afford them whatever pleasure he could in making his poems more readily available, or it might be that in assuming the editorship of the *Evening Post* he felt, as he had once before when he entered the law, that he had reached a place in his life's journey, one of his favorite figures of speech, where two roads diverged and he could not follow both. The book could be left as a marker for the road not taken. The writing of poetry, if he was to write it at all, would be done as an avocation.

Bryant in his brief introduction to the book was typically diffident about his poems:

> The favor with which the public have regarded them, and of which their republication in various compilations seemed to the author a proof, has induced him to collect them into a volume. In preparing them for the press, he has made such corrections as occurred to him on subjecting them to a careful revision. Sensible as he is that no author had ever more cause of gratitude to his countrymen for the indulgent estimate placed by them on

---

*The young poet John Greenleaf Whittier appealed to Bryant to cease writing his "daily twaddle" in behalf of factional politics as well as his coadjutor on the *Evening Post*, William Leggett, and another poet, James Lawson of the *Mercantile Advertiser*, and return to wooing the Muse, in a poem, "To a Poetical Trio in the City of Gotham," in the Haverhill *Iris* of Sept. 29, 1832. One of the stanzas on Bryant went:

> Men have looked up to thee, as one to be
>   A portion of our glory; and the light
> And fairy hands of woman beckoning thee
>   On to thy laurel guerdon; and those bright
> And gifted spirits, whom the broad blue sea
>   Hath shut from thy communion, bid thee, *"Write,"*
> Like John of Patmos. Is all this forgotten,
> For Yankee brawls and Carolina cotton?

his literary attempts, he yet cannot let this volume go forth to the public without a feeling of apprehension, both that it may contain things which did not deserve admission, and that the entire collection may not be thought worthy of the generous and partial judgment which has been passed upon some of the separate poems.

In choosing the poems for his first major collection, Bryant included only five that had not previously appeared in print. He found nothing in his juvenilia to publish—such work also having been omitted from his 1821 volume—and the earliest of the poems he resurrected was "The Burial-Place," which he had written in 1818 at Great Barrington at the age of twenty-four. This is a fragment of fifty-seven lines, a blank-verse effort dealing with the theme of death, written during the period when he was still working on "Thanatopsis." The most interesting of the earlier unpublished poems is "Oh Fairest of the Rural Maids." This was a poem written to Frances Fairchild in 1820. Frequently quoted in anthologies, the poem has had the appeal to many readers that it had for Poe, who considered it "a gem" and "of the very loftiest order of Poesy."[2] While editing the *New-York Review* and *United States Review,* Bryant had been hard pressed to find poetry worth printing. It is therefore puzzling that he had not before printed "The Massacre at Scio" (1824), one of several poems written on the Greek struggle for freedom, and "The Journey of Life" (1826), an expression of one of his moments of despair in his early days in New York. It may have been that he had not revised them to meet his standards for a public appearance or that he had overlooked them. "To the Fringed Gentian," composed in 1829, is a companion-piece to Bryant's earlier "The Yellow Violet." The violet was the first of the flowers to bloom after the departure of winter, the fringed gentian the last before the season's arrival. Bryant evidently had the contrast in mind in the second stanza:

> Thou comest not when violets lean
> O'er wandering brooks and springs unseen.

In his introduction Bryant said that he had subjected the poems to "a careful revision," but his changes were not extensive. His care was exercised chiefly in matters of nuances—in the choice of word or figure of speech and in meter. This was characteristic of Bryant's revision of the first printed versions of his poems throughout his life. He seldom completely rewrote a poem. To do so would violate his idea of what poetry was. To him, as he said in his lectures on poetry, "the great spring of poetry is emotion" and as to taste and discernment "strong feeling is always a sure guide." He held this view throughout his life, declaring thirty-eight years later that the poet who would "touch the heart or fire the blood" must write only when his own "lips quiver" and his "eyes o'erflow." His method, if "I Cannot Forget with What Fervid Devotion" is a truthful statement, was to let his emotions form his expression when they were aroused by a natural object:

> And the thoughts that awoke, in that rapture of feeling,
>   Were formed into verse as they rose to my tongue.

Nevertheless, Bryant's practice in composition was not to warble as a bird does, for he held that poetry not only appeals to "the passions and the imagination" but also to the understanding. Thus, though emotion is the spring of poetry its course after overflowing is controlled by thought.[3] As the history of the repeated reworkings of "Thanatopsis" before it attained its final form has demonstrated, Bryant was a reviser—and a thorough one. The manuscripts of his early poems reveal that a poem often began with the writing down of stray thoughts on a subject. Tremaine McDowell discovered in his study of these manuscripts: "Entire poems appear in two, three, or even four versions; individual stanzas or lines appear in two, four, eight, or more forms." This extensive revision was not so common in Bryant's later poems, the reason being, according to McDowell, "that when Bryant was writing poetry regularly he did not find it necessary to warm himself to the task by jotting down preliminary drafts and . . . that practice had now made him more expert and more fluent in composing."[4]

The minor alterations in the 1832 volume, therefore, were all that were needed since before committing his poems to print he had already reworked them. The slight emendations he now felt called upon to make were due to his being a perfectionist. Although Bryant against much of the critical opinion of his time defended the trisyllabic foot in carefully specified circumstances, he liked an even flow of numbers; hence, he often improved upon his meter. A precisionist in the use of words, he sought for one that conveyed his exact meaning. For example, Dana questioned his use of "disappeared" in a stanza in "The Past":

> Full many a mighty name
> Lurks in thy depths, unuttered, unrevered;
>   With thee are silent fame,
> Forgotten arts, and wisdom disappeared.

Bryant replied that he was not certain the word was a defect: "I have sometimes thought it was a boldness. Disappeared is used nearly in the sense of vanished, departed, passed away; but with more propriety than vanished, since that relates to a sudden disappearance. At all events, I do not find it easy to alter the stanza without spoiling it."[5]

Bryant's precision in finding the right figure of speech is similarly finely drawn. In "To a Waterfowl," he had first written:

> As, darkly painted on the crimson sky
> Thy figure floats along.

He had successively sought for the right image, using "limned upon," "shadowed on," and finally "seen against." Dana pleaded with him to restore "painted," but Bryant protested:

> I was never satisfied with the word "painted" because the next line is
> Thy figure *floats* along.
> Now, from a very early period—I am not sure that it was not from the very time that I wrote the poem—there seemed to me an incongruity between the idea of a figure being painted on the sky and a figure moving, "floating," across its face. If the figure were painted, then it would be fixed. The incongruity distressed me, and I could not be easy until I had made the change. I preferred a plain prosaic expression to a picturesque one which seemed to me false.[6]

Yet Bryant could not remain fully satisfied that he was doing the right thing in making revisions, even slight ones, in poems he had once published. It was a question that came to his mind very often over the years. After the publication in 1832 of his collected poems he exchanged several letters with Dana in which they discussed infelicities in each other's verses, both agreeing that alterations in small matters tended to weaken the emotion out of which a poem was written. Bryant wrote that in attempting to improve a criticized passage in "Forest Hymn" he had marred the effect, adding: "The truth is, that an alteration ought never to be made without the mind being filled with the subject. In mending a faulty passage in cold blood, we often do more mischief, by attending to particulars and neglecting the entire construction and sequence of ideas, than we do good." On another occasion he wrote: "I have sometimes been conscience-smitten at wasting so much time in making a crabbed thought submit to the dimensions of the metre. . . . I fear that the process has been attended with a loss of vigor and freshness in the composition."[7] Bryant's practice seems to be summed up in a piece of advice given his brother

John, who had sent him copies of poems printed in the *Illinois Herald*.[8] He said: "What you write . . . you should not write lazily, but compose with excitement and finish with care, suffering nothing to go out of your hands until you are satisfied with it."

On the whole, Bryant had reason to be pleased with the reception of his book, and he was except for some querulous complaints expressed to Dana. William Ellery Channing, writing in the recently established *American Monthly Review*,[9] greeted the collection as giving an opportunity to renew an "acquaintance with one of the great poets of our age." The book extended Bryant's reputation to the South, where the critic Hugh Swinton Legaré wrote in the *Southern Review*[10] that he had heard "Mr. Bryant advantageously spoken of" but had seen none of his verse. He found the volume "the most faultless, and we think, upon the whole, the best collection of American poetry which we have ever seen." There were dissents to these sentiments, of course. William J. Snelling, in the *North American Review*,[11] did not find Bryant "a first-rate poet" but he granted that he "has great power, and is original in his way." The most severe condemnation came in the *American Quarterly Review*[12] at Philadelphia, whose critic, James McHenry, included Bryant among the poets discussed in a venomous attack on "American Lake Poetry." He conceded, however, that Bryant was the least offensive of the American members of the school.

Reviewers generally agreed on what was admirable in Bryant's poems and what was bad. Channing, praising their spiritual qualities, did not consider the author guilty of mysticism: "he always seems to be talking of what he has fully experienced in the most natural exercise of his faculties." Likewise, Legaré found that Bryant did not think "mysticism any element of the true sublime" or that the "finest poetry" was "at all inconsistent with common sense." Of Bryant's preoccupation with death, neither Channing nor Snelling considered him to be gloomy. Mentioning "Thanatopsis," "The Death of the Flowers," and "June," Channing spoke of them as being "funereal" but said that there was "nothing of despondency in any of these views, nor a heartless fabrication of horrors." Bryant was, according to Snelling, "too much of a philosopher to entertain visions of gloom." Both Channing and Legaré praised Bryant's diction and versification. To Channing, Bryant's "delicate and practiced ear" made him a master of English verse, and his words were "as things felt" and his expression "luminous, easy, original." Legaré spoke of his language as being "idiomatic and racy—the language of people of this world such as they use when they utter home-bred feelings in conversation with one another around the fireside or the festive board, not the fastidious, diluted, unexpressive jargon used no where but in second-rate books, and called elegant only by critics of the Della Cruscan School."

Yet there were qualifications to the praise accorded the book even by those who admired it. Snelling pointed out that Bryant could not "lay claim to fertility of invention," explaining: "He has brought forward no hero or heroine, with whom the reader may sympathize or identify himself. . . . He tells no story; he lays no plot, which may sustain his thoughts. . . ." Similar views that Bryant had limited his greatness by making short swallow-flights rather than soaring with the eagles were expressed by Channing and Legaré. Channing, granting that Bryant had succeeded very well with short poems, nevertheless said that "the variety, involution, and invention of a great epic or play are trials and proofs of higher genius than . . . one or two hundred lines of lyric or descriptive poetry." And Legaré appealed to Bryant to extend his talents: "Let him refine them by elaborate cultivation—let him combine them in a work, calculated to display the higher attributes of genius, by sustained invention and unity of purpose. . . ."

James McHenry in the article, "American Lake Poetry," castigated all the poets he considered to be followers of Wordsworth and Coleridge. He attended first to Nathaniel Parker Willis, whom Bryant had introduced to readers in the *New-York Review,* and then turned to Bryant. His poems were marked by the peculiarities of the school but not to "such a fanatical extent" and were not "unpleasing to those who are fond of poring over sentimental stanzas or fragments in prosing blank verse." The attack coming this late against the Lake School—in the early days of the *North American Review* it would have caused little stir—was answered by the *American Monthly Review* in the May issue of 1832. Bryant himself thought the comments on his poems were instigated by Robert Walsh, publisher of the political newspaper, the *National Gazette,* as well as of the *Quarterly Review.* He wrote Dana that Walsh had said in his newspaper that the review was written at his request, adding: "Walsh has a feeling of ill nature toward me, and was doubtless glad of an occasion to gratify it, but I believe that, as you say, the article will do me no harm."[13]

Bryant was pleased with the first sales of his book, reporting to Dana in April that one thousand copies had been printed of which more than one-half had been sold. He had set the price rather high, $1.25, but he did not expect to realize much from the publication, $300 if the whole printing sold. Six months later, however, when Dana reported that Boston booksellers had asked about bringing out a new edition, Bryant complained that Bliss still had about one hundred copies on hand. "Any other book-seller," he added, "would have got off the whole before this time."[14]

In discussing the reviews with Dana, Bryant expressed disappointment that the critics had not, with the exception of Channing, said anything about "The Past." Channing had reprinted the whole poem. Bryant was most provoked, however, that reviewers so little understood the laws of versification, that is, that they would not accept his trisyllabic foot. "The tune of *rúm ti, rúm ti,* etc., is easily learned," he wrote, "but English verse not only admits but requires something more. He who has got no further than *rúm ti* knows no more of versification than he who has merely learned the Greek alphabet knows Greek." He was of half a mind to write a book "in order to set our people right on this matter, but I fear nobody would read it." The idea was supported by Dana, who wrote that he believed there was a market for such a work since nothing significant of the sort had been written.[15]

II

Although Bryant, among other literati of the times, wanted American writers to throw off British influences, he was interested in getting his book published in England. He and Dana, their letters reveal, were like others in the United States who were flattered by attention in England and who valued critical opinions from abroad, if they were favorable, more highly than those of their own countrymen. Bryant's name was not unknown in England, but he had no contacts with publishers there. In consequence, he presumed, in a letter of December 29, 1831, to ask the help of Washington Irving, then in London and highly thought of by British readers, on the basis of a letter Irving had written in 1826 to a New York friend, Henry Brevoort, praising his poems, as well as those of Halleck's, as being by "masters of the magic of poetic language." Bryant also asked Verplanck, who had been an associate of Irving before he went abroad, to write asking for his assistance.[16]

A month later, on January 26, Bryant received a reply from Irving praising the book and offering to help bring "before the British public a volume so honorable to our national literature." But Irving was not very sanguine, because, owing to a cholera epidemic, the book trade was "miserably depressed" and the publishers "shy and parsimonious" in undertaking new projects. After encountering several rejections, Irving finally prevailed upon a Bond Street bookseller, J. Andrews, to bring out the book. It was published in March of 1832.

Irving in his dedication of the book to the then highly esteemed British poet, Samuel Rogers, praised Bryant's descriptions, which like those of Cooper's were entirely American:

> They transport us into the depths of the solemn primeval forest, to the shores of the lonely lake, the banks of the wild, nameless stream, or the brow of the rocky upland, rising like a promontory from amidst a wide ocean of foliage; while they shed around us the glories of a climate, fierce in its extremes, but splendid in all vicissitudes. His close observation of the phenomena of nature and the graphic felicity of his details, prevent his descriptions from ever becoming general and commonplace; while he has the gift of shedding over them a pensive grace that blends them all into harmony, and of clothing them with moral associations that make them speak to the heart. . . .

While the book was going through the press, Andrews became alarmed over a line in the poem, "Marion's Men," that he feared would anger British readers:

> And the British soldier trembles
> When Marion's name is heard.

Irving changed the objectionable words "British soldier" to "the foeman." It was done in a spirit of goodwill to both the bookseller and the author to help the sale of the volume, and Irving explained this to Bryant in a letter on March 6 after saying that he had taken the liberty of dedicating the book to Rogers as being necessary to call attention of British readers to a volume by an author not well known to them: "I have taken the further liberty of altering two or three words in the little poem of 'Marion's Men'—lest they might startle the pride of John Bull on your first introduction to him." British sensibilities were thus protected, but several years later American patriotism was outraged when knowledge of the alteration became known.*

---

*William Leggett in the *Plaindealer,* in the issue of Jan. 14, 1837, called Irving's alteration "contemptible" because it resulted from "that unmanly timidity which is afraid to let the public see the truth." Both Bryant and Irving were embarrassed by the charge but it caused no break in their friendship. Their correspondence on the subject appears in *The Life and Letters of Washington Irving* (Pierre M. Irving, ed., New York, 1862–4), III, 102–10. Tremaine McDowell says (*Representative Selections,* p. 403) that "as recently as 1932, a prejudiced historian characterized the incident as an 'outrageous' case of 'kow-towing to English influence.' "

Considering the ferocity with which reviewers had fallen upon the work of Byron, Wordsworth, Shelley, and Keats and their attacks on later Romanticists like Tennyson, it might have been assumed that Bryant was a lamb being led to slaughter in publishing in England. But such was not the case. On the whole, the book was well received, as well as if not better than it was in the United States. The critics saw resemblances to Cowper, Wordsworth, and Rogers but not so close that Bryant was a mere imitator. They admired about the same qualities in the poems the American critics admired and they condemned about the same faults.

The first review to reach the United States was one by John Wilson in *Blackwood's Edinburgh Magazine* of April, 1832. Wilson disagreed with Irving's dedication saying that Bryant was the equal of Cooper in describing American scenery. "Bryant's genius," Wilson said, "consists in a tender pensiveness, a moral melancholy, breathing over all his contemplations, dreams, and reveries . . . and giving assurance of a pure spirit, benevolent to all living creatures, and habitually pious in the felt omnipresence of the Creator." The long review quoted passages which "could only have emanated from a genius of very high order." After reading this review, Dana wrote Bryant: "It is a little amusing to see how, with all our patriotism, our men of real genius must send abroad for their good names. Look at the miserable notices of your poems at home, and then consider how you stand in England."[17]

An article in the *Foreign Quarterly Review*[18] was less favorable. The critic was reminded of passages in Thompson, Young, Akenside, and Wordsworth, but Bryant was not truly a follower of any one of them; he had, like them, "a manner of his own, and [was], like them, original." The critic felt that Bryant excelled principally in his nature descriptions; he was an accurate observer, "with the eye of a genuine lover of natural scenery," and he described "eloquently and unaffectedly" what he saw. But fault was found with Bryant's versification, which lacked "metrical polish" in some of his measures though his blank verse was good, "more satisfactory to the ear than his other poetry." He concluded that he did not consider Bryant "a first-rate poet," but he would "assign him an honourable station in the second class."

Bryant did not like the review very much. Writing to Dana, he said he had "not the slightest doubt that the writer meant to be exceedingly kind, condescending, and patronizing, and all that" but "the misfortune was, that he did not know how to criticise poetry." "I have no right to complain," he continued, "for he wrote in a friendly spirit, and praised me enough, I believe, though not in the right place. What is the reason that none of the critics in England or America, except Channing, in noticing my things, have said a word about 'The Past'?" There were other British reviews which Bryant saw but which he did not have much to say about, "a rather extravagant but brief notice" in Campbell's *Metropolitan* and articles in the *Athenaeum,* the *Literary Gazette,* and other weekly journals —"no great authorities in matters of criticism"—which generally praised the poems and printed long extracts from them.[19]

III

While Bryant was preparing his poems for publication, he was also planning a trip to Washington. On November 21, 1831, he wrote his brother John in Illinois that he hoped to go to the capital sometime in the winter "to look at the old General and his Cabinet." "Affairs go on prosperously with me," he continued. "The *Evening Post* has increased in subscribers within the last year, and I am in hopes by making it better to obtain still more. I shall want them to pay the new debt I have contracted."[20] The last sentence would indicate that he had increased his holding in the property. One of his purposes in going to Washington seems to have been to see if he could arrange for a permanent correspondent. As a supporter of Jackson, the *Evening Post* copied articles from the President's organ, the Washington *Globe,* as well as its satellite the Van Buren organ, the *Atlas,* in Albany, and Verplanck was an occasional contributor, too occasional as Bryant complained to him in letters. But Bryant felt that his paper should be better served, for 1832 was to be an important year politically: it was a presidential election year and major controversies were building up to climaxes—the tariff, the growing movement for nullification in the South, the complex matters of Indian removal, and, what was to become the first issue in the campaign, the rechartering of the United States Bank.

Bryant reached Washington about eight o'clock on the evening of January 21 after "a journey of two hundred miles by land over bad roads and thirty miles by water over a rather high sea," he wrote Frances.[21] As usual when he traveled by water, Bryant was sick but not so fatigued that he could not the next day look about the city, in whose public buildings he found more "to strike the eye than those of New York." Bryant's second night in the capital, under the guidance of Verplanck, was spent in calls at the homes of Louis McLane, secretary of the treasury, whom he found to be "a quiet man, of small stature and unassuming manners," and Levi Woodbury, secretary of war, "a fine-looking man, with a prepossessing face, and of agreeable conversation."

The next day, accompanied by Verplanck, Bryant visited the Capitol. In the Senate gallery he got his first view of one of the men he had been castigating in his editorials, Henry Clay. He wrote Frances: "We saw Harry Clay, who has what I should call a rather ugly face. He is a tall, thin, narrow-shouldered, light-complexioned man, with a long nose, a little turned up at the end, and his hair combed back from the edge of his forehead." His word-portrait of Vice-President Calhoun, then at odds with Jackson, was equally unflattering: "He is a man of the middle size, or perhaps a little over, with a thick shock of hair, dull complexion, and of an anxious expression of countenance. He looks as if the fever of political ambition had dried up all the juiciness and freshness of his constitution." In his visit to the House gallery Bryant mentioned seeing John Quincy Adams and Edward Everett, among others, and hearing several "short speeches on trifling questions." He quickly tired of these, and ascended the dome of the Capitol for a view of the city. After a lunch attended by the other New York City Democratic representative, Churchill C. Cambreleng, and others, Bryant continued his tour. He had planned to call on Jackson at the White House but had been kept on the go so much that before he and his friends realized it the time was nine o'clock—too late for a visit since "the old gentleman" went to bed at that hour.

The meeting with Jackson came on the night of January 25. Bryant rode to the White House—in his letter to Frances, he called it a palace—with Cambreleng on a bitterly cold night at about seven o'clock. Jackson was reported to be busy upstairs, but, after Bryant and Cambreleng had talked for some time with his two personal secretaries, he came down to meet the editor of the *Evening Post*. Bryant wrote two brief accounts of the meeting. To Frances, he described Jackson as "a tall, white-haired old gentleman, not very much like the common engravings of him." They conversed about three-quarters of an hour "very agreeably." The rejection by the Senate of Van Buren's appointment as minister to England had taken place that day and "when that subject was alluded to the 'lion roared' a little."* To his brother John, Bryant wrote that the President "appears to be a sensible old gentleman, of agreeable manners."[22]

---

*Bryant was having lunch with Verplanck while the vote on Van Buren's nomination was being taken in the Senate. When Senators Daniel S. Dickinson of New Jersey and Littletown Tazewell of Virginia entered the dining room, Verplanck turned to them to ask how the vote had gone. Told that Van Buren had been rejected, he declared: "There, that makes Van Buren president of the United States." Bryant related the anecdote to illustrate Verplanck's political acumen. *Discourse on Gulian Crommelin Verplanck* (New York, 1870), p. 30.

The remaining days of Bryant's visit were spent in meeting other public officials and attending evening parties, which were marked by a new tone influenced by the austere manners of the President. Of the fashionable society, Bryant wrote John: "The only peculiarity I observed about it was the early hours that are kept—the balls beginning at eight and breaking up at eleven, and the refreshments being all light, and no supper." It had been a rewarding trip. Bryant had met most of the leading men in the administration and was favorably impressed by them, writing his brother that he considered the President's cabinet to be the best "that we have had since the days of Washington." He had heard the leaders in both houses of Congress and, though there were no noteworthy speeches made, he felt that his understanding of the men had improved. Back at his desk in New York, he was better prepared to carry on his editorial work.

The newspaper competition in the city was becoming keener. At the start of the year, the *Mercantile Advertiser* and the *Journal of Commerce,* as had the *Evening Post* with its first issue in 1831, appeared as enlarged sheets. "These changes," Bryant noted, "are indications of the prosperity of the newspaper press in this city which we are pleased to see." Bryant added a new department, "Postscripts," in which late news could be carried; sometimes the press would be stopped to throw out type to make room for a more recent report. On April 11 Bryant called attention to the fact that his paper carried on Wednesday accounts of the proceedings of Congress on Monday. It was able to do so because of the speedup in mail delivery. The morning papers of Washington, from which most of the capital news was garnered, reached Philadelphia on the day of publication and New York the following day. An evening publication, the *Post* had the news before the more numerous morning publications.

Editorially, Bryant attacked the Senate for its rejection of Van Buren as minister to England, condemned proposals for the revised tariff because they retained the protective principle, and of the threats in the South to refuse to obey the laws or to secede said that if a fair and equitable rate of duties were adopted "we should hear no more of nullification." The issue of rechartering the United States Bank had been joined when Nicholas Biddle decided to request renewal that year though the charter did not expire until 1836. Bryant did not become excited about it, however, until a congressional investigating committee revealed that the bank had been bribing editors willing to support rechartering the bank. Biddle had long been in the habit of helping editors with loans on easy terms and generous extensions when they came due, but in 1831, fearing that Jackson would effectually through the Democratic party destroy the monopoly rights of the bank, he had begun a program of direct payments to editors for printing articles favorable to it. He wrote a correspondent that "newspapers must be used, not for their influence, but merely as channels of communication with the people." He had commissioned articles about the bank for insertion in the press and would pay for their printing either in advance or as they appeared. He bought newspaper subscription lists for his own mailing of articles and paid publishers for printing extra copies of issues containing favorable pieces that might be distributed widespread.[23] Bryant was delighted when the congressional investigation turned up the names of the editors of the *Courier and Enquirer,* Colonel James Watson Webb and Mordecai M. Noah, on the list of those receiving the benefactions of the bank. His editorial on May 4 breathed fire: "Of the fact, that the bank has been guilty of bribery—that it purchased the influence of the *Courier and Enquirer,* (paying dearly for the whistle, too) no one, we think, can for a moment doubt. Its dealings . . . constitute the most palpable, barefaced, downright corruption. . . . Every step in the whole affair smells of roguery—the offence is rank."

IV

Meanwhile, Bryant was planning two more personal projects, which he announced to Dana in a letter on April 10—one to move his family from the noise and crowds of New York to Hoboken, where he would give his friend "a chamber" if he could manage a visit, and the other to go to Illinois to see his brothers. Thus, when the annual moving-day came around on May 1, the Bryants found themselves in the village of Hoboken, near Bryant's good friend Robert C. Sands. Delighting in walking, he now had a congenial companion for his strolls and wrote occasional descriptive pieces about them for the *Evening Post.* On May 19 he noted that a railroad had been completed from the ferry-landing to a place called the Elysian Fields and that a new wagon trail just built along the river bank following "the various windings of the shore" presented "a great variety of prospects." In the village the public house on the green had been taken over by a Mr. Swift, "a person of accommodating manners and gentlemanly deportment . . . who will make it an excellent and well-ordered establishment." A new acquaintance was the South Carolina poet and novelist, William Gilmore Simms, whose poems Bryant had praised a few years before in the *United States Review.* Bryant met Simms through James Lawson, an editor on the *Mercantile Advertiser* and a poet and playwright who had been corresponding with the southerner for several years. This was Simms's first visit to the North, and he joined Sands and Bryant in their walks about Hoboken.[24] It was the start of a long friendship, not only between Bryant and Simms but also between Frances and Mrs. Simms.

For his trip to Illinois Bryant chose a route that permitted him to see a great part of the country in the upper South. He would, as he wrote Dana, "go down the Ohio till it mingles with the Mississippi, and up the Mississippi till it meets the Illinois, and up the Illinois to within twenty miles of Jacksonville," where his brothers had located. He described his journey in long letters to Frances that could have been printed as travel articles in the *Evening Post.*[25] He portrayed the people he met along the way, telling how they lived and what they talked about; he noted the ugliness of the towns and the primitiveness of the dwelling houses; but above all he painted pictures like those of his friend Cole's of the rolling forests, of the broad sweep of the inland rivers, and finally of the limitless prairies whose tall grasses undulating beneath the wind looked like an ocean with living waves catching the light from the blue heaven.

Departing by boat from New York on May 22 on his way to Baltimore, Bryant whiled away the time reading Camoens, the sixteenth-century Portuguese poet. He spent the night at Philadelphia, a city whose residences lacked "that tawdriness which you see in New York houses." The low, flat shores along the Chesapeake offered little worth looking at approaching Baltimore, where Bryant reluctantly let himself be introduced to delegates to the Democratic convention which had just renominated Jackson for the presidency and chosen Van Buren as his running-mate. He enjoyed the rail trip on the new road just built across Maryland to Cumberland, noting that vegetation was only slightly more advanced than in New York. The towns along the way were mostly unattractive—Fredericktown, Hagerstown, and Cumberland in the foothills of the Alleghenies. Along the road after leaving Cumberland and passing through southern Pennsylvania, Bryant was interested in the number of emigrating families on their way west. Everywhere the handiwork of man was unlovely compared to the landscape. At Union, in Pennsylvania, for example, there was "a most beautiful and rich country of undulating surface" but the buildings of the town were "mostly mean and ugly."

At Wheeling, in Virginia, Bryant embarked by boat on the Ohio for the two-day trip to Cincinnati. He was struck by the vast continuity of the forests whose trees, in the rich soil, grew to a colossal size, and by one view a little after sunset when "each tree-top and each projecting branch . . . stood forth in strong and distinct relief, surrounded by deep shadows." The Ohio with its placid and even currents deserved the French appellation of "la belle rivière." Cincinnati, whose population was thirty thousand, was a city of fine homes and public edifices equal to some of New York's, but downriver Louisville, with half as many people, had the appearance of having more business. Below Louisville, after traversing the falls, which larger ships had to bypass by means of a canal, Bryant saw one of the new river steamers intended for the New Orleans trade. The deck above the hold had twenty-five staterooms on either side—"each as large as Fanny's bedroom in the *new house*" at Hoboken—with berths for ten persons, and the top deck for "steerage" passengers had berths for two hundred and twenty persons. On the boat went, passing the mouths of the Wabash and then the Cumberland and Tennessee Rivers until, at eventide on June 2, the Ohio and the Mississippi were joined, the swifter current of the Mississippi forcing back and discoloring the slower current of the Ohio.

Ascending the Mississippi, Bryant considered the shores to be low and unhealthy but thought the scenery was beautiful nevertheless as the river everywhere flowed through stately woods. When the boat stopped at Chester, on the Illinois side, Bryant heard that the state was alarmed over Indian raids in the north and that in consequence he would have to give up his plan to return to the East by way of Chicago. The trip continued, past the French settlement of Cape Girardeau, whose people spoke in broken English; past the junction of the river with the Missouri, which poured "thick, muddy water" into the clearer stream of the Mississippi, and on to St. Louis, where there was more talk of the Indians; past Lower Alton, where the steamer stopped to repair a boiler; and finally into the gentle waters of the Illinois for the last stage of the journey to a landing place about twenty miles from Jacksonville, which Bryant reached on June 12.

Bryant found Jacksonville to be "a horribly ugly village, composed of little shops and dwellings, stuck close together around a dirty square." The surrounding country was a "bare, green plain, with gentle undulations of surface, unenlivened by a single tree." Only Bryant's younger brother John was at Jacksonville, Arthur having returned to New England to find a wife.* The cabin on Arthur's farm—John was living in Jackson-

*William in a letter of Nov. 21, 1831, had advised John, who shared his own poetic and intellectual interests more than the other brothers, not to be "in too great a hurry to marry." "When you do," he wrote, "I hope you will take the step with wisdom and reflection. Marry a person who has a good mother, who is of good family that do not meddle with the concerns of their neighbors, and who, along with a proper degree of industry and economy, possesses a love of reading and a desire of knowledge. A mere pot-wrestler will not do for you." Goddard-Roslyn Collection and Godwin, *Biography,* I, 280.

ville and earning his living as a clerk in a store—was built of logs, even to the floors and doors of split oak. It had but two rooms, a kitchen and a parlor, separated from each other by a roofed passage "large enough to drive a wagon through."

The day after his arrival Bryant set out with his brother on a tour of the prairies by horseback. The soil was "fat and fertile" with "not a stone, a pebble, or bit of gravel" anywhere so that a plow would last a lifetime and the horses went unshod. Of the fauna, Bryant noted the prairie-hen, which at the approach of a man "starts up and whirs away from under you"; the spotted prairie-squirrel hurrying through grass which grew as high as five feet; and the prairie-wolf, "a coward and a robber" that seized the young lambs and pigs of the farmers and ravaged the hen-roosts. The prairie-wolves also invaded watermelon patches in packs, fighting over "the spoils as fiercely and noisily as so many politicians." Bryant considered the country "most salubrious" and the soil the most fertile he had ever seen but nonetheless he did not think it beautiful, though the view from the more elevated parts of the prairie "some would call beautiful in the highest degree, the green heights and hollows and plains blend so softly and gently with one another."

The next week the brothers made a more extended tour to the north, visiting Springfield and the land office there, as Bryant wished to inquire about tracts that might be for sale. From Springfield they rode northward for several days, putting up for the night at squalid farm cabins encountered by chance. At Pleasant Grove, some fifty miles from Springfield, Bryant was tempted to buy a quarter-section of land. The soil was fertile and the region healthy, and at Pekin, eight miles away, there was a convenient market. On the return trip to Jacksonville, the brothers fell in with a body of Illinois militia headed for the American army camp gathered to fight the Indians in the Black Hawk War. "They were a hard-looking set of men," Bryant wrote, "unkempt and unshaved, wearing shirts of dark calico, and sometimes calico capotes." The captain was a youth "whose quaint and pleasant talk" interested Bryant; years later Bryant learned that the youth was Abraham Lincoln.

Shortly after Bryant and John had returned to Jacksonville, Arthur and his bride arrived from Massachusetts. Bryant, writing his mother later in the year, said that they would have "a cold time of it in the winter in their little cabin unless it is repaired."[26] The next day after their arrival, Bryant set out on his return trip to New York, retracing the route by which he had come to Illinois. His letters to Frances, detailed though they were, had ·not expressed the real emotions aroused during this journey on which he saw for the first time the vast distances of his country and the level lands of Illinois under broad skies. One of his letters to Frances ended: "What I have thought and felt amid these boundless wastes and awful solitudes I shall reserve for the only form of expression in which it can be properly uttered." The trip was, the next year, to result in one of his most noble blank-verse poems, "The Prairies."

13

NO PIPE FOR POLITICIANS' FINGERS

WHEN BRYANT RETURNED TO NEW YORK ON JULY 12, 1832, he found the people in a panic over a cholera epidemic, and even at Hoboken, away from the contagion ravaging the metropolis, his family were suffering from what Frances called the "premonitory symptoms" of the plague.[1] Earlier in the year, the *Evening Post* had reported the progress of the disease across Europe, using large headlines, an unusual typographical device, when the cholera struck London and again, on June 15, when outbreaks were reported in Quebec and Montreal. Fearing that it was only a matter of time when the plague would strike New York, William Leggett called upon the people to take preventive measures. By July 3 the board of health had identified several cases of the plague. The news resulted in an immediate exodus of people. Leggett reported every departing steamboat "crowded with a dense mass of fugitives flying in alarm" and the roads in all directions lined "with well-filled stagecoaches, livery coaches, private vehicles and equestrians, all, panic struck, fleeing from the city, as we may suppose the inhabitants of Pompeii or of Reggio fled . . . when the red lava shower poured down upon their houses, or the walls were shaken asunder by an earthquake."

Two days before Bryant's return, the *Evening Post* reported 191 deaths for the previous week which, it said in an attempt to allay fears, were normal for that time of the year. But the next week, on July 17, the number of deaths had climbed to 510, which was 300 above normal. Bryant, who did not easily panic, urged people to be calm. "Let the report be scrutinized, and it will be seen that it is the intemperate, the dissolute, and the poor creatures who are too ignorant to know what to do, or too destitute to procure medical attention, that chiefly fall victims to the destroyer," he wrote. "Our safety is in ourselves, not in our place. . . . Fear but assists the action of those malign influences which exist in the air we breathe."

Going every morning from Hoboken to his office on Pine Street, Bryant saw the "same melancholy spectacle of deserted and silent streets and forsaken dwellings" and had the sad duty of "looking over and sending out to the world the list of the sick and dead."[2] There were "so many houses and shops . . . shut up, and there was such a silence in the streets that every day seemed like Sunday except that you saw no well-dressed people going to church."[3] In his own family, Frances, whose delicate health regularly caused her to leave the city during the heat of summer, was "sick abed with complaints" of the stomach, and Bryant himself was obliged to keep to his bed on one occasion for two days. The baby Julia had suffered from diarrhea, but Fanny had enjoyed perfect health. The *Evening Post* estimated on August 6 that half the city's population, 100,000 people, had fled. The plague departed as quickly as it had come, and on August 22 the board of health announced that those who had left might return without danger.

With life in the city returning to normal, Bryant turned his attention, and the columns of his paper, to the coming election, diagnosing it correctly on October 4 as being "little else than a battle between the United States Bank and the friends of the administration." He feared what the bank could accomplish with its capital of thirty millions of dollars: "The Saviour of the world was betrayed for thirty pieces of silver. The influence of the 'root of all evil' is not lessened by the lapse of eighteen hundred years, and the interests of the Union may be betrayed for thirty millions of dollars." Increasingly, as the election approached, *Evening Post* columns were devoted to political news. Bryant was jubilant over the Jackson-Van Buren victory, but he was also relieved that he could devote space to other matters. To readers, he apologized for printing almost nothing but "political discussions, exhortations and abjurations" and hoped now that right had triumphed they could look forward to more varied fare.

Despite the cholera plague and the election, Bryant found time to work with Sands and Verplanck on a collection of tales requested by the publishers John and James Harper on the order of *The Talisman*. They had obtained the collaboration of Leggett, Catharine Sedgwick, and James Kirke Paulding, and since six authors would be represented in the volume planned to call it *The Sextad.* Verplanck, however, withdrew from the project, and the authors changed the title to *Tales of the Glauber Spa,* supposed to have been narrated by visitors at a health spring just as Chaucer's Canterbury pilgrims had entertained themselves with stories during their journey. The collection in two small volumes was printed early in November. As with *The Talisman,* reviewers sought to identify the authors, and the *Evening Post* on November 20 humorously denied that its editors had ever been at the Glauber Spa in their lives. Bryant's two stories were "The Skeleton's Cave" and "Medfield," which were no improvement over his earlier tales and which were his final effort in this literary form. The book was well received, a second printing being issued on December 5. The *Evening Post,* announcing the new printing, said: "If the whole impression has already gone off—and the Harpers never print small ones—it is very likely the publishers . . . will get back the money they paid . . . for the manuscripts, with a fair profit on the outlay of capital and the trouble of publication."

A little more than a week later Bryant had the unhappy journalistic duty of reporting Sands's unexpected death of a paralytic stroke suffered while he was preparing an article, "Esquimaux Literature," for the first number of a new publication, the *Knickerbocker Magazine.* Bryant's poem, "Arctic Lover to His Mistress," was intended to be a part of the article. Sands's last spoken words were the name of his friend and next-door neighbor when, just before losing consciousness, he called out: "Oh, Bryant, Bryant."[4] In the *Evening Post* Bryant spoke of Sands as being "a man of extraordinary powers of attainments, joined to a disposition of equal humanity and goodness" and as possessed of "a quick and prolific fancy, and a vein of strong, racy, original humour." Bryant performed two more services for his friend. He wrote a memoir to accompany Sands's incompleted article on "Esquimaux Literature" in the January, 1833, issue of the *Knickerbocker* and assisted Verplanck in gathering his writings and composing an introduction for a two-volume collection issued by the Harpers in 1834.

II

In the meantime, the business of the *Evening Post* was improving after the cholera panic, which had caused the year's profits to fall to $10,220 in November. Bryant increased his share in the firm to one-third by the purchase of Thomas Gill's interest, signing a note to Mrs. Coleman for the money needed. Though Gill retired as one of the owners, he remained until the next year as a bookkeeper and clerk.[5] In a December 31 report to its readers the *Evening Post* said that the subscription lists for both the daily issue and the country paper were the largest in history and directed attention to improvements made over the year.

Although Bryant in editorials in 1832 described the *Evening Post* as being a "political journal," he showed early in 1833 that it was not a servile party follower, being accused by one Democratic sheet of not being a "party print." It was the first but not the last occasion for Bryant to be charged with disloyalty to party. In December the *Evening Post* had seen acute danger in South Carolina's ordinance of nullification of tariff duties, calling it an act of "madness" that had startled and alarmed even Calhoun partisans. It therefore lauded Jackson's proclamation against nullification and his explication of its fallacies. Bryant commented favorably on the compromise tariff of 1833, because it eased the tensions between the federal government and the dissident southerners and was based upon the abandonment of the protective principle, but he also regarded "it altogether a clumsy piece of legislation." He considered it, however, to be a victory for his newspaper in its agitation for free trade:

> This journal has persevered in the cause of free trade through good report and evil report, it has never intermitted, never slackened its exertions from discouragement, never lowered its tone for fear of going too fast for the party to which it has been attached. For this course we have received much abuse; we have been assailed by journals otherwise respectably conducted, in such terms that we have been obliged to discontinue our exchanges with them; we have been charged with being bribed by British gold, for supporting doctrines which to our understanding seemed no less clear than the principles of Christian morality, and we have been fiercely threatened with vengeance in anonymous communications from the creatures of those whose interest it was to uphold the restrictive system. None of these things, however, have moved us; we have never desponded; we always believed that public opinion would rectify itself at last. . . .

John M. Mumford's *Standard,* which he had established in the first year of Jackson's presidency, was eager to be the favored Democratic voice in New York and in March began an attack on the *Evening Post* as not being truly "a party print." Bryant, in reply, declared the independence which he would pursue on the *Evening Post:* "Our journal . . . is certainly not a 'party' print in the sense in which the Standard seems to view the phrase.

It is not a mere *party hack*—it is not a pipe for politicians' fingers to sound what stop they please.''

The quarrel with the *Standard* was conducted with words only. The *Evening Post*'s quarrel with the *Courier and Enquirer,* which had become an apostate to the Democratic party when Colonel Webb was revealed to have accepted money from the United States Bank, took the form of action. Bryant, since his attempt to chastise Colonel Stone with a cowhide whip, had sought to avoid personal animosities in attacking rival newspapers; but Leggett could not exercise such restraint. On April 9 he engaged the colonel in a fight on Wall Street. According to an account by James Lawson of the *Mercantile Advertiser,* Leggett approached Webb and said: "Colonel Webb, you are a coward and a scoundrel, and I spit upon you." This he did and they exchanged blows until pulled apart by members of a crowd that had gathered but not before Leggett spit again in the colonel's face while calling him a "contemptible puppy." The city's papers for several days discussed the fight in attempts to fix the blame and to decide which man had won.

The *Evening Post* during this interval between campaigns had the space to carry out its self-elected duty of acting as *arbiter elegantiarum* of the arts. Though book publishing had become so extensive that volumes piled up on editors' desks which they did not have time to read they nevertheless tried to keep up with the flood by short notices and occasional long reviews. Bryant found the time to write many of these notices. New Yorkers were inveterate theatergoers, and Bryant had the plays at the Park and Bowery reviewed at length. In January he served as a member of a committee which arranged a "complimentary benefit" for the impresario, the aged William Dunlap, who had managed the Park since the early 1800's. Bryant's love of painting was indicated in the frequent items about artists and the long articles carried about the exhibitions of the National Academy at Clinton Hall. When his friends Thomas Cole and Samuel F. B. Morse returned from Europe in December of 1832, the *Evening Post* welcomed them back and defended American art against criticisms that there was none, declaring that the United States had artists "equal to any in Europe" and that the country had "mountains and clouds, earth and skies as fitted to inspire the poet or the painter as Italy can boast."

But there were offenses against good taste and propriety in both the theater and the art displays that Bryant felt compelled to censure. In the print shops on Broadway and William Street pictures "which our unsophisticated maidens did not dare to contemplate in their most secret thoughts, a short time ago, are now openly gazed at without a blush, and talked of with the most perfect freedom." So it was also on the stage, and "delicate females hesitate not to look, with a steady and approving gaze, upon exhibitions, which their unsophisticated mothers would almost have died rather than witness." But for Bryant, *"Tempora mutantur et nos mutamur."* He concluded sarcastically: "The good people of this city have, within the last six or seven years, made wonderfully rapid strides in refinement. There is reason to hope, if we go on much longer at this rate, that, in a few years more, we shall be as refined as the Parisians or Neapolitans themselves."

Bryant's new affluence and the acquisition of Leggett as his associate had enabled him in 1832 to get away from the paper for his trip to Illinois. In July of 1833 he made another extended tour, this time north to Montreal and Quebec. He could now satisfy his desire for travel, and these two journeys were the first of many he would take during his long life. His trip this summer was made in company with Frances. They went first to Great Barrington, where Fanny and Julia were left with relatives in the charge of their nurse, and then took the stagecoach northward through Vermont to Vergennes near Lake Champlain, continuing by boat up the lake into Canada and ascending the St. Lawrence River to Montreal and Quebec.[6] Bryant, since he did not have occasion to write to Frances, left no extended account of this trip. Later he was to describe his travels at length in letters to the *Evening Post.*

III

Returning to his editorial desk, Bryant defended Jackson's plan to withdraw government funds from the United States Bank, declaring, for example, on July 31: "We look upon the United States Bank . . . as so utterly corrupt and profligate an institution, that we would not have it trusted a single day longer . . . with a single dollar of the people's money." But a new issue was arising, the first premonitions of one that was to divide the nation. In a long editorial on August 7, the *Evening Post* condemned the agitation in certain quarters of the northern press for emancipation of slaves. The paper saw it as politically motivated to "exasperate the south against the north, and to get up, if possible, a great southern party, the soul of which shall be a deep-rooted and invincible local jealousy." It did not believe the plot would succeed, because there was no widespread support in the North for emancipation: "That the existence of slavery in the Union is regretted by the great mass of the population of the non-slaveholding states, we believe to be true; but that there is the slightest disposition to interfere in any improper and offensive manner, except among certain fanatical persons, and those few in number, we regard to be as well settled as any fact in relation to public opinion ever discussed in the public journals."

A week later the *Evening Post* found another occasion to attack the agitation against slavery in quoting an article from a New Orleans paper describing an incident in which "a large number of colored men and boys" occupied railway cars set aside for whites and resisted efforts to remove them. The paper attributed the violence to "the intemperate declamations of the agents, lecturers, and editors of the Anti-Slavery Society." In passing, the paper took a rap at William Lloyd Garrison, then "in the capital of the British empire holding forth in public lectures against American slaveholders."

When Garrison returned to the United States in August, he announced a meeting in Clinton Hall of "friends of the immediate abolition of slavery." Garrison's speeches in England had not pleased Americans, the *Evening Post* calling them "slanders against his native land." Garrison's meeting October 2 at Clinton Hall attracted a crowd of some five thousand people objecting to the antislave forces but only twenty or thirty Abolitionists, the *Evening Post* reported the next day. The Abolitionists were denied use of the hall and moved to Tammany Hall and then to the Chatham Street Chapel. The mob was dissuaded by its leaders from going on to the chapel, and there was no violence. Bryant attacked Garrison and his movement:

> Garrison is a man who, whatever may be the state of his mind on other topics, is as mad as the winds on the slavery question. . . . As to the associates of Garrison in this city, some of them may be of good intentions, but they are men whose enthusiasm runs away with their judgment—and the remainder are persons who owe what notoriety they have to their love of meddling with agitating subjects. . . . They are regarded as advocating measures which, if carried out, would most assuredly deluge the country in blood, and the mere discussion of which has a tendency to embroil the south with the north, and to endanger those relations of good will which are so essential to the duration of the Union. . . .

Bryant, of course, was opposed to slavery and had written verse hailing the Greek soldiers in their fight for freedom, a sonnet expressing admiration for William Tell, a man of "iron heart" who could not be tamed, and a poem, "The African Chief," pitying a warrior shackled in chains in the slave market who, unable to stand the thought of captivity, went mad. His editorials in the *Evening Post* now as later did not condone slavery, or as he expressed it in an article of October 10 supporting the work of the Colonization Society, "the peculiar relation of the black and white races in this country." His first attitude toward the Abolitionists in this summer of 1833 was one that he was to maintain for years, one held by many other liberals of the North who feared that antislavery agitation would produce violence and divide the Union. Fresh in his mind was the threat to the Union by the southern nullification forces willing to resist the collection of tariff duties by arms or to set up a separate confederacy. He could not look with equanimity on a movement against a condition, evil though it was, that, because it struck more deeply into the vitals of the South than the tariff, might destroy the nation.

III

Early in September Bryant welcomed in a short editorial the establishment of a paper by Thomas Gill, whose interest in the *Evening Post* he had purchased the year before, and Mordecai M. Noah, but when the new paper, the *Evening Star,* appeared later in the month he was forced to regret Gill's association with it. The paper was an anti-Jackson sheet. The expression of regret brought a rejoinder from the *Star* attacking Bryant and Leggett, "the poets of the Post." In an editorial on September 28 Bryant lectured Noah, who did not seem "to know that newspaper personalities and vulgar abuse are now generally abominated" and that editors "are expected to be guided by the same rules of propriety and decorum, which prevent gentlemen, in their personal intercourse, from calling abusive names, and spitting in each other's faces." After this admonition, the editorial turned with ungentlemanly fury on Noah and his subservience to the United States Bank: "A professor and renegade by turns of every political faith, one who, lured by lucre, has consorted to-day with those whom yesterday he affected to despise; who has betrayed every party that ever trusted him; and as the last and closing act of his versatile career, has sold himself, for a handful of gold, to an infamous and corrupt monied monopoly—for such a man to prate of *his principles* is a piece of impudence almost as great as his venality."

The appearance of the *Star,* espousing narrowly partisan policies, was nothing new in journalism, but there were other press developments in 1833 that were to be revolutionary. One, which went unnoticed in the *Evening Post,* was the publication on January 1 of a paper calling itself the *Morning Post.* A partner in its founding was a young man, Horace Greeley, who had come to the city two years before from a New England village with ten dollars in his pocket and his personal property carried in a small sack. He applied for work on the *Journal of Commerce* as a printer, but was bluntly told by David Hale to be off since he looked like "a runaway apprentice from some country office."[7] One biographer relates that he did get a job in the *Evening Post* shop but was fired when Leggett saw him, shabbily dressed in a homespun suit, and told the foreman: "For God's sake discharge him, and let's have decent-looking men in the office at least."[8] But the gawky youth stayed on in the city, set up his own printing shop, and late in 1832 obtained backing for a new paper to be sold for two cents a copy that working people could afford. The paper was printed as planned on January 1, 1833, but a heavy snowstorm during the night kept people off the streets and there were few buyers that day and on the days that followed. The price was reduced to one cent, but still the paper did not catch on and was abandoned in less than a month.[9]

But the outcome was different when another one-cent paper, the *Sun,* appeared on the morning of September 3. Its founder was Benjamin Day, who like Greeley was a recent comer to the city from New England, had managed to start his own printing shop, and believed that a cheap paper could succeed with the masses. There the likeness ended. The *Sun* won a circulation of two thousand within two months—the equal of that of most of the prosperous sixpenny commercial papers—and five thousand within four months. Its popularity was due not only to its cheap price but also to the kind of news it carried. There were no long-winded discussions of public affairs and no vituperative political harangues. A small paper in size, seven and one-half by ten inches, it carried news items that were short and brightly written and human-interest articles obtained in the police courts that reflected the drama of life.

The *Sun* was not, as has often been said, the originator of sensational crime news or of human-interest news—both had often appeared in newspapers in the past. Just before its founding, Bryant had inveighed, in the *Evening Post* on August 28, against the "habit which certain conductors of newspapers have of filling their columns with the disgusting details of crimes." They not only served up every detail of murders, rapes, and suicides but "every anecdote which can be gathered respecting the offender's former life and associations, his conversations in prison, his personal appearance, and other circumstances of like public importance." But the success of the *Sun* was a harbinger of change. Within two years James Gordon Bennett, who had quit the *Courier and Enquirer* when Colonel Webb came out against Jackson and who was now working on the *Pennsyl-*

vanian in Philadelphia, was to return to New York to start his own paper, and the unlucky Greeley was gaining experience in a variety of journalistic projects. In a few years Day, Bennett, and Greeley were to succeed in radically changing journalism from what it was when Bryant began working on the *Evening Post* in 1825.

IV

In the last months of the year Bryant occupied a part of his time going over his poems in preparation for a new volume to appear in 1834. He had only several new poems to add, but there were individual lines in earlier poems whose meter, rhymes, and diction he wished to correct because they had been mentioned as defects by reviewers. His book and one being brought out by Dana occasioned an exchange of letters in which the two men sought each other's advice about alterations.[10] Dana, early in the year, had asked Bryant's aid in finding a New York publisher. His lack of success—Dana was finally able to get a Boston publisher to bring out his book—occasioned one of Bryant's animadversions on the lack of a market for "poetic wares": "Poetry may get printed in the newspapers, but no man makes money by it, for the simple reason that nobody cares a fig for it. The taste for it is something old-fashioned; the march of the age is in another direction; mankind are occupied with politics, railroads, and steamboats." Bryant had been unhappy with Elam Bliss as a publisher, and he asked Dana to see if Russell, Ordiorne & Metcalf of Boston would undertake the volume. Bliss had offered him $200, he wrote Dana, and if the Boston firm would make it $250 for one thousand copies he would gladly send the book out of town. The arrangement was completed, with Dana agreeing to see the work through the press.

The one major addition to the volume was Bryant's eloquent blank-verse poem "The Prairies," with which he had been tinkering since his return from Illinois As late as November 2, he had not been able to complete it, asking Dana to save space for it: "It is not yet quite finished; the conclusion gives me some perplexity. The winding up of these things in a satisfactory manner is often, you know, a great difficulty. I have sometimes kept a poem for weeks before I could do it in a manner with which I was at all pleased."

The theme of the poem is an old one with Bryant—the passage of time, the disappearance of ancient races, and their replacement by later arrivals. Only the scene is different, the rolling and treeless plains that had been unimaginable to Bryant whose first observed grandeur had been that of

217

northern forests and mountains. Though the poem was not written by Bryant on the spot, his opening lines convey the reader there:

> These are the gardens of the Desert, these
> The unshorn fields, boundless and beautiful,
> For which the speech of England has no name—
> The Prairies.

The first impression is of space and distance and, unexpectedly, of movement like the waves of the ocean. The prairies seemingly untenanted by the human race are, however, but another sepulchre for those who had once lived there—the mound builders of early times and the later hunter tribes. But the progression is destined to continue, and the poet, seeing the myriads of insects above the tall grass, birds in the sky, and bees murmuring over the gaudy prairie flowers, seems to hear

> The sound of that advancing multitude
> Which soon shall fill these deserts. From the ground
> Comes up the laugh of children, the soft voice
> Of maidens, and the sweet and solemn hymn
> Of Sabbath worshippers.

V

Though Bryant was concerned with perfecting his poems for the new edition of his works, he was being subjected at the same time to quite different winds from those of the prairies in his position as .editor of a newspaper. Jackson's withdrawal of federal funds from the United States Bank and placing them in "pet" state banks, as these depositories were called, had aroused such partisan controversy to amount to "a sort of fury," he recalled later. During the summer, Jackson had made a trip to New England in an effort to win support for his program. His reception in New York amounted almost to idolatry, the *Evening Post* editorializing on June 11 that his "personal popularity was probably never so great as at this moment." The paper noted a softening in "the acerbity of party feeling" and looked forward to "calm in the political or rather the party world which will probably last a few months—at least until the candidates for the next presidential election are brought before the nation." The calm did not last that long. Striking out at the President in the hope of making business conditions so bad that the people would come to the support of the bank, Nicholas Biddle imposed a program of "discipline," as his defender Daniel Webster termed it, by contracting loans and taking other measures to make it hard to get money. When Jackson defended his removal of the deposits in his annual message in December, Biddle increased the pressures. Money had been scarce in September and October and by December factories were shutting down and workers were thrown on the street. The diarist Philip Hone found the Christmas season in New York "gloomy" with "times bad" and a panic portending "which will result in bankruptcies and in ruin in many quarters where, a few short weeks ago, the sun of prosperity shone with unusual brightness."[11]

Biddle's rule-or-ruin policies had the desired results in New York, whose manufacturing, commercial, and financial interests commenced an outcry against the President. The *Evening Post* had been popular with city businessmen because of its militant espousal of free trade, but when Bryant and Leggett continued to support the President over the bank the paper became the object of bitter attack. The demands by the Whigs—the name now being adopted by the National Republicans and Calhoun forces —for censure, even impeachment of Jackson, were attacked by Bryant in an editorial on January 7. It was one of the first of his anecdotal beginnings of an editorial, a literary device to become so habitual with him that it led to the remark that his editorials always began with a stale joke and ended with a fresh lie. Bryant began:

> The editor of the *National Gazette* [Robert Walsh's Whig paper in Philadelphia] appears to be in the predicament of the worthy Rhode Island juror, who, after sitting out the trial of a man arraigned for a capital offence, in which his innocence was clearly established, insisted upon bringing him in guilty. His companions, who were unanimous for acquitting the prisoner, pressed him to give the reason for so strong a determination. At length it came out: "It was high time," he said, "that somebody should be hung for the credit of the state."

"In a like manner," Bryant continued, "the *National Gazette* thinks it is high time to have an impeachment of the president of the United States."

Before the end of the month, the *Evening Post* was being pressured by the business community to change its stand and was losing advertisers and subscribers. The attacks were spearheaded by what Bryant called "the contemptible bank tools in this city," the anti-Jackson press. Bryant declared in reply that the conductors of the *Evening Post* "are not of those who run to their subscription book to learn what course they ought to take on any question whatever."

The forthcoming city election, the first to choose a mayor and council by popular vote, was early recognized by the opposing forces as a test case of the popularity of the President vs. the bank, being held to be crucial not only by New York politicians but also by the Jackson leaders in Washington. The anti-Jackson forces in the city, at the suggestion of Colonel Webb in an editorial in the *Courier and Enquirer,* went into the fray under the banner of the Whig party, when the designation first received significant acceptance. The Whigs chose as their candidate Bryant's friend Gulian C. Verplanck, who as chairman of the House Ways and Means Committee had investigated the bank the year before and returned a report favorable to it. This report saying that the bank was a safe depository for federal funds cost Verplanck the Democratic nomination for reelection to Congress. He had, however, been nominated by an "Independent Jacksonian" party of which Webb was one of the leaders. Bryant, opposed to Dudley Selden, the nominee of the Tammany Democrats, as being nothing but a political opportunist, had sought to obtain a reconsideration of Verplanck. He had failed in this and Selden had defeated Verplanck in the election. In the mayoralty campaign of 1834 the Democrats nominated Cornelius W. Lawrence, a merchant whom the Whigs accused of deserting his class for public office and personal profit. Philip Hone thought the two candidates were evenly matched, writing in his diary: "This will be a fair trial of the issue,—Mr. Lawrence, the man who has for the sake of party proved recreant to the interests of the merchants, on the one side, and Mr. Verplanck, who lost his seat in Congress because he would not pursue the same course, on the other."[12]

If the New York City election of April, 1834, was crucial in a national sense in pitting the people against the vested interests, it was also crucial in a personal sense for Bryant. He declared himself unequivocally for the people. In 1829 Bryant had opposed the Working Man's party because, influenced by the doctrines of Robert Owen and Fanny Wright, it might in his opinion bring about a class war which would destroy democracy. Now a class war was developing and it was not being fomented by the workers. The *Evening Post* first took notice of it on February 11 in an editorial on a meeting of mechanics and working men called to protest firings of men favoring Jackson. The editorial hailed it as a free-speech meeting embracing "all who are opposed to the domineering spirit of a purse-proud aristocracy, and determined to hold and express their own political opinions, without regard to those of their employers." It decried the discharge of men for their opinions on the bank question, mentioning the case of a journeyman printer on the *Courier and Enquirer.* As for the *Evening Post,* it employed some thirty persons, "the political opinions

. . . of no one of whom are known to either of the conductors of this journal."

Bryant returned to the attack on March 10, declaring that bank papers were boasting of indiscreet partisans who implied that the campaign was to be carried on by "arraying the rich against the mechanics and labouring classes." He charged that large sums of money had been contributed to the campaign and that merchants were being urged not to employ any laborers who would not vote as they were told to. The election, therefore, would "be one of the rich against the poor; the idle against the industrious; of the spending and earning classes of this community; of those who contribute every thing, and those who contribute nothing to the wants and the comforts of society." Bryant declared himself on the side of the working people:

> Well, be it so. If the rich will, by their own acts, and their own choice, thus draw the line of distinction, between the two great classes of mankind, and provoke the people into self-defence by declaring war against them, they must meet the consequences. The people must make common cause against them, since they have made common cause against the people. They are called upon by every motive of self-respect, and self-preservation, to combine in one great overwhelming mass, and show those proud presumptuous dictators, that they cannot be seduced by money, or overawed by power— that they are not to be bought or sold—nor kicked, nor cuffed, nor bribed, nor starved into a desertion of their principles.

Daily during the thirty days that preceded the election on April 8 the *Evening Post* carried on the attack. It warned merchants against "the folly and danger of provoking the opposition and hostility of the labouring classes." It replied vituperatively to the "hireling presses" that accused it of being "guilty of incendiary attempts to array the poor against the rich," when just the reverse was the case. It printed long extracts, beginning on March 13, from the influential book advocating a hard-money system, *A Short History of Paper Money and Banking in the United States,* by William M. Gouge. It carried frequent reports of "proscription" incidents, of working people fired from their jobs—a carpenter, a seamstress, a cartman, a mechanic, and persons in other employments. It tagged as "aristocrats" the Jackson opposition—the National Republicans, the Independent Republicans, and the recently self-styled Whigs. The charges and countercharges had stirred the city to a high emotional pitch when voters went to the polls on the first of the three days devoted to balloting on April 8.

It was a cold and overcast day when the polls opened, and early in the morning crowds gathered in the streets. Merchants had shut up their stores, having sent, the *Evening Post* charged later, their clerks and laboring men to surround the polls to intimidate voters. But Tammany had its counter forces, chiefly newly naturalized Irish immigrants, who roamed the streets looking for trouble. There was no violence for some hours. Then a group of toughs in the Sixth Ward attacked a Whig committee room; it was well defended and a battle raged for some time. This started off a series of similar affrays that before the polls closed two days later developed into pitched battles, at times with several hundred combatants. Once Webb's *Courier and Enquirer* building was threatened by a mob of Tammanyites, but the doughty ex-soldier put up a barricade of paper bundles, mounted on the roof a band of armed supporters, and threatened to shoot any who moved toward his property. The crowd grumbled, stood around for awhile, and then dispersed. But after the war of words that preceded the election and the physical war that marked it, no real winner was revealed when the ballots were counted. The Jackson Democrats elected Lawrence mayor over Verplanck by a close tally of 17,573 to 17,393 votes, according to the *Evening Post's* report, but the Whigs won a majority in the Common Council.

The attacks against the *Evening Post* during the campaign apparently did little harm to its circulation or its advertising. Starting the second half of the thirty-third year of publication, it declared on May 16 that though it had been a victim of the "proscriptive spirit" its subscription and its revenue had never been greater. This was not an idle boast. Bryant's income for the year when the books closed on November 16 was $4,646.20.[13] The May 16 editorial said, somewhat contradictorily, that the paper's opponents "do not seem to have been aware that they were paying us indirect but high compliment to our honesty; for surely no journalist can exhibit stronger proof of integrity than by perseverance in a course which conflicts with his private interests."

Nevertheless, Bryant was economizing, for he had made plans early in the year to go to Europe. He was by no means sure that he could manage it. Frances expressed doubt of it in a letter to John Bryant on February 26: "William seems determined on going to Europe; and I am preparing our clothes as fast as possible; still I think we may not go. I do not intend to be very much disappointed if we should not be able to go in June."[14] The difficulty was that though Bryant received a good income from the paper he had gone heavily in debt in buying his one-third interest. The chief obstacle to the trip was raised by Mrs. Coleman. Bryant explained the situation to his brother Cyrus in a letter of April 14: "Mrs. Coleman whom

I have more than half paid the note she holds against me for the purchase money of the *Evening Post* establishment on being made acquainted with my design to go has demanded of me, in case I should leave the country, two thousand dollars on the principal of the note, which is more money than I can raise from my own friends and there is not much likelihood that I can get it elsewhere. If I cannot I must stay till I earn it; and by sending my family into the country I am making arrangements by a course of rigid economy to diminish my debts as fast as possible and to endeavor to get out of the power of those people who want to hamper my movements."[15]

In carrying out this plan, the family broke up housekeeping on the annual moving-day, May 1, and Bryant took Frances and the two children to Great Barrington for a brief visit and then on to Cummington. On his return to New York, he wrote Dana that he was now "without a home, ready to wander, whithersoever my inclination may lead—provided I can *raise the wind.*" Somehow he did raise the wind. Frances and the children returned to New York about June 15, and the Bryants stayed at the Leggett home until June 24, when they sailed for Le Havre in the packet ship *Poland.*[16]

The scurrilous political warfare of the first three months of the year had taken a great deal out of Bryant spiritually but not physically. He wrote Dana on April 22, a week after the election, that his health was much better than usual. He attributed it to a new regimen he was following. For some time he had gradually reduced his drinking of coffee and tea and now completely abstained from them. "I have also, by degrees," he wrote, "accustomed myself to a diet principally vegetable, a bowl of milk and bread made in my house of unbolted wheat at breakfast, and another at noon, and nothing afterward." This diet was not invariable, but nearly so. "Its effect upon me," Bryant continued, "is so kindly that, while it is in my power to continue it, I do not think I shall ever make any change."[17]

It might have been expected that Bryant, as with many Americans going abroad, would have gone to England to see at first hand the scenes with which he was long familiar through his reading in British literature and to meet the poets he admired. But such was not the case. For years he had been a student of Spanish literature and history, translating the work of many of its poets, and his plan was to spend most of his time in Spain. In first seeing "the light of distant skies" he therefore bypassed England entirely and landed at Le Havre in France on July 20. Bryant, who in his poems had stressed the antiquity of Europe as compared with the newness of America, was chiefly impressed in his first views of France on the trip from Le Havre to Paris by reminders "that we were in an old country."

The churches were vast, "venerable and time-eaten," the dwelling houses were gray and of "antique architecture," and the thatched cottages looked almost as old as the "very hills about them." Even the life of the people seemed to be that of earlier times—women riding on donkeys, "the Old Testament beast of burden, with panniers on each side, as was the custom hundreds of years since"; old dames sitting at their doors with distaffs, "twisting the thread by twirling the spindle between the thumb and finger, as they did in the days of Homer"; and shepherds attending their grazing flocks "as was done thousands of years ago."[18] Bryant had been prepared to see old things, and since he was he saw them.

14

A JOURNEY INTO THE PAST

ON THIS FIRST VISIT TO EUROPE BRYANT HAD EXPECTED TO be gone about one year. The civil war in Spain over the succession to King Ferdinand VII made it inadvisable for him to take his family to that country, as he had planned, and he went instead to Italy for the major portion of his trip. Delighting in travel and reluctant to return to the political and journalistic battles of New York, he decided while in Italy to extend his visit six more months in order to take in Germany. As a traveler, Bryant was not content with monuments and museums. He wanted to know the people and to speak their language as one of them Finding a city that interested him, he would leave his pension or hotel, and, as Frances expressed it in her travel diary, set up housekeeping for from one to four months.[1]

Bryant's first stop in France after landing at Le Havre was of course Paris. The triumphal arches of the Barrière de l'Étoile and of Neuilly, the gray pinnacles of the Tuileries and the Gothic towers of Notre Dame, the dome of the Panthéon, and other sights recalled to him France's power and magnificence, the valor of her soldiers, her "battles and victories which had left no other fruits" than her monuments. In contrast to these solemn reminders of the past, the people seemed "as light-hearted and as easily amused as if they had done nothing but make love and quiz their priests since the days of Louis XIV." Their gaiety was manifested from

225

early in the day to late at night, when Bryant was wakened by the sounds of music and dancing feet near the Tuileries where he and his family had taken lodgings.

The attractions of Paris were not the sort to hold Bryant. Italy, with its history going back to antiquity and its classical and Renaissance art that had lured from home his friends among the American painters and sculptors, beckoned him. After three weeks in the city, the Bryants left by diligence on August 21 for Chalon-sur-Saône on their way south to Italy. The coach trip of three days, according to a Bryant letter of September 27 to the *Evening Post,* provided him with views of monotonous plains of vineyards and wheatfields with few trees, whose branches had been cut off for fuel, of gloomy towns with narrow, filthy streets, of troops of beggars that surrounded the carriage whenever it stopped. The trip down the Saône to Lyons was made by steamboat, a "supremely uncomfortable" one in a dirty narrow cabin with benches on each side and a long table in the middle at which Frenchmen sat playing cards and eating *déjeuners à la fourchette* all day long. Bryant found the people of Lyons superior to those of Paris in looks and features, and he enjoyed the picturesque location of the city between the quiet Saône on one side and the swift Rhone on the other.

At Lyons the Bryants transferred to a carriage to continue their trip. Once more Bryant, the poet of "The Ages," was struck by the remains of antiquity—the remnants of feudal castles and fortresses on the heights overlooking the country and the traces of Roman colonization in gateways, triumphal arches, walls, and monuments. Marseilles, however, beautifully situated in the middle of a semicircle of mountains of whitish rock, was a thriving commercial center, animated with a bustle Bryant had not seen since leaving New York. The journey was continued by land along the coast of the Mediterranean in the heat of late summer, through Nice, Genoa, Spezia, Sarzana, and Lucca and finally to Florence, which the Bryants reached on September 12.

After two weeks at Florence, Bryant wrote that he would "return to America even a better patriot than when I left it." He noted a "contrast between a government of power and a government of opinion" forced upon the traveler at every step. Everywhere there were guards and sentinels, their places on the farms taken by women; poverty was widespread, "the effect of institutions forged by the ruling class to accumulate wealth in their own hands"; the visitor had to put up with endless examination of passports, with the "rapacity and fraud" created in people by the poverty in which they lived, with the need for resorting to bribery in dealing with customs and other officials.

Bryant, praised as a landscape poet, viewed scenery with the eye of a painter. After a week's stay at the Hotel de l'Europe in Florence, the family moved into lodgings from which they could look out upon a bridge over the Arno, already familiar in Bryant's mind's-eye since it had been painted by Thomas Cole. Bryant described the outlook from his window: "It gives . . . a view of the Arno travelling off towards the west, its banks overhung with trees, the mountain-ridges rising in the distance, and above them the sky flushed with the colors of sunset. The same rich hues I behold every evening in the quarter where they were seen by the artist when he made them permanent on his canvas." Like a painter, Bryant knew the importance of lighting as well as that of color and form, and he marveled at the clarity of the Italian atmosphere, especially "about the time of sunset, when the mountains put on an aerial aspect, as if they belonged to another and fairer world." Bryant in his sonnet to Cole on the painter's departure for Europe had exhorted him, among the new scenes, to keep bright his "earlier, wilder image" of the America he had left. Bryant himself did this. He found "no fine sweep of forest, no broad expanse of meadow," and no "rows of natural shrubbery following the course of the brooks and rivers." Instead, the hand of man had deformed the landscape. Only the mountains of the Apennines were "beyond the power of man to injure." In a poem written at this time, "To the Apennines," Bryant apostrophized the mountains whose lofty peaks wore the "glory of a brighter world" than the land below with its "graves of yesterday."

One of the attractions of Florence was the sculptor Horatio Greenough, then at work on his huge statue of George Washington commissioned by Congress for the rotunda of the Capitol. Bryant had first met Greenough in New York in 1828 when the sculptor stopped over on his way from Boston to Washington to do a bust of John Quincy Adams. During the fall of 1834 Greenough modeled a bust of Bryant that one admirer said was a fine likeness "redolent of poetry in every feature."[2] Greenough's design for the Washington figure, suggested by the Greek sculptor Phidias's lost statue of Zeus, often copied by the Romans, was being ridiculed in the United States. It showed the Father of His Country naked from the shoulders to the waist, the bottom part of the seated figure being covered by a mantle in loose folds. American artists and intellectuals considered the design sublime, but the Jacksonian Democrats objected to the partial nudity and to the portrayal of the President as an ancient Greek or Roman. A letter from Bryant, after he had gone from Florence to Pisa, is said to have strengthened Greenough's resolution not to alter his conception of the statue at the behest of American critics. "As you are to execute the statue, do it according to your own notions of what is true and beautiful, and when Mr. Public wants a statue made after his own whims, let him make it himself," Bryant wrote. "If you undertake it, give us a Greenough; the statue deserving it, the popularity will come sooner or later."[3]

II

After two months in Florence, the Bryants left for Pisa on November 18, taking lodgings at No. 700 Casa Ginoni on the Lung'Arno. Writing the *Evening Post* on December 11, Bryant contrasted the two cities— Florence a bustling place visited by throngs of foreigners from the United States, England, France, Germany, and Russia; Pisa a place of "stagnation and repose" with the rattle of carriages seldom heard in the streets.

At Pisa, Bryant heard from his brother Austin, the only one of the sons still at the homestead at Cummington, that he and his mother had decided to sell the farm and emigrate to Illinois to join the three younger brothers, Arthur, Cyrus, and John. They had first located at Jacksonville, which William had visited in 1832, but the next year had bought land to the north near Princeton in Bureau County. Gaining a living on the upland New England farm had not been easy, and Sarah Snell Bryant had been forced to borrow money. William had assumed the responsibility of keeping up the interest payments in 1832 so that she would not go deeper and deeper into debt. Writing Austin from Pisa on February 24, 1835, William regretted the decision to sell the family farm. A note appended by Frances inquiring about Dr. Peter Bryant's books said that William wished to buy them. If Austin would pack them up, William would pay for them on his return to the United States.[4] When the Bryants were leaving Pisa on March 18 and traveling south to Rome, Sarah in Massachusetts was making her final visits to relatives before leaving Cummington on May 11 on what was to be an arduous trip westward by boat on the Great Lakes from Albany to Chicago and then overland to central Illinois.

Bryant had written Austin that he could obtain news of the European trip from his travel accounts written for the *Evening Post*. But Bryant was not a regular correspondent, sending only seven reports for the paper, none of which described his visits in Rome and Naples. The family arrived in Rome on March 27, putting up at a hotel for a week before moving into lodgings at No. 57 Via Pontifici. In Rome they met the popular actor Edwin Forrest, who had made his New York debut in the handsome new Bowery Theatre in October of 1826.[5] Bryant and Forrest were fellow members of the city's literary and artistic set, but the actor was chiefly the close friend of Leggett, to whom he wrote letters about his European trip that were appearing in the *Evening Post*. After a month in Rome, the Bryants went south down the coast to Naples, which they visited from May 1 to May 26. Bryant was horrified by a story that illustrated the barbarity of some of the royal houses of Europe. It was that a brother of the king, some months before, had found an old man cutting myrtle twigs on some of the royal hunting-grounds. The offender was tied to a tree and shot to death. Visiting the spot, a beautiful place fragrant with the blossoms of white clover, Bryant commented: "You may be sure I was careful not to trim any of the myrtles with my penknife."

On a trip to Sorrento, Bryant was inspired to write the poem, "The Child's Funeral," suggested by a story he had been told: a child died and the family going to bury it found it revived and playing with the flowers that had been placed around the casket.[6] In another poem Bryant, with the evidences of Italy's ancient past all around him, was recalled to the theme expressed in "Thanatopsis" of the earth being one "mighty sepulchre." But amidst the examples of tyranny and poverty now before his eyes he wondered if the voices of the betrayed and wronged ones among the dead did not cry out in protest from the earth.* He incorporated his thoughts in a nobly written blank-verse poem, "Earth," one to set alongside "Thanatopsis," "Forest Hymn," and "The Prairies":

---

*Bryant first expressed his thoughts about the earth of Italy in rhyme, completing seven stanzas totaling forty-two lines. Dissatisfied with what he had written, he discarded them and rewrote the whole in blank verse. The rhymed version begins:

> A midnight black with clouds is on the sky;
>   A shadow like the first original night
> Folds in, and seems to press me as I lie;
>   No image meets the vainly wandering sight,
> And shot through rolling mists no starlight gleam
> Glances on glassy pool or rippling stream.

He apparently thought the exigency of rhyme made the expression too diffuse, and recast the poem to begin:

> A midnight black with clouds is in the sky;
> I seem to feel, upon my limbs, the weight
> Of its vast brooding shadow. All in vain
> Turns the tired eyes in search of form; no star
> Pierces the pitchy veil. . . .
>
> *Poetical Works* (Godwin, ed.), I, 351–2.

229

I hear the sound of many languages,
The utterance of nations now no more,
Driven out by mightier, as the days of heaven
Chase one another from the sky. The blood
Of freemen shed by freemen, till strange lords
Came in their hours of weakness, and made fast
The yoke that yet is worn, cries out to heaven.

After a year in Italy, Bryant was ready to leave a land where so much of what he saw reminded him of a cruel and repressive antiquity. From Naples he returned to Rome and then to Florence to begin, on June 16, a journey to Germany. This trip by way of Venice, which he found to be the most pleasing of Italian cities, northward across the Tyrol and the Alps to Innsbruck and Munich, permitted him to see Europe's most stupendous scenery, which he described in one of the longest prose accounts of his visit abroad. He did not tarry long in Venice, however, leaving on June 24 for the Tyrol. A newspaperman aware of local-interest angles, he reported to *Evening Post* readers that the first night's stop was at Cenada, the birthplace of Lorenzo da Ponte, who had brought the Italian opera to New York. From Cenada Bryant could see the Alps, the "rocky peaks and irregular spires of which, beautifully green with the showery season, rose in the background." On June 28 the party descended the Brenner in a snowstorm which turned to rain as the town of Innsbruck in the Tyrol was reached. From Innsbruck another mountain range was crossed, and the Byrants found themselves in the Kingdom of Bavaria. Going on, they passed through "extensive forests of fir, here and there checkered with farms," and finally came to "the broad elevated plain, bathed by the Isar, in which Munich is situated."

At Munich, where the family stayed until October 2 when they moved to Heidelberg, Bryant took up the study of German with the thoroughness with which he had learned the French, Provençal, Spanish, and Italian languages, observed the people and their customs, and investigated the country's economy and history. Early in December at Heidelberg Bryant was visited by an American traveler whose poetry he had long admired, the young Henry Wadsworth Longfellow. Longfellow had left the United States in March of 1835 to perfect his knowledge of German in preparation for becoming professor of modern languages at Harvard. He had been accompanied by his wife Mary and two Boston ladies, Miss Mary Goddard and Miss Clara Crowninshield. When Longfellow went to Heidelberg he was in low spirits bordering on despair, for his wife had died at Rotterdam on October 1. The presence at Heidelberg of Bryant, whom

Longfellow esteemed, was therefore "a very pleasant circumstance."[7] The two had never met but they had long known each other's work. They had appeared together on the same page of the *United States Literary Gazette* of November 15, 1824, which printed Longfellow's poem "Thanksgiving" and two of Bryant's sonnets, "Mutation" and "November." The next year, in the *New-York Review*, Bryant had written that no English or American periodicals had published as "much really beautiful poetry" as the *Gazette*, and he cited three poems "all by H.W.L., we know not who he is," poetry then being signed usually by a pen name or initials only. Eight years later Bryant's friend Charles Folsom had solicited his aid in behalf of Longfellow, who, dissatisfied with his teaching position at Bowdoin College, "sighs for a more public scene." Aware of Bryant's interest in education, Folsom wanted to know if a project of Longfellow's had any promise of success, that of "establishing a female school, of the higher class, in the city of New York."[8] Bryant, unhappily, had to discourage the venture. Bryant's reception of Longfellow in Heidelberg was cordial and they were frequently together, carrying on discussions in German to perfect their ability to speak the language and taking long walks over the hills outside the city.

III

For a year and a half Bryant had been permitted to follow his bent for study free from the embroglios that had taken up his time and exhausted his spirit in New York, but the responsibilities of newspaper ownership were recalled to him early in 1836 by a letter, dated November 6, 1835, from Michael Burnham,[9] giving the disquieting news that William Leggett had become ill in mid-October and had not been out of bed since. Burnham expressed his surprise that no one at the *Evening Post* had informed Bryant of what was happening. Since Leggett's illness, Theodore Sedgwick, Jr., who during the past year had contributed articles to the paper under the name of "Veto," was writing the leading political editorials and Henry J. Anderson, Bryant's associate on the *New-York Review*, was writing frequently on political economy.

So bad did the situation appear that Bryant decided to return at once to the United States. Making arrangements for his family at Heidelberg, he left for Le Havre on January 25, expecting to sail February 2 on the packet ship *Francis I* for New York. The ship was delayed five days at Le Havre and, after finally getting under weigh, was driven by a gale into Plymouth harbor, where it was delayed for seven more days. Bryant was able to get ashore twice for his first glimpses of England. The transatlantic crossing was a rough one, and fifty days after leaving Heidelberg, Bryant sailed into New York harbor on the evening of March 26. On landing he went immediately to the American Hotel, where he left his baggage, and then to Michael Burnham's home to find out what he could about the situation. He was shocked to learn that Burnham had died on January 20. The next day he called on Leggett, who was still seriously ill and, though improving, would not be able to return to work for some time.[10] Only little by little during the next few weeks did Bryant learn what had happened to the *Evening Post* during his absence.

Sharing the responsibility of editing the *Evening Post* had led to an unusual relationship between Leggett and Bryant. In many respects opposites in character, they influenced each other in ways that brought them close together in their views. When Leggett joined the newspaper, he had disavowed any interest in politics and wished to devote himself entirely to the literary content. But he quickly absorbed Bryant's free-trade principles and his strong belief in Jacksonian democracy. Where Bryant had learned to control his feelings, Leggett was tempestuous. Bryant was the man of sense, Leggett of sensibility. The stands taken by the *Evening Post* in early 1834 pitting class against class—the working people against the aristocracy—were indicative of Leggett's influence on the older man. Leggett changed Bryant from an advocate to an agitator. Free from the restraints that the prudent Bryant would normally impose, Leggett during his partner's absence became more and more radical. Day after day in long editorials that became increasingly denunciatory, he carried on his attacks against the bank interests and the special privileges given corporations and defended with equal ardor the working men's movement and the Abolitionists. When he became ill, exhausted by his daily output of editorials that would have been a week's writing for most men, he was considered by half the city to be crazy. Yet though Bryant on his return found the financial condition of the paper in chaos because of Leggett's disregard for money and many former friends now his enemies, he expressed no word of complaint. Nor did he ever. He admired Leggett and for years after his death in 1839 recalled his power of thought and expression, his fearlessness, and his honorable character in editorials in the *Evening Post.*

Leggett's editorials declared few policies and opinions that had not already been espoused by Bryant, but he went further than Bryant would have gone and he expressed himself in more forceful and offensive language. Always a rapid writer, carried along on the strong current of his emotions, Leggett wrote at length, so that his editorials tended to flood over the bounds of a single column and to become a series. Though written in the heat of controversy, the editorials, as Bryant declared, "brought public measures to a rigid comparison with first principles." They were philosophical as well as political but so eloquently written, Bryant said of them, the reader "found himself seized and carried forward by something of the same warlike enthusiasm which courageous and high spirited men may be supposed to feel in the heat of battle."[11]

Leggett's first serious editorial controversy arose early in July of 1835 when Bryant was only a few days on the high seas en route to Europe. An outbreak of rioting that required the militia to subdue was provoked by a fight on July 7 between whites and Negroes at the Chatham Street Chapel. The Negroes had obtained permission to celebrate a belated Fourth of July there, but the Sacred Music Society claimed that it had the use of the chapel that night. When the Negroes refused to leave, fighting broke out. Leggett the next day condemned the accounts of the melee in the morning papers as being inflammatory and warned both the Abolitionists and their adversaries of the dangers of fanaticism by either side. On July 9 and 10 there were riots involving at times as many as two thousand people. Leggett allocated the blame between the Abolitionists and certain of the city's newspapers. Though disavowing, as Bryant had done before him, agreement with the Abolitionists, Leggett maintained that they were entitled to the protection of the laws.

The next year Leggett again defended the constitutional rights of the Abolitionists of free discussion when President Jackson's postmaster general Amos Kendall ruled that postmasters in the South could confiscate Abolitionist literature to prevent attacks upon them by slave-owners. "Neither the General Post Office nor the General Government itself possesses any power to prohibit the transportation by mail of abolition tracts . . . ," he declared. "If the Government once begins to discriminate as to what is orthodox and what heterodox in opinion, what is safe and what is unsafe in its tendency, farewell, a long farewell to our freedom." Just as Bryant before him had defended the rights of the Abolitionists though considering their agitation against slavery pernicious, Leggett attacked the institution of slavery as "the foulest stigma on our national escutcheon." But where Bryant believed the South could be conciliated Leggett believed that this was now impossible. He declared on September 9 that he would rather see the Union dissolved, a tenet Bryant would never accept, than "that its duration should be effected by any measures so fatal to the principles of freedom as those insisted upon by the south."

Leggett's humanitarianism was evidenced in two other editorial themes

233

during 1835, the right of workmen to organize into unions and the right of immigrants, mostly of Irish origin, to vote. Both were closely allied to his and Bryant's fundamental political belief, that of equal rights for all. Though editorializing almost daily against monopolies and against combinations that would interfere with the operation of laissez faire, there was a basic inconsistency in his attitude toward labor unions which anti-Jackson papers were quick to point out. Leggett's defense was not a very strong one. "We are opposed to the principle of combination entirely and strongly," he wrote on May 2; "but we are constrained to say that of all combinations, that between the journeymen and different mechanick callings is the least reprehensible." A month later he defended a strike of Philadelphia coal heavers to reduce their working day from twelve to ten hours. "For our own part," he declared, "we should be glad if a general strike of all classes of labouring men in our country could be entered into and maintained until the hours of labour should be fixed at eight, or at most nine hours in the day." As to voting rights for immigrants, Leggett in a series of editorials in June attacked inflammatory articles against the Irish appearing in the Whig papers. Eight years before nativist sentiment led to the forming of the American Republican party in 1843, he urged that immigrants be given the same voting rights as all citizens.

As a supporter of President Jackson's opposition to the United States Bank and the use of government funds for internal improvements, Leggett was naturally the target of the Whig newspapers. But he equally became the target of the Democratic newspapers because of his attacks on monopolies of any sort, even of chartered state banks, and because of his defense of the working men's political movement and of the rights of the Abolitionists to have their say. Few papers heaped such vitriol on him as Martin Van Buren's Regency paper, the *Argus,* in Albany and the Democratic *American* in New York. Before the end of 1835 he was to be denounced also by the Washington *Globe,* the Jackson organ run by the Kitchen Cabinet.

In the first days of the new year, Leggett asked disconsolately, on January 3: "What have we done or said, that we should be denounced as incendiaries, striking at the very roots of society?" All he advocated was that protection of property is one of the first functions of government, that "all grants of monopolies, or exclusive or partial privileges to any man or body of men, impair the equal rights of the people." In almost daily editorials Leggett had attacked the *Argus,* which retaliated by calling him a Jack Cade, the Kentish man who had led a revolt in England in 1450. This opprobrious label was picked up by other papers.* But Leggett could

*The opprobrious term caught on because of the popularity of R. T. Conrad's play, *Jack*

top such slanders against him. To a charge of the *Argus* that he was an apostate of Democracy, he said that the paper might "as well save its breath to cool its porridge"; it did not have the power to "excommunicate" him since the great body of the people were with him. But Jack Cadism was a mild epithet and soon the opposition papers were calling him "crazy," a description also adopted by his enemies among the Democrats.

Bryant, in an account of Leggett's career, described him as "a man of middle stature, but compact frame, great power of endurance, and constitution naturally strong, though somewhat impaired by an attack of the yellow fever while on board the United States squadron in the West Indies."[12] Nevertheless, after more than a year of living so intensely for the *Evening Post*, Leggett's energies began to flag. The charge that he was crazy disturbed him, and he addressed himself to the matter in a long editorial on September 29. "If true," he wrote, "the charge is brutal; if false, it is base." He asked only that his opinions be judged on their merits: "Even a mad man's arguments ought to be respected, if they cannot be refuted, or their absurdity exposed." On October 21 and 22 the *Evening Post* carried no editorials. The reason was explained next day in an announcement that the editor was ill and confined to his bed. Notices that he was expected to return continued until November 7, when it was announced that "a temporary arrangement" for the editorial department had been made.

Leggett's surrogate was Theodore Sedgwick, Jr., the twenty-four-year old son of one of the Stockbridge brothers who had helped Bryant get away from Great Barrington. Sedgwick had been graduated from Columbia College in 1829 and admitted to the bar in 1833. He was appointed an attaché of the United States legation in Paris, where he formed a friendship with Alexis de Tocqueville. On his return to America in 1834, he began contributing articles to the *Evening Post* under the name "Veto." Sharing Leggett's beliefs, Sedgwick made no change in the paper's editorial stand. When at the primary meetings in New York in October the radical wing of the Democratic party broke away from the regular wing, or Tammany, and nominated their own slate under the banner of the Equal Rights party, Sedgwick sided with the dissidents. The radicals became known as Locofocos from an incident occurring on October 29 at a meeting at Tammany Hall. The regulars, over the protests of the Equal Rights men, declared their ticket carried and adjourned the meeting.

Cade, the Captain of the Commons, which transformed the fifteenth-century revolt into the issues of Jacksonian democracy.

When the rebellious men refused to leave, the Tammany stalwarts turned out the gas lights. Having warning beforehand that this would happen, the Equal Rights men had come prepared with candles, which they lit with the new self-igniting friction matches called locofocos. They proceeded to draft their own platform and to name their own ticket.

Leggett being ill at the time, the *Evening Post* had said nothing about the split in the party. What Leggett would have written, Sedgwick wrote on November 9 in his first editorial, "The Disorganizers Hold the Balance of Power." Of the new movement, Sedgwick said: "After exhausting all other terms of vituperation, the friends of ten per cent dividends have at length found that we are something yet more odious; and having illuminated the firmament with the discovery that we are agrarians and infidels, at length proclaim us to be—disorganizers." He accepted the appellation with pride: "We will disorganize—disorganize—disorganize, until the people, whom you mislead, see through the folds of the bandage with which you would blind them, and until you yourselves are compelled to acknowledge our strength, and yield that to fear which you refuse to justice."

By November 20 Leggett was sufficiently recovered to return to the paper but only for a short time. During the last month of the year the editorial page, which was also the main news page, consisted principally of reprinted material, and political commentary was confined to articles contributed by correspondents. On December 26 a notice was printed that because of Leggett's protracted illness the editorial department had been placed "under the charge of another gentleman" until Leggett's recovery or the return of Bryant from Europe. He was Charles Mason, an attorney who had written letters for the paper under the pen name "New Yorker." A graduate of the United States Military Academy in 1829, Mason had served in the engineer corps two years before resigning to study law. When he became the temporary editor of the *Evening Post,* he had been in New York City less than a year, having gone there from Newburgh, where he had practiced law two years. Mason's editorials during the three months before Bryant returned from Europe were devoted to the antimonopoly, antibank, and anticorporation themes that had been dominating the paper's discussions of public affairs but they lacked Leggett's fiery spirit. Bryant, writing his wife on July 4, said that the paper had been "a sad, dull thing during the winter" after Sedgwick's departure and that the people had grown tired' of it. His main effort had been to raise it to its former standards to get it "talked about and quoted,"[13] an effort carried

236

on unassisted since Leggett was to be away from the paper for three more months.

IV

Because of Leggett's championship of so many unpopular causes, the *Evening Post* was in disrepute with much of the city's polite and prosperous society. Bryant's friends among the writers and artists rallied to his support with an invitation on March 31 to a dinner in his honor. The signers included the writers Irving, Halleck, and Paulding, the artists Durand, Morse, and Inman, old friends like the Sedgwicks and Henry James Anderson, and a dozen other well-known persons in the city. Bryant declined the invitation with the excuse that during his absence he had spent his time "only in observation and study" and had done nothing to merit such a distinction.[14] The fact was that he did not have time: he had to arrange for living quarters and to devote his best effort to restoring the prestige of the *Evening Post*. In letters to Frances during April he wrote that friends had been hospitable and he did not want to impose on them, but the boarding houses were all full and furnished rooms all taken. It was "very important that the paper not again be left in the state in which it had been for the last six months," he said in making it clear to Frances that there was no possibility of his being able to rejoin the family in Europe.

The *Evening Post* had been quickly labeled a Locofoco paper because of Sedgwick and Leggett's support of the Equal Rights party. Bryant's editorials were not of the sort that would remove the label. On May 31 he wrote the first of several attacking the conviction and sentencing of twenty-one tailors indicted for a conspiracy injurious to trade for refusing to work at the low wages they were offered. Bryant declared the law was "tyrannical and wicked." When the conviction was appealed, he wrote other editorials attacking the law, and when it was upheld by the Supreme Court declared angrily, on June 13, of the verdict against the tailors:

> They were condemned because they had determined not to work for the wages that were offered them. Can any thing be imagined more abhorrent to every sentiment of generosity or justice, than the law which arms the rich with legal right to fix, by assize, the wages of the poor? If this is not SLAVERY, we have forgotten its definition. Strike the right of associating for the sale of labour from the privileges of a freeman, and you may as well at once bind him to a master, or ascribe him to the soil. If it be not in the colour of his skin, and in the poor franchise of naming his own terms in a

contract for his work, what advantage has the labourer of the north over the bondman of the south?

In July and August, Bryant was aroused to wrath over news reports that a meeting was held in Cincinnati at which plans were made to put down a newspaper to be established by the Abolitionist James G. Birney. Bryant thundered: "So far as we are concerned we are determined that this despotism shall neither be submitted to nor encouraged. In whatever form it makes its appearance we shall raise our voice against it. We are resolved that the subject of slavery shall be as it ever has been, as free a subject of discussion and argument and declaration, as the difference between whiggism and democracy, or as the difference between the Arminians and the Calvinists." When a mob destroyed Birney's plant and, without interference from police, dragged the furnishings through the street, and sought out the Abolitionists themselves, Bryant raged:

> It was only when the fury of the multitude, in searching for one of its victims, seemed likely to endanger a building in which there were two banks that the civil authorities thought proper to interfere. The disturbance of the peace was nothing, the act of breaking open the dwelling of a private individual was nothing, the plunder and destruction of his property was nothing, the hue and cry after his life was nothing, but when the hoards of a monied institution are in peril, the majesty of the law wakes from its slumber and interposes its shield. When the mayor who had looked on quietly while all these outrages were committed, comes forth and tells the mob in a "determined manner" that he will order the police to shoot the first person who offers violence to the building, what a commentary on the depraved state of public feeling!

Bryant's editorial stands brought additional attacks from the Whig papers and from the Democratic papers speaking for the national administration. He took note of the latter, on August 16, in reply to a charge of the *Argus* that the *Evening Post* was "the organ *ad interim* of the Loco foco party." He asserted, as he had on previous occasions when accused of being a party organ, that the *Evening Post* was "responsible only, for the opinions of its editors." "It never was," he continued, "and, under its present conductors, never will be,

——a pipe for *party's* finger
To play what tune she pleases on."

Bryant's aligning himself with the Locofocos in many of their aims was something of an embarrassment, for the *Evening Post* was supporting Martin Van Buren for President in 1836. He discussed the political situation with Van Buren at a conference in July. "I found the little magician at the Astor House," Bryant wrote Frances on July 20. "He was in a parlor facing the south; the sun was blazing against the shutters, which were nearly closed, and the room was a furnace of heat. I told [Judge Thomas J.] Oakley, who was with me, that I believed this was a contrivance to shorten the calls of his visitors. These politicians, you know, are politic in everything; they even 'drink tea by stratagem.' "[15] He had to perform something of a balancing act to reconcile his support of the Locofocos with his support of the administration. His July 20 editorial expressed agreement with the policies of the Locofocos but disapproved of their methods. "A good cause may be unskillfully or injudiciously supported," Bryant wrote. "We regret the violent censure pronounced by the Loco focos against Mr. Van Buren, not only because we think it was unmerited, but because we perceive that the friends of monopolies are taking advantage of its evident injustice, to get up a prejudice both against the antimonopolists and their opinions." As the election approached, the *Evening Post* campaigned for Van Buren, considering his victory, however, a foregone conclusion, as it was. "Our adversaries give us nothing to do," Bryant said in pointing out the weakness of the opposition.

V

Bryant's long vacation in Europe had resulted in his having less inclination than ever for continuing in journalism. He was now forty-one years old and thoroughly dissatisfied with his life, having been "chained to the oar these twenty years," he wrote Dana, "drudging in two wrangling professions one after the other."[16] He thought of selling the paper once he got it back on its feet and he could dispose of it at a profit. Since the departure of Charles Mason at the end of May, Bryant, while searching for "some young man to relieve me of a part of the drudgery,"* as he wrote Frances, had been assisted by Anderson, who, since he was a professor at Columbia College, had to keep his connection a secret. Writing to Frances on July 14, Bryant said that Anderson had promised to find a purchaser. "I think, from the attention he pays to politics, visiting fre-

---

*Bryant obtained an assistant in the fall, Henry Ulshoeffer, son of a New York City judge. Because of ill health, Ulshoeffer resigned the next year. On his death in 1840 the *Evening Post* described him as "a man of kind heart and amiable deportment."

239

quently, talking much, and coming to the office to read the papers we receive in exchange, that he may possibly become a purchaser himself," Bryant wrote.[17] If he sold the *Evening Post,* Bryant had, however, no definite plans in mind. He wrote his brother John in September:

> I have had my fill of town life, and begin to wish to pass a little time in the country. I have been employed long enough with the management of a daily newspaper, and desire leisure for literary occupations that I love better. It was not my intention when I went to Europe to return to the business of conducting a newspaper. If I were to come out to Illinois next spring with the design of passing the year there, what arrangements could be made for my family? What sort of habitation could I have, and what would it cost? I hardly think I shall come to Illinois to live; but I can tell better after I have tried it. You are so distant from all the large towns, and the means of education are so difficult to come at, and there is so little literary society, that I am afraid I might wish to get back to the Atlantic coast. I should like, however, to try the experiment of a year in the west.[18]

When Bryant left Heidelberg, the plan had been for Frances to start for America in the spring, but, disliking to travel alone, she decided to stay on and return with Longfellow, who had taken the family under his wing, later in the year. Bryant wrote on April 14 that he missed her and the children "every hour of the day" but was reconciled to their absence as being best for them: "Fanny will go on with her music and German and make some proficiency . . . in other studies, and Julia will learn thoroughly the language of the country."[19] Some of his letters were scolding ones, for Frances did not write regularly. On July 20 he took his wife to task because she had not entered Julia in school to learn to read German. "You complain that she has nothing to do that interests her," he wrote. "Well —Germany is full of excellent children's books, she knows the language and would very shortly read it. Do you mean to put the trouble of teaching it upon me, after you return?"[20] In June his family, in company with Longfellow, made an excursion to the baths at Ems. On their return to Heidelberg, Longfellow left the group to go to Switzerland and to Tyrol, planning to pick up his charges in August and go to Paris to sail for the United States. Of these responsibilities, Longfellow wrote his father on September 8 from Paris: "It is much pleasanter than being alone, though it has some inconveniences. It diverts my thoughts, however, from myself in some degree; and so far has a good effect."[21] They sailed from Le Havre on September 12 and reached New York on November 10.

As the summer progressed, Bryant discovered that Leggett's management of the paper had left a tangled financial situation. The circulation, though it had fallen off, was still respectable, but the revenue, through loss of advertising, was hardly more than a quarter of what it had been before. Some of the businessmen were alienated by the paper's defense of the Abolitionists, and, in making a change in format on November 23, 1835, reducing the size from seven to six columns, Leggett had lost many of the advertisements of shipping and real estate firms by discarding the cuts used as illustrations.[22] Leggett was chiefly in difficulties, in his own financial affairs, with Mrs. Coleman. He had not paid over to her the dividends she should have received in November and she brought suit against him in May. The matter was settled, Bryant wrote Frances on July 4, by Leggett's assigning to Mrs. Coleman his entire one-third part of the paper. This would give Mrs. Coleman a voice in the control of the *Evening Post,* but Bryant had no objection since Leggett sometimes needed "a curb." He was to be employed at a salary of $1,000 a year with the option of repurchasing his one-third interest in three years.[23] In the meantime, Leggett had left the city to take a place in the country at New Rochelle to recuperate from his illness, being assisted financially by loans from Edwin Forrest.

Handling these financial problems and getting out the paper kept Bryant at his desk from seven o'clock in the morning until about four o'clock in the afternoon. He was able to get away from the city for the Fourth of July, going to Orange Spring in New Jersey. It was so hot, however, and the mosquitoes so "very numerous and very hungry" that after one day Bryant left for New York. Leggett returned to the office in September, and Bryant was able to get away for a week to go to Great Barrington. The trip had been tentatively planned in June when the poet and novelist William Gilmore Simms had come up to New York from South Carolina. The weather of western Massachusetts was cool, and Simms enjoyed rambles about the countryside with Bryant and seeing such scenes described in his poetry as Monument Mountain and Green River.[24]

The eight year association of Bryant and Leggett ended on November 1, when Leggett, apparently wanting a freer voice than he was allowed on the *Evening Post,* issued a prospectus for a new weekly political newspaper, the *Plaindealer,* to begin publication in December. On the same date the *Evening Post* carried a notice that the partnership of Mrs. Coleman, Bryant, and Leggett had been dissolved. Since the retirement of the elder Burnham, the shop had not been well managed, and to improve the situation a practical printer, William G. Boggs, was employed with the option that he could purchase Leggett's one-third interest. The *Plaindealer* was to be a sixteen-page paper containing discussions of public affairs to be "distin-

241

guished by such boldness and directness as the title chosen implies"—a promise that Leggett was to carry out. Though Leggett had been a thorn in Bryant's flesh, he nevertheless regretted, in an editorial on November 3, his leaving the paper. Bryant praised Leggett's "large and comprehensive views of public policy, his ardour in the cause of truth, his detestation of oppression and unjust restraint in all their forms, his perspicacity in discovering abuses and his boldness in exposing them without regard to personal consequences, and the manly, unstudied eloquence which riveted the attention and persuaded the judgment of the reader." There was a need, Bryant continued, for men in public life not afraid to adopt a minority view and when public opinion is wrong or tyrannous for men to "boldly take it by the beard and tell it the things it ought to do." Such a man was Leggett.

15

WEATHERING FINANCIAL STORMS

WHILE STRUGGLING IN 1836 TO PUT THE *Evening Post* BACK
on its feet, to get it "talked about and quoted," Bryant also engaged
himself in a project of the Harper brothers, who had published *Tales of
the Glauber Spa,* to bring out a new edition of his poems. He wrote Dana
that journalism did not give him time for poetry—he was "a draught-
horse, harnessed to a daily drag" and he had so much to do with "legs
and hoofs, struggling and pulling and kicking" that if there was anything
of the Pegasus in him he was too much exhausted to use his wings.[1] But
the offer from the Harpers was so attractive that he went over the edition
of 1834 to make "a few corrections" suggested by criticisms of friends and
reviewers.[2] He wrote Frances in May that the book would be stereotyped
and 2,500 copies printed; he was to be paid $625 outright and to receive
twenty-five cents a copy for books sold.[3] The artist R. W. Wier was doing
an engraving for the title page, a scene at West Point to illustrate the lines
from "Inscription for the Entrance to a Wood":

> . . . enter this wild wood,
> And view the haunts of nature. . . .

With one exception, "The Hunter of the Prairies," a poem suggested
by Bryant's trip to Illinois, the dozen new poems added were written in

1835 and 1836. All, with the exception of "Catterskill Falls," had been published in George Pope Morris's weekly *New-York Mirror*. These included five poems written in Europe, the philosophical "To the Apennines" and "Earth"; "The Strange Lady," a ballad based on a German legend heard at Heidelberg; and "The Count of Greiers," a translation from the German of Uhland.

Since Bryant's national reputation had been established with the first thin edition of his poems published in 1821 and a critical evaluation of his accomplishment had been made possible with the collected edition of 1832, the new volume produced no extended commentary by reviewers. An exception was Edgar Allan Poe, who had become editor of the *Southern Literary Messenger* in May of 1835 and who now wrote an elaborate criticism. Bryant's poems of course were well known to Poe. He had written a brief note on the 1834 edition for the January, 1835, number of the *Messenger,* in which he commented on Bryant's fame as a poet of "uncommon strength and genius" but noted that his Muse lately had "languished probably for want of that due encouragement, which to our shame as a nation be it spoken, has never been awarded to that department of literature."

Now, for the January, 1837, number of the *Messenger* Poe was able to write one of his painstaking dissections of American poets often touching upon minute points. Of Bryant's favorite poem, "The Past," Poe disliked the word "womb" in the lines:

> And glorious ages gone
> Lie deep within the shadow of thy womb.

"The womb, in any just imagery, should be spoken with a view to things future," Poe declared; "here it is employed, in the sense of the tomb, and with a view to things past." He ridiculed Bryant's repeated use of "old" preceded by another adjective, citing "proud old world," "grey old rocks," "wide old woods," and others. But Poe defended Bryant's use of the trisyllabic foot. Mentioning precedents for Bryant's employment of it, as well as his occasional substitution of a trochaic foot for an iambic one, in Milton, Wordsworth, and even in that master of regularity Pope, Poe said that such devices to avoid monotony were "a merit and not a fault." The review paid especial attention to Bryant's more recent poems. "The Prairies" and "Earth" were examples of "fine imagination" and "noble conception"; "The Strange Lady," "The Hunter's Vision," and "Catterskill Falls" were excellent narratives; and "The Living Lost" had a "high ideal beauty." Poe even found something favorable to say about Bryant's humorous poems, "To a Musquito" and "A Meditation on Rhode Island Coal": they were both "droll." He praised Bryant's most famous pieces, "To a Waterfowl," "A Forest Hymn," and "Thanatopsis," but he liked most "Oh, Fairest of the Rural Maids," whose chief quality was a "rich simplicity" and whose conception was of "the very loftiest order of true Poesy." Poe said that no writer, living or dead, could be said "greatly to surpass" Bryant as a master of the art of versification and that he excelled in his descriptions of nature and in his moral vision. But for the greatest poetry more was demanded. Bryant had all the minor merits and was the first poet of America, but he lacked the spiritual qualities that would place him among the highest ranks of poets with Shelley, Coleridge, Words-worth, and Keats.

In January of 1837 Bryant's friendship with Washington Irving was clouded by an attack made on Irving by William Leggett in the *Plaindealer*. In seeing Bryant's *Poems* through the press in England, Irving had changed the line, "The British soldier trembles," in "Song of Marion's Men" to "The foeman trembles in his camp." Leggett, never one to compromise, wrote in the January 14 number that the alteration was "contemptible" and showed an "unmanly timidity which is afraid to let the public see the truth." Irving had returned to the United States in 1832 after seventeen years abroad and was living quietly in the country. He was shocked by the unexpected attack and replied in a letter which Leggett published two weeks later, prefaced by a note absolving Bryant of any blame for the criticism. Irving explained that he had made the alteration in the spirit of friendship, since the British publisher had suggested that the line "might be felt as a taunt or bravado, and might awaken a prejudice against the work." Hence, Irving was "little prepared to receive a stab" from Leggett, Bryant's "bosom friend." Bryant, too, was shocked by the violence of Leggett's remarks and in the next issue of the *Plaindealer* wrote that though he himself would not have made the change he had never com-plained of it. Bryant expressed surprise, however, that Irving in referring to the fact that the criticism had come from his "particular friend and literary associate" seemed to connect him with the attack. Irving disa-vowed any such implication in a letter to the New York *American* and regretted that the change had not met with Bryant's approval. It was a liberty, he said, "the least excusable with writings like yours, in which it is difficult to alter a word without marring a beauty." Thus, with apologies and expressions of mutual respect, any rancor that might have been created by Leggett's "plaindealing" was erased.[4]

II

One of Bryant's immediate problems—that of obtaining a reliable assistant on the *Evening Post*—was solved when he persuaded a twenty-year-old "briefless barrister," Parke Godwin, later to be his son-in-law and biographer, to try his hand at journalism.[5] The two met at the boarding house on Fourth Street where Bryant had taken rooms after his return from Europe and where his family joined him in November. Godwin, whose father was a man of some prominence in Paterson, New Jersey, had graduated from Princeton College at the age of eighteen in 1834. He read law in the office of a Paterson attorney and then went to Louisville, Kentucky, where he was admitted to the bar. He was so horrified at what he saw of slavery in the South that he gave up his plan of opening a law office. He went to New York early in 1836 to see what opportunities the city offered and was living quietly at the boarding house. One evening in May the owner, a native of Great Barrington, introduced him to a gentleman, whose name Godwin did not catch, with the statement that he would soon become one of the boarders. Godwin gave his first impressions of Bryant:

> He was of middle age and medium height, spare in figure, with a clean-shaven face, unusually large head, bright eyes, and a wearied, severe, almost saturnine expression of countenance. One, however, remarked at once the exceeding gentleness of his manner, and a rare sweetness in the tone of his voice, as well as an extraordinary purity in his selection and pronunciation of English. His conversation was easy, but not fluent, and he had a habit of looking the person he addressed so directly in the eyes that it was not a little embarrassing at first. A certain air of abstractedness in his face made you set him down as a scholar whose thoughts were wandering away to his books; and yet the deep lines about the mouth told of struggle either with himself or with the world. No one would have supposed that there was any fun in him, but, when a lively turn was given to some remark, the upper part of his face, particularly the eyes, gleamed with a singular radiance, and a short, quick, staccato, but hearty laugh acknowledged the humorous perception. It was scarcely acknowledged, however, before the face settled down again into its habitual sternness. . . .

In the weeks that followed Godwin saw little of Bryant, catching only glimpses of him when he left early in the morning for his office at the *Evening Post* and when he returned late in the afternoon after one of his long walks taken to maintain his health. Bryant usually spent the evenings alone in his room. When Mrs. Bryant and Fanny and Julia joined him, he was more sociable. Godwin found Mrs. Bryant to be a person of lively sympathies and breezy cheerfulness that drew her husband out of his reserve so that at times he became chatty and even playful. He showed a great fondness for his children, treating them with consideration though always requiring their obedience. He was interested in forming their minds, and much of the family talk was carried on in the languages all of them had learned—French, Spanish, Italian, and German.

Several months later Godwin was surprised one day when Bryant informed him that his assistant, Henry Ulshoeffer, was leaving the *Evening Post* because of ill health and asked if he would like to go to work on the paper. Godwin protested that he had never been inside a newspaper office in his life and believed he would make a poor journalist. "Well, you can learn," Bryant told him; "and I think you are the very man for it." Thus Godwin became the third person on the staff, a general reporter being employed to obtain the routine news of the courts and commerce. Godwin clipped the exchanges for news of other parts of the country, wrote the theatrical notes, and compiled the foreign news which filled the paper whenever a ship arrived with publications from abroad.

The newspaper situation in New York when Godwin joined the *Evening Post* was described in a book by a British traveler, J. S. Buckingham.[b] Like most visitors from abroad—Harriet Martineau, Mrs. Trollope, Captain Marryat, and Charles Dickens—he considered the American press to be depraved. He reported that "the party of the rich," the Whigs, had the greatest number of papers—five morning and five evening dailies. There were only two Democratic ones, the *Evening Post* and the *American,* both of which, of all the city's papers, gave "the greatest attention to literary subjects." He thought the penny papers—the *Sun* now had a circulation of 30,000—to be poor things. Taken chiefly by the "humbler classes," their chief attraction was first the price and second their police reports of crimes and quarrels. Bryant himself, in the summer of 1836, had devoted three and four columns daily to the trial of Richard P. Robinson for the murder of the prostitute Helen Jewett, the case whose exploitation by James Gordon Bennett made his *Morning Herald,* founded in 1835, the talk of the town and furthered his career as the most enterprising newsgatherer of the century. When the trial ended, Bryant had said he was "glad that our columns are relieved of this disagreeable subject." Buckingham wrote of Bryant: "The *Evening Post* . . . is at present under the editorship of one of the most celebrated poets of the country, William Cullen Bryant, who may fairly rank with our Campbell, the author of "The Pleasures of Hope"; and, like other great poets, Milton, Byron, Campbell,

247

and Moore, he is an extreme Liberal in his politics. In talent, wit, taste, and, above all, in gentlemanly fairness of argument, this paper appeared to me to possess great superiority over most of its opponents. . . ."

III

The year 1837 was one of hard times brought on by the suspension of specie payments by the banks, and the *Evening Post* suffered along with other businesses. Bryant, on February 1, blamed the panic on the market in money, comparing the city to the condition of an unlucky bon vivant who has "quaffed deeply of the intoxicating cup of speculation and is now suffering with the headache of the next morning." "There are many who are for adopting a too common remedy," he continued, "that of getting tipsy again as soon as they can. Some of them are asking for new state banks; these are the petitioners for petty grog shops and small distilleries. Others are signing memorials for a national bank; these are persons who desire to quench their thirst on a more magnificent scale, and are for opening a mighty gin palace, in which the whole nation may get fuddled together."

On February 11 of an announced meeting in the park at City Hall to inquire into the reasons for the high prices of rent and food, Bryant wrote that they were already apparent: the increase in the circulation of bank notes. In his discussion of economic principles, Bryant had the ability to write in terms of the experience of the ordinary man, as in this explanation of the price situation: "When there is a glut of cotton cloths in the market, it is idle to suppose that you can get as much bread in exchange for ten yards of sheeting, as you can when cotton cloths are scarce. It is exactly the same with rag money." After the meeting, mobs broke into warehouses of Eli Hart & Co. and dragged out and destroyed in the streets several hundred barrels of flour and a thousand bushels of wheat. Then they sacked other warehouses and business concerns. Whig newspapers blamed the rioting on the *Evening Post's* notice of the meeting. Denying the charge on February 14, Bryant pointed to the paper's consistent stand against violence. Its notice did not exhort anybody to attend the meeting —it merely announced that the meeting was to be held.

Though often at odds with the national administration, Bryant praised Jackson as one of the great men in the nation's history when the President gave his farewell address on March 4. His "very character," Bryant wrote, "has in some measure stamped itself on his countrymen, and given to the popular feeling a higher, more generous cast than it has exhibited since the heroic age of the revolution." Jackson's support came from the people, who never "ceased to trust him amid all the tempests of party, in spite of an organized system of detraction and calumny" against him. He went into retirement, "our old Roman president," with the "blessings of millions of freemen."

During the summer Bryant continued to editorialize on the financial situation, playing over and over the themes of past years and giving support to the Van Buren administration. In September he endorsed the President's calling a special session of Congress to legislate on bank and money matters, urging a complete separation between the government and the unsound state banks and the adoption of a general bankruptcy law to apply to all corporations, associations, and individuals engaged in the business of issuing notes.

Bryant's sense of outrage at the use of violence to put down the Abolitionists was aroused again in November when reports were received from Alton, Illinois, that the Rev. Elijah P. Lovejoy, editor of the antislavery paper the *Observer,* had been murdered by a mob. The *Evening Post's* account came from the *Missouri Argus* of St. Louis, which began: "The infatuated editor of the Alton Observer has at length fallen a victim to his obstinacy in the cause of the abolitionists." Bryant was as much shocked by this attitude as he was by the actions of the Alton mob. He wrote angrily:

> The right to discuss freely and openly, by speech, by the pen, by the press, all political questions, and to examine and animadvert upon all political institutions, is a right so clear and certain, so interwoven with our other liberties, so necessary, in fact to their existence, that without it we must fall at once into despotism or anarchy. To say that he who holds unpopular opinions must hold them at the peril of his life, and that, if he expresses them in public, he has only himself to blame if they who disagree with him should rise and put him to death, is to strike at all rights, all liberties, all protection of the laws, and to justify or extenuate all crimes.

Although Bryant could be aroused to passionate utterance in dealing with public affairs, his characteristic editorial approach in the years after his return from Europe was one of urbanity and wit. Unlike Leggett, who required two or more columns to express his opinions, Bryant usually could say what was needed to be said in a half column. Thought out between interruptions at his desk and written on whatever scraps of paper came to hand—the backs of letters or the reverse side of used copy paper —his editorials were nevertheless perfectly organized and always clear.*

---

*Of Bryant's writing on the backs of letters, John Bigelow said: "It was not to save money but merely the logical consequences of his theory of human responsibility. His table was

Bryant wrote slowly and carefully, with many erasures and corrections, but his handwriting was so neat and his ideas so carefully expressed that he made few changes when his articles were set in type and he received the proofs.[7] Once asked how it happened that his prose style, though his newspaper articles were written in haste, was marked by such purity and clarity, Bryant replied: "If my style has fewer defects than you expect, it is for the reason, I suppose, which Dr. Johnson gave Boswell for conversing so well: I always write my best."[8]

Because of Bryant's wide reading and his interest in collecting anecdotes illustrating the quirks and quiddities of people, he had in stock a wide choice of quotation and example to enliven his editorials. When Nicholas Biddle explained that he could not resume specie payments at his bank because it would not be in the public interest and he had to protect the financial system, Bryant quoted a couplet by George Barrington about some English criminals sent to Botany Bay for picking pockets:

> True patriots we, for be it understood,
> We left our country for our country's good.

Biddle, Bryant wrote, had improved upon Barrington, who "did not urge in his defense that he was impelled to pick pockets by the ardor of his patriotism." The Whig papers, in the summer of 1838, saw a sinister plot in President Van Buren's choosing a Virginia watering-place to a northern one to visit to escape from Washington's heat—that he was seeking support in the South for his policies. Bryant's editorial on the fear of the Whigs began: "It is said by an Italian naturalist that the reason why the ass, in drinking, is careful not to dip his muzzle into the water, but cautiously and gingerly touches it with the tip of his lips, is, that he is afraid of the shadow of his own long ears reflected from the surface." So were the Whigs as easily alarmed over the President's simple choice of a spa to visit.

Bryant's sarcasm and wit could be as offensive as the cruder name-calling that went on in the political and editorial quarrels of the time and that sometimes provoked challenges to duels. He himself received such a challenge in 1838. It came from Dr. William Holland, editor of the New

---

filled with old letters on their way to the paper mill. They were as serviceable for his editorial work as if they were fresh from it. He used them because he believed that everybody in the world was made the poorer by everything that is wasted, and no one so much as he who wastes, for he experiences a waste of character as well as of property." Century Association, *Bryant Memorial Meeting of the Century* (New York, 1878), p. 50.

York *Times,* a Democratic morning sheet published in the interest of Senator Nathaniel P. Tallmadge, who made a speech defending Biddle's bank that was ridiculed by Bryant. Incensed by some remarks about the ·*Times* being an instrument of men like Tallmadge, Holland demanded an apology. Bryant made light of the affair, writing to Frances, who as usual was spending the summer in Great Barrington, that his friends were congratulating him on being alive.[9] One morning, Bryant related, he was called upon by an emissary of Holland with a message asking for an explanation of his remarks against the *Times.* Bryant wrote a noncommittal reply which did not satisfy Holland. When the emissary returned for a fuller explanation, Bryant told him that while Leggett, "a gentleman of strict honor," was editor of the *Evening Post* he had called Holland a "scoundrel," an epithet which he chose to take quietly. Holland would have to settle the affair with Leggett before Bryant would "consider whether his note deserved any further reply." "My friends are much amused at my having got into such a scrape," Bryant wrote, "and laugh heartily at the idea that a popinjay who curls his whiskers should think to engage me in a duel." Bryant's stratagem worked, and Holland did not pursue the matter.*

Bryant was persuaded to write an ode to be sung at a program on April 30, 1839, conducted by the New-York Historical Society on the fiftieth anniversary of the inauguration of George Washington as President. Bryant frequently turned down requests to write poems on special occasions, but he agreed to compose one for this affair even though John Quincy Adams was to be the orator. He was willing to share the limelight with Adams, whom he had often attacked, because he understood the speech would be on the Constitution and include a plea for national unity in the face of the growing split between the North and South over slavery. Even such an affair could not soften party spirit. The diarist Philip Hone, a Whig, wrote of Bryant's effort: "The ode, in my judgment, is very so-so, considering it is the production of the crack poet of New York."[10]

Most of Bryant's editorials were day-by-day commentary on events as they occurred, but on occasion he took a historical view to write on the promise of America as the New World experiment in democratic govern-

---

*The *Evening Post* announced the demise of this New York *Times* on Oct. 17, not without sorrow: "We do not exult that an adversary print has ceased to exist; we would rather that the 'conservatives,' as a faction of nominal democrats call themselves, who though few, are as a class wealthy, active and intriguing, should have their journal, in order that we may understand what are their plans, and what they are doing to maintain and propagate their opinions."

ment. In August, for example, he wrote several editorials expounding on what he called the first principles of democracy. He regretted the growth of an "aristocratic party" which distrusted the mass of people and opposed the popular tendencies of the times. "Start a new plan of civil or political reform and a croaking, louder than the chorus that rises from the margin of a fresh water lake on summer evenings, instantly begins," Bryant wrote. "They see in it only the cause of wide calamity. It is fraught with nothing but ruin and distress. It is a plot against property, a scheme directed at the very being of society, urged by the worst men, and appealing to the basest passions." The *American,* commenting on these "homilies of the Evening Post," said that Bryant was living in "a world of theories and dreams" and was "absolutely ignorant" of what was happening.

Bryant's call for a nobler view of politics was thus ridiculed, and he himself quickly descended to the level of his foes. In December the Whigs at Harrisburg, Pennsylvania, bypassed their most famous names—Daniel Webster and Henry Clay—to nominate the military hero William Henry Harrison for President, his chief qualifications being that he had no program and no enemies. Bryant wrote on December 14 that before Harrison's nomination most Whigs looked upon him as "a tiresome, stupid old gentleman." "Let the Whigs be grateful that matters are no worse," Bryant said. "Let them call to mind the philosophy of the honest Dutchman, who having broken his leg, told the bystanders that it was a mercy that he had not broken his neck." The convention might have nominated "a baboon or made the Whigs vote for the bear at the show of beasts in the Bowery" but it had shown great moderation: it had "been reasonable enough to nominate a thing in human shape, though by no means, as far as intellect is concerned, a favorable specimen of the human species."

IV

During 1838 and 1839 one of Bryant's personal concerns was for William Leggett. He had been forced to suspend the *Plaindealer* in October of 1837, and his friends sought some means by which he could continue to expound his views and to make a living.* On January 21, 1839, Bryant announced in the *Evening Post* that through their efforts the

*Leggett's chief financial supporter in publishing the *Plaindealer* had been his friend, the popular actor Edwin Forrest, who is reported to have lost fifteen thousand dollars in the enterprise. He had also set Leggett up in his house at New Rochelle and had paid some of his debts. W. R. Alger, *Life of Edwin Forrest* (Philadelphia, 1877), I, 373.

Plaindealer would be revived. Subsequent notices in February and March said that copies of a prospectus for the paper could be obtained at the office of the *Evening Post,* where subscriptions would also be taken. But Leggett's health was so bad that he was unable to return to the arduous life of a journalist, and his friends obtained for him an appointment from Van Buren as a confidential agent to go to Guatemala to negotiate a trade agreement, hoping that the sea voyage and residence in a warm climate would help him. The mission was assailed by Colonel Webb's *Courier and Enquirer,* and Bryant, on May 27, wrote an angry response: "We should pass it by with the usual degree of notice which we give to the crazy declamations of that paper, did it not contain a gross misstatement which it may be proper to correct for the benefit of such of our readers as may have happened to see it." But the appointment came too late to help Leggett. He died at his home in New Rochelle on May 29 at the age of thirty-nine. In an obituary editorial, Bryant praised Leggett as being "a sincere lover and follower of truth" who "never allowed any of those specious reasons for inconsistency, which disguise themselves under the name of expediency, to seduce him for a moment from the support of the opinions which he deemed right, and the measures which he was convinced were just."

Another friend whose support by Bryant was welcome at this time was James Fenimore Cooper. When Cooper had gone to Europe in 1826, he was a national hero whose pioneer tales and sea stories were widely read. When he returned in 1833, he found that his popularity had waned, his later books with European settings having been adversely reviewed. Moreover, he had affronted American patriotism by engaging in a controversy at Paris over the relative cost of government of the French monarchy and the American democracy—democracy was more expensive. Both sensitive and pugnacious, Cooper reacted by denouncing his detractors. A part of his trouble was that the America to which he returned was changed, in his opinion, for the worse in manners, morals, and national spirit. Women no longer maintained an elegant or dignified deportment. Gentlemen of the old school had been supplanted by the "wine-discussing, trade-talking, dollar-dollar set" of the day. The simplicity of the architecture was replaced by tawdry and pretentious new designs. In 1834 Cooper had published a pamphlet, *Letter to His Countrymen,* replying to newspaper criticisms of his later books. He had followed this the next year with a satirical fable, *The Monikins,* comparing to the disadvantage of America her social and political life with that of England. Then, in 1837, he had brought out his *Home as Found,* a novelized attack on American people and institutions. Of this book, Cooper's friend Horatio Greenough had protested that he would "lose hold on the American public by rubbing down their shins with brickbats." It was an understatement. It aroused the people's wrath and the newspapers attacked him with ferocity. "By the end of 1837," one biographer wrote, "Cooper had pretty sedulously improved every opportunity of making himself unpopular."[11]

Bryant had noted the change in Cooper on his own return from Europe. Cooper was no longer living in New York, having several years before moved to the old family estate at Cooperstown on the shore of Otsego Lake, but he always called on Bryant at the *Evening Post* when in the city. In a letter to Frances while she was still in Heidelberg, Bryant had written that Cooper appeared "quite discontented" and talked of returning to Europe, and he noted the same in a letter to Dana on February 27, 1837.[12] When the press fell with fury upon *Home as Found,* Bryant published on November 22, 1838, a letter of Cooper's responding to an attack on him and the book in the *Courier and Enquirer* and in December two more letters protesting "libels" against him in other newspapers. Bryant wrote Dana that the *Courier and Enquirer* comment was "a very malignant notice indeed" and that Cooper in his letter gave warning that he would prosecute Colonel Webb. "It is a favorite doctrine with him just now that the newspapers tell more lies than truth," Bryant continued, "and he has undertaken to reform the practice so far as what they say respects him personally. He has several law suits with publishers of newspapers already on his hands, and I have no doubt that he will perform his promise of prosecuting the *Courier.*"[13] These two or three libel suits were the first of many which Cooper was to bring in the next five years, a time when Bryant continued to open the columns of the *Evening Post* to Cooper's protests against the attacks on him by other newspapers.

Bryant by no means shared all of Cooper's views. He agreed with him that the American people's seeking after success and money was deplorable, but in other respects the two men were opposites. Bryant was a free-trader, Cooper a protectionist; Bryant was a supporter of the Jacksonian principle of government by the people, Cooper an opponent of such leveling; Bryant was a realist in his approach to economics and politics, Cooper a romantic who still clung to an ideal past. By spirit and belief, Cooper should have been a Whig; but it was the Whig papers what attacked him most viciously. Bryant defended Cooper in a long editorial on January 11, 1839. One of the criticisms of *Home as Found* was that it would make people of other countries think badly of the American character. Bryant replied to this:

Without staying to examine whether all of Mr. Cooper's animadversions on American manners are perfectly just, we seize the occasion to protest against this excessive sensibility to the opinion of other nations. It is no matter what they think of us. We constitute a community large enough to form a great moral tribunal for the trial of any question which may arise among ourselves. There is no occasion for this perpetual appeal to the opinions of Europe. We are competent to apply the rules of right and wrong boldly and firmly, without asking in what light the superior judgment of the old world may regard our decisions.

The editorial went on to condemn the eagerness of Americans to read books by foreign travelers in this country to see what they had to say about it. This indicated a weakness, that Americans despite their habit of talking of the greatness of their own country at bottom had no confidence in it. For his part, Bryant admired and honored "a fearless accuser of so thin-skinned a nation as ours." And he concluded, "It is bad enough to stand in fear of public opinion at home, but if we are to superadd the fear of public opinion abroad, we submit to a double despotism."

V

The English traveler J. S. Buckingham had mentioned the *Evening Post* and the *American* as the two New York newspapers that gave the most attention to literary matters. Because of this, Ralph Waldo Emerson, in assuming the task of promoting the sale of Thomas Carlyle's *French Revolution* and *Miscellanies* in the United States, specified that copies be sent to these two papers, and in letters to his brother William in New York emphasized the importance of making sure that Bryant received them.[14] With only two regular staff assistants, however, Bryant had little time to read and comment on the books coming in increasing numbers from publishers. "I see the outside of almost every book that is published," he wrote Dana, "but I read little that is new."[15]

Bryant was not sympathetic to Carlyle and did not himself review his books. He wrote Julia Sands, sister of his friend Robert C. Sands, somewhat mockingly of Carlyle: "Have you read Carlyle's Miscellanies? You will like them better than his History. In Boston they are all agog after him, and they will take up Kant next."[16] Emerson's correspondence reveals his disappointment that Bryant had chosen politics over poetry. He wrote Margaret Fuller, after seeing Bryant in New York, that "his poetry seems exterminated from the soil, not a violet left—the field stiff all over with thistles & teazles of politics." Sent some lines of Bryant's by his brother, Emerson thought that they betokened "the death of his muse."[17]

255

The reference may have been to "The Future Life," published in the *United States Magazine and Democratic Review* of March, 1839, in which Bryant said:

> For me, the sordid cares in which I dwell,
> Shrink and consume the heart, as heat the scroll.

Because of Bryant's interest in Spain, he wrote a long review of William H. Prescott's *Ferdinand and Isabella* on April 3, 1838, calling it a "work highly honorable to our literature, and one of the best histories produced in the language." He enjoined an old family friend, Miss Eliza Robbins, vacationing at Nahant where she met Prescott, to write him all she could about the historian.[18] The *Evening Post* recognized the importance of Alexis de Tocqueville's *Democracy in America* and praised it as being an exceptionally acute analysis, in a review of the first United States edition on June 2, 1838: "De Tocqueville appears to have had a clearer insight into the nature and peculiarities of our institutions, and their effect upon society, than any other foreigner who has written of this country, and . . . he has traced these peculiarities and their consequences with more clearness, precision and minuteness than any of our own writers have done."

Bryant had two occasions to resume his acquaintanceship with Longfellow. In January of 1839 Longfellow stopped for several days in New York while en route to and from Washington. He was then completing his prose romance *Hyperion,* whose hero followed in the tracks of Longfellow's travels in Europe a few years before. When the novel appeared in July, the *Evening Post* noted it favorably. It was "tinged with peculiarities derived from the author's fondness for German literature" and its strain of meditation "now and then passes into the grand dimness of German speculation," but on the whole the book was pleasing: "Upon the slender thread of his narrative the author has hung a tissue of agreeable sketches of the different parts of Germany, supposed to be visited by the hero, delineations of character, and reflections upon morals and literature." Longfellow's first book of poems, *Voices of the Night,* published in December, was praised in a review signed J.Q.D.: "These voices of the night breathe a sweet and gentle music, such as befits the time when the moon is up, and all the air is clear, and soft, and still." In January of 1840 Longfellow was invited to give three lectures on Dante before the Mercantile Library Association, a series on which Dana also was scheduled for lectures on Shakespeare. Bryant was host at a dinner to the two visiting lecturers, at which Halleck was also present. Parke Godwin, reporting the affair, said that "thus the four most famous poets that our literature had produced were brought together."[19]

In 1839 Dana asked Bryant's opinion of a book manuscript by his son Richard Henry, Jr. The young Dana, suffering from eye trouble, had been advised by physicians to interrupt his studies at Harvard and undertake an ocean voyage. Like many New Englanders, young Dana had been from boyhood fascinated by the sea; he signed up as a sailor on the *Pilgrim*, which was to sail around Cape Horn to California to pick up an unglamorous cargo of cattle hides. His account of the trip was the book Bryant was asked to read. Like thousands of later readers, Bryant was caught up by the spirit of the voyage, the lively account of a sailing ship breasting the waters, the descriptions of the ocean in its stormy and calm moods, and the book's symbolism found in his own poetry—life as a journey. When Bryant took the manuscript to his own publishers, the Harper brothers, in June, they hemmed and hawed that times were too bad to bring out a work by an unknown writer. They might do it in the autumn, but now they could not undertake it. Bryant met with the same negative response when he submitted the work to three other New York publishers and to a Philadelphia firm. Convinced that the book should be published, Bryant returned to the Harpers in January of 1840 to ask them to reconsider. As Bryant had always done in dealing with publishers of his own books, he was prepared to haggle to get the best bargain he could when the Harpers agreed to publish the journal as a volume in their School District Library. They offered to pay the author $200. Bryant argued that the book was not just a school work but one that would have a wide sale, mentioning the popularity of travel books. The bargaining continued like a Yankee horse trade. Bryant proposed a payment of $500, then was willing to accept $300, and finally agreed to the $250 which the Harpers said was the most they could offer. For the trade edition the brothers agreed to include the journal in their Family Library.[20] Thus did Bryant succeed in bringing to the public a book that was to become an American classic, *Two Years Before the Mast*.

As for Bryant's own literary pursuits, he still wrote verse occasionally, though in a letter to Dana he declared that his work on the paper gave him "no leisure for poetry." "The labors in which I am engaged would not, perhaps, be great to many people," he said, "but they are as great as I can endure with a proper regard to my health. I cannot pursue intellectual labor so long as many of a more robust or less nervous temperament. My constitution requires intervals of mental repose. To keep myself in health I take long walks in the country, for half a day, a day, or two days.''[21] Nevertheless he submitted his 1836 volume of poems to a "few corrections" and added several poems completed more recently for a new edition of his work brought out in 1839 by the Harpers.

Bryant was now giving first publication of his sparse poetic output to the *United States Magazine and Democratic Review,* the first number of which appeared in October, 1837. To be continued for more than twenty years as a supporter of Democratic party principles, the magazine attracted contributions from many of the country's chief literary figures—Hawthorne, Whittier, Simms, Longfellow, and Lowell—and published some of the early prose of Walt Whitman. Among Bryant's poems at the time were "The Battle-Field," written in 1837, which celebrates the warrior for truth in political strife, the reference to Bryant's editorial battles being clearly apparent. He paid tribute to his former editorial colleague in a stirring poem, "In Memory of William Leggett," and wrote "The Death of Schiller," probably suggested by a series of lectures on the German poet given by Dr. Charles Follen in New York which Bryant attended and liked so much that he became a friend of this libertarian Harvard professor, a friend also of Longfellow. Except for "Oh, Fairest of the Rural Maids," Bryant had not printed any of his poems to his wife. Now, in the March, 1839, issue of the *Democratic Review* he published "The Future Life," in which he wonders if their earthly love will continue after death:

> In meadows fanned by heaven's life-breathing wind,
>   In the resplendence of that glorious sphere,
> And larger movements of the unfettered mind,
>   Wilt thou forget the love that joined us here?

His major poem of the time was another of his blank-verse views of history, "The Fountain," which was to furnish the title for a small collection of poems to be published in 1842.

VI

Despite the opposition of New York merchants to the *Evening Post's* Locofoco policies, the new competition of the cheap popular press, Benjamin Day's *Sun* and James Gordon Bennett's *Herald,* and the financial panic of 1837, Bryant within four years after returning from Europe had succeeded in putting the paper back on its feet financially. His letters reveal that it had not been easy. Writing Frances on May 22, 1837, that he wished with all his heart that he could join her at Great Barrington, he said: "But of that it is idle to think, I have enough to do, both with the business part of the paper and the management of it as editor to keep me constantly busy. I must see that the *Evening Post* does not suffer by these hard times and I must take that part in the great controversies now going on which is expected of it." He reported that the dividend for the six months ending in May was the smallest he had known, "not over $2,000." William Boggs, the "practical printer" who had taken over the management of the shop, had talked of buying into the firm, but they could not agree on terms.[22] Later in the year, however, Boggs did purchase an interest and relieved Bryant of some of the business office burden. On October 25 Bryant wrote his brother John that his hope of spending a year in Illinois as an experiment in country living could not be realized. There was no possibility of selling the paper because of difficulty in making collections and the income did not represent the real value of the property. He thought prospects were improving, however, but there was no reflection of this in his own personal affairs. "I have taken a house in town at as moderate a rent as I could find," he said, "and expect my family from the country in a few days. I am obliged to practice the strictest frugality —but that I do not regard as an evil. The greatest difficulty lies in meeting the debts in which the purchase of the paper has involved me."[23]

Bryant made several changes to cut expenses and improve the paper's competitive position. In April of 1836 he had moved the office from William Street around the corner to 43 Pine Street. He made a second move in April of 1837, to 27 Pine Street opposite the Customs House. In an effort to get additional subscribers, he began printing what he called a second edition in January of 1837 to get in news from Washington and the South via the government's express mail. This edition went to press at two o'clock in the afternoon. To advertise it, Bryant in September illustrated the "second edition" column of the latest tidings with a picture of a post rider blowing a horn while passing a milestone labeled New York.

By June 28, 1838, Bryant could see the glimmerings of success in his efforts. He wrote Dana that to recover the losses incurred by the paper during his absence in Europe he had been forced to give careful attention "to the *business* of the paper properly so called." He had several times thought of giving up the paper "and going out into the world worse than penniless." "Nothing but a disposition to look at the hopeful side of things prevented me," he added, "and I now see reason to be glad that I persevered."[24] Observing the commencement of the thirty-eighth year of the

Evening Post on November 16, 1838, Bryant wrote an editorial pointing out the persecutions the paper had undergone because of his liberal policies and declared that, nevertheless, the circulation and advertising had increased. Of the efforts to destroy the paper, he said:

> For four years we have had to contend with the enmity of a class whose hostility, when directed against a daily journal, could hardly help making itself felt. We allude to the New York merchants, a class of men whose just and essential interests we have never assailed, nay, whose just and essential interests we have ever vindicated. . . . Yet because we would not go along with them in denouncing measures which we held to be just, democratic, wholesome and necessary, because we would not bend our cherished principles to their imaginary interests, our journal became the object of the most intolerant hatred, and an attempt was made to trample it out of existence. . . .
>
> For our own part, we feel that we have maintained the truth . . . and we are certain that what was meant for evil by our enemies is now working for our good. . . . The hostility which at first did us harm is now become to us a principle of growth. We have been persecuted into the good opinion of many. Enmity on the one side has gained us friends on the other.

Bryant invited readers to look for evidence of the paper's victory in its columns. It was to be found in the higher number of advertisements, so great an increase that on December 26 the *Evening Post* was forced to use smaller type to maintain the volume of news for readers. The progress continued during the next year, and, recounting it in December, Bryant announced the purchase of a new press "of the most perfect construction and the most rapid execution."

16

VARIED INTERESTS AND ISSUES

DURING THESE YEARS WHEN BRYANT WAS "HARNESSED TO A daily drag" by the *Evening Post* he followed a rigorous program to maintain his health. Sickly as a boy and subject to pulmonary troubles as a young man, he could not afford to neglect it. He took long walks for exercise and ate simply and sparingly. "By this means I enjoy a health scarcely ever interrupted," he wrote Dana, "but when I am fagged I hearken to Nature and allow her to recruit."[1] During the week his walks were confined to nearby places on Manhattan and Long Island or across the river in New Jersey; on week ends and over holidays and during the summer they extended to the Palisades on the Hudson, the Delaware Water Gap, the Catskills, and, when joining Frances and Fanny and Julia at Great Barrington, among the scenes familiar to his youth in the Berkshires.

A companion on a hike in 1837 from West Point to New York was an English visitor, Ferdinand E. Field, who described Bryant as "the most indefatigable tramp" that he ever "grappled with."[2] Bryant was able to get along on "a baker's biscuit and a few apples" and he "put up cheerfully with the rude fare of wayside inns and laborers' cottages." In an account of this trip to Frances,[3] Bryant related that after leaving West Point, he and Field walked through the woods six miles to Fort Montgomery, then entered a pleasant path along the Hudson, descending the river about fifteen miles to Caldwell's Landing, which they reached in a drizzling rain. After taking tea there, they continued on to Stony Point, arriving a little after sunset. Five more miles over muddy roads brought them to Haverstraw in the darkness, but they went on until about nine o'clock, stopping for the night at a "wretched tavern." They were up at five o'clock the next morning to complete, during the day, the journey to New York. "The excursion was one of the pleasantest I ever made," Bryant wrote. Mention of this hike was made by James Lawson, the poet, playwright, and editor, in an article on Bryant written for the *Southern Literary Messenger*.[4] Lawson felt that Bryant was "temperate in his living almost to abstinence" and indulged in "athletic exercises almost to labor." He related that at an evening party Bryant left early, remarking to his host that he felt a little fatigued, because he had walked the day before rather farther than usual —"from Haverstraw to New York, by the banks of the river, a distance not much short of forty miles."*

Bryant occasionally wrote on the pleasures of walking for the *Evening Post.* Hikers, wearing "brown linen jackets and pantaloons, straw hats, stout Oxford shoes with strong soles studded with nails," were well repaid "for the fatigues of the journey—repaid with spirits as fresh and airy as the country they traverse, with sound sleep, a keen appetite, a freedom from care as great as that of a strolling gipsy, and a stock of health and strength that increases every day." He listed favorable areas for excursions: "The Palisades on the west side of the Hudson stretching up to the Highlands . . . ; the more gentle and cultivated declivities of the eastern bank; the mountainous region of New Jersey from the Ramapough Mountains along the ridge from the western slope of which the springs supply the streams that feed the Schuylkill; the northern shore of Long Island with its beautiful bays, hills and woodlands, all offer a succession of the most picturesque and varied scenes, which he must be uncommonly diligent who can exhaust in several seasons."

---

*Lawson described Bryant: "Retiring in his habits, modest in his deportment and unostentatious in all his actions, he shuns the public gaze and seldom mingles in society. In the company of some chosen friends, in the solitude of his study, or, in many exercises in the country, he employs the hours not necessarily devoted to his daily occupation. When chance, or circumstance, places him among strangers, he is reserved and taciturn. He never leads conversation, but occasionally, in a subdued tone of voice, takes an unpretending part." Lawson disagreed with those who said that Bryant lacked warmth: "Those who meet him occasionally and know him slightly, think that he is cold and unsocial—nay, repulsive—but those who know him best, praise his generous heart, his ardent feelings and unwavering friendship." "Moral and Mental Portraits: William Cullen Bryant," *Southern Literary Messenger*, Jan., 1840.

In 1840 Bryant's excursions included a walking tour of the Berkshires, a trip in midsummer to the Catskills with the painter Thomas Cole, and later in the year a visit with Mrs. Bryant to the Moravian settlement at Bethlehem in Pennsylvania. In joining his family at Great Barrington, Bryant went to New Milford, Connecticut, by steamboat and railroad. He walked the last fifty miles along the Housatonic through Kent, Cornwall, Canaan, and Sheffield. From Great Barrington Bryant made an excursion to Pittsfield and thence, he wrote Dana, "to Worthington, where I studied law, and to Cummington, where all that is left of my father rests in a burying-ground, on the summit of one of the broad highlands of that region."[5]

Bryant's visit to the Catskills with Cole marked perhaps the closest intimacy of the poet and the painter, "Kindred Spirits," as they were portrayed by Asher B. Durand in his picture of the two standing on Table Rock projecting three thousand feet above one of the magnificent "cloves" or valleys in the Catskills, a stream brawling down the center of the gorge and in the background mountains fold on fold receding into the distance until they are lost in the sky.* Cole after his return from Europe had retreated from the city to a country home in the Catskills and during 1840 was completing his series of paintings called "The Voyage of Life," whose conception Bryant considered "a perfect poem."[6] Bryant wrote for the *Evening Post* two articles describing views from Table Rock. One was shortly after dawn when the sun was ascending the sky and, on the rock above the valley he and Cole looked out over it with "mingled bewilderment, delight and awe" and, leaning over the precipice, listened to the breezes down below. The second was at evening while a storm was gathering when the "dark summits of the distant mountains penetrated the sky until the whole seemed like one continuous wall of black."[7]

Bryant's chief literary effort in 1840 was compiling at the request of the Harper brothers an anthology, *Selections from the American Poets,* for the firm's Family Library. Published two years before Rufus Griswold's important and influential collection, *Poets and Poetry of America,* which revealed to Americans that they possessed a substantial poetic literature of their own, Bryant's more modest book was a pioneer assessment of the nation's verse. A duodecimo volume of three hundred and sixteen pages,

---

*The picture was commissioned by the New York merchant Jonathan Sturges soon after Bryant delivered his oration on the death of Cole on May 4, 1848. In presenting it to Bryant, Sturges wrote: "I think the design, as well as the execution, will meet your approbation, and I hope that you will accept the picture from me as a token of gratitude for the labor of love performed on that occasion." Godwin, *Biography,* II, 37.

it included poems by seventy-eight authors. Bryant wrote only a short introduction, in October, and did not set forth his standards for inclusion except that he had decided to leave out "amatory poems and drinking songs," which, whatever their skill in writing or spirit, he did not think appropriate for a book to be placed in the hands of young people. He apologized for the probable omission of some worthy poets on the ground that he had been given only a short time to assemble the volume and was unable to search through the magazines for their work, often unsigned but whose authorship might "with due pains" be ascertained.

In his survey of American poetry written for the *North American Review* in 1818, Bryant did not have very much that was favorable to say about early versifiers, and his judgments then are reflected in the anthology. The volume begins with Philip Freneau, represented, not by his nature poems, but by two ballads and two poems on Indian themes. The Hartford writers of patriotic epics, Joel Barlow, Timothy Dwight, and John Trumbull, are given short shrift; rather than extracts from their grandiose works, Bryant printed Barlow's "The Hasty Pudding" and Dwight's "The Country Schoolmaster." Most of the book is devoted to poets who began writing after Bryant himself had published. An unexpected judgment in the collection is the inclusion of six sonnets by Jones Very, a highly mystical poet and a favorite of the New England Transcendentalist circle of Emerson and Margaret Fuller.

II

For almost fifteen years since joining the *Evening Post,* Bryant had stood out, among the partisan editors of the time, as an independent. On the whole he had supported the Democratic party of Jackson and Van Buren, especially in the battles against the United States Bank, against a protective tariff, and against internal improvement at federal expense. These stands were not so much political as philosophical. They coincided with his strong belief in individual liberty and the rights of man. Good government was that which governed least; personally against gambling, he opposed laws to regulate lotteries. Truth would emerge from free discussion in the market place of ideas; personally against the Abolitionists, he defended their right to be heard. All men were created equal; he was therefore against all special privilege. As an editor, he had seen the accomplishment of a revolution in values in which political power had been shifted from the propertied man to the common man. He was not prepared for the campaign of 1840 when the Whigs in a counterreformation seemed to be the spokesmen for the common people.

Defeated nationally in the last three elections, a new breed of Whigs had emerged, typified by the wily Thurlow Weed of Albany. They were interested in success at the polls instead of doctrinal policy; they realized that they had to get the vote of the masses if they were to win in 1840. Seeing that the people were for the independent treasury, they turned against the national bank. Seeing that aristocratic manners repulsed the voters, they decided to look and talk like plebeians. At Harrisburg in 1839 they nominated for the presidency a nonentity who could be made over into the image of a candidate of the people to run against Van Buren, who was renominated by the Democrats. A Democratic newspaper at Baltimore, on March 23, 1840, unwittingly supplied the Whigs with their campaign theme. It had written "that upon condition of his receiving a pension of $2,000 and a barrel of cider, General Harrison would no doubt consent to withdraw his pretensions, and spend his days in a log cabin on the banks of the Ohio." Here, then, ignoring Harrison's aristocratic Virginia background and his wealth, was a man of the people—a sturdy pioneer, a dweller in the humblest of houses, a log cabin, and a tippler of the drink made on every farm, hard cider.

In the hobbledehoy Horace Greeley, struggling to keep alive his weekly paper the *New Yorker*, Wood found the right publicist for the Harrison campaign. Two years before Greeley had shown his political acumen when Weed invited him to Albany to get out a campaign sheet in the state election. Greeley named it the *Jeffersonian*. At first startled by the proposal, Weed soon saw it as a stroke of genius—using the name of the statesman associated with the Democratic party as a banner for the Whigs. It was pure political chicanery, but the *Jeffersonian* helped elect William H. Seward governor. In this campaign paper, though it had been an effective one, Greeley saw where he had failed: it was dull reading, there was too much instruction. He did not make this mistake with the Harrison campaign sheet, the *Log Cabin*. It was readable in both typography and content. Woodcuts, cartoons, and slogans in large type were used; at the top of the first page was a drawing of Harrison's fictitious log cabin, with barrels of hard cider at the door. The general's Indian battles were related in colorful detail, and other articles portrayed him as a man of the people. Songs and jingles which aroused enthusiasm at the rallies for Harrison, where cider was abundant and log cabins displayed with latchstring out, were printed and new ones created, such as "Old Tippecanoe; or, the Working Man's Election Song":

> The President boasts of his Palace and "chink,"
> And says a Log Cabin won't do,

And sticks up his nose when Hard Cider we drink
To the health of good Old Tippecanoe.

In a campaign in which the standard-bearer of the opposing party was presented as the hero of Tippecanoe mounted on a horse, as a togaed Cincinnatus at the plow, as a frontiersman clad in homespun greeting visitors at his log cabin, as an Indian chief paddling toward the White House in a canoe, always with the accompaniment of songs and cheers and fife and drum music, Bryant was at a loss to know what to write about in his editorials. At first, he tried to get the Whigs to reveal their policies, but this they would not do. He thought ridicule would shame them into addressing themselves to issues, but in this he failed. Finally, his editorials resorted to vituperation at a level to which Bryant seldom sank. On March 10 Bryant advised Democrats not to be taken in by the Whigs' effort to divert attention from principles to irrelevancies like the hero of Tippecanoe or his life in a faked log cabin. "The question is," he declared, "what he and his party will do if they obtain the power." Of hard cider as a drink, Bryant had no objection. "There is, doubtless, much virtue in hard cider," he wrote, "but it is worthy of inquiry whether it will impart the proper qualifications for the presidency, even to him who drinks it diligently."

The *American* charged that the *Evening Post* had "calumniated and scandalized the past services and deeds of General Harrison." Bryant denied the allegation: "We are not in the habit of resorting to personal abuse, in our political controversies, and should disdain it especially in this instance, when there are so many better weapons to be wielded against the party to which the *American* is attached." It was true that the *Evening Post* had said Harrison was "notoriously unfit for the presidency" and that it had spoken of him as "a harmless and imbecile old gentleman," but in this the paper had the sanction of Harrison's most intimate acquaintances: "They have placed him in a ludicrous attitude before the people, and we have laughed at the ludicrous exhibition, as is our wont, when any thing particularly amusing chances to turn up."

The election was won, of course, by "Tippecanoe and Tyler, too," but in a way it was a victory for the Democrats, since the Whigs, though the campaign was carried on with ebullient duplicity, had made their appeal to the people, as Jackson had done. And Bryant, whatever his misgivings about the new party in Washington, had the satisfaction of knowing that Van Buren had carried New York City by a bigger majority than he had in 1836.

The tumult and the shouting by the Whigs over the inauguration of Harrison as President on March 4 had scarcely ended when Old Tippecanoe died as a result, the *Evening Post* said in an editorial, of the festivity and excitement of the ceremony which were too much for the aged man. Bryant was criticized for failing to turn the column rules in the paper— the customary sign of mourning for the death of a notable.* The *Evening Post* had merely used a heavy border, or rule, at the top and bottom of the editorial. Bryant explained in reply that he had discontinued the practice of the turned column rules several years before, not even resorting to it when William Leggett died. "If we had ever departed from our usual practice," Bryant wrote, "then was the time to do it, when a truly eminent man, of great virtues and great talents, a fearless champion of truth, illustrious beyond any renown that high station could give, suddenly departed from among us." In truth, Bryant said, "we look upon the practice as a piece of typographical foppery, and, therefore, have not conformed to it."

Bryant's obituary editorial speculated about Tyler, pointing out that he was known to belong to the Clay faction, was an enemy of the protective system, and was opposed to a national bank. Two days later he could not refrain from twitting the Whigs about Tyler in a mock congratulatory editorial: "As abolitionists they have elected a slaveholder for the acting President of the United States: as manufacturers, they have chosen an anti-tariff man: as merchants, an opponent of the national bank: as federalists, a strict constructionist and states rights man. Surely, surely, it was worth while to unite to produce such results." Bryant refused to give Tyler the title of "President," arguing that he "was elected vice president, that is, an officer who upon the happening of certain circumstances, acts as the substitute for president."

Under either title, Tyler was not a man the *Evening Post* could find much good to say about in his first months in office. In his appointments the "veriest scamps of party" were raised to high stations, his intimate circle, the Corporal's Guard, included "the notorious perpetrators or abettors of the most infamous frauds of the age," and altogether he gave only "feeble indications of that ability and virtue, which some had fondly hoped would translate him from the ranks of little to that of great men." The best thing

*The diarist Philip Hone wrote of Bryant's attitude toward Harrison: "The newspapers were clothed in mourning, all but the *Evening Post,* whose malignant, blackhearted editor, Bryant, says he regrets the death of General Harrison only because he did not live long enough to prove his incapacity for President." *The Diary of Philip Hone* (New York, 1927), II, 536.

that Bryant could say of the "vice president's" message to Congress of June 1 was that it had "the rare merit of being short." Tyler's effort to form his own middle-of-the-road party between the liberals among the Whigs and the conservatives among the Democrats was described by Bryant: "He stands between the two parties, like the ass in the famous argument of the schoolman, attracted with equal force on both sides, and therefore unable to move towards either." But in September and August when the "acting president" vetoed two Whig bills to incorporate a Second Bank of the United States, the *Evening Post* cheered him. Finally, on September 6, Bryant in a short editorial was able to write the obituary of the United States Bank:

> Departed This Life,—at eleven o'clock, on Saturday morning, after a linger-ing illness, the United States Bank. The patient was originally of weak constitution, but succeeded by a course of high living to give itself an appearance of florid vigor. Its habits, however, soon degenerated into in-temperance, which brought on successive fits of delirium tremens, and a consequent debility of which the poor patient, after suffering the last agonies of distress, died. . . .

III

For several years Bryant had been wanting to go to Illinois to visit his mother, who had gone there at the age of sixty-seven in 1835, and his brothers, all settled on land near Princeton in Bureau County. Leaving Julia with Frances's sister at Great Barrington, the Bryants set out on May 22, following the route that Bryant had taken in 1832. Since Bryant's first visit to Illinois, his brothers had prospered. Their log cabins had been replaced by frame or brick houses and the once unbroken prairies of mile on mile of waving grass had been put to the plow, and wheat and corn fields and orchards dominated the former wilderness.

In a letter to the *Evening Post,* dated June 21 at Princeton, Bryant wrote of an excursion to Rock River in the northwestern part of the state in a still unfenced region.[7] There wildlife was abundant—quails, prairie-hens, rabbits, and prairie-squirrels frequently being startled into flight by the travelers. There were few memorials of the Indians who once occupied the region, the most remarkable being their trails across the grasslands or alongside the rivers, "narrow and well-beaten ways, sometimes a foot in depth, and many of them doubtless trodden for hundreds of years." Bryant developed a fancy about these former dwellers of the region in his one poem inspired by the trip, "The Painted Cup." The scarlet blooms were not "bright chalices" to "hold the dew for fairies" but rather, if the poet wished to use his imagination, they were "bright beakers" offering "the gathered dew" to the ghosts of Indians who had disappeared long ago.

In this letter, and in another written on July 2, Bryant wrote at length about "Lynch law" on the sparsely populated frontier. The most common crime was horse-stealing, a great number of horses being bred and allowed to graze in herds on the open prairies. The stealing operations were so well organized and law enforcement agencies so weak that citizens had formed companies of "regulators" to drive out the miscreants. The regulators set a pattern of dealing with lawbreakers that was followed by the better known vigilantes of the Far West in later years. Though the punishment meted out was of a rough-and-ready sort, floggings being the most common, some of the formalities of courts of justice were followed, the accused being allowed to make his defense and witnesses examined. In one incident that Bryant reported, there was a manhunt for a trio suspected of murder who, when they were caught and convicted, were shot to death on the spot. Bryant did not condemn the work of the regulators nor did he approve; he merely reported a condition that existed where no effective law enforcement agencies existed.

The Bryants returned to the East by way of Chicago and the Great Lakes, reaching New York early in August. During Bryant's absence the issues he had been sturdily fighting for years were revived in a set of resolutions Clay introduced June 7 calling for repeal of the Independent Treasury Act, for the incorporation of a bank, and for a tariff high enough to provide adequate revenue. When Tyler signed the measure repealing the independent treasury, Bryant was reminded of an old legend of a man chased by wolves who pulled off his coat and threw it to them hoping to check their pursuit: "The hungry herd . . . snuffed for a moment at the vacant garment and then followed on with a faster pace and fiercer cry. It is in vain that Mr. Tyler has flung down to the wolves of party this repeal of the subtreasury. . . . They want the body and will not be put off with the coat." But he was able to rejoice a week later when Tyler vetoed the measure creating a Fiscal Bank of the United States. By the end of August Bryant could sit back and look with complacence upon a divided Whig party.

During this respite in the political battle, Bryant made an excursion to Lebanon Springs in company with Samuel J. Tilden, one of the young liberal lawyers of the city strongly enough attracted by the policies of the

Evening Post to become contributors.* The first had been Theodore Sedg-wick, Jr., who had written for it for several years under the name of "Veto." More recently he had worked with Bryant in collecting the political articles of William Leggett, published in two volumes in 1840, and at Bryant's request had written in 1839 an elaborate analysis of the legal aspects of the *Amistad* case. This involved African Negroes who had been taken to Cuba and sold in the Havana slave market. While being transported in the ship *Amistad* to their buyer's plantation they had muti-nied and killed the captain and several of the crew and had compelled the others to sail the vessel, as they supposed, back to Africa. Instead, the ship was directed to the American coast and captured by a U.S. naval vessel off Long Island. Sedgwick's legal argument that the Negroes should be considered freemen was upheld by the courts.

Another of these lawyers was John Bigelow, who first became ac-quainted with Bryant while serving in the office of Robert and Henry Sedgwick. Bigelow attempting to establish his own practice was also trying his hand at writing, and Bryant obtained a commission for him to put into shape the manuscript of Benjamin Moore Norman's *Rambles in Yuca-tan.*[8] Bigelow and Tilden had met at a boarding house where both were rooming, and in 1841 Tilden had written for the *Evening Post* at Bryant's request a series of articles exposing the part played by Edward Curtis, collector of the port, in frauds in the election of Harrison. Tilden and Bryant had "kept up a hot fire on Curtis," the young lawyer wrote his father, and the articles "made a great sensation."[9] Both Bigelow and Tilden were friends of Parke Godwin and they and others had formed a club of young liberals who met for debate and social intercourse. In going with Bryant to Lebanon Springs, Tilden served as a guide as well as a companion, since it was near the place of his birth.

Bryant's chief purpose in making the excursion was to visit Martin Van Buren, now retired to his farm at Kinderhook. It was a country estate where the former President led a life that Bryant had been dreaming of for years. He described it in an article in the *Evening Post* of September 18. Van Buren lived in a plain but commodious house built in 1797, and he spent his time in cultivating recently purchased farm land that had been neglected for years. A large garden had been laid out, a greenhouse erected, fruit trees planted, and a spring made to supply water for a

---

*Tilden, a precocious politician, had written his first article for the Albany *Argus* at the age of eighteen in 1832. He began contributing to the *Evening Post* in 1838. John Bigelow, *The Life of Samuel J. Tilden* (New York, 1895), I, 72 ff.

succession of fish ponds. Van Buren began his day with a horseback ride of ten or fifteen miles; after breakfast he was engaged with his workmen in directing farm operations; when tired of this he would read and study in his library. "I was glad to find him so free from the pedantry of party men," Bryant wrote, "and to know that his mind could so readily command resources beyond the occupations in which so large a part of his life has been engaged."

Bryant on his return from Lebanon Springs began a new project for the *Evening Post,* the publication of a weekly edition, primarily for out-of-town circulation, in addition to the daily and the semiweekly, which had been printed since the early 1800's. The announcement of it on October 14 said: "It is intended that it shall contain all that variety of matter which shall make it a useful and entertaining family newspaper. In politics, it will embrace the democratic side; but it will be more devoted to the spread of sound political principles than to the support of a party." The *Evening Post* on March 30 of the previous year had been enlarged from seven to eight columns. Bryant had apologized for making the change, for the smaller sheet was more convenient for readers, but the increase in advertising had made it necessary. The enlargement not only indicated the growing prosperity of the *Evening Post* but also Bryant's willingness to compete in size with the commercial papers. In a few years they were to increase to nine, ten, and eleven columns, to become so large that the name "blanket sheets" was applied to them. In contrast, the "cheap" penny or twopenny papers were modest in size—Benjamin Day's *Sun,* James Gordon Bennett's *Herald,* and Horace Greeley's *Tribune,* which he founded as a daily after his successful Log Cabin campaign on April 10, 1841.

IV

A leading political issue in the winter of 1841 and 1842 was a local one —a measure before the legislature at Albany to permit public funds to be allocated to the Roman Catholic parochial schools. It had been proposed in 1840 by Governor William H. Seward in his annual message in an attempt to win for the Whigs the support of the seventy thousand Irish Catholics in New York City, who had been welcomed by the Democrats into their party. The bishop of the New York diocese was John Hughes, an astute politician who called upon the Democratic assemblymen to vote for the bill under a threat to organize the Catholics as an opposition bloc in the city's mayoralty and aldermanic election in April. The bishop's action placed Bryant on the horns of a dilemma. Strongly believing in the separation of church and state, he could not endorse the idea of using public funds for parochial schools; but, being a Democrat, he could not look with equanimity upon a Whig election victory brought about by the disaffection of the Catholic vote. Moreover, he saw trouble portending if Bishop Hughes persisted in his scheme. In Bryant's first editorial on the school question on October 28, 1841, he thought it "absurd" to think that the Catholics would ever obtain a portion of the school fund. "The community will not consent to be taxed," he wrote, "that children may be educated according to certain religious distinctions, any more than they will consent to be taxed for the religious instructions which grown men receive from the pulpit." Later, after Bishop Hughes had presented his own slate for the city election and had received the endorsement of the Tammany faction of the Democratic party, Bryant warned: "When the church goes to ward meetings, and calls her flock to the polls, her person is in danger of being jostled, and her sacred vestments of being rudely plucked by her great enemy—the world."

For several years there had been a strong Native American movement in the city directed against the Irish both because they were "foreigners" and because they were Catholics. Bryant, opposing public support of the church schools, was thus placed in the unpleasant position of being on the same side in this issue as the bigoted Native Americans. The same was true of another editor, a young man from Long Island, Walter Whitman, who in March had assumed the editorship of a new twopenny paper, the *Aurora,* which had been established in November of 1841. Whitman, then twenty-three, had only recently come into notice in New York. In July of 1841 the *Evening Post* had given prominence to an address he had made at a Democratic rally, and on March 5, 1842, in an article about the *Democratic Review* had praised his tale in the magazine, "Last of the Sacred Army," as being "a very neat and fanciful performance."

The articles of the two editors on the school question reflected their opposing natures—Bryant's disciplined and judicious, Whitman's unrestrained and emotional.[10] Bryant wrote conciliatory editorials in support of the Democratic party, because he saw no chance that the Public School Society, which disbursed the funds, would ever contribute to the Catholic schools; the measure passed by the legislature merely permitted such aid, he pointed out, and did not prescribe it. Whitman, working for a paper which in its opening announcement had declared its sympathies with the Native American movement, wrote editorials that were diatribes against "a gang of false and villainous priests" and "tattered, coarse, unshaven, filthy, Irish rabble." The result of the agitation was that the city was rocked by anti-Catholic rioting during the election, with pitched battles taking place between the Irish and the Native Americans and Bishop Hughes's home being stoned. Bryant condemned the violence and placed the blame on such papers as the *Aurora*. Whitman applauded the routing of the "bog trotters" and the stoning of Bishop Hughes's home, saying that if it had been "the reverend hypocrite's head, instead of his windows, we would hardly find it in our soul to be sorrowful." The election was a divided one —the Democrats named the mayor but the Whigs a majority to the Common Council.

A literary event of the winter was the American visit of Charles Dickens, since the time of Sir Walter Scott the most popular author in the country, whose books were pirated by publishers and widely sold. One of the purposes of Dickens's visit was to urge the adoption of an international copyright law. When the noted author arrived at Boston the first week in February, the *Evening Post* printed several columns about his reception and publicized the elaborate plans for his New York visit that included a ball at the Park Theatre on February 14 and a dinner February 18 at the City Hotel with Washington Irving presiding. Bryant, infected by the popular enthusiasm, called upon Dickens twice after he had checked into the Carlton House but was unable to see him. Dickens made amends in a note to Bryant on February 14:

> My Dear Sir: With one exception (and that's Irving) you are the man I most wanted to see in America. You have been here twice, and I have not seen you. The fault was not mine; for on the evening of my arrival committee-gentlemen were coming in and out until long after I had your card put into my hands. As I lost what I most eagerly longed for, I ask you for your sympathy, and not for your forgiveness. Now, I want to know when you will come and breakfast with me: and I don't call to leave a card at your door before asking you, because I love you too well to be ceremonious with you. I have a thumbed book at home, so well worn that it has nothing upon the back but one gilt "B," and the remotest possible traces of a "y." My credentials are in my earnest admiration of its beautiful contents. . . .[11]

The breakfast duly occurred, those present being one of Dickens's American hosts, Professor Charles Felton of Cambridge, and Fitz-Greene Halleck. Felton, writing of the affair, said that Dickens's "exuberant animal spirits and frank boyishness of manner, to say nothing of his wit and nice observation, took direct hold of Mr. Bryant's quieter temperament."[12] Subsequently Bryant entertained Dickens at his own home and even went so far as to attend the ball for him in the Park Theatre.

The *Evening Post* continued to report Dickens's triumphal visits to Philadelphia, Washington, and other cities and was the vehicle chosen by him for an address to the people to obtain their support for the copyright law. Dickens sent the address to Bryant from Buffalo and it appeared in the *Evening Post* on May 9 with an editorial asserting that the law would benefit American authors as much as British ones, mentioning the work of Cooper, Bancroft, Irving, and Prescott among others. Bryant's editorial ended:

> The plea against an international copyright, that it gives our publishers an advantage over those of Great Britain, is not true, or if true, is true for the present only. If our publishers enrich themselves at the expense of British authors, British publishers enrich themselves at the expense of ours, and will continue to do so, from year to year, until the advantage will be shifted from our side to theirs. The policy of our country is to secure for its authors the benefit of an international copyright before that time arrives.

Later in the year a letter by Dickens in the London *Chronicle* attacking Americans who opposed the international copyright and his book *American Notes* disparaging the people and their habits prompted indignant editorials by Bryant. Berating pirating publishers of the United States, Dickens had said that for the most part they were men whose only interest was in what they could gain in money by republication of English works and that they were also men "of very low attainments and of more than indifferent reputation." In an editorial on August 2, Bryant declared that this was false. "We know many very respectable men,"·he wrote, "respectable in their attainments, and respectable in their position in society, who condemn the proposal to establish an international copyright. . . . They do so . . . from an earnest desire to promote the real interests of American literature." The next day, quoting Dickens as saying "the uncouth manners, and the unmitigated selfishness, which meet you everywhere in America, made my journey one of a good deal of annoyance," Bryant commented: "We should like to know if these were Mr. Dickens's sentiments when he was flourishing his fine compliments at the dinner tables. Either he was disreputably insincere then, or he is most lamentably inconsistent now."

Three weeks after Dickens's appearance, New York had another distinguished visitor, Ralph Waldo Emerson, who arrived to expound the new doctrine of Transcendentalism that the intelligentsia had been hearing about—"so much dreaded and so little understood among us," as the *Evening Post* said in announcing the six lectures on "The Times" at the

Society Library. Of the opening lecture, Bryant wrote in a short notice on March 4 that the visiting sage was probably not a popular speaker but he was "an extremely interesting and instructive one." "His language is bold and striking," Bryant wrote; "his manner direct, earnest and impressive; and his matter is original and important." Bryant could not consider himself qualified to judge Emerson's doctrines: "We cannot say that we precisely apprehend what they are. Now and then, in listening to his discourses, or reading his essays, we have fancied that we caught glimpses of great and novel truths—truths that seemed to reveal to us an entirely new existence, and that certainly gave a fresh impulse and elevation to our moral nature. It is, at least, pleasant in these days . . . to find a man who is faithful to his own mind and independent of the minds of others."

Bryant wrote nothing more on the lectures until the series was completed on March 14. Summing them up on March 16, Bryant felt that Emerson "often failed to carry with him the convictions of his hearers," but "invariably succeeded in ministering to a high and rare intellectual enjoyment." Bryant, however, had some adverse criticism:

> His doctrines, original and profound as they are, seem to us wanting in coherence and completeness. He never elaborates a system; he seldom argues; he flings out his thought and leaves it at once to its fate. His own convictions rest on his intuitions and so appeal mainly to the intuitive perceptions of others. He seems to feel that his best and deepest sayings, to borrow the peculiar phrase of his own doctrine, are only the spontaneous and unobstructed utterance of the *one soul* which dwells in *all men,* and that thus whenever they are authentic, they must, of necessity, be recognized and received.

In another speaker, this might have produced only "dull dogmatism" but not so in the case of Emerson.

Emerson respected Bryant as a man and a poet, but he could not bring himself to like him. On March 9 the Rev. Henry W. Bellows, since 1839 minister of the First Unitarian Church, which Bryant attended, was host to Emerson at a dinner. Among the guests were Bryant and his old friend from Stockbridge, the novelist Catharine Sedgwick. Emerson, writing his wife Lidian of this affair, said that Bryant "was just as gentlemanlike good easy dull man as ever." The next day, writing to Margaret Fuller, he said: "I have seen Miss Sedgwick, and Bryant, but believe I have nothing to tell you of them. Bryant is greatly interested in homoeopathy and is himself an active practitioner. The cold man gets warm in telling his stories of his cures. He is always to me a pleasing person so clean and unexceptionable in his manners, full of facts, and quiet as a good child, but Miss Sedgwick complained of his coldness, she had known him always and never saw him warm."[13]

Emerson's observation that Bryant was capable of being aroused from his usual reserve to manifest enthusiasm in describing his homoeopathic cures reveals his growing interest in medicine. Just when Bryant first read the work of S.C.F. Hahnemann, the German physician who advanced the theories of homoeopathy in 1796, is not known. By the mid-1830's he was sufficiently familiar with them to accept them. In 1836 he had written his brother John that the practice of medicine in New York had undergone considerable revolution. "Physicians begin to think that a vast many patients have been drugged out of the world within the last fifty years," he said, "and the let-alone system is becoming fashionable. I am so far a convert to it that I distrust a physician who is inclined to go to work with large quantities of medicine."[14] On December 23, 1841, physicians advocating the new doctrine organized the Homoeopathic Society of New York Physicians. Bryant was elected president and delivered an inaugural address in which he attacked the uncertainty of the then prevailing system of medicine in contrast to the empiricism employed in the homoeopathic system. This began the formal association of Bryant with the homoeopathic medical group to continue for the rest of his life.[15] Of the popularity of the new medicine, Bryant on January 11, 1842, wrote his friend the Rev. Orville Dewey, the Unitarian minister, who was in Europe, that it was "carrying all before it."[16]

Another scientific matter which aroused Bryant's interest was hypnotism, or animal magnetism as it was then called. In writing Dr. Dewey of the happenings stirring New York, Bryant mentioned the popular demonstrations of animal magnetism. "It is quite the fashion for people to paw each other into magnetic sleep," he wrote. "Physicians somnambulize their patients and extract teeth literally without pain." Scientific and medical interest in it had been aroused by the work of the Viennese physician F. A. Mesmer, who theorized that a vital magnetic fluid became stored up in living bodies and, through the instrumentality of one person, could be made to act upon another. Bryant had become so interested in the subject that in 1837 he had translated from the French a long report by the Academy of Medicine on its investigation of the scientific validity of the phenomenon and printed it on November 1 of that year. In an editorial announcing the article Bryant said that the manner in which the committee of physicians had exposed the fraudulence of a practitioner's experiments was "quite amusing." Writing to Julia Sands about the article, he said: "I have no doubt that animal magnetism is the flam of flams."[17]

In the autumn of 1842, a new theory called neurology was advanced by a Louisville physician, a Dr. Buchanan, in a series of lectures reported in the *Evening Post.* Bryant was named to a committee of three to investigate the phenomena produced by Dr. Buchanan in his demonstrations. Dr. Buchanan's method of influencing his subjects, according to the committee's report, largely written by Bryant, was by exciting various functions of the nervous substance, which he called Neuraura, by the pressure of his fingers on the cranium of a person. In one experiment, Dr. Buchanan applied his fingers to the right side of his subject's forehead, causing his hands to quiver and the fingers to clutch convulsively. In another, he relaxed the muscular system of his subject to produce feebleness and eventually "animal sleep." The committee's report was open minded: There was sufficient evidence to indicate that Dr. Buchanan's views had a rational experimental foundation and that they opened a field of investigation promising important future results to science and humanity.

V

On May 12, 1842, the close-knit Bryant family was broken up by the marriage of Fanny to Parke Godwin. Little mention of the wedding is made in the personal correspondence of the family, and the reason may be that Bryant opposed the match. The relations between him and his son-in-law seem never to have been marked by affection. In fact, the reverse was true. Three years after his marriage, in 1845, Godwin was writing his friend Charles Anderson Dana, then living in the Transcendentalist socialist community of Brook Farm, that Bryant lacked "human every day sympathies" and was "a little malignant" and the next year that Bryant was "a cold, irritable and selfish man."[18] Letters and incidents of later years reveal continued incompatibility, and Bryant in his will directed "that the property given to my daughters shall be settled upon them in such a manner as to be free from any intermeddling or control of the husband of either of them."[19] The clause was directed at Godwin, since Julia was unmarried.

At the time of the marriage the family were living in a rented place on Ninth Street, which Bryant described as "a comfortable two-story house, quite new and very convenient."[20] Fanny was twenty years old, an accomplished young lady whose education Bryant had supervised since Mrs.

277

Bryant, more easygoing than he, did not insist upon the perfection of the girls in their studies that her husband demanded. It was rigorous educational regime to which Bryant subjected his daughters. He wanted them to share his appreciation of nature; to be proficient in several modern languages—French, Spanish, Italian, and German; to be accomplished musicians; and to have a thorough knowledge of literature and history. In rambles in the country with his daughters, Bryant was a moral guide and attempted to teach them an enjoyment of nature that went deeper than pleasure over a pretty scene.

Over the years Bryant's letters to the girls were written in the languages they were studying, letters to Fanchette or Giulina, and they learned their nursery rhymes and tales in translations made by him. As they grew older, Bryant suggested books for them to read and extracted their critical opinion of them. When Fanny had complained of nothing to do at Great Barrington, Bryant admonished her to "make yourself amends for it by passing more of your time in that society of the wise and good of all ages which you will find in your mother's library."[21] Such homilies were frequent in his letters. When Fanny was fifteen, he wrote:

> You will never, I hope, allow a dislike of exertion or a love of amusement and frivolous occupation to obtain the ascendancy over you. You are now arrived at "years of discretion," as they are called—the time of life when your own reason is strong enough, if you will follow it, to show you what you ought to do to form your own character and intellect. You have, as we all have, three enemies to contend with—laxness, selfishness, and ill-temper —and you must master them, or they will master you. Now is the time to put them in chains for the rest of your life. After you have once fairly subdued them, they will give you no further trouble. . . .[22]

When Godwin became acquainted with the Bryant family in a New York boarding house in 1836 after their return from Europe, Fanny was a schoolgirl of fourteen years and he a young man of twenty. Six years later, at the time of their marriage, she at the age of twenty was if not a learned woman at least a well-read one with a knowledge of several languages and possessed of an interest in literature and history which they could indulge in together.

If Bryant opposed the marriage, this may explain Godwin's leaving the *Evening Post* the next month to establish his own newspaper. The reason may also have been a temperamental incompatability revealed in Godwin's own correspondence. An outgoing man in contrast with the self-controlled Bryant and a man with ideas of his own, Godwin chafed under the editorial rein maintained by Bryant. Both were Democrats, but Godwin was strongly attracted to the socialistic theories of the Fourierists, and these Bryant considered to be nonsense. Moreover, as Godwin later complained to Charles A. Dana, he was underpaid for his work on the *Evening Post.*

Godwin's departure from the *Evening Post* was revealed on June 16 in the announcement of a new paper, the New York *Morning Post,* to be published by P. Godwin & Co. at No. 21 Ann Street. It proclaimed the creed of "equal rights of man" and "perfect freedom of trade." It was to be a "cheap" paper, selling for two cents, and despite the name was to have no connection with any other paper. Bryant, in an editorial saluting the new paper, recalled to readers that Godwin had been associated with the *Evening Post* for several years and, in the absence of the senior editor, had been its sole editor. The *Morning Post,* Bryant said, would be an "enlightened advocate of political doctrines which are essential to the welfare of the nation." But before a week was up Godwin dropped plans for the *Morning Post.* The *New Era,* which had been established in 1836 as a Democratic paper, came on the market when Levi D. Slamm, a party stalwart, left as editor to establish with Clement Guion a new daily, the *Plebeian.* Godwin, in announcing his purchase of the *New Era,* which appeared under his editorship on June 23, said that it had been thought best to "build on the foundation of a journal already in existence." Bryant gave his blessing to the enterprise in these words: "That Mr. Godwin, the editor, whose assistance in this journal we lose with regret, will conduct the paper with uncommon ability; with spirit, knowledge and eloquence; and, at the same time, with fidelity to the loftiest standard of political morality, we need hardly say to our readers."

VI

During the three years since the 1839 edition of his *Poems,* Bryant had continued to write verse occasionally. His eminence among American poets and his popular appeal led the shrewd and enterprising publisher, George R. Graham, to conduct a campaign to obtain him as a regular contributor to *Graham's Magazine.* In May of 1842 the magazine's literary editor, Edgar Allan Poe, had been replaced by Rufus Griswold, a young journalist who had worked on two or three of the city's weeklies and had just published his anthology, *Poets and Poetry of America.* He was the prime mover in the effort to get Bryant to contribute to *Graham's.* Graham began his campaign to obtain Bryant's name in his magazine's table of contents by offering him fifty dollars a poem or a flat rate of six hundred dollars a year for a poem every month. When Bryant did not reply, Graham wrote him again saying that space was being reserved for him in the August number if he would send in something.[23] Bryant finally obliged with "The Maiden's Sorrow." Bryant could not, as he had done for the *United States Literary Gazette* when he was at Great Barrington, agree to supply poetry regularly, but he did send in poems for three subsequent numbers.

Among Bryant's poems of 1842 was a hymn sung at a memorial service in New York on October 15 for the apostle of Unitarianism, William Ellery Channing. In an obituary editorial on October 5, Bryant had chosen to discuss not Channing's theological opinions but his political writings. Channing's aims, Bryant wrote, had been "to recall the practice of government . . . to the strictest conformity with the highest standard of right," and his prose style was of the highest and, though unadorned with figures of speech, nevertheless had a "poetic effect, and an irresistible power of kindling emotion in the reader." His hymn mourned the loss of such a speaker and worker for the good.

In July the firm of Wiley & Putnam published a collection of fifteen of Bryant's poems written since his return from Europe, titled *The Fountain and Other Poems.* In the introduction Bryant said that some of the poems were written "as parts of a longer one planned by the author, which may possibly be finished hereafter." He was more specific in an afternote to "An Evening Revery," in which he said: "This poem and that entitled 'The Fountain,' with one or two others in blank verse, were intended by the author as portions of a larger poem, in which they may hereafter take their place." Besides these two poems, there are three other blank-verse poems in the collection. Only one of these is sufficiently like the two Bryant mentioned in spirit and theme that it would seem to be a component of a longer work.* It is "The Antiquity of Freedom," written in the same year, 1842, as the poem "Noon," not printed in *The Fountain* but later in Bryant's collected work identified by him as being from an unfinished poem. Fitting into such a master scheme also is another poem of 1842, "A Hymn of the Sea," which also found its way into Bryant's later collected works.

---

*The other two blank-verse poems are "The Painted Cup," which describes a prairie flower Bryant saw on his visit to Illinois, and "The Old Man's Counsel," a recollection of his Grandfather Snell, who

> taught me much
> That books tell not, and I shall ne'er forget.

If these five poems can be considered as parts of a single work, they reveal that Bryant had made progress toward fulfilling the request of Dana and some of the critics that he should test his stature as a poet by composing a long poem. They constitute three hundred and ninety-nine lines of fluent blank verse that though never perhaps attaining great poetic heights nevertheless show a writer in control of his material and his method. This was the feeling of Dana, who wrote Bryant on December 2: "Have you a poem with some few passages of more stir and passion (I don't mean, of convulsions) than these? If your poem is long, it will need have here and there a peak thrown up out of the level."[24]

Since Bryant's manuscripts do not show that he gathered these fragments together in any sort of order so they could be considered a unit or contain notes about his plans for the poem, his major theme and its development can only be surmised. Of Bryant's conception, Godwin wrote:

> Having travelled a great deal in all parts of our country, he was familiar with the experiences of settlers in different regions, and it may be conjectured that he contemplated a poem in which the aspects of American nature and life as they are seen from the shores of Massachusetts to the prairies of the great West should be presented in a series of pictures connected by a narrative of personal adventures, as Wordsworth has connected the principal parts of his *Excursion* by the story of his pedler. He never, however, discussed his plan to any one, and even this suggestion is mere guesswork.[25]

It is probable that Bryant did have in mind a philosophical poem on the order of *The Excursion,* in which Wordsworth gave his views on man, nature, and society, or his unfinished *The Recluse,* but the fragments indicate a much broader scope than a mere portrayal of American nature and life through personal experience. Instead, they indicate a cosmic view of nature suggested by Bryant's knowledge of the science of geology. In his longest poem up to this time, "The Ages," Bryant had sought to show "from a survey of the past ages of the world, and of the successive advances of mankind in knowledge, virtue, and happiness, to justify and confirm the hopes of the philanthropist for the future destinies of the human race." In his later poems on man's history in the universe, a steady rise from savagery to higher civilization is not seen as inevitable. The key poem of his changed view is "The Fountain." The fountain, which illustrates God's bringing "from the dark and foul the pure and bright," is set up against a history that includes its pristine years when only animals— "the quick-footed wolf," the deer, and "the slow-paced bear"—were known to it; afterward came the white settlers of a pastoral age followed by increasing numbers when it became a resort of occasional visitors, having lost its centrality in the environment. But the confirmation of the hopes of the "philanthropist" expressed in "The Ages" is not found in "The Fountain." Instead, the forces that brought the spring into being are seen as capable of destroying it, in lines that recall Bryant's descriptions of the landscape of Europe:

> Is there no other change for thee, that lurks
> Among the future ages? Will not man
> Seek out strange arts to wither and deform
> The pleasant landscape which thou makest green?
> Or shall the veins that feed thy constant stream
> Be choked in middle earth, and flow no more
> For ever, that the water-plants along
> Thy channel perish, and the bird in vain
> Alight to drink?

The contradiction between Bryant the poet of nature and Bryant the political editor was pointed out in some of the reviews of this little volume of one hundred pages. Charles C. Felton of Harvard, in the *North American Review*,[26] wrote that Bryant in his editorials dipped "his pen daily in bitterness and hate" and produced "torrents of invective," yet was "able to turn at will from this storm and strife and agony to the smiling fields of poetry, where not a sound of the furious din with which he was but just surrounded strikes upon the ear." "We gaze with wonder on the change," Felton added, "and can scarce believe the poet and the politician to be the same man."

17

THE CONFLICT OVER TEXAS

APPROACHING HIS FIFTIETH BIRTHDAY, BRYANT, ON AN excursion to Weehawken in 1842, was led to reflect upon his reaching "the noon of human life." From the brow of a rock overlooking the Hudson, as he wrote in the fragment "Noon," he was led to regret that

> in this feverish time, when love of gain
> And luxury possess the hearts of men

he was so seldom able to pause to refresh his spirit with contemplation of "the calm and beautiful" as in his youth. For twenty years as a magazine and newspaper editor, he had been limited to occasional periods of escape on his hikes about the countryside and his trips during the summers when journalistic pressures were eased; but though he could not look forward to fulltime retirement to the country, he could, now that the *Evening Post* had become so prosperous, afford to buy a rural retreat which would be his own. He exultantly announced his plans to his brother John in a letter of February 5, 1843: "Congratulate me! There is a probability of my becoming a landholder in New York! I have made a bargain for about forty acres of solid earth at Hempstead Harbor, on the north side of Long Island. There, when I get money enough, I mean to build a house."[1] He had at last found a place to alight permanently after years of moving almost every spring from one boarding house or rented place to another with little more tenancy than a migrant bird's.

But the move could not be made at once, and, in fact, more than a year passed before Bryant was able to install his family in their own place. In March and April Bryant made a trip to the South and on his return completed the purchase of the land. His first plan had been to build a new house, but on the place was a large structure of plain architecture, put up by a Quaker in 1787, that appealed to him because of its location and that could be renovated to suit his needs. It stood on a rise overlooking Long Island Sound and before it was a lawn with a small lake fed by springs. There were many old trees and the terrain was rough—a visitor in later years, Walt Whitman, said it was "a beautiful place" but "somewhat cliffy —rather cliffy."[2]

Bryant's trip to the South with Frances was one that he had been wanting to take for several years to satisfy his curiosity about the people and their way of life. Moreover, he had received urgent invitations from William Gilmore Simms to visit his plantation, Woodlands, near Charleston. On Simms's trips to New York to arrange for publication of his books he had become one of Bryant's most intimate literary friends, and he remembered with pleasure their walks and talks when Bryant and Robert C. Sands occupied nearby cottages at Hoboken. Writing Bryant on January 10, 1841, Simms could not offer him much "imposing scenery," the country being too level, but there were other attractions, the mystery that "seems to clothe the dense & tangled masses of forest, that lie sleeping around you" or the fancy coming to mind that "in the flitting of some sudden shadow . . . the old Indian is taking his round among the graves which hide the bones of his family."[3] Bryant found it possible, in March of 1843, to "steal off for a month [actually two months] and cheat the public & the paper" to visit his South Carolina friends and, as a journalist, to write seven travel letters for the *Evening Post*.[4]

In his first letter dated March 2 at Richmond, Bryant reported passing through Washington, which he had visited in 1832. Looking in on a session of the House of Representatives, he found that proceedings were conducted with less decorum than a decade before, and in the Senate he was disgusted at the sight of an American practice that had revolted Mrs. Trollope and Dickens: preparing to make a speech, a senator blew "his nose with his thumb and finger without the intervention of a pocket-handkerchief." Bryant added sarcastically: "The speech, after this graceful preliminary, did not, I confess, disappoint me." Bryant found Richmond to be a beautiful city and he was impressed by the gardens in which the finer homes were situated. With his mortuary interest, Bryant, as he usually did on his travels, visited the burying-ground, "where sleep some of the founders of the colony, whose old graves are greenly overgrown with the trailing and matted periwinkle." In the St. John's Episcopal church on one of the hills of the city he recalled that it was here Patrick Henry on March 23, 1775, had made his well-remembered speech with its ringing declaration: "Give me liberty or give me death!" Bryant studied the economics of the tobacco industry and visited a factory where some eighty Negroes were engaged in rolling the leaves of tobacco and cutting them into plugs. There was "a murmur of psalmody running through the sable assembly," and Bryant was told that the slave-owners encouraged singing—the slaves worked better to the sound and rhythm of the sacred hymns they preferred.

From Richmond Bryant traveled to Charleston, most of the way by railroad, through the vast pine forests of North Carolina. Negroes extracting turpentine from the trees had made blazing fires everywhere of the resinous wood, for the temperatures were freezing and ice coated the road and patches of swampy ground. Bryant condemned the turpentine industry as a "work of destruction" and foresaw that the long-leaved pine soon would become "nearly extinct in this region, which is so sterile as hardly to be fitted for producing any thing else." He was glad to note that where the trees were destroyed they were replaced by loblolly pines, which had little commercial value to attract the destroyers. Bryant reached Charleston on March 6 and did not send back to the *Evening Post* another letter until March 29, after he had passed three weeks in the interior of South Carolina, visiting Columbia, the capital, and staying with the Simmses at Woodlands—he had "been out in a raccoon hunt; had been present at a corn-shucking; listened to negro ballads, negro jokes, and the banjo, witnessed negro dances; seen two alligators at least, and eaten bushels of hominy."

At the corn-shucking the Negroes worked by the light of a log fire, "singing with great glee . . . , keeping time to the music, and now and then throwing in a joke and an extravagant burst of laughter." Unlike the singers in the Richmond tobacco factory, these slaves sang songs of a comic character. One of them, however, was sung to "a singularly wild and plaintive air" which Bryant thought should be reduced to notation:

> Johnny come down de hollow.
> O hollow!
> De nigger-trader got me.

285

O hollow!
De speculator bought me.
O hollow!
I'm sold for silver dollars.
O hollow!
Boys, go catch de pony.
O hollow!
Bring him round de corner.
O hollow!
I'm goin' away to Georgia.
O hollow!
Boys, good-by forever.
O hollow!

Bryant was amused by another song in which various animals were represented as being a member of a profession:

De cooter is de boatman.
John John Crow.
De red-bird de soger.
John John Crow.

And so until the slaves tired of the game.

Bryant in his first look at slavery at close hand reported nothing that would feed the fire of the Abolitionists. "The blacks of this region are a cheerful, careless, dirty, race, not hard worked, and in many respects indulgently treated," he wrote. "It is, of course, the desire of the master that his slaves shall be laborious; on the other hand it is the determination of the slave to lead as easy a life as he can. The master has the power of punishment on his side; the slave, on his, has invincible inclination, and a thousand expedients learned by long practice." Bryant considered the result to be "a compromise in which each party yields something, and a good-natured though imperfect and slovenly obedience on one side, is purchased by good treatment on the other."

Bryant cut short his visit at Woodlands, perhaps because it was a damp and chilly spring, the season being, he was told, three weeks later than usual, to go farther into the South.[5] He left Charleston by steamer on March 30, following the inland waterway to Savannah. He found the city beautifully laid out, commenting that "Oglethorpe seems to have understood how a city should be built in a warm climate." Continuing his journey, Bryant spent a day at Picolata, East Florida, where he wrote his first letter giving his impression of Savannah for the *Evening Post,* and on

April 8 reached St. Augustine. This city, the oldest in the United States, fascinated him. He noted its narrow streets paved with an "artificial stone" of shells and mortar, its old stone houses having attached balconies of wood, and its luxuriant growth of trees—the pomegranate, the orange tree then fragrant with flowers, and the fig verdant with broad luxuriant leaves. Always a student of languages, Bryant was interested in the dialect of Spanish still spoken in the city. On the eve of Easter Sunday he heard a group of serenaders who sang a hymn in honor of the Virgin in the dialect. A native of the city wrote down the words for him, and he translated them into Castilian Spanish, as he did also a song soliciting the customary gift of cakes or eggs.

Bryant started his return trip north on April 24 after two months of pleasant experiences with the people of the region. Simms wrote him, regretting that he had not yet seen the real South, much of the trip having been in the "most wealthy" regions where "the lands & people are most cultivated," and inviting him to return the next year.[6] Bryant's friends had feared, because of the agitation against slavery in the North and the *Evening Post* editorials inveighing against the institution, he would encounter some hostility among the planters. But this was not the case. He had been received everywhere with friendliness, and his failure to write adversely against slavery may have been because he thought it was unbecoming in a guest to attack his hosts. "Our visit to the South," Bryant wrote Dana, "was extremely agreeable. New modes of life and a new climate could not fail to make it interesting, and the frank courteous, hospitable manner of the southerners made it pleasant. Whatever may be the comparison in other respects, the South certainly has the advantage over us in point of manners."[7]

Back in New York, Bryant busied himself on the *Evening Post* and consummated the deal for the purchase of the land on Long Island. His chief assistant on the newspaper was a lawyer, William J. Tenney, who had graduated from Yale College in 1832 and had practiced before the Rhode Island bar before going to New York in 1840; Tenney afterward joined the publishing firm of D. Appleton & Company, and edited *Appleton's Annual Cyclopaedia* besides writing several historical volumes. Parke Godwin may also have worked on the *Evening Post* during 1843. His own launching out into publishing a daily newspaper had apparently failed, for on February 25 the *Evening Post* announced the first number of the *Pathfinder,* a weekly, with him as editor. The paper was published at the *Evening Post* plant at 25 Pine Street. Modeled after William Leggett's *Plaindealer,* its political department proclaimed the slogan of "freedom and progress" and its literary department was to comprise "high-toned and carefully prepared criticism of new publications, choice extracts and anecdotes from new books and magazines, short tales, and a faithful register of the latest literary intelligence."

The *Evening Post*'s own literary material had been curtailed because of the volume of advertising. In reprinting poetry, Bryant in the past two years had been most hospitable to Longfellow and Whittier. Reviewing Whittier's *Lays of My Home and Other Poems,* Bryant wrote on June 2: "Whittier's verses, we think, grow better and better. With no abatement of poetic enthusiasm, his style becomes more manly, and his vein of thought richer and deeper." In commenting on new books and periodicals, Bryant usually noted the quality of the printing and production. He condemned the binding of the Whittier volume: "The book . . . comes out in that fair cream-colored paper binding with which it is now the fashion for our publishers to clothe the volumes of our poets, and which is sullied almost by the slightest touch. Do these publishers expect that their books will not be read, or read only in boudoirs, by gloved ladies?"

For about three weeks in July Bryant was able to get away for a tour of parts of New England that were unknown to him—Vermont and New Hampshire. His route took him north to Saratoga Springs and then to the canal joining the Hudson with Lake Champlain. Several years before on his trip to Canada Bryant had sailed the length of the lake and now, to see more of the northern part of Vermont, he chose to go by wagon overland across the mountainous country. He noted that French Canadians had settled along the shores of the lake and that additional ones came only for the summer to work on the farms. After a week in northern Vermont, Bryant traveled crosscountry from Middlebury through Rutland and Bellows Falls to Keene in southwestern New Hampshire. At Keene he visited with an aunt, Charity Bryant, the youngest sister of his father. Bryant ended his two letters describing the trip to *Evening Post* readers by saying he would "gladly have lingered, during a few more of these glorious summer days, in this wild country" but his commitments in New York would not permit his doing so.[8]

II

The chief political issues of the year were two long-simmering ones that were to come to a boil in the presidential election of 1844—American claims to Oregon territory between the Rocky Mountains and the Pacific Ocean from the forty-second parallel to fifty-four forty north and the annexation of the Republic of Texas, which, under President Sam Houston, was eager to join the United States. Bryant would have been glad in both instances to extend the boundaries of the United States, but he found himself contradictorily upholding American claims to Oregon against those of Britain and opposing the incorporation of Texas into the Union.

As to Oregon, Bryant in an editorial on January 6, 1843, approved a Senate bill providing for extension of United States laws into the northwestern territory. He pointed out that the question had often been raised in Congress in the past twenty years and condemned the delay in taking decisive action. His statement was an expression of "manifest destiny":*

> It is a duty which the United States owes to mankind, to assert inflexibly its title to its proper territory, to guard it religiously from all encroachments by the powers of Europe, that it may become the home of men living under democratic institutions, framed after the pattern of our own. We hold this territory in trust for future governments, and we have no permission either to surrender it voluntarily, or let it pass from our hands through our own negligence. We have no right to give up a foot of the domain in which Providence has put under our charge, to the evils of a colonial, or an aristocratic government. We should early mark out our just limits, and take early measures to hold them sacred against the invasion of the governments of the old world.

On the Texas question, Bryant from the first had been against annexation. In June of 1836 when Texas declared its independence of Mexico, Bryant opposed even recognition of it as a nation. To do so, he wrote, "our government would lose its character for justice and magnanimity with the whole world, and would deserve to be classed with those spoilers of nations whose example we are taught as republicans to detest." During subsequent years he joined with Abolitionists in objecting to annexation because the drive for admitting Texas was spurred by southerners wishing to divide it into slave states. On December 7, 1843, Bryant had changed his view to the extent of agreeing with President Tyler, who in a message to Congress stated that the United States had a right to treat Texas as though its independence had been recognized by Mexico. But he opposed coming to the aid of Texas against armed attacks from Mexico and taking it into the Union. The Tyler administration, with John C. Calhoun now

---

*The term was first used by John L. O'Sullivan, in an editorial in the *United States Magazine and Democratic Review,* to which Bryant had contributed poetry and prose, July-Aug., 1845. O'Sullivan used the term again in editorials in the New York *Morning News,* which he established with Samuel J. Tilden, on Aug. 21, 1844, as a Democratic organ.

serving as secretary of state, moved steadily toward adopting a treaty of annexation, and Bryant, on March 22, 1844, warned that the admission of Texas would increase dissension between the North and the South, keeping alive "a war more formidable than any to which we are exposed from Great Britain or any other foreign power." He followed this in April with a series of six articles, written by "Veto," Theodore Sedgwick, Jr., in which all aspects of the question were explored. The central overriding issue, according to Sedgwick, was simply this: should Texas, equal to one-sixth of the present United States, be added as a slave-holding territory from which five or six states could be formed?

In the meantime, Bryant acted as chairman of a committee of antiannexationists in calling a meeting on April 24 at the Broadway Tabernacle to oppose the treaty. The gathering was not a quiet one and the *Evening Post* the next day condemned outrages committed by rioters trying to break it up. On April 27 Bryant devoted the whole of the front page and five columns on page four to the draft of the treaty with Texas and the government's correspondence, none of which had been made public. This unauthorized printing resulted in the appointment on April 30 of a Senate committee to investigate how the paper obtained the material, and Bryant's business partner, William G. Boggs, was subpoenaed as publisher to appear before it. On May 1 Bryant demurely explained that he had found on his desk a copy of the treaty and had not known its source. He had hesitated about publication "under an apprehension that it might have been improperly procured against the resolution of secrecy imposed by the Senate," but on hearing that copies were circulating in Washington and New York had put it in type and printed it. Then, becoming serious, he referred to Secretary of State Abel P. Upshur's letters in the past year on the subject of annexation, "alternately coaxing and threatening Texas," and other "curiosities" in the correspondence. "After reading this paper," Bryant declared, "the people of the United States will not hesitate in making up their minds in respect to the infamy of the project."

On May 6 the paper's Washington correspondent reported that the Senate investigation had been completed and that the owners would "not be subjected to the punishment of hanging and quartering, which was the mildest proposal for them before the examination took place." Bryant could treat the Senate investigation with amusement, but when under terms of the treaty, which had been signed by Tyler though not ratified by the Senate, the President on May 16 ordered troops to the Mexican border and a naval expedition to Vera Cruz to protect Texas from attack he became serious: the actions amounted to a declaration of war.

While Bryant was agitating over the Texas question, he did not ignore other editorial campaigns. A measure introduced in Congress in February of 1843 to forbid private express companies to carry newspapers caused him to renew his attacks on monopoly. He pointed out that the two private expresses between Boston and New York were faster than the United States mail. The arrest next year of the carriers of one company brought the protest that such power exercised by the government was odious. In 1844, Bryant wrote a series of editorials showing how the Black Tariff of 1842 was increasing the cost of products. His fight against the United States Bank was recalled when Nicholas Biddle died on February 27, 1844, and eulogies were carried in a number of papers. Bryant wrote that he would have been pleased to remain silent about Biddle's death but the "praise of goodness bestowed upon bad men" was an "offence to morals" and should not be allowed to pass unquestioned. Then, in one of the most embittered statements against a man that Bryant ever wrote, he declared of Biddle: "After bringing thousands to utter poverty, by the frauds and extravagances of his bank, he passed the close of his life in elegant leisure at his country seat on the Delaware. If he had met with his deserts, he would have passed it in the penitentiary."*

III

Over the years Bryant had played the gadfly in urging municipal improvements and in attacking corruption and mismanagement in the city government. In the two decades he had lived in New York, the city had grown from about 200,000 population to almost 500,000. As was to be expected during such a rapid increase in the number of people occupying Manhattan Island, life became more difficult. *Evening Post* editorials attacked the "insufferable" filth of the streets, and urged that they be swept daily by machinery; the reason why they were not cleaned with horse-drawn brooms was that hand-brooms gave jobs to gangs whose votes the politicians needed at election time. The city's numerous fires, holocausts almost, with their huge destruction of property and life, caused Bryant to

---

*The diarist Philip Hone, quoting this sentence from the *Evening Post*, declared of Bryant: "This is the first instance I have known of the vampire of party spirit seizing the lifeless body of its victim before its interment, and exhibiting its bloody claws to the view of mourning relations and sympathizing friends. How such a blackhearted misanthrope as Bryant should possess an imagination teeming with beautiful poetical images astonishes me; one would as soon expect drops of honey from the fangs of a rattlesnake." *The Diary of Philip Hone*, II, 686–7.

inveigh against the volunteer fire-fighting system and to urge a paid force. The volunteer companies were made up of young men little better than "blackguards" who gathered nightly at the engine-houses to engage in drinking, ribaldry, and fighting. They levied blackmail against merchants to obtain money for their ruffianly sports, they stole valuables dragged out of burning buildings, and their rivalry with other companies led to bloody street affrays. Because of the inadequacies of law enforcement, people were helpless victims of thieves, robbers, and murderers. The city was protected by a body of watchmen, and Bryant urged its replacement by a uniformed police force. "Our city swarms with daring and ingenious rogues . . . who find no difficulty in exercising their vocation here with perfect impunity," Bryant declared.

Reforms in fire and police protection, improvements in sanitation, and paving of streets and sidewalks that Bryant sought would no doubt have come about in the course of time, though he was often attacked for urging them. Godwin recalled that the *Evening Post*'s advocacy of a uniformed police force, as had been established by Sir Robert Peel in London with success, was ridiculed. Opponents said it was but following "the Chinese custom of hunting criminals with a brass band," the reference being to the rattle that watchmen in China carried to scare away evildoers. A uniform worn by a policeman would perform the same function—the malefactor could see him coming and make off.[9] But another improvement sought by Bryant probably might not ever have been realized had he not urged it in the paper. It was that, before all the land in the growing metropolis be lost to business and industry, an area be set aside for a large uptown park. Bryant's proposal, advanced in an editorial on July 3, 1844, was the first recognition of the need for such a retreat where people could escape from crowded and noisy streets and find relief among trees and meadows and brooklets of a sylvan region. Godwin recalled: "It seems astonishing at this day that such a proposition met not only with criticism, but with the bitter opposition of people who considered a park such as Mr. Bryant proposed a reckless and wicked waste of public money."

Bryant in his walks about the city must have frequently had the idea of setting aside an area for a park, but the inspiration for the July 3 editorial apparently was an incident involving one of the several small parks in the city. Opposed to any government interference with the private lives of people, he was angered that the city was arresting sellers of peanuts and apples at the parks on Sundays. In an editorial titled "Blue Law Legislation" he wrote that the "spirit which in ancient Connecticut forbade the making of beer on Saturday, lest it should work on the Sabbath, seems to be fast reviving in this city." Not only was the city stopping people from biting into an apple or eating a peanut on Sundays, it had also "discovered it is wicked to allow water to run on Sundays, and will soon be seized with scruples as to the propriety of sunshine." His reference was to the stopping of the fountain in Union Park and the halting of the business of an old woman who rented chairs to visitors. "Both acts must be regarded as outrages upon common sense, no less than the comforts of our citizens," Bryant perorated.

This short editorial was followed by a longer one titled "A New Public Park." Bryant described an area on the road to Harlem, between Sixty-eighth Street on the south and Seventy-seventh Street on the north and extending from Third Avenue to the East River which he said constituted "a tract of beautiful woodland, comprising sixty or seventy acres, thickly covered with old trees, intermingled with a variety of shrubs." He continued:

> The surface is varied in a very striking and picturesque manner, with craggy eminences, and hollows, and a little stream runs through the midst. The swift tides of the East River sweep its rocky shores, and the fresh breeze of the bay comes in, on every warm summer afternoon, over the restless waters. The trees are of almost every species that grows in our woods—the different varieties of ash, the birch, the beech, the linden, the mulberry, the tulip tree, and others; the azalea, the kalmia, and other flowering shrubs are in bloom here in their season, and the ground in spring is gay with flowers. There never was a finer situation for the public garden of a great city. . . . If any of our brethren of the public press should see fit to support this project, we are ready to resign in their favor any claim to the credit of originally suggesting it.

Bryant understated the size of the tract—it was about one hundred and sixty acres—but he had conceived the idea of the park and given it to the public; and though a different site was eventually chosen for the city's great Central Park his suggestion was sufficient for others to take up the project.*10

The stream of Bryant's poetry in these political years had been reduced to a trickle, but it still flowed. Since the publication of *The Fountain* in

*Allan Nevins credits Bryant with being the first to propose the idea for the park: "In Edward H. Hall's scholarly history of Central Park . . . the plan is said to have originated with Andrew J. Downing, editor of the monthly *Horticulturist,* in a letter contributed to that magazine in 1849. Charles H. Haswell, in his *Reminiscences of an Octogenarian,* also gives Downing the credit. . . . But the real originator was the poet-editor." *The Evening Post,* p. 193.

1842, he had written about a dozen poems. In that year Rufus Griswold had sought to obtain his work exclusively for *Graham's Magazine* by his liberal payment of fifty dollars a poem and thought he had done so. In December, 1843, however, George A. Graham, the publisher, was chagrined to see a poem by Bryant in *Godey's Lady's Book* for January, 1844. Though Griswold had left *Graham's,* the publisher sought his aid in bagging Bryant.[11] Griswold wrote Bryant that Graham was surprised to see one of his poems in such a magazine as *Godey's.* "Mr. Godey's system of giving one number each year for *men,*" Griswold wrote, "and eleven numbers for milliners, was supposed to be so well understood as to prevent the better class of writers from furnishing him articles." Griswold held out the lure to Bryant that Graham had been waiting "with his fingers upon his purse strings" ready to pay the "highest price" for a poem. So persistent was Griswold that Bryant, in a letter of May 12, 1844, wrote that he had no objection to entering into an agreement to contribute exclusively to *Graham's.* Such an arrangement might furnish not only an answer to solicitations from other magazines but he could derive satisfaction from appearing in such good company as *Graham's* offered.*

At the same time, Bryant was prevailed upon by Evert A. Duyckinck to make a small collection of his work to inaugurate a series to be called the Home Library. Later to become a leading critic and editor, Duyckinck was known to Bryant as editor of the short-lived but brilliant *Arcturus, a Journal of Books and Opinions,* which he had established in 1840. Bryant's new collection of twenty-five pages bound in yellow paper covers appeared in 1844 with the title *The White Footed Deer.* The title poem was suggested by the account in John Davidson Godman's *American Natural History* of specimens of a deer collected in one of Stephen Harriman Long's western expeditions having a white band just above the hoofs.[12] From this Bryant created a story of such a deer, reverenced a century ago by the Indians, according to legend, that had become the pet of a "cottage dame." On one occasion her son, failing to get any game on a hunting trip, shot the pet deer. The next night avenging Indians, long gone from the area, returned, burned the cottage, and killed its occupants. The poem has little interest other than as another example of Bryant's effort to find literary material in the past of the Indian, and the others in the volume with the exception of the fragment "Noon" and "Hymn of the Sea,"

---

*The agreement with *Graham's* continued for about ten years, but since Bryant's output was small the magazine had the benefit of original publication of only nine or ten of his poems, about one a year.

written in 1842 while Bryant was visiting Dana at Cape Ann, likewise cannot be considered among his major works.

IV

Though Bryant had escaped for a time the pressures of daily journalism in his trips to the South and New England, he had inevitably to turn his attention again to politics. The Texas question was clearly the most important issue in the forthcoming election campaign of 1844, and it created difficulties for Bryant and the Democrats. His old friend Van Buren, though retired to his country place since his defeat in 1840, had not given up political ambitions, and as the heir of Jackson, was the favorite for the Democratic nomination. But the southern wing was aware of his opposition to annexation and had obtained from the old general a letter favoring the policy, which had been published in March to force Van Buren's hand. Van Buren realized, of course, that he would endanger his strong New York support if he came out for acquisition of Texas. Henry Clay's bid for the Whig nomination created no similar problem. Faithful chiefly to his own ambitions, he could oppose annexation with the expectation of getting the Whig vote in the North and need not worry about it in the South since it did not amount to much there anyway. Both, ignoring the underlying issue of slavery, made public letters in April opposing annexation on the ground that it would result in war. Tyler, playing both ends against the middle since becoming President, was a man without a party except for about 150,000 Democrats whose support he had obtained through patronage.

As was expected, Clay, with Theodore Frelinghuysen of New Jersey as his running mate, received the Whig nomination at Baltimore on May 1. Following the precedent of the Harrison campaign four years before, the Whig platform avoided issues, being silent about the Texas and national bank questions. But things were different on May 27 when both the regular Democrats and the Tyler Democrats gathered at Baltimore. There was no question that Tyler's followers would enter him in the race, and the *Evening Post* disposed of his nomination in an editorial on May 29 by calling it a "farce" in which the players performed their "parts with admirable congruity." Realizing that revival of the two-thirds rule being urged at the convention would hurt Van Buren, Bryant wrote against it. He was correct, of course, when Van Buren received 146 votes on the first ballot to 83 for Lewis Cass and 24 for Richard M. Johnson. After that Van Buren's vote dwindled until, none of the candidates winning a two-thirds majority, the convention decided on the ninth ballot to nominate a political unknown who in the last two elections in Tennessee had lost his race for governor—James K. Polk, an "also-ran" in his own state as well as the first "dark horse" to head a presidential ticket.

The nomination of Polk and George M. Dallas of Pennsylvania created a dilemma for Bryant. In his first editorial on the convention, he recognized that Polk was a "man of handsome talents, of fair and manly character, and right views in regard to the questions on which the two parties of the nation are divided," but he was "deplorably" wrong on the Texas question. Bryant could not accept the convention resolution which had declared for annexation "at the earliest practicable moment," but equally he could not accept the certainty that, with a Clay victory, the national bank would be reestablished, the 1842 tariff "with all its oppressions and abominations" would be continued, and the proceeds of the public lands would be distributed among the states and "scrambled for by speculators and jobbers." He was placed in the position—and the Whig papers were quick to point it out—of supporting "the Texas candidate," Polk, while hanging back on annexation itself. He sought to resolve the dilemma of northern Democrats in an editorial on July 6 titled "How Shall I Vote?" His answer was that annexation was not a certainty and that immediate annexation was not possible. Northern Democrats, therefore, should stay with the party and then later work out differences by compromise among themselves. This was not very realistic, for, as Bryant himself pointed out on May 31, compromise had been sought at Baltimore but it was a compromise in which the concession was all on one side—that of the southern delegates, who were ready to support any man who might be named— "the thinnest and feeblest shadow of a candidate"—provided he agreed with them on the slavery question.

But Bryant was not willing to let the matter end with an editorial. He joined six other Democrats in writing a confidential letter to party members they thought to be of like mind for backing Polk but rejecting the party plank on Texas and "supporting at the next elections the nomination for Congress of such persons as concur in these opinions." The letter declared that Van Buren had been defeated for the nomination on an issue which had no relation to the principles of the party and that the convention had gone beyond the authority delegated to its members in adopting the resolution since before their selection they had not been instructed on this issue. "In this position what was the party of the north to do?" the letter asked. "Was it to reject the nominations and abandon the contest, or should it support the nominations, rejecting the untenable doctrine interpolated at the convention, and taking care that their support should be accompanied with such expression of their opinions, as to prevent its being misinterpreted?'' The second alternative, the letter declared, was the preferred one.

Such a letter could not be kept secret and, somewhat to Bryant's dismay, was published in Levi D. Slamm's *Plebeian* on July 24 with a statement that the signers should be expelled from the party unless they declared themselves in favor of annexation. Bryant replied that the *Evening Post* for a number of years had opposed annexation and its stand had not been called into question as failing to conform to party principles. "The letter contains only the expression of opinions which are frequently repeated in the *Evening Post* and will be repeated hereafter," Bryant wrote; "but we claim a right to correspond privately on political subjects, when we choose, and if our letters are pilfered and published, we merely ask the community to mark those who are concerned in the act, as spies and thieves." Bryant's editorial closed, somewhat inconsistently: "With regard to the personal abuse with which we are assailed in the *Plebeian,* we give the same answer which we always return to such attacks, profound silence."

Continuing the fight against annexation, Bryant on August 19 gave prominent display to a circular to Democratic voters prepared as a result of the committee's sounding out opinion on supporting Polk but rejecting the annexationist plank. Editorially he said that the joint letter had been "judicious and well-timed" and that the committee had "from all quarters . . . received assurances of concurrence in their position." The effect of this circular, if it had much of an effect, was to widen the rift between the reform and conservative segments of the Democratic party in New York. The reformers were led by Van Buren and Silas Wright, who had resigned from the United States Senate to run for governor. They were known as "Barnburners" after the Dutch farmer who burned his barn in order to destroy the rats. The conservatives were called Hunkers, from the Dutch word "hunkerer," meaning a self-seeking person, and in reference to politics designating a person who "hunkered," i.e., "hungered" after office.* The split was to widen in the next three years. Bryant's refusal to bolt the Democratic party on the annexation issue was wise political strategy, for if Polk had lost in New York its thirty-two electoral votes

---

*Bryant gave his own explanation of the origin of "Hunker" in a humorous editorial on Oct. 7, 1847. It was derived, he said, from "Henker," which was German for "hangman." Bryant thought the appellation was appropriate, saying that the Hunkers, if given enough rope, would hang themselves.

would have gone to Clay and given him the presidency. The circular had no apparent effect in restraining those who favored annexation. President Tyler, recommending to Congress in December a joint resolution approving annexation, gave as one of his arguments the vote in the presidential election which demonstrated that "a controlling majority of the states have declared in favor of immediate annexation."

Although Bryant saw that annexation was almost inevitable, he continued to fight it up to March 1, 1845, when Congress adopted President Tyler's proposal that the treaty be accepted. His obstinacy provoked some of his best friends, including Samuel J. Tilden and John L. O'Sullivan, one of the founders of the *United States Magazine and Democratic Review*. Tilden and O'Sullivan had established a morning Democratic paper, the *News*, in New York City on August 21, 1844, and its appearance had drawn from Bryant the praise that the Democracy should be congratulated "upon the possession of a morning journal upon whose statements they will be able to rely, and whose discussions of current topics will be manly, dignified, and honest." On January 18, 1845, Bryant replied to an attack in the *News* calling him a "fanatic" for his opposition to annexation. "The term 'fanatic' among friends, is hardly parliamentary," he wrote, "and we hope that our contemporary used it only in a Pickwickian sense."

Early in 1844 Bryant entered happily into his project of getting into shape the house at Hempstead Harbor for occupation by moving day on May 1. Replying on January 16 to an invitation from Dana to visit him at Cape Ann, Bryant wrote: "It is true that I have house and lands on Long Island—a little place in a most healthy neighborhood, just upon the sea water—a long inlet of the Sound, overlooked by woods and hills—and near a village skirting several clear sheets of fresh water fed by abundant springs which gush from the earth at the head of the valley." If Dana would visit him there, he would have "fruits of all kinds in their seasons" and "sea-bathing, if you like it." He himself had found sea-bathing beneficial to his health the previous summer.[13] On March 30 Bryant wrote Dana that the family was in the process of moving. His plan was to spend three days a week at Hempstead Harbor and the others in New York, probably taking rooms in Brooklyn. "The winter," he said, "we shall pass in town, trusting to chance to get lodgings when the cold weather comes."[14]

After the move, living for half the week away from home, Bryant maintained communication with Frances by short notes, hundreds of which are found among his papers. They contain homely details about his day-to-day existence. On August 6, 1844, for example, he beseeched his wife: "Will you be so good as to see where all my *new socks* have gone to? I found but one in my drawyer this morning." And again, on September 9: "I suppose you have found out before this time that I gave you no money on Monday morning to pay Mr. Seek. Another time you must seize me and rob me."[15] These notes at first were addressed to Springbank, Hempstead Harbor, but before long the village was given the name Roslyn. Walt Whitman recalled that the place when Bryant moved there was known also as Mosquito Cove, but "when the wealthy New Yorkers came along there with their handsome stately villas, Mosquito Cove had a plain rude sound, which they changed to Roslyn."[16] The name was changed by Bryant himself, according to another account, because the British evacuating the island in 1781 had marched away to the tune of "Roslyn Castle."[17] Bryant chose the euphonious name Cedarmere for his own estate.

18

A SECOND VOYAGE TO EUROPE

LATE IN FEBRUARY OF 1845, JUST BEFORE THE CHANGE OF administrations on March 4, Congress by the unusual method of a joint resolution acceded to President Tyler's request that the treaty for annexation of Texas be approved. Since Bryant's near-bolt from the Democratic party in the election had been his opposition to the convention plank urging annexation at the earliest practicable period, he was left with no quarrel with his party. His editorials on Polk's inauguration were as favorable toward the new administration as any partisan could ask. He expressed his relief that the Tyler administration, corrupted as he thought by the use of government patronage, was at an end: "We think we can already perceive somewhat of a purification of the political atmosphere; we are beginning already to respire a better air." He described Polk's inaugural address as being marked by "a tone of modesty, understanding and dignity" and praised his promise of strict construction of the Constitution. The editorial ended: "Of the impartiality, the fairness of intention, and the magnanimous elevation above narrow party views, with which Mr. Polk . . . engages to administer the affairs of the nation, we entertain no distrust, and we shall rejoice to see the principles he so frankly avows, made the rule of executive practice."

Bryant made it a practice to be at the helm of the *Evening Post* during a national election. Once the votes were counted, he was willing to leave its guidance to other hands. He now began to arrange for a suddenly conceived visit to Europe of five or six months. Such a trip had seemed impossible in September, when he wrote Ferdinand E. Field, the Englishman who had hiked with him years before from West Point to New York, that he would have been delighted to have accompanied him on his walking tours in Britain. "But these are dreams," Bryant wrote in self-pity; "the probability is that I shall never visit England nor you come to New York. I shall go on, a mere journalist until I am worn out. . . ."[1] Not long afterward, however, one of the members of the Sketch Club, the merchant and art patron Charles M. Leupp, told Bryant that he was planning a trip to England and invited his companionship. Bryant had no feeling of guilt about neglecting his editorial duties for such a trip, but he did about leaving his family. He expressed these qualms in a letter to his old friend Charles Sedgwick, from whom, a few days before sailing, he received a letter encouraging the project. Sedgwick admitted that it was "a hard thing for a domestic man to be separated from his wife and children" yet he held "it to be impossible for a man to get rid of care by going abroad with his family."[2]

Bryant now had no worries about the financial situation on the *Evening Post*. Advertising had been increasing and to provide more space for it he had reduced the type size in the news columns. But still the advertising grew, and on March 19, 1844, he had enlarged the paper to nine columns, making it the equal, he boasted, of the largest in the city. All was well with the business operations, but in going abroad Bryant was faced with the problem* of what to do about the editorial management, since Parke Godwin had left the paper after his marriage to Fanny. Converted to the Associative Movement based on the theories of Charles Fourier and expounded in the United States by Albert Brisbane, he had been attempting to develop journalistic projects of his own to promote the new doctrine.** Bryant was out of sympathy with the movement, considering ridiculous

---

*Bryant also had a financial problem, revealed in a letter to George R. Graham, publisher of *Graham's Magazine,* on Feb. 26, 1845: "Poets as you know are always in want of money, and I, one of the tribe, am at this moment particularly so, being about to make a journey of some length and duration. You have published two poems of mine in your magazine, and also two of my brother's. For the four the amount which I was to receive is a hundred and twenty dollars. If you will be so kind as to send me the $120 within the next fortnight I shall be much obliged." Bryant-Godwin Collection.

**The *Evening Post* on April 2, 1844, carried a notice of a pamphlet by Godwin, *A Popular View of the Doctrines of Charles Fourier.* The brief comment was: "It is a full, although concise exhibition of the subject on which it treats; all the doctrines of Fourier, good or bad, as the reader may think them, being clearly stated."

the philosophy of voluntarism by which the cooperative communities, or phalanges, hoped to reform society, and the relations between the two men were cool.

Godwin had made his first attempt to establish an Associationist paper with the *Pathfinder* in 1843. It was a short-lived publication, although he had obtained a circulation of five hundred "paying subscribers" in three months, as he wrote Charles A. Dana. Godwin's efforts to further reform through a paper and his dislike for his father-in-law are revealed in a series of about forty letters written Dana between 1844 and 1846.[3] Dana was a member of the Brook Farm experiment founded by George Ripley. It had attracted the interest of such literary people as Emerson, Hawthorne, and Margaret Fuller, and it was enthusiastically praised by Greeley in the *Tribune.* Dana was the editor of the Brook Farm paper, the *Harbinger,* to which Godwin was a contributor, and much of their correspondence was devoted to plans for Dana to come to New York and with Godwin get out an Associationist daily. In April of 1845 Godwin was named chairman of the executive committee appointed at a general convention of the Associative Movement to propagate its ideas through lectures and tracts. While busy with the movement, Godwin was also a leader in starting a new party, the National Reformers, composed largely of working men, and he was one of the party's nominees for Congress in the election of 1844.[4]

After the collapse of the *Pathfinder,* Godwin suffered a spell of deep depression. He wrote Dana on May 17, 1844, that he envied him at Brook Farm. "My own life here is like the snail's," he said, "when many grains of sand come between it and its shell; it is agony that we even *crawl.*" His spirits were not much changed in the spring of 1845, when he wrote that he was "occupied every minute, making money to get rid of my chains." Needing to get out of doors and engage in physical exercise—he had been influenced enough by the somewhat hypochondriac Bryant to fret about his health—he had obtained through friends a job as a weigher of customs, hoping also to rid himself of his "money embarrassments in a short time." He was attracted by the idea of going to Brook Farm, where he could "escape worldly care, discipline the body and think out the Truth." His dislike of his father-in-law was revealed in a letter on August 1 in connection with a projected article for the *Harbinger* on the newspaper press. Godwin considered Greeley the best editor in the country, "the freest, boldest, and most industrious, consistent, vigorous" though he also had the faults of being "cunning" and displaying "vulgarism in the shape of mean dirty-mouthed prejudices." Bryant was "the most accomplished editor, and by odds the most varied and beautiful writer—but his heart is not in it, he wants human every day sympathies, and is a little malignant." And so the letters continued for another year and a half while the two young reformers tried to realize their dream of a daily newspaper devoted to the Associationist cause of a society living in "harmonious cooperation" and guaranteeing "perfect Justice to every man, woman and child, of general abundance and universal education, and the extension of the highest social privileges and advantages to all."[5]

Not being able now to leave the paper in Godwin's hands, as he had done before, Bryant solved the problem of his absence abroad by engaging Charles E. Anderson, the brother of his friend and former associate on the *New-York Review and Atheneum*, Henry J. Anderson, to take over the editorial management with complete authority to determine policy, reaching such an agreement—or so he thought—with William G. Boggs, the publisher and head of the business office, and Timothy Howe, who had become a part owner in 1844 and supervised the printing department. William J. Tenney, who had filled in for Bryant when he made his tour of the South in 1843, would continue on the staff as Anderson's assistant. With these matters taken care of Bryant embarked on the packet ship *Liverpool* on April 22 for England.

II

After leaving New York harbor, the *Liverpool* was delayed for several days off Sandy Hook awaiting a favorable wind. Bryant spent the time in reading, talking with other passengers, and playing shuffleboard on deck. Because of his susceptibility to seasickness, the voyage was an unpleasant one. "I cannot express to you with what intensity I wished myself on shore again in the early part of the voyage," Bryant wrote Frances from the Adelphi Hotel at Liverpool on May 26 after a crossing of twenty-eight days from Sandy Hook. "To leave so many objects of interest to purchase five or six months of fatigue at the expense of a month of misery, which besides for all profitable purposes was almost a blank, seemed to me little short of madness. I do not view it quite in that light now, but I think of you constantly and pray that this wandering of mine which shall be the last I take without you, may yet end happily for us both."[6] He wrote Dana that he beguiled "the qualms of sea sickness" as he lay in his berth by thinking about improvements for his home at Roslyn "such as planting a fruit tree here and a shade tree there and clearing away the growth of shrubs about some fine young pear trees that had sprung up in a corner of my field."[7]

Little of this tribulation of travel was reflected in Bryant's first letter to the *Evening Post* describing his journey. The *Liverpool* was "one of the strongest, safest, and steadiest of the packet-ships" and she "slid along over a placid sea, before the gentlest zephyrs that ever swept the ocean."[8] Nevertheless, even for his larger public than his family and friends, Bryant rejoiced when the Irish coast came into view "like a faint cloud upon the horizon" and later, after "beating about for several days in . . . the Chops of the Channel" he saw the mountains of Wales and their reflection in the sea as if on a dull mirror so realistically that he was ready to take out his "pocket-handkerchief to wipe the dust and smoke from its surface."

Now recognized as America's foremost poet, his work being familiar to many British readers through the 1832 edition sponsored by Irving and a later edition that included his newer compositions, Bryant was received almost as a literary lion on this, his first real visit to England. In a month and a half in the British Isles during which he saw most of the major tourist attractions in England, Scotland, and a part of Ireland, Bryant met some of the leading literary figures in London, Cambridge, Oxford, Edinburgh, and Dublin. Between visits with poets, critics, and historians, Bryant inspected factories and mills, studied governmental institutions, and investigated economic and social problems. Since this was an art tour, he took in the exhibition galleries and visited with American painters and sculptors who had gone abroad for instruction and inspiration.

At Liverpool Bryant called upon the Rev. James Martineau, a young Unitarian clergyman, and they talked of this religious movement as it was expounded by its leaders in the United States and England. Bryant was told that Liverpool was more like an American than an English city: it was "new, bustling, and prosperous." The streets crowded with huge drays carrying goods, the docks where ships from all parts of the globe were tied up, the shops which had "for the most part a gay and showy appearance" convinced him of the truth of the observation. Interested in establishing a public park in New York, Bryant visited the Zoological Gardens and Prince's Park, then in the process of construction. His preoccupation with death led him to visit St. James's Cemetery, which, situated in the midst of the populous city, he found to be one of "the most remarkable places in Liverpool." While there, he attended a funeral service in the chapel, so badly conducted, he thought, that it constituted profanation of the beautiful ceremony. Having in mind the development of his estate Cedar-mere, Bryant availed himself of the opportunity to look over some of the fine country homes. At one he admired the number of shrubs in full flower, "rhododendrons of various species, flushed with bloom," azaleas of different hues, one species of which he recognized as American, and many others.

On a side-trip Bryant visited the walled town of Chester, but even here he found that no ancient monument—the town's walls were said to have been erected as early as the time of William the Conqueror—was allowed to stand in the way of progress: workmen at one corner were "tumbling down the stones and digging up the foundation to let in a railway." Leaving Liverpool for a tour of Derbyshire, Bryant on May 30 went to the industrial city of Manchester, where, among other places, he visited a huge textile plant. In a three-day tour of the countryside, he traveled over the mountainous area called the Peak, the scene of Sir Walter Scott's novel about the ancient family of the Peverils, and he wondered if a ruined castle he came upon might not be the one mentioned in the book. On this trip Bryant heard his first English skylark. "The little bird, so frequently named in English poetry," he wrote, "rose singing from the grass almost perpendicularly, until nearly lost to the sight in the clouds, floated away, first in one direction, then in another, descended towards the earth, arose again, pouring forth a perpetual, uninterrupted stream of melody, until at length, after the space of somewhat more than a quarter of an hour, he reached the ground, and closed his flight and his song together." At Derby, Bryant was eager to see the Arboretum, a gift to the town by Josiah Strutt. He found the eleven acres planted with every kind of tree and shrub which grew in this northern English climate. "Shall we never see an example of the like munificence in New York?" he ended his letter to the *Evening Post.*

Going to London about June 1, Bryant was called upon a day or two after his arrival by the United States minister, Edward Everett, who had been among those present when Bryant delivered his Phi Beta Kappa poem, "The Ages," at Cambridge in 1822. Not friendly to Bryant's poetry as editor of the *North American Review,* Everett, now welcoming one of his country's most distinguished literary figures, invited him to a breakfast to meet some of London's men of letters. At this then popular version of the levee in England, Bryant met the poet Samuel Rogers, who had greeted favorably the first British edition of his poems; the Irish poet noted for the sweetness and music of his verse, Thomas Moore; R. Monckton Milnes, a member of Parliament and also a poet and critic; and John Kenyon, the poet and philanthropist. It was the first of a series of breakfasts at which Bryant was a guest, for Rogers, Kenyon, and Milnes, as was

Henry Crabb Robinson whom he met shortly afterward, were rivals in collecting interesting people for their morning repasts where conversations were more important than comestibles. Bryant did not mention these social gatherings in his *Evening Post* letters, recording only his brief impressions in a pocket diary in which he noted his comings and goings. "Rogers," Bryant wrote, "was very kind; he took me to his house and to my lodging, talked of poetry, etc., and gave me a general invitation to his breakfasts." Rogers, whose poetic talent was slight but whose charm was great, had during his life a reputation scarcely warranted by his verse. His home in St. James's Street, Westminster, with its fine collections of pictures, books, and antiquities, was famous and this "Nestor of living poets" had no difficulty in assembling distinguished guests. He knew everybody —Coleridge, Wordsworth, Southey, Tennyson, Hallam, Lamb, Thackeray, Dickens—as did Milnes, Kenyon, and Robinson, and Bryant was regaled with talk about these writers whose works had been long known to him.

In a letter to the *Evening Post,* Bryant wrote that his readers should not expect him to give them what they could find in guidebooks, but his diary showed that he took in all the sights—Westminster Abbey and Westminster Hall, the new houses of Parliament, the British Museum, Windsor Castle, Hampton Court, the National Gallery, and the art exhibitions. It was the last that interested him most, and New York did not suffer in comparison. He wrote at length of the statue, "The Greek Slave," by the American sculptor Hiram Powers, a work which when exhibited in the United States so shocked the prudish that separate viewings were held for men and women. "The statue," Bryant wrote, "represents a Greek girl exposed naked for sale in the slave-market. Her hands are fettered, the drapery of her nation lies at her feet, and she is shrinking from the public gaze. I looked at it with surprise and delight; I was dazzled with the soft fullness of the outlines, the grace of the attitude, the noble, yet sad expression of the countenance, and the exquisite perfection of the workmanship." It had made Powers's reputation in England, and the owner had been offered two thousand pounds sterling for it. The Royal Academy show, Bryant found, had "nothing in it to astonish one who has visited the exhibitions of our Academy of the Arts of Design, except that some of the worst pictures were hung in the most conspicuous places." The latest pictures of Joseph Turner, "a great artist and a man of genius," did not please Bryant: "they were mere blotches of white paint, with streaks of yellow and red, and without any intelligible design"; and Benjamin R. Haydon had "spoiled several yards of good canvas with a most hideous picture of Uriel and Satan." On the whole the exhibit was uninteresting, for British artists conformed to a general model in style and coloring that allowed no freedom for the individual "to attain excellence in the way for which he is best fitted." Bryant was somewhat put out that several pictures by Americans listed in the catalog were "all hung so high as to be out of sight."

In Bryant's opinion, the art of oratory did not reach a high level in Parliament, at least on the days he visited the House of Lords and the House of Commons. His diary of June 16 gave his impression of a debate in the House of Lords on making a grant of money to a Roman Catholic college in Maynooth, Ireland, strongly opposed by the English and Scotch Protestants:

> Lord Campbell was making a speech in favor of the Maynooth grant—feeble and affected. Bishop of Landaff spoke on the other side—plain and pretty well. Lord Ellenborough spoke afterward in a sounding oratorical manner. Lord Shrewsbury, a Catholic, made a set speech in favor of the bill, which he sung like a Baptist preacher. The Duke of Manchester said a few words wretchedly enough. The Duke of Newcastle spoke against the bill—a deplorable stammerer. Wellington defended the bill; articulation imperfect, like that of a drunken man; hesitation and stammering; but he spoke pithily and to the point, and was listened to with the deepest attention.

The speakers in the House of Commons, which Bryant visited on June 23, were similarly unimpressive. The manner of Lord John Russell was "not good"; Lord Morne "spoke badly"; and John O'Connell "very badly." Bryant was better pleased by the speaking at an Anti-Cornlaw League meeting at Covent Garden. Richard Cobden, who had "a certain New England sharpness and shrewdness," presented such a clear argument with such feeling that his speech was "uncommonly impressive," and William S. Fox, the leading orator of the league, was "one of the most fluent and ingenious speakers" Bryant had ever heard. Fox alluded to Bryant's presence in the audience and quoted his "Hymn to the City," a reading that received enthusiastic applause in the crowded theater.

Writing to the *Evening Post* on June 24, Bryant devoted most of his letter to topics touched upon in editorial campaigns he was carrying on. London's parks were so extensive, he wrote, that their size could not be comprehended until a person "tried to walk over them." He described his visits to them—St. James's Park, Hyde Park, Kensington Gardens, Regent's Park, and Primrose Hill—around whose "immense inclosures presses the densest population of the civilized world." He exhorted New

Yorkers to follow London's example before it was too late, to set aside land "for a range of parks and public gardens along the central part of the island . . . to remain perpetually for the refreshment and recreation of the citizens."

London also did a better job than New York of keeping the streets clean, and Bryant described a horse-drawn machine which consisted of brushes turning over a cylinder that swept the dust of the streets into a box, a machine so efficient that the pavement was left "almost as clean as a drawing room." Bryant, who had urged reform of the New York police department, pointed to London as a model. So efficient were the policemen that burglaries were almost unheard of and the shutters of windows on the ground level of houses were unclosed during the night. "The windows of the parlor next to my sleeping-room open upon a rather low balcony over the street door," Bryant wrote, "and they are unprovided with any fastenings, which in New York we should think a great piece of negligence."

The day after Bryant's visit to the House of Commons he went to Cambridge to attend a meeting of the British Association. He visited Peterhouse, heard a service at the chapel of King's College, was a guest of honor at a luncheon at Trinity College, and at Christ's College was presented with a facsimile of Milton's handwriting by the vice-chancellor. That night he was entertained at a dinner, attended an evening party at the Senate House, and ended a busy day during which he had met the university's chief scholars and scientists—the historian Henry Hallam, the geologist Charles Lyell, and others—with a visit to the university's observatory where the astronomer James Challis permitted him to look at a double star through the telescope. Next day the round of visits continued, closing with a dinner at Trinity College and a meeting of the British Association in the Senate House at which the noted astronomer Sir John Herschel presided.

Bryant spent the first days of July as the guest of a brother of Ferdinand Field, Alfred Field, at Leamington in the heart of Warwickshire. By pony carriage, he visited Coventry, Oxford, the Blenheim estates, the ruins of Kenilworth, Byron's home at Newstead Abbey and his burial place at Hucknall Church, and the spot most glorified in English literature, Stratford-on-Avon. But Bryant, in his eagerness to see all that was possible, did not allow the attractions of Warwickshire to hold him long, and he started a journey to Scotland, planning to take in the Lake Country of the poets Wordsworth, Coleridge, and Southey on his way.

On his trip north he stopped at the Commercial Inn at Ambleside, near

Wordsworth's home at Rydal, on July 10. His diary briefly records his impressions of "craggy mountains, half covered with heath, green dells, and rapid brooks." In London Crabb Robinson had urged Bryant to call upon Wordsworth, and prepared the way by writing a letter of introduction. Bryant's only written account of his meeting the poet was contained in his travel diary. He drove from Ambleside to Rydal and sent in his card with Robinson's letter. "Mr. Wordsworth was in the garden, in a white broad-brimmed, low-crowned hat," Bryant wrote; "he received me very kindly; showed me over his grounds, his study, etc. Beautiful view of Windermere from his house, and of Rydal Water from part of his grounds. At six o'clock took tea with him, after having first looked at Stock Ghyll Force. He showed us the fall of the Rothay in Rydal Park, belonging to Lady Fleming. Left his house at ten o'clock in the evening." Then seventy-five years old and illiberal in his views, Wordsworth probably was not a person Bryant would find congenial despite the esteem he held for the poet of *Lyrical Ballads*. In later years Bryant often alluded in conversation to his pleasant visit with Wordsworth, but he also entertained his intimate friends "with imitations of Wordsworth's reverent manner of repeating his own verses."9

Before leaving Ambleside, Bryant called on Harriet Martineau, whom he had met several times in 1836 during her tour of the United States and whom he had found to be a person "of lively, agreeable conversation, kind and candid."10 She had visited Bryant's haunts at Great Barrington and Stockbridge as a guest of the Sedgwicks, and he was pleased to see her own chosen countryside at Waterhead a mile and a half from Ambleside and the place she had selected to build a cottage.

Bryant spent less than two weeks in Scotland, delighting most in visiting spots described by Scott and Burns, whose works served him as a Baedeker. Writing the *Evening Post* from Edinburgh on July 19, Bryant said he had been told Edinburgh would be "the finest city" he had ever seen. It was true insofar as its situation was concerned. The magnificent Firth of Forth was visible from any of the eminences of the town, and the high and massive buildings of stone quarried almost at the site of construction were impressive. But the plight of the poor was another matter. More than half the population, he was told, lived in squalid misery, "sickly-looking, dirty people," who were crowded into the wynds, or alleys, between the broad streets.

Leaving Edinburgh by boat, he sailed inland to Stirling and then went by coach to Callander in the highlands. He traversed storied Trosachs Valley by foot, for a description of which he referred his readers to the first canto of Scott's *Lady of the Lake.* From a boat on Loch Katrine, he saw the place in the Trosachs where Fitz James lost his "gallant gray," the island where Douglass concealed his daughter, the rock, covered with heath, on which Fitz James "stood and wound his bugle," and other scenes of incidents in the poem. Farther along, on the north shore where the hills had a gentler slope, there was a solitary dwelling, the birthplace, so Bryant was told, of Rob Roy. From Loch Katrine, the travelers went by foot through a craggy valley to Inversnaid, on Loch Lomond, where they boarded a steamboat that took them the whole length of the lake, and at Renton, on the way to Glasgow, Bryant saw the place where the novelist Tobias Smollett was born.

A day or so after reaching Glasgow, where he noted crowds of people with "that squalid appearance which marks extreme poverty" though the city was prosperous and growing rapidly, almost as fast as New York, Bryant made an excursion to Burns's birthplace at Alloway. Passing through Ayr on the way, Bryant recalled Burns's dialogue between the "auld brig" of Ayr and the new, the former predicting that the time would come when its rival would, too, become old and dilapidated. It was true: the new bridge had begun to give way and workmen were shoring up its arches. The river Doon, which Burns described as "bonnie," deserved the adjective, and Bryant stopped at the bridge crossed by Tam O'Shanter on the night of his adventure with the witches. He was disgusted with the monument erected to the poet here, "an ostentatious thing, with a gilt tripod on its summit." But he found some of the mementoes of Burns to be interesting, among them the Bible given him by Highland Mary. He saw bonnie lassies of whom Burns might have sung, one a barefoot beauty who came down a grassy bank among the trees with a pail and who, after washing her feet in the swift stream, filled the vessel and returned to her cottage hidden behind a hedge of wildrose and woodbine; and another at the inn who served him a dish of strawberries and clotted yellow cream. Passing through Ayr again on the return trip, Bryant fancied that he saw the sequestered spot on the banks of the river "where Burns and his Highland Mary held the meeting described in his letters, and parted to meet no more."

Leaving Glasgow on July 22 to sail on a steamer to Ireland, Bryant had one last reminder of Burns, a view of the coast of Ayr and the cliffs near the poet's birthplace. He wondered why Burns, born so near the coast, drew so little of his poetic imagery from the sea. Bryant's explanation was that, gaining his living from work in the fields, Burns's thoughts "were of those who dwelt among them, and his imagination never wandered where his feelings went not." The journey across the channel to Belfast took nine hours, and Bryant saw little of the city since he had planned to go by mail-coach the next morning down the coast to Dublin. He was chiefly impressed by the evidences of poverty along the highroad—the dirty hovels in which the people lived, even in fertile farm areas, and the swarms of beggars who gathered around the coach whenever it stopped, the "wittiest beggars in the world," however, and "the raggedest, except those of Italy." The one literary shrine in Dublin that Bryant noted was the house where Swift had been born, standing "in a narrow, dirty lane called Holy's court . . . its windows . . . broken out, and its shutters falling to pieces."

III

Two days later Bryant was back in London, where, on July 28, he wrote the *Evening Post* another letter, which he devoted chiefly to a visit at the Lunatic Asylum at Hanwell, an institution conducted along advanced lines so that the inmates were kept in order by "the law of kindness." With the letter written, Bryant was off to Paris, where he spent almost two weeks before starting a hurried tour, on August 10, of the continent. Before he returned to Paris, he traveled through Belgium and Holland, ascended the Rhine to Wiesbaden and Mannheim and then crossed over to Heidelberg, and next, after having seen Dresden, Prague and Vienna, passed over the Styrian Alps to Trieste, where he took a steamer to Venice. He went through Padua, Ferrara, and Bologna to Florence, where he had spent so much time during his first trip to Europe, and then on to Rome and Naples. Returning north, he went to Genoa, Milan, and the Alps, which he crossed to Geneva on his way back to Paris. Writing to Ferdinand E. Field from London on November 3, Bryant said: "We have made a rapid but most fortunate journey through Europe. We have had good health, good weather, and the opportunity to see almost everything we desired; we have met with no misfortunes, no accidents, and no disappointments, scarcely anything which could be called annoyances."

Bryant informed *Evening Post* readers of the work being done by American painters and sculptors who were thronging abroad. In Paris, he renewed his acquaintance with John Vanderlyn, long a resident of the city, and reported on the huge picture, "The Landing of Columbus," which the painter hoped to complete in eight or ten weeks for the rotunda of the Capitol at Washington. The grouping of the figures—the great navigator with his officers taking possession of the newly found country, crewmen scrambling about in their search for gold, and the native redmen seen among the trees in attitudes of wonder—was, in Bryant's opinion, a happy one, "the expression and action skillfully varied," and the coloring agreeable. At Antwerp Bryant noted in the churches the paintings of Flemish artists hung wherever space allowed and in particular Rubens's "The Descent from the Cross," which proved "what one might almost doubt who had only seen his pictures in the Louvre, that he was a true artist and a man of genius in the noblest sense of the term."

At Düsseldorf studying at the Royal Academy was another friend, Emanuel Leutze, then twenty-eight years old, as well as the young Boston painter, William Morris Hunt, then twenty-one, both of whose fame lay in the future.* Leutze was working on a picture of John Knox reproving Queen Mary. Bryant said it promised to be a capital work. "The stern gravity of Knox," he wrote, "the embarrassment of the Queen, and the scorn with which the French damsels of her court regard the saucy Reformer, are extremely well expressed, and tell the story impressively." Leutze accompanied Bryant to Cologne to arrange for him to view his painting, "Columbus before the Council of Salamanca." Bryant was happy to report to Americans that Leutze ranked high in Germany as a man of promise.

Revisiting Florence, Bryant found Horatio Greenough at work on another huge statuary piece, his "The Indian and the Hunter," designed for the east front of the Capitol in Washington. It portrayed an American settler rescuing a woman and her infant from an Indian, who had just raised his tomahawk to murder them; the settler had approached the Indian from behind and grasped his arms so that the man was powerless. Bryant saw it as representing "an image of the aboriginal race of America overpowered and rendered helpless by the civilized race."

Also in Florence was Hiram Powers, whose statue "The Greek Slave," Bryant had so admired in London. In Powers's Florence studio Bryant saw the original model, from which Powers's workmen were cutting two copies in marble. A new sculpture he had completed was a bust of Proserpine, a figure of "great sweetness and beauty." Bryant admired some allow me to refer to what I should have done, had I remained in charge

*Leutze had been born in Germany on May 24, 1816, and taken at an early age by his parents to Philadelphia. He later had gone to New York. His best known paintings are two huge canvases, "Westward the Star of Empire Takes Its Way" and "Washington Crossing the Delaware." Hunt, who studied under Jean François Millet, was dominated by French influences and turned the new generation of American painters toward Paris.

copies from Titian executed by another American, Henry Peters Gray, and some landscapes by G. L. Brown. He regretted that Brown, who painted nature so beautifully, chose not "to represent her as she appears in our own fresh and glorious land, instead of living in Italy and painting Italian landscapes." His chauvinism even led him to dislike an exhibition by Italian artists. Except for some landscapes that reminded him of those of Thomas Cole, he found the pictures "decidedly bad"; the landscapes were "wretched" and of the portraits some "were absolutely hideous, stiff, ill-colored, and full of grimace."

Rome, too, had its colony of American artists, most of them copying the classic sculpture of the Greeks and Romans and the paintings of the Renaissance and pondering over artistic and moral questions that were raised a few years later by Nathaniel Hawthorne in *The Marble Faun*. Of the American expatriates, Bryant liked most the sculptor Henry K. Brown. He was at work on two figures that differed from the usual run of sculpture, one a statue of Ruth gleaning in the fields of Boaz and the other of Rebecca at the well. In the studios of the English sculptors Richard James Wyatt and John Gibson, Bryant disdained the "sleek imitations of Grecian art, their learned and faultless statues, nymphs or goddesses or gods of the Greek mythology." Brown's Ruth, not inferior in perfection of form, was marked by "a deep human feeling" much more to his taste. Two painters whose work pleased him were the Americans Thomas P. Rossiter, whose illustration of the story of Naomi and her two daughters-in-law Orpah and Ruth he considered "well composed"; and Louis Lang, whose picture of a young woman being arrayed by attendants for her bridal and another of a marriage of a quite different sort, a neophyte taking the vows of a nun, he considered "entirely agreeable."

IV

While in Rome Bryant was reminded that he had responsibilities in connection with the *Evening Post* when he received a letter from his interim editor, Charles E. Anderson, complaining that the other two owners, William G. Boggs and Timothy Howe, were objecting to the editorial policy. Bryant reassured Anderson on October 1 that it had been his intention that he would have "the entire control and responsibility of its columns."[11] On the road so much in his travels, Bryant had seldom seen the paper, but he was well pleased with the copies that did reach him. "I liked its fairness and independence," he wrote Anderson. "If you will

of the paper, I must say that I should have maintained a sturdier tone on the Texas question, and that I should not have noticed certain newspapers which you thought proper occasionally to controvert or to quote." In any case, Anderson was told that the original agreement of his having control of the editorial columns still stood, though Bryant planned to set out immediately for New York and expected to be home within a few weeks.

Returning to New York about the middle of November, Bryant found the nation filled with talk of war—possible conflicts with England over the Oregon question and with Mexico over Texas. Of the prospects of the latter, Bryant was not greatly worried. President Polk had sent a commissioner, John Slidell, to Mexico with instructions going beyond the settlement of the boundary dispute that had been the cause of agitation, namely an offer of five million dollars for the purchase of New Mexico and twenty-five million for the purchase of California. Bryant believed that Mexico was too weak to provoke the United States and that therefore the issues between the two countries could be settled.

As to the Oregon matter, Bryant contended that the United States should assert her claims even at the risk of war. On November 28, he declared: "No man cancels a note of hand because he is afraid that a demand of payment may give offence to the choleric drawer. No man says to himself—'My neighbor looks hard at me; I must send him a deed to the northwest corner of my farm, or perhaps I shall catch a flogging.' If we were to yield what we believe to be our just title to the northwestern coast of our continent, on so slight and shadowy a menace of danger as that which exists, we should deserve to be classed with the most cowardly and abject races of men that ever lived."

Of Polk's first message to Congress, Bryant on December 3 praised the part that said the matter of annexation of Texas should be disposed of early in the session, but he criticized the speech for not being "equally communicative" on other points of the dispute with Mexico. As to the Oregon question, Bryant approved the President's proposed abrogation of the agreement for joint occupation of the territory, but he objected to a plan of offering grants of land to American settlers. He declared this was a war measure: "A farm to every man with a rifle would cause the wilderness of Oregon to bristle with rifles." In subsequent editorials, the *Evening Post* discounted the chances of war, however. The paper printed in full Secretary of State Buchanan's correspondence with England setting forth the claims of the United States, and Bryant asserted that the argument was irrefutable and must be recognized by England.

During December Bryant was persuaded by Rufus Griswold, who had

1. Bryant around the age of sixty, a portrait by Charles Loring Elliott. In the collection of The Corcoran Gallery of Art.

3. Andrew Jackson

4. Samuel J. Tilden

5. William Coleman, editor of
the *New York Evening Post*.

6. William Leggett, Bryant's partner.

7. Parke Godwin,
Bryant's son-in-law and partner.

8. John Bigelow, another of
Bryant's business partners.

9. The title page of the Townsend edition of "A Forest Hymn," one of many gift editions of Bryant's poems published during his later years.

10. An engraving of Bryant
as "The Poet of Our Woods,"
from *Appleton's Journal*,
December 18, 1869.

Ye have no history.   I cannot know
Who, when the hillside trees were hewn away,
Haply two centuries since, bade spare this oak,
Leaning to shade, with his irregular arms,
Low-bent and long, the fount that from his roots
Slips through a bed of cresses toward the bay.

11.   One page of Putnam's
1874 edition of Bryant's
poems, showing part
of "Among the Trees."

12. An engraving from an 1860 *Harper's Weekly* shows part of Central Park, which Bryant played a large part in founding.

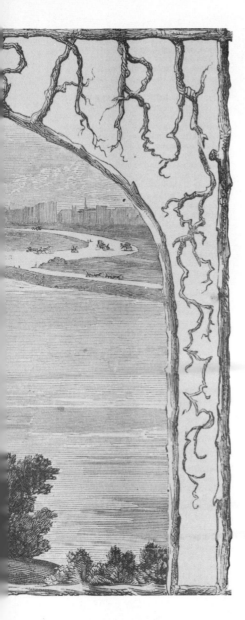

"HERITAGE OF NEW YORK"
THIS HOUSE WAS THE RESIDENCE,
FROM 1867 TO 1878,
OF
WILLIAM CULLEN BRYANT
(1794-1878)
POET, EDITOR, AND ORATOR.

FROM HERE HE REGULARLY WALKED
TO HIS NEWSPAPER OFFICE AT THE
EVENING POST, NEARLY THREE MILES
DOWNTOWN. HERE HE WAS BROUGHT
TWO WEEKS BEFORE HIS DEATH AT 83
AFTER SUFFERING A SUNSTROKE WHILE
DEDICATING A MONUMENT IN CENTRAL
PARK TO THE ITALIAN PATRIOT,
GIUSEPPE MAZZINI. THE PERORATION
OF HIS FINAL ADDRESS PRESAGED
A COMING OF CIVIL AND RELIGIOUS
LIBERTY "WHEN THE RIGHTS AND
DUTIES OF HUMAN BROTHERHOOD
SHALL BE ACKNOWLEDGED BY ALL
THE RACES OF MANKIND."

PLAQUE ERECTED 1967 BY
THE NEW YORK COMMUNITY TRUST

13. *Above right:* A plaque marks the house on Sixteenth Street in New York, where Bryant lived.

14. *Below right:* A silver vase, paid for by public subscription and presented to Bryant on his eightieth birthday.

15. The aged poet in his study, at his country house in Roslyn, Long Island.

16. Bryant's house at Roslyn.

pursued him indefatigably to obtain his poems exclusively for *Graham's Magazine,* to let the firm of Carey & Hart of Philadelphia bring out an illustrated edition of his poems. Griswold, whose own *The Poets and Poetry of America* had been published by the firm with immense success, had written Bryant as early as June 20, 1844, suggesting the volume. Bryant replied on August 18 that he was under contract with the Harpers, who had stereotyped the 1839 edition at their own expense, allowing him a royalty on each copy printed. "When I choose to put an end to the engagement I must pay them for the plates," he said. "I cannot publish an illustrated edition without either obtaining their consent or taking the plates and paying for them."[12]

With Griswold serving as an intermediary, an agreement was worked out and Bryant set himself to revising and correcting poems printed in earlier editions and those that had appeared more recently in magazines. For this he obtained the assistance of Dana in December. "I suppose you have read them all," Bryant wrote, "and that they have left some impression, favorable or unfavorable, which, in looking them over again, you will be apt to remember, without taking the trouble to read them a second time. If your former impressions were unfavorable in regard to any one of them, you will counsel me, of course, to omit it."[13] To illustrate the volume, Carey & Hart commissioned paintings by Bryant's friend Emanuel Leutze, with whom he had visited at Düsseldorf. Leutze was not unknown as an illustrator, having painted scenes for Irving's *The Sketch Book* and Cooper's Leatherstocking tales. The project turned out to be a long one of which Bryant wearied before it was over, and the sumptuous volume was not printed until November 2, 1846.

19

FREE-SOILER AND BARNBURNER

DURING THE EARLY MONTHS OF 1846 BRYANT CONSIDERED settlement of the Oregon question and not the Texas question to be the first priority of the government. He stood behind President Polk in claiming the whole of Oregon, and he demanded that England be notified immediately of termination of the treaty of joint occupation. He denied Whig arguments that such a notice would amount to a declaration of war and attacked those who would give up the territory as being "timid commercial men of the Atlantic cities, trembling for the fate of their goodly argosies." When, in February, Britain offered to submit the question to arbitration, the *Evening Post* upheld the President in his refusal to do so. Arbitration, the paper said, would give "all the advantage to England"; and, if she were granted a port on the Pacific, one would be denied the United States. The long debate on the question in Congress provoked from Bryant the warning: "It is evident that delay only tends to increase the difficulty, and though we have no apprehension that England will venture on a war . . . still the nature and position of the controversy call loudly for energetic and decisive action."

But the dispute with Mexico could not be ignored. In 1845 General Zachary Taylor, commander of U.S. forces in the Southwest, had been ordered to Texas to be in a state of readiness in case of an invasion of Mexican troops. The *Evening Post* discounted reports from New Orleans that immediate hostilities between the two countries impended. "We would remind the New Orleans journals which manifest so much impatience for a brush with their feeble neighbor," Bryant wrote on February 2, "that when we shall have adjusted the Oregon question, with that great and powerful nation which claims the northwestern territory against us, it will be early enough to think of going to war with Mexico."

Bryant had additional grounds for supporting Polk when the House passed the independent treasury bill, recommended by the President, and he considered Senate approval a foregone conclusion. He was happy, he wrote on April 4, to see the change in thinking on the measure that Martin Van Buren had been unable to obtain. "The people have looked at it on both sides," Bryant said, "viewed it both theoretically and experimentally, examined it as an assay master would examine a piece of gold, and at last have deliberately put their stamp upon it. It is undoubted bullion, and will pass without question for the next hundred years." This was a fair prediction, for it was the chief basis of the United States fiscal system until the Federal Reserve Act of 1913 and the abolition of subtreasuries established under the 1846 bill in 1920.

In the first week in May newspapers carried reports from New Orleans of skirmishes between General Taylor's troops and Mexican troops that had crossed the Rio Grande. Stating on May 8 that bloodshed was to be expected from forces of the two countries occupying neighboring positions, Bryant urged that the United States withdraw hers from the disputed territory. A war with Mexico, he warned, would be "vexatious and expensive and slow in reaching its termination."

But three days later, on May 11, when Polk sent his war message to Congress, Bryant quickly supported it and the action of the House the next day in declaring a state of hostility existed. He wrote: "The promptness with which the House of Representatives has answered the call for the means of protecting our frontier and the gallant little detachment of men on the Rio Grande, does them honor. There should be neither hesitation nor delay when either our territory is invaded or our countrymen in danger from an enemy." Many northerners, including close friends of Bryant, opposed the war with Mexico, considering it a move by southerners to extend slavery into new territory to be obtained by conquest, New Mexico and California, but Bryant did not discuss this argument in his early editorials on the conflict. Instead he wrote, on May 20, that "a large majority of both political parties in this part of the country at least, are disposed to give support to the administration in its prosecution," partly because the people "are weary of the amphibious state in which our relations towards Mexico have so long remained,—a state which is neither war nor peace." Bryant's was a patriot's view: his country had been attacked, and the enemy should be repulsed. Hence, he declared it was not "a wise policy to prosecute the war feebly" and he urged the nation to make "such demonstrations of vigor as shall convince Mexico that we are in earnest." Thereafter, during the first months of skirmishing, Bryant refrained from comment either approving or disapproving of the war in general.

The *Evening Post*'s war coverage consisted of dispatches by its Washington correspondent, "Civis," who filed regular reports, printed on arrival up to press time under the heading "Postscripts" on page three, and of reprints from other papers. The latest news was contained in "Civis's" letters, dated the day preceding publication at first but later the same day when the last gap in the telegraph line from New York to Washington, that between Philadelphia and Baltimore, was spanned. The chief sources of information, other than the government, were the New Orleans papers, which had their own correspondents in the field who sent the news by ship from the Mexican and Texan coasts. As the war dragged on, the leading papers maintained pony expresses between New Orleans and the southernmost extension of the telegraph at Richmond. News of the Army of the West, the expedition of General Stephen W. Kearny to New Mexico, arrived much later from St. Louis, being brought by the long and difficult route overland on the Santa Fe Trail.

II

Bryant found what relief he could from the tensions of war in continuing the work already begun on revising his poems for the new collection commissioned by Carey & Hart. After the publication of *The White-Footed Deer,* his fountain of poetry had almost ceased to flow. His output in 1844 was only one poem and that of 1845 only two poems. During the next decade, when the nation was at war with Mexico and the issue of the extension of slavery brought the Union nearer and nearer to division, he continued to have little heart for poetry, some years writing none at all. In asking Dana for suggestions for poems that might be omitted from the new edition as well as for suggestions for improving those to be retained, Bryant indicated a realization that his work, in so elaborate a volume, would be subject to critical reassessment. Since he had first appeared in print and established his reputation, a new generation had arisen with tastes differing from those of his earlier admirers. The public ear was ·

attuned to new voices, Longfellow and Whittier, to the young Lowell, and to Poe, whose poem "The Raven" created a sensation when it was printed in the New York *Evening Mirror* of January 29, 1845, and whose volume, *The Raven and Other Poems,* in the fall was immediately popular.

Dana, however, was reluctant to leave anything out, being, as Bryant wrote him on January 13, 1846, inclined if he erred to err "on the side of mercy."[1] About two weeks later Dana sent Bryant a critique of twenty closely written pages in which he subjected the poems, one by one, to careful scrutiny. Individual words, lines, stanzas, whole poems were challenged—for lack of clarity, for harshness of sound, for nobility of conception. Dana feared that if Bryant did not include everything that had appeared in earlier volumes the sale of the new edition would be hurt, and he repeated his admonition in a letter of February 1: "And now, my dear sir, let me beg you to leave out none of these pieces; depend upon it, if you do, it will cause a feeling of dissatisfaction, and people will call the edition an incomplete edition."[2] Bryant replied that, though it had been his purpose "to prune out some of the poems," he would follow his friend's advice, as he had done in making minor changes.[3] "You have shown me faults which I was amazed should have escaped my notice," Bryant wrote; "for example, that passage in 'The Ages' where I talk about vampires and their net. Such nonsense I could hardly believe I had written. . . ." The reference was to the penultimate stanza in which Bryant had said:

> Europe is given a prey to sterner fates,
> And writhes in shackles; strong the arms that chain
> To earth her struggling multitude of states;
> She too is strong, and might not chafe in vain
> Against them, but shake off the vampyre train
> That batten on her blood, and break their net. . . .

The figure of speech of enchained Europe was made consistent by altering the lines to

> Against them, but might cast to earth the train
> That trample her, and break their iron net.

Bryant's concern about his reputation may have been reflected in a letter to Longfellow on January 31 after receiving his *The Belfry of Bruges and Other Poems,* which had just come from the press of Carey & Hart.[4] "I have been reading aloud to my wife some of the poems that pleased me most," Bryant wrote, "and she would not be content till I had written to express to you something of the admiration which I could not help manifesting as I read them." And Bryant added: "I am not one of those who believe that a true poet is insensible to the excellence of his writings, and know that you can well afford to dispense with such slight corroboration as the general judgment in your favor could derive from an opinion of mine. You must allow me, however, to add my voice to the many which make up the voice of poetic fame."*

Bryant must have considered as justified his efforts to perfect his own lines, with the careful counsel of Dana, when *Godey's Lady's Book* for April appeared. It contained an article by Poe which gave the verses the same close study that he himself had been giving them and commented on the lack of esteem in which Bryant was held by the younger critics. The article was one of a series of studies of American authors that Poe had projected for a book. Going to New York from Philadelphia in 1844, Poe had been struggling, between bouts of illness, to support himself, his frail wife Virginia, dying of tuberculosis, and her mother, Mrs. Maria Clemm, in a cottage at Fordham a few miles from the city. Poe had obtained occasional work on several literary journals and was a contributor to the leading magazines. Because of the popular and critical reception of his collections of his tales and poems, both printed in 1845, Poe's commentary must be taken into account even if Bryant could not like him as a person or admire the perversity of his work.**

The New York literary circle was a small one, and Bryant and Poe had met each other occasionally. Parke Godwin recalled that Poe had visited the *Evening Post* office in 1837 and that he had seen the two together, very likely in 1845 after Bryant's return from England,[5] at an evening party

*Longfellow replied on Feb. 5, expressing his indebtedness to Bryant: "In return, let me say what a staunch friend and admirer of yours I have been from the beginning, and acknowledge how much I owe to you, not only of delight, but of culture. When I look aback upon my earlier years, I cannot but smile to see how much in them is really yours. It was an involuntary imitation, which I most readily confess, and say, as Dante says to Virgil: 'Tu se lo mia maestro e il mio autora.'" Godwin, *Biography,* II, 25.

**Dana, an admirer of Poe's poetry, recommended that Bryant seek him out to know him better, but Bryant replied in a letter of Sept. 12, 1848: "You have much to say of Mr. P., of whom I think very well in many respects, but who has some peculiarities in his character which show it, perhaps, not to be quite a healthy one. I shall be glad to be useful to him in any way; but how can you, who know me, ask me to *get* acquainted with anybody? I do not know that I ever got acquainted with anybody of set purpose in my life. The three things most irksome to me in my transactions with the world are, to owe money, to ask a favor, and to seek an acquaintance." Goddard-Roslyn Collection; Godwin, *Biography,* II, 37–8.

given by Mrs. Caroline Kirkland, whose sketches and tales of life in the West—she had lived in Michigan—were charming and deservedly popular. Poe in his *Godey's Lady's Book* article painted one of the best word-portraits we have of Bryant:

> He is now fifty-two years of age. In height, he is, perhaps, five feet nine. His frame is rather robust. His features are large but thin. His countenance is sallow, nearly bloodless. His eyes are piercing gray, deep set, with large projecting eyebrows. His mouth is wide and massive, the expression of the smile hard, cold—even sardonic. The forehead is broad, with prominent organs of ideality; a good deal bald; the hair thin and grayish, as also are the whiskers, which he wears in a simple style. His bearing is quite distinguished, full of the aristocracy of intellect. In general, he looks in better health than before his visit to England. He seems active—physically and morally energetic. His dress is plain to the extreme of simplicity, although of late there is a certain degree of Anglicism about it.

The statement about Bryant's "prominent organs of ideality" refers to the popular method of character analysis by phrenology and that about the whiskers worn in "simple style" is somewhat misleading—Bryant then did not have a beard but let his hair grow from his temples down to his chin in full, wavy sideburns. Like many who knew Bryant intimately, Poe thought his reputation for frigidity to be false. "The peculiarly melancholy expression of his countenance has caused him to be accused of harshness, or coldness of heart. Never was there a greater mistake. His soul is charity itself, in all respects generous and noble."

Taking cognizance of the adverse view of Bryant held by some of the younger critics, Poe wrote: "It will never do to claim for Bryant a genius of the loftiest order, but there has been latterly, since the days of Mr. Longfellow and Mr. Lowell, a growing disposition to deny him *genius* in *any* respect." To be sure, Bryant was a writer of "high poetical *talent*" and he was very "*correct,*" after the "old-school manner of Cowper, Goldsmith and Young," but these opinions did not reflect the whole truth. "Mr. Bryant has genius, and that of a marked character, but it has been overlooked by modern schools, because deficient in those externals which have become a measure symbolical of those schools." Bryant was condemned as being too skilled in the art of poetry and too lacking in the expression of passion that touches the heart. Poe disagreed with this. "Passion proper and poesy are discordant," he declared. "Poetry is elevating, tranquilizes the *soul*. With the *heart* it has nothing to do." He cited as an example Bryant's "June," the poem in which he expressed the hope that when he died it would be in this lovely month: "The thoughts here belong to the highest class of poetry, the imaginative-natural, and are of themselves sufficient to stamp their author a man of genius."

Such lines were by no means rare in Bryant's poetry, and Poe went on for several hundred words to quote like utterances of genius drawn from a score of poems. But Poe had some faults to report in the department of poetry in which Bryant was considered most adept, his versification. His lines were "occasionally unpronounceable through excess of harsh consonants"; in his anapaestic rhythms he sometimes got so out of depth that the result was "sad havoc"; even his pentameters were sometimes "inexcusably rough"; he was not often guilty of "merely grammatical errors" but faulty constructions were "frequently chargeable to him." Nevertheless, in the "minor morals of the muse," Bryant excelled, and Poe could only find these "flaws" with difficulty.

During the spring and early summer Bryant continued to exchange letters with Dana over revisions and by mid-July he had the completed manuscript ready to send to his publisher. He had chosen a new arrangement in the plan of the book, printing the poems in the order of composition, with the exception of the longest poem, "The Ages," which appeared first. In a short introduction, he mentioned his original idea of omitting certain poems that had been in earlier editions but asked "leave to plead the judgment of a literary friend, whose opinion in such matters he highly values, as his apology for having retained them."

III

With the collection of poems readied for the press, Bryant planned another trip, with Frances and Julia a visit to his mother and brothers in Illinois. The problem of what to do about the *Evening Post* had an immediate answer, for Parke Godwin, though still disaffected with his father-in-law and still writing Charles A. Dana of plans to start an Associationist publication in New York, had returned to the paper. In August of 1845 Godwin had written Dana urging him by all means to come to New York.[6] There was a chance that he could get a job on the *Tribune,* since Horace Greeley was enthusiastic over Fourierism, and Godwin assured his friend that if he could obtain a salary of five hundred dollars he could manage to live upon it and supplement it by writing for the magazines. "I shall live in the hope of having one companion at least," he added, "in this cold and dreary wilderness." As to establishing an Associationist paper, Godwin felt it would be best to have a penny daily for "regular bushwhacking," but he also had in mind a liberal magazine. "With the original materials that we have in our heads—a great deal of which I have put already on paper—we could in the dignified form of a monthly produce an impression on the mind and heart of this country that would tell," he wrote.

Bryant, as he had done on previous travels both at home and abroad, sent back letters to the *Evening Post,* writing eight between the first on July 24 and the last on August 20.[7] Such travelogues were a feature of the paper in the 1840's, for the people were eager to learn all they could about their expanding and rapidly-filling country. From nearby, correspondents in New York, Connecticut, Massachusetts, and Pennsylvania sent letters describing the watering places and summer vacation spots in great detail —Bryant himself a few years before had pointed out places to visit for their scenery in his accounts of his walking trips. But equally popular were the reports of travelers in the South and in the West and those written by Bryant's friends on their European travels. Navy officers supplied accounts of their cruises to remote places, and the *Evening Post* had several correspondents among the fighting forces in the Mexican War.

In this trip to the West Bryant took passage July 24 on a steamer sailing from Buffalo to Chicago, whence he went by stagecoach to Princeton. On the return trip, reaching Chicago on August 8, he sailed to Mackinac Island and then to Sault Ste. Marie, which two years before had been only a military outpost in the midst of a village of Indians and half-breeds. He left the latter place on August 19 for the return trip through the lakes to Buffalo. This trip was notable for Bryant's observations among the Indians: their improvidence in living, their addiction to drink, their relations with missionaries and their corruption by white settlers, and their crafts and arts—the different construction of wigwams by the Chippewas and Pottawatomies, the birch-bark canoes, "the most beautiful and perfect things of the kind constructed by human art," the woven blankets, and the embroidery with porcupine quills.

At Buffalo Bryant was reminded of the war in which his country was engaged by an examination of a new fort at the entrance of the Niagara River, one with walls of "prodigious thickness." "It is curious," he observed, "to see how, as we grow more ingenious in the means of attack, we devise more effectual means of defence." And he was led to ask: "Do not these more dreadful engines of attack on the one side, and these more perfect means of protection on the other, leave the balance just where it was before?"

When the steamer stopped to take on wood on the Canadian side of the

St. Clair River after passing Detroit, Bryant was told of efforts to get the Chippewas to change their tribal ways. The Canadian government had built them log houses and furnished them with horses and cattle and farm equipment. But the Indians did not readily accept the life of the white man. The squaws planted a little corn and a few beans, and the braves, when they were not idle, which was much of the time, hunted and fished. At Chicago, Bryant discovered that the town, which contained about five thousand people when he was last there five years before, had now grown to fifteen thousand. On the trip from Chicago to Princeton the stagecoach overturned while fording the Illinois Canal where a bridge had been washed out in a heavy rainstorm and nearly drowned the travelers. Four of the nine passengers were trapped inside beneath the turbid water. "We extricated ourselves as well as we could," Bryant wrote the *Evening Post*, "the men waded out, the women were carried, and when we got on shore it was found that, although drenched with water and plastered with mud, nobody was either drowned or hurt."

Bryant was struck by the changes made since his previous visit. "Frame or brick houses in many places had taken the places of log-cabins," he wrote; "the road for long distances now passed between fences, the broad prairie, inclosed, was turned into immense fields of maize, oats, and wheat, and was spotted here and there with young orchards, or little groves, and clumps of bright-green locust-trees, and where the prairie remained open, it was now depastured by large herds of cattle, its herbage shortened, and its flowers less numerous." At Princeton, he found his mother, now seventy-seven years old, still alert and vigorous. A tall, strong woman with a long face, high brow, and sharp chin, she shared the hypochondria of the Bryant family, and her letters often gave details of headaches, colds, coughs, and other ailments. She had been influenced by her son's interest in homoeopathy, and like him had her own treatments for minor ills with medicinal herbs raised at home.[8]

After about a week at Princeton, Bryant returned to Chicago and sailed to Sault Ste. Marie, which he reached on August 13. At a brief stopover at Southport, in the new state of Wisconsin, he was interested in the way the Indian women gathered a variety of wild rice that served as the winter food of the Menonomee. Two to a canoe, one of the squaws paddled the frail craft over the marsh water while the other grasped the heads of the rice plant and knocked the grains off with a stick. He wondered if this cereal could not be cultivated in the grassy shallows of Eastern rivers.

At Sault Ste. Marie occurred another of Bryant's adventures that he described for *Evening Post* readers. Here the waters of Lake Superior and Lake Huron were joined by the St. Mary River, rushing and foaming for almost a mile over rocks. A visitor was expected to want to enjoy the thrill of descending the rapids in a canoe manned by Indians, and Bryant determined at once to meet the requirement. At the first wigwam he entered to obtain the services of canoeists he found three men and two women, all drunk, the "squaws . . . speechless and motionless, too far gone . . . to raise either hand or foot" and the braves, though able to raise themselves from the ground, inclined to be truculent. Most of the men of the village were in about the same state of intoxication, but Bryant finally found two willing to pilot the canoe down the falls. He marveled at their dexterity in keeping the craft in the smoothest part of the water. "At one time," he related, "we would seem to be directly approaching a rock against which the waves were dashing, at another to be descending into a hollow of the waters in which our canoe would be inevitably filled, but a single stroke of the paddle given by the man at the prow put us safely by the seeming danger."

When Bryant returned to New York late in August, the papers noted his arrival, one of the longer items appearing in the Democratic Brooklyn *Eagle,* of which a young Barnburner, Walter Whitman, had recently become editor after having had several "sits," as he called them, on New York papers.[9] He described Bryant for his Brooklyn readers: "Sometimes, walking across the Park in New York, or along one of the thoroughfares of the city, you may meet a plainly dressed man of middling size, considerably beyond the younger age of life, with rather bloodless complexion, sparse white hair, and expressive grey eyes." This man, according to the Brooklyn editor, who himself had written some verse in conventional rhymed stanzas and had contributed tales and articles to the magazines, was "a poet who, to our mind, stands among the first in the world." Then, turning to politics, he declared: "It is an honor and a pride to the Democratic party that it has such a man to conduct one of its principal newspapers—to be an expounder of its doctrines, and act as one of the warders to watch the safety of the citadel." Whitman deprecated the lack of appreciation for Bryant as a poet by the current "literary quacks," and asserted vehemently on this theme:

> We have called Bryant one of the best poets in the world! This smacks so much of the exaggerated that we are half a mind to alter it, true as we sincerely believe it to be. But we will let it stand. We know the prophet has but little fame in his own country, and that there are among us those who

think no author's worth established till he has been endorsed by European approval. Bryant, indeed, has been thus endorsed.* Moreover, there will come a time when the writings of this beautiful poet shall attain their proper rank—a rank far higher than has been accorded to them by many accomplished men, who think of them by no means disparagingly. We allude to such as, like the critic of American poetry in the *Democratic Review,* place Mr. Bryant "not in the first, or second, but in the third or fourth rank". . . . Foreign appreciation of American literary talent is sometimes truer than native.

One of the first tasks that faced Bryant after his return was correcting the proofs of his book, but publication was being delayed by Leutze's slowness in doing the illustrations and the engravers in reproducing them. "I grow fastidious in regard to illustrations," Bryant wrote Dana; "there is scarcely one in a score, in the books of poetry that I take up, which does not displease me. I have seen eight of those intended for my book, and, with one or two exceptions, cannot say I take much delight in them." Though Bryant admired Leutze as a painter he could not understand how he as an artist could do well if he worked to order. "What sort of verses should I make if I were to sit down to put his pictures into verse?" Bryant asked.[10] Bryant was pleased, however, with a black-and-white crayon portrait of him done by the artist Seth Wells Cheney and the engraving by his brother John Cheney and thought it would be "the best thing in the book." When the volume came out late in the year, Dana disagreed. "I have occasionally seen you with the look that the Cheneys have given you," he wrote, "but it is not characteristic of you—at any rate, not your higher self."[11] Perhaps the reason Bryant liked it and Dana did not was that it showed a less severe expression on his face than most of his portraits. He is not smiling but is about to smile, and the face is lighted up as the sky is by the sun emerging from behind a cloud.

Bryant's displeasure over Leutze's illustrations is understandable, for they did not reflect the American quality of his poetry. The proper illustrator would have been one of the American landscape painters—Thomas Cole, Asher Durand, or Henry Inman, the men who shared his delight

---

*Whitman may have had in mind *Graham's Magazine,* Oct., 1845, which carried a translation of an article, "American Literature and the Arts," published in the *Journal* of Augsburg, Germany. Contrasting Bryant with the "too provincial" writers of Boston, the article said: "When the New Englander leaves his native place, and explores either the regions of the West or South, he becomes a thorough American, and . . . a national poet." Such a one was Bryant, whom the writer called "the first lyric poet in the English language." The writer found him, however, "a little monotonous, like the prairies and primeval forests which he so beautifully depicts."

in panoramic views from the heights along the Hudson River, the brawling streams rushing down rocky glens, and long vistas of mountains shading off imperceptibly into the sky. Instead, Leutze chose such Old World figures to portray as the Greek partisan and the Greek boy, the Swiss champion of liberty William Tell, and the Biblical mother Rizpah. Even the illustrations for the poems with American people and settings were European, the Indian maidens of "Monument Mountain," for example, having classical Greek faces and wearing draped Greek robes. The "fairest of the rural maids," Bryant's Frances of his Great Barrington days, resembled a Valkyrie more than a backwoods American girl.

IV

Bryant had planned his return to New York so that he would be on hand to direct the *Evening Post* during the fall elections. A hard-fought campaign for the governorship was in the offing because of the split between the New York Democrats. The radical wing of the party to which Bryant belonged, the Barnburners, or "Softs" as they were called in opposition to the conservative wing, the Hunkers, or "Hards," succeeded in controlling the state convention and renominating Silas Wright. But the Hunker opposition to Wright was as effective as that of the Whigs in bringing about his defeat. The Softs, rankled over their failure to nominate Van Buren for president at the Baltimore convention in 1844, felt that Polk should have used his political patronage to strengthen their faction of the party. Instead, Polk had used his influence, he hoped, to bring the factions together. Naturally, he pleased neither, and indeed the Barnburners believed that the national administration had opposed Wright.

Bryant at the close of the year, despite the failure of the national administration to come decisively to the support of Wright, had not shifted his allegiance from President Polk. In an editorial on December 9 he defended the President's thesis, set forth in his annual message to Congress, that the war with Mexico could not have been avoided. "It will satisfy the people, we believe, that the annexation of Texas in the manner finally decided upon, necessarily drew after it a conflict of arms with Mexico, who had never relinquished the idea of recovering that province," the editorial concluded. A week later the *Evening Post* defended the President against charges of the Whigs that organizing temporary governments in the occupied areas of California and New Mexico was unconstitutional. Bryant wrote: "The authority to go to war with another nation, necessarily implies the right to invade its territory; the invasion of its territory necessarily implies an occupation of it, temporary if no more; and the right of occupation necessarily draws after it the right to ordain, in the stead of the hostile government already existing, a new set of authorities acknowledging allegiance to the invading nation. If the constitution permits war, it permits these secondary consequences of war."

V

Bryant was more and more pleased with his rural retreat at Roslyn during this period of war tensions. A picture of his home life is given in a letter by Catharine Sedgwick, who had been a guest of the family in May.[12] It was "a generous, old-fashioned house" with piazzas and was enclosed by trees, "dark, solid pines" and oaks and chestnuts with "lovely branches of light spring foliage." Bryant's grounds encompassed a terraced garden that descended to the water of Great Neck Bay, a pond formed from springs, and a "green ravine" spanned by a bridge leading to a cottage occupied by the Godwins. "But better than any outdoor life, nobler gifts of God than hill-sides and their rich borderings of trees, clear streams, and bays, we have within," she wrote, "and delightfully we have spent the day, though it has been cloudy and dripping."

Although Godwin had returned to the *Evening Post* and occupied a pleasant cottage near his father-in-law, he was still desperately unhappy, regretting his inability to establish with Charles A. Dana their Associationist publication. Moreover, he was worried about his wife. Fanny, he wrote Dana on August 12, had "as the Germans say *a good hope*" and he was concerned over "the near approach of what has delayed itself now for some four years." He wrote again of Fanny's "precarious health" on September 29. The approach of the birth of his first child had intensified his feeling of guilt that there was so much to do to help humankind and he had not been able to do anything. "I have never felt such a high and profoundly religious zeal on this subject of the Organization of Labour as I now do," he wrote Dana on November 16 after Fanny had been delivered of her first child. "Perhaps the new relation in which I am placed has made me more thoughtful of the realities of life; for when one comes to think that every individual of this poor, suffering, distracted, much abused race of ours has been to some of our fellows the subject of the same deep care, anxieties, and affections with which I now contemplate my helpless little one, the sense of duty towards all men impresses me with an awful weight."[13]

To escape from the paper, Godwin had written the historian George Bancroft, Polk's secretary of the navy who years before had thrown in his lot with the Jacksonians and had supported the workingmen's movement, about getting a government appointment in Europe. Bancroft wrote that he had repeatedly spoken of Godwin to the President, but warned him that "the salary of a secretary is for a married man in a foreign land so inconsiderable that it merits consideration."[14] Nothing coming from this effort, Godwin decided to leave the *Evening Post* to accept an appointment as collector in the custom house. He wrote Dana of the decision on December 5.[15] He would have quit before but he was so indebted to the firm that he could not get away, but in the last two years he had been able to pay $1,800 toward his "emancipation." "The association with Bryant, who is a cold, irritable and selfish man (*entre nous* all this) was distasteful," Godwin wrote, "and things have happened lately to make it intolerable." He did not explain what these things were, but they may have been Bryant's objection to his inserting Fourieristic articles in the paper when left in charge. At any rate, Godwin would stay with the custom house until he could find literary work.

With the departure of Godwin, Bryant was impelled again to look about for an assistant. There had been a change in the internal management of the paper on October 29 when the name of William G. Boggs was removed from the masthead as publisher and that of the William C. Bryant & Company was substituted. The reason for this is not known. It may have been that Bryant had purchased more of the paper's stock or that he wanted to give Boggs less authority since his partner had borrowed heavily on the credit of the paper for personal business dealings. The most promising prospect Bryant found for his assistant was John Bigelow, who as a young lawyer interested in government reform had contributed frequently to the paper, most recently articles on the state's constitutional convention. The older and the younger man had become familiars in May of 1847 when Bryant took rooms in a house at 4 Amity Place, occupying the first floor and Bigelow having rooms on the second.[16] Bigelow had devised a movable shower bath, a utility so ingenious that it fascinated Bryant. They were able to share it to the mutual convenience of both, for Bryant, who began his work on the paper by eight o'clock, was gone from the house before Bigelow arose. Bryant, first through an intermediary and later personally, offered Bigelow the position at whatever salary he might ask. But Bigelow, who had just formed a partnership, in 1845, with a progressive lawyer, Edgar H. Seeley, was not willing to quit the law to go into journalism.[17]

VI

Bryant had been on his Great Lakes trip when, on August 8, a young Jacksonian Democrat from Pennsylvania, David Wilmot, introduced an amendment to an appropriation bill of two million dollars sought by President Polk to negotiate with Mexico over the territories of New Mexico and California that was to crystalize the divided sentiment of the nation. The amendment, the Wilmot Proviso, would have barred slavery in any part of the territory acquired through the war. Losing in the Senate by the adjournment of Congress on August 10, the amendment did not furnish occasion for editorial comment by Bryant when he returned to the paper. Revived in the new Congress, it was, however, to be a main editorial theme during 1847, to be climaxed on October 28 when the *Evening Post* emblazoned on the masthead above its editorials the slogan of the Barnburner wing of Democratic party: "Free Soil, Free Labor, Free Trade, and Free Speech."

Early in the year, however, the complex political situation in New York, with the Whigs taking the lead in the protest against extension of slavery and the Democrats in a precarious position because of the split between the Barnburners and the Hunkers, led Bryant to temper his editorials on the issue. On January 25 in an editorial on "Slavery in California" he argued that it would be better for the Union to content itself with its old limits than to add new slave territory under the Missouri Compromise rule. He this early advanced the "squatters' sovereignty" theory. He pointed out that emigrants were already beginning to settle in California and argued that when the time came for taking the territory into the Union she be admitted "at her own desire, into the bosom of the confederacy, a free state." Two days later he protested against the doctrine that any new territory be divided equally between slave and free territory on a premise not likely to appeal to southern Democrats: it was a mistake to regard all people of the South as slaveholders since more than half of them owned no human beings in bondage. "Exempt the new territory that may be acquired from the curse of slavery," Bryant urged, "and you not only open it to emigration from the north, but you make it a place to which the citizens of the south not owning slaves may emigrate, with a prospect of attaining that social equality which the laboring portion of them do not possess at home."

A month later Bryant saw that no sort of compromise seemed probable when John C. Calhoun submitted four resolutions in which he asserted that any law interfering with slavery would violate the Constitution. "We thank Mr. Calhoun for playing so bold and open a game," Bryant said sarcastically. "It is a manly stand that he has taken. He declares, that if any new territory is annexed to the Union it instantly becomes, by the operation of the constitution, a territory in which slaves may be taken as merchandise, and that Congress shall have no power to direct otherwise by any compromise or division of the territory. Our only safety lies in anticipating this argument, and refusing our consent at the earliest period to the annexation of a rood of territory in which men are to be regarded as merchandise." When the Wilmot Proviso again was attached to the appropriation measure asked by President Polk and was defeated in March, the *Evening Post* printed the names of the five free-state senators who voted against it and anathematized Daniel S. Dickinson, the New York Democrat who cast a "nay" vote despite a New York assembly resolution instructing for the prohibition of slavery in new territories.

Later in the month Bryant perceived what he called "a new form of nullification" in resolutions adopted by the Virginia legislature declaring that it would under no circumstances recognize as binding any enactment by the federal government which had as its object barring slavery from any territory acquired either by conquest or treaty. Bryant, mindful of the nullification movement over the Tariff of Abominations of 1828, declared: "A plainer and more direct threat of organized and forcible resistance to the laws, even to the extent of dissolving the Union, could not be made." The *Evening Post*'s copy of the resolutions was reprinted from the Washington *Union,* the newspaper which Polk had adopted as his organ after breaking with Francis P. Blair, whose Washington *Globe* had been the voice of the party since the days of Jackson. Bryant commented that the paper had not condemned them as it should have as the acknowledged organ of the executive. When the *Union* replied that it had merely "commended" the resolutions to the attention of Wilmot Proviso advocates with the hope that they would see the need for conciliation to preserve the harmony of the Democratic party and to prevent sectional discord, Bryant, on March 30, set forth what he considered the only basis for compromise:

A man who does not approve of slavery in the abstract may tolerate it where it exists, from the want of constitutional authority to extinguish it, or from regard to the actual conditions of society, and the difficulties of change; but how can he justify himself in instituting it in new communities, unless he believes with Mr. Calhoun, that it is in itself a "great good"? . . .The federal government represents the free as well as the slave states; and while it does

331

not attempt to abolish slavery in the states where it exists, it must not authorize slavery where it does not exist. This is the only middle ground— the "true basis of conciliation and adjustment."

VII

While deeply concerned about what was happening to the nation in the growing division between the North and South, Bryant was disturbed by the news from Illinois of the serious illness of his mother. She had suffered a fall during the winter, and John wrote him on April 4 that her condition was "very bad, her strength failing very fast, and her mind . . . in a great measure gone."[18] She died on May 6 at the age of seventy-nine. Bryant, in a letter to John, sought to assuage their grief in these words: "To have lived in benevolent work and contentment, and, for the most part, in health the full number of years allotted to the human race, may be accounted as singularly fortunate. We have reason to be grateful that such was the case with our mother."[19] But grief is not so easily erased from the mind, and two years later, with the return of another May, Bryant in the poem, "The May Sun sheds an Amber Light," recalled his boyhood when with his mother he observed the "new-leaved woods" and listened to the singing of the birds in the morning.

For his summer trip of 1847 Bryant was able to get away from the *Evening Post* for less than a month, beginning the last week in July, for a tour of parts of the country he had not seen before. After spending several days in Boston, he took the railroad for Portland, Maine. In a letter to the paper, he commented on the growing industrialism of New England, and wrote at length on the new town of Lawrenceville, founded only a year before by the manufacturer Abbot Lawrence and now a bustling place of six thousand inhabitants.[20] Sailing up the Kennebec River to Augusta, he noted details of the fishing industry and ship-building, keels for new vessels being laid wherever a stream or creek was large enough to float a ship. After crossing Maine by coach into New Hampshire, Bryant traveled through the White Mountains, which, except for the absence of glaciers and snow-capped peaks, he found comparable to the Swiss Alps. "The depth of the valleys," Bryant wrote, "the steepness of the mountain-sides, the variety of aspect shown by their summits, the deep gulfs of forest below, seamed with the open courses of rivers, the vast extent of the mountain region seen north and south of us, gleaming with many lakes, took me with surprise and astonishment."

Within a week after Bryant's return to New York, the man about whom those opposing extension of slavery had rallied, Silas Wright, died, on

August 27, at his home at Canton, where he had lived quietly after his defeat in the governor's race the year before. Bryant's editorial on his death reflected the sentiment of the northern wing of the Democratic party: "We deplore the loss of such a man at such a time . . . when so few can be found in public life who refer their conduct to the same high standard. We lament that services so valuable have ceased—that an example so instructive is withdrawn, and we feel that the political world is worse than it was yesterday, by the deduction of so much virtue as has departed with the removal of one of its brightest ornaments."

Though seldom a participant in party councils, Bryant was enough of a practical politician to realize that the Barnburners could triumph at the state Democratic convention only if they worked from the ward level on up. In April he had called for reform in the nomination system, proposing that the selection of tickets by committees be abolished and that a direct primary in each election district be established. "For some years," he wrote, "our friends have been struggling between their desires to keep the party unbroken, and to keep unfit persons out of office. They will bear no longer; and if the nominations are not reformed, the party in this city will be dissolved."

Bryant's prediction was borne out in part when the Democrats gathered at Syracuse on September 28. Dominated by a small Hunker majority, the convention voted down resolutions against the extension of slavery and refused to yield on other points. The Barnburners, embittered by their defeat through what Bryant called "chicanery and misrepresentation" here and by what they considered to be the betrayal of Van Buren in 1844 and Wright in 1846, walked out of the meeting and called a "mass convention" to be held at Herkimer on October 26. Bryant considered this meeting an inspiring instance of democracy in action. "The people were there by thousands," he wrote on October 28, "and thousands more would have been present, had not the roads of the northern part of the state been rendered impassable by inundations. The strong men of the democracy were there, the men whose voices stir the blood like the sound of a trumpet." The principles set forth in the Herkimer resolutions, he declared, "will be referred to as the commencement of a new era in the politics of the state, that era in which the democratic party shook off the conservatives and their corruption, and rescued the highest principles of the party from the disrepute in which men who had falsely assumed the democratic name are striving to merge them." The real party slogan henceforth would be: "Free Soil, Free Labor, Free Trade, and Free Speech."

333

20

A NEW PARTNERSHIP

THE *Evening Post* IN 1848 OCCUPIED A DRAB TWO-STORY building at 18 Nassau Street across the way from an equally dilapidated building that still bore in faded letters a sign neglected for a dozen years: "Aaron Burr: Counsellor-at-Law." Bryant had moved the paper to this location in March of 1847 to obtain more space, but the building was by no means commodious. He occupied a tiny office on the second floor reached by a narrow flight of stairs. Since Parke Godwin had again left the paper late in the previous year, Bryant was getting along with a regular staff of two men: a city reporter, who gathered the news of the courts and the Common Council, and a business and financial reporter, whose services were shared with another afternoon paper, the *Commercial Advertiser.*

The *Evening Post's* biggest labor cost was for the force of compositors who set the type by hand.[1] The paper began the year with a smart clean appearance, readers being told on January 7 that new type had been obtained, a large size, minion, for the main editorial matter and a smaller size, agate, for advertisements and miscellaneous news material. William G. Boggs, assisted by a clerk, Isaac Henderson, had charge of the accounting office as well as the printing operations. An ancient double-cylinder press cranked by hand occupied most of the dark basement. Two flyboys lifted each of the nine-column double sheets from the bed of the press as they were printed. These were then folded for distribution to subscribers.

Bryant could be found in his cubicle of an office before eight o'clock every morning at work writing his editorials and checking copy at a big desk piled up to a height of from twelve to twenty inches by letters, manuscripts, pamphlets, and books. Like "paper-paring" Alexander Pope, Bryant wrote his articles on the backs of letters and rejected manuscripts, using a quill pen which he sharpened with a jackknife retained from his boyhood. In bringing out new editions of his poems, Bryant went over them repeatedly to smooth their texture and clarify their meaning. He gave almost as close attention to his editorials. Working under pressure to meet deadlines, however, he could not, as he often did in composing his letters, write several drafts of his articles, but he made so many changes and corrections on his manuscripts that they could be read only with difficulty even by those familiar with his handwriting.[2] One reader, the historian W. H. Prescott, regarded him as a "very great artist" in prose. The praise was conveyed to Bryant in a letter from Dana on June 23, 1848. "Frequently in his editorials," Prescott was quoted as saying, "I see the same qualities that mark his poetry, the peculiar stillness of great passions not merely controlled, but utterly vanquished, and the power of making common epithets tell."[3]

Bryant considered it a duty of an editor to be a guardian of the language. The danger of being a journalist, he was to write a few years later, was that his style was "apt to become, in consequence of much and hasty writing, loose, diffuse, and stuffed with local barbarisms and the cant phrases of the day." [4] During his more than twenty years on a newspaper he had frequently directed attention, in editorial comment, to these faults of the press, and later on sought to eliminate them from the *Evening Post* by establishing an *index expurgatorius* of undesirable words and expressions for the guidance of young staff members.* So insistent was he that the paper be a model of literate English that he would reprint as a correction a paragraph containing a typographical mistake that made hash of the meaning.

Bryant sought to keep separate his newspaper work and his home life, and almost never wrote anything for the *Evening Post* in his town lodgings or at Cedarmere.** Journalism might occupy his day but not his evenings,

---

*Containing but eighty-six items, the index excluded colloquialisms like "gents" for "gentlemen"; inflated words like "inaugurate" for "begin"; and doubtful usages like "above" and "over" for "more than." But chiefly the index was a device to obtain simplicity and unaffectedness in writing, and thus more than one-third of the list barred such words as "decease" for "death"; "devouring element" for "fire"; "rendition" for "performance"; and "repudiate" for "reject." Nevins, *The Evening Post,* p. 348.

**When Bryant undertook the writing of a history of the *Evening Post* for the paper's

which he usually devoted to study and to his family. Busy during the mornings with the dozens of tasks confronting an editor, Bryant sometimes did not have his editorial ready by one o'clock. Boggs once asked him if he could not get it done earlier, but Bryant protested that he was too occupied with other matters to get down to writing it. "Why not write it the evening before?" Boggs asked. "Ah," replied Bryant, referring to his use of his evenings for study, "if I should empty out the keg in that way it would soon be exhausted." Boggs then suggested that Bryant come earlier to the office, and he agreed that he could do this. A few months later, mentioning to Boggs his earlier arrival, Bryant said: "I like it. I go through my gymnastics, walk all the way down, and when I get here I feel like work."

Bryant had begun his physical exercises in the 1830's after joining an athletic club conducted by a prizefighter. Boggs described Bryant's routine: "Every morning, for half an hour, he would go through a series of evolutions on the backs of two chairs placed side by side. He would hang on the door of his bedroom, pulling himself up and down an infinite number of times. He would skirmish around the apartment after all fashions, and once, he told me, under the table. Breakfast followed, then a walk down town; and then he was in the best of spirits for the writing his editorial article for the day."[5]

Though soon to be lampooned by James Russell Lowell as being

as quiet, as cool, and as dignified,
As a smooth, silent iceberg, that never is ignified

Bryant did not entirely live in "supreme iceolation."* In January of 1847

fiftieth anniversary on Nov. 15, 1851, John Bigelow suggested that he do it at Roslyn so that he would not be subject to interruptions. "He rejected the proposal as abruptly as if he had been asked to offer sacrifices to Apollo," Bigelow related. "He would allow no such work to follow him there. Not even the shadow of his business must fall upon the consecrated haunts of his muse." *William Cullen Bryant* (Boston and New York, 1890), p. 109.

*Lowell may have borne Bryant some personal malice in writing about him in *A Fable for Critics*. He was miffed when he learned that *Graham's Magazine*, which had offered him twenty dollars a poem if he would become a contributor, was paying Longfellow and Bryant fifty dollars. Leon Howard, *Victorian Knight-Errant* (Berkeley and Los Angeles, 1952), p. 265. In a letter of May 12, 1848, to a friend, Charles F. Briggs, editor of the *Broadway Journal*, Lowell said, however, that his section on Bryant was "funny, and as far as I could make it, immitigably just." Briggs had written him that Bryant was saying that Lowell's "To the Past" was derived from his own poem "The Past." Lowell angrily denied that he had been influenced by Bryant: "*I* steal from him indeed! . . . Does he think that he *invented* the Past and has a prescription title to it? Do not think I am provoked. I am simply amused. If he attended a meeting in the rotunda of the New York Gallery of Fine Arts at which the Century Club was formally organized as a successor to the Sketch Club, which for twenty years had been the outlet for his gayer hours when he could forget politics and the problems of government. There were forty-two charter members of the Century—old friends like Verplanck, Halleck, Inman, Durand, and Charles Leupp—and the former spirit of drollness and lightheartedness that had marked the meetings of the Sketch Club, for it had become primarily a social club, was not entirely lost in the new organization that had a constitution, bylaws, and club-rooms. There were billiards and bowling for those who wanted them, but the early Knickerbocker love for genial talk still prevailed in this organiza-tion whose members were made up, "like Joseph's coat, of many colors" —painters, poets, lawyers, editors, clergymen, merchants, physicians, and scientists. Bryant's former collaborator Verplanck was elected president, holding that office until 1864. During the first year the membership grew to eighty and shortly afterward to the one hundred persons, or Centu-rions, to be admitted.[6]

Bryant was also an occasional visitor at the literary salons where charm-ing hostesses with the inclination if not the talent to be writers welcomed their guests. Among these hostesses was his friend Caroline M. Kirkland. It was at one of her open houses that he first met a young admirer, Bayard Taylor, who was editing a weekly newspaper in Phoenixville, Pennsyl-vania. Taylor had been in Europe in 1845 while Bryant was there and the two were in Florence at the same time in October. But Taylor had been too diffident then to introduce himself. "I did not wish to call on him directly," he related, "but went to the galleries, hoping to meet him."[7] Taylor had returned to the United States and described his trip in a book, *Views Afoot,* and in the first number of the Phoenixville *Pioneer,* which he established in 1846, had reprinted from *Graham's Magazine* Bryant's "O Mother of a Mighty Race." On a trip to New York in the summer of 1847 Taylor was fortunate enough to meet Bryant at one of Mrs. Kirkland's gatherings. "Bryant is her most intimate friend, and she gave me a deep insight into his character," Taylor wrote to a friend. "Bryant I found calm

---

he had *riled* me, I might have knocked him into a cocked hat in my satire." A few years later, in a letter to the art critic William J. Stillman, Lowell admitted that he had been unfair: "I am quite sensible now that I did not do Mr. Bryant justice in the 'Fable.' But there was no personal feeling in what I said—though I have regretted what I *did* say because it might seem personal." *Letters of James Russell Lowell* (Charles Eliot Norton, ed., New York, 1894), I, 131, 221.

and cold, as I had expected, but having the stamp of greatness in his countenance."*[8]

Another salon at which Bryant was sometimes a visitor was that of Anne Charlotte Lynch, the striving poet who had gone from Providence to New York in 1845 to teach English composition at the Brooklyn Academy for Women. Her home in Waverly Place soon became a center for intellectual and social life, where Miss Lynch in one of the two upstairs parlors welcomed her guests, the ladies elaborately coiffured and wearing hoopskirts beautifully embroidered and the gentlemen somberly clad in black. Bryant's old friends like Miss Sedgwick, Mrs. Kirkland, Halleck, the Rev. Orville Dewey, and many others attended the salon, but there he also met the younger literati—Poe, Margaret Fuller, Richard Henry Stoddard,** Griswold, and the women poets whom Poe overpraised in his magazine reviews. It was at one of these gatherings that Bryant had the idea of asking a friend of several years' standing, Mrs. Eliza Farnham, to sound out John Bigelow about joining the *Evening Post*. Mrs. Farnham had been head of the women's prison at Sing Sing, and Bryant shared her views on penal reform, including the abolition of capital punishment, advocated strongly in the paper's editorials since a bill to do away with the death penalty was introduced in the state legislature in 1841. Escorting Mrs. Farnham home one night in February of 1847, Bigelow, a friend since the days when he was inspector of prisons, was told that there was a place for

---

*Taylor, after his return to Phoenixville, wrote Bryant Oct. 19, saying he wished to give up his weekly paper and asking what the prospects were for his getting a situation in New York. Goddard-Roslyn Collection. Bryant replied on Nov. 30, apologizing for his delay because he could not make up his mind what advice to give. There were advantages to living in New York—"the intellect is incited to greater exertions, is invigorated by collision with other intellects, and finds more abundant aliment"—but there were disadvantages also— literary employment was uncertain and the rewards were scanty. *Life and Letters of Bayard Taylor* (Marie Hansen-Taylor and Horace E. Scudder, eds., Boston, 1885), I, 105.

**On Dec. 1 Bryant noted in the *Evening Post* the receipt of Stoddard's first collection of poems, *Footprints*, accompanied by some lines in manuscript:

> This little offering is my first, in sooth
> I know not what its worthiness may be;
> A wreath of wildest flowers and pleasant weeds,
> The growth of nature and the simple seeds,
> Scattered with prodigal hands by careless youth,
> I cast it at the feet of poesy. . . .

Bryant praised the little volume, saying he had read it "with uncommon pleasure" and thought the author wrote from "the true poetic instinct."

him on the paper if he were interested. He was, but not to the extent of giving up his law practice for only a salaried journalistic position.[9]

During the winter of 1847–1848 Bryant was concerned over the serious illness of Thomas Cole, an illness that resulted in his death on February 12. In an editorial that might have been applied to his own poetry, Bryant praised Cole as being the first artist to portray on canvas "the wild magnificence" of American scenery and to give it "a moral interest." He was led to write an extended memoir of his friend when the National Academy of Design asked him to deliver a funeral oration. Bryant worked on the address—the first of similar tributes he was to pay to old friends, Cooper, Irving, Halleck, and Verplanck—during April. He gave the oration, which ran to about ten thousand words, on May 4, and it was printed as a pamphlet by D. Appleton & Company for the academy. Dana liked it as a whole, he wrote Bryant on June 23, but he thought Bryant's comparison of Cole's death to the sudden disappearance before one's eyes of one of the Catskill mountains or the blotting out of the night sky of a planet like Hesperus or Jupiter a little "over-strong." Bryant replied that the criticism might be just but explained: "It was written in very sincere and deep grief for his loss; I did not stop to measure my phrases."[10]

II

With the capture of Mexico City in September of 1847, it was clear that the war with Mexico was all but ended and that the chief political issue of the presidential campaign year of 1848 would be the extension of slavery into the new territories of New Mexico and California. In the debate over whether United States troops should be evacuated immediately from central Mexico or garrison forces should be maintained, Bryant argued for the latter since they were needed to support the government against revolution. On June 9 he expressed satisfaction with the terms of the peace treaty negotiated by President Polk, but he thought that the purchase price of the new territory by war was too high even when the moral issue was disregarded.

Early in 1847 Bryant had believed that the question of slavery in the territories could be left to the decision of those who settled the country, but before the year was out he realized that there was not much chance of a compromise on this issue with the South. He therefore urged that Congress forbid the extension of slavery into the new lands, wholeheartedly supporting the Wilmot Proviso. But even early in 1848 Bryant did not appreciate the strength of the southern position. When General Lewis

339

Cass, a foe of the Wilmot Proviso and a prospective presidential candidate, gave his views in a long letter carried in the *Evening Post* on January 3, Bryant could not agree with him that Congress should not interfere in the matter because to do so would breed dissensions between the North and the South. "It is for Congress to do what is its duty, without a sickly uneasiness or regard to consequences," Bryant declared. Despite the nullification movement in Virginia and South Carolina, Bryant maintained that there was no danger to the Union. The South had acquiesced in the Missouri Compromise, and there was no reason to believe that it would not acquiesce in barring slavery from California and New Mexico. Bryant ridiculed Cass's argument that Congress had no constitutional power to forbid slavery in the territories. "If this be the proper construction," Bryant wrote, "General Cass must take it with all its consequences. According to such a construction, it is unconstitutional to appoint governors and secretaries of our territories, as we have done for the last sixty years. It is unconstitutional to frame a government for the territories; it is unconstitutional to give them a legislature by act of Congress." Bryant's sarcastic conclusion was that "nobody ever dreamed of such a construction of the constitution until recently."

The Democratic party put together by Andrew Jackson was hopelessly split over the issue of slavery, and efforts were being made to form a coalition of free-soil men in the North to act as one in the presidential election. There was much talk of forming a new party, bringing together the antislavery Democrats of the North and dissident Whigs, but political leaders doubted that one could be formed and doubted even more that one could succeed. Salmon P. Chase, a former Whig who was working with the Liberty party in Ohio, had written the Democratic senator from New Hampshire, John P. Hale, in 1847 wondering if a third party could not be got together. He was doubtful, suggesting that it might be better to support all antislavery men in the major parties. Bryant likewise did not believe that anything could be accomplished through a new party, writing his brother John on February 7, 1848: "All parties formed for a single measure are necessarily short-lived, and are as much subject to the abuses and vices of party as any other—I have sometimes thought more so. I never mean to belong to any of them unless I see some very strong and compelling reason for it. The journalist who goes into one of these narrow associations gains by it no increase of independence in discussion, while he parts with the greater part of his influence. . . ."[11]

As for the Democrats of New York, Bryant believed that no candidate not against extension of slavery would receive a vote in the state. "We

... will contend for the measures and principles we think right, let what will come of it," he declared. He was convinced, however, that the state had the key role in the presidential election, declaring in several editorials that the Democrats could not expect to win without the thirty-six electoral votes of New York. "New York must be conciliated," he asserted on April 13, "and given a candidate the people can vote for."

Martin Van Buren, since his failure to obtain the presidential nomination in 1844, had retired again to his agricultural pursuits, taking pride, however, in the witty and incisive attacks of his son John, the most popular spokesman of the Barnburners after giving the main address at the Herkimer convention in October. The father, since the death of Silas Wright, was the one man, however, who had the prestige and the experience to lead the liberal cause. Late in the winter of 1848 he had written a manifesto setting forth the Free-Soil view, the manuscript of which he had given to Samuel J. Tilden to put into "proper shape" for presenting to the public.[12] The occasion determined upon was to issue it as an address of the Democratic members of the New York legislature on April 12. The question of slavery, the address declared, could no longer be evaded or postponed. A slave-labor and a free-labor system could not coexist, and it was the duty of the government to protect the laboring masses "in their rights to political and social equality and in the secure enjoyment of the fruits of their industry." This address was the platform which the Barnburner delegation bore to the national Democratic convention at Baltimore on May 22.

The *Evening Post* had two correspondents at the convention whose dispatches were sent to New York by telegraph. Bryant was outraged when reports of the first day's proceedings revealed that neither of the New York delegations was seated, and he expressed the fear that the state would have no voice in the nomination at all. He could not see why the Barnburner delegation was not seated at once, writing of the Hunker delegation chosen at Albany: "The agents in so notorious a fraud should have been turned from the door with very little ceremony." When the convention tried to resolve the problem by admitting both delegations and splitting the New York vote, Bryant praised the Barnburners for refusing to be seated. He chose to consider as a "nullity" the nomination of General Cass for President and General William O. Butler of Kentucky for vice-president. "It is entitled to just as much consideration, and no more," he declared, "as if it were an accidental meeting of persons on board a steamboat, taking a vote to ascertain who was the favorite candidate of the greatest number of individuals present."

341

Though opposed in principle to a third-party movement, Bryant praised the decision of New York Democrats to hold a convention to nominate their own candidates, and he was one of the twelve hundred signers of a call for a mass meeting in the city on June 6 to protest the Baltimore convention. Most of page two of the *Evening Post* was taken up with a report of the event. The Whig nomination of General Zachary Taylor for President and Millard Fillmore of New York for vice-president at Philadelphia on June 7 convinced Bryant that the election was already virtually settled. Taylor would sweep "the south from Cape May to Key West and from the Ohio to the Rio Grande," and his prospects were scarcely less satisfactory in the North. Nevertheless, Bryant consulted frequently with the young Barnburners—John Van Buren, Tilden, Bigelow, and Preston King—in planning the Utica convention at which Martin Van Buren was nominated for President and General Henry Dodge of Wisconsin for vice-president. He regretted editorially on June 23 that the convention did not have "more of a national character" and worked closely with the leaders of the movement to bring together all the antislavery forces for the national Free-Soil convention at Buffalo on August 9. When Salmon P. Chase wrote John Van Buren on June 19 to find out about the Buffalo meeting, the free-territory men of Ohio being in doubt about what course would be pursued there, it was Bryant who dictated the letter of reply signed by Tilden. It was to be merely a mass convention, a "voluntary assemblage of individuals," and there would be no attempt to apportion delegations as at a party convention. As to the choice for President, the New York Democrats would accept no one but Van Buren though they were not so strongly committed to General Dodge for vice-president.[13] In editorials Bryant made it clear that the Utica meeting had been attended only by dissident New York Democrats; the Buffalo meeting was a national convention of Free-Soilers. The meeting, which attracted several thousand delegates—Barnburners, Liberty party men, Conscience Whigs, and others on the outs with things as they were—was held in a huge tent under a broiling sun. Bryant praised the nomination of Van Buren and Charles Francis Adams, a Conscience Whig from Boston: "We have candidates with whom we are satisfied, whom we can trust—in electing whom we cannot be deceived, and from whom we are not obliged to invent or imagine a creed suited to the latitude in which we live."

Since Bryant had not expected Van Buren and Adams to win, he was not greatly disturbed by their defeat in November. He was disappointed that many Free-Soilers defected and voted for Taylor in order to defeat Cass, but he considered the Free-Soil balloting "large enough to show that a powerful anti-extension party has been formed." In a later editorial on "the moral of the election" Bryant, who had heretofore given nominal support to Polk, turned his sarcasm loose on the President. The country, Bryant said, should be grateful to Polk for his misuse of patronage. "There is one service which any officer be he never so weak and never so wicked can always render the public," the editorial declared. "He can so abuse the discretionary powers with which he is invested as to animate his constituency with a common purpose of reform, by which the possibility of the recurrence of such abuses will be prevented forever. The more wicked or foolish the officer, the greater will be the service he is thus likely to render."

III

Except for weekends at Roslyn and one trip of a few days to the Berkshires, Bryant throughout 1848 had been tethered to his desk at the *Evening Post.* To obtain a longer range, he must obtain someone to serve as his assistant, and he turned again, with Tilden acting as his emissary, to lure the thirty-one-year-old John Bigelow into joining the staff. The older and the younger man held the same political principles and Bigelow had proved himself an excellent expounder of them in his contributions to the paper; Bigelow had impressed Bryant as a practical man of affairs, moreover, in his work with the New York constitutional convention, his services as inspector of Sing Sing prison, and his activities in the Free-Soil party; he was, therefore, just the man needed as his substitute as well as his associate on the *Evening Post.* But Bigelow was firm in his refusal to accept a salaried position. "Unless they want me in the firm, they don't want me enough to withdraw me from my profession," he told Tilden. Even for a partner, the *Evening Post,* despite its prestige, offered no great financial attraction for an ambitious and confident man. Not one to go into any project blindly, Bigelow found that since 1839 the firm's average annual earnings had been $37,360.76 a year and the average dividends had been $9,776.44 a year. But he did not like the law and he thought he would like journalism.

Finally, during the early fall, William Boggs, embarrassed by heavy borrowings to carry on personal business projects, offered to sell his three and one-tenth shares in the firm for $15,000. The deal was completed when Bryant agreed to pay Boggs $12,500 in regular installments at seven per cent interest to come out of Bigelow's earnings and Bigelow was able to borrow $2,500 to cover Boggs's immediate needs. The transfer was

announced on December 5. Bryant was the controlling shareholder and Bigelow and Timothy Howe, who became business manager in place of Boggs, held equal shares. Bigelow estimated his income under the arrangement would amount to about $1,500. It was less than he earned as a lawyer but he thought he had made a good bargain. "I had so much confidence . . . in my ability, with Mr. Bryant's assistance, to render the paper more productive," he wrote in his *Retrospections*, "that I did not quarrel with the price, though in it the proprietors seemed to be discounting its prospects. They were so anxious, however, to secure what they hoped would prove a more useful partner than Mr. Boggs that they acceded to terms which they would probably have rejected."[14] This view might very well be true, but Bryant's overriding interest in the sale was that with Bigelow as his associate he could get away from the *Evening Post* more often and for longer periods. In any case, he wasted little time in resuming his travels. Within two and one-half months after Bigelow joined the staff, Bryant left on March 21, 1849, with Charles M. Leupp on a trip to the South and to Cuba, returning to New York in May, and then after only three weeks he was off again with Leupp, on June 13, to Europe for a six months' tour.

During the past year Bryant had made a careful study of public opinion in the South on the slavery issue, reprinting editorials from its newspapers and carrying reports of the speeches of its politicians and governors' messages under a heading, "The Voice of the South." But he did not make this trip with a view to getting information at first hand. Because of his editorials against slavery, he was hated too widely to expect to talk freely with the South's leaders.* As a matter of fact, his Free-Soil stand had hurt the business of the *Evening Post* in New York. "Southern business men resented anything with an abolition tinge," Bigelow recalled, "and most of our advertisers looked to the South for business. It was enough for a Northern merchant to report in the South that a rival firm advertised in the *Evening Post* to close accounts between such firm and any of its Southern customers, to whose notice the fact was pretty sure to be brought. Some of the oldest and best friends of the *Evening Post* gave this as their

---

*On Jan. 16, 1849, the *Evening Post* replied to an attack made on it by President Polk's organ, the Washington *Union*, which had complained of its "insulting taunts upon the South." "The *Post* is certainly not aware of the mischief which such insulting language is calculated to inflict," the *Union* had said. "It contributes to make the South only the more determined in any purpose which she may adopt. . . . We beg the *Post* to forbear." Bryant answered that the *Evening Post* would not forbear "until New Mexico and California are closed to slavery by act of Congress, or as long as slave interests are able to dominate the Democratic party and elect proslavery men to office."

excuse for withdrawing their advertisements."[15] Bryant, therefore, planned only to visit William Gilmore Simms in South Carolina before going on to Cuba. His interest in the island was one of long standing, dating from his first years in New York when, living in the home of a Spanish-speaking family, he had met a number of Cuban visitors and had written his tale, "A Story of the Island of Cuba," for the 1830 volume of *The Talisman.*

The voyage from New York to Savannah on the new ship *Tennessee* making her first trip out to sea was a delightful one.[16] Bryant described humorously in his first letter to the *Evening Post* some of the passengers: two young brides "too happy to do anything but laugh, even when suffering with seasickness," and who, after retiring to their staterooms, could be heard "shouting and squealing"; two "long-limbed gentlemen" who spent most of the time on sofas, "each with a spittoon before him, chewing tobacco with great rapidity and industry, and apparently absorbed in the endeavor to fill it within a given time"; and "a robust old gentleman" who had interminable tales to tell of his home-place, Norwalk, Connecticut. From Savannah, Bryant sailed back up the coast to Charleston, and then went by train to Augusta before going on to see the Simmses in the Barnwell district. Though he visited a fine Georgia plantation, one of ten thousand acres and large enough for a German principality, he was most interested in the newly established textile mills which turned out a coarse cotton cloth. These mills furnished the first employment ever open to the "crackers" outside of farming, and Bryant saw in them a way to a better life for these people. The mill owners had at first tried to work the poor whites alongside the blacks but the effort failed and the use of slave labor in them was abandoned.

Sailing from Charleston on the steamer *Isabel,* Bryant reached Havana after four days. On his first visit to the tropics, he found that it required "a greater effort of resolution to sit down to the writing of a long letter" than it would have been in the North. He felt "a temptation to sit idly, and let the grateful wind from the sea, coming in at the broad windows, flow around me." But he found the energy to take in all the sights. He wrote in detail about the Campo Santo, or public cemetery, where the coffins of the more opulent dead were placed in niches in the thick surrounding wall and the bodies of the less opulent were thrown into foul trenches to be devoured by quicklime. At the cockfights, the principal diversion of the island, he watched the screaming bettors enjoying the brutal sport, and could not help thinking that soon they would lie in the pits of the Campo Santo; and at a masked ball, where Spanish dances were gracefully performed, the same thought came to mind that these gay celebrants of the end of Lent too would ultimately find their way to that indiscriminate burial-place.

Additional letters to the *Evening Post* described the vegetation of the Cuban countryside, then not at its best because it was the dry season, the coffee estates near San Antonio, and the sugar estates southeast of Matanzas. Bryant's last letter, written at Havana on April 22, gave an account of the execution, by *garrote,* of a slave who had killed his master. The event took place about half past eight in the morning before a huge crowd. The victim, his wrists bound together, was led to a platform and seated before a post fixed with an iron collar which was placed about his neck. A screw attached to the side of the collar was so arranged that when turned it would push forward an iron bolt against the back of the neck and crush the spine. "After a few turns, the criminal gave a sudden shrug of the shoulders," Bryant related; "another turn of the screw and a shudder ran over his whole frame, his eyes rolled wildly, his hands, still tied with the rope, were convulsively jerked upward, and then dropped back to their place motionless forever." Bryant said he had never intended to see an execution, but he had been led to attend because of the unusual method of inflicting death and his desire to note the behavior of the people. "The horror of the spectacle," he confessed, "now caused me to regret that I made one of a crowd drawn to look at it by an idle curiosity."

Bryant also reported on slaves in Cuba, trade in which, though illegal, was being carried on openly, with several hundred being landed at a time by boats from Africa. The ease with which fresh slaves could be obtained to replace those who died or became too old to work had resulted in poorer treatment of bondmen than some years before when the trade in human merchandise had been halted, for there was no need to look after their welfare. "The whip is always in sight," Bryant noted. But black slaves from Africa were not the only ones imported. Indians of Yucatan, taken prisoner by white settlers, were sold to Cuban slavers, and Asians brought in as contract labor were also treated as bondmen. While Bryant was in Havana, the newspapers printed an ordinance governing the handling of these—how much maize or rice and other food they should receive daily and the number of lashes by cowskin that could be administered for misbehavior. Though sanctioning such barbarity, the government, Bryant observed, "betrays great concern for the salvation of the souls of those whom it thus delivers over to the lash of the slave-driver." The American Indians were to be treated as Christians already, but the Asians must be carefully instructed in the doctrines of religion.

Bryant and Leupp landed at Liverpool on June 23 after a voyage of less than two weeks on the steamer *Niagara*—the trip being very pleasant, Bryant wrote Frances—and went on immediately to London.[17] Bryant's friend and admirer, the poet Samuel Rogers, then in his eighties, greeted him enthusiastically. "You look hearty and cheerful," Rogers told Bryant; "but *our* poets seem to be losing their minds." Then, without malice, for Rogers was the most agreeable and kindest of persons, he went on to say that Thomas Campbell's son was in the madhouse and that, if the father had been put there during the last years of his life, it would have been the proper place for him. Robert Southey had died in 1843, *his* mental powers gone. Thomas Moore, then in London, was showing signs of going the way of these two. Meeting Moore, Rogers had asked how long he had been in town. "Three or four days," he replied; but when Rogers protested that Moore had not let him know, he had put his hand to his forehead and said, "I beg your pardon. I believe I came to town this morning." But Bryant would not find Wordsworth changed. "He still talks rationally," Rogers said.

Having seen the standard tourist attractions on his previous trip, Bryant spent most of his time viewing the art exhibitions. In his 1845 visit Bryant had been most impressed by the excellence of English artists in their watercolors, and he wrote now to the *Evening Post* at length of those exhibited in Pall Mall. "The English may be almost said to have created this branch of art," he said. Of the annual exhibition of the Royal Academy, he said that "its general character is mediocrity, unrelieved by any works of extraordinary or striking merit."

By July 11 Bryant and Leupp were in Edinburgh on their way to the Orkney and Shetland Islands, the "farthest Thule" of the Romans. Bryant delighted in the wild and magnificent landscape of the islands, often hidden in fog, and at Bressay ascended the towering rock called the Noup of the Noss. The heights were the gathering place of thousands of sea birds, a cloud of them constantly in the air, and the face of the rocks was "tapestried" with flowers—"daisies nodding in the wind, and the crimson phlox, seeming to set the cliffs on flame; yellow buttercups, and a variety of other plants in bloom." Bryant, seeking vaster distances to view, continued his climb to the summit, where, in a cold mist and a wind so strong he could hardly stand, he looked down upon the dizzy depths below and out to sea where he had a prospect before him of green island summits with "their bold headlands, the winding straits between, and the black rocks standing out in the sea."

After the trip to the northern islands, Bryant visited at various places in Scotland—Aberdeen, Inverness, Glenshacken, Oban, Glasgow, and Edinburgh—before returning to London to cross the channel to France on

August 9. His account of his travels on the continent was an unrelieved description of suppression of the people by the military following the democratic and nationalistic revolutions of 1848. "Whoever should visit the principal countries of Europe at the present moment," Bryant wrote the *Evening Post* from Paris on September 13, "might take them for conquered provinces, held in subjection by their victorious masters, at the point of the sword." During 1848 Bryant had published full accounts of the uprisings of that year. He had not been optimistic that the people could throw off their centuries-old chains, although he had been inclined to think that the revolution in France might succeed. But, taking the long view expressed in his poem "The Ages," Bryant had written Dana on April 8: "That earth is to become a paradise in consequence of any political changes that may or can be made, I do not believe but I believe it to be in the order of Providence that republican institutions will come in with a higher and more general civilization, and that their effect is good and wholesome."[18] There was, however, no immediate prospect of such amelioration in Europe in 1849. In Paris, soldiers filled the streets and marched before the churches whose cornices bore the inscription "Liberty, Equality, and Fraternity." Going into Germany, Bryant found the cities along the Rhine crowded with soldiers, and at Heidelberg, pleasant memories of which Bryant held because of earlier sojourns there, he was appalled to find it occupied by Prussian troops. He left as soon as possible for Stuttgart, but conditions were no different there, nor were they in Munich, where news arrived of the fall of the Hungarian republic. "So perishes the last hope of European liberty," a Bavarian said to Bryant. Leaving Munich, Bryant went to the border town of Lindau, where he took passage on a steamer across the Lake of Constance to Rorschach in Switzerland. Not a soldier was to be seen. "Nobody asked for our passports," Bryant related, "nobody required us to submit our baggage to search. I could almost have kneeled and kissed the shore of the hospitable republic."

IV

When Bryant returned to New York in December, he could see that he had exercised good judgment in bringing Bigelow to the paper, for its editorial sentiments had been expressed as he would have expressed them, with decorum and decisiveness; the news coverage had been improved; and the firm's business was good, despite a cholera epidemic in the summer, with increases in revenue from the job-printing department and the advertising and circulation. From the Free-Soil vice-presidential candidate of 1848 came a letter on December 25 inclosing a payment of twenty dollars for a subscription in which Charles Francis Adams called the *Evening Post* "the best daily journal in the United States."[19]

Bigelow took an interest in both the business and editorial sides of the paper. He had turned the lagging job-printing department into one of the firm's best assets in January when he decided to seek the legal printing in the city. A law had been passed requiring that all court cases submitted on appeal be printed. With Bryant's concurrence, Bigelow inserted a notice at the head of the editorial column on January 24 directing attention to the firm's "well appointed book and job printing establishment." Aggressively going after such printing and doing the work speedily, the firm before several years passed handled most of the city's legal printing. Bigelow recalled that in 1848 the job-printing office had a net income of only $150 but in a year or two after he joined the firm it was bringing in $10,000 and continued to do so year after year. Bigelow saw that Timothy Howe was not much of a business manager, and before long he was able to place the clerk Isaac Henderson in charge of the accounts of both the job-printing department and the newspaper.[20] The discovery of gold in California in January of 1848, the first report of which was printed in the *Evening Post* on December 4, impelled scores of thousands of people to rush to California. Bigelow took advantage of this, beginning in November of 1849, by issuing "extras" for circulation in Central America, California, Oregon, and the Sandwich Islands to give the news of Europe and the United States. To increase the circulation of the twice-a-week and weekly editions of the paper, he began printing the names of representatives authorized to solicit and collect for subscriptions throughout the country.

As a participant in the councils of the Free-Soilers and Barnburners and carrying on a large private correspondence with public figures, Bigelow heard much political gossip that could not be printed as news or used in editorials. He hit upon the idea of getting such information into print by inventing interviews with a character, "John Brown, Ferryman," an illiterate but shrewd observer who reported what he heard from congressmen, governors, and other public men whom he carried back and forth on the ferry between New York and New Jersey. Published usually once a week, the articles became perhaps the most popular feature of the *Evening Post.* These pieces, as well as Bryant's anecdotal editorials, made the paper interesting reading, at least for a sixpenny political and commercial sheet, though of course it had little appeal to the multitude, which preferred James Gordon Bennett's spicy and sensational *Herald.*

21

CURRENT STRIFE AND ANCIENT SCENES

ADMIRING BRYANT'S *Evening Post* LETTERS ABOUT HIS THIRD trip to Europe, Richard Henry Dana suggested that these, with his earlier travel reports, should be gathered into a book. Bryant found that the New York firm of George P. Putnam would be interested in such a volume, travel books being eagerly read in the 1840's, and he went through the files of the paper to assemble his letters. The volume that appeared early in 1850, *Letters of a Traveller,* contained fifty-three reports published during the fifteen years intervening between the first, written in Paris on August 9, 1834, and the last, written in the same city on September 13, 1849, a total of about one hundred and thirty thousand words.*

Going through the files to obtain the letters, which were published in the book with no major revisions, Bryant was led to contemplate the *Evening Post's* history since he had been connected with it. He summed up his thoughts in a long editorial on March 14, 1850, in which he proudly set forth the principle of independence by which it had been conducted

---

*Bryant in his short introduction said his letters might have been more interesting if he had "spoken of distinguished men to whose society he was admitted." He did not write of them because he feared to overstep the limits of propriety if he made such personal references. He wrote Dana on July 4, 1850, that it had sold fairly well, which should please the booksellers, and that the newspapers had been "civil" in their reviews. Goddard-Roslyn Collection; Godwin, *Biography,* II, 53.

and defended it against its current enemies who objected to its Free-Soil doctrines and its caustic attacks on the defenders of slavery.**

The country was deeply stirred by the great debate taking place in the Senate provoked on January 29 when Henry Clay introduced his compromise resolutions designed to preserve the Union by settling the differences between the North and South. The debate was to be the last appearance together on the national stage of the three men who had played such notable parts in the historical drama of the past quarter century—Clay, Webster, and Calhoun. Bryant delayed editorial comment on the resolutions until February 6, when the complete text became available for publication. The paper's Washington correspondent had earlier described them as "an octagon, presenting sides and angles enough to challenge attention of men of all shades of sentiment." When Clay rose to open the debate on February 5, the ladies, according to the correspondent, took possession of the upper chamber by storm, displacing all with the exception of senators and reporters. Never friendly in the past to Clay, Bryant now expressed admiration for his bold stand as a senator from a slave state in asserting that slavery had no legal existence in the new territories and that Congress had the authority to legislate on the question. The editorial condemned the policy of President Taylor of doing nothing. "The politician and the warrior seem in this instance to have changed characters," Bryant wrote. "Mr. Clay gallantly beards the disunionists; General Taylor avoids the responsibility and skulks from the danger."

The *Evening Post,* as it had with Clay's speech, printed in full Calhoun's speech of March 4. Although Bryant did not regard Calhoun's address as contributing anything to the solution of the slavery problem and believed him wrong in saying the Union could not continue if the Clay plan or the administration plan for the admission of California were adopted, he praised him for the earnestness of his endeavor:

> Its illustrious author is standing upon the brink of the grave; he has been struggling with a disease which has confined him to a sick chamber for several months, and with which he does not expect much longer to contend successfully. Regardless of the hours or days which the excitement may abbreviate his mortal career, he totters to his seat in the body of which he has for so many years been a distinguished ornament, and submits, in

**On June 17 the *Evening Post* reporter was barred from a dinner at which Senator Daniel S. Dickinson, a Hunker Democrat, spoke in favor of Clay's compromise bills. Bryant wrote that it was a long speech "in which the cold meats of the banquet presented every day in Congress were served up."

writing, to his countrymen, a speech which he had not strength to read, and which contains what is probably destined to be his last public declaration upon the subject of slavery.

But for Webster, who spoke on March 7 in support of the Clay resolutions, Bryant had nothing but scorn. Beginning with the first comment on his speech and continuing during the summer, the paper attacked him in terms of unmerciful ridicule. In arguing that climate and geography would prevent extension of slavery into the new territory, Webster showed less percipience than Calhoun, who saw that if there were no legal barriers against slavery the slave owners would "take care of the rest." When the Washington *Union* praised Webster's "manly speech" in which he had the "moral courage to risk himself for his country," Bryant was outraged: "Mr. Webster's 'manliness' and 'moral courage' consist in attempting to turn the battle into a universal defeat for the north; he is 'bold' enough to offer to run away from every point which the enemy wish to gain." The paper on May 6 reprinted from the *National Era,* which later was to publish Harriet Beecher Stowe's *Uncle Tom's Cabin,* Whittier's poem "Ichabod" decrying Webster's apostasy. To expose Webster more fully as a betrayer of principle, the paper reprinted earlier statements of his against slavery. In this project it had the enthusiastic aid of Charles Sumner, then being backed by a coalition of Massachusetts Free-Soilers and Democrats for the Senate. Sumner had first met Bryant in 1841, but in the attack on Webster he worked with John Bigelow, supplying him with ammunition in a half dozen letters in the spring and summer of 1850.[1]

During the summer, while Clay's select committee of thirteen was considering the resolutions, Bryant maintained that the purpose of the compromise—to preserve the Union—was pointless, since there was no danger of the South's seceding. He was confirmed in this belief when the Nashville convention of southern advocates of separation was dominated by moderates and in June merely recommended extension of the Missouri Compromise line westward to the Pacific. Its resolutions, Bryant wrote, "were but faint and reduced copies of those passed by the legislatures of several of the slave states—a revised edition of a bad farce, with the only tolerable jokes left out."

Of the measures passed in September that made up the Compromise of 1850, the *Evening Post* objected most strenuously to the Texas and New Mexico Act, which organized New Mexico as a territory without restriction on slavery and paid Texas ten million dollars, as the paper said, "for fixing the boundary" of the state, and the Fugitive Slave Act, which placed the problem of slaves fleeing the South under exclusive federal jurisdiction. The paper delayed comment on the Fugitive Slave Act, passed on September 4, until October 2, waiting to see how it would be enforced. The occasion to attack the law came when a Negro, James Hamlet, was seized in Pennsylvania and carried off to Maryland. As summarized in an editorial, under the law "any man of ambiguous color" in the North might be seized, taken instantly before a commissioner, and without a trial by jury, without counsel, without cross-examination of witnesses and on testimony of men unknown in the community, be transported to another place. This procedure violated all principles and practices of American justice, the paper declared, and no worse tyranny could be found in any place on earth. From then on, the paper publicized all instances that came to its notice of the seizure of fugitive slaves and denounced the law that made this ruthless violation of freedom possible.

II

During the first two months of 1850 Bryant was without the services of Bigelow on the paper. Since Parke Godwin had returned to the staff, Bryant could have made one of his usual summer trips, but because of the momentous debate over Clay's compromise measures, he chose, as he wrote Dana, to remain "grinding wearisomely at the mill."[2] Bigelow had left on January 3 for Jamaica to study the conditions in which the free Negroes there lived with the idea that he might contribute something to the discussion of emancipation in the United States. His twelve articles, published between February 20 and May 24, were issued as a book, *Jamaica in 1850; or, the Effects of Sixteen Years of Freedom on a Slave Colony.*

While caught up in the mainstream of political events, Bryant became personally involved in one of the most distasteful situations in his life in January when he was asked to serve as an intermediary between the actor Edwin Forrest and his wife Catherine in their negotiations for a divorce.[3] Bryant and his family, especially his daughter Fanny, who was a bosom friend of Catherine, were intimates of the actor and his wife. Like Othello, the role he played in his New York debut at the Park Theatre in 1826, Forrest had nursed suspicions of his wife for several years. These seem to have been confirmed when he discovered a love letter to Catherine from the minor actor George Jamieson. Told by Forrest that she must leave his house, Catherine confided her troubles to the Godwins in April of 1849. They insisted that she stay with them until a formal separation could be effected. But the matter dragged on, and she moved for a time to the household of the littérateur Nathaniel Parker Willis, one of the men that Forrest later accused of being intimate with his wife, and then stayed with the Bryants at Roslyn. Forrest employed Theodore Sedgwick, Jr., to represent him in a divorce action, and Catherine, upon Godwin's advice, employed Charles O'Conor. Bryant was brought into the disagreeable situation when Forrest and Sedgwick asked him to serve as their intermediary in communicating with Mrs. Forrest. He was unsuccessful, however, in getting the two parties to agree on procedures.

Despite efforts to keep the affair a secret, it reached the newspapers, and Forrest's feelings were exacerbated by what was printed. On June 16, he encountered Willis in Washington Square and attacked him. Two days later, meeting Bryant and Godwin on Broadway, he angrily asked which of them had put in the *Evening Post* a story saying that the attack had been made from behind. Godwin, as he later testified in a suit brought by Willis for assault, said that it had been printed on his responsibility. In November Mrs. Forrest filed suit for divorce in New York, accusing her husband of infidelities. The trial, however, did not begin until December 16, 1851. It lasted six weeks, ending with a verdict for Mrs. Forrest, during which newspaper readers were regaled daily with thousands of words of testimony about all-night parties, hotel and bawdy house assignations, and bedroom embraces of some of the city's most fashionable people.

With the exception of a meeting of the Sketch Club in the late spring at the home of the Rev. Orville Dewey at Sheffield, Massachusetts, Bryant made no trips during 1850. Although members of the Sketch Club had helped found the Century, they were unwilling to give up their pleasant social meetings at the homes of members, and the group continued on its irregular way for several years. Bryant spent the Fourth of July at Roslyn, writing Dana that he dreaded going back to "the foul, hot, noisy town."[4] On October 25 he wrote his brother John that he and Frances had planned a trip to Illinois, but she did not much like the idea of such a journey and he did not want to go alone. Bryant reported on his autumn harvest, Cedarmere being more than just a country retreat: there were good crops of hay, wheat, and corn; the potatoes, although a little injured by disease, were excellent; and the yield of berries and fruits—strawberries, raspberries, cherries, pears, and peaches—was on the whole abundant.[5]

III

After the excitement in 1850 of the debate over the Clay compromise resolutions and their enactment into law in September, the nation was fairly calm politically during the next year. The *Evening Post* continued to follow the incidents, or "kidnapings" as it called them, in the enforcement of the Fugitive Slave Act. The strongest resistance was in Boston, whose citizens resorted to violence in freeing captured Negroes. In February a group broke into a courtroom and spirited away a Negro, one Shadrach, and President Fillmore issued a proclamation authorizing use of the military to prevent such deliverances. Denouncing the order, the *Evening Post* warned: "Proclamations against popular feeling in our country are a puff against the tempest." On May 23 it defended Emerson against an attack made upon him in the Boston *Daily Advertiser* for lectures given at Worcester and Fitchburg opposing the infamous law.

With both Godwin and Bigelow on the staff during 1851, the *Evening Post* made notable advances in the quality of news and editorial material and in its business affairs. Bigelow made a popular contribution to the paper's intellectual material on December 14 of 1850, when he introduced a literary character who had a different appeal from his "John Brown, Ferryman," articles relaying political gossip. To express views that would be inappropriate coming from him, Bigelow created the character Friar Lubin, whose lucubrations were printed under the heading "Nuces Literariae." Godwin, too, was finding an outlet in the paper for his literary work, including a two-part biography of the naturalist and artist James Audubon, who died on January 27.

One of the contributors during the year was the Brooklyn Free-Soil Democrat Walter Whitman, as he still called himself formally. Like Bryant, Whitman had suffered from being at odds with the conservative wing of the party, having been fired as editor of the Brooklyn *Eagle* in 1848. He had gone to New Orleans to work for a time on the *Daily Crescent* and, returning to New York, had edited the short-lived *Freeman*. With no regular employment thereafter, he wrote several articles for the *Evening Post*. In one he lauded several obscure Brooklyn artists and in another he noted changes taking place as the city grew in population. A trip to the eastern end of Long Island produced an article praising it as a better place than Saratoga and Newport for a summer visit, and in two articles he described the joys of sea-bathing and commented on boarding house life. His final article was a rhapsodic account of an opera at Castle Garden and the singing of Bettini. Whitman, in the garrulity of his old age at Camden, New Jersey, referred to walks with Bryant on Long Island and conversations with him. Whether the two men were familiars in the summer of 1851, however, is not known.

During the year advertising increased so much that on occasion supplements to the regular four pages were printed. This situation was taken care of in part on October 7 when a smaller type face for the advertising was adopted, giving five additional columns of space. Formerly, the literary material had consisted of reprints from other publications. The paper's new affluence permitted it to announce on November 24 that, to add to its "attractions as a family newspaper," the fourth page would be devoted to original stories written expressly for it and to "interesting literary and biographical miscellany." "We indulge the hope," the paper said, "that the female portion of our readers will henceforth concede that their tastes have not been disregarded." During the past several years, the paper said on November 24, more than ten thousand dollars had been spent for improvements in equipment and services.

Late in October Bryant undertook the task of writing a history of the *Evening Post* in observance of its fiftieth anniversary November 16. Running to more than ten thousand five hundred words, his "The First Half-Century of the Evening Post" told of its founding by William Coleman as a Federalist newspaper in 1801, his stormy career as an editor, and Bryant's reminiscences of the quarter century in which he had been the editor. Closing his article, Bryant said that one of the chief temptations of an editor was to "betray the cause of truth to public opinion" by falling into the views held by the majority. The *Evening Post,* he declared, had not often yielded to this temptation.

After completing this history, Bryant set off, in mid-September, on a trip to Illinois, accompanied only by Julia, now twenty years old, since Mrs. Bryant preferred her quiet life at Cedarmere to an arduous journey. On this trip Bryant wrote only one letter to the *Evening Post,* dated from Rochester on September 19 where an agricultural fair was being held.[6] Something of a farmer himself at Roslyn, Bryant compared the fruit of the western part of the state with his own products. The western fruits were better. "The apples which Atalanta ran for," he wrote, "could not have been fairer than hundreds of those ranged on the tables in the building appropriated to fruits and flowers." He wrote also about the short-horn breed of cattle becoming popular with stockmen and marveled at the new mechanical farming equipment—reapers, drills, winnowing machines, and plows.

Shortly after returning to New York, Bryant attended, on September 24, a meeting of literary men to plan a tribute to James Fenimore Cooper, who had died on September 14. Bryant had last seen Cooper in the spring when the novelist came to the city to receive medical treatment. "He has grown thin, and has an ashy instead of a florid complexion," Bryant wrote

Dana.[7] The meeting to plan a memorial brought together, for the first time in years, the leading survivors of the older group of Knickerbocker authors—Irving, Halleck, Paulding, and Verplanck. They united in choosing Bryant to deliver a memorial address sometime during the winter.

During December the city was excited over the forthcoming visit of the Hungarian fighter for freedom, Louis Kossuth, who was one of the chief inspirations in the 1848 revolutions in Europe. Kossuth's exile from Hungary to Turkey and his voyage from there to England had been publicized in American newspapers, the *Evening Post* devoting several columns daily to his enthusiastic reception in London. Since Kossuth had edited liberation papers, New York editors considered him one of their own and met on November 20 to plan a reception in his honor. Henry J. Raymond, who only in September had established the New York *Times,* welcomed by the *Evening Post* because he was a leader in the Free-Soil branch of the Whig party, presided. Bryant was chosen chairman for a banquet which the press would give for Kossuth on December 15.

The banquet was one of the most glittering affairs ever held in the city, and the *Evening Post* devoted five columns to it. In the choice of viands the owners of the Astor house had furnished profusely "every luxury imaginable in or out of season" and likewise had spared no expense in the decorations of the banquet room for the ladies who were admitted, "three hundred strong," when the speeches began. Bryant in his introduction of Kossuth compared him to the great men of America's Revolution and recalled his trip to Europe in 1849 when, while he was in Munich, Russia had intervened in the revolt in Hungary led by Kossuth and crushed it. Bryant hoped that the leader in exile would be "cheered and strengthened with aid from this side of the Atlantic," a hope that came true when Kossuth was met by huge throngs when he continued his tour of the country and received an outpouring of adulation seldom given a foreign visitor.

Three days after the *Evening Post*'s accounts of the city's salutes to Kossuth, readers were regaled by reports of another sensation—the divorce trial of Catherine and Edwin Forrest. Heretofore, the paper had tended to mention only briefly the lurid events that the twopenny papers and especially James Gordon Bennett's *Herald* gave in detail. During the thirty-three days of the trial, however, the *Evening Post* printed most of the testimony, devoting to it from four to seven columns daily. The explanation for this may be that, since Bryant and the Parke Godwins had been involved in the early negotiations between the actor and his wife, Bryant felt that, mortifying though it was, he must publish what the other papers published to prevent criticism of the *Evening Post*. Fanny, a loyal friend of Catherine, accompanied her to court on the opening day and was with her on many subsequent days, and the roles that Bryant and Godwin had played as friends of the couple were brought out in testimony. Reporting the verdict in favor of Mrs. Forrest on January 26, Bryant was glad that the trial with its daily exposure of "foul details" was over. "Thus ends one of the longest, most bitterly litigated, and in some respects one of the most disgusting trials that ever was held in this country," an editorial commented.

Happy to forget the Forrest trial, Bryant devoted himself to completing his eulogy of Cooper, to be given at Tripler Hall on February 25 with Daniel Webster presiding.[8] Bryant sought to explain Cooper's war with his countrymen in the address as well as to praise his literary accomplishments. Cooper had the ability to describe the grandeur of his country in his tales of the forests and the prairies, he was "in the highest sense of the word a poet," but he was a proud man who took as a personal affront the abuse heaped upon him for his criticism of the American society. "With a character so made up of positive qualities—a character so independent and uncompromising," Bryant said, "and with a sensitiveness far more acute than he was willing to acknowledge—it is not surprising that occasions frequently arose to bring him sometimes into friendly collision, and sometimes into graver disagreements and misunderstandings with his fellow-men." Nevertheless, Cooper had a great capacity for friendship: "His character was like the bark of the cinnamon—a rough and astringent rind without, and an intense sweetness within." In criticizing Cooper's novels, Bryant noted, and accepted, the faults commonly found in them: inconsistencies in his plots and carelessness in his writing. He observed that Cooper's popularity in Europe was due to the fact that his excellences, chiefly his ability to tell a story that carried the reader along, were translatable—they passed "readily into languages the least allied in their genius to that in which he wrote, and in them he touches the heart and kindles the imagination with the same powers as in the original English."

IV

Since 1852 was a presidential election year, Bryant and Bigelow began preparations early for covering the nominating conventions and the campaign. Both the Democratic and Whig parties had been fragmented by the quarrels over slavery, and there was a tendency for their leaders to hope that the Compromise of 1850 would have the same effect of the Missouri

Compromise, which had banished the slavery issue from campaigns for a quarter century. The Fugitive Slave Act, however, stood in the way of this, though Bryant hoped that it might be repealed or modified. After having supported the Free-Soil party in the previous campaign, he early in the year decided to return to the Democratic party since, with the exception of the southern slave faction, it still stood for most of the things the *Evening Post* had supported in years past. To a gibe from Henry J. Raymond in the *Times* that the *Evening Post* had lost its solicitude for Free-Soil principles, Bryant replied on May 13 that he stood with the southern Democrats on the question of states' rights. The Fugitive Slave Act, he declared, was "the most fatal blow ever struck to the doctrine of state rights." Because the North and the South could not agree upon slavery, he hoped that the Democrats at their Baltimore convention would say nothing about it. Bryant merely asked for "a candidate whom both sections of the party, having so many interests, sympathies, principles and recollections in common, may support without compromising their respective positions."

The nomination of the dark horse Franklin Pierce by the Democrats in the first week in June on the forty-ninth ballot met with Bryant's specifications. In fact, he had not thought the Democrats would do so well, Bryant wrote on June 7. "Instead of taking a candidate from among those who have been sedulously patching and piecing, taking in and letting out, their political creed to suit the fashion of the day, like an economical housewife with a twice-turned gown," Bryant said, "we have a man who has done nothing to purchase the presidency, retired for the present from political life, and uncommitted on the questions which for the last three or four years have divided the Democratic party." As to the platform, which accepted the Clay compromise measures and affirmed opposition to renewed agitation over slavery, Bryant said it was adopted with indifference by the delegates, many of whom did not stay to debate the issues or to vote.

The Whigs, meeting at Baltimore on June 16, nominated the hero of the Mexican War, General Winfield Scott and adopted a platform that in the sections on slavery was the same as that of the Democrats. The issues in the campaign for Bryant, therefore, were the personal qualities of the two candidates and the old and tired slogans the *Evening Post* had been repeating for years—states' rights, free trade, and freedom from government interference in the private affairs of the people. As to Scott's fitness for office, he believed the general as a commander of armies had a claim upon the gratitude of the country, but nothing in his experience had prepared him for the position of its chief executive.

Bryant's belief that a party got up with only one aim in view, a sort of ad hoc organization, would prove ineffective seemed to have been borne out in the Free-Soil movement. He had already announced his support of Pierce and the Democrats when the Free-Soilers on August 11 nominated John P. Hale of New Hampshire for President and George W. Julian of Indiana for vice-president. Explaining to John Bryant why he supported Pierce, Bryant said that the Free-Soil party had not accomplished much, though, with thirteen members in Congress, it held the balance of power. "Its representatives in Congress have wasted their time till all chance of repealing or modifying the fugitive slave law is gone by, if there ever was any," Bryant wrote.[9]

Another reason why Bryant supported the Democratic rather than the Free-Soil ticket was given in an editorial on September 20 when he replied to newspaper criticisms that the *Evening Post* seemed to have forgotten its earlier stands against slavery. Bryant declared that the paper was just as strongly opposed as ever to slavery and added: "But we are also aware . . . that hostility to slavery goes but short way—a very short way—in making a true Democrat, or even a sound economist." When the federal treasury was raided by Congress in granting subsidies to steamship companies for the European ocean mail service and made valuable land grants to railroads, the "free democrats" had voted along with the Whigs. "The history of the present Congress alone," the *Evening Post* declared, "was enough to destroy all our faith, which was never much, in that democracy which rests upon the anti-slavery sentiment alone. We have not found in that sentiment any protection against the most profligate and lawless schemes of public extravagance."

Looking forward to the close of the *Evening Post*'s books on November 16, Bryant wrote Frances at Roslyn that things were going on well with the paper. "We shall have a thumping dividend this half year," he said.[10] It had been indeed a good year for the paper. Its political news had improved, Bigelow himself attending the conventions to provide it with exclusive coverage; documents relating to the campaign, of which a dozen were issued in pamphlet form, had been popular; and special rates offered for the weekly and semiweekly editions had increased the circulation throughout the country. Bigelow's records show that the daily circulation was now about 1,900, not large compared with the "cheap" papers like Bennett's *Herald* but very good for a sixpenny commercial publication, and the combined circulations of the editions for the country were in excess of 9,000. Bigelow's own income had risen from the $1,500 he received during his first year with the paper to $6,000.[11] Bryant, since he held more than fifty percent of the shares, therefore had earned more than $12,000.

V

With the election over and the Democrats returned to office in Washington, Bryant embarked on the steamship *Arctic* on November 13 with the companion of some of his earlier travels, Charles M. Leupp, on the longest journey of his life—one that would take him to London and Paris and thence to Italy and from there to lands of even greater antiquity, Egypt, the Holy Land, and Greece.

During the crossing to Liverpool Bryant obtained information about the lands of the Near East from Captain William Francis Lynch of the United States navy, whose report on his explorations of the Dead Sea had been printed by order of Congress and whose personal narrative had also been published. Bryant had not planned to write the *Evening Post* a letter from London, but he was so vexed by the seizure at the customs at Liverpool of books copyrighted in Britain and printed in the United States that he thought it worthy of mention.[12] Captain Lynch's American copy of his narrative of the Dead Sea expedition was seized as was a volume of Bryant's poems he wished to present to a British friend. Staying only a short while in London, Bryant saw few friends there. His travel diary records an evening spent at the home of the publisher John Chapman. There Bryant met the poet, the Rev. Thomas J. Upham, with whom he had carried on a correspondence, and "a blue-stocking lady, who writes for the *Westminster Review*." This was Mary Ann Evans, later to become famous under the pen name of George Eliot.

In Paris, which Bryant reached on December 1, he found that the spirit of French gaiety had not been destroyed by the revolution which he had described for *Evening Post* readers three years before and the re-establishment of the empire by Louis Napoleon. The shops were again open, "glittering with showy wares and thronged with customers," and the theaters, public ballrooms, and other places of entertainment were crowded. The day after his arrival he was a spectator when the newly proclaimed emperor, Napoleon III, was conducted to the palace of the Tuileries by a military escort. "A few cries of *Vive l'Empereur* arose, which he answered by taking off his hat and bowing to the people," Bryant related. "He appeared of shorter stature than most of the officers of his suite, but he sat his horse well, a spirited creature, which pranced and curvetted, and seemed proud of bearing the sovereign of the French

Empire." Bryant believed that public opinion supported the new regime, since the emperor had already embarked on a program to promote prosperity though at the same time he was suppressing the people's freedoms. "What the people now want," a hotel attendant told him, "is the opportunity of earning their livelihood by their labor in peace. That they now have, and they are not ambitious of anything beyond it."

At Paris Bryant and Leupp were joined by John Durand, son of the artist, whose interest was in literature rather than in painting, and they made a leisurely trip south to Marseilles. Bryant reported that in the south of France he found, as he had at Paris, that the people accepted the empire. "It is characteristic of the French race," he observed, "that it conforms itself easily to any change of circumstances, provided you do not interfere with its amusements." Leaving Marseilles for Naples on December 14, the trippers had a pleasant passage by steamer to Genoa, where they had a day to see the palaces and churches; but, because of repressions that followed the revolutions of 1848, there were unpleasant delays at other stopover points, Leghorn and Civitavecchia, passports having to be brought out for inspection. At Naples they were taken before police authorities on landing and had to obtain a written permit to remain for twenty-four hours and then to get another permit either to stay longer or leave. They chose to stay for a time, making side trips to Pompeii, Salerno, Amalfi, and Paestum. They then left for Malta, where Bryant wrote a travel letter for the *Evening Post,* and sailed on December 30 to Alexandria.

Bryant's first view of Egypt, the ancient land of the Pharaohs, was of Alexandria rising above its low flat shore through a driving rain. On landing he had no opportunity to recall Alexandria's storied past, if he had wanted to, because the passengers found their way blocked by a mob of shouting men offering donkeys for hire to carry them to their hotels. "As there was apparently no alternative," Bryant related, "I took the [man] who stood immediately before me by the throat, shoved him out of my way, and then attacked the next in like manner, till I made my escape out of the crowd." The Mussulmans smiled at being "thus unceremoniously handled by an infidel," and Bryant, when he was clear of them, jumped upon one of the best looking of their animals. It trotted off through the muddy streets, followed by its scolding owner, who sped it on its way by thwacks from a stick.

The travelers spent a day in Alexandria during which Bryant stored up impressions of a strange people in their still stranger costumes and, adapting himself to the common mode of transportation, the donkey, went to view Cleopatra's Needle and Pompey's Pillar. Then they embarked on a boat that took them by a newly opened canal to the Nile for the river trip to Cairo. Bryant's letters describing the capital and its people, both those written to the *Evening Post* and those to Frances, were typical accounts of any tourist. He was struck most, perhaps, by the noise: "human voices, greeting, arguing, jesting, laughing, shouting, scolding, cursing, praying, and begging, mingled with the bleating of camels, the braying of asses, and the barking of innumerable dogs." It was a mistake to think of the Oriental as grave and solemn, for everything that went on in Egypt, at least, was accompanied by noise. If readers of Bryant's "The Ages" expected him to be inspired to the expression of sublime thoughts by the pyramids, they were disappointed. "It is almost the first business of travellers in Egypt to visit the pyramids of Ghizeh, and we made it ours," Bryant wrote; "but do not suppose that I am going to weary you with a description of them."

The travelers, after a week examining the monuments in and near Cairo, completed arrangements with a dragoman to conduct them by way of what was called the Little Arabian Desert to Jerusalem. But they were persuaded to postpone the expedition when an opportunity presented itself to ascend the Nile by a government steamer which had just been fitted up for such trips. Heretofore, the journey had to be taken by sailboat, and the winds being uncertain, its duration never could be determined in advance.

Bryant was more deeply impressed by the temples at Karnak and Luxor and the tombs and colossal statues along the riverside than he had been by the pyramids at Cairo. "As I sat among the forest of gigantic columns in the great court of the temple at Karnak," he wrote Frances, "it appeared to me that after such a sight no building reared by human hands could affect me with a sense of sublimity." The trip up the Nile had not exhibited any dramatic landscapes worth describing, but Bryant, because of his botanical interests, could always find something interesting in the vegetation he saw. The Nile valley, he wrote, was "a green stripe dividing the wilderness of rock and sand." At Aswan, however, there were more picturesque sights. "Here the Nile breaks its way through rocks, forming rocky islands, of which Philae, the sacred island of the Egyptians, is one," Bryant related. "The granite cliffs are piled upon each other in pinnacles, and the river pushes rapidly between them."

Returning to Cairo, Bryant, Leupp, and Durand, with a fourth American who joined their party but who was not identified in Bryant's letters, each mounted on a donkey, set out in the afternoon of January 31 on their journey to Jerusalem. Their dragoman, Emmanuel Balthas, an Athenian, had sent the camels with the baggage on ahead in the morning, and the party was to join the caravan that night at the village of Khankia. Balthas was linguistically well equipped as a dragoman, speaking both ancient and modern Greek and being fluent in Italian, Turkish, and Arabic; he was intelligible in French but knew only a little English. He was a "little man with the manners of a nobleman," eager to serve his employers, but, as it turned out during the trip, "a little too much given to flogging his Arabs."

With a village crowd watching them, the travelers prepared to leave early the next morning. "I placed myself on the back of the camel destined for me," Bryant related, "and was nearly thrown over his back, and then over his head, as he lifted me up by three different jerks to the height of nine feet in the air." The caravan consisted of two donkeys and thirteen camels. There were two tents; four camp bedsteads with mattresses, pillows, and bedclothes; a table; four camp stools; mats and carpets for the floor of the tents; and table linen and cutlery. The stock of provisions included a hen coop crowded with chickens, which the cook, Vincenzo, plucked and prepared for roasting as he was carried along on the high back of his camel. At the head of the column rode the dragoman Balthas, armed with a saber, a rifle, and two horse-pistols. The courier, John Muscat, a Maltese, also wore a sword, which he assured Bryant he was ready to use against any brigands that might show up on the road to Syria. Also in the group were the four Arabs who owned the camels and watched over them and a cousin of the dragoman, whose duties, if any, were not revealed by Bryant.

The first day of the journey, at the close of which the travelers were still able at eventide to see the rocky heights east of Cairo, the tall minarets of the mosque of Mohammed Ali gleaming in the sunlight, was typical of those that followed. They broke camp at sunrise, stopped for lunch at noon, dining in the shade of umbrellas from mats spread on the ground, and set up their tents at night near some village or at a waterhole. The motion of the camel, tossing its rider backward and forward like the pitching of a ship at sea, was fatiguing, and it was customary for travelers to wear a belt which supported the muscles of the back. Bryant, after the second day however, laid aside his belt, since he found he could avoid fatigue by varying his position on the back of the animal, sitting sometimes astride and sometimes with both legs on one side and dismounting occasionally to walk.

Bryant's walks gave him an opportunity to indulge his interests as a naturalist. The desert, he found, had a greater variety of animal life than strangers to it might have thought. There were lizards that skittered out of the way of the camels; moths and butterflies fluttering above the flowers; snails clinging to every shrub; and land tortoises, chameleons, beetles, and other fauna that he recorded in his notebook. There were also traces of animals that he seldom saw, the burrows of jackals in the hillocks and the traces of the jerboa, or leaping rat, and less often the delicate triangular footprint of the gazelle. Of avian life the most familiar sights were of herons rising from a pool of brackish water as the caravan came near and ravens nearly always hovering overhead. But that the desert was an inhospitable place to life was indicated by the skeletons of camels and other animals scattered along the way.

Never far from the Mediterranean, following the long curve of the coast of northern Egypt and western Syria, the caravan encountered daily other travelers—pilgrims returning from Mecca and caravans bearing silks and other goods to Cairo—and frequently passed by or stopped at villages of Bedouin Arabs. After leaving El Arish, a primitive village on the coast, the travelers encountered a new vicissitude of travel, the tribute levied by the sheiks to protect them from robbers, or as Bryant expressed it, their solicitation of the tribute as compensation for the robberies they themselves would otherwise commit. It was all conducted very systematically as if established by law: three piastres for each traveler but nothing for the servants.

Entering Syria at Khan Yunis on February 10, the travelers were told that, as with all persons arriving from Egypt, they would be in quarantine five days, the first to be spent in the lazaretto there and the others, including the day spent en route, at Gaza. It was a numerous company that left Khan Yunis next day—pilgrims, dervishes, Arab families, and European tourists—and all were herded into the lazaretto, a compound with high walls. Bryant spent the time writing up his notes for his travel letters later to be dispatched to the *Evening Post*.

Released from quarantine, the caravan proceeded to Jerusalem, Bryant taking notes on the ruins of the city of Askelon over which the sands of time had drifted; the town of Ramleh, the center of a vast circle of huge old olive trees; the plain of Sharon, green and fresh but no longer beautiful with roses; and other places described in Biblical literature. "At length, after crossing a bleak table-land, where the soil seemed to have been washed away by rains from the spaces between projecting rocks," Bryant wrote, "we came in sight of the walls, the towers, and the domes of the Holy City. The ancient metropolis of Palestine, the once imperial Salem, had not lost all its majesty, but still sat like a queen in her place among the mountains of Judea."

Bryant's letters describing the caravan trip of twenty days constituted

365

the longest sustained account of any of his travels thus far, running to more than twenty thousand words, most of which he set down at Jerusalem. He did not tell in detail of his impressions of the ancient city, not wishing, he wrote, to attempt "the description of a place described so often." With Leupp and Durand, he did the usual things that visitors to the Holy Land did—they penetrated all niches and corners of the city, they went to Nazareth, Mount Carmel, and other places mentioned in the Bible, and they bathed in the waters of the Jordan River and the Dead Sea. Then they went north to Beirut, crossed Lebanon to visit Damascus, and, returning to the coast, took an Austrian ship to Smyrna, where on March 29 Bryant wrote another letter for the *Evening Post,* the first in more than a month since leaving Jerusalem. The Turkish government was so weak, Bryant said, that Smyrna was "a sort of prison watched by a guard of robbers" and it was unsafe to go outside its environs. From Smyrna the travelers sailed to Constantinople and then to Athens. During a stop at the island of Siros, Bryant was able to get in touch with the American consul, C. Evangelides, who thirty years before as a boy had been brought to the United States from Greece by a ship's captain to be educated and about whom Bryant had written the poem, "The Greek Boy." Bryant told of the meeting in his *Evening Post* letter, reporting that Evangelides had been a leader in developing the schools of his native land.

Familiar with the grandeur of Rome, Bryant had looked forward to seeing the glory of Greece. At first he was disappointed. The country was so drained of color, the herbage being meagre and the soil leached out to whiteness, that it took time for him to perceive the real beauty and harmony of the scene. Because of this, Bryant felt, the beauty of the mountains about Athens made a deeper and more durable impression than more dramatic landscapes. He was moved to write of the city:

> The remains of ancient art, which are to be seen at Athens, have the character of the surrounding scenery—repose and harmony. Of all that antiquity has left us in the way of architecture, they are the only ones which fill and satisfy the mind. Here is nothing too large or too little, no subordination of the whole to the parts—all is noble, symmetrical, simple; there is not a grace that does not seem to arise naturally out of the general design. It is wonderful how time has spared them. They are mutilated, defaced, and in great part overthrown, yet the marble, in many places, is as white as when it was hewn from the quarries of the Pentelicum Mount, and the outlines as sharp and clear as when the chisel had just finished its task.

During the last week of April the travelers sailed among the Greek islands, stopping for three days at Corfu, "a fertile and beautiful spot," Bryant noted, and then on to Trieste. They proceeded to Venice and Florence and went on from there to Rome where, on May 17, Bryant wrote another *Evening Post* letter, giving the news of the artists and the American colony. Returning to Paris by way of Marseilles, Bryant wrote his last letter of the trip on June 1. The party crossed to London, where they spent a day or two, and then took passage on the steamer *Humboldt* for New York.

While traversing the desert from Cairo to Jerusalem, Bryant had let his beard grow, and he was amused, so he wrote Dana on July 3, that a clerk sent from the *Evening Post* to help him with his luggage at the wharf did not recognize him.[13] "I went down to my place on Long Island," he related, "put on a Turkish turban and gown, and had a long conversation in broken English with a young lady, our next-door neighbor, who really thought that I was an oriental." Bryant's long flowing beard familiar in the portraits of him in his later years dates from this time.

Although nearing his sixtieth birthday, Bryant had endured the rigors of the trip as easily as his two younger companions. Durand found him a pleasant traveler, "always in elastic spirits, always cheerful and chatty, always keenly alive to the peculiar beauties of the scene." Bryant's knowledge of botany enabled him to point out interesting aspects of the vegetation that would be hidden to the ordinary person and his knowledge of literature enabled him to quote a poem or cite a passage from prose that provided a relevant background for scenes viewed. "No matter where we might be," Durand recalled, "whether wandering through the beautiful gardens of Egypt, crossing the wide plain of Esdraelon sprinkled with anemones, watching the 'wild gazelle' on approaching 'Judah's hills,' amid the willows on the banks of the rapid Jordan, or sitting by the fountain which gives such life and beauty to Damascus—always some shrub, tree, or flower elicited a fact or a poem to augment the interest of the various objects and landscapes."[14]

22

FORMING THE REPUBLICAN PARTY

WHEN BRYANT RETURNED TO NEW YORK IN JUNE OF 1853 from his tour of the Near East, he found the *Evening Post* housed in a building which Bigelow had bought and enlarged. It was a prosperous period in the nation, and the paper was sharing in the gains. The city had a population approaching the one million mark, Broadway was more than four miles long, and Fifth Avenue was being extended into the open country above Thirty-fourth Street. Exulting in its growth, the city that year held its Exhibition of the Industry of All Nations in the beautiful and sparkling Crystal Palace, copied after the famous showplace in London. Theodore Sedgwick, Jr., was president of the association putting on the exposition, and the *Evening Post* devoted long columns to describing its embellishments and the amazing new machinery exhibited.

The first issue of the paper printed in the new plant at the northwest corner of Nassau and Liberty Streets, one block north of the former location at 18 Nassau Street, appeared on April 7. Bigelow had added a fourth story to the building for the prosperous book and job-printing department, the composing room and five cubicles for the editorial staff occupied the second floor, the business and accounting departments opened on the street on the ground floor. The basement housed the latest type of fast-printing cylinder press manufactured by Hoe & Company. The new press had been expected to go into operation on May 1, but it was not ready, however, until July 25. The delay was due to Bigelow's fascination for a "caloric" engine devised by the Swedish naval engineer John Ericsson. Bigelow became interested in it in January when Ericsson invited a group of editors to sail down the bay on a vessel powered by his engine, which made use of compressed hot air instead of steam. Bigelow was proud to announce that Ericsson had agreed to manufacture one to run the *Evening Post* press, the first other than the demonstration engine to be built. It did not work, however, and Bigelow had to confess that it was nothing more than an "ingenious toy."[1] He replaced it with one of the "powerful lightning engines" of the Hoe company, which increased the press run to seven thousand copies an hour.

The *Evening Post's* circulation was small compared with that of its two-penny rivals, the *Herald, Tribune,* and *Times,* of between 25,000 and 35,000, but its income was respectable, the dividends now ranging between $35,000 and $40,000 a year. Parke Godwin attributed the paper's prosperity to its advertising rather than its circulation. It charged higher rates than the "cheap" papers and was "the organ for the most exclusive and expensive advertising, that which appeals chiefly to well-to-do people and investors."[2]

Bigelow from his first association with the paper had no high opinion of the business abilities of Timothy A. Howe, whose incompetence was demonstrated further in his failure to cope with problems created in buying the new building and moving the plant. When Bryant returned from his trip abroad, Bigelow called a meeting of the three partners and bluntly declared that the concern would have to get a new business manager. He did not wish to crowd Howe out, he said, but he did not propose to continue as a partner with him conducting the business. He named a figure at which he would either buy Howe's share or would sell his own. Recalling the session, Bigelow related that Bryant was embarrassed, refusing to look up from papers on his desk. Howe, his face white, looked at Bryant "to see whether there was any comfort there, but he did not find any." Finally, he stammered: "Very well, I see that Mr. Bryant is with you in the matter, and I will go." Bigelow's ultimatum prepared the way for Isaac Henderson, who had been a clerk in the accounting department since 1839 and had demonstrated his proclivity for making money, to buy into the firm. Five years before Bigelow's one-third share was valued at about $15,000. Henderson cheerfully paid $17,083 for Howe's share plus six percent of the semiannual dividends for the next five years.[3]

During Bryant's absence Godwin had continued to contribute to the paper, but in January of 1853 he joined *Putnam's Monthly Magazine,* established by George Palmer Putnam with Charles F. Briggs as editor and Godwin and George William Curtis as associate editors. Godwin's position was that of political editor. A reformer and agitator, Godwin employed a pen dipped in acid, and his invective—he spoke of certain political leaders as being "flatulent old hacks," for example—made the magazine read and talked about. At the same time Godwin was attempting to obtain an appointment as a professor of history at Columbia College, appealing in letters to a number of distinguished people for their support.[4] He apparently still bore some resentment toward Bryant, probably sharpened by the fact that Bigelow had been made a partner when the opportunity to become an owner might have been opened to him, and sought to free himself from having to rely on the paper for employment.* Except for his newspaper and magazine writing, Godwin had published little—two pamphlets on Fourierism and the Association movement in 1844, two translations from the German, one of them Goethe's *Autobiography,* in 1845 and 1846, and a *Hand-Book of Universal Biography* in 1852. His efforts to be named to the Columbia College faculty came to nothing. To replace Godwin, Bigelow, upon the recommendation of Charles Sumner, employed a young New Englander who had done some writing, William S. Thayer.**

II

Bryant in making his more extended trips timed them for the periods of quiet just after elections when no important policy decisions had to be made and he could leave the *Evening Post* to his second in command. The Compromise of 1850 and the election of Pierce had justified Bryant's long journey to the Near East, because these events seemed to foretoken a

---

*Fanny Godwin sought Bryant's help in getting her husband the appointment. He wrote her on March 31, 1857, however, not to have "too strong hopes of success," promising to speak in Godwin's behalf to the trustees he happened to know. Bryant's friend, the Columbia professor Henry J. Anderson, had told him he thought Godwin would be a good man for the position but warned "you know the prejudices of those people—the trustees." Goddard-Roslyn Collection.

**Thayer later became the paper's Washington correspondent and was an intimate of Charles Sumner, whose views he expressed in many of his dispatches. Thayer was invited by the military adventurer William Walker to accompany him on his filibustering expedition to Nicaragua in 1855–7. The *Evening Post* had exclusive coverage of this foray in which Walker was able to set himself up as dictator and to have his government recognized by the United States.

period of truce between the North and South. Shortly after his return he was happy to report the fruition of a long-standing campaign when the legislature at Albany approved two New York City park measures. One provided for Jones's Wood Park of one hundred and fifty-three acres along the East River and the other for Central Park of seven hundred and fifty-nine acres. But party politics were merely quiescent and the *Evening Post,* though it had supported Pierce in the election, was attacked in midsummer by two administration organs, the Richmond *Enquirer* and the Washington *Union,* for its criticisms of the administration and its continuing strictures against the South.

To the *Enquirer's* request that he leave the party, Bryant replied in a long editorial on July 14 giving the reasons why he still considered himself a Democrat. It was the party whose principles had been laid down by Jefferson of "as little government, as little patronage, as little expenditure as the structure of civil polity can subsist with"; it was a party which he had helped form and had supported, in the main, for a quarter of a century; and it was "the party of the people." Though there were knaves in it, he said, there were also honest men who were in the majority, and he would remain to work with them to drive out the rogues. A derisive comment in the Washington *Union* that the *Evening Post* was not on the patronage list of the Pierce administration brought from Bryant the riposte on July 25 that this was true but it was equally true that the paper had never received patronage from any administration. "Its existence, its prosperity, its influence," Bryant said, "do not depend in any manner upon the men who have ever been, or may now be in office. It has never been for a moment in their power to build up such a journal as ours or to pull it down." A jeering remark that slaves directed at free Negroes was applicable to papers like the *Union* which gloated over the *Evening Post's* receiving no political patronage: "Oh, you poor debbel, you got no massa."

Though Bryant in midsummer was still able to proclaim his allegiance to the Democratic party in the belief that it could be reformed, by fall he was beginning to express his doubts publicly. On September 29 he noted a growing disaffection with the Pierce administration among the older Democrats and interpreted this as meaning that a new party was forming. His own belief that the Free-Soilers who had returned to the party to help elect Pierce had been wrong was sharply stated in an editorial on October 20. The Abolitionist *National Era* of Washington commented that it feared the *Evening Post's* confidence in the administration was beginning to be shaken. Bryant replied that he saw no occasion for the remark. Citing earlier editorial objections to the President's use of patronage and the plunder of the treasury for private interests, Bryant declared with his typical sarcasm: "Our confidence in the wisdom of the administration is as strong now as it has been for many months back."

Bigelow, working hard during the past year to move the *Evening Post* to its new quarters, to improve its content, and to reorganize its business operations, felt the need of a vacation in the latter part of 1853 and sailed on November 23 to Haiti. His mission was the same as the one that had taken him to Jamaica—to study and describe an experiment in free government by Negroes. Bryant was therefore without the support of his energetic assistant when the fight against extension of slavery met a new challenge on January 4, 1854. It came from the ambitious Democratic senator from Illinois, Stephen A. Douglas, who almost as much as Clay had been responsible for securing the Compromise of 1850. Given the sobriquet "the Little Giant" because of his short stature—he was about five feet tall—and his large head and broad shoulders, Douglas now proposed not only to set this compromise aside but also to repeal the Missouri Compromise of 1820. As chairman of the committee on territories, first in the House and later the Senate, he had been in the forefront in organizing them as soon as possible for admission to the Union as states. The January 4 measure which he reported from his committee dealt with the organization of the Nebraska territory, amended later in the month to divide the territory into two states, Nebraska and Kansas. Calling the bill "a new scheme for disavowing an old bargain," Bryant in his first editorial on the plan attacked Douglas as being "a convenient agent when any game of petty cunning is to be played."

The Kansas-Nebraska bill was to succeed in making strange editorial bedfellows. In New York such enemies as the usually magisterial Bryant, the shrill and scolding Horace Greeley, the cool and calculating Henry J. Raymond, and the strutting and belligerent James Watson Webb were as one in anathematizing the Douglas plan. They were joined at Albany by the clever political manipulator Thurlow Weed, sponsor of the career of William H. Seward; and at Silver Spring, Maryland, by Francis P. Blair, a member of Jackson's Kitchen Cabinet and editor of his organ, the Washington *Globe,* who came out of retirement and declared angrily of the bill: "I hope there will be honest patriots enough found to resist it." Bearing the scars of many party battles, they were now agreed on one issue and soon were to be among the most important of the men who brought together in 1855 and 1856 the splintered antislavery factions into one party—the Republican.

During January and February Bryant wrote almost daily editorials denouncing the Douglas bill as the beginning of a series of agitations to extend slavery. On January 25 he printed in full the important manifesto urging opposition to the measure, "Appeal of the Independent Democrats in Congress to the People of the United States," signed by Salmon P. Chase, Charles Sumner, Joshua R. Giddings, and other Free-Soilers. In support of the manifesto, Bryant declared: "If we allow ourselves to be beaten in this first engagement, there is no hope for us in the remainder of the warfare; we are a routed army, and must expect to be ingloriously chased from one post to another." He was one of the signers of a proclamation calling a mass meeting on January 30 to protest the Douglas plan and, as one of the honorary vice-presidents elected for the occasion, sat on the platform.

When the bill passed the Senate on March 3, Bryant was appalled. He did not, however, give up the fight. He continued his furious editorial onslaughts against it and on March 14, again assuming a public role that he disliked, was one of the promoters and vice-presidents of a meeting at the Broadway Tabernacle to arouse the people to express their opposition. On April 24 he was optimistic enough to believe that the House would not dare pass any bill repealing the Missouri Compromise, but he warned the President, who seemed "to have reconciled himself and some of his friends to the odium which they have incurred from their connection with the Senate bill," that if it became a law opposition to it would not die down as had opposition to the 1850 compromise. The only hope of maintaining the Democratic party in the North, Bryant wrote, was for the President to see this. "To persist in the foolish scheme of Senator Douglas," Bryant's editorial continued, "can only result in whittling away the Democratic party into shavings; in multiplying abolitionists, and in making the president ridiculous." Bryant's hope that the northern segment of the party could be saved was destroyed when the House passed the Douglas measure on May 22, for he felt that the "dishonor" of its adoption was upon the President and his party.

III

A member of a "routed army" with the passage of the Douglas bill, Bryant made plans to get away immediately from the newspaper, to start out with Frances at the last of May on a journey to Illinois. Bigelow had returned from his trip to Haiti the second week in March with a series of articles on the situation on the island, and what could be done in the

struggle against slavery could be done as well by him. Writing Dana of the trip, Bryant expressed his dejection: "It seems to me that never was public wickedness so high-handed in our country as now."[5]

Since Bryant's return from the Near East he had again revised his poems, correcting faults of diction and versification, for a two-volume edition brought out in 1854 by D. Appleton & Company of New York, henceforth during his lifetime to be the publisher of all the editions of his work. Early in the next year the firm of R. Clay in London had brought out a one-volume edition with illustrations by British artists. Bryant had not been happy about the illustrated edition printed in 1847 by Carey & Hart, which in 1849 issued an edition without the illustrations, and of the new illustrated edition planned by Appleton he said in his letter to Dana: "As to my poems with illustrations, that is an idea of my bookseller. There is, I suppose a class of readers, at least book-buyers, who like things of that kind; but the first thing which my book-seller—it is Appleton—has promised to do, is to get out a neat edition in two volumes, *without* illustrations. The illustrated edition is to be a subsequent affair, and, though I have as great a horror of illustrations as you have, they will, I hope, hurt nobody."

The new volumes contained only seven poems which had not appeared in the 1847 edition. Three, "The Unknown Way," "The Land of Dreams," and "Oh Mother of a Mighty Race," had been written in 1845 and 1846, and the others since 1849. *Graham's Magazine* had continued to print Bryant's poems exclusively until January of 1854, when he permitted the new *Putnam's Magazine,* of which Godwin was an associate editor, to have "The Conqueror's Grave." One of Bryant's most popular poems in later years, printed in all the school readers, "The Planting of the Apple-Tree," written at Roslyn in 1849, was not included in the new collection, its first appearance being in the *Atlantic Monthly* of January, 1864.

A pleasant association of Bryant's during this year of political turmoil was with the painter and art critic William James Stillman, who contributed criticism to the *Evening Post.* Stillman was planning an art magazine, the *Crayon,* with John Durand and obtained from Bryant a poem for the first number to appear on January 3, 1853. When Bryant gave Stillman the verses, they bore no title and to the request that he supply one replied: "I give you a poem, give me a name." Stillman called it "A Rain-Dream," which, though not very suitable, was retained as the title when the poem appeared in Bryant's collected works.

Stillman believed that Bryant's reputation for being a cold man not only in his poetry but in his personal relations was false. "He impressed me as a man of strong feelings, who had at some time been led by a too explosive expression of them to dread his own passions, and who had, therefore, cultivated a repression which became the habit of his life," Stillman recalled. "The character of his poetry, little sympathetic with human passion, and given to the worship of nature, confirmed the general impression of his coldness which his manner suggested. I never saw him in anger, but I felt that the barrier which prevented it was too slight to make it safe for any one to venture to touch it."[6]

Stillman, also a friend of James Russell Lowell, believed he was the means of softening the enmity between the two men caused by the portrait drawn in *A Fable for Critics*. In planning the *Crayon*, Stillman had been helped by Lowell, who found sponsors for the magazine in Boston. Just before Lowell sailed from New York for Europe in 1854, Stillman gave a dinner for him attended by Bryant and Bayard Taylor. "Lowell laid himself out to captivate Bryant," Stillman related, "and did so completely, for his tact was such that in society no one whom he desired to interest could resist him; and our dinner was a splendid success." Later Stillman was embarrassed when he discovered that he had received poems from both Bryant and Lowell for the first number of the *Crayon* and he had space for only one of them. When told of the contretemps, Lowell wrote Stillman from London: "But, my dear sir, if Bryant has given you a poem you should put *that* in your first number by all means. It will do you more good than many of mine. . . ."[7]

The trip of Bryant and Frances to Illinois was a hard one for her, and she was ill when they returned to Roslyn, so much so, in fact, that on August 15 in declining an invitation from the Rev. Orville Dewey for them to visit at Sheffield, Massachusetts, Bryant expressed the wish that he was not encumbered by his country property, "more on my wife's account than any other," since he was compelled to be away from her most of the week because of his work on the paper. He added a hasty qualification, however: "But I am not sure that she would get well any faster anywhere else than here, where we have a pretty genial climate, and sea-bathing, which I think does her a great deal of good."[8]

IV

Bryant's vacation from politics was a brief one, and during the summer and fall he drearily devoted himself to the candidates and issues arising in the 1854 campaign. The New York political picture had been cut into a jigsaw puzzle and how the pieces would be fitted together, if they could at all, no one could foretell. In the Democratic party there was still the old division between the Hard Shells and Soft Shells, who were further split by those favoring the Pierce administration and those opposed to it. The Whig party was not so badly split up, but it was now out of office, its policy of getting a maximum of votes for a minimum of principles having led into a dead end. It had been bifurcated by the issue of the 1850 compromise, the radicals led by Seward and the conservatives led by Francis Granger, whose gray hair, conspicuous when he walked out of the state convention that year with his followers, had given his faction the name of "Silver Grays." As the summer progressed, other political bits and pieces were to emerge—the Native American or Know-Nothing party, the Liberty party, and the Free Democrats.

Immediately after the passage of the Kansas-Nebraska Act, a movement developed rapidly in the North and West for a coalition of all the anti-Nebraska people in a new party. It had started even earlier, when Whigs, Free-Soilers, and antislavery Democrats met on February 28 at Ripon, Wisconsin, and urged a new party to be called the Republican. Such a coalition under the Republican name came into being at a meeting at Jackson, Michigan, on July 6, to be followed quickly by like coalitions in Ohio, Wisconsin, Indiana, and Vermont. Neither Whig nor Democratic leaders in New York looked with favor upon the establishment of the new party, and their newspapers, with the exception of Horace Greeley's *Tribune,* likewise held back in supporting the Republicans.

Averse to political adventurism in principle, the failure of the Free-Soil party perhaps being in the back of their minds, and critical of all the present party organizations, if they could be considered such, Bryant and Bigelow could do little other than watch developments during the summer. They made the *Evening Post* a sounding-board for a proposal of Preston King, a supporter of the Wilmot Proviso and a Barnburner, that the antislavery forces unite behind a ticket made up of Thomas H. Benton of Missouri for President and William H. Seward of New York for vice-president. Benton, who stood for Jacksonian principles, would draw the support of the old-line Free-Soil Democrats, and Seward the anti-Nebraska votes of the Whigs. The *Evening Post* took the proposal seriously enough to carry an editorial on it on June 8 but only to condemn it as being a "disjunctive conjunction": it would not do to try to start a party with personal leadership that had only one point of agreement in common. During July and August the *Evening Post* carried news reports of Republican organizations as they were formed in the northern states, but it did not endorse them editorially though agreeing with their anti-Nebraska aims. Only once did Bryant seem to have a hope that the new party or fusionist movement could accomplish its aims. He urged the people on August 8 to attend a mass meeting in the Park that night and do something practical to prevent sending a northern man to Congress who could be bent to the will of the slave interests and to stigmatize those who had voted for the Nebraska bill. Bryant was elected one of the honorary vice-presidents, but next day he editorially regretted that nothing material was done except for naming delegates to a statewide anti-Nebraska convention at Saratoga on August 16.

The paper carried full reports of the nominating conventions of the parties and the pieces of parties formed around special issues, but its editorial comment generally reflected an attitude of chilly aloofness. The Hard Shells, meeting at Syracuse on July 12, were the first in the field. They approved the nefarious Nebraska scheme, repeal of the Missouri Compromise, and adoption of the law prohibiting liquor which Governor Seymour had vetoed in 1853. Their nominee for governor was the distinguished jurist Greene C. Bronson. Referring to the Hards' stand on slavery, Bryant commented: "They have occupied the ground in advance, and seem fairly entitled to all the few votes which can be got in this state by coming out in favor of a measure so generally odious throughout the North."

On the day before the anti-Nebraska people convened August 16 at Saratoga at the height of the season in this popular resort city the *Evening Post* recommended that it adopt a platform of a single plank: "No More Slave States." The convention, formed as the paper described it, of "heterogeneous materials" as to former party associates, was controlled, however, by Seward, Weed, and Greeley, a reluctant collaborator since he had received little support from the other two members of the triumvirate in his own political aspirations. It adopted a program, entirely satisfactory to Bryant, denouncing the Kansas-Nebraska Act and the policy of popular sovereignty and approving the colonization movement to send northern emigrants into the territory. But the Whig leaders at the meeting were not ready to establish a new party and the delegates temporized on the selection of candidates by setting a second convention for September 26 after other parties had acted.

On September 4, two days before the Soft Shells were to meet at Syracuse, the *Evening Post* warned that this faction of the Democratic party must speak out boldly against extension of slavery, "the issue which has convulsed the country for thirty years," if it were not to "cover itself with contempt and ridicule." When the convention, dominated by "office-

377

holders and their dependents," adopted a weak resolution declaring the Kansas-Nebraska Act to be "inexpedient and unnecessary," Bryant lost his last faint glimmering hope that the party could be saved. At the convention, the antislavery men, led by Preston King, withdrew, and the resolutions on the great issue of the day were, in Bryant's words, "spiritless and cowardly."

The Whig convention at Syracuse on September 20 nominated an antiliquor man, Myron H. Clark, for governor, largely through the machinations of Thurlow Weed working behind the scenes and providing free liquor and cigars in abundance. Clark was known for his fanatical advocacy of temperance and had been elected to the Senate chiefly because of his promise to submit an antiliquor law modeled on one adopted in Maine. He had succeeded in forcing his bill through the legislature, but it had been vetoed by Governor Seymour on the ground that it was unconstitutional. When Weed succeeded in getting Henry J. Raymond the nomination for lieutenant governor, Greeley, who had sought the honor and had been refused Weed's support, was humiliated though he was to continue as a member of the triumvirate for several months more. The *Evening Post* in commenting on the convention could do little more than praise the Whig resolutions that condemned the devices to extend slavery.

When the mixed bag of anti-Nebraska, anti-popular sovereignty, and antislavery men held their delayed nominating convention at Auburn on September 26, they indorsed the Whig slate approved the week before at Syracuse. This insured for the Whigs, Bryant editorialized on September 27, the principal state offices in November. Referring to the Soft Shell convention, Bryant declared: "the consequence is now before us—men who have all along been faithful to the democratic party are exasperated, disown its nomination, and join in the acclamation by which a whig is nominated as governor of the state."

On August 16 the *Evening Post* had noted the resurgence of the Know-Nothing party, which in less than a year had come into prominence "with no public meetings, no loud boasting of its strength, apparently with none of the ordinary instruments of electioneering, and without the countenance of any of the leading politicians, who generally are not slow in observing which way the cat is about to jump." The paper felt, however, that the party would be short-lived, though by attracting dissidents of other parties it might "confound the shrewdest political calculations." On October 6 Bryant printed an editorial consisting of two sentences on the party's convention: "The Know-Nothings yesterday nominated Daniel Ullman, Esq., as their candidate for governor. If he should be elected, he will be the first Know-Nothing governor we ever had." Thus did he show his disdain for this movement, but later, on October 23, he was forced to take cognizance of it in noting that many Democrats, disgusted with the Pierce administration, had become "either members of the Know-Nothing lodges or inclined to favor their objects."

In trying to explain the confused political alignments for his readers Bryant resorted to an analogical anecdote in an editorial on September 30. A builder had instructed an Irish worker on how to drill and blast a large boulder so that it would split in a certain way. When he returned to ask how it had broken, the Irishman answered: "Illigantly intirely, divel a bether; it is *quarthered exactly in three halves."* "Both the old parties," Bryant wrote, "are quartered into three halves 'intirely.' " He pointed out that there had been seven conventions, representing as many parties, and four slates of candidates had been nominated. Likewise there were four main issues: support of the administration, encouragement of slavery propagandism, enforcing temperance by legal restraints, and exclusion of aliens and Catholics from public office. The *Evening Post* could not approve of any of the slates and so told its readers on October 30. Informing readers on November 6 just before the election that he had no advice to offer, Bryant wrote caustically: "A voter may have a triumph in supporting any one of the candidates, for whichever is elected will involve the defeat of the others, each of which, for some good reason, deserves no better fate."

Bryant's warning in August that the Know-Nothings might "utterly confound the shrewdest political calculations" was borne out in the election. Ullman, their candidate, polled 122,000 votes to the approximately 156,000 each received by Clark and Seymour and the 35,000 received by Bronson. Clark squeaked through to a victory by a plurality of fewer than 200 votes over Seymour. The triumph of the Know-Nothings, Bryant wrote on November 20, was due less to their anti-Catholic and antiforeign principles than to "the popular dissatisfaction with the way in which the old parties have been managed by mischievous and place-seeking officeholders." He declared that he did not believe, therefore, that they could be converted into "a grand fusion."

V

Bryant's doubt that the people searching for a party would find one which they could join in large numbers continued throughout most of the next year. He wrote ironically on the question of fusion on September 13,

1855. Fusion was, he said, "the rage of the day" like the latest fashion for men of long-skirted frock coats and for women of trailing dresses. The Know-Nothing party was a fusion of Whigs and Democrats; and the Republican, which had been scoring some victories in the northern states, a fusion of Whigs, Democrats, and Free-Soilers. But there were other people looking for some crucible into which they could jump to be melted. The Hard Shell Democrats, for example, might let themselves be melted into an association with the Know-Nothings and Silver Grays or it was equally likely that they might merge with the friends of President Pierce.

But the situation in Kansas, which was in a state of civil war between slave and free settlers, had the effect of drawing together the antislavery people no matter what their beliefs on other matters—the beliefs that once stood for party principles. A party label no longer meant anything. "Men who have acted together in the same party their whole lives long find themselves suddenly dissociated," Bryant wrote on September 10; "men who never acted together on political questions before, rush into each other's arms." Thus Bryant was ready for fusion when the opportunity presented itself in September. It came when the Whig and Republican state committees arranged for the two parties to hold their conventions at Syracuse at the same time to facilitate a formal union of all antislavery voters. Though meeting in separate sessions, the two groups worked together in adopting platforms and dividing their tickets between men of Whig and Democratic antecedents. On the last day the Whigs marched in a body to the Republican convention hall. Seward had written a supporter who had inquired which convention he should attend that it did not make any difference. "You will go in by two doors," he said, "but you will come out through one."

Bryant's decision to join the Republicans was equivocally stated in his first editorial comment on the union of the two parties. He could not suddenly bring himself to calling himself a Republican but that he had accepted the label was indicated from what he said. The delegates at Syracuse had succeeded in effecting the "grand fusion" he had doubted a short time before—one that took in three-fourths of the antislavery men of New York—and they had adopted resolutions and nominated men so that the party's stand for "the nationality of freedom and the sectionality of slavery" was unmistakable. Speaking as much for himself as for the Democrats at Syracuse, Bryant said: "They have been constrained to form new, and, to some extent, perhaps uncongenial associations by the course pursued by their old friends, and to take upon themselves the responsibility of commencing the dissolution of an organization which has ceased to serve the cause of freedom and justice." But he was upset that this dissolution had come about, perhaps because a Whig, Seward, was the leader of it, writing: "We cannot look with indifference upon old personal and political friends, whose joys have been our joys and whose sorrows have been our sorrows,—men whose honor and patriotism are above suspicion, arrayed against each other, with their swords crossed and ready, we had almost said, to spill fraternal blood." His decision became firm late in the year. When the Democrats called a state convention at Syracuse to elect delegates to the national convention in 1856 at Cincinnati, Bryant wrote on December 26: "Our advice to our readers, is to take no part in the election of delegates. Let there be no attempt to modify what we cannot possibly control. As we can hope nothing right from the Cincinnati convention, let us not make ourselves parties to its results, or in any way constructive accomplices in acts at which the entire spirit of the free states will revolt."

VI

During the year Frances had sufficiently recovered from the illness which had afflicted her after the trip in 1854 to Illinois to leave Roslyn and join Bryant in the city, taking quarters at 35 Lexington Avenue for the summer, so Bryant wrote his brother John on March 10, in order to "have a place to receive her friends."[9] Bryant wrote Dana that she was "gradually coming up to the old mark." During her illness, which Bryant described as a "nervous attack," she had given up the care of the household, but, he continued, "it is now again in her hands, though we try to prevent her from encumbering herself with too many matters at once and to moderate her zeal for keeping every thing in order."[10] During the early part of June they were visited at Roslyn by their old Berkshire friends, Catharine and Charles Sedgwick. Writing to tell Bryant how much he enjoyed the visit to Cedarmere, Sedgwick said: "Life there seemed as near right as I could fancy it; as well prepared as wisdom can prepare it for longevity; and as well secured as righteousness can secure it against the pangs of survivorship."*[11] Sending Catharine a recipe for beer, Bryant

---

*In less than a year Charles Sedgwick himself was to die. Bryant, deeply affected, wrote Catharine Sedgwick on Aug. 8, 1856, that his own "natural reserve would have dictated a silence which, if less demonstrative, would have been equally full of sympathy," but he was persuaded by Frances to write. "Yet I may be allowed to suggest," Bryant said, "that the very virtues which make his friends grieve are the sources of their consolation, when they reflect that the more they have lost in him, the more he is sure to have gained." Goddard-Roslyn Collection; Godwin, *Biography,* II, 90–1.

related that he had been engaged in brewing his own since passage of the state antiliquor law under Governor Clark. He had "compounded" some beer according to the recipe but would have to wait a week to find out if it were fit for drinking, summer being too warm for "the happiest cerevisial fermentation." He may also have had in mind making some cider, an occupation so prevalent in New England homes during his boyhood, for he wrote: "We must go back to what we can make in our households. It is to be hereafter with drinks as it would be with tissues if all the cotton and woolen mills were stopped by law, and we were obliged to wear linsey-woolsey and other homespun cloths."[12]

Such escapes from urgent political questions, however, were only temporary, and Bryant when he returned to his desk at the *Evening Post* pored over the news reports and prepared his editorials supporting the new party alignment and attacking President Pierce. He was disheartened by the civil war in Kansas, which had set up a dual government of legislatures chosen by the contending proslavery and antislavery forces, and aroused to indignation when the President, in his annual message to Congress, temporized on the issue, saying that the people of the territory had the right to determine their own institutions. "It is some comfort to know that Mr. Pierce admits that the doings of the Missourians in Kansas have not been quite regular," the *Evening Post* declared on January 2. "Shooting people dead without provocation is, he acknowledges, not quite the thing, and though not to be called by so horrid a name as assassination, it may be safely styled a proceeding 'prejudicial to order.' "

In Washington the battle between the proslavery and antislavery forces was being waged in the House of Representatives over the election of a speaker. It went on for almost two months, requiring one hundred and thirty-three ballotings, before the Republican nominee, Nathaniel P. Banks of Massachusetts, emerged as the victor. Supporting Banks's election, the *Evening Post* rejoiced: it was the first Republican victory, "the first triumph achieved by the party of the people over the party of the slaveholders." Now a national leader through his election, Banks became active in organizing the Republicans for the 1856 presidential campaign. The problem, as he saw it, was to agree upon a candidate who could "incarnate" Republican principles. On a trip to New York to talk with party leaders, he visited the *Evening Post* and conferred at length with Bigelow and took him to meet John C. Frémont, who was staying at the Metropolitan Hotel. The meeting resulted in Bigelow's being brought into the inner councils of the Republicans, and he was during this election year to become one of the party's most indefatigable campaigners, bringing with him to the Frémont campaign Bryant and the newspaper.

In considering men to "incarnate" the new party, Banks had ruled out Chase and Seward. They had been too active in oposition parties to unite all the antislavery people. General Sam Houston, whom the *Evening Post* had spoken favorably of the year before, was too noncommittal on Kansas and too friendly to the Know-Nothings. By this process of elimination, Banks concluded that Frémont would be the best candidate. He was the son-in-law of Senator Thomas Hart Benton of Missouri, whose support he thought—erroneously as it turned out—could be expected; he had no previous political history to embarrass him; and he had a national reputation because of his explorations and surveys and his role played in California during the Mexican War. Bigelow was persuaded by these arguments and moved to organize New York behind Frémont by inviting a few former Whigs and Democrats to his home to meet the dean of the Jacksonian Democrats, Francis P. Blair, whose support Banks had earlier obtained for Frémont.[13]

Thus far the Republican party had been organized only on a state basis; it was not a national organization. To correct this deficiency, five state chairmen issued a call in January for a meeting at Pittsburgh on Washington's birthday to bring the state units together into one association that would represent all the antislavery factions of the North. Blair had been persuaded to attend, and apparently considerable effort was made to get Bryant to attend also, for he wrote his brother John on February 15:

> I cannot go to Pittsburg. I do not like public meetings. I do not like consultations. I am surfeited with politics in my vocation, and when I go from home I cannot bear to carry them with me. If I were not a journalist, perhaps the case would be different. . . . That the consultation at Pittsburg will be among honest men is provable enough, but I am not a very firm believer in the honesty of parties. All parties include nearly all sorts of men, and the moment a party becomes strong the rogues are attracted to it, and immediately try to manage it. . . .[14]

At first the Pittsburgh convention, attended by former Democrats, Know-Nothings, Abolitionists, Whigs, and Free-Soilers, seemed unlikely to agree on anything, but as proceedings went on the differences that separated the factions were forgotten in the one desire to prevent the extension of slavery. Blair was elected president, and Bryant referred to this indirectly in an editorial on February 25 praising the accomplishments of the convention at which members of the older parties and new men coming into prominence with few loyalties to these organizations had united. "One of the remarkable features of the convention," Bryant wrote, "was the part taken in conducting its deliberations by some of the sturdiest democrats in the Union, men who had stood by the side of General Jackson in all his battles with the whig party, who loved his sincerity, courage and ever-wakeful sense of right, as much as they admired his political principles, and who learned from his example to make no compromise with wrong and injustice." But after this last look at the past, Bryant faced the future: the convention gave those opposed to slavery new confidence and new strength for the battle to come. "The waters that are dispersed in a thousand little rivulets are of no use to the manufacturer," Bryant said. "Gather them into one mighty stream, and they move the most ponderous machinery."

More than two months before the Republican nominating convention was to open on June 17, the anniversary of Bunker Hill, the *Evening Post* began to campaign for Frémont. On April 9 the paper gave prominent display to a letter Frémont had written to the free-state governor of Kansas, Charles Robinson, offering him his support. The next day, an editorial commented: "Mr. Frémont, as our readers know, has been spoken of among those who are likely to receive the nomination for the presidency at the Philadelphia convention. This letter gives him a high and prominent place in the list of those distinguished persons from whom a selection is to be made." Additional publicity was given him the next day when the paper carried a compilation of editorial comment from other papers on the letter. Frémont continued to receive favorable comment in the *Evening Post,* and on May 19 Bigelow began publication of a biography of the "Pathfinder" on which he had been working.

Loath to appear before the public as a political spokesman, Bryant merely sent a letter to be read when he was invited to speak at a mass meeting at the Broadway Tabernacle on April 28 to hear a report of the state delegates attending the Pittsburgh convention. The call for the meeting carried more than three thousand signers, the names being printed in the *Evening Post.* But Bryant's reluctance to attend such meetings was overcome by his indignation when Charles Sumner, making personal attacks against several senators in a powerful speech known later as "The Crime against Kansas," was brutally beaten on May 22 while sitting at his desk by Preston Brooks, nephew of Senator Andrew P. Butler of South Carolina, exacting vengeance for insults to his uncle. At a mass meeting on May 30 at the Tabernacle to protest this outrage, Bryant attended and was chosen to introduce the officers elected for the occasion. According to the *Evening Post's* report, Bryant came forward to the platform and was compelled to stand silent for some minutes "by reason of the deafening cheers that rose at his appearance." Later in the year he spoke in behalf of the Republican nominee, and on August 26 called a meeting at Roslyn of all those in "favor of Kansas being a free state" which he addressed.[15]

On the day that the Republicans had held their preliminary convention at Pittsburgh, the American party, or Know-Nothings, had met at Philadelphia. It had become divided, as the Whigs and the Democrats before it, over the slavery issue. The southern group seceded from the convention for a time when it appeared that their interests would not dominate, but they returned when it became apparent that Millard Fillmore would get the nomination. He was of course acceptable to them because of his support of the Compromise of 1850 and his efforts to enforce the Fugitive Slave Act. Bryant took satisfaction in this "purely southern" nomination. Whomever the Democrats nominated at Cincinnati—be it Pierce or James Buchanan—he would find Fillmore "already on the ground, prepared to dispute with him the votes of every southern state in which the Whigs had at any time held the ascendancy."

The meeting of the Democrats at Cincinnati on June 2 was preceded by an editorial blast in the *Evening Post* against the party which "in its zeal for the extension of slavery holds falsehood, robbery and manslaughter to be lawful when employed for that purpose." The defeat of Pierce and the nomination of James Buchanan of Pennsylvania, Bryant wrote on June 6, indicated that even in the eyes of the Democrats the President's subservience had shown him unfit for another term of office. The slaveholders, he added, "want a fresh man to spoil."

Two weeks later Bryant, resorting to ridicule, wrote that Buchanan was the nominee of a party without a name, since it would be a misuse of the language to call it Democratic; likewise it could not be called the Administration party, since it had repudiated Pierce. For one reason or another Bryant discarded other names—Pro-Slavery, Disunionist, Doughface, Federal. He proposed to label the party the "Bucaniers," spelled "Buchaniers" in later editorials. The name had the advantage of identifying the party with its leaders and it additionally identified Buchanan with the last great measure of his public life, "the piratical manifesto from Ostend" in which as minister to Great Britain he had urged that the United States take over Cuba from Spain.

When the Republicans convened at Philadelphia on June 17, the way had been prepared for the nomination of Frémont, though both Seward and Chase had enthusiastic supporters. Seward wanted the nomination but would not allow his name to be presented, because Thurlow Weed did not think the Republicans could win their first national campaign and his protégé would have a better chance in 1860. Chase's supporters followed suit in withdrawing his name, and upon a motion of James Watson Webb of the New York *Courier and Enquirer* Frémont was elected by acclamation. The cheer that greeted the nomination became the chief slogan of the party in the campaign: "Free Speech, Free Press, Free Men, Free Labor, and Frémont."

Bigelow hastened home from the convention, which he had attended as one of New York's delegates, to work for Frémont, dividing his time between the *Evening Post* and the Republican campaign headquarters. Bryant had already placed the paper firmly behind Frémont with an editorial on June 19 in which he hailed the nomination as an instance in which the politicians had answered the voice of the people. They saw in Frémont the qualities needed in a "Chief Magistrate of the Nation," a man of "unshaken courage, perfect steadiness of purpose, and ready command of resources."

The Republicans' campaign for Frémont was reminiscent in its rollicking spirit and ebullient meetings of the Whigs' Log Cabin campaign for "Tippecanoe and Tyler, too," and the ordinarily staid *Evening Post* forgot its dignity in its enthusiasm at the hustings. Just as the Whigs had tried, as Bryant had written in 1840, to "sing" General Harrison to victory, the Republicans raised songs to Frémont. The *Evening Post* offered two hundred dollars in prizes for the best songs submitted, and printed scores of the entries, sometimes devoting a whole page to the jingles. Altogether, there were more than two hundred entries. The Young Republican Clubs, calling themselves Wide-Awakes, had fife and drum corps that filled the air day and night, glee clubs entertained audiences gathered to hear party speakers, and as many as fifty bands marched in some of the huge parades. Bryant was right in calling the nomination an expression of the people's voice. The crowds assembled to hear the party orators—George William Curtis, William H. Seward, Abraham Lincoln, David Wilmot, Joshua Giddings—were mammoth—10,000, 15,000, 35,000 and even 50,000 when Sumner, not recovered from the attack by Preston Brooks, was given a rousing welcome in Boston.

But despite all the tumult and the shouting, the Republicans trailed in the popular vote. Frémont received 1,335,264 to Buchanan's 1,838,169 but he was far ahead of Fillmore with his 874,534. The defeat did not dishearten Bryant. In an editorial, "The Duty of the Republican Party," the *Evening Post* called upon the members to act through their state legislatures, since nothing to halt the extension of slavery could be expected from the President or Congress, and to make liberal provision to help send emigrants to Kansas. "They must go armed," Bryant said, "in such numbers and array that to allow their entrance will be the part of discretion. All this is in our power; and if, with our large resources, and our vast and enterprising population, we neglect to use that power in the amplest manner, we shall deserve to wear the yoke of the southern oligarchs forever." This, however, was nothing new, for the paper had been advocating aid to the emigrants all year, running frequent notices informing persons that they could leave their contributions at its office at Nassau and Liberty Streets. The popular minister, Henry Ward Beecher, had said that a Sharpe's rifle was a greater moral agency than the Bible in arming the emigrants. Bryant accepted this opinion on the persuasive power of "Beecher's Bibles," as the guns came to be called. In the fight for a free Kansas, Bryant, though in the past he had condemned any violence, seemed not now averse to shedding blood.

23

SHADOWS OF THE GATE OF DEATH

DURING THE POLITICAL AGITATION OF THE SUMMER AND fall of 1856, Bryant, now in his sixty-first year, impressed the irregularly employed journalist, Walter Whitman of Brooklyn, as being a busy and preoccupied man as he was seen walking about the streets of New York. The year before Whitman had set up in type himself and published a book with the odd title *Leaves of Grass* containing even odder poems that mystified the few who read them. Whitman was writing a series of articles for *Life Illustrated,* in one of which he described notables encountered on the streets. Bryant with "a dry, spare, hard visage" and "a huge white beard of somewhat ragged appearance" strode along "regardlessly and rapidly, a book in his hand, a thought—and more too—inside his head, a most rustical straw hat outside of it, turned sharp up behind and down before, like a country boy's, and a summer coat streaming flag-like from his shoulders."[1]

Among Bryant's preoccupations not known to Whitman was a personal one, worry about the health of his wife. A year before she had seemed to have recovered from her illness of the fall and winter of 1854, but now her condition had again become cause for apprehension. "She cannot lie down on account of a feeling of oppression in the chest and a troublesome cough and her ankles and feet are much swollen," Bryant wrote his brother John. "Her symptoms give us intense anxiety."[2] During the winter she suffered an attack of what Bryant called "acute or inflammatory rheumatism," and in April of 1857, he wrote Dana, he decided upon a sea voyage, a trip to Europe, in the hope of aiding her recovery.[3]

In the meantime, Bryant continued to worry about what was happening in the country. The uncompromising attitude of the North toward the South was emphasized for him in November when, with George Bancroft, he arranged for the Young Men's Lecture Association a series of addresses by William Gilmore Simms. Simms avoided current problems in choosing his subjects, but even views on noncontroversial matters could not get a hearing for a southerner in New York. He gave only one lecture, "South Carolina in the Revolution," on November 18. The others were canceled because the first provoked such rancorous feeling that the association "could not only sell no tickets, but could not succeed in *giving* them away." The *Tribune, Times,* and *Herald* commented adversely on the lecture and only the *Evening Post* defended Simms. "He is neither a politician by habit or profession," the paper said. "He holds no office, nor is an applicant for any. His pursuits are purely literary."[4] Part of the hostility to Simms was due to the attack by his fellow South Carolinian, Preston Brooks, on Sumner, but Bryant could not see why the novelist and poet should share this obloquy.

While making arrangements for the trip to Europe, Bryant was aroused to wrath when, two days after James Buchanan was inaugurated President, the United States Supreme Court announced its decision on the appeal of the Negro slave Dred Scott, who had sued for his liberty in the Missouri courts on the grounds that his owner had taken him to the free state of Illinois and the free territory of Wisconsin. The decision was that Scott was not a citizen and therefore could not sue in the federal courts; that his temporary residence in free territory did not entitle him to liberty when he returned to Missouri, where slavery was permitted; and that the Missouri Compromise was unconstitutional because the Fifth Amendment prohibited Congress from depriving persons of their property without due process of law. Bryant gave Chief Justice Roger B. Taney's opinion close scrutiny in a series of editorial leaders on eight successive days and found it to be a willful misreading of the Constitution, an interpretation so "superficial and shallow" that it should be respected nowhere. The "peculiar institution" of the South was now declared a federal institution, he wrote, and the United States should now be designated the Land of Bondage and its flag the flag of slavery.

In April Bryant took Frances to Great Barrington for a visit with her sister before they left with Julia and a friend of hers, Estelle Ives, on a sailing ship for Europe, chosen instead of a steamer, he wrote Dana, because the longer voyage would give the invigorating sea air a better chance to restore Frances's strength.[5] On a trip to Cummington Bryant found that the monument on his father's grave had broken and fallen on the ground, and he arranged for a new stone to be put up with the plain inscription:

Peter Bryant
a studious and skillful
Physician and Surgeon
and for some time a member of the
State Senate
Born at North Bridgewater
August 12th, 1767
Died March 19th, 1820[6]

II

Reaching Le Havre on May 30 after a "for the most part not unpleasant passage,"[7] the Bryants remained only overnight before going on to Paris. In a letter to the *Evening Post* dated June 11, Bryant described the Palais de l'Industrie, the French exposition similar to New York's Crystal Palace exposition of 1853.[8] He complimented the French on their way with flowers, finding the palace beautifully decorated with growing plants in bloom about which smartly dressed Parisian ladies hovered like butterflies. He was not displeased to report that the New York maize displayed was much better in quality than the European product.

Charles Sumner was in the city recovering from Preston Brooks's attack on him. "He was looking exceedingly well—too fat, rather," Bryant wrote Julia Sands; "in fact, he had lost something of the intellectuality of his expression, which was exchanged for a comfortable, well-fed look." His health was mending slowly, however, though the injury to his spine prevented him from taking exercise by walking. Sumner was pleased to hear Bryant's report that the Dred Scott decision was being disavowed in the North, that only "a few old bigots to judicial infallibility acknowledged the decision to be law."[9]

By July 14 the travelers were in Heidelberg after a tour of Belgium and Holland, the most noteworthy part of the trip being Bryant's visit to a pauper colony in the province of Overijssel, which he described in a personal letter to W. S. Thayer and also wrote up for the *Evening Post*. One of Bryant's favorite European places, Heidelberg was especially enjoyable because of the presence of the Unitarian minister, the Rev. Robert C. Waterston, whom Bryant had first met in Boston, and his wife and their seventeen-year-old daughter Helen. Bryant and Waterston climbed the hills about the city and wandered among the castles and ruins. Long afterward Waterston remembered vividly their walks. "The history and character of every shrub were familiar to him," he related, "while with these was a sense of beauty and harmony that quivered through his whole being, an emotion all the deeper because of its calmness. . . ."[10]

Twice before while Bryant was in Europe political conditions had deterred him from going to Spain. Now he made plans to visit the country whose language he had learned on first going to New York and whose literature he had studied and translated. Leaving Heidelberg, he bent his way toward that country, making a leisurely trip across Switzerland and the south of France to Bagnères-de-Luchon in the French Pyrenees near the border late in August. Frances benefited from the warm sulphur springs that brought many invalids to the spa, but it held other attractions. "Luchon is the most attractive summer residence I have seen on this side of the Atlantic," Bryant wrote the Rev. Orville Dewey. "Here we have cool airs and extensive promenades of deep and ample shade, a fresh and flowery turf, rapid streams, cascades, clear brooks, picturesque mountains, and the greenest valleys winding away in almost every direction, and all this under the glorious sunshine of the south of France."[11]

By September 28 the Bryants had traversed the Pyrenees to the west coast, after brief stops at Bagnères-de-Bigorre, Pau, and Bayonne, and had crossed the border to San Sebastian in Spain. They were in the country of the Basques, and Bryant noted their appearance as the party traveled by diligence deeper into Spain—"the men in flat blue caps, short jackets, and wooden shoes, many of the younger wearing scarlet sashes" and "the women for the most part barefoot, their heads bound with gay cotton kerchiefs, and their petticoats tucked up for the convenience of walking in the wet roads." The party broke their journey to Madrid by a week's stop in San Sebastian, taking rooms in a squalid hostelry where sleep was impossible because of the fleas. But the beauty of the town's location compensated for the discomfort of the lodgings. "The two sublimest features of nature are the sea and the mountains," Bryant wrote the *Evening Post;* "and it is not often that in any part of the world you see them in their grandeur side by side." Such a splendid view was offered by San Sebastian.

Continuing on toward Madrid, the party stopped several days at Burgos, where, on October 14, Bryant wrote another letter to the *Evening Post,*

391

describing visits to Las Huelgas, a Cistercian convent, and La Cartuja, a Carthusian monastery. Burgos, which Bryant estimated had a population of 30,000, was agog over the final bullfights of the season, and he was persuaded by a Spanish friend to attend. He was impressed by the color and drama of the spectacle, reporting it in detail for his New York readers; but he was appalled when the horse ridden by a picador was attacked by the bull and its bowels ripped open. His horror was provoked not so much by this cruelty as by the fact that the horse had been blindfolded in order that it might not get out of the way. Seeing the dispatch of two bulls satisfied Bryant's curiosity about the Spanish national sport, and he left the arena before the fights were over.

The Bryant party departed from Burgos on October 14 and after a four-day journey marked by stops at squalid inns reached Madrid. Thus far in Bryant's journey through Spain letters of introduction given him by Archbishop John Hughes of New York had resulted in his meeting Spaniards, who hospitably served the party as guides in the towns where they stopped. In Madrid there were acquaintances to introduce him to leading writers and public figures, Calderon de la Barca, former Spanish minister to the United States; the American minister to Spain, A. C. Dodge; and a former secretary of the American legation, Horatio Perry, who had married the well-known Spanish writer, Carolina Coronado. The Bryants spent about four weeks in Madrid before going on to the south of Spain.

Shortly after reaching Madrid, Bryant had been disturbed by a letter from John Bigelow, dated October 12, reporting a financial panic in the United States, the worst since 1837.[12] The business situation had become shaky in midsummer due, Bigelow had explained in editorials, to speculation. The real panic started in August when the New York branch of the Ohio Life Insurance and Trust Company, which held a half million dollars of country bankers' deposits lent to unsound railroad companies was forced to close. On October 10, Bigelow wrote in the *Evening Post:* "Business of all kinds is more completely suspended than it would have been two months ago if a hostile fleet had anchored in our harbor, or if a pestilence were sweeping the land." But in his letter to Bryant, Bigelow was able to report that the paper had not been so adversely affected as other businesses. Advertising had held up and the circulation of the daily, semiweekly, and weekly papers was greater than ever, fluctuating from day to day but rising from 5,040 early in September to 7,000 on October 10. Bigelow was, however, having staff troubles. Thayer had been away from the paper for a month because of illness and the law reporter had quit to become night editor of the *Tribune.* One young man taken on as a replacement had to be fired because of incompetence and another proved to be not much better. Bigelow had obtained a new Wall Street reporter, one Gibbons, but they had not yet agreed on terms, Gibbons wanting $2,000 a year and Bigelow willing to pay only $1,500. He now was assisted by a staff of five, including one Cutler, who did the book criticisms for a salary of ten dollars a week. But insofar as the affairs of the paper were concerned the most interesting news was that Judge William Kent, son of the famous Chancellor Kent, wished to buy into the firm. He had contributed some articles, mostly on legal topics, and had suggested that he purchase "a small interest as an excuse for devoting himself to editorial work."*

Bryant found the Gallic influence great in Madrid, members of the court speaking the French language, reading French books, and attending performances of French plays. "Madrid," he was told, "is not a Spanish city; it is French—it is inhabited by *afrancesados,* people who take pains to acquire French tastes, and who follow French fashions and modes of living." Nevertheless, there were old Spanish customs that interested him, especially the daily promenades, the chief Spanish social institution, on the Prado. His greatest interest, however, was in the Royal Museum, where there were more than two thousand paintings, works by such masters as Murillo, Raphael, Valasquez, Ribera, Titian, Veronese, and Guido Reni. He wrote the *Evening Post* of the museum:

> At the very first sight of it, I could hardly help assenting to the judgment of those who call it the finest gallery of paintings in the world. The multitude of pictures by the greatest masters the world has produced, amazed me at first, and then bewildered me. I was intoxicated by the spectacle, as men sometimes are by sudden good fortune; I wanted to enjoy all this wealth of art at once, and roamed from hall to hall, throwing my eyes on one great masterpiece after another, without the power of fixing my attention on any. It was not till after two or three visits, that I could soberly and steadily address myself to the contemplation of the nobler works in the collection.

The Bryant party left Madrid on November 18 by train on the first leg of their journey to the south of Spain, regretting that they did not have the opportunity to visit the ancient Moorish city of Toledo and thinking

---

*Nothing developed from Kent's offer, though he repeated it on Sept. 7, 1858, in a letter to Bigelow. He wrote that though he was retiring from the law he still wished to keep himself busy and that if he became one of the owners he would "enter into the work heartily and industriously." Bryant-Goddard Collection. Allan Nevins said that Isaac Henderson opposed bringing a fourth partner into the concern. *The Evening Post,* p. 340.

of other places they would have to miss—Bilbao, Salamanca, Zaragoza. Bryant described the landscape for *Evening Post* readers, noting that the Spaniards had not preserved the forests. As a result, streams and rivers were shrinking and topsoil was being washed away by the rains. Don Quixote's La Mancha had a look of cheerlessness and poverty, and dust-clouds filled the air blown by the wind that turned the windmills as it had in the days when the mad knight charged them as an enemy host. The railroad ended at Almanza, and Bryant had to find other transportation to their destination, Alicante, facing the Mediterranean on the southeast coast. The only vehicle that could be hired was a small rudely constructed cart, a two-wheeled conveyance with no springs but provided with cushioned seats and covered by an awning of painted cloth. Their luggage, mounted at the back, occasionally touched the ground as the *carrito* bounced over the rough road, tossing the passengers backward and forward and from side to side. The sixty-mile journey required two days.

Alicante, though a town of great antiquity, did not have much interest for Bryant, and, bored after several days waiting for a ship on which to sail to the coastal cities, he decided to go alone overland to Cartagena, where he would join his wife, Julia, and Miss Ives on their arrival by sea. After the dreadful trip to Alicante, the women would not subject themselves to travel again over roads that they were told were just as bad. The roads were indeed so bad that the diligence scheduled to carry travelers was canceled and they were loaded on a *galera,* a sort of market-wagon without springs, drawn by eight mules. Three days after Bryant reached Cartagena, the ship with the remainder of his party arrived, and they sailed on to Malaga, reaching port on December 1.

After the hardships suffered since leaving Madrid, the Bryants were delighted with Malaga, enjoying during their stay weather so soft and serene that it reminded them of New York in June. They investigated the labyrinthine streets, so narrow that it was proverbially said that a priest could not turn around in them without knocking off his hat. Bryant visited the Protestant burial ground, which had recently been established through the efforts of the British consul, bodies of non-Catholics heretofore having been interred in the sands of the sea-beach at low water mark. The party made a side trip of several days to see the Moorish splendor of the city of Granada, whose story Washington Irving had told in *The Conquest of Granada* and whose chief place of interest, the summer palace of the Moors, he had described delightfully in *The Alhambra.* Bryant's first view was that of the ancient city from a distance, magically coming into sight "on a hill-side, with her ancient towers rising over her roofs and her woods, and towering far above all . . . the snow summits of the Sierra Nevada." He was not, however, about to describe Granada, he wrote in his *Evening Post* letter: "After what Irving has written of it, I should as soon think of attempting a poem on the wrath of Achilles in competition with Homer." But saying this, he could not resist the attractions of the city. It was situated at a place "where you hear on all sides the sound of falling waters and the murmur of rivers; where the hill-sides and water-courses clothe themselves with dense woods; where majestic mountains stand in sight, capped with snow; while at their foot . . . lies one of the fairest and most fertile valleys that the sun ever shone upon."

On December 12, regretting that they did not have time to visit Cadiz, Seville, and Gibraltar, the Bryants took passage on a French steamer bound for Marseilles by way of Oran and Algiers. Shortly after leaving port, she collided in the darkness with another ship and, only slightly damaged, remained in the vicinity, tossed by a violent wind that had arisen, for the remainder of the night as the captain sought to discover what happened to the other vessel.

At Oran, the Bryants had two days ashore, with opportunities to see the Moorish city and its motley people: Arabs in loose garments of dirty white, Zouaves strolling about in Oriental garb, soldiers in French uniforms, Jews in black caps or turbans and black tunics, Spaniards in ample cloaks, and Franciscan monks in brown gowns and Dominicans in white. A few days later the ship entered the port of Algiers, which Bryant discovered, in contrast to the color and variety of Oran, to be a "mere French town" in its lower part but having all the mystery of the Orient in its older section. Entering the Kasbah, Bryant found himself "in a sort of twilight, in narrow winding lanes, into which the sun never shone, where the wind never blew." So quietly did the people move about and so dimly were they perceived that Bryant could almost fancy himself "in a city of the dead, walking among the spectres that haunted it." It was with a feeling of relief that after wending his way through the maze of dark lanes he emerged into the broad streets of the new city. It seemed that he had returned from "the abodes of death to the upper world."

III

Arriving at Marseilles the day before Christmas, the Bryants, after the glorious sun of southern Spain and northern Africa, thought the city with its damp and frosty winds and sunless streets a "gloomy and dreary abode." Mrs. Bryant becoming ill with the grippe, their departure by sea to Naples was delayed several days until she recovered. But Naples was also unseasonably cold, Neapolitans saying that they could not recall such unfavorable weather, and the city was swept by an epidemic of fever which, Bryant wrote his friend Alfred Field in England, "swept off the people like the cholera, sometimes four hundred in a day."[13] Mrs. Bryant, still not fully recovered from her illness at Marseilles, caught the fever and for four months was so prostrated that Bryant feared she could not recover. Bryant himself was her physician and nurse and, writing his brother John after the ordeal, said he was inclined to think that "if she had had an allopathic physician" he could not have brought her alive out of Naples. He attributed her recovery to "the gentle methods of the new system," homoeopathy.[14]

Bryant had mixed feelings about Naples. He wrote John that it was "the same noisy place, full of beggars and blackguards," it had been twenty-three years before when he first saw it and "just as badly governed," but in his letter to Fields he described the beauty of the spring, "the orange trees . . . full of ripe fruit and fragrant with blossoms" and the countryside brightened by the verdure of trees and grain. There were fewer Americans than usual in the city, travelers having rushed home when news of the financial panic reached them. There were friends, however, to give him sympathy and encouragement during the worst part of Frances's illness and to take his mind off his worries—the American chargé d'affaires Robert Dale Owen; the Baltimore novelist John Pendleton Kennedy, whose woodsman Horse Shoe Robinson was often likened to Cooper's Natty Bumppo; Mrs. Robert Sedgwick and her daughters; and most helpful of all, the Rev. Robert C. Waterston and his wife and daughter. Bryant spent a great part of his time reading, his travel diary mentioning Dante, Schlegel's *Italian Art,* the *Pensées* of Pascal and Nicole, and many others, including two manuscripts given him by Owen, a work on spiritualism and his father's autobiography.

Three years before in a poem, "The Twenty-Seventh of March," Bryant had addressed lines to Frances on her birthday, developing the theme that she was born in the season

> When March, just ready to depart, begins
> To soften into April

and that the first issuing flowers, the periwinkle, the ground-laurel, and the squirrel-cup, brought into being by "an hour's sunshine," still faced the danger of frost. The following lines may have recurred to him when, in April, Frances seemed on the way to recovery:

> Well hast thou borne the bleak March day of life.
> Its storms and its keen winds to thee have been
> Most kindly tempered, and through all its gloom
> There have been warmth and sunshine in thy heart;
> The griefs of life to thee have been like snows,
> That light upon the fields in early spring,
> Making them greener.

Apparently in a similar mood of thanksgiving, he sent, on May 23, a note to Dr. Waterston saying there was a subject he wished to discuss and asking for a meeting.[15] The next day they walked in the Villa Reale, the park overlooking the Bay of Naples, and Bryant, mentioning that he had never joined the church, said that he felt he would like to do so now. "Never can I forget the beautiful spirit that breathed through every word he uttered," Dr. Waterston has related, "the reverent love, the confiding trust, the aspiring hope, the deep-rooted faith. . . . Anxiously watching, as he had been doing, in the twilight boundary between this world and another, over one more precious to him than life itself, the divine truths and promises had come to his mind with new power."

The reason why Bryant had not until now united with a church is one of the more difficult complexities of his character since he was a regular attendant at religious services. Though brought up in the Congregationalist faith, his failure to subscribe to that belief as a boy can probably be attributed to his rationalist father, who was an early Unitarian. Rationalism, however, was never enough for Bryant, as he declared in the poem "The Conjunction of Jupiter and Venus," written in 1826:

> I would not always reason. The straight path
> Wearies us with the never varying lines,
> And we grow melancholy. I would make
> Reason my guide, but she should sometimes sit
> Patiently by the way-side, while I traced
> The mazes of the pleasant wilderness
> Around me. She should be my counsellor,
> But not my tyrant. For the spirit needs
> Impulses from a deeper source than hers. . . .

Bryant, as most of his poetry testifies, found this deeper source in nature and in his conception of the past, the present, and the future as constituting a process that, though set in motion by the Creator, was in a constant state of renewal. The great religious dispute of his time was over the Trinity, denied by the Unitarians. Bryant mentioned the idea of the Holy Spirit only once or twice in his work, and it may be concluded that the doctrine of the Third Person of the Trinity was not one into which he cared to enter. He was more interested in Christ, not however because of his deity but because of his humanity, a person not to be worshiped so much as one to serve as a guide for conduct. Though in much of his verse Bryant employed conventional religious diction, referring to God as a personal deity, his views were by no means orthodox although some of his readers may have been misled into considering them so. Such definitions of God as "eternal change," "the Great First Cause," "the Scourge of Wrong," "the Bestower of health," and other epithets employed by Bryant make it clear that he was eclectic in his beliefs. Though no one could call Bryant irreligious, he was heterodox according to the prevailing theology of his times. The doctrines of no church, therefore, could fully satisfy him spiritually or philosophically. The poet who found that the groves were God's first temples could worship in one institution as well as another when no choice was available as he did in the Congregational church in Great Barrington and in the Presbyterian at Roslyn, though in New York he was a pew-holder in the Unitarian.

The morning after the meeting in the Villa Reale, Dr. Waterston baptized Bryant into the Unitarian church in the presence of his family and one or two friends. "With snow-white head and flowing beard," Dr. Waterston related, "he stood like one of the ancient Prophets, and perhaps never since the days of the Apostles has a truer disciple professed allegiance to the Divine Master." Hymns were sung, a selection from the Scriptures was read, and the Holy Communion enacted. The next year in the poem, "The Song of the Sower," Bryant wrote of

> The consecrated bread—
> The mystic loaf that crowns the board,
> When, round the table of their Lord,
>   Within a thousand temples set,
> In memory of the bitter death
> Of Him who taught at Nazareth,
>   His followers are met,
> And thoughtful eyes with tears are wet,
>   As of the Holy One they think,
> The glory of whose rising yet
>   Makes bright the grave's mysterious brink.

After the service Bryant stood with Frances looking out over the bay where the island of Capri stood in relief against the sky and recited lines by John Leyden which he said he had always loved and which seemed to express his religious emotion of the moment:

> With silent awe, I hail the sacred morn,
> That scarcely wakes while all the fields are still;
> A soothing calm on every breeze is born,
>   A graver murmur echoes from the hill,
>   And softer sings the linnet from the thorn.
> Hail, light serene! Hail, sacred Sabbath morn!

But Bryant's thanksgiving was greater than the words of another poet could reveal and later in the month in "The Life That Is" he welcomed "back to life's free breath" his wife who "so long had pressed the couch of pain," concluding with the conventional religious sentiment that though death had been postponed he and his wife would be reunited in the future life:

> Twice wert thou given me; once in thy fair prime,
>   Fresh from the fields of youth, when first we met,
> And all the blossoms of that hopeful time
>   Clustered and glowed where'er thy steps were set.
>
> And now, in thy ripe autumn, once again
>   Given back to fervent prayers and yearnings strong,
> From the drear realm of sickness and of pain
>   When we had watched, and feared, and trembled long.

His wife's recovery had so uplifted Bryant's spirit that he wrote three other poems during the remainder of their stay in Naples, one "A Sick-Bed," in which he described the care he had given Frances during her illness, shifting her in her bed so that she lay more comfortably, smoothing her pillow, and cooling her fever with draughts of water from a spring and a moistened handkerchief placed across her brow. His belief in the restorative power of time and nature was embodied in "The River, by Night," a recollection of the Hudson with its

> ministry that never rests
> Even while the living slumber.

The Bay of Naples inspired "A Day-Dream" in which, watching the billows whitening toward the shore, he fancied he saw sea-nymphs taking form who sang a song regretting that they were lost to the eye of modern and disbelieving man before they dissolved again in the dancing spray and only waves ran "murmuring up the beach."

While in Naples Bryant was kept informed of political and financial developments at home in letters from Bigelow. On December 28 Bigelow wrote that in spite of the panic the *Evening Post* had continued to do well, the daily's circulation averaging more than four thousand, and that the November dividend would be about as usual. By the end of the year the decline in business had been halted, and, though there was suffering among the poor in the city, Bigelow could write with some confidence that the economy was fundamentally sound. On February 11 he again reported increases in circulation and advertising. The firm's affairs were in such good shape that he was negotiating with Moses Taylor to purchase the buildings the paper occupied, the one on Liberty Street for a down payment of $10,000 and an adjoining one on Nassau for $3,000. The next week Bigelow reported that he was about to conclude a deal to lease the buildings for five years with the option of buying them at any time for $45,000, but on March 22 he wrote that he had decided to abandon the idea of purchasing them now, preferring not to take such an important step without Bryant's concurrence. Later, on June 12, he reported semiannual dividends in May of $22,560, the largest ever paid. The daily paper's circulation was 4,404, the weekly's 5,591, and the semiweekly's 2,279.[16]

IV

During Frances's illness, Bryant had received several letters from the artist John Gadsby Chapman urging him to come to Rome, since the city's mild climate would be better for an invalid than Naples.[17] They were unable to make the journey until the early part of May, however, stopping first for a week at Castellamare on the mountainside by the seashore south of Vesuvius, and then proceeding by easy stages to the capital, which they reached on May 16. Since it was the first trip to the Eternal City for Julia and Miss Ives, Bryant spent much of their stay of about two weeks in sightseeing. In a letter to the *Evening Post* dated May 21, he reported that there was a "passion for excavation" and that everywhere the earth was being dug into to uncover pieces of ancient Greek sculpture and the buried foundations of buildings. "Rome has its rich collection of ancient art in the Vatican," Bryant said, "but there is still a richer museum in the earth below."

In Rome at the time was the novelist Nathaniel Hawthorne with his family, and Bryant called upon him on May 21. They had met only once before, at Lenox in the Berkshires, when Bryant accompanied by the Sedgwicks had stopped by the Hawthornes' cottage to exchange greetings. "He presented himself now with a long white beard," Hawthorne wrote in his *French and Italian Notes,* "such as a palmer might have worn as the growth of his long pilgrimages, a brow almost entirely bald, and what hair he has quite hoary; a forehead impending, yet not massive; dark, bushy eyebrows and keen eyes, without much softness in them; a dark and sallow complexion; a slender figure, bent a little with age, but at once alert and infirm." The Hawthornes gathered around Bryant, who told them of his travels, speaking, so Hawthorne recorded, "with readiness and simplicity." He was now eager to get back to the United States though his "gals," as he called Julia and Miss Ives, "dragged him out to see the wonders of Rome again." Hawthorne found his manners were "very particularly plain, though not affectedly so" as though "in the decline of life, and the security of his position, he had put off whatever artificial polish he may have heretofore had, and resumed the simpler habits and deportment of his early New England breeding." He nevertheless was "a man of refinement, who has seen the world, and is well aware of his own place in it."

When Hawthorne introduced the subject of Kansas, it seemed that Bryant's face "forthwith assumed something of the bitter keenness of the editor of a political newspaper while speaking of the triumph of the administration over the free-soil opposition." But neither in talking about Kansas nor about Charles Sumner, whose appearance in Paris he described to Hawthorne, did Bryant display excitement. "He uttered neither passion nor poetry," Hawthorne related, "but excellent good sense, and accurate information, on whatever subject transpired; a very pleasant man to associate with, but rather cold, I should imagine, if one should seek to touch his heart with one's own."[18]

The Bryants left Rome on May 28 to begin their trip home, planning to stop only a day or so at a time in the cities they must pass through to reach Paris. At Florence, where Bryant had spent so much of his time on earlier visits to Italy, he had another encounter with Hawthorne, when both were guests of Elizabeth Barrett and Robert Browning, along with another American couple and the English poet Felicia Hemens, at Casa Guidi. Hawthorne, describing the occasion, said that Browning was very efficient in keeping the conversation going and seemed "a most vivid and quick-thoughted person, logical and common-sensible" in his talk. "Mr. Bryant, as usual, was homely and plain of manner," Hawthorne related, "with an old-fashioned dignity, nevertheless, and a remarkable deference and gentleness of tone in addressing Mrs. Browning. I doubt, however, whether he has any high appreciation of her poetry or her husband's, and it is my impression that they care as little about his." When the guests were leaving at ten o'clock, Mrs. Browning asked Bryant if he planned to revisit Europe. Tugging at his white hair, Bryant replied: "It is getting rather too late in the evening now." Hawthorne went on to describe Bryant:

> If any old age can be cheerful, I should think his might be so; so good a man, so cool, so calm, so bright, too, we may say. His life has been like the days that end in pleasant sunsets. He has a great loss, however—or what ought to be a great loss—soon to be encountered in the death of his wife, who, I think, can hardly live to reach America. He is not eminently an affectionate man. I take him to be one who cannot get closely home to his sorrow, nor feel it so sensibly as he gladly would and, in consequence of that deficiency, the world lacks substance to him. It is partly the result, perhaps, of his not having sufficiently cultivated his emotional nature. His poetry shows it, and his personal intercourse, though kindly, does not stir one's blood in the least.[19]

At Aix-les-Bains, where the travelers stopped for a day, Bryant wrote, on July 1, a letter to the *Evening Post* describing the northern cities of Italy through which they had passed: Bologna, where he found the cloisters of the Campo Santo to be "the most sumptuous repository for the bodies of the dead" he had ever seen; Venice, invaded by Germans from Austria bringing with them "Vienna beer, sausages, and sourcrout"; Milan, not so Germanized but with the people submitting gloomily to the domination of Austria; and Turin, where he visited a fair exhibiting the products of Sardinian industry. More than thirty years before, Bryant, in "Hymn of the Waldenses," had assailed the persecution of the Protestants by both the French and Italians; now at Turin, under the new system of religious freedom, he was able to attend the Sunday services of the Waldenses, one in the morning for the French-speaking members of the church and one in the afternoon for the Italian-speaking members.

At Paris, which the party reached in mid-July, Bryant received a letter from Bigelow and Isaac Henderson giving continued favorable accounts of the *Evening Post.* "My best way, I am inclined to think is not to go near a concern which is so much the more prosperous without me," Bryant wrote Bigelow on July 15. Similar progress Bryant could not report about his wife's health. She had improved but more slowly than he wished and was not equal to the task of sight-seeing.[20] At Paris also the Bryants heard from the Waterstons, who were still at Naples; they had been unable to leave because of the serious illness of Helen. "My wife bids me say that she was ill at Naples a longer time than your daughter has been," Bryant wrote them, "and that she did not think she could recover, and yet she was raised up." He begged the Waterstons to keep him informed of Helen's condition.*[21]

Going on to England, the Bryants had planned to stay only a short time, but their visit was extended to almost a month during which they were guests of the Edwin Fields at Stratford-on-Avon, the Ferdinand Fields, near Evesham, a village in the farming district of Worcestershire, and the Alfred Fields, who lived in the village of Edgbaston, "just out of the smoke and jar" of Birmingham, Bryant wrote the Rev. Orville Dewey on September 9 after his return to the United States.[22]

It was while visiting in the English countryside that Bryant first felt confident that his wife would recover. There, as he wrote Dr. Dewey, she "gained strength every day," and on their return to the United States he was able to report: "I brought back Mrs. Bryant nearly as well as she was when I carried her off to Europe, and gaining strength so steadily that I have great hopes of seeing her even better than she was there." Bryant was still optimistic on October 13 when he wrote Dana: "Frances, I am glad to say is gradually improving in health and with her health she is regaining her cheerfulness. Perhaps she is hardly as strong yet as when I took her abroad, but if she makes the same progress as she has done since she began to recover, I am sure she will be better than she has been at any time for more than three years past."[23]

---

*While in England the Bryants heard that Helen Waterston's illness had terminated in death. Bryant was so affected that in sending the *Evening Post* an obituary notice he accompanied it with an article about the girl. "Some of the pleasantest as well as some of the saddest recollections of my present visit to Europe, relate to the charming young person and her premature death . . . ," he wrote.

24

ELECTING LINCOLN PRESIDENT

DURING BRYANT'S ABSENCE ABROAD THE DIFFERENCES between the North and the South had become so irreconcilable that a gangling and little-known politician addressing the Illinois Republican convention on June 16, 1858, expressed his fears for the country in the words: "A house divided against itself cannot stand." Receiving the nomination for United States senator, the politician, Abraham Lincoln, challenged his Democratic opponent, Stephen A. Douglas, to debate the slavery question. In contrast with Lincoln, Douglas was nationally known and, though he had been oppugned in the North when he introduced his Kansas-Nebraska bill, he now had wide support because he had broken with the national administration when President Buchanan asked Congress to approve a constitution adopted at Lecompton, Kansas, admitting the territory as a slave state. Douglas opposed the Lecompton constitution because it violated the doctrine of popular sovereignty.

Bryant had not returned when the first two of the debates were held at Ottawa, Illinois, on August 21 and at Freeport on August 27, but he was back on the *Evening Post* for the five others between September 15 and October 15. John Bigelow had early recognized the significance of the Illinois senatorial campaign when on July 13 he reprinted from Chicago papers an address given by Douglas replying to Lincoln's "house divided" speech. Taking no sides, Bigelow wrote that both Lincoln and Douglas were regarded by their friends as material from which presidents should be made. The *Evening Post* coverage continued to consist of reprints from Chicago papers until August 16, when it had its own correspondent on the scene, Chester P. Dewey. Under the name "Bayou," Dewey sent in vivid reports that placed readers on the scene among the backwoods crowds gathered in the dust and heat to hear the two debaters. In his first he described Lincoln for eastern readers: "A native of Kentucky, where he belonged to the class of 'poor whites,' he came early to Illinois. Poor, unfriended, uneducated, a day-laborer, he has distanced all these disadvantages, and in the profession of law has risen steadily to a competence, and to the position of an intelligent, shrewd and well-balanced man." He was familiarly known as "Long Abe" and though "a cautious, thoughtful politician" was capable "of taking a high position as statesman and legislator." His nomination meant that Illinois Republicans were determinedly against Douglas and "no latter-day conversion of his, however luminous it might appear to some eastern eyes, could blind them to the fact that in him were embodied the false and fatal principles against which they were organized." "Bayou's" pro-Lincoln bias in his first report continued to be shown in later reports, which were so detailed that they ran to as many as fifteen columns and had to be printed on successive days.

Bryant did not regard Douglas's election as senator by the Illinois legislature a setback for the Republicans. He attributed the victory to the state's having been apportioned to give the Democratic party the power in the legislature. Douglas had the legislature but not the people—he had yet to gain Illinois. Elsewhere in the North, Republican victories made Bryant confident that the party would win the 1860 presidential election. In New York Edwin D. Morgan, with the support of Thurlow Weed, obtained the Republican nomination for governor and defeated his Native American opponent, Lorenzo Burrows, and his Democratic one, Amasa J. Parker, in the election. Cheered by the New York victory, as well as Republican advances in other states, Bryant proclaimed that freedom was national in the United States and slavery was sectional. Citing the *Evening Post*'s recent role, Bryant predicted on October 22: "The Republican party, which has fought the good fight against countless discouragements, is the party which will soon be called to distribute the political honors of this nation, and no one can complain of our agency in allying them to its fortunes."

The *Evening Post*'s prosperity had enabled Bigelow shortly after Bryant left for Europe in 1857 to purchase a farmhouse and twelve acres of land on the Hudson about two miles below West Point and to engage the young English architect Calvert Vaux to remodel the building. Upon Bryant's return, Bigelow felt that he could afford a trip to Europe, and with his family he sailed on November 13, a journey that was to keep him away from the paper for eighteen months. In addition to watching over political developments and writing his commentary on them, Bryant now was forced to meet problems created by the paper's growth. Its success on occasion was more than he could bear. The November dividends were as satisfactory as they had been in the past and Bryant was pleased, but the advertising, he wrote Bigelow on February 15, 1859, had expanded until it had become "a perfect nuisance," causing a continual war between the composing room and business office, Isaac Henderson's domain, and the news room, William S. Thayer's domain as managing editor. Writing Bigelow on April 11, Bryant reported that Henderson was wont to put on a serene look in which satisfaction was mingled with resignation, to gaze off into the air, and say quietly: "The *Evening Post* is prosperous—very prosperous."[1] Bryant felt that the paper had not been edited since Bigelow's departure "except by the advertisers," and on April 4 he increased the size of the already overly large blanket-sheet from nine to ten columns.*

Bryant continued to take an interest in the progress made toward the completion of Central Park, visiting it frequently to report on what was being done. On February 19 he commended the park commissioners for employing Vaux as the architect for the buildings, the landscaping being superintended by Frederick Law Olmsted, who with Vaux had submitted the prize-winning design for the project. The thousands of men at work blasting rocks, making roads, rearing embankments, and planting trees reminded him of Virgil's description of Dido and her people building Carthage.[2] On November 12 after a walk through the Ramble of the park, Bryant praised the designers for having seen the desirability of representing the wildness of the native landscape, especially its forests. They had seen no need, he said, to "torture American scenery into an imitation of European."

---

*Isaac Henderson began more and more to wield influence on the paper, largely because of his part in improving its financial position. Bryant did not let the balance sheet affect his editorial policies, but he appreciated Henderson's contributions, as did Bigelow, who wrote Henderson on Dec. 23, 1859, from Paris: "You have done wonders for the *Evening Post.* You have supplied what no amount of editorial ability could have dispensed with. There is no change in the times or in the literary or political management of the paper which can explain the renewed prosperity of the paper since 1855, and I state an obvious truth when I concede the credit of it mainly to you." Bryant-Godwin Collection.

With Bigelow in Europe and Thayer quarreling with Henderson over the crowding out of news and literary material in the paper, Bryant was unable during the summer to get away from the city for his usual trips. Whenever he could, he went to Roslyn to work at improving his garden and orchard. He found Cedarmere an especially pleasant retreat in April when Edwin Forrest, carrying on his vendetta with Nathaniel Parker Willis over his part in the divorce of several years before, sued him for libel. In Bryant's April 11 letter to Bigelow he had written: "At present I am hiding. The suit of Forrest against N. P. Willis . . . is in the court and Forrest wants me for a witness. I find it convenient to be out of the way as I do not want to be questioned about the old difficulties between Forrest and his wife." Bryant wrote the Rev. Orville Dewey on May 6 of the beautiful weather he was enjoying at Cedarmere. "The sunshine is pure gold," he said, "and there are floods of it, poured over a wilderness of blossoms, like cream over strawberries."[3]

II

The South created a new provocation for editorials condemning slavery in May when the Southern Commercial Convention at Vicksburg urged repeal of laws against the trade in blacks followed by speeches by Jefferson Davis and William L. Yancey defending the institution both as a constitutional right and a moral right. On October 17 the nation was startled by news from Harpers Ferry that an armed band of Abolitionists had taken possession of the federal arsenal. The accounts illustrated the changes that the telegraph had brought about in reporting the news. Formerly, papers printed full accounts of events taking place elsewhere copied from local papers days and sometimes weeks after they had occurred. Now the news came piecemeal in brief telegraphic dispatches sent sometimes at hourly intervals.

The *Evening Post*'s first dispatch from Harpers Ferry that the "insurrectionists were reported numbering about 250 whites, aided by a gang of negroes," was greatly exaggerated, there being only eighteen persons involved. It was several days before full details became known. On October 19 Bryant wrote that John Brown's "crazy attempt to excite the slaves of Virginia to revolt" had been much misrepresented in the Democratic papers. He denied their charges that the Republicans counseled or countenanced violence. Instead, the slaveholders were the ones addicted to violence and Brown was "only a disciple" of this school. On October 25, replying to statements in the southern press that the revolt had been instigated in the North, Bryant declared: "The danger is not in the north but in the south. It springs out of the slave institution itself. . . .The great body of the northern people have no desire nor intention to interfere with slavery within its present limits, except by persuasion and argument. They are unalterably opposed to the spread of it, as the south ought to be, but they are willing to leave the extinction of it in the states to the certain influences of commerce, of good sense, of the sentiment of justice and truth, and the march of civilization."

Bryant was not prepared to sanctify John Brown as a hero and martyr, as were many Abolitionists, but his sense of justice was outraged by the unseemly speed with which Virginia indicted him for treason and brought him to trial nine days after his futile raid. "It is not the usual course of justice," Bryant declared, "to hurry men in this way to the gallows." After the conviction, Bryant urged that appeals be made to the Virginia legislature to commute the death penalty on the ground that Brown was insane. "Treason and bloodshed, we do not believe, he ever contemplated," Bryant wrote; "his only object was to run off slaves to a place of security; but the method he adopted for doing this was so thoroughly impracticable and absurd as to show at once the twist in his intellect." Bryant was deeply affected by the manifestations of mourning at the hour of Brown's execution—the prayers said in the churches of the North, the tolling of the bells in the towns, the firing of minute guns. These expressions of pity by half the nation for "the old man's fate, the sympathy which almost everyone seemed glad to avow for his simple and manly virtues" were not to be dismissed with newspaper paragraphs; instead, it was "an event in our national history which warrants every thoughtful man amongst us in pondering over it deeply."

During the winter a major political activity was getting up rallies to save the Union. Bryant approved the sentiment as much as anyone, but he viewed the rash of meetings sardonically. Discussing a forthcoming Union meeting in New York on December 9, he said that disunion was the chronic terror of the United States just as invasion by the French was that of Great Britain. "We have a fit of it every four years," he wrote, "and, curiously, it always comes on just before a presidential election, as the sea-serpent was always seen off Newport at the beginning of the summer season." He believed that the people of the North should hold the meetings to show their goodwill toward the South, but nevertheless they should realize that "every attempt at disunion that has ever been made has originated at the south." Since the Union meetings were arranged by Democrats and Republicans were excluded, they failed in their object,

Bryant wrote in December. "Indeed the threats of dissolution seem to increase in number and violence just in proportion to the frequency of northern meetings of condolence and sympathy," he said. Bryant's satirical comments on the current passion for Union did not go down well with many *Evening Post* readers. "The Union-savers, who include a pretty large body of commercial men, begin to look on our paper with a less friendly eye than they did a year ago," he wrote Bigelow.[4]

Bryant's lack of sympathy for the Union meetings was due to his having reached the conclusion that the South could not be mollifed. Therefore, his editorials set forth the view that there could no longer be any compromise in the selection of a Republican candidate and in the adoption of a policy: the issue was the extension of slavery and the party candidate and the party program must be against it. As to Bryant's choice for the nomination, he neither expressed his formal endorsement of nor opposition to those being discussed before the convention in Chicago on May 16. His personal letters and his editorials made it clear, however, that he could not willingly support Seward. Not only had Bryant never liked Seward but now he was scandalized by Thurlow Weed's machinations in the recent state legislature in giving away city railway charters in return for money for Seward's campaign. Writing Bigelow, Bryant expressed the fear that if Seward were elected president Weed would be "viceroy over him." In any case, he said, he would not be surprised "if the names which have been long before the public are put aside for some one against which fewer objections can be made."

The opportunity for Bryant to meet such a one came in February when the Young Men's Central Republican Union invited Abraham Lincoln to address a New York audience. James A. Briggs, in charge of business arrangements for the speech, was responsible for obtaining Bryant to introduce the speaker from the West,[5] a man whose name was widely known because of newspaper coverage given his debates with Douglas but who otherwise was a stranger to New Yorkers. In two notices preceding the address at Cooper Union on February 27, the *Evening Post* promised "a powerful assault upon the policy and principles of the proslavery party, and an able vindication of the Republican creed." Lincoln had recognized the importance of the occasion and came to the city with a carefully prepared speech and with a new broadcloth suit of clothes in which to appear before his sophisticated audience. It was an asset that he was to be introduced by Bryant, the nation's foremost poet and a highly respected editor. In accepting the invitation to introduce the speaker, Bryant placed the *Evening Post* ahead of the city's other Republican newspapers in recognizing the importance of Lincoln as a presidential candidate. In editorials on the forthcoming campaign, Greeley had followed an eccentric course in the *Tribune,* first puffing Douglas after he broke with Buchanan over the admission of Kansas under the Lecompton constitution, a strategy which Greeley conceived to divide the Democrats but which the Republicans could not understand, and then advancing the interests of the aged, white-bearded Edward Bates, a Missouri Whig with antislavery leanings who had long ago gone into retirement and had not been heard from since 1836. Henry J. Raymond had also been friendly to Douglas in the hope that he could exert a national leadership that would minimize the sectionalism of the Republican party, but Raymond, as an associate of Thurlow Weed, was committed to the candidacy of William Seward. In contrast, Bryant had assailed Douglas repeatedly and marked himself a strong "Black" Republican in his recent editorials attacking the Union movement as being futile and in declaring that there was only one issue on which the Republican party could stand—opposition to the extension of slavery.

A heavy snowfall on the day of the speech made it hard to get through the streets to Cooper Union, but nevertheless a large audience of 1,500 persons, who paid twenty-five cents for tickets, gathered to hear the speaker, filling the hall, the *Evening Post* reported. Lincoln, wearing the new suit still showing the creases of being carried across the country in a satchel, was escorted to the stage by Bryant and another former Democrat, the lawyer David Dudley Field. They were greeted by cheers, and Bryant's short introduction was interrupted five times by loud applause. Bryant stressed the importance of "the great west in the battle which we are fighting in behalf of freedom against slavery and in behalf of civilization against barbarism." "These children of the west," Bryant declared, "form a living bulwark against the advance of slavery, and from them is recruited the vanguard of the mighty armies of liberty." He presented Lincoln as "a gallant soldier of the political campaign of 1856" in his support of Frémont and "the great champion" of the antislavery cause in Illinois two years later when he would have been elected senator if it had not been for the state's "unjust apportionment law."

Lincoln sought to refute Douglas's popular sovereignty doctrine, argued that the Republican party rather than being radical was conservative in that it upheld the policy of Washington, Franklin, Hamilton, and others of the founding fathers, condemned northern extremism and appealed for sectional understanding, and, though he did not minimize the southern disunionist threats, declared there could be no compromise with principle on the extension of slavery. Lincoln had gone to New York fearful of cutting an awkward figure before the smart New York audience, but his clarity and logic and his occasional racy sallies were just as effective in the splendor of Cooper Union as they were at the hustings in Illinois. The hall frequently rang with shouts of applause for a point well made and roars of laughter at a witticism drolly delivered. One of the most enthusiastic of Lincoln's listeners was Greeley, who, perhaps envious that it was Bryant who had first perceived the appeal of the tall, gaunt westerner, rushed to Lincoln after the speech to get his manuscript for next morning's *Tribune.* If he had started the race late, he would at least be first in carrying the speech to the people. On the morning of February 28, the *Tribune* said that since the times of Clay and Webster "no man has spoken to a larger assemblage of the intellect and mental culture of our city" and the next day it described Lincoln as "one of Nature's orators."

Bryant's regard for the speech was just as high as Greeley's but his expression of it was less ebullient. It was a "deeply interested and enthusiastic audience" that attended the speech, which was well worth the close hearing they gave it. Bryant particularly liked the portion which placed "the Republican party on the very ground occupied by the framers of our constitution and fathers of our republic." There was nothing really new in what Lincoln had to say in this respect but, Bryant continued, "it is wonderful how much a truth gains by a certain mastery of clear and impressive statement." Bryant found more novelty in the consequences which Lincoln saw as following from the demands of the southerners. "What they require of us," he declared, "is not only a surrender of our long-cherished notions of constitutional rights, inherited from our ancestors and theirs; not only a renunciation of freedom of speech, but a hypocritical confession of doctrines which revolt both our understanding and our conscience, a confession extorted by the argument of the highwayman, the threat of violence and murder." Commenting to Briggs on the reception given by New York newspapers to the speech, Lincoln said: "It is worth a visit from Springfield, Illinois, to New York to make the acquaintance of such a man as William Cullen Bryant."[6]

Although Bryant did not put the *Evening Post* behind the nomination of Lincoln at Chicago nor of Salmon P. Chase, whom he also thought highly of, hailing in February his return to Congress as senator from Ohio and praising him as a man of "admirable moral constitution" and of notable "gifts of intellect," his political position was of some concern to Seward's supporters. The *Evening Post*'s endorsement would be of immense help to Seward, guaranteeing the favor of the old-line antislavery Democrats who were uneasy, as Bryant was himself, in their alliance with the Whigs in the Republican party. Because of Bryant's attacks against the railway charters granted by the New York legislature, Seward's friends knew it would be of no use to ask Bryant directly to support him or even to be neutral. In consequence, they sought to influence Bryant through Bigelow, the former Democrat Preston King acting as their spokesman. As early as April of 1859, King had written Bigelow expressing his anxiety over what stand the *Evening Post* would take, though the course of the paper thus far had been "discreet and just" and Bryant had assured him that he would acquiesce in supporting the Republican choice.[7] The next year King wrote Bigelow several letters urging him to return to the United States to serve as a delegate at the Chicago convention, both Seward and Weed wanting his help. Bigelow was half-persuaded to return but decided not to cut short his trip.[8] His decision was probably determined by a letter from Bryant coldly rejecting Bigelow's argument for supporting Seward. "I admit that you have made your reasons for nominating Mr. Seward clear by your explanation," Bryant wrote him on April 13, "but I do not care to enter into the argument now. His friends I have reason to believe are not dissatisfied with the course of the *Evening Post,* and whether he be nominated or not depends on causes of another kind. If you were here I think you would better understand some parts of the question than you can at a distance."[9]

III

Bigelow had been delighted in his trip, writing long and enthusiastic accounts of his impressions for the *Evening Post.*[10] Arriving in Paris, he spent several weeks there before going on to Italy. In Rome he viewed the exhibition of marbles excavated by the Marquis de Campana and, hearing that they were on the market, proposed to Bryant that the *Evening Post* start a campaign to raise money to purchase them for the new Metropolitan Museum of Art, of whose founding Bryant had been one of the principal promoters. The marbles could be had for a million dollars. Bryant printed Bigelow's description of the collection and his plea that they be obtained for America, but he regretfully had to report that no such sum could be raised.[11] Returning to Paris, Bigelow was caught up in a social whirl, among his triumphs being an invitation to a ball at the palace where he and Mrs. Bigelow were presented to the emperor. He also met the city's leading literary figures and was so impressed by the critic Sainte-Beuve that he sought to obtain him as a correspondent for the *Evening Post,* offering him twenty dollars a letter, the translation of which would cost another ten dollars. Caught up in his enthusiasm over the French, Bigelow outlined to Bryant a program of spending $960 a year for correspondence, of which $260 would be for translations. Sainte-Beuve wrote one letter for the paper, on Béranger, and then decided that he could not do additional ones because of his old age and ill health.[12] Bryant considered Bigelow's contributions a little too high-toned even for the *Evening Post* and too long—an essay on Buffon, for example, took up four and one-half columns on each of two successive days. "Your letters respecting the policy of the emperor are eagerly read and much talked of," he wrote Bigelow. "Those on literary subjects, I am afraid, frighten people by their length. The first sell the paper; the others I cannot find have caused the sale of a single one."[13]

A year after Bigelow had gone to Europe, Bryant still had not solved his management problems on the paper. He wrote Bigelow on March 22, 1860: "The old trouble of too many advertisements and too little reading matter has returned upon us." There was a fight every day between the editorial room and the composing room, with the shop foreman, Henry Dithmar, "the sturdy friend of the advertisers parrying all attempts to displace advertisements by reading matter."* On March 27 the paper began issuing a third edition, printed at 4:15 P. M., carrying mail and telegraphic news up to that hour and the latest market reports.[14] These gave the paper as late financial news as businessmen found in next morning's papers. The third edition, however, was no help in solving the problem of finding room for both news and advertising. The bitterest wrangles were between Thayer, the managing editor, and Henderson. To Bryant's report of these difficulties, Bigelow replied that he had come to the belief that Thayer's days of usefulness to the paper were numbered. "If his continuance with us is not agreeable to Mr. Henderson," Bigelow wrote, "he had better be put in the way of finding other employment as soon as possible though I should be loth to lose entirely the services of a man whom we have trained so long and who can if he chooses be useful."[15] The problem with Thayer shortly solved itself. During the winter he had been away from the office for six weeks with an inflamma-

---

*Dithmar, a cultivated man who knew both German and English literature, was greatly admired by Bryant, and they often discussed poetry and philosophy. He was, however, a tyrant in the shop. William Alexander Linn, who joined the paper in 1871, recalled that if enough material was in type to get out a paper Dithmar would refuse, in the interest of economy, to set later news articles sent to the composing room. *Evening Post,* 100th anniversary issue, Nov. 16, 1901.

tion of the lungs; when he returned, his health continued to deteriorate and he left the paper early in July. Parke Godwin had returned to the paper after Bigelow's departure, but his work was interrupted first by the death of his mother and then by an attack of rheumatic fever which confined him to his home at Roslyn. Bryant's detailed accounts of his troubles were no doubt designed to get Bigelow to return, but Bigelow, though writing to regret that the paper was shorthanded, was having too interesting a time to abandon his trip.

During the past winter Bryant had been led to think again upon the subject that was never far below the surface in his consciousness—human mortality—by the death of several close friends. As a journalist, he recorded on November 29, 1859, the death of Washington Irving. A suggestion had been made that a memorial should be erected in his memory, and Bryant proposed that there be placed at his home, Sunnyside, on the Hudson, a statue with a pedestal depicting scenes from the tales and essays. Shortly afterward, on December 9, he wrote of the death of Theodore Sedgwick, Jr., at Stockbridge, whose articles signed "Veto" had appeared in the *Evening Post* almost from the first days of Bryant's connection with it. "His political essays . . . were remarkable for their noble and independent spirit," Bryant said, "their soundness of judgment, and their clearness and vigor of style." There were other deaths of friends —Benjamin F. Butler, attorney general under Presidents Jackson and Van Buren, and the companion of his travels, Charles M. Leupp. One of the saddest was that of his grandson, Alfred Godwin. "He was about three years old, quite a favorite of the family, waggish, playful, and of quick sensibilities," Bryant wrote Dana.[16]

Reading Bryant's poem, "The Cloud on the Way," which had appeared in the February, 1860, number of the *New York Ledger*,* Dana wondered if it had not been written with a premonition of Alfred's death. "Some-

---

*The *Ledger* was a moribund mercantile newspaper when it was taken over by the sensational publisher Robert Bonner in 1855 and converted into a literary miscellany devoted chiefly to popular fiction. Through an unparalleled advertising campaign, Bonner ran its circulation up to a phenomenal 400,000 in a few years. He paid large sums to such literary figures as Bryant, Longfellow, and Bancroft to get them to contribute. Bryant was invited to do so on April 14, 1859, in a letter from one of the *Ledger's* editors, William O. Bartlett, who wrote: "I beg leave to remind you that any time you will appoint to meet me . . . I shall be pleased to hand you a check for one thousand dollars, as compensation for a few poems for the *Ledger,* to be furnished only when you feel the inspiration and leisure to write them." Bryant-Godwin Collection. Bryant had seven poems printed in the paper between the first, "A Sick-Bed," in the issue of July 23, 1859, and the last, "Our Country's Call," in the issue of Nov. 2, 1861.

times death and troubles do cast their shadows before," he wrote Bryant. "In your case, it may not have been from any such mysterious communication and influence; for the grave and life beyond the grave have been too often the subjects of verse with you for that."[17] Dana's interpretation of the poem, however, was wrong; instead it was addressed to Frances. The cloud is the realm of death that travelers see before them in the journey of life and when they enter it they are "gathered to the past."

A finer poem expressing Bryant's thoughts on death at the time is "Waiting by the Gate," which contains the boldest and most original of his figures of speech declaring the end of all men. Now in his sixty-fifth year, Bryant could view his own entrance into the realm of death with some equanimity in contrast with his youthful dread:

> Beside the massive gateway built up in years gone by,
> Upon whose top the clouds in eternal shadow lie,
> While streams the evening sunshine on quiet wood and lea,
> I stand and calmly wait till the hinges turn for me.

The hinges turn for the aged one whose "allotted task is wrought," for the youth who in passing through throws back a "look of longing," and for the child whose "sprightly shout" is stilled forever for all of mankind, some of whom approach in fear and some of whom in the confidence of religious faith approach in joy. But the poet is unmoved by any of these:

> I mark the joy, the terror; yet these, within my heart,
> Can neither wake the dread nor the longing to depart;
> And, in the sunshine streaming on quiet wood and lea,
> I stand and calmly wait till the hinges turn for me.

Irving's death was commemorated on his birthday, April 4, by the New-York Historical Society with orations by Edward Everett and Bryant. Writing the Rev. Dr. Dewey of his reluctance to speak at the Irving memorial, Bryant commented ruefully upon his advancing years: "Among other symptoms of age, I find a disposition growing upon me to regard the world as belonging to a new race of men, who have somehow or other got into it, and taken possession of it, and among whom I am a superfluity. What have I to do with their quarrels and controversies? I, who am already proposed as a member of the same club with Daniel Defoe and Sir Roger L'Estrange?"[18]

In delivering the eulogy of Irving,[19] Bryant was conscious that he spoke of another American who had lived beyond his time, a man born in 1783 a few days after the news of the treaty with Great Britain acknowledging

American independence had been received. Irving was born, he said, at a fortunate time, when he grew up with the noble examples before his eyes of the men of "steady rectitude, magnanimous self-denial, and cheerful self-sacrifice." Reflecting the spirit of much of Irving's own writing, Bryant said of his passing: "It is as if some genial year had just closed and left us in frost and gloom; its flowery spring, its leafy summer, its plenteous autumn, flown, never to return."

Bryant recalled his own delight in first coming upon Irving's *Knickerbocker's History.* "I was then a youth in college," Bryant related, "and, having committed to memory a passage of it to repeat as a declamation before my class, I was so overcome with laughter, when I appeared on the floor, that I was unable to proceed, and drew upon myself the rebuke of the tutor." Having recently reread the history, Bryant found that it had not lost its freshness. He believed that Irving's power of expression was as great in his last years as in his earlier ones though it was of a different sort. Irving's *Life of Washington* set forth a profound philosophy and it gathered together miscellaneous materials in such orderly arrangement that Bryant compared him to a skillful commander who from "a rabble of raw recruits, forms a disciplined army, animated and moved by a single will."*

IV

By the time the Republicans gathered in Chicago May 16 to name their candidates for president and vice-president, indications were clear that their choices would be endorsed at the polls, for no effective opposition seemed to be in the offing. The Democrats had been hopelessly divided at Charleston on April 23 when the moderates dominated the convention and the delegates from eight southern states withdrew. But even those who remained could not agree on a candidate after fifty-seven ballots, though Douglas had been sure that he would win on the first, and they adjourned with plans to reassemble at Baltimore on June 18. The remnants of the Whig and American parties had met at Baltimore on May 10, a collection the *Evening Post* described as consisting of "somewhat superannuated" though for the most part of "well-seeming politicians." In forming the National Constitutional Union party, they had shown themselves "excessively senile and ludicrous," Bryant wrote, since no party in the country except for "a handful of Garrison abolitionists and Yancey

---

*Bryant wrote Bigelow of the Irving memorial: "The Irving meeting was a grand affair, so far, at least, as the concourse that attended was concerned—an immense audience, and very attentive. Professor Green's speech, the latter part at least, was not heard; the audience was impatient for Everett, who delivered his remarks with more vehemence of manner than usual." Godwin, *Biography,* II, 134.

fire-eaters" had any quarrel with the Constitution or the Union.

The Seward supporters gathered in Chicago in force, thirteen railroad cars of them, confident of victory. Thurlow Weed set up headquarters at the Richmond House, where he dispensed champagne and cigars while his imported band paraded the streets. Judge David Davis, Lincoln's campaign manager, had also seen the importance of a cheering section, and had occupied the Tremont House from which he directed the hundreds of downstate young bucks brought to town to root for "Honest Old Abe." In lesser numbers were the supporters of Salmon P. Chase and Edward Bates. The population of Chicago, now numbering more than 110,000, was increased by some 40,000 visitors, only a fraction of whom could crowd into the Wigwam, the huge building erected especially for the deliberations of the 466 official delegates.

Bryant, in his office at the *Evening Post,* followed the proceedings from the long accounts filed by telegraph by the paper's correspondents. The party platform denounced the Harpers Ferry raid, the doctrine of popular sovereignty, and the Lecompton constitution; declared that neither Congress nor a territorial legislature could give legal existence to slavery in a territory; and favored a tariff to encourage the development of the industrial interests of the whole country. Bryant, in an editorial on May 18, found little wrong with it except that he felt it was too long. With "a wise and upright man" for president, he could get along very well with it.

One of the more conspicuous among the delegates was Horace Greeley, the oracle whose weekly *Tribune* was the most widely read paper in the country. Bent on defeating Seward since the breakup of the triumvirate of Seward, Weed, and Greeley, he roamed the hotel corridors and gathered groups about him when he presented his argument that Seward could not win the doubtful states. Greeley's efforts against his former political ally bore fruit when Seward, unable to win a majority on the first ballot, saw his early lead dwindle as delegates, at first one by one and later delegation by delegation, ranked themselves behind Lincoln. Bryant, in his first editorial on the nomination, expressed himself as being somewhat surprised by the zeal which Lincoln had been able to arouse. He did not think it was misplaced. "There are many points in his character," he wrote, "fitted to call forth the enthusiasm of his party and to unite upon him the support of that numerous class who float loosely between the two parties, and are found sometimes on one side and sometimes on the other, as the popular qualities of one candidate or another attract their suffrages." Two days later, on May 21, Bryant hailed Lincoln as the representative American. "Whatever is peculiar in the history and development of America," he said, "whatever is foremost in its civilization, whatever is grand in its social and political structure finds its best expression in the career of such men as Abraham Lincoln."

Bryant immediately put the *Evening Post* strongly behind Lincoln and his running-mate Hannibal Hamlin. Bryant had met Hamlin in 1843 and they had maintained cordial relations over the years as leaders in the Free-Soil movement.[20] Announcing special cheap rates for the semiweekly and weekly issues on June 2, he said: "The Evening Post means to do all the good it can during the coming presidential canvass. It means to elect Lincoln and Hamlin if it can. It means to turn out the present most corrupt of administrations, and install an honest administration in its stead." The next week the city's Republican editors made a display of unity when Bryant, Webb, Greeley, and Raymond served as vice-presidents for a Republican rally held at Cooper Union.*

Bryant took a greater interest in Lincoln's career than he had in that of any political figure since Jackson and Van Buren, giving him advice in a series of letters on how to conduct himself and proposing policies to be adopted and men to be appointed to his cabinet. On June 16 he gave counsel from an "old campaigner who has been engaged in political controversies for more than a third of a century." He said that Lincoln began his campaign with the advantage of not being "encumbered with bad associations" and "a ruck of political confederates who have their own interests to look after." Lincoln would stand the best chance of winning if he avoided political commitments, Bryant advised, urging that he "make no speeches, write no letters as a candidate, enter into no pledges, and make no promises, nor even give any of those kind words which men are apt to interpret into promises."[21] Lincoln wrote a note in reply on June 28, thanking Bryant for his interest and declaring: "I appreciate the danger against which you would guard me; nor am I wanting in the *purpose* to avoid it."[22]

Bigelow returned to New York on June 11, his presence being welcome by Bryant, as he wrote Dana, for the opportunity it would give him to spend more time at Roslyn.[23] Bigelow did not enter into the campaign

---

*James Gordon Bennett wrote in the *Herald* on Nov. 8: "Without New York journalism there would have been no Republican party," explaining that several of the papers, "possessing revenues equal in amount to those of some of the sovereign states," were independent of outside influence and that their news and opinion were carried by the telegraph and the locomotive "to the remotest corners of the land in constantly increasing ratio." At the time the *Tribune* had a daily circulation of about 55,000, but its weekly edition went to about three times as many readers. The *Times* had a daily circulation of about 35,000, the *Evening Post* almost 20,000, the *Herald*, pro-South in the controversy over secession, about 77,000, and the *Sun* about 35,000.

with any enthusiasm. He had hoped that Seward would be the Republican nominee, though he had not seen fit to cut short his trip abroad to help him at the convention, and he did not warm to Lincoln. After meeting the urbane politicians of Europe, he felt that Lincoln, with his backwoods manners, his awkward appearance, and his delight in improper jokes, did not have the dignity that the chief executive of the republic should have. Nevertheless, he wrote a British friend, he was persuaded by Bryant that Lincoln's election was desirable. He had "a clear and eminently logical mind, a nice sense of truth and justice and a capacity of statement which extorted from Mr. Bryant the declaration that the address he delivered in this city last winter was the best political speech he ever heard in his life."[24]

Early in the summer Dana urged Bryant to visit Boston, and Bryant replied that though he had often thought about such a trip he did not feel up to it. "To go to any country place is an entertainment to me," he wrote; "to go to a large town I find myself, for what reason I can scarcely say, reluctant. I shall not find Boston what it is when I knew it, and the change, I am sure, will not strike me pleasantly. . . . Most of my old friends there and in its neighborhood are gone."[25] Nevertheless he did get away late in September with Frances and Julia to visit the Waterstons in Chester Square. Among the guests at one evening affair was Longfellow, who made a brief entry about it in his journal on September 28. "Bryant looks old and shaggy, with his white beard," Longfellow noted. "Mrs. B. seems very little changed, and J. is charming."[26]

A week after the Boston trip Bryant set off with Mrs. Bryant, Julia, and Fanny to visit an old friend, John A. Graham, who had moved from New York to Mount Savage, Maryland, in the Cumberland coal and iron district. Bryant had been in the region twenty-eight years before, when its natural beauty, unspoiled by progress, had charmed him. He wrote for the *Evening Post* an account of the trip that appeared on October 22, beginning with a description of a new iron ship that he had seen at Baltimore. Shaped like a "segar," one hundred and eighty feet in length and sixteen feet in width, it was capable of such high speeds that, so he was told, it could cross the Atlantic in five or six days. At Mount Savage, Bryant visited a coal mine, the workers, who wore a lamp in their caps and were blackened by dust, suggesting to him that they were demons with flaming horns coming from the womb of the mountain.

Though the Republicans had begun the political campaign confident of victory, Bryant and Bigelow, realizing that New York was a pivotal state, warned that the party could not take things easy. They estimated that the ticket should win in the state by a 46,000 majority but maintained that this was too slim for comfort. Their fear was not of the Democratic party, which was fractured when Stephen A. Douglas received the nomination for president and the southern states seceded and nominated John C. Breckenridge of Kentucky, but of the National Constitutional Union party formed by northern fusionists who got behind John Bell of Tennessee. The *Evening Post* editors feared that the new party of anti-Lincoln men led by Mayor Fernando Wood, a devious but for a time successful politician in manipulating New York dissidents, would divert votes from Lincoln and throw the election into the House of Representatives.

The *Evening Post*'s attacks on the fusionists, or "Dry Goods" party, as the paper called them, led to a break between Bryant and Bigelow and their long-time political ally, Samuel J. Tilden, who feared that Lincoln's election would lead to civil war. On October 8 the fusionists held a rally in Cooper Union at which Tilden, the first speaker, was shouted down by the crowd, which had come to hear Mayor Wood. In a mocking editorial, the *Evening Post* referred to past associations with Tilden as a Free-Soiler, regretted that he had not been able to give his speech, and offered to print it in full, as his friends would "be glad to know by what process so clever a man has reasoned himself into such bad company."

A few days later Tilden called on Bigelow in his office at the *Evening Post*, "pale, haggard and preoccupied." With Bigelow were several Republican friends, and they twitted Tilden over the gloomy prospects of the Constitutional Union party. Tilden remained silent until he rose to leave and declared with a fervor that sobered the group: "I would not have the responsibility of William Cullen Bryant and John Bigelow for all the wealth in the subtreasury. If you have your way, civil war will divide this country, and you will see blood running like water in the streets of this city."[27]

Bryant had for years maintained that the southern talk of secession was not serious, being part of the bullying tactics that the slaveholders had employed to gain their way in national politics. In his editorials on the campaign he argued that further bowing to the slave interests was impossible. For fifteen years their wishes had been granted, and, if this were the proper method of attaining amity, the work would have been accomplished long ago. The more the North gave in, the greater grew the demands of the South. Bryant drew an analogy from the nursery in expressing his view:

> The slave interest is a spoiled child; the federal government is its foolishly indulgent nurse. Everything asked for it has been eagerly given it; more

420

eagerly still if it cries after it; more eagerly still if it threatened to cut off its nurse's ears. The more we give it the louder its cries and the more furious its threats; and now we have northern men writing long letters to persuade their readers that it will really cut off its nurse's ears if we exercise the right of suffrage, and elect a president of our own choice, instead of giving it one of its own favorites.

Bryant's first editorial reaction on November 7 to the election of Lincoln was to congratulate the country, which, after a long and dreary struggle, had declared "boldly and firmly" for "justice and humanity." Not only did a large majority in the free states have reason for rejoicing but so also did a large minority in the slave states, hitherto "trampled under the iron heel of an oligarchy which has shown itself as impatient of the freedom of thought as any of the despotisms of the Old World." He saw the vote in the border states for John Bell as a favorable sign. He did not minimize the difficulties that still faced the nation, however, warning that the victors must follow a course of "strict regard to the rights of the states" and of "a careful abstinence from every doubtful exercise of authority" if distrust was to be changed to confidence and "hostility disarmed of its weapons." The next day he served as chairman of a celebration of the victory at Stuyvesant Institute by the Young Men's Central Republican Union. Describing the political victory as a moral victory, Bryant told his audience: "I have been long an observer of public life, though never in it; and never have I seen any course of right steadily pursued without public opinion coming round to that course, and crowning those who pursued it with a final triumph."

But in the midsts of these rejoicings, firm in his belief that the South would not go so far as to secede, Bryant learned by telegraph that both houses of the South Carolina legislature had called a convention, as he put it in an editorial on November 8, for the purpose of "raising the flag of rebellion." Bryant opposed demands of Lincoln supporters that he issue a policy statement "to quiet alarms at the South and compose the public mind." His reasons were that Lincoln was only the President-elect and not yet the nation's chief magistrate and that in any case his views were already known. As to the threats of secession, Bryant took the same stand that he had taken in the nullification controversy in the early 1830's over the tariff. President Jackson in his proclamation to the people of South Carolina had termed nullification an "impractical absurdity" and declared that no state could leave the Union and to attempt to do so by armed force was treason. Bryant used almost the same words on November 12 in an editorial entitled "Peaceable Secession an Absurdity." The government could not tolerate the doctrine of peaceable secession, he declared, for it could have no credit or future. If a state seceded, it was in rebellion and the seceders were traitors.

A week later the *Evening Post*'s correspondent in Illinois obtained an hour-long interview with Lincoln in which he discussed his views, his "fullest utterance" on public affairs, Bryant said in an editorial, since his election. The correspondent found Lincoln engaged in studying the history of the nullification movement of 1832, paying especial attention to the Force Bill and President Jackson's proclamation. Lincoln had received many anonymous letters from the South threatening him with death, some "ornamented with sketches of executions by the gibbet, assassination by the stiletto, or death by lightning-stroke." The interview indicated that Lincoln was following the course recommended by the *Evening Post*, or so Bryant interpreted it. He summarized Lincoln's views in an editorial: he would conduct his administration according to principles already laid down in speeches, he would make no further public declarations until assuming office, he approved Jackson's course in the nullification controversy and would "act as much like him as difference in circumstances" would permit, and he would choose for his cabinet political friends and persons subscribing unreservedly to the policy of the Republican party. Bryant considered all of these points right and proper.

While defending Lincoln in his policy of reticence as to what he would do on assuming office, Bryant was concerned that he should select for his cabinet only men of unimpeachable integrity and that former Democrats should have a place in the new government. The election votes had hardly been counted when Bryant, on November 10, wrote Lincoln suggesting that Salmon P. Chase be named secretary of state, an appointment which would please members of the party in the East. "He is regarded as one of the noblest and truest of the great leaders of that party," Bryant declared, "as a man in all respects beyond reproach—which you know few men are."[28] A short time later, Bryant was a member of a delegation that called on the Illinois senator, Lyman Trumbull, who had stopped in New York on his way to Washington, to object to Seward's being named to the cabinet. Trumbull wrote Lincoln on December 2 that Bryant feared that Seward, because of his political associations with members of the recent corrupt New York legislature, would cause the Republicans to lose the state elections if not repudiated. Lincoln replied the next week regretting the anxiety of "our friends" in New York but adding: "it seems to me the sentiment in that state which sent a united delegation to Chicago in favor of Gov. S. ought not, and must not be snubbed, as it would be by the omission to offer Gov. S. a place in the cabinet."[29]

Bryant was worried that Lincoln might be improperly influenced when he heard that, as he wrote on December 24, he had been visited "by a well-known politician of New York who has a good deal to do with the stock market and who took with him a plan of compromise manufactured in Wall Street." Bryant said that the financiers were willing to compromise on the slavery question in the interest of maintaining trade with the South. "Any . . . concession recognizing the right of slavery to protection or even existence in the territories would disgust and discourage the large majority of Republicans in the state and cool their interest in the incoming administration down to the freezing point," Bryant warned. He insisted that the cabinet include members of the old Democratic party, declaring: "It would be most unfortunate if the cabinet were to be so constituted as to turn the policy of the administration into the old whig channels." As a long-time free-trader, Bryant feared that a protectionist would be named secretary of the treasury, and he deplored the possibility.[30] His reference to a well-known politician was to Thurlow Weed, who had consulted with Lincoln on December 20. Lincoln replied that Bryant was wrong in thinking that Weed had proposed a compromise, and said he would be as fair as he could be in his office appointments.[31]

Bryant's fear about who would head the Treasury Department was increased when a report came out that Simon Cameron of Pennsylvania was the choice. In some agitation, he answered Lincoln's letter of January 3. He praised the principle Lincoln had set forth in forming his "council of official advisers" but he believed that the appointment of Cameron would diffuse feelings almost like despair among many people. His objection to the appointment was his distrust, shared by many, of Cameron's "integrity—whether financial or political." "Only let us have honest, upright men in the department—whatever may be their views of public policy," Bryant pleaded.[32] As a matter of fact, Lincoln had offered Cameron the post but on the same day that Bryant was writing him he notified Cameron that things had developed which made it impossible to take him into the cabinet. Lincoln did not want to recall the offer openly and asked Cameron to write declining the appointment as he had no objection to its being known that it was tendered. "Better do this at once," Lincoln said, "before things so change that you cannot honorably decline and I be compelled to withdraw the tender."[33] Bryant's letters to Lincoln, especially the emotional one objecting to Cameron, bore great weight with him in Springfield. On January 7 Lincoln wrote Trumbull that it was a "propriety" and a "necessity" for Chase to be secretary of the treasury. "His ability, firmness, and purity of character," Lincoln said, "produce the propriety; and that he alone can reconcile Mr. Bryant, and his class, to the appointment of Gov. S. to the State Department produces the necessity."[34]

Bryant in writing his suggestions to Lincoln was the spokesman for former Free-Soil Democrats with whom he conferred frequently on how they could set the President-elect right on his appointments. Three of them decided to call on Lincoln at Springfield to give their views in person. They were George Opdyke, who was one of the candidates for mayor defeated by Fernando Wood in the last election, Judge J. T. Hogebrom, and Hiram Barney, who had worked for Lincoln's nomination at Chicago. To introduce them, Bryant wrote Lincoln on January 10 asking him to give them an "attentive hearing." "They represent the anticorruptionists of the Republican party in our state," Bryant said; "they speak for that class of men who thought it unsafe to nominate Mr. Seward for the presidency on account of his close association with a class of men of whom want of principle in our state legislature last winter gave such a melancholy proof."[35]

Barney, reporting by letter to Bryant on the meeting at Springfield, said Lincoln had a quarrel on his hands over his request that Cameron refuse the appointment offered him and had decided to make no more decisions regarding his cabinet until he went to Washington sometime in February. Although Lincoln thought well of Chase and wanted him in the Treasury Department, Barney said, he was holding off on an offer until the row over Cameron could be settled to the satisfaction of Pennsylvania Republicans.[36]

When Opdyke returned to New York and Bryant learned further details of the conference, he was disturbed at the delay in offering Chase the treasury post. He wrote Lincoln on January 22 urging immediate action. "The appointment of Mr. Chase," Bryant said, "would give a feeling of security and confidence to the public mind which the rascalities of Mr. Buchanan's cabinet have made exceedingly sensitive and jealous, and would, it seems to me, settle the point in advance that the new administration will be both honored and beloved." Bryant did not regard the hope of pacifying Cameron as justification for delay by Lincoln: "One thing . . . is perfectly clear, that by failing to secure the services of Mr. Chase in the Treasury Department, both the country and the Republican party will lose infinitely more than the incoming administration can possibly suffer from the enmity of Mr. Cameron and his adherents."[37]

Bryant wrote one more letter to Lincoln about cabinet choices before the President-elect left Springfield for Washington. This was on January 24 to introduce Richard C. McCormick, a member of the Young Men's

Central Republican Union, who represented a group desiring to see Cassius M. Clay as head of the War Department. "The manly bearing of Mr. Clay in his visits to our city has prepossessed the people greatly in his favor," Bryant said, "and throughout our part of the country his courage, disinterestedness, and generous, unquenchable enthusiasm in the cause of liberty and humanity have given birth to a feeling of admiration that amounts almost to personal attachment. Whatever politicians may say, his appointment would be exceedingly popular with the mass of the people, who think that his energy and spirit fit him in these perilous times in a peculiar manner for that place."[38]

The times were indeed perilous, for the threats of secession had become an actuality and federal forts and arsenals had been seized; the national administration, rocked by scandals in the Treasury Department, was discredited throughout the country and because of sympathy with the southern cause had announced the impotence of the government to use force to stop the disruption of the Union; and the President-elect, if he had chosen to reveal his policy, could not through words have changed the course of events. When South Carolina on December 20 announced its separation from the Union, to be followed within a few weeks by five other states of the Deep South, the question of what action should be taken was hotly debated in the North. It was couched in either-or terms of coercion or secession. Bryant, who had adopted the Jacksonian policy that no state could leave the Union, did not see fit to change his view when the actuality occurred. He argued, however, that action taken against the secessionists would not be "coercion," writing on December 20: "The United States government cannot recognize secession, assent to it, or negotiate with it or its agents, in any manner whatsoever; neither can it surrender its own power or acquiesce in usurpation. If the people of any state or district determine to do so, they may compel it to defend itself and its possessions with a strong arm; but this will be very different from attempting to enter and over-run a state with United States forces." Again, on February 2, he expressed the view that if the federal government used force to bring back the seceding states it could not be held guilty of starting a war: "No one doubts that if the people of those states should transfer them back to Spain or France, the United States would be prepared to recover them at all the hazards of war; and, for the same reason, she will recover them from the hands of any other 'foreign powers' under any other names." No, the government did not intend war, but if war came, begun by the South, the South should understand that "eighty years of enterprise, of accumulation, and of progress in all the arts of warfare have not been lost upon the North."

25

WHAT DOES THE PRESIDENT
WAIT FOR?

IN THE TWELVE YEARS OF JOHN BIGELOW'S CONNECTION with the *Evening Post*, beginning when he was a moneyless lawyer of thirty-one, he had become a man of considerable affluence. He owned a one-third interest in a property valued at $175,000 and had an annual income of about $25,000. With the paper increasing its advertising and circulation, he could look forward to becoming a wealthy man. But more important than the money had been his enjoyment of journalism. He never regretted taking the chance, when it was offered him, of quitting the law to become a part owner of the *Evening Post*. His proposal in December of 1860 to sell his interest in the firm to Parke Godwin, therefore, astounded his partners and friends.[1]

In a way it was a surprise to Bigelow himself, for he made the offer spontaneously when Godwin came into his office one day and asked his aid in getting an appointment under the Republican administration. None of Godwin's editorial or writing projects had been successful and he had been employed on the *Evening Post* for the past two years at a weekly salary of fifty dollars. In approaching Bigelow, Godwin indicated a reluctance to ask a favor of his father-in-law, who was being besieged by office seekers well aware of his influence with Lincoln in the dispensation of patronage in New York. Godwin sought from Bigelow a letter to Salmon P. Chase recommending him for a position with the government, probably at the custom house, since he had worked there before.

"For God's sake, Godwin, don't go back to the custom house," Bigelow recalled telling him. "That is not a suitable place for you. Do anything but that." Godwin, who had only recently recovered from an attack of rheumatic fever, replied that his health was bad and that he had been unable to make his living by writing. He was overwhelmed when Bigelow told him: "Godwin, buy out my interest in the *Evening Post* and come here and make your fortune." Bigelow had only a vague notion of how much the property was worth, but Godwin, whatever its value, realized that even if Bigelow was serious in wanting to sell he himself was an unlikely buyer. "You know I have no money," he said.

This did not seem insuperable to Bigelow, who said that the partners, as in his own case, would allow him to pay for his share out of the dividends.* After a week or so of negotiation, Bigelow on January 5, 1861, made an offer in writing to sell his interest in the firm at a figure less than its real value, $121,000, including $75,000 for the *Evening Post*, $25,000 for the job office, and $21,000 for the buildings at Liberty and Nassau Streets.[2]

The change in ownership took place on January 15, but no announcement was made until January 30, when a brief notice was printed to put down rumors about what Bigelow intended to do. There were a number of stories in city gossip about his plans, one that reached print in the *Tribune*. It was that Bigelow with Thurlow Weed would buy the *World*, which had been established in June of 1860, and convert it into an organ of the Republican administration. Weed had indeed made such a proposal, but Bigelow, having just left an established paper, was not interested in a new journalistic project. At Bigelow's request, Bryant published a notice of his retirement which said, "That there may be no misunderstanding as

---

*Godwin relates in his reminiscences for the 100th anniversary issue of the *Evening Post*, Nov. 16, 1901, that Lincoln promised him the consulate in Paris on his first visit to New York after the inauguration. When Bryant was told of it, the account continues, he protested that Godwin could not leave the paper. Bigelow, consulted by the two about the matter, is said to have offered to sell Godwin his share in the *Evening Post* if Lincoln would change the appointment, naming him to the consulate, since he would like to go to Paris. This story cannot possibly be true, since contemporary evidence—Bigelow's letters to friends and one to Godwin—shows that the discussions of the sale were conducted in December and the announcement of it was made in the *Evening Post* on Jan. 30, more than two months before the inauguration. Bigelow's version in his *Retrospections of an Active Life*, therefore, has been followed here. Bigelow received notice of his appointment as consul general from Secretary of State Seward on Aug. 14, 1861.

to the cause of this change, it may perhaps be well to say that Mr. Bigelow, having fully realized all the ends which he proposed to himself in embracing the profession of journalism, desires to betake himself to pursuits more consonant to his tastes." One of these pursuits was to complete a biography of Archbishop Fénelon, whose career had so fascinated Bigelow while he was in Europe that he had collected material about him as the basis for a work on the relations between church and state. While the storm clouds of secession were breaking over the nation, Bigelow retired to the Squirrels, his home on the Hudson, to work on his book and, in the role of a country squire, to improve his property by building a road and starting an orchard.

In editorials in the *Evening Post* in the first months of 1861 Bryant had continued to assail President Buchanan and his cabinet as traitors for allowing the seceding states to seize government property and delaying in sending reinforcements to the aid of the garrison at Fort Sumter to which troops had withdrawn in December when South Carolina had taken over the arsenal at Charleston. When the six original secessionist states formed a confederacy by a "species of Caesarian operation," Bryant resorted to ridicule in condemning them. They had written a constitution little different from the charter of the United States, one designed "to coax the border states into the new Union." This bribe was accompanied by blackmail: if the wavering states refused to join they would face tariff barriers that would destroy their commerce. The secessionist debate over the design of a national ensign prompted Bryant to recommend the original palmetto emblem showing a rattlesnake twined around the trunk of the tree. As a tree, the palmetto bore no fruit, and the rattlesnake, when disturbed, wound itself into a coil and rapidly vibrated its rattles. The South was similarly unproductive and similarly resorted to making noises to frighten a potential enemy.

Just before Lincoln started on his trip to Washington, an *Evening Post* correspondent interviewed him at Springfield, reporting that his forbidding face was now covered with whiskers. "The gaunt, hollow cheeks, and long, lank jawbones are so enveloped as to give fullness and rotundity to the entire face, and, if he escapes the barbers, Mr. Lincoln will go to Washington an exceedingly presentable man," the article said. On Lincoln's arrival at New York, one of his callers at the Astor House was Bryant. No record was left by either of the conference, but on Lincoln's departure on February 21 Bryant wrote an editorial praising both his physical appearance and his political policy. Bryant was amused by the remarks of the crowd as Lincoln rode through the streets. Instead of the "horrid caricature" circulated during the campaign, the people found a man with a "highly intellectual face" that refuted all the slanders about his ugliness.

Lincoln's inaugural address on March 4 drew the praise from Bryant that it was wholly admirable, "convincing in argument, concise and pithy in manner, and simple in style." He liked Lincoln's views on conciliation with the South: "Mr. Lincoln thoroughly refutes the theory of secession. He points out its follies and warns the disaffected districts against its consequence, but he does so in the kindly, pitying manner of a father who reasons with an erring child." But he was also a stern parent, and he was "perfectly resolute in his enunciation of purpose to enforce the laws." Bryant might have had reason to cavil at Lincoln's cabinet, but, in the manner of the conciliatory inaugural address, he wrote temperately of the selections, implying that he did not like some of them but did not object to any of them.

Although Godwin had avoided seeking Bryant's help in getting a patronage job, this diffidence was not manifested by Isaac Henderson. He wanted to be named navy agent for the city, and Bryant supported his partner's request. In respect to this appointment, Secretary of the Treasury Chase wrote Bigelow on March 11 that his wishes, for Bigelow also supported Henderson's request, would be gratified "unless Mr. Byant presents some other gentleman as his choice." Bryant's own name figured frequently in the press as a seeker for office, usually as a United States minister abroad. Chase perhaps had this in mind when he wrote Bigelow: "If Mr. Bryant wd. go to Europe (say Paris) & take Mr. Godwin as Private Secretary he should have my voice."[3] So persistent were the reports of Bryant's seeking an office that he had a denial published on April 1: "Those who are acquainted with Mr. Bryant know that there is no public office from that of the President of the United States downwards which he would not regard it as a mistake to be obliged to take. They know that not only has he asked for no office, but that he has not allowed others to ask for him—that he has expected no offer of any post under the government, and would take none if offered. He has not visited Washington to influence any of the appointments which have been made, though he has cheerfully borne his testimony in writing to the merits and qualifications of others." The notice went on to say that requests for his aid had become so numerous and importunate that he had been obliged to go out of town to avoid them. The trip mentioned was one which he had taken to Boston and Cambridge to visit the Waterstons, Danas, and Deweys and which, he wrote Frances on April 12,[4] he planned to extend at the insistence of

Willard Phillips, who along with Dana many years before had recognized the greatness of "Thanatopsis" and had printed it in the *North American Review*. During the visit Bryant and Phillips called on Longfellow, who noted in his diary on April 14: "I never saw Bryant so gentle and pleasant."[5]

II

Lincoln had been in office less than a month when two of the Republican newspapers in New York, Greeley's *Tribune* and Raymond's *Times,* joined the antiadministration press, which was urging compromise with the South or letting the secessionist states depart, in attacking him. During the first weeks of the crisis, Greeley had wavered in his views, sometimes arguing that coercion could not be employed to maintain the Union, since it would mean war, and sometimes arguing that the southern states should be allowed to leave if they wished. Raymond, on the other hand, maintained steadily that the Union should be preserved, short of war preferably but by war if necessary. When Lincoln did nothing to reinforce the garrison at Fort Sumter and the seceding states had established the Confederacy, both Greeley and Raymond, as if by prearrangement, came out on April 3 with editorials assailing him for indecision and inactivity. "Come to the Point!" the *Tribune* exhorted in the title of its editorial, and the *Times* advertised: "Wanted—a Policy." Greeley did not know what he wished the President to do except that he ought to make up his mind— to announce a decision that he intended either to maintain the Union or let the seceding states go their own way. Raymond charged that the President had "spent time and strength in feeding rapacious selfish politicians, which should have been bestowed upon saving the Union." Bryant replied the next day in a mild editorial called "Republican Grumblings." He pointed out that "it is not so very easy to decide what course of policy is best suited to the emergency" and that thirty days were not a great deal of time to obtain a consensus in a cabinet made up of men of different views. The only offenses of the administration were "a little delay and no publicity" and to get excited over them was absurd.

On the night of April 9 the telegraph brought to the morning newspapers the report that Lincoln had dispatched an expedition to provision the Fort Sumter garrison. Bryant interpreted the President's order as meaning that he had decided "to defend at all odds the trust the nation conferred upon him on the 4th of March"—to preserve, protect, and defend the Constitution. He had ended a wearisome period of five months of "suspense and inaction." If the rebels fired on the unarmed supply ship, on their heads would fall the responsibility of war. If war came, then immediate action must be taken to put down the rebellion. Any delay would merely result in the shedding of more blood.

The suspense over what would happen in Charleston harbor ended two days later when information reached the city that at 4:30 on the Sabbath morning of April 12 shore batteries under the command of General Pierre G. T. Beauregard had opened fire on Fort Sumter. Bryant's first editorial reaction was to ridicule the idea of southern chivalry exemplified in the rebels' spending four months collecting an army of five thousand troops and ringing Fort Sumter with scores of batteries to dislodge "eighty pale, patient, loyal soldiers from a federal fortress." "If there was an atom left of that chivalry of which South Carolina boasts so loudly," Bryant wrote, "even traitors would have respected the bravery of Sumter's garrison, and turned their battle, if battle they *must* have, to another point. But they glory, in cowardly glee, in their thousands hunting to death the loyal eighty. They have well learned the ignoble lessons in their blood-hound hunts of defenseless slaves." Bryant was confident that the North would gather behind the President to put down the treason forever. "It will not grudge the men or the money which are needed," he said. "We have enjoyed for eighty years the blessings of liberty and constitutional government. It is a small sacrifice we are now to lay upon the altar."

The *Evening Post* had not engaged in the frenetic competition for news that had marked the careers of Bennett, Greeley, and Raymond. Bryant, as were Bigelow and Godwin, was a scholarly man who believed his main duty as an editor was to give his considered judgment on the events of the day in his editorial leader. He knew, of course, that a paper must have readers and that to get readers it must print the news, before other papers if possible, but he was willing to leave to others the task of gathering the trivia and sensations of the hour that attracted readers by the scores of thousands. But civil war presented a different problem, for it furnished serious news that if the *Evening Post* was to maintain its position it must obtain and print.* Fortunately, with the departure of Bigelow, Bryant had

*John Bigelow wrote of Bryant's attitude toward news before the Civil War: "Mr. Bryant was not a journalist in the modern sense of the word; he had, like most editors of the period, but an imperfect appreciation of the financial importance of news for a newspaper. He had always been a leader-writer. . . . The *Evening Post's* influence was always considerable; but news had never been . . . its chief or even a conspicuous feature. . . ." *Evening Post,* Nov. 16, 1901, 100th anniversary issue.

employed a managing editor who had the enterprise to conduct the news operation in a way to accomplish this aim.

The new managing editor was Charles Nordhoff, who had spent nine years in the navy and merchant marine before turning to literature and journalism and who still had something of the sailor in his talk and his manner. He came to the *Evening Post* from the publishing firm of the Harper brothers, where he had been employed for several years as an editor. Bryant may have been attracted to him because he reminded him of William Leggett, also a sailor and man of action with strong opinions vigorously expressed. Nordhoff had led an adventuresome life, having visited many exotic ports in his days as a sailor, and he had recorded his experiences on a man of war, merchant ships, and a whaler in several briskly written books eagerly read by boys hearing the call of the sea. Nordhoff, born in the province of Westphalia in Germany on August 21, 1830, was brought to the United States at the age of four when his father, a wealthy liberal, was forced to leave Prussia. The family visited from place to place for several years in the Mississippi Valley before taking up residence in Cincinnati, where the father died in 1839. At the age of thirteen Nordhoff was put into a printing office to learn the trade by his guardian, the Rev. William Nast. Disliking the religious discipline to which he was subjected, Nordhoff took the opportunity when his guardian was on a trip to Europe to run away to Baltimore to ship out to sea. Considered a scamp and a runaway boy by the captains he approached, he was unable to get a berth either at Baltimore or at Philadelphia. To earn his living meanwhile, he found a job as printer's devil on the Philadelphia *Sun* and not long afterward was able to persuade the commander of the frigate *Columbus* to let him join the navy. The cruise of the *Columbus* took him around the world. After getting his discharge at Norfolk in 1848, Nordhoff spent several years in the merchant marine, visiting Europe, Asia, South America, the South Sea Islands, and Australia; he also made one cruise on a whaler to the Indian Ocean and for a time worked on fishing boats sailing out of Cape Cod. Turning to journalism in 1853, he was employed on papers in Philadelphia and Indianapolis and wrote his realistic books about his life at sea.

Nordhoff shared Bryant's belief that the Union must be preserved and that the war must be prosecuted energetically. Though unlike in character and manner, the two men worked together without conflict during the disheartening years of the war. A later associate on the paper, John Ranken Towse, compared them: Bryant always studiously courteous in communicating with the juniors on the staff, conveying the impression of being cold and distant; Nordhoff, brusque, authoritative, quick-tempered.

"There was much of the sailor in his free and easy manner and his quick decision," Towse wrote of Nordhoff. "He was an inveterate smoker of big and strong cigars, which held in the center of his mouth and as he wrote—with characteristic, unhesitating energy—he used to envelop himself in such clouds that it was a marvel sometimes how he could see either pen or paper." [6]

During the first days of the war the *Evening Post* was unable to print papers fast enough to meet the demand. Its city circulation rose to almost double that of the previous year, in excess of twenty thousand, and apologies were printed for the delay in delivery to subscribers. Press time for the three editions was moved up to an hour earlier—to 1:30, 2:15, and three o'clock—and advertisers were notified to have their copy in by ten o'clock to get their notices on the first and fourth pages and by 12:30 for the second and third pages. An order was placed for an eight-cylinder press in November, but it was not installed until July 19, 1862.

In early editorials on the war, the paper called for a blockade of the coast of the Confederate states, for the military occupation of Maryland, and then for a demonstration against Richmond because it was a supply center for the South. It took the lead in starting a subscription fund to support families of New York volunteers, receiving contributions at its business office, a notice saying that the money would be paid over "by Mr. Bryant to Mr. Theodore Debon, treasurer of the committee formed for that purpose." In an editorial on May 15, "No Occasion for Hurry," the paper attacked the public demand for an immediate and decisive blow at the South. This could not be done without "ample and cautious preparation," the policy being pursued by General-in-Chief Winfield Scott.

In the latter part of May, Bryant got away from the newspaper for two weeks to visit his brothers in Illinois, making the entire trip by the railroad which only a few years before had been completed to Chicago and from there to Princeton. "Your mother bore the journey remarkably well," Bryant reported to Fanny Godwin on May 25. [7] Over the years his brother John had continued to be an Illinois correspondent for the *Evening Post*. He had helped form the Republican party in the state and was a supporter of Lincoln in his campaign against Douglas for United States senator, writing him in September of 1858 that Bureau County was safe for a handsome majority for the Republicans. [8] A more radical antislavery man than his brother, John had maintained a station on the underground railroad during the fugitive slave agitation of the 1850's, and he was a close friend of the Abolitionist Owen Lovejoy, brother of the martyred Elijah P. Lovejoy, killed by a mob at Alton in 1837.

The visit to Illinois apparently turned Bryant's attention to the matter of emancipation, which thus far had not figured prominently as one of the aims of the war. On his return to New York, he arranged for a meeting at Cooper Union on June 16 to be addressed by Owen Lovejoy, now a member of Congress from Illinois, on the subject. Introducing Lovejoy, Bryant recalled the murder of Elijah Lovejoy and the destruction of his press and hailed the brother as a man "equally fearless and resolute" who had "never ceased since that day to protest against an institution upheld by suppressing the liberty of speech and by assassination."

Thus early in the war Bryant placed himself among the radical Republicans and the Abolitionists who demanded immediate freedom for the slaves and, before the year ended, he was writing editorials critical of Lincoln, who in trying to retain the loyalty of the border states temporized over the question. On July 19 in an editorial, "A War for Emancipation," he declared that the Rev. William Henry Channing, in a talk at the Harvard Divinity School, was wrong in saying that the British had turned a cold shoulder to the North because it had not made the war to free the slaves. This was not the real explanation, Bryant said; his reading of British publications indicated that some of the people of England would delight in the overthrow of the republic and some feared the conflict would interfere with the importation of cotton. Bryant concluded that "though not a war directly aimed at the release of the slave," it "must indirectly work out the result in many ways." On September 2, after General Frémont issued his proclamation freeing the slaves of Missourians taking up arms against the nation, an order quickly modified by Lincoln, Bryant declared that Frémont had "done what the government ought to have done from the beginning." Bryant became angry, however, in October when the *World* classed the *Evening Post* with such Abolitionists as Owen Lovejoy and Wendell Phillips. He denied that his paper had ever asserted that emancipation was the chief object of the war but on the contrary had sustained the government in its aim of restoring the Constitution and the Union. But, he argued, the institution of slavery should not be allowed to stand in the way of this end and military exigency could justify its abolishment. Certainly soldiers risking their lives in a great cause should not be degraded into becoming "slave-catchers and beadles" in compliance with the military order that commanders should respect southerners' property even to the extent of returning fugitive slaves. As for freeing the slaves, he argued, when their "disloyal masters are converting their strong arms into powerful instruments of rebellion, either in the camps or in the corn-fields, we say that their masters should from that moment, and forever afterward, forfeit all right to their services."

Finally, on December 4, Bryant expressed disappointment over Lincoln's indecision about what to do with the slaves, revealed in his message to Congress. "His evident eagerness to dispose of the slavery question without provoking any violent convulsion is honorable to his feelings of humanity," Bryant wrote. "But with all this, it will be felt universally that he does not meet either the necessities or the difficulties of the case with sufficient determination." The President seemed to be "painfully aware" that something must be done about the slaves in the insurgent states but his view of practical solutions was "limited and perplexed." His hints of possible colonization struck Bryant as not making much sense. The nation needed the labor force that the slaves could provide, and it was inconsistent to suggest sending them out of the country while welcoming immigrants to do its work. Always a strict constructionist of the Constitution, Bryant the next day argued that slaves could be freed as exigency required without violating the nation's charter. In ordinary times, neither the President nor Congress had authority to interfere with slavery. But these were not ordinary times. The war had altered the relations between the national and the state governments. Under martial law Congress had the power to confiscate the property of the rebels and since slaves were property they could be seized to be dealt with as the government saw fit.

III

Although Bryant advocated carrying on the war vigorously, urging no delay in raising men and money, he did not join in the strident demands for an immediate onslaught against the South. He was confident that the North could put down the rebels in a short war but he counseled against hasty action with unprepared troops. On July 16 he warned against the war cry raised by Greeley's *Tribune* on June 26 and eagerly taken up by the people: "Forward to Richmond! Forward to Richmond!" Bryant predicted that should an early engagement result in a disaster the war would be prolonged by a year and he spoke out against an immediate confrontation on the battlefield.

When federal troops under General Irvin McDowell were defeated at Bull Run on July 21 and began a retreat that ended in a panicky stampede, Bryant's ability as a seer and strategist seemed to have been demonstrated. However, he put the best face on the rout that he could. The first stories of the "shameful flight" were told by persons who had gone out from Washington to view the spectacle and who, half-frightened to death, magnified the disorder of the retreat. As a matter of fact, Bryant said, the

soldiers had performed bravely and successfully until General Beauregard's forces were joined by those of General Joseph E. Johnston and only
then, greatly outnumbered, had they moved back. The lesson of the
disaster was that it must be repaired by "new exertions and new sacrifices." In an adjoining editorial, the *Evening Post* took delight at the
discomfiture of the "general" of the *Tribune,* Horace Greeley, who in a
signed article pledged himself in the future to refrain from ordering
military movements and from criticizing those engaged in by legitimate
commanders. Two days later Bryant outlined what he considered the
responsibility of the press in the war. It was not to "organize armies or
to conduct campaigns" nor in its criticisms should it reveal to the enemy
any weaknesses, either military or political. Nevertheless, "gross and
obvious blunders on the part of those in power" ought to be denounced.
Bryant set forth his paper's policy:

> The *Evening Post* . . . has been the consistent advocate of an unlimited
> freedom of discussion; it will still continue to point out notorious instances
> of inefficiency; and to urge the government to its duties, whenever it is
> lethargic or lax. But it will remember that secrecy in war is often vital to
> success; that great measures cannot be carried out in a day; that it is no less
> important to inculcate upon a naturally impatient people patience and confi-
> dence in those who have the control of affairs, than to watch the conduct
> of the authorities, and lay open all instances of incompetency. And finally,
> it will remember that blind and sweeping censure, made, necessarily without
> a sufficient knowledge of facts, can do only injury to the best interests of the
> nation.

Twice during the summer Bryant turned to poetry to rally the country
to live up to its promised greatness during this hour of peril. In "Not
Yet," printed in the popular literary weekly, the *New York Ledger,* he
wrote that the time had not come for his country, the "marvel of the
earth," to be laid low by traitors; and a short time later, in "Our Country's
Call," he appealed for recruits for the army, calling upon men of all
pursuits, the farmer, the woodman, the seaman, the city worker, to answer
their country's need. Stalwart though Bryant was in heeding his country's
call, striving through his editorials to point to the path for it to follow and
to inspire it to fulfill its duty, he could not forget, in the bitter autumn of
1861, that his own lifetime had reached its autumn. In a poem on his
birthday, "The Third of November, 1861," at the age of sixty-seven, he
wrote:

> Dreary are the years when the eye can look no longer
> With delight on Nature, or hope on human kind;

Oh, may those that whiten my temples, as they pass me,
Leave the heart unfrozen, and spare the cheerful mind!

Bryant since his days as a young lawyer at Great Barrington had studied economic theory and applied it in his discussions of the affairs of business and government during the thirty-five years he had edited the *Evening Post.* Now he was worried about what the government would do to the economy in its efforts to finance the war. He felt a personal responsibility, since he had urged upon Lincoln the appointment of Chase as secretary of the treasury. During the first half of 1862, when financing measures were before Congress, he devoted editorial after editorial to consideration of how the war should be paid for. He set forth his views in letters to Chase and met with him once early in January when the secretary was in New York.[9] He also sought the opinions of businessmen and bankers, and exchanged letters with the Boston merchant and financier, John Murray Forbes, who endorsed his views and wrote for the *Evening Post* under the pen name "Justice." With the people avid for news of campaigns and battles, Bryant realized that they would find economics dry but, as he wrote on January 15, "we will make ourselves as clear and be as little tedious as we can." The resulting editorials were remarkably lucid discussions of a difficult subject, illustrated with homely example and interesting analogy.

From the first, Bryant advocated a pay-as-you-go war by means of direct taxes. There was no need for "desperate remedies." The country had entered the war with no national debt and its resources were such that it could well afford taxes on industry and trade. Bryant believed that the people were willing to accept the burden of taxation. "The same spirit which has prompted the flower of our young men to volunteer for the war makes those who remain at home willing to be taxed for the purpose of paying them their wages," he wrote.

Bryant had several serious objections to a bill introduced early in the year to establish a national banking system, but his principal concern was over a move that began early for the issuance of paper money as legal tender, a proposal that he fought strenuously in editorials and that, when approved by Congress, he appealed personally to Lincoln to veto. He began his attack on January 15, pointing out that "there is a large class of persons in this country who are always ready to favor any scheme for givng us a currency the value of which shall grow less and less." These were "the speculating gentry—men whose brains are teeming with projects to make their own fortunes at the public expense." In subsequent editorials he

437

dealt with the dire results of issuing such legal tender. History did not record an instance, he wrote on January 25, in which currency did not depreciate in value, and the most disastrous effects would be upon the working people and the poor.* In editorial after editorial Bryant warned that once the leak in the dike began it would not be long before the ocean poured in and the country would be flooded by the worthless currency, prices would rise, and the credit of the nation would be destroyed.

Secretary Chase attempted to reconcile Bryant to the need for the legal-tender clause in the banking act, writing him on February 4 that he shared Bryant's repugnance for it but that he considered it indispensable as a temporary measure.[10] Bryant was unconvinced and in an editorial on February 12 answered the "financial philosophers who favor the paper money scheme." "They agree with us perfectly that paper money is a bad thing," he wrote, "but *this* paper money is to be an exception to all other schemes of the kind. All others have ended disastrously; but this is a most innocent, carefully considered scheme, and is certain to end well." The idea, he declared, was nonsense.** But the legal-tender clause passed Congress and in a final supreme effort to prevent it from going into effect Bryant addressed Lincoln in a long editorial, "A Word to the Chief Magistrate of the Union," on February 17 urging him to veto the measure. The appeal failed.

IV

Though never giving up his belief that the first goal of the war was to put down the rebellion and restore the Union, Bryant continued to urge

---

*This editorial seems to have been suggested by John Murray Forbes, who wrote Bryant on Jan. 22, 1862: "I have not seen set forth so distinctly as it deserves the point that while speculators, and gamblers, and indeed shrewd men in active business can take care of themselves, no matter how vicious the currency tinkering may be, it is the women and minors, the helpless and the poor generally, upon whom a vicious currency and its consequences are sure to fall the hardest." *Letters and Recollections of John Murray Forbes* (Sarah Forbes Hughes, ed., Boston and New York, 1900), I, 282.

**Secretary Chase's report to Congress in December drew from Bryant a sharp rebuke in an editorial, "The Financial Ideas of Mr. Chase." Chase replied in a letter on Dec. 13 in which he said he "was not a little pained" to read the article. "A public man, in times of terrible trial, must often adopt expedients, not inherently immoral, which he would in a normal condition of things, avoid," he wrote. "This would, I think, justify my support of a national system of banking associations, even were the plan intrinsically defective." He wondered if it was "quite right," when he was struggling with "almost overwhelming difficulties," to be attacked in the *Evening Post.* Bryant-Godwin Collection; Godwin, *Biography,* II, 185–6.

immediate emancipation not only in editorials but also in speeches given at Abolitionist rallies. In editorials he repeatedly pleaded with the President not to delay in declaring the slaves free and condemned him when he failed to act. On March 7, 1862, Bryant was one of the vice-presidents elected at a mass meeting assembled at Cooper Union to hear Carl Schurz, the Wisconsin lawyer who had supported Lincoln's nomination for President and was now a brigadier general of volunteers in the army, on the undesirability of any longer tolerating slavery. Lincoln's message to Congress proposing graduated and compensated emancipation was read to the throng. "Nobly did that message crown the proceedings of the meeting," Bryant wrote, "and those who attended it went home with the assurance in their hearts that in listening to its plain and direct words they had heard the death knell of slavery." He hailed the action of Congress in April in barring slavery from the District of Columbia as being a declaration of the United States that "wherever its jurisdiction rightly extends the subjects of it shall be freemen." Bryant could still applaud Lincoln on June 12 in introducing Owen Lovejoy as the speaker before the Emancipation League at a meeting in Cooper Union. The blood shed by Elijah P. Lovejoy in Illinois had not been shed in vain, for that state had given the nation a "chief magistrate who urges upon the slave states the policy of emancipation." Bryant again rejoiced on July 12 when Congress passed the confiscation act liberating slaves of all persons who committed treason or supported the rebellion, an earlier one extending only to slaves employed in arms or labor against the nation. But two days later he had become disillusioned with the President. "Mr. Lincoln should be informed that the people are becoming impatient for the execution of the important laws just passed by Congress," he wrote. "The legislature has put a sword into the hands of the President, with the general approbation of the country, and everybody is wondering why he delays to strike."

Although Bryant learned of it only later, on the day that his editorial appeared Lincoln had submitted to his cabinet a tentative draft of an emancipation proclamation. He was persuaded by Secretary Seward to delay it until a more propitious time—when the Union armies, now suffering a series of defeats in Virginia, had a victory to announce. When the story got out, being reported to the *Evening Post* by its Washington correspondent, Bryant in an angry editorial on August 4 demanded the names of those who were responsible. "Was it Chase, or Stanton, or Welles, or Seward, or Blair, or Smith, or Bates?" he asked. Then speaking in the Old Testament terms of the prophets he resembled with his shaggy gray hair and beard, Bryant urged: "Let the country know who are the champions of slavery that surround the President, and they will demand, in a voice of thunder, that the traitors be dismissed and sent to join the cabinet of Jeff. Davis. God grant that the President may follow his own instincts, and fling off the evil influence of corrupt politicians and disloyal states that would deter him from the faithful execution of his high duties!''

Lincoln's reply to the fulminations of the emancipationists was made not to the *Evening Post's* attacks but to one by Horace Greeley, who in the *Tribune* on August 20 printed his ''The Prayer of Twenty Millions,'' in which he pleaded with the President to carry out the confiscation acts. Lincoln released to the press a letter to Greeley in which appeared his memorable statement: ''If I could save the Union without freeing *any* slave I would do it, and if I could save it by freeing *all* the slaves I would do it; and if I could save it by freeing some and leaving others alone, I would also do that.'' Bryant in his editorial comment agreed in principle with Lincoln's statement of the need for saving the Union and approved his expression of abhorrence of slavery but he did not accept his statement that emancipation now would harm the cause. He believed with nine-tenths of the loyal North, he declared, that nothing would be more effective than ''stripping the insurgents of their laborers.'' Once the word was abroad, and it would reach southern plantations with the speed of the telegraph, the flow of supplies to the army, now provided by slave labor, would stop, workers at home would resist the call to join the government forces, and soldiers would leave the battlefield to guard their endangered firesides. When Lincoln did issue, on September 22, his preliminary emancipation proclamation after the Union victory at Antietam Creek in Maryland, there was little for Bryant to say. It might have been more opportunely issued at the time of the passage of the confiscation act in July, he wrote, but he was satisfied that the step had at length been taken.

In the newspaper competition for war news the *Evening Post* under Charles Nordhoff made only a respectable showing. He relied heavily on the reports of the Associated Press and maintained only about a dozen correspondents in the field, a much less extensive establishment than the popular morning newspapers, the *Tribune, Herald, Times,* and *World.* These engaged in a ruinous competition, spending huge sums for telegraph tolls and for printing the increased number of papers demanded by an avid public. In October, replying to a published statement that probably not one newspaper in the city had an income equal to its increased costs in wartime, the *Evening Post* declared itself an exception. The other papers did not operate on a sound business basis; they were sold at a price below the cost of printing and each increase in circulation only added to the financial loss. Yet Bryant and Henderson were willing to spend money and did so—more than $40,000 to acquire two adjoining buildings for expansion of the printing plant and installation of the new Hoe press ordered early in the war, "the largest and most efficient eight-cylinder newspaper press that has ever been constructed," the paper boasted on July 19, 1862.

As to the freedom of the press to print the war news, Bryant saw the need for some sort of censorship to prevent publication of plans and troop movements that would help the enemy, but he was opposed to such restriction in principle. He regretted, for example, the power given the President to take over the telegraph lines, because it was "too much like the practices of the absolute governments of the world." On May 27 he praised the work of the "Bohemian Brigade," the war reporters who shared the danger and the privations of soldiers in order to get the news, but he warned that all of them were not equally "enterprising and trust-worthy" and that their sometimes false reports were mischievous. Nevertheless, he inveighed strongly against efforts to bar them from the battlefield. On June 2 the *Evening Post* argued that the army was part of the nation and "the wives and mothers, fathers and brothers of our brave soldiers will not be content to depend upon a government reporter for intelligence of their acts and their sufferings." Later in the year, when the city became excited over a false rumor that General John Pope had been forced back to Alexandria on the outskirts of Washington, the paper sharply attacked the policy of exclusion of reporters. By barring them, the government "deprived the people of the one source of intelligence on which, imperfect as it may be, they have been taught by experience to count as the most generally trustworthy, the most unfailing, and the quick-est."

V

In the summer of 1861 Bryant had protested against the public opinion that demanded an immediate invasion of the South, holding that an army must be trained and equipped before it could begin to fight. Early in 1862 he felt that this task of preparation should have been completed. The time had come for aggressive action. But there was none. Temperately at first and then with growing anger as the months passed, marked by hesitant decisions, costly blunders, and military defeats, Bryant inveighed against the army and the administration, centering his fire in the latter part of the year on Lincoln as being chiefly at fault.

Bryant supported the radical Republicans in Congress who late in 1861 had formed a Joint Committee on Conduct of the War to press the administration to take the initiative, and he demanded the removal of General George B. McClellan, who had succeeded Scott as general-in-chief, declaring that McClellan was a man more interested in his political prospects than in prosecuting the war. It seemed to be McClellan's belief, Bryant said, that the wisest way of conducting the war was to weary the South with delay. Contrasting the inaction of the eastern army with the battles being waged by the western army, the paper declared on January 11: "The success of our arms and the energies of our generals seem to increase as we get farther away from the capital; the men of the west do not stand upon ceremony with the enemy. They regard rattlesnakes as rattlesnakes, and treat them accordingly." A month later Bryant replied to criticisms in other papers of the severity of the *Evening Post*'s attacks on the conduct of the war in the East. The paper's strictures had been harsh, he admitted, but they were made only with the view of the best interests of the nation.

Writing on "The Conduct of the War" on February 28, Bryant said that Lincoln at the start had given his subordinates carte blanche for preparations, but now he had assumed the full responsibilities of commander-in-chief. But despite the President's order of March 8 reorganizing the Army of Virginia into four commands followed by one on March 11 relieving McClellan of supreme command and putting him at the head of the Army of the Potomac, the Union forces in the next three months made no headway. McClellan, charged with taking Richmond, advanced by way of the peninsula between the James and York Rivers. The campaign, costly in lives, failed the last week in June when McClellan was able only by withdrawing to the James to save his army. In the meantime, General Thomas J. "Stonewall" Jackson had fought his way up the Shenandoah Valley and compelled the Union troops to retreat across the Potomac. Now he posed a threat to Washington.

Since early in the war Bryant had maintained that capturing Richmond would serve no end, for the capital could easily be removed elsewhere. He had outlined a strategy as early as October 5, 1861, which he was to urge thereafter. It was to concentrate the Union's heaviest forces in drives down the Appalachian valleys running south through Virginia and Tennessee into the heart of the Confederacy. When McClellan, even with vastly superior forces to those of the rebels, reeled back from the attack on Richmond, Bryant on July 1 assailed the "fatal error" of the attempt to take the Confederate capital:

General Scott first laid the egg, and incubated it all the time he was in command. It was the object of McDowell when he marched into the fatal snares of Bull Run; it was the sublime study of McClellan for eighteen months, when he undertook the campaign of the Peninsula. . . . For the same end we have tried it in front, we have tried it from behind, we have tried it from the sides, and, though always in vain, though we have been repulsed a dozen times, and sacrificed fine armies in the effort, the official mind at Washington still clings to it as the one thing needful. . . . It is our fixed idea, our enchantment, our pleasant illusion, our fatuity.

By July 22 Bryant was willing to confess that he had perhaps been wrong early in the war in ridiculing newspaper "generals." Mentioning the disastrous summer campaigns, he concluded that the editors could scarcely have committed worse mistakes than the generals. The next day, in a long editorial, Bryant related how the hopes of the people had again and again been raised by the promise of action in Washington only to fall when nothing happened. Of Lincoln's war orders earlier in the year, for example, Bryant had written: "Everybody was delighted at the prospect: Mr. Lincoln has at length, they said, aroused from his slumbers; the drowsy influences of border state opiates have been shaken off, the fascinations of the great serpent of slavery, which has paralyzed the brains and arms of the Executive have been resisted, and we are now to see the war carried on as a war against desperate and malignant enemies should be." But the people had been disappointed then and again later on as the President failed to summon up the will to proceed with energy and dispatch. Bryant returned to the theme again on August 1, writing:

A deep lethargy appears to have fallen upon the officers of our government, civil and military, from which they must be aroused, or it will prove the sleep of death. Our duty as public journalists will not permit us to remain silent longer; we have kept our peace perhaps too long already; we will not cease now to warn the people of the dangers that threaten them; we counsel them to take heed of those who are conducting their affairs; and we demand of the government an energy and will of which it has yet shown no sign.

Bryant's growing impatience with Lincoln worried old friends, some of whom remonstrated with him. The Rev. Orville Dewey, for example, wrote him on August 1 that he was "very much troubled" about the *Evening Post's* stands. "Even if its strictures were perfectly just," he wrote, "it seems to me that there should be some reserve in making them just now. The papers that I have been reading . . . must be a dash of cold water upon our recruiting.''[11] Bryant defended himself in a long letter two weeks later. He was in direct communication with several army officers —General James Wadsworth and General E. A. Hitchcock, among others —and he wrote Dewey that he knew officers of great merit who shared his beliefs about McClellan's mismanagement. "I *know* this," he said in emphasizing that his sources were military men themselves. As to the bad effect upon recruitment, Bryant said: "The mischief was done before the *Evening Post* began to criticize. A gloomy and discouraged feeling prevailed, throughout this city and this state at least, which seemed to make the raising of the necessary number of volunteers hopeless."[12] Bryant did not mention it to Dewey, but he had seen months before that an adequate army could not be raised from volunteers and had urged a manpower draft repeatedly in the *Evening Post.*

Two weeks before writing the letter to Dewey, Bryant had exerted himself to go to Washington to protest personally to Lincoln for his failures, as Bryant thought, in conducting the war. With others in the city, he had formed a Committee on National Affairs, one of whose purposes was to promote the enlistment of troops. His trip was taken as a member of a group appointed to call upon the President. What the *Evening Post* had been saying in editorials, Bryant wrote Dewey, had been "said in still stronger terms to Mr. Lincoln himself." Lincoln had admitted General McClellan's major fault as a commander: "No man organizes or prepares an army better, but when the time for action comes he is greatly deficient." In another account of the trip, in a letter to the Rev. H. N. Powers of Chicago, Bryant wrote: "I saw Mr. Lincoln, and had a long conversation with him on the affairs of the country, in which I expressed myself plainly and without reserve, though courteously. He bore it well, and I must say that I left him with a perfect conviction of the excellence of his intentions and the singleness of his purposes, though sorrow for his indecision."[13]

During the last months of 1862 Bryant vented his dissatisfaction with the President in a series of virulent editorials. On September 4 he said, for example, of Lincoln in accusing him of failure to exercise leadership:

He has been drifted along by the current rather than controlled it, has made war on peace principles, and guided the army by old political traditions rather than military law. Rebels, the most malicious and desperate the world ever saw, were not to be conquered but conciliated; border states, which prayed Good Lord today and Good Devil tomorrow, were not to be forced to do their duty, but coaxed or bribed to it; and, strangest of all, the one primary, radical, efficient cause of the rebellion, its main material support, its animating genius or demon, without which the revolt would have no motive or impulse, was not to be touched, except with furred gloves and the nicest delicacy. Slavery, the hideous monster, which is hurling these masses of brothers and fellowmen in wild and sanguinary fury upon each other, was to be allowed to lie concealed in its horrible pit, grinning all the while with a kind of fiendish exultation at the insane folly of its victim.

Occasionally Bryant departed from his Old Testament style of denunciation to ridicule. When the telegraph carried the news that a New York chiropodist had operated on McClellan's feet to remove corns and bunions, the *Evening Post* commented: "It may be that in this . . . we have the key to the mysteriously slow movements of the 'Young Napoleon,' and that, as these vexatious *impedimenta* have been removed, we shall have a series of rapid and brilliant movements, which will justify the plaudits of his admirers." On October 22 Bryant again made a personal appeal to Lincoln, this time in a letter. The government's course of vacillation seemed to Bryant "little short of absolute madness," and he warned: "If what is apparently the present military policy of those who conduct the war be persisted in, the Union in our view is lost, and we shall resign ourselves to the melancholy conviction that the ruin of our republic is written down in the decrees of God."[14]

In contrast with his despair over the war in the East, Bryant was pleased with the fighting in the West, holding up General Ulysses S. Grant as a model for other officers. After Grant's victory at Corinth, the *Evening Post* said on October 8 that he was a leader "able not only to shake the tree, but to pick up the fruit," and returning to the theme on October 21, inspired by southern accounts which had just been received, declared: "The rebel fox left more than his tail in Grant's trap, he left there large pieces of his carcass; and he will not soon be able to walk into another Union barn-yard." Bryant was aware of the stories about Grant's drinking and made the effort to check their truth. John Murray Forbes, the Boston financier with whom Bryant was in frequent correspondence, wrote him in October of his fear of "drunken generals." Bryant replied that he had "in a drawer a batch of written testimonials as to Grant's sobriety" and that it was "a cruel wrong" to think of him otherwise. "Whether he drinks or not, he is certainly a fighting general," Bryant concluded, "and a successful fighter, which is a great thing in these days."[15]

Bryant was pleased when Lincoln issued his preliminary emancipation proclamation on September 22 and when, on November 7, he replaced McClellan with Major General Ambrose E. Burnside; but he was made sick by the November elections, in which gains were made by the Democrats and in New York Horatio Seymour, whose election Bryant had written Lincoln on October 22 would be "a public calamity," was made governor, and by the huge Union losses suffered at Fredericksburg when the 113,000 troops led by Burnside were shattered by 75,000 Confederates. Shocked by the "massacre," Bryant wrote his most despairing editorial of the year on December 18:

> How long is such intolerable and wicked blundering to continue? What does the President wait for? We hear that a great horrible crime has been committed: we do not hear that those guilty of it are under arrest; we do not hear even that they are to be removed from the places of trust which they have shown themselves so incapable to fill.* What does the President wait for? *He* knows who was in fault; *he* knows whose ignorance, or incapacity, or treason it was which has brought this needless shame and sorrow upon the American people. Let him do his duty, and that at once; let him show the people, who look to him, that he conceals nothing, that he protects no guilt, that he favors no incapacity, that he stands between no criminal and justice.

In the past when overwhelmed with daily cares or appalled by thoughts of the ancient evil of the world, Bryant had found relief from his depression in nature. In the midst of the terrible destruction of life in 1862 he found it by escaping into fancy of an olden time when men peopled the sea with nymphs and the forest with fairies. Several long poems written in these months are unlike anything he had done before. They are stories contrasting the real world with imaginary ones underneath the waters of the sea, on the mountain heights where the snow is created, or in cloud-land with its edifices built of vapor and mist. In "Sella" he invites the reader:

> Hear now a legend of the days of old—
> The days when there were goodly marvels yet,
> When man to man gave willing faith, and loved
> A tale the better that 'twas wild and strange.

And, in "The Little People of the Snow," the children plead:

> One of your old-world stories, Uncle John,
> Such as you tell us by the winter fire,
> Till we wonder it is grown so late.

The maiden Sella puts on the magic slippers found by the river that enable

*Lincoln replaced Burnside with General Joseph Hooker on Jan. 25, 1863.

her to frolic with the nymphs that inhabit the waters; a girl, Eva, joins the Little People of the Snow who from their mountain home toss the spangles of frost upon the land; and another girl, Mary, is attracted to the creatures of the sky

> Whose dwelling is the cloud, who guide the shower
> From vale to vale, and shed the snows, and fling
> The lightnings.[16]

Varied though the tales in setting, all have the same theme: the desire to enter an imaginary realm of innocence and the impossibility of doing so because human beings must always come back to the real world. Pleasant though these sojourns in fancy were for Bryant, the moral was plain: he must heed the admonition of the mother in "A Tale of Cloudland" to meet his "daily duty":

> Life has its cares . . . graver cares
> That may not be put by.

26

GLORY TO THE LORD OF HOSTS!

IN THE FIRST WEEK OF FEBRUARY OF 1863 BRYANT WAS IN-
vited to attend a private meeting at Delmonico's to discuss what its sponsors
called a most important subject, "the diffusion of political information at
the present crisis." It was signed by fourteen of New York City's leading
business and professional men, including two close friends of Bryant, Samuel F. B. Morse and Samuel J. Tilden. Bryant, unable to attend, sent a reporter in his stead. The *Evening Post's* story about the meeting shocked
the city when it appeared on February 7 accompanied by an angry editorial
by Bryant.

Instead of being a meeting to diffuse political knowledge, Bryant wrote,
it was called "to raise a fund for the circulation of political ignorance, as
of treasonable newspapers and speeches." The rich men of the city would
supply the money and the Copperhead editors of the *World, Express,* and
Journal of Commerce the brains for "an active and unscrupulous campaign
against the government of the nation, and in behalf of a body of rebels
now in arms." For some time Bryant had been concerned about the
danger posed by the Copperhead press, which he believed was endeavor-
ing to demoralize the people and to build up opposition to the war. Now
he had evidence of a conspiracy "to break down the loyal party of the
nation, and to hand the government over . . . to the malignant and
slaveholding oligarchs."

Why Bryant was asked to join the secret group is unknown though one of the leaders (it has been suggested that Morse was responsible for his getting the invitation)[1] might have thought that, because of the *Evening Post's* acid criticism of the conduct of the war, he could be persuaded to join those wishing to end it by an armistice. Bryant's first reaction was to express his horror of what he considered treason. His second was henceforth to devote his editorials less to condemnation of the war effort, blundering though he held much of it to be, than to rallying public support for it. He probably would have become less censorious of the administration in any case, for he had become worried about the growing peace movement in the North which might stop the strife but leave the nation still dismembered and the slaves still in bondage. Horace Greeley had expressed a widespread sentiment on January 22 when he urged that, if after three more months of fighting the rebellion still was not crushed, the North should bow to destiny and make the best attainable peace. Bryant's own fault-finding editorials, he must have realized, were of no help in stemming this movement or in overcoming the reluctance to make more sacrifices for a war which after two years seemed to have no conclusion in sight.

In his new mood Bryant did not confine his efforts to editorial exhortation. He became one of the leaders in a movement which sought to obtain support if not enthusiasm for continuing the war through greater exertions. On February 14 he attended a meeting to organize a Loyal Publication Association, in the words of one of those who attended, "in opposition to the surreptitious workings of the gang of Belmonts and Barlows and Tildens that met the other evening at Delmonico's and were undermined, caught, and haled out into the light by the *Post*."[2] He presided at a rally held March 6 at Cooper Union to oppose a negotiated peace, writing an editorial the next day praising "the determination to stand by the Union, to support the government in subduing the rebellion, and to carry on the war with the utmost energy until the last traitor has yielded." A week later he attended another meeting at Cooper Union at which the organization of the Loyal National League was completed. Bryant was one of the twenty-five council members elected to direct the organization. After a mass meeting in Madison Square on April 20, at which Henry J. Raymond of the *Times* was one of the speakers, Bryant hailed the public spirit that the Loyal League rallies were arousing, a spirit which "is binding a great free people together, till they become, in their perfect Union, an irresistible power."

Bryant's softer attitude toward the administration, however, did not mean that he intended to protect it from its mistakes. On April 6 the *Evening Post* printed the report of the Committee on the Conduct of the War blaming the failure of the Peninsular campaign upon McClellan's incompetency. So it was, Bryant said, but the ultimate blame rested upon the President, who should be expected "to know the difference between a good general and an incompetent one." A month later the paper denounced the government's suppression of telegraphic news dispatches. The people should have the news, good or bad, since they "are not children who are incapable of enduring the worst calamities that can befall a nation, as they have shown in former reverses." Again, on May 18, Bryant argued that public condemnation of the conduct of the war, contrary to the opinion expressed in the morning Republican papers, was not likely to discourage the people. If malignant and intended to mislead the public mind, criticism would be bad; if sincere and honest, intended to expose the mistakes of men in power, it would be beneficial. He considered Copperhead press criticism to be of the first type. The method was to magnify rebel successes and minimize those of the Union; calumniate energetic generals like Sherman and Grant and praise worthless ones like Halleck and Pope; declare that the nation was weary of the war and ask how long the fratricidal conflict would be allowed to continue; expatiate upon bankruptcies, high prices, and gouging profiteers; abuse the administration in two ways, saying that it was weak and incompetent and also that it was tyrannous and despotic; and condemn the draft by doubting its constitutionality and declaring it made a distinction between the rich and the poor.

Opposing an armistice and mediation by foreign powers to end the war —the *Evening Post* called the offer of Napoleon III of France to serve as an intermediary an insult to the nation and praised Secretary Seward's summary rejection of it—Bryant repeatedly urged more aggressive action by the northern armies. Through careful study of war maps and accounts by *Evening Post* reporters and letters from army officers, he made himself something of an authority on strategy. He continued to oppose the preoccupation with the capture of Richmond. The Army of the Potomac, he argued in January, should be a reserve force, available to reinforce any point which needed it. He vigorously supported Grant's campaign to control the Mississippi River. "The capture of the rebel capital would be a pretty thing to talk about," Bryant wrote on January 26; "the phrase has a magnificent sound; yet, so far as regards its substantial effect on the result of the war, the rebels dread it infinitely less than the capture of Vicksburg or the presence of a formidable Union army in East Tennessee."

450

Bryant was dismayed by the disastrous defeat of Union forces under General Joseph Hooker at Chancellorsville and condemned the strategy as incomprehensible and sometimes insane. He saw, however, that it was a costly victory for the South and predicted on May 21 that General Robert E. Lee would make a desperate attack on the free states as being less of a hazard than maintaining the defense against Hooker. "Lee will move, not in the direction of Washington," Bryant wrote with prophetic accuracy, "but of the Shenandoah Valley, with a view to crossing the Potomac somewhere between Martinsburg and Cumberland." He urged either the occupation by the North of the Shenandoah Valley in force or a new attack on Lee and advised Maryland and Pennsylvania authorities to fortify their towns and raise fresh bodies of troops. The defeat of Lee at Gettysburg, together with the surrender of Vicksburg, led Bryant to believe that the turning point in the war had been reached, that the South had suffered reverses from which it could never recover.

II

During the weeks before the draft act of March 3 was to go into effect on July 11, the "submissionist" papers, as the *Evening Post* termed the Copperhead press, had been filled with denunciation of conscription. The President was accused of "wanton exercise of arbitrary powers" and the measure was described as a despotic effort to get men to replace those that the government had slaughtered by the thousands. The *Evening Post's* account of the first drawing of names on Saturday, July 11, in the Twenty-second Ward indicated that, instead of the violence expected, the affair was conducted quietly, and even with good humor. But when the drawing recommenced on Monday in the Eighteenth Ward, the wheel containing the names of eligibles had been turning only twenty minutes when the enrolment office was attacked by a mob wielding clubs and hurling brick-bats and the building was set afire. Thus began four days and nights of rioting. Mobs roamed the city, setting fires, looting, attacking the homes and firms of antislavery men, and lynching Negroes unfortunate enough to be caught on the streets. Even the Colored Orphan Asylum on Lexington Avenue near Forty-third Street was sacked.

As supporters of the draft and the war, the *Evening Post, Tribune,* and *Times* were expected to be targets of the rioters, but only the *Tribune* was actually endangered, though hoodlums gathered before the buildings of the other two papers. Charles Nordhoff was undaunted by the threats, remaining at his desk "quietly smoking and writing while the mob howled

451

outside." To prepare against attack, he equipped the editorial rooms with hoses attached to steam pipes so arranged that a shower of boiling water could be directed from a half dozen windows down to the street below and in reserve he billeted in the building and supplied with arms twenty convalescent soldiers just arrived in the city from Gettysburg.[3] At the *Times* Henry J. Raymond prepared to resist attack by illuminating the building so that rioters could not approach in darkness and mounting two Gatling guns at windows facing the street. But at the *Tribune* Horace Greeley had forbidden his staff to set up any defenses, and in consequence mobs moved against the building about seven o'clock on the night of the 13th, shouting: "We'll hang old Greeley to a sour apple tree!" The marauders had broken into the business office on the lower floor and had started a fire of papers when they were charged by eighty policemen, according to the *Evening Post* account of the riot, and fled when billyclubs began descending on their heads.

Opposed to the mob spirit in any form, Bryant, as did Raymond in the *Times*, called for the harshest measures to suppress the riot. In his first editorial on the subject, on July 14, he denied statements of the *Herald* that the violence was a "*popular* opposition to the enforcement of the conscription" and of the *World* that the mob was made up of "the laboring population" resisting the draft. Instead, Bryant declared, the rioters consisted of a "small band of cutthroats, pickpockets and robbers" who took the opportunity during the excitement to engage in a criminal spree. The bands which burned the Negro orphanage, pillaged the stores, and attacked the *Tribune* never numbered more than two or three hundred people; most of those forming the huge crowds in the streets were there merely as spectators. This was no *popular* uprising. Bryant blamed city officials for allowing the riot to get out of hand. The situation did not require "pacificatory speeches"—officials had tried to persuade the crowds to disperse—but "a light battery, with a supply of grape and canister, half a regiment of cavalry, and two or three officers with pluck to use these means."

When quiet returned to the city, Bryant, in an editorial on July 16, had a more ominous explanation of the riot. Far from being a spontaneous protest against the draft, it was the result of "a regular conspiracy, a branch of the rebellion, and the work of those who hold communication with the rebels." The former mayor, Fernando Wood, now publisher of the secessionist *Daily News,* had plotted early in the war to separate New York City from the rest of the state and declare it a free port to provide a haven for rebel shipping. "The project has slept till now," Bryant declared, "but it has *slept* merely, and the fomenters have revived it. . . . Out of this anarchy there is very little doubt that these dreamers hoped to erect a revolutionary government." The source of Bryant's information about the conspiracy was a visit to his office by "a distinguished and sagacious member of the Democratic party," a man privy to its councils, who had told him he did not understand the character of the city's disorders. His informant —it may have been Tilden—had told him the riot had "a firmer basis and a more fixed object than we imagined" and "our wisest course would be not to exasperate them by too resolute an opposition." Bryant declared that the warning would have no effect on the *Evening Post*'s policies: the more determined the traitors the more firmly would they be resisted.*

III

Bryant's concern about the war did not occupy his whole attention. His place at Roslyn continued to receive his care, and his letters to friends spoke of the fruits of his horticulture—Osband's summer pears "just ripened for me on their dwarf trees, and very handsome, with their orange skin and scarlet cheek" and five varieties of American grapes sent in a basket to the Rev. Dr. Dewey, though Old World grapes, including Isabellas hanging around the cornice of the house "as black as a thundercloud," were also available.[4] One of Bryant's projects was building a trail through his woods, whose completion under the eye of Frances he celebrated in a poem, "The Path." For the past two or three years since James T. Fields had taken over the editorship of the *Atlantic Monthly* he had solicited Bryant for contributions, and, searching among his papers, Bryant found a poem written at Roslyn years before in 1849, "The Planting of the Apple-Tree," which he sent for the January, 1864, number. He who planted an apple tree was not planting for the present but for the future, and Bryant added the wry concluding stanza:

---

*In the autumn, when it was expected Seymour might again be the Democratic candidate for governor, Bryant published a blistering editorial accusing him of having fomented the draft riots. He referred to Seymour's famous address to the rioters as "my friends" and declared: "Surely, demagoguism could go no further. He justified their acts by proclaiming to them his disapproval of the law of Congress, resistance to which was their excuse for murder, arson, and robbery. . . . Having encouraged the rioters, he refused to guard the lives and property of New Yorkers against another outbreak of these 'friends' of his; and thus forced the government, at a critical moment, to detach troops from the army to perform this duty. . . ."

"Who planted this old apple-tree?"
The children of that distant day
Thus to some aged man shall say;
And, gazing on its mossy stem,
The gray-haired man shall answer them:
"A poet of the land was he,
Born in the rude but good old times;
'Tis said he made some quaint old rhymes,
On planting the apple-tree."

There was time also for some of Bryant's other interests, his practice of homoeopathy, for one, which had become a profession as well as a pastime. The *Evening Post* on March 5 carried a report on the commencement of the New York Homoeopathic Medical College at which Bryant, as president of the Board of Council, spoke. He had presided at the commencements for years, but now his efforts were crowned with the bestowal of the degree of doctor of medicine. On October 21 the National Academy of Design laid the cornerstone of its new building at Twenty-third Street and Fourth Avenue, and Bryant was one of the speakers. He recalled the academy's founding forty years before when, as a young lawyer-poet just arrived in the city, he had been invited to deliver a series of lectures on mythology to the young artists who, rebelling against the rigidities of the old Academy of Fine Arts, had started the new organization. Bryant was led also to think back on his earlier years when he was asked to write an ode for the fiftieth anniversary meeting of his class at Williams College. Bryant did not attend but he sent the poem, which was read by his Great Barrington friend Charles F. Sedgwick.[5] Bryant ended his poem with an expression of hope for an end to the civil war convulsing the nation:

For us, who fifty years ago went forth
Upon the world's great theatre, may we
Yet see the day of triumph, which the hours
On steady wing waft hither from the depths
Of a serener future; may we yet,
Beneath the reign of a new peace, behold
The shaken pillars of our commonwealth
Stand readjusted in their ancient poise,
And the great crime of which our strife was born
Perish with its accursed progeny.

Publication of the poem as a leaflet drew a response from a member of the 1813 Williams class, and Bryant, in replying on October 5, summed up his own half century since:

> For my own part, I have been what the world might call fortunate in life. I have been happily married, and my wife is spared to me. I have had two children; both are alive. I have been poor enough while poverty was best for me; I have now a competence at a time of life when it seems most desirable. My health is good, better of late years than formerly, and my activity of body scarcely diminished. I do not yet use spectacles, though next November I shall complete my sixty-ninth year. The world, for some reason, has always used me quite as well as I deserve. I hope I am not ungrateful for all these blessings to the Giver of them.[6]

Bryant's major private concern, however, was gathering together and revising his recent poems for publication. Thanking Bryant for sending the *Atlantic* "The Planting of the Apple-Tree," James T. Fields had expressed the hope that his own firm of Ticknor & Fields might have the volume, but Bryant had committed himself to the Appletons, who brought out his *Thirty Poems* in January of 1864.[7] In a prefatory note dated December, 1863, Bryant said that he was printing the poems in the order of composition, an arrangement "as satisfactory as any other, since, at different periods of life, an author's style and habits of thought may be supposed to undergo very considerable modifications." There was, however, little to set these new poems apart from those of earlier years. That there was no new Bryant in the poems was recognized by the reviewer for the *Independent,* who wrote:

> [Mr. Bryant] is now in his seventieth year, and after a life of almost incessant intellectual labor, in one of the most exacting and laborious of professions, he comes before us—the patriarch of our literature—in an aspect quite as extraordinary as that in which he originally presented himself to the world. With eye undimmed—with faculties unworn—with heart still eager and hopeful . . . he flings into our laps *Thirty Poems,* mostly new and all excellent. . . . It has been the singular felicity of Mr. Bryant that he has done whatever he has done with consummate finish and completeness. If he has not, as the critics often tell us, the comprehensiveness or philosophic insight of Wordsworth, the weird fancy of Coleridge, the gorgeous diction of Keats, the exquisite subtlety of Tennyson, he is, nevertheless, the one among all our contemporaries who has written the fewest things carelessly, and the most things well. . . .[8]

The "faultless periods" of Bryant led the reviewer to deplore the lack of passion in his poems, yet in the last one in the book, "The Poet," we find a protest against this conception of his work and a restatement of the early lectures on poetry in which Bryant emphasized that emotion is the essential element in verse:

> No smooth array of phrase,
>   Artfully sought and ordered though it be,
> Which the cold rhymer lays
>   Upon his page with languid industry,
> Can wake the listless pulse to livelier speed,
> Or fill with sudden tears the eyes that read.

But if Bryant's own belief that he wrote with feeling was not shared by many, there were those who realized that he always spoke out of his innermost being. After reading *Thirty Poems,* Ralph Waldo Emerson recorded in his journal:

> Bryant has learned where to hang his titles, namely, by tying his mind to autumn woods, winter mornings, rain, brooks, mountains, evening winds, and woodbirds. . . . He is American. Never despaired of the Republic. Dared name a jay and a gentian, crows also. His poetry is sincere. I think of the young poets that they have seen pictures of mountains, and sea-shores, but in his that he has seen mountains and has the staff in his hand.[9]

The volume was welcomed by Bryant's friends of many years, who wrote him of their pleasure in it. Catharine M. Sedgwick, once widely read as a novelist but now at the age of seventy-five almost forgotten and living in straitened circumstances at Woodburne, Massachusetts,* said: "My 'blue and gold' book, with its thirty pieces . . . is always beside me, whether I sit by my table, am lying on my bed of weakness, or on my couch on the piazza, watching the unfolding of the glorious spring, listening to its poetic breathings, in such exact harmony with yours, which you, master as you are of nature's language, so beautifully interpret, or illustrate in your illumined pages."[10] Richard Henry Dana thought the book "per-

---

*On July 22, 1864, Miss Sedgwick wrote the Rev. Dr. Dewey of her regret that she could no longer afford to subscribe to the *Evening Post:* "I have come to my greatest trial of self-denial from the contraction of my little income by the war. I must give up the daily *Evening Post,* which has been a great consolation to me ever since my exile from my New York friends. It has been a sort of daily intercourse with the Bryants. . . . Even my maid, witnessing my daily enjoyment of it, pleads with me to continue it; but alas! necessity, that knows no law, knows no indulgence, and this must go." *Life and Letters of Catharine M. Sedgwick* (Mary E. Dewey, ed., New York, 1871), p. 401. Writing Frances on Aug. 4, Bryant said he had received a similar message. "She said in a note to me," Bryant related, "that the war obliged her to give up pleasures and luxuries—so I ordered the 'luxury' to be continued at my expense and wrote her to that effect." Goddard-Roslyn Collection.

vaded throughout by a beautiful spirit,"[11] and Henry Wadsworth Longfellow read it "with great sympathy and delight" and found it "very consoling both in its music and in its meaning."[12] Lydia Maria Child, in the forefront of all humanitarian movements, thanked him for the book, especially for "Robert of Lincoln"—"so bird-like, so charming in its simplicity and its rollicking life"—but also for what he had done as an editor "to advance free principles."[13] Caroline M. Kirkland loved most "The Planting of the Apple-Tree," but all the poems meant something to her, and she rejoiced that Bryant still enjoyed "the mellow inward sunshine which brings such fruits to perfection."[14]

There was one poem in the collection, a translation of the fifth book of the *Odyssey*, that indicated a new drift in Bryant's interest. The translation had been done during the summer of 1862. Parke Godwin relates that going into Bryant's library he found him with a new edition of Homer's works. When he picked up one of the volumes to examine it, a few pages of manuscript dropped out. Bryant explained that he had been doing a rapid version in blank verse of some passages of the *Odyssey*. "I was only trying my hand on the Greek," he said, "to see how much of it I still retained."[15] Bryant was also led to try his hand at a translation, he indicated in a letter to Dana, because he had been looking over Cowper's translation and comparing it with the original. "It has astonished me," he observed, "that one who wrote such strong English as Cowper in his original compositions, should have put Homer, who wrote also with simplicity and spirit, into such phraseology as he has done. . . . The greater part is in such stilted phrase, and all the freedom and fire of the old poet is lost."[16] Viewing the translation, then, as something of a challenge, Bryant continued his work and, as he said in a note to the published version, completed it on November 15, 1862. In the note Bryant apologized for his presumptuousness in attempting a blank-verse rendering after that of Cowper. Cowper's translation, however, with its clumsy inversions of the English order of speech and its pretentious language was so unlike the idiomatic language of Homer that he felt justified in his endeavor "to give the verses of the old Greek poet at least a simpler presentation in English, and one more comfortable to the genius of our language."

IV

Although Bryant had believed the federal victories at Gettysburg and Vicksburg marked the turning point of the rebellion, more than a year of warfare was to follow. His editorials continued to attack the goal of taking Richmond and to demand emancipation of the slaves. In a speech on October 2, 1863, at a mass meeting welcoming to New York a delegation that had protested to Lincoln of conditions in Missouri and Kansas, he made one of his strongest pleas against the idea of freeing slaves only in areas where the federal government was in control. "Gradual emancipation!" he exclaimed. "Have we not suffered mischief enough from slavery without keeping it any longer? Has not blood enough been shed? My friends, if a child of yours were to fall into the fire would you pull him out gradually? If he were to swallow a dose of laudanum sufficient to cause speedy death, and a stomach pump were at hand, would you draw the poison off by degrees? If your house were on fire would you put it out gradually?" In February of 1864 *Evening Post* editorials endorsed Sumner's resolution in the Senate for amending the Constitution to abolish slavery in all the states.

Bryant continued to have doubts about the quality of Lincoln's leadership. He expressed these indirectly in an editorial on February 23 urging that the Republican national convention be put off from June 7 until later in the year. Mentioning the names of those being discussed for the presidential nomination—Lincoln, Chase, Grant, and Frémont—Bryant said that a great deal had to be done before the people could judge which man would be best qualified to head the nation for four years. If the spring campaigns brought victories for the North, Lincoln no doubt would get the nomination by acclamation; if not, if the war dragged on as it had been doing, then the people would oppose him. In March Bryant praised Lincoln's elevation of Grant to the supreme command of the armies, but he still maintained a wait-and-see attitude toward renominating him for the presidency. On March 16 he blamed Lincoln for heeding the wrong counselors—proslavery men in his cabinet and among the men placed in command of the armies; but on March 21 he granted that the administration, though committing such "dreadful blunders" as retaining McClellan and Halleck in commands and in making "arbitrary arrests," had on the whole been "so successful and fair" that Lincoln inspired more confidence than any untried administration was likely to. Nevertheless, Bryant maintained that the convention should be put off.

The *Evening Post's* reception of Lincoln's renomination at Baltimore was something less than enthusiastic, but it admitted that whatever might be said of the character of his administration he enjoyed the confidence of the people. "In their conviction of his complete integrity," the paper said on June 9, "of his homely good sense and honesty of purpose, they overlook his defects, they pardon his mistakes, they are prone to forgive even his occasional lapses into serious and dangerous abuses of power." He might be slow to make up his mind, he might gather about him unworthy men, there might be "nothing high, generous, heroic in the tone of his administration," nevertheless the people felt that he did somehow "reach the very best ends."

Bryant's concern over the welfare of the slaves had led him in 1863 to take the lead in helping to found the National Freedmen's Relief Association, and he was active in its affairs during the year. Presiding at its second anniversary meeting at Cooper Union on February 26, 1864, he declared in a brief address that looking after the four million slaves to be freed by the blood of northern soldiers was to be the great task of reconstruction. The role of the association, he said, was to be that of the Good Samaritan of the slave, adding: "We must bind up his wounds; we must convey him to a place of shelter; we must see that he is healed; we must set him forward on his journey, and bid him God speed."

A month later, Owen Lovejoy, one of the country's best friends of the slave, died, and Bryant, as well as his brother John, who had come east to accompany the body to Princeton, Illinois, was a pallbearer at funeral services held March 27 at Henry Ward Beecher's Plymouth Church in Brooklyn. The next month Bryant went to Princeton to attend a meeting called by John and other friends of Lovejoy to plan a monument to him. Bryant addressed the meeting and was named to a committee to choose the memorial.[17]

V

The enemies of Bryant and the *Evening Post* were delighted in the summer of 1864 when the paper, always a preacher of rectitude and during the war a sharp critic of frauds against the government by suppliers, became involved in a scandal itself. The trouble arose over the handling of purchases by Isaac Henderson as navy agent in New York. Bryant's long-time partner was accused of exacting a commission from firms selling materials to the Brooklyn Navy Yard, summarily removed from office by the secretary of the navy, Gideon Welles, and arrested on charges of committing frauds against the government.

The first hint that Henderson was implicated in any wrong-doing reached Welles on February 1 in a report from Provost Marshal L. C. Baker of the arrest of one H. D. Stover for fraud.[18] Welles was a personal friend of Bryant and a former contributor to the *Evening Post* whose work

Bryant considered as having a newspaper style "much better than that of almost any correspondent we have." He was disinclined at first to believe that Henderson was involved in any illegal dealings with Stover, he wrote in his diary, but when the publisher's name turned up again in the investigations being conducted he was not so sure.

The newspaper reports of the investigations and a speech in Congress by Senator James W. Grimes of Iowa detailing them in an attack on corruption provided the opportunity for an ancient political foe, Thurlow Weed, to attack the *Evening Post.* He did so in vitriolic editorials in his newspaper, the Albany *Journal,* in one of which he spoke of Henderson's having his "arms shoulder deep in the federal treasury." It was no worse than what the *Evening Post* had been saying for years about Weed's corrupt finaglings in Albany, but Bryant, incensed, met the abuse with abuse in editorials on June 13 and June 20.

But the situation involving Henderson was more serious than just a war of words between two political opponents. On June 20 Welles decided to remove Henderson and to file criminal charges against him, reluctant though he was "to break with old friends." Before doing so, however, he laid the case before Lincoln, who asked Welles if he were satisfied that Henderson was guilty and when told he was agreed that a dismissal letter should be sent. Henderson was arrested on June 22 upon evidence given in an affidavit by a Brooklyn hardware merchant, Joseph L. Savage. Savage deposed that in submitting vouchers to Henderson for payment for supplies he received less than the full amount of his bill, deductions being made and pocketed by the navy agent. Both in the news story reporting the arrest and in an editorial the next day the *Evening Post* maintained that Henderson was innocent and the action taken against him was part of a political plot. The paper gave no credence to Savage's allegations since he himself was "under grave charges of corrupt dealing."

So confident was Bryant of Henderson's innocence that on June 25 he wrote Lincoln requesting that the dismissal be withdrawn, since this was the most damaging aspect of the case against him.[19] The letter was sent to Welles to be delivered to the President. "The effect of these proceedings upon Mr. Henderson's reputation, hitherto spotless, cannot but be very damaging, since they imply that in the view of the government he is indisputably and grossly guilty," Bryant wrote. He declared that Henderson would be able to prove his innocence and appealed to Lincoln's "sense of justice" to reinstate him. "It is the only way of making reparation for the great injury, which he has suffered, and which I believe I know you too well to suppose that you would willingly inflict upon an honest man, and a faithful public servant," Bryant continued. Descending from this high plane, Bryant next made a political appeal: "What makes these severe proceedings the more unkind is, that Mr. Henderson has always zealously supported your administration, that he has used all his influence in its favor, and that he desired and approved your second nomination."

Smarting under the *Evening Post's* attacks against the administration, although the Navy Department had fared better than most other departments, Welles was somewhat put out by Bryant's letter, delivered to him by Representative M. F. Odell of Brooklyn, a friend of Henderson and like him a prominent member of the Methodist church. "Of course Mr. H. stimulated Mr. B. to write these letters, and, having got them, sends them through his religious associate," Welles wrote in his diary on June 27. He mentioned that former governor Edwin D. Morgan believed both Bryant and Godwin were "participants in the plunder of Henderson" but expressed doubts about Bryant, "who is feeling very badly, and thinks there is a conspiracy in which Seward and Thurlow Weed are chiefs." Welles could and should easily have disregarded Morgan's opinion, since as governor he had been linked with Weed in the *Evening Post's* assaults on the flagrantly corrupt legislature of 1859–1860.

Like Welles, and for the same reasons, Lincoln was unsympathetic to Bryant's letter. Replying on June 27, Lincoln related that when Welles had come to him with the letter of dismissal he had asked "with as much emphasis as I could": *"Are you entirely certain of his guilt?"* To Welles's assurance that he was, Lincoln had said: "Then send the letter." Lincoln told Bryant that he neither knew nor inquired about Henderson's being a supporter of his renomination for President and indicated that he was not impressed by Henderson's reputation: "I believe, however, the man who made the affidavit was of as spotless reputation as Mr. Henderson, until he was arrested on what his friends insist was outrageously insufficient evidence. I know the entire City Government of Washington, with many other respectable citizens, appealed to me in his behalf, as a greatly injured gentleman." Lincoln ended his letter with a stinging reprimand of Bryant: "While the subject is up may I ask whether the *Evening Post* has not assailed me for supposed too lenient dealing with persons charged of fraud and crime? And that in cases of which the *Post* could know but little of the facts? I shall certainly deal as leniently with Mr. Henderson as I have felt it my duty to deal with others, notwithstanding any newspaper assaults."[20]

If Lincoln was tart in writing to Bryant, Bryant could be equally tart in reply. He wrote Lincoln on June 30:

You speak of having been assailed in the *Evening Post.* I greatly regret that any thing said of your public conduct in that journal should seem to you like an assault, or in any way the indication of hostility. It was not intended to proceed beyond the bounds of respectful criticism, such as the *Evening Post,* ever since I have had anything to do with it, has always permitted itself to use toward every successive administration of the government. Nor have I done you the wrong of supposing that any freedom of remark would make you forget what was due to justice and right.

In regard to another point mentioned in your letter, allow me to say that I do not know what the standing of Mr. Henderson's accuser may be in Washington, but here it is bad enough.[21]

Bryant waged a bitter editorial campaign against the case up to the time the hearing began before the United States commissioner on July 5. He published letters by Henderson attempting to explain away the charges and in editorials ranked the case with other "arbitrary arrests" resulting from the suspension of habeas corpus, which Bryant had opposed as being a violation of constitutional rights.

The hearing, conducted with the legal formality of an actual trial, continued for six days, a transcript of proceedings being printed daily in the paper. The government's only witness against Henderson with the exception of persons questioned briefly as to operational procedures by the navy was the hardware merchant Savage, who testified that $2,000 had been deducted from bills he submitted totaling about $17,500. The government's position was that this amounted to extorting a seven per cent commission. Henderson's attorney, a former judge, Edwards Pierrepont, sought to show that the accuser was led to make his affidavit as the result of a promise of the government to free him from Fort Lafayette, where he was imprisoned on the ground of short-weighting the navy in supplies he had sold, and that in addition he hated Henderson and had attempted to enlist others in a conspiracy to get him removed as naval agent. The reason for wanting to get rid of Henderson was that he had stopped the practice of open purchase orders and required bids on supplies sought. The main defense, however, was that the $2,000 Henderson had received from Savage was interest on a loan made to him. Testimony brought out the fact that payment on vouchers by the Navy Department sometimes took several months and that suppliers, needing the money immediately, were in the habit of discounting their vouchers at banks at the legal interest rate of seven per cent. Savage was one of the suppliers nearly always in need of ready cash, and on other occasions had borrowed from Henderson at the standard discount rate. In brief, what Henderson was doing was carrying on a loan business at his office at the navy yard.

Despite the efforts of Pierrepont to get the case dismissed, the commissioner held Henderson for trial, which began almost a year later on May 23, 1865. The prosecution presented the same evidence that it had at the commissioner's hearing, but the United States Circuit Court judge ruled that it was insufficient to support the charge. When the government's attorneys offered to enter a *nolle prosequi,* Henderson's attorney refused, and the case went to the jury, which returned a verdict of not guilty without leaving their seats. The *Evening Post* editorially, on May 26, 1865, hailed the verdict: "Thus ends a prosecution which has been kept for a long time hanging over the head of an innocent and worthy man . . . and the existence of which has given occasion to innumerable malignant allusions to this journal, of which Mr. Henderson is one of the proprietors."

Although Bryant was persuaded that the charges against Henderson were unfounded, Parke Godwin was not and used the affair in an attempt to get him out of the business. The details are given in a letter to Bryant dated July 31, 1865, written, Godwin said, because he had "found writing less liable to mistake or misconstruction than what is said by word of mouth."[22] Henderson's guilt, Godwin declared, was proved by the fact that his own clerk had admitted receipts of $70,000 as commissions, Henderson's private bank account showing "very large transactions, which are believed to correspond irregularly with the entries in the books of the contractors implicated with him." But even if wholly innocent Henderson's position before the public had become such that it was a "mortification and embarrassment" to those who worked on the *Evening Post.* No criticisms of wrong-doing anywhere could now be made without having the Henderson case "flung in our face." This had happened to Godwin a dozen times, and Charles Nordhoff had told him "peremptorily and positively that he could not continue on the paper if Mr. H. retained an active part in connection with it." Godwin was also dissatisfied with Henderson's management of the paper: he now gave little time to it, being constantly engaged in outside speculations, and the publication was therefore not so prosperous as it ought to be. As a result of all this, Godwin proposed that Henderson sell his interest but his request was refused.*

---

*The dissatisfaction of the staff with Henderson's increasing domination of the paper's affairs continued and flared into open revolt the next year. Bryant, without giving details, wrote Frances on Aug. 18, 1865, that matters were "in a fair way of arrangement" and that he thought the *Evening Post* owners could "satisfy Nordhoff and the others by giving them a certain proportion of the profits without making them partners." Goddard-Roslyn Collection.

VI

Bryant's proposal early in 1864 that the Republicans hold their convention late in the year seemed to have been justified in midsummer by the immense losses suffered by Grant in his move against Richmond—the casualties of almost 70,000 in the Battle of the Wilderness, at Spotsylvania, at Cold Harbor, and at Petersburg exceeding the total forces Lee had under his command. Lincoln's popularity with the people early in the year had been manifest in the state conventions, which supported his nomination, but in late summer, when it seemed doubtful if he could be reelected, radical Republicans sought a new convention to reconsider the nomination. Bryant noted the changed political temper in a letter on August 17 to Frances, who was at Elizabethtown in the Adirondacks with Mrs. Henderson. He regretted that he could not join his wife for a trip she planned to Lake Saranac, pointing out that the Democrats would meet at Chicago the next week to make their nominations and he "ought to be on the ground to comment upon their doings." "A great many persons now say, that the advice of the *Evening Post* to postpone the sitting of the nominating convention at Baltimore until September was wise and judicious," Bryant said. "By that time the friends of the Union would probably have made up their minds as to the man whom they preferred."[23]

The failure of Grant's spring and summer campaigns had increased defeatism in the North and there was widespread clamor for a negotiated peace. In July Horace Greeley, who had advocated this earlier in the year, received a letter from William C. Jewett, a somewhat mysterious figure who had set himself up as a go-between to promote peace overtures on both sides, saying that "two ambassadors of Davis & Co." had arrived in Canada across the river from Niagara Falls with power to offer peace terms. They would be interested in discussing these with Greeley. Excited by the prospect and flattered that he was chosen as a spokesman for the North, Greeley informed Lincoln and obtained from him a letter saying that any proposal that included "the restoration of peace, the integrity of the whole Union, and the abandonment of slavery" would be considered by the government. Such terms could not possibly be acceptable to the South and the peace conference did not come off. When the story reached the newspapers, Greeley was accused of "cuddling with traitors" and being a "meddler" and "bungler." But Greeley was not the only Republican editor anxious to do something to end the war. The noise over Greeley's effort had barely died down when Henry J. Raymond, who had been a leader in promoting Lincoln's nomination at the Baltimore convention and who was chairman of the national Republican committee, proposed that the President appoint a commission to make a definite offer to the South with only one condition for peace, acknowledgment of "the supremacy of the Constitution," other issues to be settled in a "convention of the people of all the states." Coming from such a source, Lincoln could not brush aside the proposal, or lead Raymond on to make a fool of himself as he had with Greeley, and rejected it only after submitting it to some members of his cabinet.

Convinced from the start of the war that the only way slavery could be abolished was by military defeat of the South, Bryant was contemptuous of the peace proposals. On July 25 he ridiculed Greeley's belief that some good would come of the negotiations at Niagara Falls. The really effective peace meetings, Bryant maintained, "are those which Grant assembled in front of Vicksburg, which Meade conducted on the Pennsylvania plains, which Rosecrans now presides over near Tullahoma; their thundering cannons are the most eloquent orators, and the bullet which wings its way to the enemy ranks the true olive branch." Bryant was equally opposed to Raymond's peace proposal. In a letter to Frances on September 7, he said: "I wrote a protest against treating with the rebel government which you will have seen in the paper. . . . I was told from the best authority that Mr. Lincoln was considering whether he should not appoint commissioners for the purpose, and I afterwards heard that Raymond, of the *Times,* had been to Washington to persuade Mr. Lincoln to take that step, and was willing himself to be one of the commissioners."[24] Bryant's long editorial on the subject, "No Negotiations with the Rebel Government," appeared on September 6. His argument, which anticipated Lincoln's message to Congress in December opposing any conferences, was that the government could not without "deserting the cause of the people both at the North and the South" deal with the leaders of the rebellion.

Bryant's September 7 letter to Frances, as well as one to the Boston financier John Murray Forbes,[25] revealed him at about his angriest with Lincoln. His anger was not, however, so much due to Lincoln's attitude toward the Henderson affair as it was to Thurlow Weed's influence in dispensing patronage in New York. The immediate provocation was the removal of Bryant's friend and ally in the Free-Soil movement, Hiram Barney, as collector of the port of New York, the most important federal political job in the state, and his replacement by Simeon Draper, a henchman of Weed. Bryant wrote Frances that after hearing of the appointment of Draper, the "pipe layer," a reference to a scandal in which he had been involved, he refused to address Lincoln. He was a little more explicit in his letter to Forbes. Mentioning that the Seward and Weed faction was "filling all the offices with its creatures," he declared: "I am so utterly disgusted with Lincoln's behavior that I cannot muster respectful terms in which to write him."

The Henderson case, however, was not entirely out of Bryant's mind. With some malice, he had written Lincoln on August 30 of matters relating to the Navy Department. The secretary, Mr. Welles, was a man of strict honesty but there was a question about the assistant secretary, Mr. Fox. Distrust of the man's capacity and integrity was widespread and there were complaints about him of not only extreme wastefulness but gross corruption. "It is not the object of this letter to express any opinion in regard to these complaints," Bryant ended his letter. "It is enough for me to state the existence of that impatience and dissatisfaction which universally prevails in regard to the class of transactions of which I have spoken. The remedy, if there be any, and whatever it be, remains with the Executive."[26]

Whatever Bryant's personal feelings may have been toward Lincoln, he did not let them stand in the way of supporting the Republican ticket in the election. Bryant began by assailing the Democrats, who met in Chicago on August 29 and nominated General McClellan for President and George H. Pendleton for vice-president. One of Bryant's editorials, a vicious attack on the financier and banker August Belmont, a leader in the secret "diffusionist" movement Bryant had exposed in 1863, got the *Evening Post* in a libel suit. Bryant had written: "Prominent among the intriguers who sought to shape the policy of the convention was Mr. August Belmont . . . , a reputed son and accredited agent of the Rothchilds, the great bankers of European monarchs. Going about the city in his sumptuous carriage, he seemed a fitting representative of those minions of the royal and aristocratic classes of the old world. It was understood and one prominent Democrat asserted that he paid the expenses of the convention. . . ." Three days after this appeared the *Evening Post* received a letter asking the name of the author of the article.[27] It said the article was not believed to be from Bryant's pen, because it seemed unlikely "a gentleman of his refined instincts would ever engage in personalities and hazard a world-wide reputation," i.e., would declare Belmont to be of illegitimate birth. Civil and criminal suits were filed, but neither ever came to trial. In support of the party, the *Evening Post* issued a weekly campaign paper, *The Little Workingman,* to get the labor vote. Selling at one cent a copy, the paper had a circulation of more than 50,000. Despite the boost given Lincoln by General Sherman's victories in Georgia, Lincoln needed whatever newspaper support he could muster. He lost New York City by a vote of 36,673 to 78,746 for McClellan and his national majority was only 400,000 out of 4,000,000 votes cast.

VII

Even in resorting to his retreat at Roslyn Bryant could not put out of his mind the horror of the war, although life went on there as if men were not dying by the thousands on the battlefields. "Birds sing, and the cicada sounds his shrill note from the neighboring tree, and grapes swell, and pears ripen . . . and children are born, and old people and the sick die in their beds," he wrote Mrs. Charlotte Field on July 20, "just as if there were no war."[28] Two weeks later, he wrote Miss Christiana Gibson that the fruits on his farm were as plentiful as ever and that the school children of the neighborhood had enjoyed their annual feast of cake and pears on the lawn at Cedarmere.[29] But the war intruded and entered into the poetry he wrote. In "The Return of the Birds" Bryant wanted them not to go back to the Southland in their seasonal migration:

> For there is heard the bugle-blast,
>   The booming gun, the jarring drum,
> And on their chargers, spurring fast,
>   Armed warriors go and come.

The poem appeared in the July number of the *Atlantic Monthly,* and so pleased was James T. Fields with it that he immediately asked of Bryant another poem.* Complying with the request, Bryant sent some untitled stanzas which Fields published as "My Autumn Walk." But the war, too, intruded here, for the wind that swept the meadows blew from the south. "Ask me for no more verses," Bryant wrote Fields. "A septuagenarian has passed the time when it is becoming for him to occupy himself with 'The rhymes and rattles of the man and boy.' " And he continued: "Nobody, in the years after seventy, can produce anything in poetry save the thick and muddy last runnings of the cask from which all the clear and sprightly liquor has been already drawn."[30]

Bryant was not yet seventy but in less than a month he would reach that

---

*The *Atlantic* paid Bryant the premium rate for his poems. Thanking Bryant for "The Return of the Birds," Fields wrote him on May 11, 1864, that he was inclosing a check for . $100 for the poem. Bryant-Godwin Collection.

age on his birthday, November 3, 1864. It was a date that had not been forgotten by his friends at the Century Club, and they planned to celebrate it with a festival to which the nation's writers and artists were invited. Even though the country was in the throes of a war that had been going on for four years and a bitter presidential campaign was nearing its end, between four hundred and five hundred persons gathered at the Century Club on the night of November 5 for the affair.[31] The historian George Bancroft, president of the Century, was the toastmaster and in introducing Bryant as the country's foremost poet said: "While the mountains and the ocean-side ring with the tramp of cavalry and the din of cannon, we take a respite in the serene regions of ideal pursuits." Bryant, in reply, thought it para-doxical to be congratulated on living to be seventy, quoting Shakespeare who had Lear say, "Age is unnecessary," and Samuel Johnson, who had written: "Superfluous lags the veteran on the stage."

Perhaps never had so many distinguished authors and artists as well as leaders in other fields been gathered together in the country at one time. The poet Bayard Taylor had written an ode for the occasion, which was sung by a chorus, and one by one such poets as Oliver Wendell Holmes, George H. Boker, Richard Henry Stoddard, and Julia Ward Howe, whose "The Battle Hymn of the Republic" had stirred the hearts of the people, rose to read tributes to the elder poet. James Russell Lowell had planned to attend but the death of a relative prevented his doing so; but he sent an ode, "On Board the Seventy-Six," the ship whose crew wearied by battle setbacks was roused to fight on by "the Singer" in the new war for freedom now being waged. Ralph Waldo Emerson had come, charged with speaking for Bryant's Massachusetts admirers unable to attend. His words were an elaboration of his journal entry of some months before recorded after he had read Bryant's *Thirty Poems:*

> I join with all my heart in your wish to honor this native, sincere, original, patriotic poet. . . .I found him always original—a true painter of the face of this country, and of the sentiment of his own people. When I read the verses of popular American and English poets, I often think that they appear to have gone into the art galleries and to have seen pictures of mountains, but this man to have seen mountains. With his stout staff he has climbed Grey-lock and the White Hills, and sung what he saw. He renders Berkshire to me in verse, with the sober coloring, too, to which my nature cleaves, only now and then permitting herself the scarlet and gold of the prism. It is his proper praise that he first, and he only, made known to mankind our northern landscape—its summer splendor, its autumn russets, its winter lights and glooms. And he is original because he is sincere. Many young men write verse which strikes by talent, but the writer has not committed himself, the man is not there; it is written at arm's length. . . .But our friend's

468

inspiration is from the inmost mind; he has not a labial but a chest voice, and you shall detect the taste and experiences of the poem in his daily life.

The poets paid their tribute to Bryant in verse, the artists in painting. He was presented with a portfolio of almost fifty pictures by such artists as Durand, Kensett, Church, Colman, Leutze, and Hicks, many of them friends of his early days in New York and others whose work he had praised in the *Evening Post*.

While Frances was away from Roslyn in the Adirondacks during the fall, Bryant helped pass the time by going through his papers and gathering together for a little book the hymns he had written, usually upon request for a particular occasion, during the past half century. "If it were not for the hymns which keep me at work, and the sick people who keep me looking into manuals, I do not know what I should do without you," he wrote Frances on August 1. Later he wrote that he would have five hundred copies printed for private distribution.[32] In his autobiographical fragment written in 1874, Bryant related that he might be said to have been nurtured on Isaac Watts's poems for children. His own hymns, like those of Watts's, were plainly written quatrains expressing a conventional faith and trust in God. Bryant's first hymns had been written in 1820, at the request of Catharine Sedgwick, for a collection to be issued by the Unitarians. In the half century since he had written perhaps a dozen others upon request for such special events as an ordination or the dedication of a new church. To fill out the collection, he wrote five new hymns during the fall, and the book, containing nineteen selections, appeared in December.

VIII

As the new year 1865 began Bryant looked forward to a quick ending of the war in a letter "To the Union Army." Reciting victories of the North—Grant exerting inexorable pressure on Lee at Richmond, Sheridan sweeping down the valley of the Shenandoah, Sherman setting Atlanta afire and marching across Georgia to Savannah, and Thomas annihilating the rebel troops left in Tennessee—he saw "a speedy end of all formidable resistance." In editorials he pressed for a constitutional amendment freeing the slaves and continued to oppose peace negotiations. He termed the trip of Francis P. Blair, with Lincoln's permission, to talk to rebel leaders at Richmond in January a "fool's errand," and he objected to the President's leaving Washington to discuss terms with emissaries of Jefferson Davis at Hampton Roads in February. The northern victories made even more important the work that Bryant had devoted so much of his time to during the war, that of the National Freedmen's Relief Association. He stressed the urgency of helping the freed slaves in presiding at a meeting of the association on January 25, declaring that those who remained at home had duties to perform as essential to making the nation a free country as those of soldiers on the field. "What we do strikes at no life," he said, "inflicts no wound, but it is no less necessary to the cause we all have at heart."

The surrender of Lee at Appomattox Courthouse on April 9, coming after so many years of horror and despair, aroused Bryant almost to religious jubilation expressed in an editorial, "Glory to the Lord of Hosts!" The day of peace, he wrote, has come

> as every wise lover of his country wished it to come, not as a weak compromise between the government of the people and its enemies, not as a concession to an exhausted yet vital power of revolt, not as a truce between two equal forces which lay down their arms for the time, to resume them as soon as they should repair damages and recover strength—but as the result of a stern, deliberate, unyielding determination to vindicate the supremacy of the organic law over the entire territory and people of the nation.

In more fervent tones, Bryant went on:

> Glory, then, to the Lord of Hosts, who hath given us this final victory! Thanks, heartfelt and eternal, to the brave and noble men by land and sea, officers and soldiers, who by their labors, their courage, their sufferings, their blood and their lives, have won it for us! And a gratitude no less deep and earnest to that majestic, devoted and glorious American people, who through all these years of trial have kept true to their faith in themselves and their institutions . . . who have never given way to despair or terror on the one hand, or dashed out wildly on the other in a spirit of vengeance and fury, but through every vicissitude of the times have stood calm, self-reliant, determined, indomitable. . . .

Five days later the clarion trumpet tones celebrating victory were changed to the muffled drumbeat of the funeral march when Bryant was compelled to write upon the death of the President. Again the religious note was struck:

> Abraham Lincoln, the man of the people, whom the Providence of God had raised to be "the foremost man of all this world," in the flush of his success

over the enemies of his country, while the peals of exultation for a great work accomplished were yet ringing in his ears, when his countrymen of all parties, and liberal minds abroad, had just begun to learn the measure of his goodness and greatness, is struck down by the hand of the assassin. All of him that could perish now lies in the cold embrace of Death. His warm, kindly, generous heart beats no more; his cool, deliberate, wise and noble brain thinks for us no more; his services to his nation and to mankind are ended; and he has gone to the Rewarder of all sincere, honest, useful endeavor. . . .

When, ten days later, thousands of New Yorkers gathered at Union Square to mourn the death of the President, Bryant expressed their sorrow and that of the nation in a hymn read to the vast crowd:

> Oh, slow to smite and swift to spare,
>   Gentle and merciful and just!
> Who, in the fear of God, didst bear
>   The sword of power, a nation's trust!
>
>   . . . .
>
> Thy task is done; the bond are free:
>   We bear thee to an honored grave,
> Whose proudest monument shall be
>   The broken fetters of the slave.

27

LIKE ONE CAST OUT OF PARADISE

ONE OF THE TRAGEDIES OF THE ASSASSINATION OF LINCOLN, to Bryant's mind, was that it removed from the presidency a man with the qualities needed to bring the nation together again after the years of agonizing civil war. During those times of turmoil Bryant had been impatient with Lincoln's slowness to act and what seemed to be his indecisiveness, though recognizing that, as he phrased it in his obituary editorial, "his kindliness, his integrity, his homely popular humor, and his rare native instinct of the popular will" had won him a place in the hearts of his countrymen second only to Washington. The qualities Bryant had once condemned he now interpreted as skill in postponing needless troubles and resisting fanatical zeal. His death was all the greater loss, Bryant wrote, "when we reflect on the generosity and tenderness with which he was disposed to close up the war, to bury its feuds, to heal over its wounds, and to restore to all parts of the nation that good feeling which once prevailed, and which ought to prevail again."

Several leaders in the struggle to end slavery thought that Bryant, because of his long fight against the evil, was the proper person to write a biography of Lincoln. Oliver Wendell Holmes wrote him on April 27, 1865: "If you will undertake it, the whole country will be grateful to you. It would be a double monument, enshrining your dear memory as imperishably as that of your subject. No man combines the qualities required for his biographer so completely as yourself, and the finished task would be a noble crown to a noble literary life." The suggestion came also from Whittier, who on April 30 expressed his earnest wish that Bryant would undertake the work as "no one living" was likely to execute it with more satisfaction to the public, and from George Bancroft, Salmon P. Chase, and Charles Sumner. Bryant, however, could not summon up enough confidence in himself to believe he could perform the task. Replying to Holmes, he said the proposal was persuasive, but added: "There are various reasons, however, some of which are personal to myself, and others inherent in the subject, which discourage me from undertaking the task of writing Mr. Lincoln's life. It is not only his life, but the life of the nation for four of the most important, critical, and interesting years of existence, that is to be written. Who that has taken part like myself in the controversies of the time can flatter himself that he shall execute the task worthily and impartially?"[1]

Although Bryant had praised Lincoln's conciliatory attitude toward the South, he himself was unlike the President in that he found it hard to be magnanimous. He was neither quick to forgive nor forget. He considered General Lee's farewell letter to his troops a "slap in the face to loyal soldiers" and declared that he retired "from the field, as unrepentant and as foolishly defiant as his master Davis." As for the president of the Confederacy, Bryant deplored the fact that Davis had allowed himself to be captured alive, "sneaking away like any ordinary criminal" in the disguise of a woman. Had he chosen to die, his "last act would have reflected upon him a color of heroism." But Bryant's anger was toward the leaders and not the people of the South. On April 21 he declared his agreement with President Andrew Johnson, who believed that treason was a crime and, like all other crimes, ought to be punished; for the people, however, the President felt "as every compassionate man must, the profoundest sympathy." Later in the year, on October 23, the *Evening Post* summarized Johnson's policy of reconstruction and endorsed it: universal suffrage, with former slaves who served in the war, those who could read and write, and those who were freeholders being admitted to the vote at once; ratification of a constitutional amendment forbidding slavery; legislation to secure equal rights for the colored people; repudiation of the debts of the Confederacy; punishment for the leaders of the rebellion; and delegation to the states the reconstruction of their own local governments subject to the supervision of the federal government.

As usual during the summer, Frances had left the city to seek the mountain air which did so much for her health, and Bryant joined her at

Great Barrington in July. It was upon this trip that he decided to purchase the family homestead at Cummington and remodel it as a summer place. The homestead had passed out of the family in 1835, being purchased and operated as a farm by Welcome Tillson.[2] On a brief visit to Newport, Bryant wrote his British friend Ferdinand E. Field of his plans: "I have repossessed myself of the old homestead and farm where my father and maternal grandfather lived, and have fitted it up and planted a screen of evergreens, from ten to twenty feet in height, back of it, to protect it from the northwest winds—though that is of little consequence in summer. . . . The region is high—nineteen hundred feet above the level of the sea; the summers are cool, the air Swiss-like, and the healthiness of the country remarkable. . . ."[3] He made arrangements for a local resident, a descendant of early Cummington settlers, T. H. Dawes, to manage the property. The addition to the farmhouse that Dr. Peter Bryant had equipped for his office had been detached and moved down the hillside to the bank of the Westfield River; Bryant arranged to have a new wing constructed as like his father's office as possible to be used as his library. Nothing now remained of the district schoolhouse he had attended, in which he had received his first public acclaim as a poet when he recited the verses composed in honor of the graduating class, except for a hollow that once was the cellar; but the little brook which he celebrated in "The Rivulet" still ran through the homestead, and the forest to the south which suggested "An Inscription for the Entrance to a Wood" still offered in its "calm shade" a retreat from the "guilt and misery" of the world. When Bryant returned to New York, he wrote his brothers in Illinois to bring their families for a reunion during the next summer at the old homestead.

In the debates over reconstruction of the South, the *Evening Post,* after Bryant's early editorials declaring that no mercy should be shown the leaders of the rebellion, generally supported President Johnson's lenient policies. Bryant gave his reconsidered views in a long editorial on January 9, 1866. He did not agree with the extremists—Thaddeus Stephens, who believed the rebels should be considered a hostile and foreign people and that the southern states should be treated as conquered provinces, or Charles Sumner, who believed that the states in seceding had destroyed themselves as entities. Instead, he sustained the President's opinion that since the secession was unconstitutional the states reverted to their status before the war and their laws and constitutions were still in effect. The question, therefore, was not one of dealing with states as states but with "bodies of individuals, who tried to subvert the government and failed." How these people should be dealt with depended upon their conduct, whether they persisted in their crime or whether they recanted.

But Bryant's chief concern was for the welfare of the former slaves. Their rights must be protected and they must be given suffrage as soon as they were capable of exercising it. He thus emphasized in his editorials and in his letters the necessity of continuing the work that he had labored so hard at during the war through the National Freedmen's Relief Association, succeeded now by a government agency, the Freedmen's Bureau. Bryant's attitude toward reconstruction was not entirely clear to some of his friends, and in a letter to Mrs. R. C. Waterston on March 3, he attempted to clarify it.[4] First, he said, he strongly favored Negro suffrage; the right should be conferred immediately upon the colored people in the District of Columbia and in the states as soon as they could be prepared for it. Until the Negroes were given the vote, they should not be counted in any state as a basis of representation in Congress. He objected to Sumner's plan to force Negro suffrage upon the whites of the South and to keep the states under the rule of the federal government until they agreed to it, believing this would only increase the South's hatred of the North and require a large standing army with turmoil and bloodshed likely to result.

II

Bryant's concern with the affairs of the nation were turned in the late spring of 1866 to a personal one, the serious illness of his wife. In May the newspapers carried reports about her condition, and these brought forth inquiries from friends. Writing to Dana on June 6, Bryant said that Frances was "alarmingly ill." According to her physician, the disorder was "an obstruction of the bile . . . with water on the heart." Breathing was so difficult for her that she had not been able to lie down during a period of more than a fortnight, but she nevertheless bore her suffering with "great patience" and her thoughts were "employed on the comfort and convenience" of others almost as much as when she was well.[5] A month later Bryant was able to report to Dana that her pain had lessened. "Nobody could have endured physical suffering with gentler resignation," Bryant wrote, "and now that the pain is past, if I could say that the danger also is over, that would be to me a day of rejoicing."[6] Frances's illness meant giving up the reunion at Cummington although John and Arthur Bryant had gathered there with their families. They, with Cullen, were the only surviving brothers, Cyrus having died in 1865 and Austin early in 1866.

Three weeks after reporting his wife's partial recovery to Dana, Bryant had the sad duty of announcing her death at eleven o'clock in the morning of July 27 to the brothers at Cummington.* Throughout Bryant's life he had contemplated death, arriving at a stoic acceptance of it as a part of nature and in accordance with his Christian beliefs hoping for a reunion with departed ones in the afterlife, but personal loss is not necessarily lessened by philosophy or religion. What his wife had meant to him Bryant expressed in letters to each of the brothers. "We have been married more than forty-five years, and all my plans, even to the least important, were laid with some reference to her judgment or her pleasure," Bryant wrote Arthur. "I always knew that it would be the greatest calamity of my life to lose her, but not till the blow came did I know how heavy it would be, and what a solitude the earth would seem without her." And to John he said: "Bitter as the separation is, I give thanks that she has been spared to me so long and that for nearly half a century I have had the benefit of her counsel and her example."⁷ Writing to Dana later in the year, Bryant said that he was like "one cast out of paradise and wandering in a strange world."

The letters of condolence that came to Bryant brought out the closeness that had existed between him and his wife. "Never, never," wrote the Rev. Dr. Waterston, "did a poet have a truer companion, a sincerer spiritual helpmate, than Mr. Bryant and his wife." Mrs. Waterston considered the union to be "a poem of tenderest rhythm." And the Rev. H. W. Bellows wrote: "All the world knew the beauty and strength of the tie that has just been broken, but none who had not the happiness of a personal acquaintance with the loveliness of that gentlest of her sex can appreciate the loneliness in which you are left."⁸ These might be considered just conventional expressions of sorrow except for the assurance that one gets from knowing of the lives of Bryant and Frances that they could only be true. The two had lived up to the vow made in the unusual prayer spoken when they became engaged at Great Barrington in 1820.

A month after his wife's death Bryant went to Cummington to look after matters there though, as he had written John after Frances's death, he now had little interest in the place or the remodeling which he had planned

---

*In writing Dana on June 6, Bryant expressed some irritation that his wife's illness was reported in the newspapers, where Dana first learned of it. The only report of her death to appear in the *Evening Post* was in a paid obituary notice under "Deaths" in the classified advertising section, marked for two insertions on July 28 and 29, which said: "Bryant—on the 27th instant, at Roslyn, Long Island. Frances Fairchild Bryant, wife of William Cullen Bryant, in her seventieth year."

primarily for her "comfort and convenience."* On his return to Roslyn, Bryant found no peace at Cedarmere and he was moved to write the poem, "October, 1866," in which he spoke of his and his wife's home:

> I gaze in sadness; it delights me not
> To look on beauty which thou canst not see;
> And, wert thou by my side, the dreariest spot
> Were, oh, how far more beautiful to me!

During this time Bryant had only Julia, who was prostrated by her mother's death, to share his sorrow, for the Godwins had gone abroad early in the winter and were away from home when Mrs. Bryant died. In November Bryant and Julia themselves departed from their desolated home on a trip to Europe that would last almost a year.

Bryant's sixth trip to Europe, however, was taken reluctantly. "I did not leave home for my own delectation, nor to get rid of the associations of the place," he wrote Catharine Sedgwick; "indeed, I felt some unwillingness to come away; but Julia, whose health is quite delicate, desired to come abroad, and her physician thought it might do her much good. So we came, taking the resolution rather suddenly."9 Bryant's letters to friends and his travel reports for the *Evening Post* reveal that on the whole he found the journey a dreary one, his thoughts constantly returning to Roslyn.10 The transatlantic voyage on the *Périere* was a quick one, taking only nine days. He and Julia, with a friend who accompanied her, landed at Brest, which Bryant found to be "a fine, picturesque, old Breton town," and went immediately to Paris, where they spent two weeks. Bryant might have been expected to stay longer in Paris, for the Parke Godwins were there, and so was John Bigelow, who early in the Civil War had been elevated from consul-general to United States minister to France; but the weather was rainy and chilly and Bryant was constantly reminded of former visits there with Frances. In consequence, father and daughter left for Amélie-les-Bains in the eastern Pyrenees as soon as they could get away, not even being persuaded to stay for a farewell banquet on December 21 for Bigelow, who had resigned his post and was returning to the United States.

At Amélie-les-Bains Bryant found a benign climate which he enjoyed

---

*The agreement on the management of the property between Bryant and T. H. Dawes and his wife Melissa was signed on this trip, on Sept. 17. They were to take care of the farm and "furnish the table" for Bryant and his guests. He was to pay them $500 semiannually. Goddard-Roslyn Collection.

and a wild picturesque landscape. "I climb the crags back of the house where I lodge," he wrote Catharine Sedgwick, "and the air is fragrant with lavender and rosemary, and other aromatic herbs."*[11] But after about three weeks at this spa, Bryant became impatient and left for Valencia with the idea of seeing places in Spain he had missed during his trip nine years before. From Valencia, Bryant went by train to Cordova and then to Seville, the occasion for a long article dated January 22 on the Spanish railway system, which was badly managed, and the Spanish practice of contriving their journeys so as to travel by night, which prevented any view of the countryside. Writing to a Roslyn friend, Mrs. L. M. S. Moulton, Bryant expressed his lack of interest in his journey: "I did not expect, in visiting Europe this time, to be so much interested by what should come under observation as I had been at previous times, and I must own that I never travelled with so little curiosity to see what is peculiar or admirable in foreign countries. Perhaps this may be in part the effect of age, but that is not all; I cannot keep the thought of Roslyn out of my mind; and the sadder its memories are, the more I cling to them. They are constantly diverting my attention from what is before my eyes."[12]

There was one sight near Seville, however, that was of more than passing interest, the ruins of the ancient Roman city of Italica on the hills above the Guadalquivir River. They were much as described by the seventeenth-century poet Francisco de Rioja in "The Ruins of Italica," which Bryant had translated during his earlier visit to Spain, a poem that expressed Bryant's own views on the changes wrought by time. Bryant did not find the prostrate columns and overturned statues described by Rioja, but the amphitheater, with its rows of crumbling seats and underground passages, was still in a fair state of preservation. In the center of the arena was a marble column on which had been carved lines from Rioja's poem, translated by Bryant as:

> This broken circus, where the rock-weeds climb,
> Flaunting with yellow blossoms, and defy
> The gods to whom its walls were reared so high,

*This was the last letter of Bryant to his old friend with whom he had carried on an extensive correspondence for more than half a century. She died the next year, on July 31, 1867. One of her nieces later wrote Bryant that for some weeks before her death she scribbled brief farewell notes on scraps of paper to her friends. One of the last said: "To all, my love; God bless you all! Bryant and Whittier you have [illegible] my life; but these I shall see no more on earth." Godwin, *Biography*, II, 255. Early in 1870 Bryant wrote a memoir of Catharine Sedgwick which appeared in the *Life and Letters*, published in 1871.

      Is now a tragic theatre where Time
        Acts his great fable, spreads a stage which shows
        Past grandeur's story and its dreary close.

Bryant left Seville by train for Madrid on January 23, "at midnight, according to the usual Spanish custom," but spent only a few days in the capital. There had been changes since his visit nine years before; the city was more populous for one thing and new and splendid public buildings had been erected, but the masses of the people lived in as abject poverty as before, the raggedest, Bryant wrote the *Evening Post,* of any he had ever seen.

From Madrid, Bryant went to Zaragoza, where he wrote his last letter from Spain for the *Evening Post* on January 29, and then continued on to Italy, going by way of the southern coast of France with stops at Nîmes, Hyères, Nice and then, in Italy, at Genoa, La Spezia, and Lucca on his way to Florence, which was reached on February 20. At the prompting of artist friends at Florence, Bryant wrote the *Evening Post* a letter on February 25 opposing a bill in Congress to put a duty on foreign works of art and sent the paper also a protest written by the sculptor Hiram Powers. At Florence Bryant met the revolutionary leader Giuseppe Garibaldi, on his way to Venice to celebrate the withdrawal of Austrian troops from the kingdom, the renewal of an acquaintance that had begun in New York when the fighter for the union of Italy had visited there for a time during one of his several exiles from Italy. Bryant was invited to accompany Garibaldi to Venice but refused, because he had already made arrangements to go to Rome.

With the departure of the Austrians from Venice, Italian unity was complete with the exception of Rome itself, ruled by the pope with forces largely recruited from France. Bryant expected no immediate troubles there, and his belief was evidently shared by a great many of his countrymen, for he reported in a letter to the *Evening Post* that the city had almost become a "Yankee city" with its more than two thousand American visitors. The chief result was that the prices of everything were high and lodgings were hard to get. Seeing Pope Pius IX after a ceremony at St. Peter's, "a short and rather stout man," Bryant had the feeling that the church's temporal power in Rome would end with the pope's death.

Leaving Rome toward the end of March, Bryant journeyed northward, stopping briefly at cities familiar to him on previous visits—Venice, Trieste, Vienna, Salzburg, Munich, Nuremberg, Dresden, Heidelberg, Baden-Baden, and Strasbourg, before returning to Paris the first week in May. But pleasant though these places were, for he had happy memories of most of them, he found little pleasure in them now. "Wherever I go," he wrote Christiana Gibson from Paris, "I cannot help thinking of a place several thousand miles off, now more than ever dear to me, and at the same time saying to myself, 'How glad I shall be when I get back to it again!' "13

In Paris on June 1 Bryant met for the first time the fiery Abolitionist William Lloyd Garrison, who more than thirty years before he had said in the *Evening Post* was "as mad as the winds on the slavery question." The two men had been appointed by the American Freedman's Union Commission, headed by Salmon P. Chase, as delegates to an international antislavery conference. Bryant left no record of the meeting, but Garrison's biographers reported that the two old warriors for freedom "spent a very agreeable evening."14

From Paris Bryant crossed over to London but spent only a short time there, preferring to pass the midsummer in the north. He made a leisurely trip through the Lake Country on his way to Scotland to visit his friend and frequent correspondent, Christiana Gibson and her sister Janet, in Edinburgh. But Bryant was not fond of cities, and despite the hospitality of his friends, chose to go on an excursion to the highlands. So delighted was he with the little town of Crieff in Perthshire that he spent three weeks there, writing a long description of the place for the *Evening Post* on July 8. Later in the month, with Christiana Gibson a member of the party, the Bryants made a tour of Wales.15 Bryant completed his tour of the British Isles with a visit to the Alfred Fields at Leamington and sailed on August 24 from Liverpool, reaching New York on September 5. At Roslyn more than a month after his return he was as forlorn as when he had left almost a year before. "I find the place very beautiful," he wrote the daughter of his friend the Rev. Dr. Dewey on October 14; "the changes please me, but there is sadness in all this beauty, since the eye for which these changes were originally designed can look on them no more. It is now a most beautiful October day; the maples at the end of our little lakelet, are glowing with the hues of autumn, and over all lies the sweetest golden sunshine. I look out upon the landscape from the baywindow while I write, but in a different mood from that in which I should have beheld it formerly."16

III

For two years after Bryant returned from Europe he worked on a translation of the *Iliad* at which he had toyed intermittently since resuming his interest in Greek literature in 1865. His letters to friends often mention the progress he was making, and he published in the magazines several books of Homer's epic as he completed them. The purchase of the family homestead at Cummington had turned his thoughts to his boyhood and young manhood, and he devoted a great deal of time to improving the place, planting an orchard of apple, pear, cherry, and plum trees and a dozen varieties of berries. As a young man preparing to go into the law, he had dreaded the thought of speaking in public, but over the years he had been able to conquer his diffidence, and increasingly he accepted invitations to speak. As editor of the *Evening Post* he had usually considered politics a dreary business, and he could not now become worked up over issues, the impeachment and trial of President Johnson and the presidential election of 1868. In public matters one of his chief concerns was that the government follow what he considered sound principles of economics and he continued to speak and write in favor of free trade. Willing to turn over the day-to-day management of the paper to other hands, he only infrequently wrote the editorial leader.

The paper had continued to be a successful enterprise and advertising still restricted the space for news, editorials, and literary matter since it remained in its blanket-sheet size of ten columns of only four pages. For a time a problem was created when Parke Godwin decided to get out of the business and sold his interest to the two other partners for $200,000 early in 1868. The major part of his share was bought by Henderson, whose holdings now amounted to fifty per cent of the firm. Henderson made several overtures to John Bigelow to get him to return to the *Evening Post*, but Bigelow was being sought by the owners of the *Times*, because of the death of Henry J. Raymond on June 8, 1869, to become its editor and part owner and accepted this offer instead, taking over the paper in August.[17]

Because Godwin did not get along with Henderson, his departure probably caused Bryant no great pain, since he disliked the squabbles that arose between the two men. In any case, the *Evening Post* had got along very well while both Godwin and Bryant were in Europe under Charles Nordhoff, and in Charlton T. Lewis Bryant had found an editorial writer with the scholarly background and the broad interest in public affairs that made him an ideal choice for the position. Then thirty-four years old, Lewis had been a lawyer, a Methodist minister, a professor of languages, and deputy commissioner of internal revenue in New York. George Cary Eggleston, later literary editor, wrote of him: "Mr. Lewis was one of the ripest scholars and most diligent students I have ever known, but he was also a man of broad human sympathies, intensely interested in public affairs and in all else that involved human progress."[18] Another co-worker, J. Ranken Towse, drama editor, recalled that he wrote with "fluency, cogency, and eloquence."[19]

Before going abroad in the fall of 1866, Bryant had completed his translation of the first book of the *Iliad,* which the *Atlantic Monthly* printed in December under the title "The Contention Between Achilles and Agamemnon." He had been back in the United States only a few weeks when he heard from James T. Fields beseeching him for new contributions in a letter that ended with the postscript: "I don't care how many poems you send me, the more the better."[20] With the translating Bryant had done while abroad, he had by now worked his way through book five of the *Iliad* and sent this to Fields. It appeared in the January, 1868, number as "The Combat of Diomed and Mars." But as the year 1867 drew to a close, Bryant was still loath to bestir himself. Writing Dana on November 30, he revealed that he spent his time principally at Roslyn, seldom going into the city more than once a week. "I am in the main cheerful," he wrote, "but with some sad hours, and life to me has lost much of its flavor. I piddle a little with Homer, whose poem, I must confess, does not seem to me the perfect work that critics have made it, notwithstanding its many undeniable beauties."[21]

Though Bryant thought that Chase would be the best Republican candidate for President, he had no objection to General Grant. Writing Christiana Gibson on Christmas Day, 1867, he said: "As to politics, Grant seems fixed upon by the people for our next president, whether we like it or not. Perhaps it is best so. Grant has many sterling qualities, among which his friends claim an insight into men's characters, and great sagacity in the choice of subordinates."[22] On February 7, 1868, the *Evening Post* replied to Democratic criticisms of Grant's character. He was not, to be sure, of "ready and dazzling" intellectual powers and he had not "cultivated the arts of forensic reasoning or eloquence," but his absence of pretense and his "frank and manly mode of stating his opinions" redounded to his credit. In the controversy over the impeachment of President Johnson, Bryant chose, as he explained in an editorial on February 27, to take no part "in this unhappy quarrel, further than to counsel moderation, calmness, justice, and freedom from prejudice." Because of Bryant's long support of Grant in his military campaigns, the *Evening Post*'s endorsement of his nomination for President was expected and he received it when he was named the standard-bearer in May.

Late in January Bryant went into New York from Roslyn to attend a dinner honoring the merchant Jonathan Sturges on his retirement, giving the response to a toast on literature, the fine arts, and commerce. He himself was saluted by the American Free Trade League three days later on his retirement as president of the organization which he had helped found. Responding to a toast given by the new president, David Dudley Field, Bryant explained his interest in free trade. What he had done, he said, was merely to apply "the principles of human liberty to the exchange of property between man and man and between nation and nation." Before leaving for his summer visit to Cummington in June, Bryant presided at a meeting to establish a National Institute of Letters, Arts, and Sciences. Of the importance of such an association and its purpose, Bryant found an illustrative example in nature. "It might have been learned from the rivulets and springs of the earth, which uniting their little tributaries are gathered into mighty rivers, bearing navies and forming the great highways of commerce between realm and realm," he said. The year closed with Bryant being asked to speak, on December 28, at a dinner honoring the inventer of the telegraph, Samuel F. B. Morse.[23]

Bryant's chief preoccupation, however, was the translation of Homer, to which he now devoted his mornings. As he wrote in his introduction to the *Iliad,* when it appeared early in 1870, he worked at the task because it helped in some measure to divert his mind from the death of his wife. It was also less demanding than any original writing would be. "I find it a pastime," he wrote a friend, Professor Joseph Alden of Lafayette College,* who wanted from him more of his own poetry. "At my time of life it is somewhat dangerous to tax the brain to any great extent. Whatever requires invention, whatever compels one to search both for new thoughts and adequate expression wherewith to clothe them makes a severe demand on the intellect and the nervous system—at least I have found it so. In translating poetry—at least in translating with such freedom as blank verse allows—my only trouble is with the expression; the thoughts are already at hand."[24]

But there were times when Bryant felt that he could not go on with the *Iliad.* As a boy, when first reading Homer in Pope's translation, Bryant

---

*In 1876 Alden edited a small collection of Bryant's poems, *Studies in Bryant,* for use in the schools. In a short introduction, Bryant said: "In judging poetry the main office of criticism is to discover beauties, for it is these only which reward the search. In the process adopted by the author of this work, the reader is made to see how, in a poem, one thought grows out of another, how kindred images shine by each other's light, how a single word sometimes sets a whole picture before the imagination, and how the fancy may tinge with prismatic hues a thought, which in the utterance of any but one poetically endowed, would attract no admiration. . . ."

had been excited by the epic and reenacted with his brothers some of the battles. But now he disliked the character of some of the Greek heroes, his sympathies lying rather with the Trojans, and he disapproved of the pettiness of the gods in their interference with human affairs. Nearing the end of the sixth book, Bryant wrote his brother John that Dana had regretted that he had not chosen the *Odyssey* to translate. "I wish I had thought of this before, for I think he is pretty much in the right; but I have already proceeded so far in the *Iliad* that I cannot think of undertaking another labor," he said. "I believe that the gods behave more shamefully in the *Iliad* than in the other poem, and their conduct is so detestable that I am sometimes half tempted to give up them and Homer together."[25]

One of Bryant's purposes in writing to John was to invite him to Cummington for the summer, but before going there late in June he devoted himself to completing a translation from the Spanish for the *New York Ledger* of a tale, "Jarilla," by his friend Caroline Coronado Perry of Madrid. "When the tale is done I must go to Homer again," Bryant wrote John on June 2. "I am now arrived at the time of life when there is small chance of completing a literary work of any great length, and must make use of my faculties while I have them."[26]

IV

In Bryant's first summer visits to Cummington after his return from Europe, he had begun a routine which he was to follow for a decade. An account of his way of life is given in the recollections of Mrs. Mary Dawes Warner, the daughter of the couple managing the farm.[27] For a man with simple tastes, he arrived with something of an entourage, traveling with four household servants and a coachman, their carriage drawn by a span of horses, one black and one white—"quite the fashion at the time." The servants included a cook, laundress, and two maids.

The Dawes family would be awakened early in the morning by a series of thumps coming from Bryant's room. "Mr. Bryant was taking his 'daily dozen,' which consisted of a vaulting pole, dumbbells, and other parts of a gymnasium outfit which he brought with him from New York," Mrs. Warner recalled. "The thumps, which shook the house, were caused by the use of the vaulting pole, he jumping back and forth over his bed with it." Bryant's light breakfast was at seven, usually fruits or berries from the farm, after which he walked around the homestead, consulting with Dawes about any repairs that were needed or horticultural problems that arose. On these tours he disdained to open gates, putting his hands on the top and vaulting over them instead. At nine o'clock he went to his study, where he worked on his translations, wrote letters, or engaged in other literary activity. He ended his work at noon, and after a light lunch would take long walks about the countryside with one or the other of his brothers, who were usually there for the summer, or other visitors. After Bryant's tramp, often of ten or fifteen miles, he returned to the house between five and six o'clock, had supper at seven, and by nine was in bed.

Bryant returned to New York earlier than usual from Cummington in the summer of 1868, feeling, as he had always felt in the past, that he should be on hand for the final months of the presidential campaign, though he had no doubts about the election of Grant. But he was less inclined than ever to interest himself in new matters, writing Dana on December 12 of the deaths among his old friends. He perhaps had in mind Fitz-Greene Halleck, who had died on November 19, 1867; Bryant was one of Halleck's literary associates who honored his memory by erecting a monument to him in 1868 in his native town of Guilford, Connecticut. "New friends acquired in old age," Bryant wrote Dana, "can never be like the old ones, nor is it easy to form new friendships as we are about to step into the other world. There is always a certain distance between the old and the young which makes itself felt."[28]

The friends and admirers of Halleck prevailed upon Bryant to deliver a discourse in his memory, which he did before the New-York Historical Society on February 2, 1869. It was more of a personal memoir than a commentary on his life and works like the discourses which Bryant had given at the memorials for Cooper and Irving. Bryant recalled that on first meeting Halleck in 1825 he was struck "with the brightness of his eye, which every now and then glittered with mirth, and with the graceful courtesy of his manners." Later Halleck contributed poems to the magazines which Bryant edited and to *The Talisman*, and there were memories also of rambles with him about the countryside and of meeting him at literary gatherings.

The occasions when Bryant was asked to speak at public gatherings now came with increasing frequency. On January 8 he was elected chairman of a meeting at Cooper Union called to enlist support for the revolution of the Cretans against the Turks. He followed this on February 8 with an address to patrons of the Newsboys' Lodging-House, a project which the *Evening Post* had aided, and on February 23 he spoke to a very different group, a dinner of Harvard alumni. These were minor talks given for the occasion. He made a major address on May 10 at a mass meeting at Cooper Union called by the American Free Trade League to seek revenue reform. In late June, while on his summer visit to Cummington, he attended the Williams College commencement and was honored, though not a graduate, by being elected president of the alumni association. He ended the year of public speech-making by presiding at a gathering on November 24 called to organize a campaign to establish the Metropolitan Museum of Art. [29] In his travels, Bryant said, he had seen collections on the market that could have been bought at a low cost and brought to America if there had been a museum to house them. But more than a museum for display of pictures of the Old World, Bryant was interested in one that would support the development of New World art. Young American painters had to go abroad to learn their craft and to get their inspiration. For its student painters, then, the United States needed a museum at home "which shall vie with those abroad, if not in the multitude, yet in the merit, of the works it contains."

V

In the meantime, Bryant had made steady progress, at his rate of about forty lines a day, in his translation of the *Iliad.* On February 10, in a letter to John, he revealed that he had completed twelve books and had about seven thousand lines to do before his task would be over. His translation would be shorter than Pope's, for using blank verse there was no occasion for padding lines as Pope was sometimes forced to do.[30] His "The Flight of Diomed," from the eighth book, had been printed in the January number of *Galaxy,* and this, with the appearance of other books in the magazines, had created interest in his translation, and in the spring newspapers carried the announcement that it would be printed by the firm of Fields & Osgood of Boston. Bryant had overcome his earlier objections to the work and, writing Dana on April 8, said that he now approached his daily task with a good deal of pleasure.[31] While busy with his Homer, Bryant also found the time to compile from the *Evening Post* his letters written on his trip to Egypt, the Holy Land, Turkey, and Greece in 1852, and they were published in the fall by Putnam's. In December Bryant wrote an introduction for his translation of Homer and sent to his publisher the first twelve books of the epic. They formed the first volume of his work published in February of 1870, but Bryant had now gained so much facility in translation that he was able to complete the second twelve books in time for publication of the second volume in June.

Although Bryant's translation of the *Iliad* can be criticized on many counts, its popularity in his own time and later attests to his success in achieving his purpose in an English rendering. He stated his aim to a

Stockbridge friend, John H. Gourlie: "I intended, if I had the power, to make a translation which it would not be a labor to read. I did not make it for those who are familiar with the original, for they have no occasion for it, being already in possession of something better; but I intended it for the sake of English readers, and, if I had not thought that I could give them a more satisfactory version than any of the previous ones, I never would have engaged in it."[32] Since he wanted to reach a broad reading public, he was somewhat sorry that Fields & Osgood had printed it in an expensive edition. "Democrat as I am, I would, if the matter had been left to my discretion, have published it in as cheap a form as is consistent with neatness, and a good, fair, legible type," he wrote the Rev. Dr. Dewey.[33]

In desiring to appeal to a numerous readership, Bryant felt that he was conforming to the spirit of the original. "I have endeavored to preserve the simplicity of style which distinguished the old Greek poet, who wrote for the popular ear and according to the genius of his language, and I have chosen such English as offers no violence to the ordinary usage and structure of our own," Bryant said in his introduction. This purpose was his justification of a blank-verse translation rather than a rhymed one or one employing Greek hexameters. Rhyme would have resulted in artificialities and infidelities to the original, and the hexameter line was not a natural one in the English language. "I therefore fell back upon blank verse," he said, "which has been the vehicle of some of the noblest poetry in our language; both because it seemed to me by the flexibility of its construction best suited to a narrative poem, and because, while it enabled me to give the sense of my author more perfectly than any other form of verse, it allowed me also to avoid in a greater degree the appearance of constraint which is too apt to belong to a translation." It was for a similar reason that Bryant employed the Latin names of the gods—Jupiter rather than Zeus, Juno rather than Hera, and Venus rather than Aphrodite. They were the ones most familiar in English and had, as it were, been naturalized in the language.

In attempting to put the *Iliad* into natural English, Bryant did not, however, take liberties with the sense of the original. Familiar not only with other English translations but also with German, Spanish, and Italian ones, he consulted these for their interpretation of disputed passages. In reading the proofs, Bryant discovered that he had omitted by oversight a number of lines. Though, as he wrote his publisher, these would not be noted by casual readers or destroy the meaning, they made the translation less faithful than he thought it ought to be; he therefore subjected his work to a careful revision, making a line-by-line comparison with the original.[34]

Bryant's translation brought him many letters, not only from friends delighted with the work, but also from strangers. Among the letters of goodwill, Bryant probably was as pleased as any with those from William Gilmore Simms. Their long friendship had been distrupted by differences over the Civil War, but now they were reconciled with, as Simms put it, an *entente cordiale* being established. Bryant had heard from Simms in 1865, when Simms on a visit to New York wrote asking him for copies of his books, his own autographed ones having been lost when his plantation house Woodlands was burned by stragglers from Sherman's army. "At our advanced periods of life," Simms wrote Bryant now, "we cannot well obliterate the associations of near forty years, nor is it the policy of age or wisdom to do so. Nothing which has occurred, or which may occur, can ever make me forget, that 'such things were and were most precious to me.'" Receiving a signed copy of the Homer, Simms wrote praising its simplicity and directness. "Above all," he said, "I rejoice, though I did not doubt, that you would choose the good, stout, manly English heroic blank verse as your medium of translation. *That* is the great verse of our language. . . ."[35]

Rather than resting after the publication of the *Iliad,* Bryant undertook a new literary project, assisting with the selection of material for an anthology, *The Library of Poetry and Song.* He was asked by the publisher, J. B. Ford & Company, to write an introduction, but he insisted on having a free hand in excluding and adding poems according to his own judgment. This was not the first project of the sort for Bryant, since in 1840 he had compiled an anthology, *Selections from the American Poets,* for the Family Library published by Harpers. One of the principles he applied in this volume he felt should be applied also in the new compilation. He did not think that "amatory poems and drinking songs," whatever the skill or the spirit of their writing, belonged in a work to be placed in a school or family library, where they would be read by young persons.[36] The huge collection was arranged topically, with such headings as Childhood and Youth, the Affections, Sorrow and Adversity, Religion, and Nature. It contained a great deal of trash but also a great deal of major poetry, since the whole of English and American literature was surveyed. Bryant's letters to the publisher contained little comment on his reasons for rejecting certain poems. One frequently given was poor versification. He objected to a poem by Mrs. Browning as being "one of her crudest, in expression and versification," and to the "bad rhymes" in another. He suggested that more of the poems of Jones Very be included as they were "quite remarkable" and proposed the addition of several by Richard Henry Dana, whose work had been overlooked by the original compilers.[37]

Bryant in his introduction, "Poets and Poetry of the English Language," set forth his belief that the proper office of poetry was to fill the mind with "delightful images" and to awaken the emotions. In consequence he objected to long poems and therefore condemned some of the greatest poems of the language for their length, the pleasure they gave being in no degree proportionate to their plan. Chaucer, for example, even in *The Canterbury Tales*, was prolix, the descriptions being excessively detailed, and the personages, though they talked well, talked too much. He found in Spenser's *Faerie Queene* the English language used with a perfection perhaps never surpassed, but the poem, going on and on and on, was tiresome to read. In Shakespeare was to be found "every conceivable kind of poetic excellence," but the metaphysical poets that followed the Elizabethan age Bryant disliked, their effort being chiefly to startle by ingenious conceits and wit "in rugged diction, and in numbers so harsh as to be almost unmanageable by the reader." Bryant disliked too much "luxuriance of poetic imagery," in the poems of Keats, for example, and extreme subtleties of thought "remote from the common apprehension." "To me," he wrote, "it seems that one of the most important requisites for a great poet is a luminous style. The elements of poetry lie in natural objects, in the vicissitudes of human life, in the emotions of the human heart, and in the relations of man to man. . . ."

Bryant's work on *The Library of Poetry and Song*, however, was not a project that could hold him long, and by July 1, 1870, he was writing John that he was immersed in a translation of the *Odyssey*, though he did not plan to be as diligent at the task as he had been with his translation of the *Iliad* and though he had only a few years remaining to finish it. "But it will give me an occupation which will not be an irksome one," he said, "and will furnish me with a reason for declining other literary tasks, and a hundred engagements which I want some excuse besides old age for declining."[38] He did not, however, pursue the task in such a desultory way as he had started it. By April of the next year he had completed the first twelve books. Announcing this to James T. Fields, who had exhorted him to get on with the work, Bryant wrote on April 25: "I have been as industrious as was reasonable. I understand very well that, at my time of life, such enterprises are apt to be brought to a conclusion before they are finished, and I have therefore wrought harder upon my task than some of my friends thought was well for me. . . . I do not think the *Odyssey* the better part of Homer, except morally. The gods set a better example, and take more care to see that wrong and injustice are discouraged among mankind. But there is not the same spirit and fire, nor the same vividness of

489

description. . . . Let me correct what I have already said by adding that there is yet in the *Odyssey* one more advantage over the *Iliad*. It is better as a story. In the *Iliad* the plot is, to me, unsatisfactory; and there is, besides, a monotony of carnage—you get a surfeit of slaughter."[39] While the first volume was in press, Bryant wrote Dana, on June 19, that he was well into the second half of the epic. "I do not feel quite so easy in this work as I did in translating the *Iliad*," he said, "for the thought that I am so old that I may be interrupted in my task before it is done rises in my mind now and then. . . ."[40] So assiduously did Bryant apply himself, however, that he was able, on December 7, to send the twenty-fourth book to his publisher. In six years, though still watching over the *Evening Post* and contributing to it and speaking frequently in public, Bryant had completed, and completed well, a tremendous work of translation. With time's wingèd chariot hurrying near, he had forced himself; yet, as he wrote in the introduction to his *Odyssey,* he considered his work only the "gentler exercise of the intellectual faculties," something more suited to his old age than original composition.

28

THE YEARS OF BUSY FAME

COMPARED WITH OTHER NEW YORK NEWSPAPERS, THE *Evening Post* in the first years after the Civil War operated with a small staff, Bryant or Parke Godwin and, after 1868 when Godwin left the paper, Charlton T. Lewis, writing the editorials and Charles Nordhoff directing the news department. As it entered the 1870's, however, the growing volume of news it had to print to maintain a competitive position with other dailies forced it to expand its staff. A paper could no longer fill its columns with reprints of articles from the exchanges, nor could it rely upon contributors for literary or political articles, although John Bigelow and Samuel J. Tilden continued to write for it. One of the first newcomers to the staff after Godwin sold his interest, to become shortly afterward editor of *Putnam's Magazine*, was J. Ranken Towse. He recalled that in 1870 when he joined the paper even the volume of telegraphic news was small and the transatlantic cable, which had been completed in 1865, was an expensive luxury and used as sparingly as possible.[1]

Towse and William Alexander Linn, who joined the paper in 1871, recalled that the offices at Nassau and Liberty Streets were in an "old and rickety building" and the editors were cramped for space to work in. "Mr. Bryant had a little room, from which he could escape unwelcome callers by means of a rear staircase," Linn recalled. "There were only three other editorial rooms, but, on the other hand, there were not many editors."[2]

To maintain the *Evening Post's* reputation as a newspaper for cultivated readers, Bryant employed as literary editor the poet and former editor of the *Southern Literary Messenger,* John R. Thompson, who joined the paper in 1868; and a music, drama, and art critic, William F. Williams. Other editors were an assistant managing editor, a city editor, a telegraph editor, and a financial editor. But the reporting staff was small, only one salaried man and one space man paid according to the amount of copy turned in. The paper had its own correspondents in Washington and Albany, but relied chiefly on the Associated Press for out-of-town news.

Bryant had never tempered his editorial views to the financial interests of the paper, but in the 1870's he was away from the office a great deal and, with Isaac Henderson owning half the stock, the business office was able to exert pressure on the news staff. For years Nordhoff had quarreled with Henderson over his interference and resigned in 1871 when he was requested to soften his hard-hitting attacks against the Tammany boodlers of William M. Tweed.* The *Evening Post* did not stop its editorial attacks on the Tweed ring, but these were less vigorous than they might have been under Nordhoff. Nordhoff's friends believed that his attacks on Tweed caused him to be fired, and in 1876 one of them blamed Bryant, or was so quoted, in an article in the *Press* of Portland, Maine. According to the story, Nordhoff was summoned by Bryant and "sternly rebuked for printing an article which was calculated to injure the business of the paper." The *Evening Post* carried Nordhoff's denial of the calumny on April 21, 1876. The article, Nordhoff said, had been submitted to Bryant before being printed and was approved by him.

One of the leaders in the fight against Tweed was Tilden, who called on Bryant in 1870, outwardly "moved from his usual calm and quiet demeanor," Bryant related. Tilden explained that his errand was to make sure that Bryant understood a new city charter which "Tweed and his creatures" were interested in getting adopted would make it easy for the ring to steal from the city. "The *Evening Post,*" Bryant said, "did not require Mr. Tilden's exhortations to oppose the bill, but we proceeded, by the help of the additional light given us, to hold up the charter to the severest censure."[3]

Accounting office pressure was also exerted by William G. Boggs, now

---

*Nordhoff left the *Evening Post* in April of 1871, taking a leave of absence which turned out to be a permanent separation from the paper. During the summer he wrote for it about a dozen travel letters about a trip to the west coast. After two years of travel, he returned to New York, becoming Washington correspondent of the New York *Herald* in 1874, a position he held until 1890.

the advertising manager, who had a wide acquaintance with businessmen and politicians. "He was the most familiar representative of the publication in the editorial rooms," Towse said, "and manifested a special interest in the suppression of any paragraph, or allusion, that might offend the dispensers of political advertising, which in those days was an important source of revenue."[4]

When Henderson was arrested and tried for extorting bribes from navy suppliers during the Civil War, Parke Godwin had attempted to put Bryant on guard against his partner. He made another attempt in February of 1870 when he had second thoughts about the sale of his interest in the paper and decided he had been cheated. He prepared a statement of the case for Bryant. Receiving no reply, he wrote Bryant on February 9 saying that he had no "desire to escape the consequences of a bargain once made, however foolishly made" and "wished merely to get at the truth." "I regard Mr. Henderson as a far-seeing and adroit rogue," he continued; "his design from the beginning has been and still is to get exclusive possession of the *Evening Post,* at much less than its real value, which I expected to prove was more nearly a million than a half million dollars. Mr. Henderson, as well as any man in the city, would not at this time take $450,000 for his half interest." Godwin regretfully concluded that though his protest had been made more in Bryant's interest and that of his children than in his own he would not take up the subject again.[5] Bryant replied on the same day that he had not taken up the matter with Henderson, believing that the statement was intended for himself only and that Godwin intended sending it to Henderson later. Bryant promised to consult with Henderson and ended his letter: "I do not want to defraud you in the purchase and I am perfectly willing to make any amends so far as I am conscious for any advantage that I may have inequitably gained."[6] From this, it is apparent Bryant was not persuaded by Godwin's charges, and he continued to have confidence in his old associate, who was a personal friend as well and who, with his wife, had been a prop during the last illness of Frances.

Godwin's worry about what was going on at the *Evening Post* was shared by Tilden, who wrote him on September 14, 1871, suggesting that he propose to Bryant returning to the editorship during the prosecution of the case against Tweed. Tilden said that with the inexperience of the present writers for the paper, the influence brought to bear on them by the business office, and the absence of "the firm will and clear intelligence of Mr. Bryant as a counterpoint," the paper was drifting badly. "Now it would be indeed lamentable," he continued, "if that renown acquired by

493

forty years of uprightness, honor, and courage and sacrifice of interest should be surrendered by Mr. Boggs and Mr. Henderson."[7]

II

Bryant's fame was now so great that he suffered from the demands on his time from the public. At the *Evening Post* there were frequent visitors and, disliking to rebuff them, he sometimes, according to Towse, fled from them by the back exit from his office. He often requested Towse to deal with the callers, and Towse, in addition to his duties as city editor, became "a sort of amateur Cerberus."[8] Bryant wrote Dana of the people seeking his attention:

> They keep me writing letters at too much expense of time. Now it is an autograph that they want, then my opinion of a poem which they have written and they send me a manuscript; at one time I am asked to write an ode for an anniversary, at another time a letter in favor of somebody who wants an office. Then I must answer somebody who wants to be a correspondent of the *Evening Post* or a place on its editorial staff, and again I must write to decline an invitation to attend a public meeting and make a speech, or a public dinner, and next I am asked what is the meaning of some verse which I have been so unfortunate as to write. I dare say others are pestered like me with these little annoyances. They are like musquitoes in your room at night; they break your quiet whether they bite you or not.[9]

Bryant's speeches while working on his translations of Homer were frequent—before reunions of Williams College alumni, before meetings of the Free Trade Association, pushing its program of revenue reform, before an anniversary celebration of the Mercantile Library, before an Italian society celebrating the unification of Italy, and before a group observing the anniversary of Robert Burns.

On two occasions Bryant addressed audiences gathered to honor two of his oldest New York friends, Gulian C. Verplanck and Samuel F. B. Morse. Verplanck had died on March 18, 1870, at the age of eighty-four, and he and Bryant, in recent years, had no longer been the companions of former times due in part to differences over the Civil War. Verplanck had refused to be drawn into the Republican party and had been accused of having Copperhead sympathies, being retired in 1864 as president of the Century Club. The same coolness existed between Bryant and Morse, who had been a leader in the Copperhead movement. Bryant was reluctant to speak at the memorial service for Verplanck held by the New-York Historical Society on May 17, 1870, and at the unveiling of a statue of

Morse as the inventor of the telegraph on June 9, 1871, in Central Park. But writing the Rev. Dr. Dewey about the request that he speak on Verplanck, Bryant said that as "he was an old, and at one time a very intimate friend" he could not excuse himself,[10] and to Dana about the Morse affair he said that he found it impossible to refuse on the ground it might be thought he was unwilling "to say a good word for an old friend."[11]

Partly to get away from the demands on his time but primarily because the completion of the *Odyssey* translation left him at loose ends, Bryant sailed January 25, 1872, on a trip to Nassau, Cuba, and Mexico. He was driven to it, he later wrote Dana, because he was "uneasy when unemployed."[12] Accompanying Bryant on this journey were Julia and a cousin of hers, Anna Fairchild, his brother John, and the companion of his trip to the Holy Land, John Durand. On the day that the party sailed on the *Morro Castle* for the Bahamas, the *Evening Post* carried an announcement that Parke Godwin would join the editorial staff during Bryant's absence. This notice apparently aroused some speculative talk in the city, for the next day the paper explained that this did not mean a change in the regular staff and that Godwin would serve only as "an adjunct and advisory editor."

The party arrived at Nassau on January 30 after one of the worst sea voyages ever experienced by Bryant. In his report to the *Evening Post,* dated February 5, he described, as was his custom, the people and their way of life and the island's scenery.[13] He was struck by the brilliant blue of the sea, brighter even than that of the Mediterranean, glowing as from an "indwelling beam." After a fortnight at Nassau, the party sailed to Havana, which Bryant found "a third larger and twice as bustling" as when he had visited the city twenty years before. The *Evening Post* reported on March 1 that Bryant at a dinner attended by important members of the government had been asked to convey to the United States the desire of Cuba and Spain for a reciprocal trade treaty. Godwin in a long editorial urged the treaty upon President Grant. The next day the paper reported that the proposal made through Bryant had been formally presented to the Department of State by the Spanish minister.

Leaving Julia and her cousin at Havana, Bryant with his brother and Durand sailed on the British steamer *Corsica* for Vera Cruz, a three-day "holiday" compared with the voyage to Nassau, the "airs the softest that ever blew, the sea like a looking-glass." Bryant was welcomed at Vera Cruz like a state visitor by the minister of finance, Matías Romero, whom he had met in New York when Romero was the Mexican minister to the

United States. Spending only a day at Vera Cruz, for an epidemic of yellow fever raged in the city, Bryant and his party left for Mexico City, the first seventy miles traversed by train to Forten, where the journey was resumed by stagecoach. At Orziba Bryant debated with his companions whether, because of bandits attacking travelers, they should continue on to the capital, but they decided to take the risk.

From Mexico City, which Bryant reached on March 1, he wrote six long letters to the *Evening Post.* He described the capital, where direst poverty existed alongside splendor and luxury; the impressive sights such as Chapultepec and the Floating Gardens; the government archives, where he was interested in documents and reports dealing with the war between Mexico and the United States; and his visits to schools, churches, and cemeteries. On March 9 Bryant was made an honorary member of the Mexican Geographical and Statistical Society at a reception attended by members of the ministry of Benito Pablo Juárez, by the justices of the supreme court, by representatives of the consulates and embassies of other countries, and by artists, and literary men. The newspaper *El Correo del Comercio* in reporting the affair mentioned Bryant's "clear, sonorous, and magnificent Castilian," but as a matter of fact he talked only briefly in Spanish to apologize for being unable to speak the language with ease and gave his response in English.[14]

Bryant spent the day of March 10 at the cemeteries, the American one where there was a monument to soldiers who had died in the Mexican War, "a war in which I take no pride," he wrote in a letter to the *Evening Post,* and the San Fernando cemetery, where he attended the funeral of a general killed in the current revolution. The next day Bryant visited President Juárez at his office in the palace. Juárez, "a man of low stature and dark complexion, evidently of the Aztec race, square built and sturdy in figure," received him courteously. They talked of the revolution, which Juárez believed was about over, and of the state of the country, which Juárez thought would be peaceful for a year or two, when there would be "another *pronunciamiento* and another revolt, and fresh robberies on the highways."

When Bryant left Mexico City on March 13, the English-language paper *Two Republics* remarked that "no foreigner ever was the subject . . . of a warmer, a more sincere and elegant reception" in the capital. For Bryant's return trip to Vera Cruz he was supplied, as a distinguished and respected visitor, with a military escort as protection against bandits. Returning to Havana to pick up Julia and her cousin, Bryant was back in New York early in April, ready, as he had always been, for the quadrennial turmoil which the country went through in a presidential election year.

III

Respectful of Grant as a military leader and as a man of character but dubious of his ability to serve as president, Bryant very soon after the election of 1868 had seen that under his administration the ideals that had gone into the founding of the Republican party were being lost. *Evening Post* editorials attacked the retention of the protective wartime tariff, the abuses of the civil service, the unconstitutional decrees governing reconstruction, the lenience toward monopolies, and the yielding of vast public land tracts to corporations. As the paper had time and again before been read out of the Democratic party because it condemned the national administration, it was now assailed as being no longer Republican. Bryant had used the Free Trade Association as a vehicle for political reform, addressing its New York meetings and writing pamphlets for distribution under its imprint. The association was the nucleus about which the Liberal Republican movement that came into being in 1872 had been formed in the East. Bryant looked with sympathy on its convention assembled at Cincinnati on May 1 by such disparate reformers as Carl Schurz, the St. Louis editor, with the young Joseph Pulitzer, of the *Westliche Post;* Charles Francis Adams, the epitome of New England rectitude; E. L. Godkin, the transplanted British intellectual of *The Nation* magazine; Gideon Welles, the former secretary of the navy; and Lyman Trumbull, the senator from Illinois. But there were others than these leaders present, as the young Louisville editor Henry Watterson, noted, "emissaries from New York— mostly friends of Horace Greeley, as it turned out," brisk westerners from Chicago and St. Louis, and "a motley array of southerners." Rather than Salmon P. Chase or Charles Sumner or Adams or Trumbull, the self-appointed delegates nominated Horace Greeley, a protectionist though the platform called for a lowered tariff, for President.

William A. Linn recalled that when the telegram announcing Greeley's nomination reached the *Evening Post* on May 4, Bryant was talking with some of the editors about the convention. He related that Bryant remarked, with a twinkle in his eye: "Well, there are some good points in Grant's administration, after all." The discussion over what the *Evening Post* would say about the nomination, according to Towse's recollections, was ended when Bryant said, "I will attend to that editorial myself," and promptly shut himself in his office to do so.[15] The lead editorial, however, was not Bryant's but one written probably by Charlton M. Lewis, entitled "The Fiasco at Cincinnati." It declared that the convention, which had opened on a high level, had ended with the delegates descending to "commonplace chicanery, intrigue, bargaining, and compromise" and predicted that the only result would be to harm the Republican party since Greeley could have no hope of winning the election.

Bryant's own editorial which followed, "Why Mr. Greeley Should Not Be Supported for the Presidency," was a personal attack in which he gave vent to a long-standing animosity.* Greeley's nomination, he wrote, had about it "a certain air of low comedy," but it was so important that it had to be treated seriously. Greeley's first disability for the office of President was that he lacked courage, firmness, and consistency, shown in his attitudes toward the South and slavery when he was willing to let the states secede, when he was all for carrying on a vigorous war, and when he intrigued for a negotiated peace. "His whole career during the war," Bryant declared, "was irresolute and cowardly, and his counsels impolitic and unwise to the last degree." Greeley's political associations were so bad, Bryant said, that his election would result in a corrupt administration. Of no settled political principles, Greeley would drift "backward and forward upon the shifting currents of expediency." Especially hateful to Bryant was Greeley's tariff policy: he was "a thorough-going, bigoted protectionist, a champion of one of the most arbitrary and grinding systems of monopoly ever known in any country." Finally, Greeley was objectionable because of the "grossness of his manners." Bryant summed up his opinion of the candidate: "With such a head as is on his shoulders the affairs of the nation could not, under his direction, be wisely administered; with such manners as his, they could not be administered with common decorum; with such associates as he has taken to his bosom, they could not be administered with common integrity."

Bryant, of course, was not alone in believing that Greeley's nomination was a catastrophe and that, with no better candidate in the race, Grant would be duly renominated and reelected and misgovernment would continue. He therefore collaborated with others who felt betrayed by the nomination in calling a mass meeting on May 30 in Steinway Hall in New York of citizens "in favor of the overthrow of our present enormous and oppressive system of taxation and opposed to the trickery of the Cincinnati

---

*In attacking the policies of other newspapers Bryant in recent years had avoided personal vituperation of their editors, considering the practice ungentlemanly. He never got over an editorial of Greeley's in 1849 in reply to something appearing in the *Evening Post* that began: "You lie, villain! wilfully, wickedly, basely lie!" E. L. Godkin relates that in the spring of 1864 he was invited to a breakfast at which Wendell Phillips, Bryant, and others were guests. When Greeley entered, Bryant was talking with the host and ignored the rival editor. The host whispered to Bryant, "Don't you know Mr. Greeley?" In a louder whisper Bryant replied: "No, I don't; he's a blackguard—he's a blackguard." *Life and Letters of Edwin Lawrence Godkin* (Rollo Ogden, ed., New York and London, 1907), I, 169.

convention." It was a huge and enthusiastic rally at which Bryant was elected chairman. Partly as a result of this popular demonstration in behalf of reform, Bryant, Schurz, and several others mailed a confidential letter on June 6 to various leaders known to be opposed to the Grant administration inviting them to attend a conference June 20 at the Fifth Avenue Hotel to canvass ways of replacing Greeley or putting another ticket in the field. Bryant presided at the conference, but no agreement could be reached. Bryant's own name was mentioned frequently in the press as being the candidate preferred by the dissidents, and he acted to stop the speculation by printing a card at the top of the editorial column on July 8:

> Certain journals of this city have lately spoken of me as one ambitious of being nominated for the Presidency of the United States. The idea is absurd enough, not only on account of my advanced age, but of my unfitness in various respects for the labors of so eminent a post. I do not, however, object to the discussion of my deficiencies on any other ground than that it is altogether superfluous, since it is impossible that I should receive any formal nomination, and equally impossible, if it were offered, that I should commit the folly of accepting it.

Even before the Democrats met at Baltimore and endorsed the Cincinnati convention reform slate and its platform, Bryant had decided to put the *Evening Post* behind the election of Grant as being the lesser, though not by much, of two evils. As for Grant, the *Evening Post* stated on June 27, not a single act of his administration could be said to have been of any particular credit though it might be asserted that, considering the times, he had done no great harm and what harm was done was done through ignorance rather than design. Not expecting any good to come of Grant's election, the people were at least forewarned and therefore might protect themselves against any positive evil. On the other hand, "it would be positively dangerous to choose Mr. Greeley President, because he is influenced far more by caprice than by principle; because his ways are devious and past finding out, and because he is already surrounded and supported—and will be still more so—by men who flock to him instinctively, as birds of prey scent afar off a promised field of disaster, corruption, and death."

So ran the paper's editorials during the campaign, ridicule of Grant on the one hand so that he would probably have been happier without its support, and malignant denunciation of Greeley on the other. When Grant won by an overwhelming vote in November, the *Evening Post* could not exult in a Republican victory. Nor, when Greeley died within a month after the election, his strong body worn out by the strain of the campaign and his brilliant and inquisitive mind destroyed by the failure of his ambition, could the *Evening Post* sum up his career in a mean spirit. His faults and his virtues were those of the American people, the obituary editorial of November 30 said, and continued:

> Without family, money, friends or any of the usual supports by which men are helped into eminence, Mr. Greeley won his place of influence and distinction by the sheer force of his intellectual ability and the determination of his character. By good natural abilities, by industry, by temperance, by sympathy with what is noblest and best in human nature, and by earnest purpose, the ignorant, friendless, unknown printer's boy of a few years since became the powerful and famous journalist, whose words went to the ends of the earth, affecting the destinies of all mankind.

IV

In August of 1872 while Bryant was at Cummington, he received a letter from Dana, who was nearing his eighty-fifth birthday and who had for a quarter of a century led the life of a literary recluse, expressing amazement that Bryant could be so active at his age: "I look out upon you from my silent twilight cave with admiring wonder. There you are, as if the sun were at high noon upon you, and all astir around you, and you in the fresh vigor of early manhood."[16] Bryant replied that Dana somewhat exaggerated his activity but went on to explain: "Though while employed I am not much haunted with the consciousness of being old, yet the fact is almost always present to my mind that the time of my remaining here is necessarily short, and that whatever I am to do must be done soon, or it may not be done at all."[17]

This may be as good an explanation as any of Bryant's busyness during his last years. He needed to fill up his days and, having lost any enthusiasm he ever had for politics and journalism and unable to devote himself to original poetry, he was willing to prepare short speeches for scores of public occasions;* to supervise the editing and to write introductions for

---

*Bryant frequently received invitations to give formal lectures. Asked by James T. Fields if he would give one in Boston, he replied: "I have been often asked to deliver public lectures, and I always answer that I never do it. I sometimes make little dinner speeches, and now and then speak at public meetings, when some important matter is up for discussion, but I never give lectures." His reason was that these required more preparation than he was

such pretentious publishing projects as an oversized collection of British and American poetry, a two-volume lavishly illustrated work on his country's landscape, a four-volume history of the United States, and a new edition of Shakespeare's plays; to travel incessantly back and forth between Roslyn and New York and Cummington as well as to make one trip to the southern states; and to accept the honors that an admiring people wished upon him as a venerable poet and revered sage and to endure the invasion of his privacy by callers and letter-writers. All these things were not done without some grumbling but they were done.

Bryant was scarcely through with his work on *The Library of Poetry and Song* when he was persuaded by the publisher George S. Appleton to work with one of the firm's editors, Oliver B. Bunce, on a sumptuously illustrated book that cost more than $100,000 to produce, *Picturesque America*, the first volume of which appeared in 1872 and the second in 1874. The idea was one that Bunce had kept in mind since 1863 when he edited a volume of engraved paintings illustrating lines by American poets, *In the Woods with Bryant, Longfellow and Halleck*. An admirer of American scenery whose poems had inspired many of the country's landscape painters, Bryant took up the task of editing the textual material commissioned by Bunce with interest but soon tired of it, writing the Rev. Dr. Dewey that he could not recall having engaged in a literary task so wearisome, since "the mere description of places is the most tedious of all reading."[18]

Bryant's next literary project was to collect, at the request of the publisher George P. Putnam, his public addresses and orations in a volume issued in July of 1873. It included his well-received funeral discourses on his friends Cole, Cooper, Irving, Halleck, and Verplanck. James T. Fields wrote him that he thought it "the most eloquent and interesting book of speeches in the English language,"[19] but Bryant, though flattered, replied that the praise encouraged him only to believe he had "not committed a folly in gathering these compositions into a volume."[20]

In the autumn of 1874 the publisher J. C. Derby, in a conversation with Bryant, suggested that he should write his autobiography. After thinking the matter over, Bryant wrote Derby that he was disinclined to do so as he could not remember the people with whom he had been thrown into contact "so minutely and accurately" as he could wish and that if he wrote only of himself the work would make a "mere egotist" of him. He con-

---

willing to give to them. "The people of New York are accustomed to my defects as a speaker, and bear with me," he continued. "I could not expect from Boston the same indulgence." Goddard-Roslyn Collection; Godwin, *Biography*, II, 327.

cluded: "If I write anything of the kind it must appear after I have disappeared, provided that anybody shall then think worth while to publish it."[21] Bryant did begin the story of his life, however, writing about 12,600 words about his boyhood and his school days up to the summer of 1811, when he returned to Cummington after leaving Williams College.*

Another firm interested in getting Bryant's name on the title page of an elaborate publishing project was that of Scribner, Armstrong & Company. It was *A Popular History of the United States* on which Bryant would collaborate with Sidney Howard Gay, who had become the managing editor of the *Evening Post* in 1872. An Abolitionist, Gay had edited antislavery publications before joining Greeley's *Tribune* in 1855, serving as managing editor during the Civil War. He resigned in 1866 because of ill health but two years later went to the Chicago *Tribune*, remaining there until 1871, when he returned to New York. It was to be a well illustrated work in four quarto volumes. In a letter to John Bryant on May 11, 1874, Bryant said he was busy on the introduction. "I write somewhat against the grain," he said, "though I think that I have some good thoughts to ventilate."[22] Though the first volume was published in May of 1876 with Bryant listed as joint author, he actually did very little work on it except for writing the introduction and going over Gay's manuscript. As he had written his brother: "The real hard work of writing the history itself is to be done by Mr. Gay, but is all to pass through my hands." The completed work in four volumes, again with Bryant listed as coauthor, appeared in 1878.

Another publishing project promoted also with the idea of making capital of Bryant's name was a new edition of Shakespeare to appear with original illustrations. Bryant's collaborator was the scholar and literary historian Evert A. Duyckinck. Again, Bryant's role was to serve as an adviser, the detail work of collating the text with the folio edition of 1623 being done by Duyckinck, and to write the preface. Bryant completed this in May of 1875, receiving a letter from Duyckinck praising it and thanking him for his cooperation in these words: "Let me add to this note the expression of my sense of your generous courtesy and kind interpretation of my part in the work, with my congratulations to you on the good health and spirits which have carried you so readily through this, certainly, somewhat onerous undertaking."[23] Because of difficulty in obtaining the illustrations, the work was not published until 1886.**

*The first part of the autobiography, "Boys of My Boyhood," was published in *St. Nicholas* magazine in Dec., 1876.

**Harriet Monroe, founder of *Poetry: A Magazine of Verse*, attacked Bryant's memory for these literary activities in his later years, saying he "used to sell his name, along with his

In these later years of Bryant's greatest fame he was so popular a speaker that in New York no public function was considered to be complete without his presence. The practice during the time at these gatherings was to elect a chairman or president for the occasion and to honor others by electing them vice-presidents, oftentimes a dozen or so. Whether it was a protest meeting against some iniquity in government, a meeting got up to establish an art museum or a library, or a meeting to honor a distinguished visitor, Bryant was almost the invariable choice for chairman. "He was always the honored guest of the evening," George Ripley, literary editor of the *Tribune,* wrote, "and the moment in which he was to be called upon to speak was awaited with eager expectation that never ended in disappointment." Yet Bryant, who as a young man had dreaded becoming a lawyer because he would have to speak in public, never mastered the art of oratory, at least the stentorian tones, the dramatic gestures, and the high-flown imagery, of a Webster, a Clay, or an Everett. His manner was quite different, never folksy or conversational but nonetheless relaxed and easy. Ripley described his appeal: "He was singularly happy in seizing the tone of the company, no matter what were the circumstances or the occasion; his remarks were not only pertinent but eminently felicitous; with no pretensions to eloquence, he was always impressive, often pathetic, and sometimes quietly humorous, with a zest and pungency that touched the feelings of the audience to the quick."[24]

As in his editorials, Bryant in his speeches made use of the humorous anecdote to illustrate a point; he drew upon his wide reading in history and literature for interesting parallels; and he often resorted to poetic imagery to heighten the effect of what he had to say. The young Moses Coit Tyler, going to New York in 1873 as literary editor of the *Christian Union,* was eager to see and hear Bryant. Of Bryant's speech, Tyler noted in his diary that his tones were "just a little angular and sharp, with a trace

---

venerable portrait, as the author of books which he never wrote nor edited." He did so to such an extent, she declared, that he was known among New York publishers as "the great tone-imparter." "To have done one's best work in youth is proof that one has lived downward rather than upward," Miss Monroe continued. "Long is the roll of artists, who beginning with more genius than character, shuffle off this glory like a rich garment and sink down in rags—or broadcloth—to a sordid feast. . . . There is only one code of honor for an artist —to be true to his vision. Bryant preferred to lead a comfortable life, and be a good journalist rather than a poet. . . . Bryant was, in short, a man born to be a poet who sacrificed the muse, not to those violent enemies, the flesh and the devil, but to that more insidious one, the world —or, in other words, comfort and respectability. Now and then a brief flash of inspiration disturbed his placidity, but gradually the light went out, until in his tone-imparting old age, he could not even see that he was sitting in darkness." "Bryant and the New Poetry," *The Dial,* Oct. 14, 1915.

of New England inflection." Bryant seldom spoke extemporaneously, writing out drafts of his addresses before delivery; but he did not read them or refer to notes. In a conversation with Bryant, Tyler was told that any address he wrote was immediately imprinted on his mind and that if all his poems were burnt up he could replace them from memory.[25] The poet Edmund Clarence Stedman believed that Bryant owed something of his prestige with the multitude not so much to his being a poet but to his being a prosperous man of affairs. This brought him near to the Philistines, who saw "him visibly haloed with a distinction beyond that which wealth and civic influence could bestow." Stedman continued: "Besides, even Philistia has its aesthetic rituals and pageantry, and it was with a gracious and picturesque sense of the fitness of things that he bore his stately part in our festivals and processions."[26]

The high esteem in which Bryant was held was shown on his eightieth birthday on November 3, 1874, in a celebration that took on a national character. His friends some weeks before in discussing how the occasion should be observed decided on what seemed to them a suitable measure —not a public dinner with speeches but a more permanent memorial in the form of a silver vase, in its ornamentation and design to symbolize the character of his life and writings.[27] The vase, to be paid for by popular subscription, was to be placed in the Metropolitan Museum of Art. On his birthday Bryant worked at his office at the *Evening Post* until noon. Shortly after he returned to his home on Sixteenth Street, a delegation of some of the city's leading men—public officials, merchants, artists, writers, and ministers—called on him and presented an address, written by Dr. Samuel Osgood and signed by thousands of well-wishers not only of New York but all parts of the country. In presenting the address, the merchant Jonathan Sturges praised Bryant as a writer who had given the people "the best thought and sentiment in the purest language of the English-speaking race," as a journalist who had for fifty years "vindicated the duties as well as the rights of men," and as a citizen and patriot who had "stood up manfully for justice and humanity." In reply Bryant spoke of the improved condition of mankind that had taken place during his lifetime—of a wider freedom throughout the world, of the attention now given to "the liberties and rights of the humbler classes" by government, and of the extinction of slavery in his own country which he had not expected to live to see. He hoped that the time would come when the world would prepare "for a universal peace by disbanding the enormous armies which they keep in camps and garrisons" and would send "their soldiery back to the fields and workshops."

The birthday was observed by literary societies throughout the country —the Bryant papers contain dozens of letters notifying him of his election as an honorary member of such groups—and by encomiums in the newspapers and magazines. At Chicago, the Literary Club celebrated the occasion with a dinner at which Bryant's two surviving brothers, Arthur and John, spoke of his early life. For days after the birthday, the *Evening Post* printed columns of editorial tributes to Bryant.* It was an outpouring of praise for a man that many editors considered the nation's most noted citizen, but the chief significance may perhaps be found in a comment of the New York *Observer:* "In the midst of this materialistic age, when sentiment is subordinated to money, and men are absorbed in trade and politics, there is something peculiarly refreshing in the fact that the birthday of a great poet, in the commercial metropolis, and in the midst of a hotly contested election, should command the respectful attention of the most eminent of our fellow citizens."

The commemorative vase, executed by James H. Whitehouse of Tiffany's, was not completed until 1876, when, on June 20, it was presented to Bryant at a public meeting at Chickering Hall.[28] In form, it was copied after Greek models, but the decorations were of American flowers twining themselves about it and over the medallions portraying Bryant and his life. It is a crowded and complicated piece of work, containing a portrait bust, a printing press, a lyre, a waterfowl in one group of medallions and the boy-poet with his father, the young student of nature, the editor of middle years, and in old age the translator of Homer in another group. There are other decorations—American farm products, broken shackles to symbolize Bryant's fight against slavery, the line from Bryant's "The Battle-Field," "Truth crushed to earth shall rise again," the waterlily as an emblem of eloquence, and a circlet of primrose and ivy to represent youth and old age.

A few months after the birthday celebration, Bryant was the object of another outpouring of praise in—of all places—the New York assembly.[29] As an editorial writer for a half-century, he had never had much except abuse to say about the state legislature, but this was disregarded when the

---

*In Bryant's later years the *Evening Post* reported fully on his public appearances and printed his speeches. He did not object to this personal publicity or to that of the printing of the birthday encomiums. However, when a supplement illustrated with a large portrait engraving of him and carrying many of the editorial tributes to him was issued on Dec. 19 he disavowed it in a notice a few days later: "I wish the readers of this journal to understand that the supplement . . . was issued by the publishing department without previous consultation with me, or knowledge on my part of its contents. I say this because I do not wish to be responsible for the extreme egotism with which I might otherwise be charged."

politicians took the grand old poet to their hearts while he was a guest of Governor Tilden in February of 1875. Largely because of his success in breaking up the Tweed ring, Tilden had been elected governor in 1874. A Democrat, Tilden had only the tacit support of the *Evening Post* in his campaign—Bryant had written he was the "best possible" candidate the *Democrats* could put up for office—but nevertheless the governor invited his old friend to visit him at the capital. Both houses of the assembly on February 9 held receptions for him. Taken by Tilden to the governor's office, Bryant was called upon by a committee of senators at noon and escorted to the upper chamber of the legislature, receiving a standing ovation when he was introduced as "the most distinguished citizen of our state—I might say of our country" by the chairman of the welcoming committee. Bryant was cheered when he compared his reception to a joke known to the Greeks two thousand years before, the story that a Greek was so overwhelmed when a large concourse of people came together for the funeral of his child that he felt called upon to apologize for the smallness of the corpse. After the exchange of compliments in the senate, Bryant was taken to the house, where his humor again won over his hearers. He was valued, if he was valued at all, he said, because old age was a rarity, adding: "If pebbles were scarce, they would not be picked up and thrown at dogs."

V

In 1871 in response to an inquiry about how he maintained his health and vigor at his age Bryant wrote a letter describing his daily regimen that received wide circulation after being published in the *Journal of Health*.[30] His habit, he said, was to rise at half past five in the morning, earlier in the summers, and to exercise for an hour "with dumb-bells—the very lightest—covered with flannel, with a pole, a horizontal bar and a light chair swung round my head." After a bath, he took breakfast consisting of hominy and milk, and sometimes brown bread, oatmeal, or wheaten grits. He was then ready for work, his literary studies if at Cedarmere or, if in New York, his editorial writing or checking of copy in his office at the *Evening Post* after a three-mile walk from his house on Sixteenth Street. This walk in summer's sunshine or rain and in winter's snow, year in and year out, made him one of the familiar sights in the city, for he was a striking figure as he strode briskly along, his white beard reaching to his chest and his hair to his shoulders. Arriving at the *Evening Post* building, Bryant would run up the stairs to his office—after 1875 when the paper occupied a new ten-story building with the editorial rooms on the top floor Bryant disdained to use the elevator—and before entering sometimes would grasp the lintel of the door and raise and lower himself by his arms for a minute or so.

Bryant, in his relations with members of the staff, was always "studiously courteous," according to J. Ranken Towse, and to some conveyed "the impression of being cold and distant."[31] Another staff member, George Cary Eggleston, named literary editor in 1874, also noted Bryant's formality. "He never called even the youngest man on his staff by his given name," Eggleston said, "or by his surname without the prefix 'Mr.' " But Eggleston did not believe this was due to any coldness in Bryant's nature. "The lack of warmth usually attributed to Mr. Bryant," Eggleston wrote, "I found to be nothing more than the personal reserve common to New Englanders of culture and refinement, plus an excessive personal modesty and a shyness of self-revelation." Eggleston considered Bryant's quiet exterior misleading, for there were hidden fires in the man. Bryant in these years left most of the editorial comment to his editorial writer, but when a topic appealed strongly to his own feelings he would write the leader himself. "He was an old man and one accustomed to self-control," Eggleston said, "but when his convictions were stirred, there was not only fire but white-hot lava in his utterance."[32]

Bryant's last travel letters for the *Evening Post* were written early in 1873 when he made a trip to Florida in company with his daughters, their cousin Anna Fairchild, and John Durand.[33] Eight years after the Civil War, he was interested in seeing what had been done in the way of healing the wounds suffered in the conflict and improving the lives of the people. In Florida, where he wrote letters from Palatka on March 18 and Green Cove Spring on March 28, he discovered a new type of northern invasion— visitors who like himself had gone south to escape the winter and had taken all the rooms in the hotels and whatever spare ones were available in homes.

Bryant's observations of the South were superficial and he gave only hints of conditions. At Green Cove Spring he noted that the freed Negroes did not seem so healthy and vigorous as the slaves he had seen on his visit to Florida thirty years before. He was unable to report any significant advances in agriculture and industry and, as a matter of fact, the only improvement he could discover was in education. Writing to Janet Gibson on April 13 from Richmond, he said: "What has most impressed me in my visit to the South . . . is the effort, which I have witnessed everywhere, to educate for usefulness both the black and the white population. . . ."[34] At Charleston Bryant found that he was held in as high esteem as a poet as he was in the North. The leading people of the city turned out for a reception given him, according to a report in the Charleston *News,* as "their loved 'Poet of the Woods' " and as the author of "Song of Marion's Men," which often "warmed the hearts of soldiers at many a Confederate campfire."[35] Although admitting that he did not have much opportunity to judge, Bryant wrote the *Evening Post* that he had heard "only the expression of a desire to be on friendly terms with us of the Northern states."

29

WAITING BY THE GATE

FOR SOME YEARS *Evening Post* STAFF MEMBERS AND FRIENDS
of Bryant long associated with the paper, Bigelow and Tilden in particular,
had felt that Isaac Henderson, with his eyes ever looking to profit and ever
watching out to protect commercial interests, had destroyed the paper's
independence. Godwin, in addition, feared that Henderson wanted to get
control of the paper. In 1873, when the partnership was converted into
a stock company, Henderson had obtained half the shares; his son-in-law,
Watson R. Sperry, who had joined the paper in 1872 after graduating
from Yale, was made managing editor in 1875; and his son, Isaac Henderson, Jr., was being trained to succeed his father as publisher. Henderson's
proprietary interest was further shown when he personally erected at a
cost of $750,000 a new building for the paper at Broadway and Fulton
Street. The move was made on July 1, 1875, into what the paper described
as "one of the most stately structures in the metropolis" and the best-
equipped newspaper plant in the country. It was a sign of prosperity that
inordinately pleased Henderson.

An editorial on the removal noted that it took place on the fiftieth
anniversary of the day that Bryant joined the paper, which owed its
principles of independence and concern for freedom to him. But now
there was doubt if these principles prevailed. Charles Nordhoff had resigned after years of wrangling with Henderson over his interference with

the news department, and J. Ranken Towse related that for the same reason Arthur G. Sedgwick, a son of Bryant's friend Theodore Sedgwick, Jr., resigned as managing editor in 1872 after only several weeks on the job. Towse said that he had written at Sedgwick's request an editorial about graft in the Parks Department raising questions about the associations of the parks commissioner, who had escaped criticism because he was a social leader in the city and had been a liberal dispenser of advertising patronage. Henderson denounced the article when he read it in the first edition as being scandalous and libelous. When he had it killed in later editions, Sedgwick resigned the same afternoon, returning to the staff of *The Nation,* which he had left to come to the *Evening Post.*[1]

To Bryant's friends and the news staff the test of who controlled the paper's policies came in the election of 1876 when Tilden, whose friendship Bryant valued and whose integrity he had never questioned, received the Democratic nomination for President, and the Republican party, which Bryant had for years been attacking as corrupt, nominated Governor Rutherford B. Hayes of Ohio.

The campaign came at a period in Bryant's life when he was disgusted, as he had so often been in the past, with the two dominant political parties. Early in 1876, in an editorial on February 24, he asserted that the "two most formidable dangers of the republic" were its two parties, standing in the way of "every practicable reform of admitted and glaring political evils." The Republicans, both in New York and in the nation, were allied with thieves plundering the government and the Democrats were "rotten to the core with financial heresies." As he had done in the 1872 campaign, Bryant sought to alter the party of his nominal allegiance rather than to swing over to the opposition party or to form a new party. Thus he allied himself with the liberal reform leaders among the Republicans, attending on May 16 and 17 a conference at the Fifth Avenue Hotel, held to advance principles on which the campaign should be conducted. He approved the general statement of reforms needed and the decision not to support any candidate who had countenanced or taken part in corrupt practices in an editorial on May 17, predicting that the movement would "gather force and effect" as the political canvass went on.

When the Republican convention nominated Hayes at Cincinnati in June, the *Evening Post* praised its action. It could have made a fatal error in a choice such as James G. Blaine but instead had chosen a man against whom nothing could be said. Subsequently, after the Democrats at St. Louis nominated Tilden, the paper believed that "the better forces" had again prevailed. "The Republicans have nominated a citizen of good character who has served well as governor of his state for three terms," the paper said on June 29. "The Democrats have nominated a citizen of good character who has served well as governor of his state for one term. . . . We shall have an election reasonably free from vicious personalities, and there will fortunately be opportunity for dispassionate discussion of broad political principles. . . ."

While Bryant was a guest of Tilden at Albany, he had proposed a toast to his friend's health in which he said that since he had made a good governor the people would not be displeased if this were to prove a stepping stone to a more elevated position. This toast had been printed in the newspapers, and it was speculated that the *Evening Post* would support Tilden. But the paper's editorials were unenlightening. The policy announced on June 29 of discussing policies rather than men was followed. But Bigelow, who had switched to the Democratic party in 1875 to run for New York secretary of state to support Tilden's reforms, being defended for his apostasy by Bryant in the *Evening Post,* was now Tilden's campaign manager. He wanted Bryant, whom he believed personally to favor Tilden, to come out publicly in support of him. When this was not forthcoming, he wrote Bryant, summering at Cummington, on August 27 expressing the hope that he would head the Tilden electoral ticket in November. "The course of the *Evening Post,* of course, somewhat disappoints me," Bigelow said, "and others who like me embarked in this effort at administrative reform for no mere personal ends. To all such it would be an unspeakable satisfaction to know that you would not decline to charge yourself with the duty of taking their vote to Washington and depositing it for the candidates who in their judgment represent the best hope of the country."

Bryant answered immediately, expressing his "utter surprise" at the request and stating that there were many reasons, which Bigelow should know, why he could not allow his name to appear on the ballot as an elector. His letter ended: "It gives me great pain to refuse anything to the friends of a man whom I esteem and honor as I do Mr. Tilden, whom I know to be so highly accomplished for the most eminent political stations . . . and who, so far as he is not obstructed by the party to which he belongs, will . . . act not only with ability and integrity, but with wisdom, in any post to which the voice of his countrymen may call him."[2]

But Bryant's friends saw a darker meaning in the *Evening Post*'s stand, or lack of one—that Henderson was now in complete charge. This view was set forth in a letter by the publisher J. C. Derby to Bryant on August 23. He wrote that in a conversation with Henderson he had mentioned "the impression that prevailed that he was now the editor in fact, as his son-in-law, Sperry, was managing editor of the *Post.*" Henderson had denied this, saying that Bryant was "the responsible editor, and inspired as he controlled the political course." In view of Bryant's friendship for Tilden, Derby wrote, a good many people "want to know if Mr. Bryant and the *Post* are still as of yore one and the same."[3]

Bryant's reply was more explicit than his reply to Bigelow. As between Tilden and Hayes, Bryant regarded Tilden as "the best, the most of a statesman, the soundest and most enlarged in opinion, and . . . of the firmest character." But as to party, Bryant said while neither was good the Republican was sounder on financial policy and probably would be more effective in civil service reform. The greater number of dissatisfied Republicans who attended the Fifth Avenue Hotel conference, Bryant continued, had acquiesced in the nomination of Hayes. Though the Cincinnati convention did not give them all they wanted, it came near enough and they were content not to leave the Republican party. As to Derby's question about Henderson's direction of the *Evening Post* policy, Bryant made no specific denial, ending his letter with a statement of his concurrence in the decision of other reform Republicans.[4]

Despite this statement of Bryant's preference for the Republican party, *Evening Post* editorials continued to be noncommittal. William Alexander Linn noted in his diary of September 13 that much curiosity had been expressed about the paper's position by those who knew Bryant's personal admiration for Tilden and that the staff had urged him to make public his letter to Derby, which Bryant did not do.[5] A month was to pass before the paper's unequivocal endorsement of the Republican party was set forth, on October 13, in an editorial entitled "Why Hayes Should Be Elected." On November 4, just before the election, the *Evening Post* in another editorial, "How to Vote and Why," repeated its firm approval of Hayes.

Although Bryant had stated in his letter to Derby that it was his decision to give the *Evening Post*'s support to Hayes, Bigelow was unconvinced, believing that it was Henderson's. In fact, he considered the exchange of letters between Derby and Bryant as confirming his belief, writing in his diary on August 31, 1876: "I am sorry he has written, for [the letters] show that instead of his editing the *Post,* the *Post* is editing him."[6] Earlier, in July, he had talked with Henderson about the campaign and found him afraid of the effect upon the paper's prosperity if it associated itself with the Democratic party. Writing to Tilden on July 14, he said: "I can hardly trust myself to talk about the *Post.* . . . But the *Evening Post* that you and

I have known and honored, which educated us and through which we have educated others in political science, I fear no longer exists. . . . I only wish Mr. Bryant had his name stricken out of it."[7]

There was additional evidence of Henderson's influence on policy. When Republicans promulgated the charge that Tilden had falsified his income tax returns during the Civil War, Bryant, at Cummington, wrote a stinging rebuttal, sending it to Sperry with the injunction that it should be published in its entirety, whatever might have appeared previously on the subject in the paper.* It did not appear for, as Julia Bryant wrote apologetically to Tilden on September 30, her father was persuaded to kill it to protect Henderson from attacks being made on him in the *Times*. On May 2 the *Times* had charged that the *Evening Post's* circulation was declining and that Henderson, as well as Boggs, trimmed its editorial sails to the winds of financial interest, an allegation which the paper described as a falsehood. Since the *Times* was playing up the income tax scandal, it was attacked in Bryant's article, and Sperry and Henderson thought publication of it would be followed by more abuse of Henderson, "abuse more violent than ever before," Julia wrote. "It was *urged* that my father should not persist in publishing that which would cause such distress to Mr. Henderson, already so worn by his troubles," she continued. "On this score my father felt that he must yield, but he did it most unwillingly and quite ungraciously." Julia's letter revealed that the *Evening Post's* editorials on the campaign were written without much consideration given to Bryant's views. He had given orders, she said, that Tilden should "not be treated in the *Evening Post* otherwise than with respect," but it required his "constant watchfulness" to keep attacks on him out of the paper.[8]

Many years before when Bigelow had been one of the owners of the *Evening Post,* he had given Henderson the chief credit for making the paper a successful property. It had made a fortune for him, he said, and he had never examined the books kept by the business manager. This confidence in Henderson was also shared by Bryant, who gave his attention only to the editorial and news pages. Parke Godwin, however, especially after the Civil War scandal involving Henderson's activities as naval agent, distrusted the man. His suspicions were further aroused in the

---

*Bryant, in a letter to Bigelow on Sept. 21, 1876, declared he was disgusted by the attacks on Tilden. "There was no need of asking me to see that a fair and just treatment of his statement in refutation of the story about the income tax should be accorded him in the *Evening Post,"* Bryant wrote. He said that he had written Sperry that the paper should express as great indignation at the slander as if it had been spoken of the Republican candidate. *Letters and Literary Memorials of Samuel J. Tilden* (John Bigelow, ed., New York, 1908), II, 466.

1870's when Sperry was named managing editor and Isaac, Jr., was being trained to become the business manager. In 1877 Godwin persuaded his wife and Julia that the business affairs of the *Evening Post* should be investigated, and they prevailed upon their father to agree. Bryant apologetically wrote Henderson of this decision on March 16, 1877. Saying that he was unable to make clear to his daughters "the precise situation of my affairs, more especially those which relate in any way to the *Evening Post* and the Job Office," he announced that he was appointing Andrew H. Green as his attorney to act in his place. He stated that this action should raise no doubts in Henderson's mind as to his confidence in him nor should it in any way be considered a terminus to the "good understanding" which had for so long existed between them.[9]

The investigation revealed a shocking state of affairs in which Henderson, who had overreached himself in putting up the new *Evening Post* building and who had lost heavily in other investments during the business depression following the panic of 1873, had transferred the firm's money to his own account. Bigelow, kept informed of the investigation, recorded in his diary on February 27, 1878, that $200,000 had been wrongfully charged against Bryant, $105,000 in a single item. Another attorney brought into the case to represent Bryant, John J. Monnell, informed Henderson that he must secure Bryant for this by a mortgage on the property or surrender his shares if he was to avoid a criminal prosecution. A public scandal was avoided when Henderson pledged thirty of his shares to Bryant as security for the misappropriated money and twenty to Godwin, who also received twenty shares from Bryant on an advance of money to the firm. Under the reorganization, Monnell became the president of the corporation and Godwin a trustee. Isaac, Jr., succeeded his father as publisher but Bryant continued as editor.[10]

II

Bryant, feeling that original poetry was beyond his powers in his later years, had devoted himself chiefly to his translations of the *Iliad* and *Odyssey* insofar as his literary effort was concerned. As he was besieged with requests to give speeches he was also besieged with requests from magazine editors for contributions and by organizations wanting some lines for a special occasion—the celebration of Whittier's birthday, the annual reunion of Williams College alumni, the nation's centennial celebration at Philadelphia in 1876. He ordinarily declined these invitations, giving age as his excuse. "Who looks for Japan lilies and heliotropes when the ground is stiff with frost?" he asked in writing the editors of *Scribner's Monthly** that he had no new poems to contribute, though he promised that if he could find "a stray marigold in bloom" he would send it.[11] He made a similar reply to the request of Williams College alumni: "You write as if I had nothing to do, in fulfilling your request, but to go out and gather under the hedges and by the brooks a bouquet of flowers that spring spontaneously, and throw it upon your table. If I should try, what would you say, if it proved to be only a little bundle of devil-stalks and withered leaves, which my dim sight had mistaken for fresh, green sprays and blossoms?"[12]

But Bryant had not entirely given up interest in his own poetry. In 1876 he busied himself with gathering together his latest work for a new edition of his poems, the first since 1871. As was his custom when Bryant was engaged in such a project, Richard Henry Dana urged him not to destroy his poems' original freshness by too much revision. Replying on September 13 that there was not much need for the exhortation, Bryant told a story of the painter Benjamin West related to him by Samuel F. B. Morse. West, in his old age, sought to improve his pictures painted years before by retouching them, "going over them all and spoiling them." His friends, however, immediately afterward would remove the paint and so the pictures were preserved.[13]

The new edition contained seven poems written since 1872. Two of them, "Tree-Burial" and "A Legend of the Delawares," both composed in 1872, marked a return to Indian themes which had interested Bryant years before as a young man. "The Two Travellers" of 1874 and "Our Fellow-Worshippers" of 1875 as well as "Christmas in 1875" dealt with religious faith, a subject that more and more in Bryant's later years occupied his mind. During the summer at Cummington, where Bryant was of course always reminded of the days of his boyhood, he was led to write the autobiographical poem, "A Life-Time." The poet, as he sits at twilight gazing on the fields around him, seems to see the gathering shadows of the night swept away by brightly lighted scenes in which his whole past is displayed before him until he returns to the present and the airy figures fade.

The major poem of the recent past was a meditation on death in blank verse, "The Flood of Years," which can be considered an answer to the religious doubt expressed in the great poem of his youth, "Thanatopsis."

---

*Bryant's last major poem, "The Flood of Years," had appeared in *Scribner's Monthly*, July, 1876.

In this later poem the "innumerable caravan" of mankind of the earlier poem is described as being swept on to death by a tumultuous flow:

> A Mighty Hand, from an exhaustless Urn,
> Pours forth the never-ending Flood of Years,
> Among the nations. How the rushing waves
> Bear all before them!

But those who are overwhelmed by the flood are carried to a region beyond the life that is:

> So they pass
> From stage to stage along the shining course
> Of that bright river, broadening like a sea.
> As its smooth eddies curl along their way
> They bring old friends together; hands are clasped
> In joy unspeakable.

In his final years Bryant completed a dozen other poems, including a translation from the German and two from the Spanish; several hymns, including "The Star of Bethlehem," written for the fiftieth anniversary of the Church of the Messiah on March 19, 1875, since he was an early member of the congregation of which the Rev. Dr. Dewey was the pastor; and a hymn for the nation's centennial celebration at Philadelphia.

He had been invited to write an ode for the opening ceremonies of the centennial but declined with his usual explanation that he was too old. On May 11, 1876, Bryant spoke to the Young Women's Christian Association, having been invited, he told the members, to read his centennial ode. He had no apology to make for having no ode to deliver. That matter had been taken care of by a younger poet—Bayard Taylor. He promised, however, that if he lived to another nineteen years, when he would be as old as the nation would be on July 4, he would "compose such a centennial ode as has never been written since the world stood." Not up to the eloquence of writing an ode for the celebration, Bryant did, however, supply a hymn. He was disinclined to attend the affair because of the crowds, but he visited the exposition grounds before they were opened to the public. "I expect soon to see things better worth looking at than any World's Fair—this world, I mean," he wrote Christiana Gibson.[14] Bryant's last two completed poems were written early in 1878. He celebrated George Washington's birthday in "The Twenty-Second of February," in a poem that was printed in the *Sunday-School Times*. His final poem seems to have been "Cervantes," written for a festival by the Spanish residents of New York in honor of the great satirist on April 23, 1878. Cervantes was an author whom Bryant had always delighted in and whose shafts flung at folly he found still "keen and bright" after three centuries.

In the early months of 1878 Bryant continued to play the role of the distinguished elder citizen, braving one of the worst snowstorms of the winter to speak January 31 at a reception of the Geographical Society for the Earl of Dufferin; addressing a meeting March 10 at the Newsboys' Lodging-House honoring John E. Williams, one of the founders of the Children's Aid Society; taking part in the series of affairs given in April for Bayard Taylor on his leaving the country to become the American minister in Germany; and appearing before the Clergymen's Club at a breakfast in May.

Increasingly in his later poems Bryant had expressed the conventional Christian belief in an afterlife, a belief that sometimes was questioned by readers of "Thanatopsis." When "The Flood of Years" appeared in *Scribner's Monthly* in July of 1876, a man wrote saying that he had found consolation in the closing lines but that he wondered if they expressed the true faith of the poet. Bryant replied on August 10, saying: "Certainly I believe all that is said in the lines you have quoted. If I had not, I could not have written them. I believe in the everlasting life of the soul; and it seems to me that immortality would be but an imperfect gift without the recognition in the life to come of those who are dear to us here."[15]

A friend of his later years, Joseph Alden, who had edited a collection of Bryant's poems for study in the schools, also questioned Bryant on this point. Some years before Bryant had suggested to Alden that his ideas on personal religion would be useful if set forth in a book. Alden said he would write the book if Bryant would provide an introduction. Discussing the introduction in May of 1878, Alden asked Bryant if the sentiment expressed in "Waiting by the Gate" was habitually felt by him. Bryant repeated the passage alluded to—

> yet these, within my heart
> Can neither wake the dread nor the longing to depart—

and said that this was so. "He then with great simplicity and humility expressed his entire reliance upon Christ for salvation," Alden later recalled.[16] At Roslyn during the summer Bryant worked intermittently on the introduction to Alden's book, *Thoughts on the Religious Life,* the manuscript of which he had received the previous December. It was to be one of Bryant's last writing endeavors, one which he did not live to complete, and in it he reiterated his acceptance of the Christian system of belief.

III

Another project engaging Bryant's attention at this time was writing an address to be delivered in Central Park on May 29 at the presentation to the city of a bust of the Italian liberator Giuseppe Mazzini. Bryant was somewhat depressed, suffering from a head cold and considering himself neglected because the Godwins were in Europe and Julia several weeks before had gone to Atlantic City to recuperate from a slight attack of malarial fever. On May 26, the Sunday before he was to go to New York to give his speech, Bryant attended the morning church services at Roslyn and had dinner at the home of Dr. John Ordronaux, who occupied one of the cottages on the Cedarmere estate. It was a pleasant occasion, for Bryant was charmed by a guest, "a lady of rare culture and endowments," according to Dr. Ordronaux's account, whose conversation melted his reserve. "He became genial and communicative to such a degree as to fascinate us all with the exuberance of his criticisms upon the men he had met and the countries he had visited," Ordronaux related.

Afterward Ordronaux walked home with Bryant along one of his favorite paths beside the bay, but the older man was preoccupied with his own thoughts and the two proceeded in silence until at last Bryant exclaimed: "Oh! I wish they would excuse me from delivering that Mazzini oration. I don't feel equal to it." Ordronaux replied that Bryant at his age surely could with good grace decline to speak, but Bryant expressed his unwillingness to go back on a promise. Another period of silence followed until Bryant remarked: "I wish my daughter were at home; I am very lonesome without her." He then, Ordronaux related, "changed to some private matters which seemed to burden his heart," mentioning "certain painful business experiences"—evidently the misappropriation of money by his partner Isaac Henderson. On reaching Cedarmere, Bryant was loath to let Ordronaux depart, saying: "Won't you come in? You see how lonesome I am!" But Ordronaux declined and left Bryant on the porch, gazing out over the bay, his white hair and beard lifted by a passing breeze.[17]

Going into the city on May 29, Bryant spent the morning in his office at the *Evening Post* checking proofs and conferring with staff members. The literary editor George Cary Eggleston related that Bryant came into his room with two poems sent by a woman who wanted his opinion of them.

Bryant gave them to Eggleston to read and asked what he thought of them. On Eggleston's reply that he thought them "extremely poor stuff," Bryant said: "I suppose so, and now I shall have to write her on the subject." Then for more than an hour the two men talked about American literature and criticism.[18]

After a light luncheon, Bryant was driven in his carriage to Central Park, where the Mazzini bust by the sculptor G. Turini was to be placed on the West Drive opposite Sixty-seventh Street.[19] Arriving thirty minutes before the program began, Bryant took shelter from the sun under the shade of some elm trees and conversed with the author and biographer James Grant Wilson, whom he had known since Wilson took up residence in New York after serving in the Civil War as a brigadier general. "The Central Park this afternoon looked at its brightest and best," the *Evening Post* said in reporting the affair. "The trees wore their richest foliage, and the dark green was in pleasing contrast with the bright costumes of the ladies present."

When the ceremonies started, Bryant took his place with other speakers on the platform. There were several preliminary addresses before Bryant moved to the front in the glare of the sun to give his oration. His delivery was described as beginning somewhat haltingly and feebly but increasing in strength as he spoke, his concluding apostrophe to the bust of the Italian patriot was spoken in impassioned tones: "Image of the illustrious champion of civil and religious liberty, cast in enduring bronze to typify the imperishable renown of thy original! Remain for ages yet to come where we place thee, in this resort of millions; remain till the day shall dawn— far distant though it may be—when the rights and duties of human brotherhood shall be acknowledged by all the races of mankind."

After delivering his address, Bryant returned to his seat and listened to the closing speech given in Italian by one of the sponsors of the affair. When the crowd was dispersing, Wilson approached Bryant and suggested that he come to his home at 15 E. Seventy-fourth Street for some refreshment. Bryant refused Wilson's proposal that they take a carriage, saying, "I am not tired, and prefer to walk." He was a little offended, also, when as they started off, with Wilson's small daughter hand in hand with Bryant, Wilson raised an umbrella to shade him from the sun. "Don't hold that umbrella up on my account," Bryant said. "I like the warmth of the sunshine." Crossing the park, they conversed on various topics—of the death the day before of Lord John Russell at the age of eighty-six; of Fitz-Greene Halleck and Samuel F. B. Morse, whose statues they passed by in their walk; and of the visit the previous year of President Hayes for the dedication of the Halleck statue when Bryant delivered the memorial address to the popular Knickerbocker poet.

Reaching Wilson's home about four o'clock, they ascended the steps to the vestibule and Wilson went ahead a few paces to unlock the inner door leading to the house. While Wilson's back was turned, Bryant fell, striking his head on the stone paving. Carried unconscious into the parlor, Bryant recovered after a few minutes and insisted on going to his own home at 24 W. Sixteenth Street. There he was left in the charge of his niece, Anna Fairchild, while the family physician, the venerable homoeopathist Dr. John F. Gray, was sent for. Other physicians were called in for consultation. Though considering the injury to the head, a brain concussion, as being very serious, they believed he would recover. Bryant, only partly conscious, resisted the efforts of the physicians to examine him, even refusing to let his pulse be taken.

In the days that followed the *Evening Post* published regular bulletins on Bryant's condition. On June 1 he had improved to such an extent that his physicians had hopes that he would entirely recover, welcome news to Julia, who arrived on this day from Atlantic City. These hopes faded a week after his illness, during which Bryant had been able to leave his bed and to converse with his family and physicians, when he suffered a stroke that paralyzed his right side. "His coma became more decided," Dr. Gray reported in a statement about Bryant's last illness; "he spoke with difficulty, but gave no signs of recognition or intelligence; he grew weaker and weaker." On June 10, summoned by a telegram from Julia, John Bigelow called at the home, finding Bryant unconscious although able to take a little nourishment of milk fed to him with a spoon. By then no one expected Bryant to live, and Julia sought Bigelow's advice on funeral arrangements. Repeatedly in recent months Bryant had told her that he wanted his funeral to be conducted as quietly as possible, with burial beside his wife at Roslyn; but the Rev. Dr. Bellows in whose Church of All Souls Bryant had long been a communicant protested on the ground that Bryant was a public man and a private funeral would be inappropriate.

Bigelow proposed a compromise, that the body be taken to the church before the service, without a procession or pallbearers, and that the attendants be dismissed by Dr. Bellows upon completing his sermon; the body then would be taken to Roslyn for a graveside ceremony conducted in the presence of the family and a few friends.[20] Julia, however, could not agree, wishing to follow her father's injunction about a quiet burial.* After

*In his diary Bigelow related that he sought to convince Julia that a private funeral would

Bigelow's visit, Bryant's vitality continued to diminish until at 5:35 on the morning of June 12 he died while asleep in the presence of his daughter Julia, his niece Anna Fairchild, and his grand-daughter Minna Godwin.

Julia only reluctantly agreed to the desire of Bryant's friends that a funeral service be conducted at the Church of All Souls, and indeed the rite, despite the efforts made to preserve dignity, was of such a character that Bryant would have been horrified. An hour before the service was to begin at ten o'clock on the morning of June 14, the church was surrounded by a multitude of people. When the coffin was brought to the church from the Bryant home, police were unable to clear a passage, and it was forced through the crowd. As the doors were opened, the people pushed forward, the police being unable to control the mob, and the church was immediately filled, with a crush of standees in the aisles and at the sides, in the balcony, and in the lobby outside the auditorium.

Once the scramble for getting into the church was over, the funeral service was conducted quietly and impressively. The coffin before the pulpit was draped in a black cloth bearing the inscription: "William Cullen Bryant, born November 3, 1794, died June 12, 1878." Below this were several palm leaves bound together with a white ribbon. A request had been made that no flowers be sent, and the only floral tribute was a large pillar of immortelles, white roses, and calla lilies in the baptismal font, bearing the card: "From his employeés, who loved him." The only other decorations were two baskets of flowers on the communion table. After the prelude, the andante from Beethoven's "Seventh Symphony," and the singing of a hymn by a quartet, the Rev. Dr. Bellows read the King's Chapel Service for the dead, offered a prayer followed by another hymn, and then gave his address, ending with the recitation of Bryant's poem "June" beginning:

> I gazed upon the glorious sky,
>   And the green mountains round,
> And thought that when I came to lie
>   At rest within the ground,
> 'Twere pleasant that in flowery June,
> When brooks send up a cheerful tune,
>   And groves a cheerful sound,
> The sexton's hand, my grave to make,
> The rich, green mountain-turf should break.

---

show disrespect to the world at large, adding that he felt it was impossible to bury "so large a personality as if he were merely a favorite horse or dog." *Retrospections of an Active Life,* V, 375.

The service ended with the singing by the choir of Bryant's own hymn, "Blessed Are They That Mourn," and the recital of the Lord's Prayer.

A special train bore the coffin and members of the funeral party, the family and a few close friends, to the cemetery at Roslyn. Situated about one mile east of the village, the cemetery lay on the western slope of a hill, a peaceful spot shadowed with many trees and brightened by shrubs. Gathered there were many of the villagers, including children, who had often been guests of Bryant at Cedarmere. Bryant's grave was beside that of his wife Frances which was marked by a granite obelisk. For the graveside ceremony, Dr. Bellows chose to read passages from Bryant's own poems on death. After the coffin was lowered into the grave, girls from the Sunday school class in the Roslyn church which Bryant attended walked in a circle around it and tossed flowers into the yawning cavity.

SOURCES

INDEX

PICTURE CREDITS

SOURCES

THE MANUSCRIPT MATERIALS AVAILABLE FOR A LIFE OF WILLIAM
Cullen Bryant are quantitatively great from the time his father, Dr. Peter Bryant,
began practicing medicine in Cummington, Massachusetts, in 1792 to Bryant's
death in New York in 1878. They are to be found in about two dozen sizable
Bryant collections in libraries and scattered among the papers of scores of men and
women with whom he corresponded—writers, artists, politicians, ministers, and
friends.

An important, though incomplete, descriptive guide to the materials is found
in "Manuscript Resources for the Study of William Cullen Bryant," by Herman
E. Spivey (*Bibliographical Society of American Papers,* XLIV [3rd Quarter, 1950],
254–68). The collections which I have made most frequent use of and which are
referred to by abbreviations in the chapter source citations are:

Goddard-Roslyn Collection (GRC). These materials were assembled by
Bryant's son-in-law Parke Godwin for his two-volume biography, which re-
produces hundreds of letters in whole or in part and cites diaries and journals kept
by Bryant and Mrs. Bryant on their travels. The collection also includes hundreds
of manuscript versions of Bryant's poems and memoranda. This huge collection
is in the custody of one of Bryant's descendants, his great-grandson, Mr. Conrad
G. Goddard of New York City. The materials have been made accessible to
scholars in eight microfilm reels in the New York Public Library.

Bryant-Godwin Collection (BGC) in the New York Public Library. This includes letters to and from Bryant and correspondence of Godwin and members
of his family.

Bryant Family Papers (BFP) in the New York Public Library. This is made up
of the correspondence of members of the Bryant family.

Bryant Miscellaneous Papers (BMP) in the New York Public Library. There are relatively few letters in this collection, but it contains a manuscript court docket kept by Bryant of his law cases as well as other materials.

Berg Collection (Berg) in the New York Public Library. Chiefly valuable are letters to Gulian C. Verplanck and Bryant's marked copy of the *New-York Review and Atheneum Magazine.*

Not listed by Spivey is a huge collection, the Bryant Family Association Papers (BFAP), in the museum of the Bureau County Historical Society at Princeton, Illinois. This collection is especially valuable for information about Bryant's childhood years in the letters of Dr. Bryant to his family and his own father, for Bryant's letters to his mother, and for the correspondence of members of the family.

Other collections cited less frequently than the foregoing are given in the chapter source notes.

No complete bibliography of the writings of Bryant has been prepared. The fullest is by Henry C. Sturges, *Chronology of the Life and Writings of William Cullen Bryant with a Bibliography of His Works in Prose and Verse* (New York, 1903). Useful also is Tremaine McDowell's *William Cullen Bryant: Representative Selections, with Introduction, Bibliography, and Notes* (American Writers Series, New York, 1935).

The principal editions of Bryant's works referred to in the text and notes are:

The Embargo, or Sketches of the Times. A Satire. Boston, 1808; 2nd ed., 1809. (Both are reproduced in *The Embargo. Facsimile Reproductions of the Editions of 1808 and 1809,* Thomas O. Mabbott, ed., Scholar's Facsimiles and Reprints, Gainesville, Fla., 1953.)

Poems. Cambridge, Mass., 1821.

Poems. Philadelphia, 1847. (Bryant brought out editions of his poems every few years, adding works composed since the previous edition. This 1847 edition was preceded by a half dozen editions. It is the first in which the arrangement of poems is chronologically by year of composition. He followed this arrangement in all subsequent editions.)

Letters of a Traveller. New York, 1850.

Letters of a Traveller. Second Series. New York, 1859.

Letters from the East. New York, 1869.

The Iliad of Homer. Translated into English Verse. 2 vols. Boston, 1870.

The Odyssey of Homer. 2 vols. Boston, 1871, 1872.

Poems. New York, 1876. (This is the last edition which went through Bryant's hands and which has been followed in the versions of poems quoted.)

The Poetical Works of William Cullen Bryant. Parke Godwin, ed. 2 vols. New York, 1883. (Published as Vols. 3 and 4 of *The Life and Writings of William Cullen Bryant.* Godwin added hymns, translations, and uncollected poems not included in earlier editions as well as some unpublished poems and fragments. He made slight textual changes, gave the dates of composition and first publication of poems, and supplied notes supplementing those given by Bryant in the editions which he supervised.)

The Prose Writings of William Cullen Bryant. Parke Godwin, ed. 2 vols. New York, 1884. (Published as Vols. 1 and 2 of *The Life and Writings of William Cullen Bryant.*)

In addition to the foregoing, Bryant's works included contributions to the magazines which he edited and to other magazines; contributions to volumes of joint authorship such as *The Talisman* and *Tales of the Glauber Spa;* separate publications of orations and addresses; and the introductions to volumes which he edited. Bibliographical information about these will be found in the chapter source notes. The only publication of many of Bryant's speeches was in the columns of the *Evening Post,* which, especially in his later years, carried them in full or in part.

Citations from the *Evening Post* of Bryant's editorials and other contributions are so numerous that they are not given in the chapter source notes. The date of publication, or approximate date, however, is usually given in the text. I am indebted to the Pennsylvania State University Interlibrary Loan office for obtaining microfilm copies of the *Evening Post* files from 1825 to 1878 as well as for many other services.

No full-length biography making use of original materials about Bryant has appeared since Parke Godwin's *A Biography of William Cullen Bryant with Extracts from his Private Correspondence* (2 vols., New York, 1883). It is frequently cited in the chapter source notes. John Bigelow's *William Cullen Bryant* (American Men of Letters Series, Boston and New York, 1890) has original material relating to Bigelow's personal associations with Bryant. Allan Nevins's *The Evening Post: A Century of Journalism* (New York, 1922) is informative about Bryant's editorial career. Credit for biographical information obtained in articles in magazines and scholarly journals, in memoirs of Bryant's friends, and in other works is given in the chapter source notes.

Criticism and reviews of Bryant's writings in magazines and scholarly journals and in books are frequently cited in the text and in the chapter source notes. The fullest critical treatment appears in *William Cullen Bryant,* by Albert F. McLean, Jr. (Twayne's United States Authors Series, New York, 1964).

Chapter 1. Lights and Glooms of Boyhood
1. Details of Bryant's death and tributes to him are taken from contemporary newspapers.
2. *Evening Post,* June 12, 1878.
3. Vernon Louis Parrington, *Main Currents in American Thought* (New York, 1930), II, 238–9.
4. Parke Godwin, *A Biography of William Cullen Bryant, with Extracts from His Private Correspondence* (New York, 1883), II, 216. (Hereafter cited as *Biography.*)
5. "Lines on Revisiting the Country."
6. "An Autobiography of Mr. Bryant's Early Life," in Godwin, *Biography,* I, 1–37. Subsequent quotations from Bryant in this chapter, unless otherwise indicated, are from this "Autobiography."
7. "They Taught Me, and It Was a Fearful Creed," in Tremaine McDowell, *William Cullen Bryant: Representative Selections* (New York, 1935). (Hereafter cited as *Representative Selections.*)
8. "The Burial-Place—A Fragment."
9. "The Two Graves."
10. The diary is cited in Godwin, *Biography,* I, 57–8. Quotations from it also appear in John W. Chadwick, "The Origin of a Great Poem," *Harper's New Monthly Magazine,* Sept., 1894; and in Amanda Mathews, "The Diary of a Poet's Mother," *Magazine of History,* Sept., 1905.

11. Bryant gave a brief account of his ancestry in his "Autobiography," and there is an autograph genealogy among his papers in the Library of Congress. The genealogy is given in Godwin, *Biography*, I, 47–52. The most complete account is in Tremaine McDowell, "The Ancestry of William Cullen Bryant," *Americana*, Oct., 1928.
12. Godwin, *Biography*, I, 52–4.
13. Donald M. Murray, "Dr. Peter Bryant: Preceptor in Poetry to William Cullen Bryant," *New England Quarterly*, XXXIII (1960), 513–22.
14. BFAP.
15. Sept. 24, 1793, BFAP.
16. Godwin, *Biography*, I, 42.
17. Murray, "Dr. Peter Bryant."
18. Godwin, *Biography*, I, 55.
19. BFAP.
20. Godwin, *Biography*, I, 55.
21. Much has been written about the Bryant homestead: "The Bryant Homestead," *Appleton's Journal*, Feb. 8, 1873; Julia Hatfield, *The Bryant Homestead Book* (New York, 1870); Arthur Lawrence, "Bryant and the Berkshire Hills," *Century Magazine*, July, 1895; and Theodore F. Wolfe, "In the Footprints of Bryant," *Lippincott's Magazine*, Nov., 1900, and *Literary Shrines* (Philadelphia, 1895).
22. Godwin, *Biography*, I, 59–61.

Chapter 2. Apprenticeship to Poetry
1. This and other quotations from Bryant's writings, unless otherwise indicated, are from the "Autobiography," Godwin, *Biography*, I, 1–37.
2. Donald M. Murray, "Dr. Peter Bryant: Preceptor in Poetry to William Cullen Bryant," *New England Quarterly*, XXXIII (1960), 513–22.
3. Tremaine McDowell, "The Juvenile Verse of William Cullen Bryant," *Studies in Philology*, Jan., 1929. The poem is reproduced in facsimile along with the 1808 and 1809 editions of Bryant's *The Embargo* under the editorship of Thomas O. Mabbott by Scholars' Facsimiles and Reprints (Gainesville, Fla., 1953).
4. Godwin, *Biography*, I, 76.
5. McDowell, "Juvenile Verse."
6. McDowell, "Juvenile Verse."
7. *The Embargo . . . and Other Poems*, facsimile edition.
8. *Ibid.*
9. The account of the composition of *The Embargo* is based on letters of Dr. Bryant in BFAP; the "Autobiography"; Godwin, *Biography*, I, 70–4; Murray, "Dr. Peter Bryant"; and McDowell, "Juvenile Verse."
10. Excerpt printed in McDowell, *Representative Selections*, 363.
11. Charles T. Congdon, *Reminiscences of a Journalist* (Boston, 1880), 33. The visit of Dr. Bryant and his son at New Bedford is reported in a letter to Mrs. Bryant, July 30, 1809, in BFAP.
12. Godwin, *Biography*, I, 75.
13. John Bigelow, *William Cullen Bryant* (Boston, 1890), 16.

Chapter 3. The Bard at School
1. BFAP.
2. *Life and Poems of John Howard Bryant* (E. R. Brown, ed. Elmwood, Ill., 1894), 8.
3. Bryant, "Autobiography." Other quotations from Bryant in this chapter, unless otherwise indicated, are from this work.
4. Besides family letters and the "Autobiography," details of Bryant's life at North Brookfield are found in Godwin, *Biography*, I, 77–80, and Tremaine McDowell, "Cullen Bryant Prepares for College," *South Atlantic Quarterly*, April, 1931.
5. Godwin, *Biography*, I, 77.
6. Godwin, *Biography*, I, 77–8; Tremaine McDowell, "The Juvenile Verse of William Cullen Bryant."
7. Godwin, *Biography*, I, 79; McDowell, "Cullen Bryant Prepares for College."
8. McDowell, "Cullen Bryant Prepares for College"; Leverett Wilson Spring, *A History of Williams College* (Boston and New York, 1917), 118.
9. Godwin, *Biography*, I, 80; McDowell, "Juvenile Verse."
10. Godwin, *Biography*, I, 61, 104.
11. Sept. 8, 1810, BFAP.
12. Sources for Bryant's life at Williams College are Calvin Durfee, *A History of Williams College* (Boston, 1860), 54–125; Godwin, *Biography*, I, 33–6, 85–101; Tremaine McDowell, "Cullen Bryant at Williams College," *New England Quarterly*, Oct., 1928; James Grant Wilson, *Bryant and His Friends* (New York, 1886), 26–34.
13. Godwin, *Biography*, I, 30.

Chapter 4. O'er Coke's Black Letter Page
1. *Bryant Centennial/Cummington/August the Sixteenth/1894* (Springfield, Mass., 1894).
2. Godwin, *Biography*, I, 94–5.
3. The list of references discussing the writing of "Thanatopsis" is too long to give completely. Godwin's extended account, followed by most subsequent biographers and scholars, appears in *Biography*, I, 97–101. Among the principal discussions are William Cullen Bryant, II, "The Genesis of 'Thanatopsis,'" *New England Quarterly*, June, 1948; John W. Chadwick, "The Origin of a Great Poem," *Harper's New Monthly Magazine*, Sept., 1894; Tremaine McDowell, "Bryant's Practice in Composition and Revision," *Publications of the Modern Language Association*, June, 1937, and *Representative Selections*, 389–392; Albert F. McLean, Jr., *William Cullen Bryant* (New York, 1964), 65–81; Carl Van Doren, "The Growth of Thanatopsis," *The Nation*, Oct. 7, 1915.
4. Godwin, *Biography*, I, 101–3; Tremaine McDowell, "William Cullen Bryant and Yale," *New England Quarterly*, Oct., 1930.
5. Godwin, *Biography*, I, 105.
6. McDowell, "Bryant and Yale."
7. Feb. 29, 1812, BGC; Godwin, *Biography*, I, 105; McDowell, "Bryant and Yale."
8. Godwin, *Biography*, I, 103–4.
9. GRC; Godwin, *Biography*, I, 124–5.

10. The story is told by Godwin in *Biography*, I, 107–14, who quotes many of the poems written during this period, none of which appear in Bryant's collected works. These poems, with additional ones not cited by Godwin, are also discussed by Bryant, II, in "Genesis of 'Thanatopsis.'"
11. Godwin, *Biography*, I, 103.
12. McDowell, "Bryant and Yale."
13. Godwin, *Biography*, I, 104.
14. *Ibid.*, 120. The complete poem is printed in McDowell, *Representative Selections*, 348–50.
15. Godwin, *Biography*, I, 106–7.
16. McDowell, "Bryant and Yale."
17. BGC.
18. GRC; Bryant, II, "Genesis of 'Thanatopsis.'"
19. Dr. Peter Bryant to Dr. Philip Bryant, Aug. 2, 1813, BFAP.
20. For references to the composition of "Thanatopsis" see note three.
21. Bryant, *Poetical Works* (Godwin, ed.), I, 329–30.
22. *The British Poets* (Chiswick, England, 1822), LVII, 202–26.
23. William Ellery Leonard, "Bryant and the Minor Poets," *Cambridge History of American Literature* (New York, 1917), I, Ch. 5.
24. *The British Poets*, LVII, 279–88.
25. James Kirke White, *Poetical Works* (Edinburgh, 1856). The lines quoted are from "To the Herb Rosemary" and "Lines Written in Wilford Churchyard."
26. Godwin, *Biography*, I, 121.
27. GRC; quoted in part in Godwin, *Biography*, I, 123–4.
28. BGC.
29. BGC.
30. Sept. 19, 1814, GRC; Godwin, *Biography*, I, 124–5.
31. Godwin, *Biography*, 125–6.
32. GRC; Godwin, *Biography*, I, 128–30.
33. BGC.
34. Bigelow, *William Cullen Bryant*, letter quoted in full, 32–3.
35. GRC.
36. Godwin, *Biography*, I, 133.
37. GRC; Godwin, *Biography*, I, 134–6.
38. GRC; Godwin, *Biography*, I, 136–7.
39. BGC.
40. GRC.
41. GRC.
42. GRC; Godwin, *Biography*, I, 138.
43. BGC.
44. Aug. 8, 1815, GRC; Godwin, *Biography*, I, 139.

Chapter 5. Themis or the Muse
1. GRC; Godwin, *Biography*, I, 145.
2. These reasons are discussed by Godwin in *Biography*, I, 143.
3. BFAP.
4. William Cullen Bryant, II, "The Genesis of 'Thanatopsis,'" *New England Quarterly*, June, 1948.

5. Godwin, *Biography,* I, 142; Bryant, *Poetical Works,* I, 24.
6. Godwin, *Biography,* I, 140–1.
7. *Ibid.,* 143–4.
8. Jan. 24, 1816, BGC.
9. GRC; Godwin, *Biography,* I, 145–6.
10. BGC.
11. Bryant, in his "Reminiscences of Miss Sedgwick," in *Life and Letters of Catharine M. Sedgwick* (Mary E. Dewey, ed., New York, 1871), 437.
12. GRC.
13. GRC.
14. GRC.
15. GRC; Godwin, *Biography,* I, 147–8.
16. Godwin, *Biography,* I, 166–7.
17. GRC.
18. BGC; Godwin, *Biography,* I, 148.
19. Godwin, *Biography,* I, 148.
20. Bryant, in a letter to Charles A. Dana, Sept. 20, 1873, GRC.
21. Godwin, *Biography,* I, 148–9.
22. Circumstances of the publication of Bryant's first work in the *North American Review* are given in Godwin, *Biography,* I, 149–53; Tremaine McDowell, "Bryant and the *North American Review,*" *American Literature,* March, 1929; Robert C. Waterston, *Tribute to William Cullen Bryant* (Boston, 1878); Wilson, *Bryant and His Friends,* 37–8, 187–8. The letters cited are from BGC and GRC.
23. George Cary Eggleston, *Recollections of a Varied Life* (New York, 1910), 222.
24. BGC.
25. GRC.
26. Godwin, *Biography,* I, 152.
27. Jacob Porter, *Poems* (Hartford, 1818), quoted in McDowell, "Bryant and the *North American Review.*"
28. Godwin, *Biography,* I, 154–5.
29. BGC.
30. BGC.
31. BGC.
32. Godwin, *Biography,* I, 153–4.
33. June 20, 1818. Godwin, *Biography,* I, 156.
34. McDowell, "Bryant and the *North American Review.*"
35. BGC.
36. Godwin, *Biography,* I, 156.
37. *Ibid.,* 157–8.
38. BGC.
39. Godwin, *Biography,* I, 158–9.
40. Godwin, *Biography,* I, 159; *Prose Writings* (Godwin, ed.), I, 157n.
41. BGC.

Chapter 6. A Votary at Sundry Altars
1. BFAP.
2. GRC; Godwin, *Biography,* I, 162.

3. *Life and Poems of John Howard Bryant,* 13.
4. Godwin, *Biography,* I, 168–9.
5. *Life and Letters of Catharine M. Sedgwick,* 438.
6. *Ibid.,* 46–7.
7. *Ibid.,* 111.
8. *Ibid.,* 438.
9. Godwin, *Biography,* I, 204.
10. Both letters in BGC.
11. BGC.
12. Godwin, *Biography,* 169–70.
13. GRC; Godwin, *Biography,* 170.
14. GRC.
15. Arthur Lawrence, "Bryant and the Berkshire Hills," *Century Magazine,* July, 1895.
16. Both letters in GRC.
17. Both letters in BGC. See also, Ethel M. McAllister, *Amos Eaton, Scientist and Educator* (Philadelphia, 1941), 261–2.
18. Godwin, *Biography,* I, 170–1.
19. BGC. See also, Charles I. Glicksberg, "From the 'Pathetick' to the 'Classical': Bryant's Schooling in the Liberties of Oratory," *American Notes and Queries,* VI (1947), 179–82.
20. Bryant's note to "The Ages," *Poems,* 489.
21. Godwin, *Biography,* I, 171.
22. May 15, 1821, BGC.
23. Godwin, *Biography,* I, 177.
24. BGC.
25. GRC; Godwin, *Biography,* I, 171–3.
26. Van Wyck Brooks, *The Flowering of New England* (New York, 1936), 115; Evert A. and George L. Duyckinck, *Cyclopaedia of American Literature* (rev. ed., Philadelphia, 1881), I, 785.
27. Wilson, *Bryant and His Friends,* 189.
28. *Ibid.,* 223.
29. Godwin, *Biography,* I, 174–5.
30. Edgar Allan Poe, "William Cullen Bryant," *Godey's Lady's Book,* April, 1846.
31. Godwin, *Biography,* I, 176–7.
32. BGC.
33. Godwin, *Biography,* I, 179–80. The Oct. 10 letter is in Berg.
34. *Poetical Works,* 329–30. For other references, see Ch. 4, note 3.
35. *The Bryant Centennial* (Galesburg, Ill., 1894), 67; and James C. Derby, *Fifty Years among Authors, Books, and Publishers* (New York, 1884), 163.
36. Godwin, *Biography,* II, 337.
37. GRC.
38. BGC.
39. BGC.
40. BGC.

Chapter 7. Recalled to the Muse
1. BFAP.

2. Godwin, *Biography*, I, 182–3.
3. *Ibid.*, 185.
4. *Ibid.*, 186.
5. BGC.
6. "I Broke the Spell That Held Me Long," written in 1824.
7. BGC.
8. BGC.
9. Aug. 3, 1821, BGC.
10. Edgar Allan Poe, "Poems by William Cullen Bryant. 4th ed.," *Southern Literary Messenger*, Jan., 1837.
11. BGC.
12. Godwin, *Biography*, I, 188–9. The letter, dated Jan. 23, 1825, is in BGC. See also, Charles I. Glicksberg, "Bryant and the Sedgwick Family," *Americana*, Oct., 1937.
13. *Life and Letters of Catharine M. Sedgwick*, 147–8; also, Godwin, *Biography*, I, 190.
14. Both letters in BGC. See also, Glicksberg, "Bryant and the Sedgwick Family," and Godwin, *Biography*, I, 188n.
15. BGC.
16. GRC; Godwin, *Biography*, I, 189–90.
17. BFAP.
18. Godwin, *Biography*, I, 194.
19. GRC; Godwin, *Biography*, I, 195.
20. McDowell, *Representative Selections*, xxxvii.
21. Note to "William Tell" in *Poems*, 491.
22. Letter from Halleck, Dec. 1, 1824, BGC.
23. Glicksberg, "Bryant and the Sedgwick Family."
24. Letter from Sparks, Oct. 16, 1824, BGC.
25. Godwin, *Biography*, I, 195.
26. Glicksberg, "Bryant and the Sedgwick Family."
27. Godwin, *Biography*, I, 216.
28. *Ibid.*, 204.
29. *Ibid.*, 201–2.
30. BGC; Godwin, *Biography*, I, 200–1.
31. BGC; Glicksberg, "Bryant and the Sedgwick Family."
32. BGC.
33. BGC; Godwin, *Biography*, I, 188–9.
34. GRC; Godwin, *Biography*, I, 210.

Chapter 8. A Literary Adventurer
1. GRC; Godwin, *Biography*, I, 210.
2. BGC.
3. BGC.
4. March 5, 1825, BGC.
5. March 5, 1825, BGC.
6. GRC; Godwin, *Biography*, I, 212.
7. GRC.
8. GRC.

9. Godwin, *Biography*, I, 216.
10. *Atlantic Magazine*, May, 1824.
11. GRC.
12. *New-York Review and Atheneum Magazine*, Nov., 1825.
13. *American Athenaeum*, Nov. 17, 1825.
14. GRC; Godwin, *Biography*, I, 213.
15. BGC.
16. GRC; Godwin, *Biography*, I, 214–5.
17. GRC; Godwin, *Biography*, I, 217.
18. GRC; Godwin, *Biography*, I, 216.
19. GRC.
20. GRC; Godwin, *Biography*, I, 217.
21. GRC; Godwin, *Biography*, I, 218.
22. GRC; Godwin, *Biography*, I, 219.
23. *United States Literary Gazette*, July 1, 1825.
24. Bryant, "Reminiscences of Miss Sedgwick," in *Life and Letters of Catharine M. Sedgwick*, 441.
25. Wilson, *Bryant and His Friends*, 45.
26. GRC; Godwin, *Biography*, I, 221.
27. *Correspondence of James Fenimore Cooper* (ed. by his grandson, James Fenimore Cooper, New Haven, 1922), I, 49–50; *Letters and Journals of James Fenimore Cooper* (James Franklin Beard, ed., Cambridge, Mass., 1960), 83–4; Derby, *Fifty Years among Authors, Books, and Publishers*, 293–4.
28. Carleton Mabee, *The American Leonardo, a Life of Samuel F. B. Morse* (New York, 1943), 100; *Samuel F. B. Morse, His Letters and Journals* (Edward L. Morse, ed., Boston and New York, 1914), I, 282.
29. Bryant, "Reminiscences of the 'Evening Post,'" published in the newspaper on Nov. 15, 1851. Reprinted in Bigelow, *William Cullen Bryant*, 312–42.
30. Godwin, *Biography*, I, 207.
31. Allan Nevins, *The Evening Post*, 63 ff.
32. Bryant, *Discourse on Gulian Crommelin Verplanck* (New York, 1870), 50.
33. Frances Bryant, fragment of autobiography, GRC.
34. Letter, GRC.
35. Review of *Lectures on Geology*, by Jer. Van Rensselaer, in *New-York Review*, Nov. 1825.
36. BGC.

Chapter 9. In a Bank-Note World.
1. GRC.
2. BFAP.
3. GRC; Godwin, *Biography*, I, 222.
4. The criticism is William Ellery Leonard's in, "Bryant and the Minor Poets," *Cambridge History of American Literature*, I, 262.
5. The tale is attributed to Bryant by Godwin, *Biography*, I, 227. It appeared in the Dec., 1825, number of the magazine.
6. GRC; Godwin, *Biography*, I, 222.
7. Leonard, "Bryant and the Minor Poets."
8. The lectures are printed in *Prose Writings*, I, 3–44. Discussions of Bryant's

poetical theory appear in Gay Wilson Allen, *American Prosody* (New York, 1935); William Charvat, *The Origins of American Critical Thought* (Philadelphia, 1936); William Palmer Hudson, "Archibald Alison and William Cullen Bryant," *American Literature*, March, 1940; McLean, *William Cullen Bryant;* McDowell, *Representative Selections;* Donald A. Ringe, *Poetry and the Cosmos: William Cullen Bryant* (unpubl. diss., Harvard University, 1953); and Robert E. Spiller, *The Cycle of American Literature* (New York, Mentor Books, 1957).

9. Bryant's influence on the artists of his time is discussed in Ringe, "Kindred Spirits: Bryant and Cole," *American Quarterly*, fall, 1954, and "Painting as Poem in the Hudson River Aesthetic," *American Quarterly*, spring, 1960; and Charles L. Sanford, "The Concept of the Sublime in the Works of Thomas Cole and William Cullen Bryant," *American Literature*, Jan., 1957.

10. McLean, *William Cullen Bryant*, 108.

11. Godwin, *Biography*, I, 233.

12. *Ibid.*, 223.

13. James McHenry, "American Lake Poetry," *American Quarterly Review*, March, 1832.

14. Information in the bound files of the two magazines.

15. BGC.

16. All three letters in BGC.

17. BGC.

18. Mrs. Bryant's autobiographical fragment, GRC.

19. BGC.

20. GRC; Godwin, *Biography*, I, 229.

21. Letter to Verplanck, Aug. 26, 1826, Godwin, *Biography*, I, 229.

22. Letter from Louisa C. Bryant to Cyrus Bryant, Oct. 1, 1826, BFAP.

23. The salary is given by Mrs. Bryant in a letter of June 10, 1827, to her mother-in-law, Sarah Snell Bryant, BFAP.

24. The Folsom letters to Bryant are in BGC.

25. The Bryant letters to Folsom are in the Boston Public Library. Most of them are printed by Charles I. Glicksberg in "Letters by William Cullen Bryant," *Americana*, Jan., 1939.

26. The tale is printed in McDowell, *Representative Selections.*

Chapter 10. Politics and a Belly-full

1. Bryant, "Reminiscences of the 'Evening Post.' "

2. Nevins, *The Evening Post*, 61.

3. Bryant, "Reminiscences of the 'Evening Post.' "

4. June 1, 1827, GRC; Godwin, *Biography*, I, 233.

5. Bryant, "Reminiscences of the 'Evening Post.' "

6. Boston Public Library. See also, Charles I. Glicksberg, "Letters by William Cullen Bryant," *Americana*, Jan., 1939.

7. Boston Public Library.

8. Bryant's reviews in the *United States Review and Literary Gazette* are discussed by Charles I. Glicksberg in "New Contributions in Prose by William Cullen Bryant," *Americana*, Oct., 1936.

9. *United States Review*, July, 1827.

10. *United States Review*, Dec., 1826.

11. *United States Review,* Nov., 1826.
12. *United States Review,* Nov., 1826.
13. *United States Review,* April, 1827.
14. *United States Review,* April, 1827.
15. *United States Review,* July, 1827.
16. *United States Review,* Jan., 1827.
17. *United States Review,* Oct., 1826.
18. *United States Review,* March, 1827.
19. *United States Review,* Oct., 1826.
20. Boston Public Library. See also, Glicksberg, "Letters by William Cullen Bryant."
21. *United States Review,* Sept., 1827.
22. GRC.
23. GRC.
24. Bigelow, *William Cullen Bryant,* 69.
25. GRC; Godwin, *Biography,* I, 235.
26. Nevins, *The Evening Post,* 136.
27. *The Writings of Robert C. Sands, in Prose and Verse* (New York, 1834). The "Memoir" introducing the volume is credited to Gulian C. Verplanck, but Bryant shared in its writing, passages being taken almost verbatim from his own memoir in the *Knickerbocker Magazine,* Jan., 1833.
28. *A Discourse on the Life, Character and Writings of Gulian Crommelin Verplanck* (New York, 1870), 34, 54.
29. Bryant memoir, *Knickerbocker Magazine.*
30. Berg.
31. GRC; Godwin, *Biography,* I, 239. The joking editorial on the Latin quotations and the "John Smith" translations appeared in the *Evening Post* in Jan., 1829.
32. *New-York Mirror,* Jan. 29, 1828. Leggett reprinted the essay in his own magazine, *The Critic,* Dec. 13, 1828.
33. Jan. 16, 1828, Godwin, *Biography,* I, 234–5n.
34. GRC; Godwin, *Biography,* I, 235.
35. GRC; Godwin, *Biography,* I, 244.
36. GRC; Godwin, *Biography,* I, 245.
37. Robert W. July, *The Essential New Yorker, Gulian Crommelin Verplanck* (Durham, N. C., 1951), 142.
38. GRC; Godwin, *Biography,* I, 246.
39. Mrs. Bryant's autobiographical fragment, GRC.

Chapter 11. Vile Blackguard Squabbles
1. "William Leggett," *United States Review and Literary Gazette,* July, 1839.
2. Leggett, in an editorial reply to some of his critics, *Evening Post,* May 29, 1835. He printed the transcript of his court-martial on July 8, 1835.
3. Bryant, "Reminiscences of the 'Evening Post.'"
4. Berg.
5. Godwin, *Biography,* I, 247.
6. *Ibid.,* 248.
7. Mrs. Bryant's autobiographical fragment, GRC.
8. BGC.

9. Berg.
10. *A Funeral Oration, Occasioned by the Death of Thomas Cole* (New York, 1848), 14.
11. Berg.
12. Nevins, *The Evening Post,* 136.
13. Mrs. Bryant's autobiographical fragment, GRC.
14. *The Diary of Philip Hone, 1828–1851* (Allan Nevins, ed., New York, 1927), I, 40–1.
15. *The Letters of Ralph Waldo Emerson* (Ralph L. Rusk, ed., New York, 1939), I, 325–6.
16. Bryant wrote his mother on March 14, 1831, giving her details on how she should travel to New York. BFAP.
17. Mrs. Bryant's autobiographical fragment, GRC.
18. GRC.

Chapter 12. His Country's Foremost Poet
1. "Literary Portraits—William C. Bryant," Nov., 1831.
2. In a review of Bryant's *Poems* (1836), *Southern Literary Messenger,* Jan., 1837.
3. "Lectures on Poetry," *Prose,* I, 10–11.
4. McDowell, "Bryant's Practice in Composition and Revision."
5. Nov. 1, 1833, GRC; Godwin, *Biography,* I, 297.
6. GRC; Godwin, *Biography,* II, 289.
7. Both letters in GRC; Godwin, *Biography,* I, 297, 305.
8. Godwin, *Biography,* I, 282.
9. April, 1832.
10. Feb., 1832.
11. March, 1832.
12. March, 1832.
13. GRC; Godwin, *Biography,* I, 275.
14. GRC; Godwin, *Biography,* I, 285.
15. Both letters in Godwin, *Biography,* I, 275–6.
16. The Bryant and Verplanck letters to Irving about a London edition of the book appear in *The Life and Letters of Washington Irving* (Pierre M. Irving, ed., New York, 1862–1864), II, 471–9. Irving's letters to Bryant are in Godwin, *Biography,* I, 270–4.
17 GRC; Godwin, *Biography,* I, 284.
18. Aug., 1832.
19. GRC; Godwin, *Biography,* I, 285.
20. Godwin, *Biography,* I, 281.
21. The letters to Frances are in GRC and Godwin, *Biography,* I, 267–8.
22. GRC; Godwin, *Biography,* I, 282.
23. See *The Correspondence of Nicholas Biddle Dealing with National Affairs, 1807–1844* (Reginald C. McGrane, ed., Boston and New York, 1919), 58–198.
24. *The Letters of William Gilmore Simms* (Mary C. Simms Oliphant et al., eds., Columbia, S. C., 1952), I, xciv.
25. Published as "Illinois Fifty Years Ago," in *Prose,* II, 3–22.
26. BFAP.

Chapter 13. No Pipe for Politicians' Fingers
1. Mrs. Bryant's autobiographical fragment, GRC.
2. Letter to Dana, Oct. 8, 1832, GRC; Godwin, *Biography*, I, 285.
3. Letter to Sarah Snell Bryant, Aug. 21, 1832, BFAC.
4. Godwin, *Biography*, I, 289.
5. Letter to Sarah Snell Bryant, Dec. 17, 1832, BFAC.
6. Mrs. Bryant's autobiographical fragment, GRC.
7. Horace Greeley, *Recollections of a Busy Life* (New York, 1868), 83.
8. James Parton, *The Life of Horace Greeley* (Boston and New York, 1896), 99.
9. Greeley, *Recollections of a Busy Life*, 91–3.
10. These letters are in Godwin, *Biography*, I, 294–304.
11. *The Diary of Philip Hone, 1828–1851*, I, 106.
12. *Ibid.*, I, 120.
13. Nevins, *The Evening Post*, 136.
14. BFP.
15. BFAP.
16. Mrs. Bryant's autobiographical fragment, GRC.
17. GRC; Godwin, *Biography*, I, 304.
18. *Letters of a Traveller* (New York, 1850), 9–10.

Chapter 14. A Journey into the Past
1. Both Bryant and Frances kept travel diaries, which are in GRC. They are chiefly account books of expenses and itineraries and convey little information about the places visited or personal affairs. Bryant wrote seven letters to the *Evening Post*, describing his trip. With one exception, they are reprinted in *Letters of a Traveller*. The letter not reprinted was written at Heidelberg on Dec. 9, 1835, and appeared in the *Evening Post* on Jan. 26, 1836. It complained of the adverse commentary on American democracy that he read in continental newspapers and heard in conversation, most of it concerning "exaggerated stories of riots, lynch trials, and violence of various kinds committed in the United States."
2. Nathalia Wright, *Horatio Greenough* (Philadelphia, 1963), 104.
3. Godwin, *Biography*, I, 310.
4. BFAP.
5. Richard Moody, *Edwin Forrest* (New York, 1960), 120.
6. Note to the poem in *Poems*, 496.
7. *The Letters of Henry Wadsworth Longfellow* (Andrew Hilen, ed., Cambridge, Mass., 1966), I, 530.
8. Aug. 18, 1833, BGC.
9. BGC.
10. Letter to Frances, April 1, 1836, GRC.
11. "William Leggett," *United States Magazine and Democratic Review*, July, 1839.
12. Bryant, "Reminiscences of the 'Evening Post.'"
13. GRC; Godwin, *Biography*, I, 318–9.
14. GRC; Godwin, *Biography*, I, 312–3.
15. GRC; Godwin, *Biography*, I, 321.
16. May 21, 1836, GRC; Godwin, *Biography*, I, 317.
17. May 23, 1836, GRC; Godwin, *Biography*, I, 319.

18. GRC; Godwin, *Biography*, I, 322.
19. GRC; Godwin, *Biography*, I, 313–4. The portion quoted is omitted from Godwin.
20. GRC; Godwin, *Biography*, I, 320–1. The portion quoted is omitted from Godwin.
21. *Letters of Longfellow*, I, 565.
22. Bryant, "Reminiscences of the 'Evening Post.' "
23. GRC; Godwin, *Biography*, I, 319.
24. *Letters of William Gilmore Simms*, I, 109–13.

Chapter 15. Weathering Financial Storms
1. Feb. 27, 1837, GRC; Godwin, *Biography*, I, 355–6.
2. Introduction to the 1836 edition.
3. GRC; Godwin, *Biography*, I, 316.
4. *Life and Letters of Washington Irving*, III, 102–10; Godwin, *Biography*, I, 342–3.
5. Godwin gives his personal reminiscences in *Biography*, I, 333–42.
6. J. S. Buckingham, *America, Historical, Statistic, and Descriptive* (London, 1841), I, 65–7.
7. Godwin, *Biography*, I, 340.
8. Century Association, *Bryant Memorial Meeting of the Century* (New York, 1878), 48–9.
9. Aug. 21, 1837, GRC; Godwin, *Biography*, I, 359–60. Bryant relates the incident in "Reminiscences of the 'Evening Post,' " and the story is told by Frederic Hudson, *Journalism in the United States, from 1690 to 1872* (New York, 1873), 222.
10. *Diary of Philip Hone*, I, 391–2.
11. Thomas R. Lounsbury, *James Fenimore Cooper* (Boston and New York, 1882), 171.
12. Both letters in GRC; Godwin, *Biography*, I, 317, 355.
13. GRC.
14. *Letters of Ralph Waldo Emerson*, II, 187, 192.
15. Feb. 27, 1837, GRC; Godwin, *Biography*, I, 355.
16. Godwin, *Biography*, I, 370.
17. *Letters of Emerson*, II, 129, 201.
18. Godwin, *Biography*, I, 372.
19. *Ibid.*, I, 376.
20. The story is told in letters to Dana of June 24 and Oct. 2, 1839, in GRC. See also Godwin, *Biography*, I, 374–6, and Eugene Exman, *The House of Harper* (New York, 1967), 20–1.
21. GRC; Godwin, *Biography*, I, 363.
22. GRC; Godwin, *Biography*, I, 356.
23. GRC; Godwin, *Biography*, I, 362.
24. GRC; Godwin, *Biography*, I, 363.

Chapter 16. Varied Interests and Issues
1. June 28, 1838, GRC; Godwin, *Biography*, I, 363.
2. Godwin, *Biography*, I, 366.
3. July 6, 1837, GRC.

4. "Moral and Mental Portraits: William Cullen Bryant," *Southern Literary Messenger*, Jan., 1840.
5. Sept. 12, 1839, GRC; Godwin, *Biography*, I, 383–4.
6. *Funeral Oration, Occasioned by the Death of Thomas Cole*, 26, 33, 39.
7. Bryant wrote only two letters to the *Evening Post* on this trip. They appear in *Letters of a Traveller*, 55–64, 64–9.
8. Bigelow relates his first acquaintanceship with Bryant in *Retrospections of an Active Life* (New York, 1909; Garden City, N. Y., 1913), I, 48 ff. (Hereafter cited as *Retrospections*.)
9. John Bigelow, *The Life of Samuel J. Tilden* (New York, 1909), I, 98–9.
10. Whitman's editorials appear in Joseph J. Rubin and Charles H. Brown, *Walt Whitman of the New York Aurora* (State College, Pa., 1950), 57–82.
11. Godwin, *Biography*, I, 395.
12. *Ibid.*, I, 396.
13. *Letters of Ralph Waldo Emerson*, II, 26, 29.
14. GRC; Godwin, *Biography*, I, 323.
15. Ernest Risley Eaton, "William Cullen Bryant, Homoeopathist," *Quarterly of Phi Alpha Gamma*, Feb., 1934.
16. Godwin, *Biography*, I, 392–3.
17. *Ibid.*, I, 361.
18. Aug. 1, 1845, and Dec. 5, 1846, BGC.
19. Bigelow, *William Cullen Bryant*, 343–7.
20. To Ferdinand E. Field, May 16, 1840, Godwin, *Biography*, I, 381.
21. June 18, 1837, GRC; Godwin, *Biography*, I, 358.
22. Sept. 9, 1837, GRC; Godwin, *Biography*, I, 358.
23. Joy Bayless, *Rufus Wilmot Griswold* (Nashville, Tenn., 1943), 56–7.
24. GRC; Godwin, *Biography*, I, 399.
25. *Poetical Works*, I, 354–5.
26. Oct., 1842.

Chapter 17. The Conflict over Texas
1. Godwin, *Biography*, I, 406.
2. Horace Traubel, *With Walt Whitman in Camden* (Carbondale, Ill., 1964), V, 467.
3. *Letters of William Gilmore Simms*, I, 213–4.
4. These letters appeared in the *Evening Post* on April 1, 12, and 21 and May 4, 10, 24, and 30, 1843. They are printed in *Letters of a Traveller*, 69–127.
5. *Letters of Simms*, I, 348–50.
6. May 13, 1843, *Letters of Simms*, I, 348–50.
7. May 26, 1843, GRC; Godwin, *Biography*, I, 409.
8. The letters appeared in the *Evening Post* on July 15 and 18, 1843. They are printed in *Letters of a Traveller*, 128–43.
9. *Evening Post*, Nov. 16, 1901, 100th anniversary edition.
10. Bryant's part in establishing Central Park is discussed by Godwin in his reminiscences of the *Evening Post* in the 100th anniversary edition and by Nevins, *The Evening Post*, 193–201.
11. The story is told in Bayless, *Rufus Wilmot Griswold*, 56–7.
12. Note to the poem in *Poems*, 497.

13. GRC; Godwin, *Biography,* I, 409.
14. GRC.
15. GRC.
16. Traubel, *With Walt Whitman in Camden,* V, 467.
17. M. A. DeWolfe Howe, *American Bookmen* (New York, 1898), 71.

Chapter 18. A Second Voyage to Europe
1. GRC; Godwin, *Biography,* II, 1.
2. BGC.
3. All in BGC.
4. *Evening Post,* Sept. 26, 1844.
5. Printed announcement of the program of the Associationists drafted by the executive committee headed by Godwin and adopted at the convention of the movement held in New York in April, 1845. BGC.
6. GRC.
7. GRC; Godwin, *Biography,* II, 12.
8. Bryant's letters were printed in the *Evening Post* on June 20; July 5, 7, and 22; Aug. 1, 19, and 20; Sept. 11, 13, and 16; Oct. 21 and 24; and Nov. 5. All except that of Oct. 21 appear in *Letters of a Traveller,* 144–240. This letter, dated Dresden, Sept. 9, 1848, described Bryant's trip from Heidelberg to Strasbourg and discussed the New Catholic movement in Germany. Bryant kept a pocket travel diary, parts of which are cited by Godwin, and his letters to his wife also contain some information. Both are in GRC.
9. Godwin, *Biography,* II, 9.
10. Letter to Frances, April 27, 1836, GRC; Godwin, *Biography,* I, 314.
11. GRC.
12. Bayless, *Rufus Wilmot Griswold,* 277–8.
13. GRC; Godwin, *Biography,* II, 13.

Chapter 19. Free-Soiler and Barnburner
1. GRC; Godwin, *Biography,* II, 14.
2. GRC; Godwin, *Biography,* II, 15.
3. April 6, 1846, GRC; Godwin, *Biography,* II, 16–7.
4. *The Life of Henry Wadsworth Longfellow with Extracts from His Journals and Correspondence* (Samuel Longfellow, ed., Boston and New York, 1891), II, 31.
5. Godwin, *Biography,* I, 370, and II, 22.
6. BGC.
7. The letters appeared in the *Evening Post* on Aug. 1, 11, 13, 15, 24, 25, and 27, 1846. They are printed in *Letters of a Traveller,* 241–302.
8. Many of Sarah Snell Bryant's letters are in BFAP. See also George V. Bonham, "A Poet's Mother: Sarah Snell Bryant in Illinois," *Journal* of the Illinois State Historical Society, June, 1940.
9. Walt Whitman, *Gathering of the Forces* (Cleveland Rodgers and John Black, eds., New York, 1920), I, 260–1.
10. GRC; Godwin, *Biography,* II, 19–20.
11. Dec. 15, 1846, GRC; Godwin, *Biography,* II, 20.
12. *Life and Letters of Catharine M. Sedgwick,* 300.

13. Letters in BFC.
14. BGC.
15. BGC.
16. Bryant to Frances, May 5, 1847, GRC.
17. Margaret Clapp, *Forgotten First Citizen: John Bigelow* (Boston, 1947), 52.
18. BGC.
19. GRC; Godwin, *Biography*, II, 31.
20. The letters appeared in the *Evening Post* on Aug. 4, 13, and 18, 1847. They are printed in *Letters of a Traveller*, 320–5.

Chapter 20. A New Partnership
1. Reminiscences by John Bigelow, *Evening Post*, Nov. 16, 1901, 100th anniversary edition.
2. *Ibid.*
3. GRC; Godwin, *Biography*, II, 36.
4. Bryant, "Reminiscences of the 'Evening Post.' "
5. Reminiscences of William Boggs, *Evening Post*, June 13, 1878.
6. July, *The Essential New Yorker: Gulian Crommelin Verplanck*, 251–2.
7. *Life and Letters of Bayard Taylor* (Marie Hansen-Taylor and Horace E. Scudder, eds., Boston, 1884), I, 59.
8. *Ibid.*, 80.
9. Clapp, *Forgotten First Citizen: John Bigelow*, 56.
10. Both letters in GRC; Godwin, *Biography*, II, 36.
11. Godwin, *Biography*, II, 39–40.
12. *Letters and Literary Memorials of Samuel J. Tilden* (John Bigelow, ed., New York, 1908), I, 49.
13. *Ibid.*, 50–5.
14. Bigelow, *Retrospections*, I, 73 ff., and 100th anniversary edition.
15. Bigelow, 100th anniversary edition.
16. Bryant's letters to the *Evening Post* were printed on April 6, 9, and 16, May 26 and 30, and June 6, 1849. They appear in *Letters of a Traveller*, 336–401. GRC contains several letters from Bryant to Frances about the trip.
17. Bryant's account of the European trip is to be found in letters to Frances and a travel diary, both in GRC, and the *Evening Post* on the dates of July 28, Aug. 27, Sept. 28, and Oct. 5, 1849. With the exception of the letter published Oct. 5, dated at Paris in September, they appear also in *Letters of a Traveller*, 402–42.
18. GRC; Godwin, *Biography*, II, 35.
19. Bigelow, *Retrospections*, I, 91.
20. Bigelow, 100th anniversary edition.

Chapter 21. Current Strife and Ancient Scenes
1. Bigelow, *Retrospections*, I, 98–105.
2. GRC; Godwin, *Biography*, II, 57.
3. Moody, *Edwin Forrest*, 251 ff; Henry A. Beers, *Nathaniel Parker Willis* (Boston, 1885), 309 ff.
4. GRC; Godwin, *Biography*, II, 52–3.
5. BFC; Godwin, *Biography*, II, 54.

6. GRC contains several letters from Bryant to Frances regarding the trip.
7. April 8, 1851, GRC; Godwin, *Biography*, II, 61.
8. Bryant's *Memorial of James Fenimore Cooper* was published by the firm of G. P. Putnam's in 1852; it is printed in *Prose*, I, 299–332.
9. Godwin, *Biography*, II, 63–4.
10. GRC.
11. Clapp, *Forgotten First Citizen: John Bigelow*, 80.
12. Bryant's letters to the *Evening Post*, several of them in installments because of their length, were printed on Dec. 15 and 27, 1852, and in 1853 on Jan. 12 and 29; March 2; April 18, 19, and 30; May 14, 16, and 17; and June 1, 3, 4, 9, 10, 11, 14, and 16. They are printed in *Letters from the East* (New York, 1869). His travel diary of the trip and his letters to Frances are in GRC.
13. GRC; Godwin, *Biography*, II, 74.
14. On the publication of Bryant's *Letters from the East*, Durand wrote a long letter giving his reminiscences of the trip, printed in the *Evening Post* on Dec. 16, 1869.

Chapter 22. Forming the Republican Party
1. Bigelow, *Retrospections*, I, 90.
2. *Evening Post*, Nov. 16, 1901, 100th anniversary edition.
3. Bigelow, reminiscences, 100th anniversary edition; Clapp, *Forgotten First Citizen: John Bigelow*, 110–11; Nevins, *The Evening Post*, 237–8.
4. Letters in BGC.
5. May 26, 1854, GRC; Godwin, *Biography*, II, 77.
6. William J. Stillman, *The Autobiography of a Journalist* (Boston and New York, 1901), 217–8.
7. *Ibid.*, 225–9. See also *Letters of James Russell Lowell* (Charles Eliot Norton, ed., New York, 1894), 217.
8. GRC; Godwin, *Biography*, II, 77.
9. BFP.
10. April 20, 1855, GRC.
11. June 11, 1855, GRC; Godwin, *Biography*, II, 81–2.
12. GRC; Godwin, *Biography*, II, 82–3.
13. Bigelow, *Retrospections*, I, 141–3.
14. GRC; Godwin, *Biography*, II, 88.
15. A placard announcing the meeting, signed by Bryant and Godwin, is in BGC.

Chapter 23. Shadows of the Gate of Death
1. The article, "Street Yarn," appeared in *Life Illustrated*, Aug. 16, 1856.
2. June 11, 1856, BFP.
3. GRC; Godwin, *Biography*, II, 94–5.
4. *Letters of William Gilmore Simms*, III, 454–5, 458–9, 467–8.
5. GRC; Godwin, *Biography*, II, 94–5.
6. Letter to Bryant's niece, Ellen S. Mitchell, April, 1857, GRC.
7. Letter to Bigelow, May 30, 1857, GRC; Godwin, *Biography*, II, 95–6.
8. During the trip Bryant wrote twenty–four letters for the *Evening Post*. They were printed on the following dates in the year 1857: June 28, Aug. 1 and 28, Oct. 3, 22, and 26, Nov. 19 and 24, and Dec. 2 and 29; and in 1858:

Jan. 2 and 6, Feb. 2, 3, 10, 15, 17, 18, and 26, March 5 and 6, June 11, Aug. 5 and 26. They were collected and published as *Letters of a Traveller: Second Series* (New York, 1859).

9. June 18, 1857, GRC; Godwin, *Biography*, II, 96.
10. Waterston, *Tribute to William Cullen Bryant*, 7–8.
11. Aug. 27, 1857, GRC; Godwin, *Biography*, II, 99–100.
12. BGC.
13. GRC; Godwin, *Biography*, II, 105–6.
14. May 18, 1858, GRC; Godwin, *Biography*, II, 109–10.
15. The details of Bryant's uniting with the church are given in Waterston, *Tribute to William Cullen Bryant*.
16. Letters in BGC.
17. BGC.
18. Nathaniel Hawthorne, *Notes of Travel* (Boston and New York, 1900), III, 391.
19. *Ibid.*, IV, 72.
20. GRC.
21. July 16, 1858, GRC; Godwin, *Biography*, II, 116.
22. GRC; Godwin, *Biography*, II, 117–8.
23. GRC.

Chapter 24. Electing Lincoln President
1. Both letters in GRC.
2. Letter to Christiana Gibson, April 19, 1859, GRC; Godwin, *Biography*, II, 125.
3. GRC; Godwin, *Biography*, II, 125.
4. Dec. 14, 1859, GRC; Godwin, *Biography*, II, 127–8.
5. Briggs told of his part in getting Bryant to preside, in an article in the *Evening Post* on Aug. 16, 1867. See also Nevins, *The Evening Post*, 260.
6. Nevins, *The Evening Post*, 261.
7. April 11, 1859, Bigelow, *Retrospections*, I, 224–6.
8. Letters of March 1 and 8, April 23, and May 10, 1860, *Retrospections*, I, 284–9.
9. April 13, 1860, GRC. Comment omitted in Godwin's version of the letter, *Biography*, II, 134.
10. Bigelow gives the complete story of his travels in *Retrospections*, I, 181–289. His letters to Bryant and Isaac Henderson are in BGC.
11. A complete account with Bigelow's letters to Bryant appears in *Retrospections*, II, 198–208.
12. Letters to Bryant of Jan. 18 and Feb. 3, 20, and 28, 1860, are in BGC. See also *Retrospections*, I, 251–3.
13. Feb. 6, 1860, GRC; Godwin, *Biography*, II, 133.
14. GRC.
15. May 8, 1860, BGC. Other details of the controversy are given in letters to Henderson, also in BGC.
16. GRC.
17. Feb. 25, 1860, GRC; Godwin, *Biography*, II, 133.
18. GRC; Godwin, *Biography*, II, 134–5.
19. The oration is printed in *Prose*, I.

20. Charles Eugene Hamlin, *The Life and Times of Hannibal Hamlin* (Cambridge, Mass., 1899), 212, 250.
21. Robert Todd Lincoln Collection of the Papers of Abraham Lincoln, Library of Congress. (Hereafter cited as RTL.) A draft version is in Godwin, *Biography*, II, 142–3.
22. GRC; Godwin, *Biography*, II, 143.
23. June 14, 1860, GRC; Godwin, *Biography*, II, 137. Two letters to Dewey about the visit are in GRC and in Godwin, *Biography*, II, 138.
24. To William Hargreaves, July 30, 1860. Quoted in Clapp, *Forgotten First Citizen: John Bigelow*, 136–7.
25. June 14, 1860, GRC; Godwin, *Biography*, II, 137–8.
26. *The Life of Henry Wadsworth Longfellow with Extracts from His Journals and Correspondence*, II, 407.
27. Bigelow, *Retrospections*, I, 292.
28. RTL.
29. *The Collected Works of Abraham Lincoln* (New Brunswick, N. J., 1953), IV, 149; Horace White, *The Life of Lyman Trumbull* (Boston and New York, 1913), 139–41.
30. RTL.
31. *Collected Works of Lincoln*, IV, 163.
32. RTL.
33. RTL.
34. *Collected Works of Lincoln*, IV, 171.
35. RTL.
36. Nevins, *The Evening Post*, 277–8.
37. RTL.
38. RTL.

Chapter 25. What Does the President Wait For?
1. Bigelow, *Retrospections*, I, 319–25.
2. BGC.
3. Bigelow, *Retrospections*, I, 348–9.
4. GRC.
5. *The Life of Henry Wadsworth Longfellow with Extracts from His Journals and Correspondence*, II, 414.
6. *Evening Post*, Nov. 16, 1901, 100th anniversary edition.
7. GRC.
8. RTL.
9. Letter to Frances, Jan. 12, 1862, GRC.
10. Godwin, *Biography*, II, 165–6.
11. BGC.
12. GRC; Godwin, *Biography*, II, 176–8.
13. Sept. 15, 1862, Godwin, *Biography*, II, 178–9.
14. RTL.
15. *Letters and Recollections of John Murray Forbes* (Sarah Forbes Hughes, ed., Boston and New York, 1900), I, 335–6.
16. From the unfinished "A Tale of Cloudland," *Poetical Works*, II, 312–20.

Chapter 26. Glory to the Lord of Hosts!

1. Mabee, *The American Leonardo, a Life of Samuel F. B. Morse,* 347.
2. *The Diary of George Templeton Strong* (Allan Nevins and Milton Haslet Thomas, eds., New York, 1952), II, 298.
3. *Evening Post,* Aug. 22, 1866, and Dec. 7, 1901.
4. Letter to Dr. Dewey, Sept. 24, 1863, GRC; Godwin, *Biography,* II, 197.
5. Letter from Sedgwick, Aug. 11, 1863, GRC; Godwin, *Biography,* II, 196.
6. To Thomas C. P. Hyde, GRC; Godwin, *Biography,* II, 198.
7. Letter to Bryant, Nov. 9, 1863, BGC.
8. Issue of Jan. 21, 1864.
9. *Journals of Ralph Waldo Emerson* (Edward W. Emerson and Waldo Emerson Forbes, eds., Boston and New York, 1914), X, 76.
10. April 30, 1864, GRC; Godwin, *Biography,* II, 209.
11. GRC; Godwin, *Biography,* II, 207–8.
12. *The Life of Henry Wadsworth Longfellow with Extracts from His Journals and Correspondence,* III, 29; Godwin, *Biography,* II, 206.
13. GRC; Godwin, *Biography,* II, 206–7.
14. GRC; Godwin, *Biography,* II, 207–8.
15. Godwin, *Biography,* II, 193. Godwin implies this was in 1863; since Bryant said he completed the translation on Nov. 15, 1862, however, the incident must have occurred in the earlier year.
16. May 14, 1863, GRC; Godwin, *Biography,* II, 192.
17. Letters to Frances May 30 and June 2, 1864, GRC.
18. *The Diary of Gideon Welles* (Howard K. Beal, ed., New York, 1960) contains frequent mention of the Henderson case: I, 518, 546, 582, and II, 54, 61, 79, 83, 104, 306. The record is also given in Richard S. West, Jr., *Gideon Welles. Lincoln's Navy Department* (Indianapolis and New York, 1943), 249 ff.
19. RTL.
20. RTL.
21. RTL.
22. BGC.
23. GRC contains eight letters, mostly dealing with trivial matters, that Bryant wrote Frances while she was on her summer trip.
24. GRC.
25. *Letters and Recollections of John Murray Forbes,* II, 101.
26. RTL.
27. The letter was written by the district attorney, A. Oakey Hall, to which was attached a clipping of an *Evening Post* editorial, "The Company McClellan Trains In," BGC. The story is also told in Croswell Bowen, *The Elegant Oakey* (New York, 1956), 46–8.
28. GRC; Godwin, *Biography,* II, 210–1.
29. GRC; Godwin, *Biography,* II, 211–2.
30. GRC; Godwin, *Biography,* II, 212–3.
31. A full account of the festival, including the speeches made and the poetic tributes to Bryant, appeared in the *Evening Post* on Nov. 7, 12, and 16, 1864.
32. Letters in GRC.

Chapter 27. Like One Cast Out of Paradise
1. May 1, 1865; Godwin, *Biography,* II, 230–1.
2. Mary Dawes Warner, *William Cullen Bryant: His Home* (pamphlet, Boston, 1930).
3. Aug. 19, 1865, GRC; Godwin, *Biography,* II, 234.
4. GRC; Godwin, *Biography,* II, 240–2.
5. GRC.
6. July 6, 1866, GRC.
7. GRC; Godwin, *Biography,* II, 244–5.
8. Godwin, *Biography,* II, 246–7.
9. GRC; Godwin, *Biography,* II, 254–5.
10. Bryant's travel letters to the *Evening Post* appeared on the following dates: Feb. 13, 16, and 27, March 14, May 4, and July 12, 1867. They have not been reprinted.
11. Dec. 20, 1866, GRC; Godwin, *Biography,* II, 254–5.
12. Godwin, *Biography,* II, 255–7.
13. May 8, 1867, GRC; Godwin, *Biography,* II, 260–1.
14. Bryant's appointment came in a letter from J. Miller McKim, corresponding secretary of the commission, dated April 4, 1867, BGC. The account of the meeting is given in Wendell Phillips Garrison and Francis Jackson Garrison, *William Lloyd Garrison, 1805–1879; the Story of His Life* (New York, 1885), IV, 193.
15. Described in a letter to Julia Sands, July 29, 1867, GRC; Godwin, *Biography,* II, 262–3.
16. GRC; Godwin, *Biography,* II, 264–5.
17. Bigelow, *Retrospections,* IV, 392 ff.
18. Eggleston, *Recollections of a Varied Life,* 129–30.
19. Quoted in Nevins, *The Evening Post,* 423.
20. BGC.
21. GRC; Godwin, *Biography,* II, 266–7.
22. GRC; Godwin, *Biography,* II, 267–8.
23. These speeches were printed in the *Evening Post* on the following dates: Jan. 28 and 31, June 12, and Dec. 30, 1868.
24. Godwin, *Biography,* II, 270–1.
25. Jan. 24, 1868, GRC; Godwin, *Biography,* II, 272.
26. GRC; Godwin, *Biography,* II, 273.
27. Warner, *William Cullen Bryant: His Home.*
28. GRC; Godwin, *Biography,* II, 275.
29. These speeches were printed in the *Evening Post* on the following dates: Jan. 9, Feb. 9 and 24, May 11, and Nov. 24, 1869.
30. GRC; Godwin, *Biography,* II, 276.
31. GRC; Godwin, *Biography,* II, 277.
32. Godwin, *Biography,* II, 292.
33. *Ibid.,* 290.
34. *Ibid.,* 284–5.
35. *Letters of William Gilmore Simms,* V, 299, 308–9, 311–2.
36. Introduction, *Selections from the American Poets* (New York, 1840).
37. Godwin, *Biography,* II, 294–6.

38. GRC; Godwin, *Biography*, II, 296.
39. GRC; Godwin, *Biography*, II, 302.
40. GRC; Godwin, Biography, II, 302–3.

Chapter 28. The Years of Busy Fame
1. Reminiscences by J. Ranken Towse, *Evening Post*, Nov. 16, 1901, 100th anniversary edition.
2. Reminiscences by William Alexander Linn, 100th anniversary edition.
3. Nevins, *The Evening Post*, 381–2.
4. *Ibid.*, 431.
5. BGC.
6. GRC.
7. BGC.
8. Towse, 100th anniversary edition.
9. GRC.
10. GRC; Godwin, *Biography*, II, 290.
11. GRC.
12. GRC; Godwin, *Biography*, II, 336.
13. Bryant wrote eight letters to the *Evening Post* on the trip. They were printed on Feb. 14, April 9 and 29, and May 4, 9, 11, 16, and 24, 1872. The paper quoted from private letters in editorials on March 1 and April 1.
14. An account of Bryant's reception in Mexico City, based on reports in Mexican newspapers, was printed in the *Evening Post* on April 1, 1872.
15. Linn, 100th anniversary edition.
16. GRC; Godwin, *Biography*, II, 336.
17. GRC; Godwin, *Biography*, II, 336.
18. GRC; Godwin, *Biography*, II, 346.
19. July 16, 1873, BGC.
20. GRC; Godwin, *Biography*, II, 328.
21. Derby, *Fifty Years among Authors, Books, and Publishers*, 156–7.
22. GRC; Godwin, *Biography*, II, 341.
23. BGC.
24. William Aspenwall Bradley, *William Cullen Bryant* (English Men of Letters Series, New York, 1926), 194.
25. Moses Coit Tyler, *Selections from His Letters and Diaries* (Jessica Tyler Austin, ed., Garden City, N. Y., 1911), 81, 83.
26. Bradley, *William Cullen Bryant*, 194.
27. The account of the birthday celebration is taken from the *Evening Post*, Nov. 4, 6, 7, and 12, 1874.
28. The account of the vase is taken from the *Evening Post* of June 20, 1876, and from a printed memorial, *To William Cullen Bryant, at Eighty Years, from His Friends and Countrymen* (New York, 1876).
29. This was fully reported in newspapers, the *Evening Post's* account appearing on Feb. 9, 1875.
30. The letter is reprinted in Bigelow, *William Cullen Bryant*, 260–2, and in Derby, *Fifty Years among Authors, Books, and Publishers*, 153–5.
31. Towse, 100th anniversary edition.
32. Eggleston, *Recollections of a Varied Life*, 188, 195.

33. Bryant wrote only three letters to the *Evening Post* on this trip. They were printed on March 24 and April 7 and 15, 1873.
34. GRC; Godwin, *Biography*, II, 331.
35. The Charleston *News* article was reprinted in the *Evening Post*, April 7, 1873.

Chapter 29. Waiting by the Gate
1. Nevins, *The Evening Post*, 432.
2. The correspondence is given in Bigelow, *The Life of Samuel J. Tilden*, I, 301–2, and in his *William Cullen Bryant*, 242–5, and in Godwin, *Biography*, II, 375–6.
3. Bigelow, *William Cullen Bryant*, 246; Derby, *Fifty Years among Authors, Books, and Publishers*, 159.
4. Bigelow, *The Life of Samuel J. Tilden*, I, 302–3, and *William Cullen Bryant*, 246–7; Derby, *Fifty Years among Authors, Books and Publishers*, 159–61; Godwin, *Biography*, II, 376–9.
5. Linn, *Evening Post*, Nov. 16, 1901, 100th anniversary edition.
6. Bigelow, *Retrospections*, V, 280–1.
7. Nevins, *The Evening Post*, 404.
8. *Letters and Literary Memorials of Samuel J. Tilden*, II, 446.
9. GRC.
10. Bigelow, *Retrospections*, V, 366 ff.; Nevins, *The Evening Post*, 420, 433–4.
11. Dec. 5, 1877, Godwin, *Biography*, II, 388.
12. Dec. 1877, Godwin, *Biography*, II, 389.
13. GRC.
14. Nov. 25, 1876, GRC; Godwin, *Biography*, II, 38.
15. Wilson, *Bryant and His Friends*, 73.
16. Joseph Alden, *Thoughts on the Religious Life* (New York, 1879), preface.
17. Godwin, *Biography*, II, 399–402.
18. *In Memory of William Cullen Bryant* (published by the *Evening Post*, 1878), 67–9.
19. Details of Bryant's illness and death are taken from contemporary newspaper accounts, from Godwin's biography, and from Wilson's *Bryant and His Friends*.
20. Bigelow, *Retrospections*, V, 373 ff.

INDEX

European trip of, 412–13
Frémont and, 386
in Haiti, 372–73
hires Thayer, 370
income of, 360
on Lincoln and Douglas, 404–5
on recession and *Evening Post,* 392–93, 400, 402
sells interest in *Evening Post,* 426–28
studies Blacks, 353
Sumner and, 352
Bion, 54
Birney, James G., 238
Black Tariff of 1842, 291
Blackwood's Magazine (periodical), 120
Blackwood's Edinburgh Magazine (periodical), 199
Blaine, James G., 511
Blair, Francis P., 331, 372, 383, 469–70
Blair, Rev. Robert, 58–61
"Blessed Are They That Mourn," 523
Bliss, Elam, 127, 129, 164, 170, 182–83, 196, 217
Boggs, William G., 241, 259, 290, 303, 313, 329, 334, 336, 343–44, 492–94
"Bohemian Brigade," 441
Bologne, 402
Bond, George, 129–30, 148
"Border Tradition, A," 153
Brainard, John G. C., 143
Branch, John, 177
Breckenridge, John C., 420
Bressay, 347
Brevoort, Henry, 197
Briggs, Charles F., 370
Briggs, Rev. James, 4, 15, 26, 33
Briggs, James A., 409
Brisbane, Albert, 301
Bronson, Greene C., 377

Brook Farm, 302
Brooks, James G., 126, 129, 148
Brooks, Preston, 384, 386, 389
Brown, G. L., 312–13
Brown, Henry K., 313
Brown, John, 407–8
Brown, Solyman, 82, 120, 143
Browning, Robert, 401–2
Bruen, G. W., 137
Bryant, Arthur, 44, 48, 54, 90, 188, 205–6, 228, 475–76
Bryant, Austin, 8, 10, 12–13, 16, 34, 36, 68, 72, 90, 155, 228, 475
Bryant, Charity, 90, 288
Bryant, Charity Louisa, 90, 189
Bryant, Cyrus, 14, 90, 188, 222, 228, 475
Bryant, Frances, 107, 130, 135, 139, 163, 181, 209, 213, 240, 246, 261, 277–78, 301, 328, 358
Bryant, Frances Fairchild, 399, 403, 475–77
  Bryant first meets, 75–76
  Bryant's Harvard trip and, 99
  cholera epidemic and, 208–9
  daughters' education and, 277–78
  European trip of, 222, 225, 228, 237, 240, 394
  Forrests and, 354
  Godwin and, 246–47
  house of, 185
  illness of, 114, 375, 381, 388–91, 396–97
  letters to, 113, 123
    on Cooper, 254
    on Evrard, 132
    on hiking, 261
    on Holland, 251
    on Illinois trips, 204, 206–7
    on Leggett, 241
    on money, 152–53
    in Roslyn, 298, 360
    on *Tales of Glauber Spa,* 243
    about trips, 303, 347, 363

PICTURE CREDITS

following page 140

1. Permanent Collection, National Academy of Design. Photograph courtesy, Frick Art Reference Library.
2. Courtesy, The New-York Historical Society, New York City.
3. Courtesy, The New-York Historical Society, New York City.
4. *Appletons' Journal,* February 8, 1873.
5. John Barber, *Historical Collections of the Towns of Massachusetts,* 1839.
6. Courtesy, The New-York Historical Society, New York City.
7. From the Personal (Misc.) Papers of William Cullen Bryant, Manuscript Division, The New York Public Library, Astor, Lenox and Tilden Foundations.
8. Henry W. and Albert A. Berg Collection, The New York Public Library, Astor, Lenox and Tilden Foundations.
9. Henry W. and Albert A. Berg Collection, The New York Public Library, Astor, Lenox and Tilden Foundations.
10. T. Hornor. *Hornor View of Broadway.* I.N. Phelps Stokes Collection, Prints Division, The New York Public Library, Astor, Lenox and Tilden Foundations.
11. Published by Bourne, New York, 1831. Courtesy, The New-York Historical Society, New York City.
12. From: *Eclectic* Magazine. Picture Collection, The New York Public Library.
13. Left to right: Permanent Collection, National Academy of Design, Photograph by Peter A. Juley and Son; Courtesy, The New-York Historical Society, New York City; Picture Collection, The New York Public Library; Courtesy, The New-York Historical Society, New York City.
14. Collections of The New York Public Library. Astor, Lenox and Tilden Foundations.

following page 314

1. Charles Loring Elliott, *William Cullen Bryant*. In the collection of The Corcoran Gallery of Art.
2. From: *Punchinello,* December 3, 1870. Prints Division, The New York Public Library, Astor, Lenox and Tilden Foundations.
3. Courtesy, The New-York Historical Society, New York City.
4. Picture Collection, The New York Public Library.
5. Picture Collection, The New York Public Library.
6. Prints Division, The New York Public Library, Astor, Lenox and Tilden Foundations.
7. Picture Collection, The New York Public Library.
8. Brown Brothers.
9. Rare Book Division, The New York Public Library, Astor, Lenox and Tilden Foundations.
10. From: *Appletons' Journal,* December 18, 1869. Prints Division, The New York Public Library, Astor, Lenox and Tilden Foundations.
11. From: *Among the Trees* by William Cullen Bryant. Designs by Jervis McEntee, New York, G. P. Putnam's Sons, 1874.
12. From: *Harper's Weekly,* October 13, 1860.
13. Reprinted with permission of COMMUNITY FUNDS, INC.
14. The Metropolitan Museum of Art, Gift of William Cullen Bryant, 1877.
15. From: *Scribner's Monthly,* August, 1878.
16. From: *Scribner's Monthly,* August, 1878.

Dec/84

a good Autaph 415.